Summer of Haight '67

DIANE SAGER

Summer of Haight '67
by Diane Sager
Copyright © Diane Sager 2014. All Rights Reserved

ISBN 13: 978-0692298213
ISBN 10: 0692298215

Edited by Felicia A. Sullivan
Cover art by Dean Samed
Interior formatting by Kody Boye

With love and gratitude this book is dedicated to:

My loving husband Russ Swallow, who puts up with all my craziness and for enduring fifteen months of 1967 during the writing of this book.

My parents, Charles and Barbara, who made endless trips to the Haight/Ashbury district of San Francisco with a very curious little girl.

My daughter Samera, who joined me on field trips to locate old stores and former homes of some famous artists contained within these pages, and for taking an unforgettable bus ride across San Francisco to research this book.

Special Acknowledgements:

The men and women of the US military who served during the Vietnam War.

The 2nd Battalion 9th Marines (Hell in a Helmet) who served bravely at the DMZ (Demilitarized Zone) during the Vietnam War.

The San Francisco Chapter of Hells Angels and the memory of Chocolate George.

The Diggers, AKA Free City Collective, who fed the needy and provided medical aid and found homes for the newcomers. They were the glue that bonded Haight/Ashbury together in 1967 and beyond.

Commander William H. Searfus MIA November 25, 1967 (Panel 30E, Line 86). He paid the ultimate price.

Felicia A. Sullivan the best editor in the business.

"This following program is dedicated to the city and people of San Francisco
Who may not know it but they are beautiful
And so is their city."

Eric Burdon and the Animals – 1967

Prelude

The so-called "Summer of Love" refers to 1967. Not only because that year saw a revolutionary new movement, but because that was the year when the media began to focus on the "hippie" phenomenon; the underground alternative youth culture that had been brewing in the United States for many years.

The epicenter of this movement was San Francisco. A city to which young people travelled from across the country and beyond, attracted by the promise of casting off conservative social values and recreating the world they lived in.

The "Human Be-In" rally took place in San Francisco on January 14, 1967, and is considered the starting point. Generation speakers and poets addressed a crowd of 20,000 people gathered in Golden Gate Park to celebrate key ideas of the new times: ending the Vietnam war, communal living, environmental awareness, and 'dropping out' of society.

The dream of the hippie era ended when the realities of 'dropping out' hit home. Thousands suffered serious drug addiction, mental problems, and homelessness. San Francisco became overrun with drug dealers and teenage runaways.

Haight-Ashbury is a district named after cross streets of the same name. Once beautiful, it deteriorated through overcrowding, homeless vagrants, and excessive crime. On October 6, 1967, a mock funeral, meant to signify the death of all that was good about the movement, was held by the original hippies who still remained. The "Death of the Hippie" ceremony signified the end to the utopia sought by so many.

Realizing that peace and love couldn't sustain them forever, some of the hippies went back to the universities, got jobs, and reentered the society they had previously abhorred.

Chapter 1

Katherine Rhodes drove through the mountain range too fast. The rain was brutal and made visibility nearly impossible. She knew she was endangering herself, especially in this weather, but she didn't care. If she crashed, so be it. In her present life there wasn't much to live for. She'd turned sixty-six years old last week and her life was a farce.

She had two grown children, both too busy in their own lives to bother with her. Her husband Mark had cheated on her numerous times during their thirty-eight year marriage. She had gotten used to the infidelity, but recently he'd actually run off with one of his "flings".

Katherine thought the novelty would wear off and he'd be back. It wasn't the first time Mark had taken off with one of his girlfriends, but he always came crawling back. It had taken her totally by surprise when she was served with divorce papers that morning.

According to a mutual friend, Mark was starting a new family and "they", meaning him and Tiffany, wanted to be married before she gave birth. A baby! The man was sixty-seven years old and the mother-to-be was twenty-six. She was younger than *both* of his adult children for God's sake.

When Katherine was presented with the divorce papers she was numbed. She had never really been happy with her marriage, of course, but she was secure. Mark had his life, his work clientele, his friends, his private vacations, and his work related trips to Mexico. She had her own friends, her hobbies, and an occasional trip to an exotic location. She knew that Mark had his girlfriends, but she had lived with his indiscretions. Never in her wildest dreams did she imagine he would divorce her.

As she sped through the hills the rain turned to hail. She didn't notice; she was lost in her own thoughts. She had made mistakes and agreed to things in her marriage even though she knew they were wrong. Looking back, she realized she had never been her own person. In her early life her father controlled her, and in later years that job had fallen on Mark's shoulders. She had let her husband have control over all aspects of her life. Mark handled her father's company and all of their finances. She had no idea how much money came in or how much money went out.

Somewhere in between getting married, raising children, and drifting further and further apart, Mark had taken complete control over her father's company. She hadn't realized until recently that she had unwittingly signed total control over to him in 2002 when her father died. All she owned now was some of the stock, but not enough to vote in the company. Mark had weaseled himself into owning everything. Until this morning that hadn't worried her, but now that he was divorcing her, what did that mean?

When she thought of the community property she shook her head. All the assets they owned—the rental property in Santa Cruz, the vacation property in the Bahamas, and their own home in the Marina District of San Francisco— according to her attorney, Mark had legally omitted her name from all the real estate. Where had she been over the past thirty-eight years? How on earth had she let him take control of her inheritance?

The blue Porsche's tail spun on one of the corners but Katherine corrected it. She saw a red Nissan in front of her and she downshifted gears, slowing to stay a safe distance away from the car. To calm her frazzled nerves, she turned the radio on and flipped channels. Finally, she tuned into a late night oldies show. She sat back, leaned her head against the headrest and listened.

"If you're going to San Francisco be sure to wear some flowers in your hair..."

The lyrics echoed through the car. She turned the volume up. That song took her back to another time and another place. A time much simpler than the one in which she now lived.

She ran her hand through her shoulder length graying hair and started to daydream. Her childhood had been a happy one. She and her younger brother had wanted for nothing while growing up; every luxury was theirs for the taking. She and Richard had been raised in a wealthy family in Antioch, California, where money was given freely, but attention and love were hard to come by.

Her entrepreneur father made massive amounts of money in the stock market, while her socialite mother stayed at home and raised the children. Patricia Searfus had been the perfect corporate wife, herself the daughter of a wealthy businessman. She was the classic stay at home mother of the 1950's, the type of woman who did what her man asked. She had stayed home, sheltered her children, attended PTA meetings, and joined the country club (where she learned to party heavily with her friends). When Katherine and Richard had entered high school, their mother's drinking had caught up with her. Patricia spent most of her days in an incoherent buzz while her children did anything they wanted.

Their father, Al Searfus, was a difficult man to live with. He was cruel, controlling, and mentally and verbally abusive. Katherine was the only member of the family who ever dared to argue with the man. Despite his many indiscretions and his abusive personality, their mother never complained. She always backed her husband, as long as she held a gin and tonic in her hand.

Katherine's brother became the "pleaser" of the family. His role in the dysfunctional mess was to appease everyone, especially their father. Richard had been a lonely child. As he grew, he strived to gain their father's love and respect. Sadly, he couldn't come close, nobody could. Al Searfus held a high status of perfection that was unobtainable. Katherine had learned that lesson early on, but her younger brother was different.

Where she was the nonconformist, the war protestor and the hippie, Richard was her complete opposite. He was a young Republican, a supporter of the Vietnam War, a puppet who blindly followed their father's instructions. Katherine had loved her brother and that was why she had always been disgusted to watch Richard beg for their coldhearted father's acceptance.

Katherine had always been the rebel in the family, and she refused to give in to his unrealistic demands. Instead, she spent many hours of her youth arguing with her father, episodes that always turned into arguments with her mother too.

Even though Patricia could barely stand during most of the fights, she always took Al's side on everything. Katherine would scream and yell and eventually storm out of the house. Sometimes she would stay away for days at a time, but eventually her brother would find her. He would beg her to come home, and with Rich's persistent pleading she would always go back to the dysfunctional household. When Katherine graduated from high school in 1966 she was finished with all of them.

At this point in her life she chose to become one of the hundreds of lost children who drifted into San Francisco. It was there, during the craziness of the hippie era, that she technically grew up. During that time, she alienated herself from her father's influence and for the first time she dared to become her own person.

Her hard earned freedom was short lived. A year and a half later her brother was killed and her father drew her back into the family, where she would remain enslaved forever.

How many promises had been made to her? And how foolish had she been to believe them? Katherine had given up her dreams, goals, values, and beliefs when she went home, rejoining the "establishment." She gave up on herself and became her parents' definition of "prim, proper and respectable."

She married the man her father wanted her to; a young executive in the company. She followed the path her father chose for her; the one society agreed with, the one all her friends said was right. She had gone home. Now, nearing the end of her life, she realized how wrong she had been; how wrong they had all been!

She had been right, all those years before, when she'd left home. She had been on the right course then. Why on earth had she doubted herself? Why had she let her insecurities get the best of her? She had been the one who allowed her belief system to cave in. She couldn't blame that on anyone else. That had been her doing.

Here she was, sixty-six years old, served with divorce papers this morning, and losing the fortune that had been promised to her.

Katherine tried to concentrate on the road. She noticed that the pounding rain was easing up. Now a misty drizzle was landing on the windshield. It was time to make her move. She had been following the Nissan far too long. On the next straight way, she swerved into the opposite lane and flew past the red car. Now the road was open in front of her. She increased her speed and switched the headlights to high beam.

The next curve was tricky but she easily maneuvered the car without sliding. Once she was safely around the bend she leaned forward and turned up the radio's volume, blasting Janis Joplin's "Take a Piece of my Heart". Katherine could feel the vibrations of the stereo through the shaking wheel that she clung to. Ahead, there was another straight way. She accelerated.

What if she crashed the car? What would the outcome be? Her children might miss her for a moment or two, but that would be short lived. Mark had already replaced her, so he wouldn't care. Both of her parents were long dead, and her brother had died before them. Who did she really have, a few friends at best? When she was no longer a corporate wife with a country club membership would they still be around?

Katherine wasn't kidding herself. There was nowhere to go from here, and very little time left to get there. Her life had been played out and it had been played out badly.

The rain became stronger. It wasn't hailing, but it was heavy enough to impair visibility to nearly nothing. Another curve. She didn't do as well on this one. The Porsche's tail spun and the car started to slide across the pavement, but Katherine corrected it before any damage was done. Another straight way and an "S" curve came up suddenly.

This time, the car skidded to the left and ran into a stone embankment. She stopped briefly but didn't get out to check on the damage. She took a deep breath and rested her head against the steering wheel for several seconds. Once she had renewed her courage she restarted the car. Katherine spun the steering wheel a hundred and eighty degrees so she could get back on the wet road going in the right direction.

The minor impact slowed her down. Her hands shook and the car rattled. She had obviously damaged the front end, but how badly she wasn't sure.

She could tell that her bumper was hanging partway off because she could hear it scraping on the pavement.

She had driven about a hundred feet when the bumper came flying off and hit a tree behind her. Luckily, the road was deserted. She looked for the car that she had passed several miles back but it was nowhere around.

With the bumper off, the car felt normal. Katherine accelerated. This time she wasn't speeding; in fact, she was going under the speed limit. Once the adrenaline wore off, however, her mind drifted and the car's speed increased.

Katherine remembered all those years she'd spent in a loveless marriage and she cringed. All the years she had dedicated to her children, forsaking herself, and the years she had been manipulated by her father and then her husband. Now she was being discarded, tossed to the side, replaced. This was her reward for giving up her life and following the path that her parents convinced her was right? She was sixty-six years old; what could she make of herself now? It was too late to change things, she couldn't start over and she couldn't go back.

There really was nowhere to go from here.

Katherine looked in her rearview mirror and saw headlights coming around the last bend. She sped up and took the next corner at a faster pace. It had started to rain again and the downpour on the road made it even slipperier. Katherine didn't care; she wasn't here to go anywhere. She was here, driving in the pouring rain on a winding roadway to weigh her options, and at the moment she didn't believe that she had any.

The Porches' headlights had been damaged in the crash. Instead of two separate beams, the two joined into one large, irregular spotlight. The result was a cross-eyed illumination pattern on the pavement. Despite new blind spots that the damage had created, Katherine ignored the danger and increased her speed. She pushed her foot lower on the accelerator and felt the car kick forward.

She turned the stereo up louder, drowning out the sound of the rain. "Mr. Fantasy" rang out. Another song that took her back to a time in her life that was much simpler. A time that was long dead and long gone. Her right foot pressed down on the accelerator and she felt the car leap forward.

Then she made a dire mistake. Thinking that she was heading into a straightway she sped up. In the next second she saw a curve that she wasn't expecting, a curve that seemed as if it had come out of nowhere. Katherine tried to downshift, hoping that her gears would slow her, but she knew she was in trouble when she glanced at the speedometer. She was traveling at sixty miles per hour. There was no way she was going to make this turn.

The tail of the car spun, and this time Katherine wasn't able to correct it. Miraculously, the car made three complete spins and didn't hit anything. Katherine thought that she might stop intact. On the fourth rotation, her luck ran out.

The car hit the guardrail and tore it off its frame, and Katherine's car plunged down the hillside. The windshield broke and small pieces of safety glass flew everywhere. Rain and debris entered the car, hitting her in the face and chest. She tried shielding herself but there was only so much she could block out.

Something hit her in the forehead and she felt warm blood running into her eyes. The top of the hillside was bare of trees, which was why the Porsche made it halfway down the embankment before she was faced with another problem. When the ravine divided into two possible paths, she realized that she wasn't going to be able to steer towards either one. She watched helplessly as her car went straight into a grove of redwoods.

Time seemed to stand still. The car hit a small tree and then it started to roll. Another twenty yards and the car collided with one of the tallest trees in the woods. The hood caved in and the air bag burst into life, knocking the wind out of Katherine.

She could tell that her legs had been shoved close to her body and she was sure that they were broken. She didn't feel pain, not at that moment, but she knew it would come.

Apart from the steam that hissed from the radiator, the woods became quiet, the car settled, and life in the forest resumed. When she realized that the car had stopped, she took inventory of her injuries. She was unaware of the extent of her wounds but she knew that she wasn't walking away from this accident.

Minutes passed. She became cold and thirsty. She tried to move her legs, but she couldn't. Then she simply gave in, closed her eyes, and drifted off as a feeling of peace washed over her, and darkness engulfed her.

***

The sound of the crash radiated through the deserted back road. Blinding rain wasn't able to drown out the sound of squealing tires and the impact the blue Boxster made as it hit the wet hillside. At first, the car seemed as if it would stop, but it was only a momentary pause. Once the mudslide started, the car rolled with the slushing mess down a thirty-foot embankment and ran head first into a giant redwood. There, the car rocked slightly as the torrent of mud and rocks continued to pour down the side of the hill. Steam exploded from the hood and the smell of hot oil filled the air.

Once the car stopped, nothing else moved. The country road became quiet, unnaturally still. Not a sound was heard except for the gush of steam that continued to burst from the engine. A car came around the curve, hesitated slightly, and then parked on the side of the road. A man and woman, who looked to be in their late 40s, got out and followed the tire marks to the edge of the cliff.

"Look there, do you see it?" Tom Shaw said to his wife, a short blonde woman who was standing a few paces behind him, trying to cover her head from the torrential rain. "Alice, it's that Porsche that was all over the road, it's down in the gully. Do you see the head lights?" Both leaned forward, looking between the evergreens and found that if they squinted their eyes just right, they could indeed see a faint light and rising steam that twinkled in the darkness.

"What are you doing, Tom?" Alice called to her husband. He was heading to a large area off the side of the road where the incline wasn't as steep.

"I'm going down! You go back to the car, call the police, and stay there." Tom found an area free of rocks and debris and he started climbing down the steep bank.

Alice pushed her soaked hair out of her face and headed back to the car. Inside, she retrieved her phone and dialed emergency services. There she stayed, waiting nervously.

Meanwhile, Tom climbed lower so he could get a closer look at the wreckage. He could smell gasoline and motor oil, and although the car didn't look anywhere close to exploding, he didn't want to take any unnecessary chances. He moved in carefully, studying the condition of the wreckage.

The front of the car encircled a tree and the engine was smoking. The trunk was open and the side door was gone. Satisfied that he wasn't going to get blown to smithereens, he moved in closer until he finally reached the ravine. There, twenty feet away, the blue Porsche sat lodged between the large tree it hit and the one beside it, which had prevented the car from rolling any further down the hill.

He could see an elderly woman trapped behind the steering wheel of the wreckage, but he couldn't tell if she was living or dead. He pushed aside wild raspberry bushes, scratching himself on the heavy thorns, until he reached the driver's side of the car. There he bent and examined the woman, whose greying head lay awkwardly against the steering wheel. He reached towards her and gently placed several fingers against her neck, smiling when he felt a pulse. He moved backwards and looked at her face; there was blood dripping from her nose and a terrible gash on her forehead. He put a shaking hand on her shoulder and rocked her gently.

"Hey, lady, are you okay? Can you hear me?" She didn't answer. "Lady, help is coming. My wife's called for an ambulance. You just hang in there, okay?"

In the distance, he could hear sirens approaching.

Tom smiled. "You see, here they come. It's the cavalry, they're coming to rescue you," he announced. He stood up straight and shivered, crossed his arms in front of his chest and stood, waiting.

Minutes passed, although in the present situation they felt like hours. Finally, Tom saw two police officers heading down the embankment. Seconds later, an ambulance arrived and three paramedics raced down the hill. When the officers reached the car, a balding cop pushed Tom to the side.

While the paramedics fastened a whiplash collar around Katherine's neck, the cop, who had steered Tom away from the accident, questioned him.

"What's your name, sir?" the officer asked.

"My name's Tom Shaw."

Behind the officer, three paramedics worked skillfully to get the unconscious woman out of the wreckage.

"Mr. Shaw, can you tell us what happened?"

Tom watched as the paramedics strapped Katherine's limp body onto a spine board, where the crew paused long enough to take her vitals.

"My wife and I saw the Porsche, maybe fifteen minutes before it crashed. We were both exiting Highway 192. Alice, my wife, commented on how fast the car was going when it passed us."

"And how fast was that?"

"She was going maybe sixty around the corners and probably close to seventy plus on the straightaways. Much too fast in this weather for this road!"

"And how fast were you driving, Mr. Shaw?" the officer asked as he wiped at his wet face with the back of his hand.

The emergency crew was heading up the hill now, scrambling in the mud so they didn't slide with the seriously injured woman. The patient, still strapped to the board, was unmoving. When they reached the top of the hill and disappeared over the edge of the cliff, Tom's attention returned to the police officer standing beside him.

"I was driving around forty, maybe forty-five. The curves were real slippery. First real rain of the season, as you know; lots of oil on that road. Taking that into consideration, plus the fact that visibility was poor, it's no wonder she went off the road."

Above them, Tom could see flashing lights, and then the siren went on and the ambulance sped away.

"Mr. Shaw, are you suggesting that the driver was trying to kill herself?"

Tom hesitated for a few seconds, considering the question carefully. Finally he nodded. "Yes, maybe I am. Even if a person had been drinking they wouldn't drive like that, especially in weather like this. So yes, officer, I think there's a possibility that she was driving that way because she wanted to crash."

Chapter 2

Frog stepped out of the yellow Victorian house on Page Street. He turned left and started up the road carrying a beat up canvas bag over his shoulder. Inside the bag he carried his livelihood.

Frog, a twenty-two year old former college student, recently turned dropout hippie, supported himself with his crafts and through skillful trade. His life was a series of business dealings. He sold his art to the tourists that drove through the Haight and then he made his daily trading rounds.

On the weekends he followed a rigid schedule, which involved getting up with the sun, organizing his things, and being out the door by 6:00 a.m. It was a proven fact in the Haight-Ashbury District that the early bird really did catch the worm. On a good Saturday he could sell out his stock by noon, head back to the house to replenish his load, and be back on the street for the evening business.

He thought of himself as one of the young entrepreneurs of the Haight. The way that he and his fellow "business minded" friends figured it, they could enjoy this crazy lifestyle while still planning for a comfortable future. A true businessman could make a killing in Haight-Ashbury. The whole area was a gold mine.

He rotated his merchandise but was sure he always had his basics; macramé jewelry, tie dyed T-shirts, and love beads. Sometimes he was able to scrape up leather remnants and he added crafted watchbands, ponytail holders, headbands, and belts to his stock. Frog would make and sell just about anything. "Anything", of course, amounted to what was popular with the tourists.

Today he was especially pleased with his merchandise. He was able to get a great buy on high quality T-shirts. The result was some vibrant tie-dye that he knew was going to be a big seller. His love beads were unique too. He'd traded some high quality hashish for a margarine tub filled with multicolored glass beads. These were not just any beads, they had come from India and they were different from any that he'd seen in the Haight.

Turning onto Divisadero Street, Frog walked up to Haight Street and made a right turn. This was the start of his normal day. First he would hit the tourists coming into the area to see the "hippies" and buy a copy of *The San Francisco Oracle,* the local hippie paper that was a favorite with the tourists.

He would walk among the cars selling his trinkets to the out-of-towners. Traffic was always heavy, making it easy to walk in between the lanes of cars. Tourists would bravely open their windows a crack to buy odds and ends as they sat patiently in their autos taking in the sights of 'freakish kids' in their natural habitat, kind of like a downtown safari.

After two or three hours of hustling his wares, he could make anywhere from $20-$80. This money made it easy to afford his plush life style. Between his trinket sales and his trade arrangements, he made an above-average income.

His favorite route would take him down the street heading west towards Golden Gate Park, weaving in and out of cars and slowly moving down the road. Generally, he would make a pit stop at the Psychedelic Shop, sometimes making purchases with his hard earned cash, and other times just visiting with his friends, Ron and Jay. Then he would continue on with his travels into Golden Gate Park, where he conducted trade agreements with the locals.

Sometimes his business arrangements would require cash, but often Frog would arrange to trade whatever he had for whatever he needed. This was where his job got complicated. Someone would trade marijuana for his trinkets, then he would use the pot to trade for food and supplies, and occasionally he would do business outside the neighborhood. These outside deals included bringing merchandise into the Haight that wasn't always considered legal, but was always highly desired in his neighborhood.

Today, he was looking for a man called Logan. Rumor had it that Logan had received a stock of fresh vegetables from one of his contacts. Since Frog was the self-proclaimed cook in his household, he always went out of his way to obtain the best ingredients.

Frog lived in a commune he shared with five other people. Each of these individuals held jobs within the household, which was how they paid their way. Rent in the Haight was inexpensive.

At one time the area had been an exclusive neighborhood with beautiful Victorian homes and quaint "mom and pop" shops. All of that changed quite suddenly when an influx of homeless youths arrived, bringing property prices down. Soon after their arrival, houses were unable to sell at all. Many owners, desperate to leave the neighborhood, simply rented out their homes or left them uninhabited.

These vacant houses became squatter communes, where a multitude of youths, mostly minors and runaways, lived. Some of these houses became drug-infested hellholes. In these houses, anyone was welcome to "flop". They were packed with kids who were filthy and strung out on drugs. The houses sometimes smelled so foul that the odors could be detected from the street. This type of housing situation wasn't acceptable to Frog.

He lived in a Victorian home that was managed by one of the inhabitants. Ron Diebel's grandmother was the actual owner. Like most of the older generation, she had vacated the residence two years ago when the "undesirables" moved in. Ron had made a deal with her; he would live in the house and maintain the property. Her main concern at the time was warding off the destruction of her home that she had witnessed in many of her neighbors' houses. Ron promised to keep the house in good condition, keep the runaways out, and only allow responsible tenants who would contribute to the maintenance and cleanliness of the home.

Ron took his promise seriously and he was strict with his tenants, which was the main reason Frog wanted to live there. Theirs was a responsible home, with good people. A safe place in the Haight, clean and respectable. It was a place where Frog felt wanted and welcome. He, as well as his roommates, wanted to keep it that way.

Ron paid the rent to his grandmother by keeping the household going. Everything was in working order and well cared for. They had running water and electricity; not all the houses in the area could claim that honor these days.

To live in the house one had to contribute to the welfare of the others. Of course, there were bills to be paid, and these were split between the inhabitants. There were chores to be divided. Frog had always been a natural in the kitchen and was thrilled to be nominated as the cook of the commune. This was a job that he took seriously, and that's why Frog was looking for Logan this morning.

Logan was a local chameleon who was able to fit in anywhere. While conducting business in Haight-Ashbury, he looked like any of the inhabitants, with long hair, love beads, torn jeans, and a faded T-shirt. But Logan did not stick to this section of the city. He also conducted business with the Hells Angels in the Dogpatch, and even some of the businessmen down on Market Street. Simply stated, Logan got around. If there was a need of any kind, and the possibility of making some fast cash, then he was available.

When dealing with Logan, there was one rule and one rule only; never ask him where he got his supplies, or who he did business with. He had seen his business acquaintances become irate on several occasions when he'd been asked either of these questions. Once he had knocked a hippie into a metal street post for that blunder. The result was a broken nose, but it could have been much worse.

The reason that Frog got along well with the fellow traders was his calm demeanor. He could get along with practically anyone. It was an art form; keeping his mouth shut, never invading another's space, especially if they were drugged-out, and minding his own business. That was why he usually got the best deals in the neighborhood. Everyone knew him, everyone liked him, and everyone knew where they could find him. It was a practical business technique that always kept Frog in the fold of everything that happened in the Haight. He knew the "in" people and he knew how to get things done, how to get items moved in or out of the neighborhood, and most importantly, how to keep his mouth shut.

Today, Logan was conducting business in an alley off Beulah Street. Generally, larger items were traded in this area, it was large enough to pull a truck into and was seldom used by the general public. There were mostly houses in the area, a few small apartments in the upper buildings, and in one corner there was a large garage that Logan often rented when he had items that needed to be displayed, such as vegetables.

To get to Beulah Street and the side alley, Frog had to walk down Page Street where old Roman's Market sat on one of the main corners. Everyone in the Haight used this small convenience store for odds and ends like cigarettes, sodas, and candy. It was also a popular place for street kids to beg money from passersby.

Frog walked past Roman's Market and then stopped in his tracks. Something looked out of place. At first he couldn't figure out what the difference was; he only knew that it existed. He stood for a few seconds and decided to walk back to the store, figuring he could use a cold drink anyway. On his way back to the market, he surveyed the corner, trying to discern why the storefront looked so different this morning. And then it struck him. Old Guthrie was not on his usual corner.

Guthrie was an old-timer who lived on the streets. He looked to be in his eighties, but he was really much younger. The streets aged you, plain and simple. Guthrie was probably in his sixties but his harsh life on the streets had taken a toll on him, and his face resembled heavily grained leather.

Guthrie was a mascot to the street community of the Haight. He lived next door to Roman's market in an abandoned doorway and had done so for years. In fact, he was there before the youth of America had claimed the area as their own. Some said he had grown up in the neighborhood, but no one knew for sure since the old man had stopped talking to anyone years before.

The owner of the market, Mike Eldridge, and some of the other locals felt sorry for Guthrie and tried to make sure that he was fed. As a result, the old man never went without food because someone would always share with him. Even the kids on the street that were down and out made sure that Guthrie was taken care of. The kids looked up to him like an elder statesman.

Today, Guthrie was missing. His shopping cart full of belongings was still in its usual spot, but Guthrie was nowhere to be seen. Frog crossed the street and searched the area. The only place that Guthrie would venture was to the tree in the back of the alley, but he wasn't there either.

Frog walked up the street and searched other doorways and then he asked some of the street kids if they had seen him. Surprisingly, no one was even aware that Guthrie was missing. Frog walked into the market, got a Coke out of the refrigerator, and placed it on the counter. In the background "White Rabbit" played softly on an old transistor radio that had tin foil wrapped around the antenna.

"Hey, Mike, did you know that old Guthrie's not out there?"

Mike was reading a newspaper and smoking a cigarette. He looked up at Frog through a haze of blue smoke. "What? Sorry man, I wasn't listening." Mike folded the paper and laid it on the counter in front of him.

"Old Guthrie, he's not out there this morning." Frog tossed a few coins on the counter and then opened his drink.

"He's probably in the alley taking a piss."

"No, I checked the alley and I even walked down the block a ways to look for him. He's not out there and none of the kids on the corner saw him walk off either. Did you see him at all today?"

Mike finished putting the coins in the register and took a long drag off his cigarette before answering. "Yeah, he was out there when I got here at 7:00. I gave him a donut and a cup of coffee. Seemed like his regular silent self, nothing out of the ordinary."

Frog walked over to the door and peered outside. "Well, he's not out there."

Mike walked around the counter over to the open door and looked outside. Then he called out to one of the kids standing on the corner. "Hey, Nate, is old Guthrie out there anywhere?"

A sandy-blond kid with greasy hair looked around and shook his head. "No man. I already told Frog that we ain't seen him for hours. None of us saw him leave either. Kerry Bug walked up the street a few times too, but now she said he's missing. His stuff is still here though, so I guess he's coming back. We'll keep an eye out for him and I'll let you know when we see him."

Mike nodded and then turned away from the door and headed back to his side of the sales counter. He took one last drag off his cigarette then disposed of it in an overflowing ashtray. "You're right, that's an oddity alright. I've owned this place for the past five years and I've never known him to wander off. Very strange. I hope nothing's happened to the old fool!"

"Listen, man, I got some business to take care of but I'll stop by later to see if he shows up. Hopefully he'll turn up unscathed. Probably just out taking a much deserved tour of the neighborhood."

"Yeah, let's hope you're right". Mike picked up his newspaper and lit another cigarette, settled himself on his stool, and resumed reading.

Frog walked out the door and looked at Nate, who shook his head. Guthrie was still missing. As Frog walked down the street he continued to look for the old man, but there was no sign of him.

By the time he hit Shrader Street, he was no longer thinking about the missing old-timer, he was planning the rest of his day. He would make this trade with Logan, stop by the house and put the vegetables away. Then he would load up his bag with trinkets and be back on the street by 3:00 p.m. That would give him a few hours of sales before he had to start dinner for the commune.

If he was lucky, he'd be able prepare dinner quickly and then work on his tie dyed shirts in the kitchen for a couple of hours. This evening he planned to stop by the Psychedelic Shop and smoke a joint or two with Ron and Jay.

This will be a good day, Frog thought.

He whistled to himself as he walked the rest of the way to Logan's makeshift market.

Frog was wrong. Today was going to be anything but ordinary. In a few minutes a series of events would take place and the whole world as Frog knew it would be turned upside down.

***

Logan's market was already crowded when Frog arrived. He wasn't concerned though. His friend always kept part of his stock for his "special customers" in the back. The only inconvenience would be the waiting time. He had hoped to pop in and out quickly, but by the looks of things, that wouldn't be happening today.

Frog took a deep breath and wove between the bodies. After a few steps, he was able to spot his business associate. In the far left corner Logan stood under a blue tarp talking to one of the other street vendors.

Cody, a weather beaten hippie in his mid-twenties, seemed to be complaining about something. When Frog walked up, Cody was scratching his sun-bleached hair in frustration. Logan turned, and seeing Frog approaching, beckoned him over with a large smile. Frog knew from experience that this was a bad sign. He was not fond of getting involved in other people's disputes and it looked like he wasn't going to be able to weasel his way out of this one.

"Hey, man, good to see you." Logan slapped Frog on the back and immediately tried to draw him into the conversation. "Listen, I was telling Cody here about interest. Last week we swapped some merchandise that cost a bit more than he had available. Being the compassionate character that I am, I graciously added the remainder of his bill to my credit list. The agreement was that the amount plus interest was to be paid before our next transaction. Well, Cody is here to conduct business, which I am more than happy to do after his last bill and the interest are paid."

Frog cringed. Now he knew that this was going to get ugly and he was right here in the middle of it.

"Fucking bull faced lie, Logan! Don't listen to him, Frog. He's full of shit."

The two men started to face-off, but Frog put his hands on both of their chests to separate them. "Wait, both of you stop for a minute." Frog eased the men apart and stood between them. He flipped his face from side to side so he could make eye contact with each of them. "Cody, tell me your side. And Logan he listened to you, so please back away and let him talk okay?" Logan didn't answer but he did take a few steps back to give Cody and Frog some room.

Before answering, Cody scratched his filthy hair again. Frog, who was now concerned about catching lice, also took a few steps back.

"Look, Frog, last week, Logan here was trading some speed for weed. We agreed on a price, but when we're meeting to make the deal, Logan tries to tell me that I misunderstood him. Suddenly the price is up and I swear it was a scam. I've been doing business with Logan here for a long time, so I let the insult go. I figured maybe it was a mistake, my mistake, so I agreed, for the sake of peace. Which, by the way, I am a defender of. I told him I would be happy to pay the new price, but he would need to give me a few days to coordinate things. See, I had already adjusted my stock so I could pay the first, or what I *thought* was the first, amount. If he wanted to change prices on me in the middle of a deal fine, but give me a few days to work on things. It's only fair, Frog." Cody stopped his story cold and stared into Frog's eyes, looking for agreement.

Frog nodded convincingly and Cody continued.

"Right, so we agree to meet today to settle things. I got what he asked me to and I'm ready to pay up. I also got a business agreement to discuss with him, and that's where the interest part suddenly comes in. I'm trying to conduct business with him and he refuses to talk to me until I pay him interest! Well, I swear man, he never said anything about interest last week, 'cause if he had, I would have told him to shove his stash up his ass. After all, he already increased the amount on me once and I overlooked that, but I'm not about to do it again. I'm not paying any fucking interest and I'm not doing business with him again. In fact, if I was you, Frog, I'd be watching my back around him because he's a cheat and a liar!"

Cody pointed at Logan and the two men approached each other. This time, Frog yelled and when he did, everyone in the market stood completely still. All eyes turned towards them and Frog felt his face turn beat red.

Great! Frog thought. *Not only am I in the middle of this shit, now everyone in the market knows it. By nightfall it will be all over the Haight. So much for my diplomatic reputation.*

Frog turned his attention away from the unwanted audience and back to the two men beside him. Now, more than ever, he was hoping for a way to resolve this embarrassment before it went any further.

"Gentlemen, please, let's talk about this, okay? There are a lot of customers around and this can't possibly be good for anyone's business!"

This comment seemed to bring both men to their senses. Frog watched their eyes as they glanced around the marketplace. Noticing that their little disagreement was being witnessed by at least twenty-five locals, they immediately calmed down. When Frog knew he had both men's attention, he addressed them in a voice that was almost a whisper.

"We don't need the whole market to watch us do we? Here's the way I see it. Logan when you quoted him a price there was obviously a misunderstanding. Now, I don't know who made the mistake, or whether anything was intentional, and I don't personally want to know. What I do want is for both of you to look at things another way. There was a mistake made. Cody accepted the new rate without question and he raised the money that you asked him to. He could have gotten mad but he didn't, he went along with the difference in price. I know that the normal way to do business is to charge interest and I fully understand why you would want to do that. But in this case, Logan, can't we just call it even? The two of you have been doing business together for a long time. Do you really want to have a huge rift with one another? After all, we do business with many of the same people. This could blow up in everyone's face if clients start taking sides. Do you know what that's going to do to our business? It means less profits, and I'm not willing to watch that disaster happen. Now, for the sake of all the business minded hippies in the Haight, and on behalf of all of us who are just trying to make a buck, how about ending this peacefully?"

The two men stood staring at each other for a few seconds and then both nodded. Frog stepped out of the way so that they could talk things over. He was able to breathe a sigh of relief. Perhaps this mess could still end peacefully and business could be restored.

"Cody, man, you made good on our deal so I guess I can drop the interest," Logan said amiably. "How about we just call this a misunderstanding and go on like it never happened?" He held his hand out in a peace offering.

"Right, I'll agree to that, Logan." The two men shook hands and peace was restored.

Frog looked around happily, noticing that they were no longer the center of attention. The market had returned to normal. Locals were shopping and trading as if the incident had never happened.

"I'm glad that you're talking to each other again, and I hate to interrupt that, but I got a lot going on today. Logan, could we finish our business? 'Cause I really got to be going, man."

"Sure thing, Frog. Cody, stick around a few minutes. Let me finish with Frog here and then we can talk about new business."

"Yeah, I can do that. Hey, Frog, thanks a lot, man." Cody took Frog by surprise when he suddenly bear hugged him. Frog wasn't sure what his response should be, so he just stood there until Cody pulled away from the embrace.

"Anytime, Cody, anytime."

With that, Logan and Frog headed to the very back of the garage. Logan opened a side storage door, and Frog handed over a package wrapped in brown paper and tied with string. Logan weighed the item with a scale and then whistled.

"Nice!"

Without another word, Logan placed the bundle in the storage compartment, shut the door and then fastened a padlock on the outside. Obviously happy with the deal, Logan pointed towards a wooden box in the corner and slapped Frog on the back.

"There's your box of first rate veggies, my friend. When will you be back for the rest that I owe you?"

Frog walked over to the corner and picked up the wooden box. He quickly checked his produce and then turned towards Logan. "I was hoping I could run an ongoing tab with you for the rest. That way when you get some fresh items in you can let me know and I can come and get them."

"Yeah, you can do that if you want. I might have some nice fruit coming in next week. Nothing exotic, just apples and pears, but if you're interested I can box some of those up for you."

The two men walked towards the front of the market. Frog was trying to hurry the conversation along in hopes of finally getting home. This market trip delay was going to cut into his evening schedule. If he hurried, he still might get some tie-dye done before going out this evening. Maybe not as much as he had hoped for, but at least he'd be able to get a few shirts finished.

"Yeah, a box of mixed fruits and vegetables would be great. Well, I'd like to stay and chat for a while but business takes me elsewhere." Logan nodded and Frog walked off. After taking a few steps he heard Logan calling his name and he turned around.

"Hey, Frog, thanks again, man!"

Frog smiled, waved and continued on. As he walked out of the alley, Frog glanced at his watch. It was 3:30p.m. He'd been at the market for nearly an hour. He shook his head. Although he was glad that he'd been able to intervene and stop a potential disaster, he was not happy that he had to adjust his schedule.

He made a left on Beulah Street, walked several small blocks, and then turned right on Shrader, heading back towards Haight Street. He walked, lost in his own thoughts, thinking about the vegetarian lasagna he was going to make for dinner, when a large shape stepped out in front of him.

Frog was startled. He jumped, and when he did the crate of vegetables fell out of his hands. The box hit the curb and spilled its contents on the roadway.

"What the fuck?"

Frog was more concerned over his spilt vegetables than with the figure before him. He knelt on the sidewalk and started gathering the tomatoes that were lying in the street. After salvaging what he could, Frog placed the remainder of his groceries back in the now broken crate.

"Hey man, what's your problem?" Frog finally looked at the man who was standing in front of him. When he did, Frog nearly dropped the crate again. Old Guthrie stood motionless, staring at him. The look on the old man's face was shocking. His skin was pale and his blue eyes were bloodshot.

"Guthrie, are you okay? What are you doing all the way down here?"

Guthrie didn't move. He just stood perfectly still, staring at Frog.

"Listen, why don't you walk with me? Mike and the kids down at the market have been looking for you, man. They'll be glad to see you're okay."

Guthrie raised his right hand and pointed his index finger directly into Frog's face. And then he did something that no one in the Haight had ever experienced before. Old mute Guthrie spoke , and when he did, his voice had a chilling quality.

"This time, Frog, you must not ignore the signs. You've been through this once before and you made the wrong choices. You have one more chance to get this right. You must have an open mind and you must believe what you see. Remember, all is not what you think it is." Guthrie dropped his arm, turned, and then headed in the opposite direction.

"Guthrie, wait! What are you saying? Where are you going? Stop for a second!" Frog gathered his broken crate, holding the cracked board securely in both hands, and started to follow the old man. He had to stop his pursuit when a second slat in the crate gave way and his groceries fell again.

"Damn. How am I going to get this lot home?" Frog removed his sweatshirt and tied it around the crate to secure it. Once he was convinced that the package was sturdy he looked up. Old Man Guthrie was gone.

Frog's generally cool demeanor was shaken. The whole day was going wrong. All he wanted was to get his groceries home in one piece and then start dinner. He shook his head and hoped that he wouldn't have any more unexpected surprises. He walked up the street slowly, cradling his vegetables in his arms. His conscience got the better of him. Instead of heading straight home, he had to stop by Old Roman's Market and check on Guthrie. Hopefully, the old man had headed back to his doorway, but the day was going so strangely that Frog wasn't certain of anything at this point.

His trip was slow going. The fragile condition of the crate required several stops to retie the sweatshirt. He was hoping to snag a large bag at the market before the whole crate gave away.

By the time he reached Roman's, he had given up the idea of working on tie-dye shirts. He would be lucky to get dinner made and cleaned up before it was time for his evening rounds.

Nate met him at the corner and helped him with his load. They set the crate down next to the building. Frog untied the sweatshirt, and then placed it over his box of vegetables. When he was finished, he looked up and noticed old Guthrie sleeping in his doorway, home.

"He got back about ten minutes ago. He went straight to his spot, settled himself down and crashed. He looks like shit too, I mean, more than he usually does. I wonder what the hell he's been up to."

"Did he say anything when he got back?" Frog asked.

Nate gave him an odd look and shook his head. "*Say* anything? You know old Guthrie doesn't talk. No, he didn't say anything. Why would you ask that?"

"Well, he talked to me!" Frog answered. "He jumped out of nowhere on Shrader Street and caused me to drop my crate of vegetables. Then he went into some 'prophesy' bullshit and walked off. Weirdest damn thing ever."

By now, Mike was standing outside of the store listening to the conversation. He took a deep drag from his cigarette and then tossed the butt down next to the doorstep.

"Talked to you?" Mike was now laughing. "What shit you been smoking, boy? Guthrie hasn't spoken in the five years that I've been here."

"Yeah, I know, man, but he sure made up for it today. Seriously, he gave me some speech about fixing mistakes. Scared the shit out of me too."

Mike lit another Camel and walked into the store. When he came out, he had several large paper bags that he handed to Frog.

"Listen, Frog, don't be telling everyone that Old Guthrie talked to you. You have a reputation to maintain. You don't want the locals around here thinking that you've lost your marbles, do you?"

"Right, believe what you want Mike, but I'm telling you that old man can talk and when he does, he's fucking spooky too."

"Yeah, I got it, Frog, he's a prophet." Mike walked back into the store laughing.

Frog took another look at Guthrie, who was sleeping peacefully in the next doorway, and then he started to bag his groceries. Nate stood back, silently watching.

"What! Aren't you gonna laugh at me too kid?" Frog ended up with two bags of vegetables. He had to dispose of several tomatoes because they were squashed and dirty. When he was done, he threw the broken crate and the unusable food items into a nearby dumpster.

"Nah, I'm not going to laugh at you, Frog," Nate said. "Strange stuff happens all the time. If he really did talk to you, maybe you should seriously consider what he told you. I mean, the guy hasn't spoken in years, right? If he decided to talk, then there must have been a damn good reason. I don't know what he told you, but consider this: Why would he talk today and why did he choose to talk to *you*? All I'm saying is, before you write this off to his mental state and a seriously freaky day, maybe you should think about it."

Frog gathered his items, handed a few tomatoes to Nate, who gladly accepted them.

"Sure, man. I'll think about it, okay? If he wanders off again, let me know." Frog turned away from the store carrying his two bags of groceries and made his way down the street.

He tried to forget about the incident with Old Guthrie but found he couldn't. Nate's words kept echoing through his mind. *Why did the old man wander off? Why did he choose today to talk?* And as Nate had so clearly pointed out, *Why did he decide to talk to me?*

Although he wanted to put the experience behind him, he decided to heed Nate's advice. Perhaps he should think about Guthrie's words, despite how bizarre the incident had been.

What if there was some strange truth hidden somewhere inside?

Chapter 3

Katherine faded in and out of consciousness. Images of the past and present drifted through her mind. For a time, she thought she was dead, then she realized that, between the blinking red lights and the loud siren, she was in an ambulance. That meant she had lived through the crash.

She could flutter her eyes but had no other muscle control. She could hear what was happening around her, but her sense of reality was surreal, as if she were in an underwater tunnel. Sounds echoed some, making little or no sense. Above all the other noises she heard the sound of the siren, blaring through the night.

As the paramedics worked to stabilize her condition, Katherine felt as if she were floating on a cloud. Her sense of sight continued to cut in and out, so that one second her world was black and in the next, she could see a distorted vision of the inside of the ambulance. Colors ran together, forming pools of new colors. Every item above her spread rainbows through the cab as they moved along the wet highway. When she could focus, she saw what must have been the medical staff, but they looked more like animals than humans and they faded in and out of their surroundings like ghosts in the night. Suddenly, the world went black and she remained in total darkness.

She could tell that she was outside of the ambulance. Someplace cold and windy, like a tunnel that was submerged in total blackness. A draft so numbing it seemed to spread icicles along Katherine's flesh continued to blow around her, wrapping its slithery wet fingers around her body in an attempt to pull her backwards. Before it succeeded, however, she broke free and again she was back in the brightly lit ambulance.

"That was close; we almost lost her. How far are we from Highland Hospital?" a male voice asked.

"About three minutes," a woman replied.

Several minutes passed. The doors flew open, Katherine was lifted out, and was met by a multitude of medical staff. They ran down a long hallway, pushing her gurney towards an empty emergency room. Once inside, they lifted her onto an examining table where a crowd of medical personnel probed and prodded her body. Despite the concern of being unable to move, Katherine realized there was no pain. Considering the ordeal going on around her, she assumed that feeling, or her lack thereof, was a bad sign.

Eventually, a young doctor, looking into her eyes with a flashlight, started to ask her questions.

"Mrs. Rhodes, can you hear me? You've been in a very bad accident and we need to take you into surgery. If you can understand me, blink your eyes."

Katherine wanted to, but she couldn't. The fluttering of her eyes was unintentional after all. Even something small like eye control was temporarily out of her reach. The doctor waited a few moments, turned sadly to the nurse beside him and said, "Let's get some blood into her and move her into the operating room. Has anyone tried to contact the family?"

"We've tried to contact her kids but they both seem to be out of the country. We finally got ahold of her husband, but he informed us that he and Mrs. Rhodes are estranged. We tried to convince him this was a real emergency and not just a, 'show for attention' by his soon to be ex-wife. He said he would continue trying to locate his children. Apparently, they're in a remote location in Asia on company business. He also refused to be a hospital contact and asked to have his name removed from our records."

"Sounds like a great guy," the doctor snorted. "Go ahead and take Mr. Frankenstein's name off of the medical records. Let's get her into surgery!"

Katherine was moved down a different hallway, up an elevator, and into a seventh floor operating room. As the gurney moved, she tried to absorb what she had heard. Even though she wasn't able to communicate, surprisingly, she could hear and understand what was happening around her. Of course they couldn't find her children; sometimes she wouldn't hear from them for months at a time. They generally only surfaced if they needed something, or at holidays when they expected something from her. Other than that, they were always away on business.

As for her husband, she knew Mark was coldhearted but she would never have expected him to be this unfeeling. She had spent thirty-eight years of her life with the man, supporting him through all of his business and personal decisions. He had robbed her dry and now he refused to be her hospital contact? Even the medical staff thought that he was a bastard, apparently, and in some dark, humorous way, she found that funny.

The operating crew met her gurney on the seventh floor and rushed her into the room that was packed with instruments and monitors. They gently lifted her crumpled body to an adjacent table and sedated her. The next thing Katherine knew she was floating in the darkness and the black icicle fingers were reaching for her ravished body again.

***

When Frog got home he was mentally drained. Today had been anything but easy. He was looking forward to putting the whole mess behind him. He anticipated a nice quiet kitchen where he could cook dinner and lose himself for an hour of therapeutic artistry. As he rounded the corner leading towards the kitchen he saw that the room wasn't empty. One of his roommates, Moonbeam, was sitting at the kitchen table with papers spread out all around her.

Frog rolled his eyes; he couldn't believe his luck. *No, no, no,* he thought, *why is everything so fucked up today?* He took a step into the kitchen and Moonbeam looked up, startled.

"Oh, sorry," Frog muttered, heading for the furthest counter in the kitchen by the avocado colored refrigerator.

He scurried along, trying desperately not to meet her gaze. He hoped that if he didn't turn around to look at her, she would disappear.

"Hi, Frog," Moonbeam said, way too cheerfully.

No such luck. Moonbeam didn't disappear. She jumped out of her chair and happily danced towards him. She hovered, waiting for Frog to turn around. He didn't. She waited a few silent seconds and then tapped him on the shoulder.

"I was hoping you'd be home soon. I was afraid you'd forgotten about tonight, Frog."

"Of course not," he lied. Not only had he forgotten about tonight, he'd made other plans that he was looking forward to! Now he would have to cancel with Roy and Jay.

Several weeks ago, Frog had agreed to take Moonbeam to a friend's party. Actually, it was payment for a favor that she had agreed to. Frog had to leave the city for a weekend on an extended business trip. Meanwhile, Moonbeam filled in for him on several of his local duties. In exchange, Frog had agreed to take her and her eccentric friend Katie to a party outside the Haight District.

Frog loved to party. He lived in the party capitol of the world, for crying out loud. That was not the problem. This party was different, however, and it was with folks that he would rather never party with, the Hells Angels.

The biker community in San Francisco frequented an area known as the Dogpatch, a part of the city that was not overwhelmingly friendly to hippies. Generally, the two groups stayed clear of each other and only interacted if they absolutely had to. There had been some nasty clashes between hippies and bikers in the past, and the hippies always came out on the losing side.

Recently, Moonbeam and her crazy friend Katie had met several bikers in Golden Gate Park. Since then, they had been building friendships within the biker community. Tonight the Angels were throwing a huge party at their clubhouse in San Francisco and, of course, Moonbeam and Katie were invited. Because the party was clear across town, and in an area where it might not be the best idea for two hippie girls to wander around by themselves, Frog had been recruited.

Frog had met the group of bikers before and all was peaceful, but tonight there would undoubtedly be a lot of alcohol and drugs. The idea of bikers, hippies, drugs, and alcohol in the same room made him a little uneasy, which was why the idea of escorting the two girls to the party was such a sour thought. But a deal was a deal. Like it or not, Frog was going to a biker party tonight.

"Don't be nervous, Froggy, you're going to have a great time!" Moonbeam said and then proceeded to dance around the kitchen.

"Frog!" he groaned.

"What?" Moonbeam stopped twirling and smiled at him.

"The name is Frog, as in I jump from project to project, completing them all I might add. The name is not Froggy. I am not a froggy that lives in a fucking creek!"

"Don't be a drag, Froggy. You agreed to go so don't be nasty because you don't want to. It will be groovy, honey, I promise."

Frog silently ground his teeth together. How someone he liked so much could get on his nerves so badly he wasn't sure. Out of all his roommates, Moonbeam was his favorite, but there were times when he just wanted to strangle her. This was one of those times.

"I'm not being nasty. I said I'd be cool about this biker thing and I will be, okay? It's just the combination of us and them; well, it kind of makes me nervous." Frog unpacked the groceries and sorted through what he needed for tonight. He placed everything else inside the crisper drawer and then shut the door with his foot. He rummaged for pots and pans in the lower cupboards while Moonbeam continued swirling around the kitchen.

"Katie will be here at six o'clock for dinner. About eight we can make our way down to the bus stop. It should take about a half hour to get to the other side of the city; perfect timing."

"Hey, Miss Go Go girl, how about you clean up the mess you made on the table while I make dinner?"

"That's not a mess, Frog. You know perfectly well that it's my astrological chartings. Want to know what the stars say about us today?"

"Not really. No wait. Yes, I want to know, but let me guess. Do they say that today will be really shitty?"

"Froggy, stop joking. I'm serious."

"So am I! Go on tell me. What do the stars say about us today, Moony?"

"They say it will be a momentous day for all of us. A life changing kind of day; isn't that groovy?"

Frog cleared his throat. Moonbeam was just way too bubbly this afternoon. For a brief second, Frog felt a chill run down the back of his neck, making him shiver. The thought of old Guthrie showing up out of nowhere and delivering his cryptic message ran through Frog's mind, but in the next second he shook the image away. Moonbeam had made many predictions based on her 'readings', and it was startling how many of them actually came true. Was this a prophecy for today, or just another coincidence?

Behind him, Moonbeam gathered her papers and personal items into a neat pile. Thank God she was going to put her stuff away. Now Frog could spread out all the ingredients and use the table.

Frog started to organize his vegetables, ready to take them over to the table area when the doorbell rang. Moonbeam bolted for the door, giving up all thoughts of cleaning the table.

"Wait, the table!" he called out after her, but of course she ignored him.

"Damn that girl," Frog muttered to himself.

Would this day ever end? It just seemed to get worse and worse as it went along.

Frog heard the front door open and then slam. He knew it was Katie because the two girls were giggling happily and commenting on each other's outfits. Several seconds later, they skipped into the kitchen holding hands and sat down at the table. To Frog's dismay, Moonbeam started to rummage through her papers again, and in the next second they were spreading out astrological charts.

"Look, Katie, let me show you the charting for today. There are conjunctions that you will not believe, very unusual."

Both girls leaned in closer to 'read' the chart, pointing at certain aspects and quickly drifting off into their own world. Frog on the other hand had just lost his workstation and was quite annoyed with the two. Sure, he could make a scene and kick them off the table but he had to spend the whole evening with them. Was it really worth it? If he made them mad, this evening could turn out to be a real fucking nightmare. He decided to play things safe. He could confine himself to the small counter top and still make dinner.

He sliced carrots and tomatoes and then put some butter into a pan to heat. The menu had changed to stir-fry tonight; fast, easy, and everyone liked it. Mealtime at the commune had no time limit. Frog would make dinner every day at 6:00.. If his housemates wanted to eat, then they were welcome. If they missed dinner when it was prepared, there was always plenty left over. They had a small toaster oven on the counter that worked great for heating small portions.

Tonight Frog would prepare dinner quickly, get the two girls and himself fed early, and when his other roommates came home they could fend for themselves. Given the choice, Frog would gladly stay here and serve dinner all evening, but that was not going to happen. No, tonight Frog was going to escort two attractive, crazy hippie girls to a Hells Angels party in the Dogpatch. Frog swallowed hard, focused on the task at hand, and chopped another carrot.

***

Annie Sullivan had moved away from the San Francisco Bay Area in the 80s. She had married an environmentalist named Jake and moved to a remote area of Washington State so she could be "one" with nature.

After twenty years of marriage, she had decided that country life was not for her, and for that matter, neither was Jake. After putting up with his crazy moneymaking schemes for twenty long years, she'd decided that she needed stability in her life. As a result, she moved back to the Bay Area, took a small apartment in Union City and a job at *The Union City Sun*, a bimonthly local paper. The job was not quite what she wanted, but it was an income.

While she lived in Eagle's Point Washington, she had tried to keep in contact with all of her friends, but most of them gradually drifted away. The only one who had stayed in her life after her moves was Katherine Searfus.

Katherine and Annie met in late 1966. They were both "lost" children, who'd migrated to San Francisco looking for a better way of life. What they found was rough times and eventual heartbreak. Annie often asked herself how things had gone so wrong. What had seemed so beautiful when they both arrived turned into one unfortunate tragedy after another.

Although they had both had wanted a life different from their parents', in the end they had both returned to the life they had abhorred. All of their visions and ideals had been abandoned and they reassembled with society, accepting the rules and restrictions that went along with it.

Annie hadn't seen Katherine in two years, but at one time they had been inseparable, another set of troubled kids who had drifted into San Francisco in the mid-sixties. Back then, they were filled with dreams of changing the world; they were sisters, they were invincible, and they believed in miracles.

This particular morning, Annie walked through the lobby of Highland Hospital in a daze. Last night she had gone to bed early and had been awakened by a disturbing phone call in the middle of the night. Mark Rhodes, Katherine's soon to be ex-husband, had called to tell her that her friend had been in a terrible accident. According to Mark, Katherine had been rushed into emergency surgery. She had made it through the operation, but was now in critical condition. The doctors said that she was in a coma and they weren't sure if she would recover.

After the call, Annie couldn't get back to sleep. She tossed and turned, waiting for daylight. Finally, she gave up, took a shower, had some coffee, and sat at the kitchen table watching the sunrise.

At 7:00 o'clock she called the paper and told her boss that she wasn't coming in. Something inside told her that she wouldn't be able to concentrate at work, not until she had seen Katherine, thinking instinctively of a power she used to believe in, a power that now told her that her friend needed her desperately.

Annie arrived at the nurses' station. Since Katherine had been placed in the intensive care unit, visitors couldn't get into that ward without checking in first. She stood waiting for several minutes. Finally, an overweight nurse with mousy brown hair arrived at the front desk.

"Can I help you?" the woman asked, without looking up.

"Yes, I'm here to see Katherine Rhodes. She's supposed to be in IC 6."

The receptionist typed Katherine's name into the computer and then she shook her head. "I'm sorry, ma'am. Unless you're family, I can't let you in to see that patient."

Annie looked at the woman's nametag before answering. "Ms. Douglas, Katherine doesn't *have* any family. I'm the closest person that she has. If you won't let me in, then she won't have anyone at all," Annie replied in a smooth, friendly voice.

Ms. Douglas continued to shake her head adamantly. "It says here family only. I can check with the head nurse if you'd like, but I don't think she's going to let you in either."

"Yes, please. I'd really appreciate it if you would do that."

The nurse grunted, obviously annoyed with the request. She rose slowly and shuffled out of the room, returning shortly with a tall red-haired woman walking behind her.

"Hello, I'm Doctor Stevens. I understand that you're here to see Katherine Rhodes." She extended her hand and Annie shook it.

"Hello, Doctor. Yes, I am. My name is Annie Sullivan, I'm a very old friend of Katherine's."

Dr. Stevens politely led Annie to a private corner of the room where they could speak without being interrupted. "Actually, I'm very glad to meet you, Ms. Sullivan. We've tried to get ahold of family members, but haven't been very successful. The only person that we were finally able to reach was her ex-husband, and I'm afraid he hasn't been very cooperative. Is there anyone else that we can contact, perhaps a sibling, even a cousin?"

"Doctor Stevens, that's why I'm here. Katherine really has nobody, as I'm sure you've discovered. Her two children are out of the country. Her parents are dead. She had one brother but he's also deceased. As far as I know, there aren't any other family members. I was hoping that I might be able to help; maybe step in as a surrogate family member?"

"Ms. Sullivan, as much as I wish you could do that, there are legal complications. I will allow you to see her at this point; I think Katherine really needs someone to be with her. We can overlook those rules. However, you can't make medical decisions for her, and legally, I can't give out information to non-family members. As you can see, we have a real problem on our hands."

"Is there any way that Mr. Rhodes can sign over his rights to me?"

"Yes, if Mr. Rhodes is willing to do that. Of course, it's a legal procedure and you'd have to hire an attorney to represent you, but it can be done."

"Doctor, I'm willing to do that. I'll get hold of Mr. Rhodes today and I'll see if he'll cooperate with me. Knowing Mark, he'll jump at the opportunity. I'm sure he'll be glad to put the responsibility on someone else's shoulders. In the meantime, may I see Katherine? I would really appreciate it if you would let me do that."

"Absolutely, I'd be happy to place you on her visitors list. Before you go in, I want you to realize how ill Katherine is. She's currently in a coma, and I'm not sure when or if she's going to come out of it. I personally believe that she can hear us, but can't respond. I've seen positive results occur when there's verbal interaction with coma patients. While you're with her, speak to her. She really can hear what you're saying."

Doctor Stevens smiled and led Annie back to the nurses' station.

"Alicia, I want you to add Ms. Sullivan to patient Rhodes' visitors list. From now on, she's allowed in the room whenever she wants to visit."

"Of course, Dr. Stevens." Ms. Douglas smiled. She updated Katherine's information on the computer and when she was finished, she told Annie that she could enter the ICU. Before entering the ward however, Dr. Stevens stopped her.

"Ms. Sullivan, if you can think of anyone we might be able to contact please let me know. If you're serious about obtaining legal rights for Katherine, keep me updated on the status. There are decisions that will need to be made in the future. If we don't have someone who can sign consent papers, then the hospital will have no choice but to file our own legal paperwork. We'll have to make Katherine a ward of the state," Dr. Stevens said weakly, and then excused herself.

Ms. Douglas gave brief directions on what to do and what not to do and then let Annie into the ICU. As she walked down the Pine Sol scented, sparkling white hall she tried not to look at the patients that were lying in the open.

Some of these individuals were barely covered with curtains, and others had no curtains at all. Everyone she saw was either damaged or broken. People of all ages with one thing in common: the look of death hanging around their bodies like a dark shroud. The weight of her surroundings engulfed her. By the time she made it to IC bed 6, Annie was overcome by a sense of loss.

When she saw Katherine, Annie gasped. She hardly recognized her friend. Katherine was hooked up to so many devices that she looked more like a mannequin than a real person. She was stark white, almost the color of the sheets that surrounded her. She had a tube down her throat that seemed to be breathing for her. She also had a feeding tube down her nose that was currently filled with rose colored liquid. Her head was heavily bandaged and her body was in a full cast, except for her arm, which had been nearly amputated in the wreck. It was in heavy bandages and suspended with wires from a frame above the bed. If it wasn't for the machines that were keeping track of her heartbeat and breathing, Annie would have thought her old friend was dead.

She pulled a plastic chair from the corner of the room and took it over to the bedside. She sat tentatively, remaining consciously aware of the devices around her. She reached for Katherine's hand, which had an IV needle protruding from the back of it. She wrapped her hand around the few fingers that were exposed.

"Hey there. Long time no see, Katie girl," she said uncomfortably. She cleared her throat, leaned in closer, and continued speaking in a soft tone that was more like a loud whisper.

"The doctor says that I can talk to you because you can hear me. Honey, if that's true then I want you to know that I'm pulling for you. I promise that I'm going to see you through this nightmare. Katherine, do you hear me? Just like we used to do. Remember all those years ago when it was you and me against the world? Remember how we used to look out for each other? We got into some nasty scraps back then, didn't we? And together, we always made it through! This is just the same, together we're going get you through this too, just you wait and see."

Tears flowed down Annie's cheeks, and she reached towards a small dresser and pulled a rough hospital tissue out of a blue and white box. She dabbed at her eyes and then blew her nose. For a few seconds she sat silently and tried to compose herself. When she stopped crying, she dropped the tissue into the trashcan, sat back in the gray padded chair and closed her aging eyes.

"Crazy how things turn out, isn't it? I never pictured us as old ladies sitting in a hospital room together, that's for damn sure," Annie said, and then laughed nervously.

"I never pictured us as ever getting old, at least not back then I didn't. We were going to be twenty forever and the Summer of Love was going to go on and on. That's what I thought for a short time anyways. Back when everything was good, you remember? When we first arrived in San Francisco and we had our whole lives ahead of us. Those were the days, Katie, weren't they?"

Annie smiled at her friend and then she touched Katherine's face and ran her hand through her hair.

"Katie Cat, too bad we can't go back and do it all again. Not the same way mind you. No, this time we'd get it right, wouldn't we? Yep, we'd get it right. We sure would."

Chapter 4

Frog managed to cook dinner, despite the space restrictions. All three of them ate and he covered the remainder of the meal and cleaned the dishes. The girls drifted off to Moonbeam's room, where they painted pink and yellow flowers on their faces.

Once the kitchen was in order, he had no excuse. It was time to get ready for the biker party that he didn't want to attend. Frog brushed his long, wavy brown hair and fixed it into a neat ponytail on the back of his head. He donned one of his homemade tie dyed T-shirts, a brown-fringed suede vest, and a pair of Birkenstock sandals. He tied a leather headband around his head, donned a string of orange and black love beads and walked into the living room where Moonbeam and Katie were laughing.

Frog looked at the two girls and sighed. Here they were, two hippie girls looking like...well, *hippies*, getting ready to go to a Hells Angel's party in the Dogpatch. He must be out of his mind to have ever agreed to do this. He and the girls were going to stick out like sore thumbs. The idea of taking a bus through the Mission District and walking into the Dogpatch to the bikers' clubhouse made him shudder. There was no use trying to explain anything to the girls. They didn't understand the division between the two groups. He hoped that tonight would go smoothly, but somehow he couldn't picture that happening.

Hippies and bikers were two groups that never mixed well. It was like adding vinegar and oil and expecting them to blend into one substance. Sure, you could mix them for a short time, but sooner or later it was obvious that the two just didn't belong together. That's what this evening was going to be like. They were going to try to mix with their opposites. They could dress in leather and try to fit in, but even that wouldn't work. Hippies and bikers, bikers and hippies, no matter how you rolled the dice, or how you dressed either group, they just didn't belong together.

The best Frog could hope for was to leave the party physically unscathed. Fortunately, he was a gifted diplomat, a talent that always came in handy. Mixed with the dread of going and the nervous gut feeling that tonight might not go as smoothly as the girls wanted, Frog knew he was going to need that skill. Bikers loved to give hippies hell, and even though he knew several of the members as business associates, he wouldn't be exempt from torment. It was going to be a very long night.

"Okay, girls, let's get this over with. Are you ready?"

Moonbeam pulled a joint out of her multi colored crocheted handbag and lit it. "Almost ready, Frog. After we smoke this. You want a hit? It will mellow you out and get you ready for the party."

"I won't ever be ready for this party, Moon. No matter how much or how often I smoke."

"Froggy, you promised to be good about this! Please don't be a drag. Otherwise, me and Katie are going to pout all night, and you know how much you'd hate that."

It was true. Frog did hate girls pouting. It was bad enough to have to take a bus through the Mission District, walk through the Dogpatch, and attend a party at the infamous Hells Angel's clubhouse, but to have to endure all that misery, plus two girls pouting the whole night, now that would be a bummer. With that thought he reached for the joint and tried to think positively.

Perhaps things would work out all right. They'd smoke some grass, ride the bus, and get to the party in one piece. The girls would flirt with bikers, Frog would smoke a little more weed, have a beer or two, and then find a quiet corner to hide in. He'd try to stay inconspicuous until it was time to go. As long as he did that, the evening would turn out all right. If anything did happen, he was good at keeping his mouth shut. As long as the girls didn't get into anything, and he doubted that they would. They seemed to get along with practically everyone.

Frog took several deep hits off of the joint. Before long, the grass had worked it's magic. By the time the three left the house, Frog was content. He still wasn't happy with this evening's plans, but he had decided to make the best of it. No more negative vibes; he was filling himself with love and peace.

They walked to the bus stop on the corner of Haight and Clayton. Perfect timing as it turned out; the bus arrived at the same time they did. The three entered, Frog paid the fares, and they took seats on the back bench. Ten minutes later they were off the first bus and were boarding the second one that would take them across the Mission District to their destination.

That's when the pot wore off and Frog got nervous. In two more stops they'd be in the Dogpatch, and it was probably another ten minutes before they arrived at the clubhouse. Frog took a deep breath and closed his eyes. Why was he dreading this evening so much? There had to be a reason beyond just not wanting to go. He wasn't afraid. Sure, he would take shit, but he knew enough of the members through his business dealings that he figured he would be safe at the party.

There was something else, a deep and heavy feeling of dread, as if he were making a huge mistake. He had the feeling that, if he were smart, he would bow out now. Take the girls to the party and then turn around and run. He had never felt that way before and he wondered if this was a premonition of some sort. The image of old Guthrie popped into his head and he felt a cold shiver run down his spine.

"What's the matter, Frog? You look like you've just seen a ghost."

Frog swallowed hard. It was a good question. *What was wrong with him?*

He looked up and saw Moonbeam and Katie standing above him. "What?"

"Time to get off the bus, Frog. Are you tripping on something you didn't share with us? Never mind, we'll talk about it later, let's go."

Moonbeam took his arm and led him off the bus. Once outside, he closed his eyes and let the fresh air wash over him. For several seconds he couldn't move. He just stood there breathing deeply. Finally, the increase in oxygen soothed him and he opened his eyes, only to see the two girls staring at him in confusion.

"What is it, Froggy?" Moonbeam stepped in for a closer inspection. "What are you on?"

"Nothing, I'm fine. I just got dizzy there for a second. No, honest I'm not on anything, but I sure could use another smoke if you've got some Mary Jane left?"

"Are you sure you're okay, Frog? You look sick." This time it was Katie who took a step towards him and stared into his eyes.

"Stop, both of you. I said I'm okay and I am. It's been a long day. I had some strange experiences, that's all. I'll be fine. How about that smoke though, if you don't mind?"

"Oh yeah, Frog baby, hang on," Moonbeam said, reaching into her bag.

She pulled another joint out of her purse and lit it. She handed it to Frog and watched as he took several long hits. Finally, he handed it off to Katie.

For several seconds he stood perfectly still, eyes closed, allowing the THC to fill his lungs, spreading peace and serenity through his body. Several deep breaths later, he was ready to face the Angels.

"I'm alright now. Let's go to the party! Start walking." He pushed Moonbeam and Katie so that they would turn and start moving, but after a few steps they stopped. They turned again and looked at him. Frog smiled convincingly and waved them along with his hand, incident forgotten, he hoped, as the three walked up the hill.

He was all right. That's what he'd told the girls, but was he really? No, not really. A sick feeling had washed over him and for a few moments he'd felt as if he might pass out. He was feeling better now that the pot was relaxing him, but he still felt a dark cloud of paranoia surrounding him.

He took deep breaths and meditated. He let the good air in and he exhaled the bad. Just like his friend Guru Ansjeet had taught him during a weekend outing. Soon he was in control and he was able to move forward with positive vibes.

He decided to ignore the whole thing. It was true, what he had told the girls, it *had* been a long day, and an unusual one. He was obviously still freaked out by the Guthrie incident. It was creepy, that was for sure. Even now, when he thought about the old timer speaking and his eerie cryptic message, he got goose bumps. He was still reacting from that. He needed to relax and stop thinking about the day. Tomorrow things would be better and tomorrow was only two hours away.

When they turned the corner onto Tennessee Street, it was obvious which of the huge houses was the Hells Angel's clubhouse. Both the front yard of the yellow Victorian and the yard of the building beside it were filled with Harley Davidson and Indian motorcycles. There were so many that the lawn and the driveway blended into a multitude of psychedelic colors. When they reached the house, Frog was in full control. The meditational breathing had done the trick. It also helped to see one of his biker friends, Skinner, outside smoking a cigarette and sucking on a bottle of beer.

"Hey, you guys made it! Welcome to our clubhouse. Come inside. Oh, by the way, Dave and Salvador have been looking for you, Frog. They said they have a business deal to discuss."

Skinner's voice was slurred and his actions were slow. Frog had never seen him this way. Although the two drank together on several occasions, he had never appeared intoxicated. Even when he was consuming large amounts of beer, the man always seemed to hold it together. From the look of him tonight, Frog realized the party must have started many hours ago.

Great, he told himself. *Wasted Hells Angels!*

Katie and Moonbeam saw their friends in the hall and squealed. They ran past Frog and Skinner, entered the large double doors, and started hugging bikers. Soon they integrated into the packed room and disappeared from Frog's sight.

"Dave and Sal are looking for me, you say? Where are they?" Frog asked.

He knew both Dave and Salvador from his dealings on the street, but he had never done business with either. If they were looking for him tonight, that was unusual. Frog's interest was tweaked. Anytime there was an opportunity to make money, a different side of Frog would emerge. He became confident and shrewd, his creative mind expanded, and he would begin to think like a calculator, numbers and possibilities flashing through his mind. If Dave and Salvador where looking for him, there must be a lot of money involved. In an instant, all of his prior fears were forgotten.

Skinner took one last drag on his cigarette and crushed it out on the patio with the tip of his black steel-toed boot. He pushed the door open.

"Last time I saw them, they were in the kitchen. Come with me, I'll take you to them."

Skinner swayed into the house. Frog followed him inside the crowed entryway, down a narrow hall, and through an old parlor. Eventually, they came to a large kitchen that was filled with people. Loud music played in the background, The Stones' 'Paint it Black'.

Skinner paused in the middle of the room in front of a dark haired girl dressed in a black leather vest and matching mini skirt, both too small for her. "Deb, you seen Dave or Sal around?"

Deb, who was busy nursing a bottle of Coors, pointed towards the backdoor that led onto a large wooden patio. Skinner nodded and headed in that direction.

Once outside, they found that the porch was filled with excitement. Ten to fifteen bikers were standing by the railing and staring into the dark yard, yelling and whistling.

Skinner pushed his way to the railing and Frog hesitantly followed. By the time they saw what was happening, the fight was in full motion. Two large men stood facing each other with broken beer bottles and the crowd was going crazy. Frog heard someone in the kitchen scream, "Fight!" and the back door was stampeded. Spectators rushed out of the house and down the narrow wooden staircase, filling the sides of the yard. Soon there were at least fifty people watching the drama, and one of those was Frog.

The largest of the two men, a beast of a biker named Abel, stood in the center of the yard making sweeping motions with a broken bottle. The other, a smaller man with long curly hair, was backing up. He too was holding a broken bottle in his hand, but he seemed calmer and his movements were smooth. Abel took another sweep with the bottle, expecting his opponent to back up, but was thrown off guard. Terry , the smaller of the two men, jabbed inward and hit him in the upper arm.

Dark blood flowed down Abel's arm. He regained his balance and then he moved faster. He swung the bottle in a rapid arc around his body, like an aura. Terry took a few steps backwards and then he lunged. This time the razor sharp bottle found it's mark and tore a large gash in Abel's side. The brute force of the blow caused Abel to tumble to the ground. He tried repeatedly to get up, but he couldn't, so he held the bottle in front of his body defensively and waited. Terry looked down at his defeated opponent and laughed.

The screen door opened abruptly, slamming against the wall. A leather clad biker emerged from the house. Big Jim, one of the officers in the MC, stormed down the steps yelling. "What the fuck is going on out here? You fucking idiots! Pull those stupid assholes apart. What the hell is wrong with all of you? Letting them fight in the backyard of the clubhouse! What were all of you thinking?"

Several bikers grabbed Terry and pulled him away from Abel, , who was still lying on the lawn holding the bottle firmly in front of him.

"Jesus Christ! If the police show up tonight, I'm going to kill both of you myself! Jonah, how bad is Abel hurt?"

Jonah, a blond man with a huge unkempt beard, bent down and examined Abel . Another biker stepped forward and took the bottle out of Abel's hand.

"Might need a couple of stitches in the arm, probably more in the side. Not too bad. Could have been a hell of a lot worse."

"Great! Just fucking great." Big Jim pointed at a young greasy haired man who was standing on the porch next to Frog. "You there, prospect, come here." The youth nodded and approached the senior biker. "Grab a few other prospects and take this moron for stitches. Be smart. Tell them he got stuck in a bar fight. Let's not mention the party."

The prospect called a few of his friends together and soon they were escorting Abel into the house and to the hospital for stitches.

Big Jim walked over to Terry and pointed a finger in his sweaty face. "What the fuck is wrong with you, man? You know not to fight here. Get on your bike and get your ass out of here! You're officially thrown out of this party." Terry said nothing, obviously expecting this. He nodded at Big Jim respectfully and headed towards the door. Big Jim turned to the crowd. "Next time there's a fight at the clubhouse, break it up. Don't just stand here like a bunch of fucking worthless imbeciles!"

He remained on the lawn, shaking his head in disgust, pulled a pack of cigarettes out of his pocket, and lit one up. Gradually, the yard came back to life. Private conversations resumed and a flood of people went back into the house.

Now that the excitement had ended, Skinner turned to Frog and patted him on the back.

"Great party, don't you think?"

Frog was tongue-tied. This wasn't like any of the parties he normally attended. Hippies were peaceful. They didn't beat on each other or use broken bottles as weapons. If Skinner thought this was a great party, he would certainly think that the parties in the Haight were dull. Frog made a mental note not to invite him to any.

"Ah, there they are," Skinner said, walking down the rickety steps, heading toward the side yard where several men were sharing a joint. "Dave, Sal, look who I found outside! Frog Boy!"

"Frog, welcome! Dave and I were hoping you'd come tonight. We have a business proposal to discuss. Well, that is, if you're interested?"

Sal, a Hispanic man in his mid-twenties, was average height, muscular, with a full beard and long black hair tied in a ponytail.

"Sure, I'm always interested in a business deal," Frog replied.

They handed Frog a joint. He took a hit and passed it to Dave, the second man of the duo. Dave was well over six feet tall, had shoulder length red hair, a matching vibrant red beard, and looked as if he'd just stepped out of a Viking movie, despite the leather attire.

"Groovy, let's go inside where we can discuss this in private, shall we?"

Sal led the way to a small office that was built in the back of a detached garage. Dave turned on an overhead light and, still holding the joint in his hand, sat at a large oak table.

"Please, Frog, have a seat, and make yourself comfortable." Frog nodded and sat in one of the overstuffed chairs. "Frog, you've made quite a name for yourself in the Haight, as well as some of the other parts of the city."

"Well, I have a large clientele, if that's what you mean."

"Yeah, true, but it's more than that. You're known to be fair, honest, and you're well liked. You're someone who can mix with just about every crowd. In fact, look where you are tonight." Dave smiled, and Frog noticed that his teeth were yellow and crooked.

"You come well recommended, my friend, and that's why Sal and I have chosen you out of all the hustlers we know. Meaning we trust you, and we think it would be easy to do business with you."

"Thank you. That's a great compliment coming from the MC, but what exactly are we discussing? I do lots of business dealings in the Haight, many different avenues. Which one are you referring to?"

"Drugs Frog. We're referring to drugs."

"There's already lots of drugs in the Haight. Are you speaking of grass, uppers, downers, acid? We have it all."

Sal and Dave looked at each other and laughed. "No man, not grass, not pills, and not acid," Dave said. "You're right, there's lots of that in the Haight. There are too many dealers to contend with and not enough money to be made in those drugs. Hell, half the time, the Diggers are giving that shit away free at gatherings. What we're proposing is much more than grass, and much more profitable. The Angels want to eventually control the drugs that are going in and out of the Haight and we want to destroy our competition in the process, but that's a long way down the road. Right now, all we want to do is to get our foot in the door. We want to offer something that isn't readily available. What we want to know is would you be interested in a marketing agreement with the MC? The market right now is small, but with a little help it will eventually replace all the other drugs in the Haight. What we're talking about is heroin. Black tar heroin from Asia. We happen to have a connection that will never dry up."

***

Katherine was floating. She felt free. There was no fear, no pain, and no memory, just the softness that surrounded her. She wanted to stay like this forever, drifting and feeling nothing, but it wasn't to be.

Out of the darkness a light appeared; a beautiful light that sparkled like gold dust. It beckoned her to come closer. When she did, she could tell that it wasn't a light at all, it was a tunnel; a golden cave that seemed to emulate peace. She could feel it calling to her as she approached it. The closer she came, the more detail she could see within the cave. She could tell that there were people standing inside. At first she couldn't make out who they were, but the closer she came the more detail she could see in their faces.

Finally, Katherine came to the doorway that led to the entrance of the golden cave. When she did she could see the faces. She was startled when she recognized all of them. They were people that she hadn't seen in a very long time, family and friends that she had loved.

Her parents where there— not old like the last time she had seen them, but young, like she had seen them in photographs, times that took place long before she was born. Her grandparents stood hand in hand, smiling. They too appeared as young adults. Her aunt Celia, her cousin Andrew, who had died as a small child, was now grown and smiling happily. Her favorite dog Owen, who she had grown up with as a child. There were friends who had died in young adulthood: Emery, Allison, and Luis. And in the very front of all these stood her brother Richard, still nineteen years old.

Katherine felt hot tears running down her face. She wanted to run to them, hug all of them, and go with them through the golden tunnel into eternal peace and harmony. But before she could take that last step, another door became visible.

This doorway didn't shine and it didn't sparkle. It didn't feel peaceful. It felt solemn and was filled with old regrets that hadn't taken place yet, where bad mistakes were yet to come. Before misery would be her constant companion; before lies would ruin her life. She was flooded with understanding that this doorway led back to a time when she was just starting out. A happy time that ended much too soon. This doorway was offering her a choice. If she chose this path there was work to be done, and it wouldn't be easy. If she took the other it would all be over. No more sorrow, no more worries, and she would be free from pain and suffering. All she had to do was walk over the golden threshold and she'd be free forever.

Katherine stared at the two paths, the golden cave where her loved ones called to her and the other, a simple wooden door that she couldn't see through. She didn't need to see inside to know where that door led.

She was being offered a second chance.

The plain wooden door started to fade in and out. Soon it would be gone and the choice would be made for her. Before it completely vanished, Katherine opened the door, and bravely walked into the darkness.

***

Moonbeam and Katie ran into the Victorian clubhouse to greet their two new friends, Joey and Dylan.

They had met the men two weeks earlier in Golden Gate Park. They had gone there to make daisy chains for their hair but were distracted when they heard two Harley Davidsons pull up, an unusual occurrence in the Haight.

After a brief conversation regarding their own personal experience with bikers, the girls discovered that neither had been on a bike, nor had they ever talked to a biker. Living in the Haight was a very different world. It was especially different from the biker community, which was across the city. The two groups were so different that they very seldom mixed. With this in mind, Moonbeam and Katie decided it was time to find out the truth. What were the Hells Angels really like? If they hated hippies, as many in the Haight crowd believed, then they wanted to find out for themselves.

The girls walked up to the bikers and asked if they could have a ride. The men turned out to be so nice that Moonbeam and Katie spent the whole afternoon on the back of their bikes. Joey and Dylan had taken them across the Golden Gate Bridge and into Sausalito and Tiburon. It had been a beautiful day and the bikers had turned out to be beautiful people.

During the last few weeks, Joey and Dylan had made several appearances at Hippie Hill looking for the girls, and Moonbeam and Katie had spent many afternoons on the back of Harleys. Recently, they'd begun to meet some of the other Angels from the San Francisco Chapter, and that's why they were invited to the party tonight.

The relationship Moonbeam had with Joey and Katie was developing with Dylan seemed to be turning into something more than mere friendship. Because of that, the girls had wanted to meet the rest of the Angels. What better place to do that than at a biker party? They'd brought Frog because he knew several of the Angels, plus he made a great escort. He was always fun to be with and he was a great diplomat. Everyone wanted Frog at hippie parties. Frog had a gift of being able to defuse heated situations. Moonbeam and Katie thought he was simply groovy and that he'd be handy at a Hells Angels party too.

When Dylan saw Katie he took her slim waist in his hands and swung her around. Her white lace maxi dress swung up revealing soiled bare feet.

"Katie, baby, you came," Dylan said happily. He placed her gently on the floor and stepped back to admire her. "Honey, you sure look cute."

Joey, who had just finished greeting Moonbeam with a very unexpected kiss, interrupted the conversation.

"Dylan, you crude asshole, where's your manners? They're adorable, both of them, they look just like little fairies!"

Katie and Moonbeam looked at each other and smiled. They *did* look cute; they had planned it that way. Katie had worn a long sleeve white gauze gown, and Moonbeam a long frayed denim skirt with an embroidered white peasant blouse.

They were barefoot and they both had pink and yellow flowers painted on their faces, and both wore peace symbols around their necks and several strands of love beads. Each of them had long hair that reached halfway down their backs, but that's where the resemblance ended. Moonbeam was barely five feet tall with straight auburn hair and a cascade of freckles that covered her cheeks and the bridge of her nose. Katie was several inches taller with wavy blond hair and sky blue colored eyes. Joey was right, both girls were cute, too cute. They didn't fit in with the biker girls at the party who were already eyeing them silently while they stood in the hall.

"You're right, Joey. Forgive my crude manners, Lady Moonbeam. You both look lovely this evening." Dylan bowed, Rhett Butler style, and the girls giggled. "Come with us, we'll fix you up with a cold beer and then we'll go out in the yard and smoke a joint."

Joey led the way through the hall and into the parlor, stopping in the large antique styled room so that he could introduce the girls to Big Jim. Big Jim was one of the officers of the San Francisco Chapter. He was a tall man, well past six feet and stocky, hence the nickname. The man was in his mid-thirties, with long ash blond hair that ended bluntly at his jawline. He wore old jeans, a white T-shirt, and his leather Angel's vest.

"Ladies, I want you to meet Big Jim McAllister. Jim, this is Moonbeam and Katie, the girls we met at Golden Gate Park, the ones we told you about."

"Ah, yes. Joey and Dylan did mention the two of you. I take it you're hippie mercenaries, here in the attempts to build a bridge between our two very different worlds," Big Jim laughed.

"Yeah, something like that," Moonbeam said with a huge smile across her pixie face.

"Well, welcome to the clubhouse, ladies. I hope you're successful."

At that moment, someone in the kitchen yelled "Fight!" and chaos erupted. Loads of people rushed for the back door and into the yard to witness the scene.

"What the fuck's happening now?" Big Jim said to no one in particular, hustling quickly through the crowd leading to the backyard. When he was gone and the room had thinned out, Moonbeam and Katie glanced at each other. This was a much different world than the peaceful one they were used to.

Finally, Dylan broke the uncomfortable silence. "Hey, do you want to see the fight?"

Moonbeam and Katie hesitated. They were stunned. They were trying to *prevent* fights, especially the big one that was taking place in Vietnam. Why on earth would someone ask them if they wanted to *watch* one? It just didn't make sense. They both shook their heads and answered in unison, "No."

"We believe in love and peace," Moonbeam said. "Fighting is just not our bag."

A brief silence resulted, where the hippies and the bikers stared at each other, saying nothing. At that moment it was evident that the huge gap between the two groups could never be fully bridged. Their whole existence was different, especially their way of thinking. They were nothing alike.

"Hey, it's okay girls, you don't have to be frightened. Fighting is a good way to let off steam. Nobody's going to get hurt."

No sooner had Joey finished the sentence than several of the MC prospects walked through the room escorting a bleeding man. They had wrapped makeshift bandages around his arm and a side wound, but both wounds were bleeding heavily. So heavily in fact, that they had bled through their wrappings. Moonbeam and Katie looked at the hard wood floors where small patches of blood were forming.

"Off to the hospital!" a short, dark haired man yelled on his way out the front door.

"It's a bitch being a prospect."

"Hey, it's supposed to be, brother," Dylan called back. "It gives you something to look forward to!" He and Joey laughed until they looked at the two little hippies who stood staring back at them.

"You don't think...I mean, he's not really hurt, not really," Dylan said, trying to rationalize with the two speechless girls.

"He's going to the hospital and he's left blood spots all over the floor. What do you mean he's not really hurt?" Katie questioned.

"Well, he's alive ain't he? If it wasn't a game, then he...well, he'd be...never mind. How about that beer?" Dylan suggested.

To his relief, the girls nodded, and the four headed into the kitchen where a full sized keg sat in a large tub of ice. Joey placed four red plastic cups in front of him and proceeded to fill them. They headed onto the back porch and down the rickety staircase. There, they found a quiet corner in the yard and Dylan lit up a joint. They had just started smoking when they saw Frog exit the garage with two Angels.

Probably his friends, Moonbeam thought. She was going to call out to him, but something in his body language stopped her. Frog was in business mode; they could tell by the way he was walking. When he was in that mindset, it wouldn't do any good to call to him, he'd ignore them anyway.

Frog and the two men entered the house just as two biker girls walked up to their small group and introduced themselves.

"Hi, I'm Eva and this is Ruby. Is this your first time at the clubhouse?" asked a tall, slim brunette.

Ruby was true to her name. Although she had long black hair, she was dressed in a red leather vest that covered a red bikini top. She had short cutoffs and red flip-flops on her feet. The hippie girls noticed that her lips and her toenails were painted a matching shade of blood red.

Eva, on the other hand, seemed to prefer the color black. She was drenched in it. She had on a black leather miniskirt, a tight black T-shirt and a black leather vest. Even her long brown hair was tied back with a black leather strap. Unlike her counterpart, Eva wore white lipstick that gave her dark skin an unnatural eerie tone.

Katie and Moonbeam nodded and smiled at the two newcomers. "Yes, this is our first time here," Katie answered.

"Far out. Well, your timing couldn't have been better. So far this party has been one of the best we've had in a long time," Eva said, and Ruby nodded in agreement.

Katie and Moonbeam shared a glance. They had mixed feelings about this party and each could tell from the other's response. Although they were glad to spend time with their new special friends, the party had proved anything but ordinary. So far, the vibes they had received were hostile. The image of Abel bleeding in the hall was still fresh in their minds. What bothered them more than the vicious battle in the backyard was the lackadaisical way the bikers had reacted.

To them, it was nothing. Everyone seemed to think that the event was normal, just part of the fun. Moonbeam and Katie were peace loving. They believed in respecting each and every person. When you were hit you turned the other cheek, just as Christ had done. In their world, you made love not war.

Everyone they associated with hated the establishment and its ungodly war. They were trying to make the world a better place. But here, just in the short time that they'd been at the party, they'd seen a completely different world. Although the Hells Angels were far from ordinary, and even though they seemed to fight against the establishment as well, the girls could tell that they worshipped the same demons. They were still following the same demigods that the establishment had taught them to follow: money, power, and violence.

"So Joey and Dylan said they met you in Golden Gate Park. Do you live there?" Ruby asked.

"Yeah, we live in the Haight District," Moonbeam answered.

"Oh, in the District? Eva and I thought you might live in the park."

"Okay, enough Eva!" Joey snapped.

"Joey, honey, I didn't mean it in a nasty way. It's just well...don't a lot of hippies live in the park, Moonbeam?"

"Sure, some people do, but Katie and I don't. We live in houses."

"Right, with other hippies? What do you call those? Communes? Is that the word? Yes, that's it. Do the two of you live in a commune?" Eva asked.

Joey and Dylan shot her and Ruby a nasty look, but the biker girls just smiled back sweetly.

"I'm sorry, Moonbeam and Katie, your boyfriends here seem to think that we're trying to be rude, but that's not true; we're just curious is all. See, we've never really known any hippies before. We've seen them around the city and all, but we've never talked to any of you before."

Moonbeam looked at Joey and smiled. "It's okay, they're just curious. We were curious too when we first met you and Dylan."

Joey nodded, but he still watched the biker women suspiciously.

"She's right, Joey, we're just curious, same as they're curious about us. There's nothing wrong with that, is there?" Ruby looked at her empty beer cup and sighed. "Ah, out again." She looked into Eva's cup and shook her head.

"Eva's cup is empty too. Hey, we're going in to get another beer. Can we get the two of you one?" Ruby asked kindly.

"No thanks. I drink slow, this one will last me for a while," Moonbeam replied.

"Well, what about you, honey, can we get you one?" Eva asked Katie.

Katie looked in her cup and nodded. "Sure, I'll take another one. I can come with you if you want?"

"No, you stay here and enjoy yourself, no sense in all of us flooding the already crowded kitchen. Just hand me your cup, unless you want a new one?"

Katie took one quick swig of beer, emptying the cup, and handed it to Ruby. "No, don't waste any more cups, it's bad for the environment. I'll just use this one again."

"Right, well we'll be back in a second. Don't smoke anything while we're gone!"

The two-biker girls strolled casually towards the back door and into the kitchen. While they were gone, Dylan and Joey started talking to a friend named Oscar. Soon they were lost in a conversation that had to do with an old '58 Harley. Apparently, Oscar had won the bike in a poker game. Although the body was in great shape, the motor was trashed. The men discussed what each felt was the best approach at rebuilding the Harley.

When Eva and Ruby returned with the beers, the men had drifted into their own group.

"Here we are." Ruby handed a full cup of beer over to Katie.

"The bodyguards have wandered off I see. Do you think you're safe with us?" Eva asked with a friendly grin on her death white lips.

"Certainly," Moonbeam said. "Why wouldn't we be?"

"Well, the way your old men were acting for one. Them hanging on your every move, like you were some type of royalty that needed protection," Ruby said, with a catlike grin on her heavily made up face.

"Oh, I don't think they meant it that way," Katie answered. She was starting to get confused. *Were* these girls being friendly? She wasn't so sure.

"Oh, yes they did. Ruby and I have known Dylan and Joey for a very long time. They don't hang out glued to the side of a chick like that unless they think you're damsels in distress. Come on, open your eyes sweetie. They were totally playing knights in…well in this case, leather armor. But don't sweat it, honey, it's all cool. We're all friends here. Ruby and I are just fucking with you a little, you know what I mean? Kind of an initiation into the clubhouse?" Eva looked into Katie's eyes and winked.

"Sure, okay. I guess I understand," Katie answered timidly.

"Well, so much for the girl time, your heroes are returning," Ruby whispered, and then she and Eva laughed.

Joey stepped into the circle, put his arm around Moonbeam, and pulled her back a few paces. At the same time Dylan took Katie's hand and gently tugged her towards him.

"Everything all right?" Dylan asked. He stared at Ruby and Eva, who seemed to be smirking.

"Sure, honey, Ruby and Eva where just welcoming us to the clubhouse. They've been ever so nice while you were gone," Moonbeam answered.

"Yeah, I bet they have," Dylan said. He was staring at the biker girls with a look of distaste on his face.

"It was nice to meet you both, Moonbeam and Katie. We'd love to stay and chat, but as you can see, we've already outstayed our welcome. We'll talk to the two of you later, maybe in the bathroom? That is, if your dogs let you go potty without them! Have a good time at the party!" Ruby smiled, took Eva's hand in her own, and the two walked off towards the back door of the house.

"Hey, what did they really say to you while we were gone?" Joey asked.

"Not really anything," Moonbeam replied. "They just tried to tell us that the two of you are being overprotective. We told them that wasn't the case."

"Are you kidding?" Joey shook his head. "You're like doves in a pool of sharks. Haven't you realized that yet? It took way too long for both of you to realize that Ruby and Eva…well, let's just say, stay away from them."

"What's their hang-up, Dylan?" Moonbeam asked.

"What do you mean hang-up? They're just bitches, that's all!"

"Nobody's *just* a bitch. There has to be a reason. Why are the two of them hung up over you?" Katie asked bluntly.

For a few seconds, nobody spoke. Finally, Joey cleared his throat nervously and then he started to talk. All the while, he kept his eyes downcast, staring at the tip of his steel toe boots.

"Up until a few weeks ago, those two were…well, they're our ex-girlfriends, okay?"

Moonbeam and Katie looked at each other as the reality hit them.

"Are you saying they were your girlfriends two weeks ago? Up until the time you met us in the park?" Katie said, shaking her head, which made the beads around her neck rattle.

"You were in relationships with them when you met us? No wonder they don't like us!"

"Let me get this straight; you broke off a thing with them because of us? Then you invite us to this party without even a warning?" Moonbeam shook her head as well, her voice starting to rise. "That's bad karma, man, real bad karma." Several bikers next to them turned to watch.

"It's not like that," Joey said as both girls sighed and rolled their eyes. "We wouldn't have done that to you! We aren't *that* stupid."

"They weren't supposed to be here tonight. They were in Los Angeles and we thought they would be there tonight. I guess we were wrong," Dylan explained.

"Is there anyone else that we should be aware of? Any other ex-girlfriends who might not like us being here?" Katie asked.

"Well, there are a few others here at the party who used to be—" Joey started to say before he was interrupted.

"So do we have to worry about meeting them in the bathroom too? Are we even safe going there to pee?" Moonbeam asked. More bikers turned to watch the scene that was unfolding.

"Umm...probably either Joey or I should walk you when you need to go, just to be on the safe side."

A few of the bikers in the yard laughed. Dylan and Joey shot them all dirty looks.

"What the fuck are you all looking at?" Dylan yelled out.

The yard went completely silent. The crowd quickly turned away. He waited until the conversations in the yard resumed and then Dylan lowered his voice.

"Look, we're sorry, it's just... well...we really wanted the two of you here tonight. We should have told you about our history, that there would be exes here. To be honest, I don't think that either of us even thought of that. Truth is, there are girls here who could be—"

"What are you saying, Dylan? That we aren't safe?"

"No, just that...Joey and I may have made a mistake by inviting you. We thought you'd be okay since Eva and Ruby wouldn't be here, but of course that's changed everything. Stay close to us and let us walk you to the bathroom when you go.

"You're going to be our bodyguards all night?" Katie asked, crossing her arms in front of her.

"Look, we don't want anything to happen to y—" Joey began.

"What are you really trying to say, Joey?" Moonbeam screeched, again bringing unwanted attention to the group. Loud laughter burst out from the porch from where Eva and Ruby stood watching.

"That's right, Joey!" Eva yelled from the porch. "What are you trying to say to her?"

Joey pulled Moonbeam gently by the hand into the darkest corner of the backyard, and Dylan and Katie followed. When they were sure that the shadows concealed them, Joey spoke, his voice low, almost a whisper.

"We can't cut out right now because we're in charge of the party. Everything considered, it might be best if the two of you played it safe and just—"

Moonbeam pulled herself away from Joey, who had been holding her around the waist.

"Are you asking us to *leave*?"

"Is this what you want?" Katie asked. She looked at Dylan, and he diverted his eyes and looked at the ground.

"Look, it's not that we don't want you here, because we do, but that's not the point. There's a lot going on now, as you can see. Everyone's drinking and there's already been one fight. Ruby and Eva are drinking heavily and they're gonna keep at you all night."

"So you *are* asking us to leave?" Moonbeam repeated.

"Only to protect you. If we could leave right now we would, but it's not possible since were on the committee to—"

"Fine! Don't bother trying to explain anymore. We'll go! The two of you can work this mess out with your ex-girlfriends or current girlfriends, whatever they are. Just don't come looking for us at Hippie Hill anymore because from now on, the two of you won't be welcome," Moonbeam snapped. She turned towards Katie, announcing loudly, "Let's go and find Frog."

Katie finished the last gulp of beer that was in her cup and tossed the plastic container into a trashcan on their way towards the rickety staircase.

"Wait! Come on, don't be angry. Can't we talk about this? It's not like you think. There's nothing between us and them, not anymore, not since...."

The two hippie girls stopped and stared at the men, dumbfounded. Both girls wondered how on Earth they had ended up in this situation.

"Well, now there's nothing between us either. Not anymore. Come on, Moonbeam, let's find Frog and get out of here. We'll go home where people care about others. Where fun doesn't mean beating up your friends. Frog was right, we shouldn't have come here tonight."

Moonbeam and Katie walked up the rickety stairs with Dylan and Joey following. When they entered the kitchen it was obvious to everyone there what they were witnessing. It was especially obvious to Eva and Ruby, who stood in the corner giggling.

"Has anyone seen Frog?" Moonbeam asked the crowd of spectators.

"I think he's in the front yard with Skinner," Jonah said, after taking a long swig out of a plastic red cup with his name written on it in permanent marker.

"Thanks," Katie said.

The two headed out of the kitchen, through the parlor, and into the hallway, avoiding the blood smears on the floor, and finally emerged on the front porch were they found Frog smoking a joint.

Big Jim also stood on the lawn. As Moonbeam started to walk down the steps, Big Jim caught her arm and turned her to look at him.

"Well, little mercenaries, does this mean you failed in your quest for peace?" he asked jokingly.

Both girls nodded. Moonbeam pulled away from Big Jim and started to walk around him. At that moment, Dylan and Joey burst out into the yard.

"Wait, just let me explain," Dylan said to Katie.

"You've already said enough. You wanted us to go home and now we are. Looks to me like you've got everything you asked for," Katie said, and turned her back on the two bikers.

Dylan grasped her upper arm, trying to stop her. That's when Frog got involved.

"Hey, man, take your hands off her. She said she wants to go home, so let her be. I think it's obvious she doesn't want to talk to you right now. Don't push the issue."

"Frog, it's not your business man. Stay out of this," said Dylan.

"Dylan, man, I have to disagree. I came to the party with these two girls. One of them is my roommate. That makes this very much my business. They want to go home and that's where I'm going to take them."

Frog walked over to both girls and pushed them in front of him. With a wave of his hand he flagged them through the yard and onto the sidewalk.

"Now I'm taking them home. If you have a problem with that, then you can hit me, because it's the only way you're going to stop me." With that said, the girls walked down the sidewalk leading the way towards the bus stop with Frog following close on their heels.

Chapter 5

Frog looked at his watch: 12:01a.m. A new day had finally begun. He frowned at his surroundings. A new day may have started, but he was still knee deep in the previous one. Two buses; that's all it would take to put this nightmare behind them.

The bus stop on the corner of 20th Street was surprisingly crowded. They were lucky to get on the first bus, but not lucky enough to get seats. This, unfortunately, was the longest part of their ride. If the traffic lights were with them and the second bus came on time, they might be home in an hour. Red lights and a missed connection might stretch it to two hours to get back to the Haight.

Frog stumbled just as the driver pulled off, then caught a pole towards the middle of the bus and steadied himself. Moonbeam snagged the pole behind him and Katie was stuck towards the front doors of the bus, where a crowd of people stood blocking her passage.

First light red. Frog sighed. He hoped this wasn't a bad omen. He closed his eyes, trying to clear any negative vibes, breathing in the good air and letting the bad air drift out slowly.

"You were right, Frog. We should have listened to you," a voice behind him said. Frog turned and faced Moonbeam, whose flower painted face was now smeared across her freckled cheek.

"If it makes you feel any better, I'm really sorry that I was right. I would have preferred a pleasant evening with the MC, but I can't say I'm surprised. Too many differences between our people, Moony, just way too many." Frog shook his head for emphasis.

Second light red. Frog leaned his head against the pole.

"Next time, when you tell me not to go somewhere, I'm going to listen, Froggy, I promise."

"No, you won't, but that's okay, Moony. You're still groovy." Frog smiled.

Several people got off at the next stop. The vacated seats were claimed quickly, but not by Frog or the girls.

Third light red. Frog looked at his watch. 12:15a.m. Twenty-one more stops and then they switched buses.

"Did you have a good night?" Moonbeam asked.

"What?" Frog asked, flabbergasted.

"Not the last part, before that. Me and Katie saw you with two guys and you looked like you were having a good time," Moonbeam said. This was her way of prying without actually prying; Frog knew that. Moonbeam was a manipulator, just like the other cute girls he knew, and she was a master at it. But Frog had grown up in a household of women and his three sisters had also been masters at the craft.

"Just a business proposition, nothing fun about it. And no, by the way, I did not have a good time. I had a fucking lousy time and so did you and Katie."

Fourth light red. Frog gave up. They were never going to get home. Another stop and more people got on; now the bus was even more crowded.

"Are you going to do it?" Moonbeam dropped the pole she'd been holding onto and moved up one, so she could hang onto the one Frog was gripping.

He had to move his hands up higher, into an uncomfortable position, to make room for her.

Let the good air in and the bad air out, he silently told himself.

"Am I going to do what?" Frog asked, smiling. He too could play the manipulation game.

"The business offer. Are you going to do it? Work with them I mean?"

"Oh that's what you're talking about." He snickered.

Fifth light red.

"To tell you the truth, I don't know. I could make a ton of dough, but working with the MC...I'm not so sure about that. It could turn out to be a real bummer."

Another stop, nobody got off.

"What do you think, Moonbeam?"

Frog's question caught her off guard. Obviously not expecting it, Moonbeam opened her eyes widely then hesitated, thinking.

The bus turned onto 16th street and made another stop.

"Hippies and bikers, you said it yourself. They don't mix well together and you'll be sorry if you get involved with them. That's what I think," she responded.

The bus continued on its long route, making several winding turns within the narrow streets of the city. Stops came and went, but Frog, Moonbeam and Katie remained standing. When the bus finally turned onto Haight, Frog smiled. The second stop was where they got off. On the corner of Haight and Fillmore, they would catch the second bus on their journey.

The first light on Haight was green, which brought a little smile to Frog's tired face. All they had to do was catch the connecting bus, travel six stops, and they would be home.

The number 70 pulled over at the curb. The only people getting off were Frog, Moonbeam and Katie. Katie was close to the front, but Frog and Moonbeam had to dig their way through the crowded bus before regrouping on the sidewalk.

The cold wind coming off the San Francisco Bay hit them full force and Frog shivered. Moonbeam and Katie wrapped sweaters around their bodies tightly, but Frog, who hadn't brought a jacket, crossed his arms in front of his body regretfully.

Six stops and we'll be home, he told himself. *Just six more stops.*

Frog looked at his watch. 12:40a.m. Either the next bus was late, or it had already left. If that were the case, they would be standing at the bus stop for the next fifteen minutes.

"Katie, are you all right?" Moonbeam asked.

Until then, Frog had been lost in his own thoughts but now he turned and looked at Katie who was, quite literally, staring at her own fingers as she dangled them in front of her face.

"I'm tracing my fingers with my mind," she said happily without looking up. She continued to wave her fingers in a manner that looked as if she were playing the keys on a piano.

"Honey, what are you talking about?" Moonbeam asked.

"Tracing them with my mind. Can't you see the orange line that's spinning around them?" Katie asked earnestly.

Frog stared into her face, which was illuminated by the streetlight at the bus stop. Her normally blue eyes looked black. The pupils were so dilated that they covered the normal sky blue color completely.

"What are you on?" Moonbeam asked her friend, who was beginning to sway awkwardly.

"On?" Katie asked, appearing quite confused.

Frog looked at Moonbeam sternly, who adamantly shook her head. "I didn't see her take anything, Frog, and I was with her the whole night."

"Well, she's definitely tripping, look at her."

Katie was flying. As well as tracing objects with her mind, she was spinning in circles on the street.

"Honey, stop that," Moonbeam said. She reached for Katie and put a hand on her shoulder. "Don't spin like that, baby, the bus won't pick us up. Come over here and we'll stand together. The bus should be here any minute and then we can go home." Moonbeam took hold of her hand and Katie followed her to the covered bus kiosk.

"I want to go home, Moonbeam," Katie said, her speech slurred.

"Of course you do, Katie, we all do," Frog said.

"The beer! God, Frog it was the beer. Those nasty biker chicks, they brought her a beer and they wanted to bring me one too!" Moonbeam turned to look at him and when she did, she saw the bus, although it was still several blocks away.

"There's the bus," Frog announced. "What are you saying, that they intentionally drugged her?"

"Yes, that's exactly what I'm telling you."

"That's fucked up. Low ass bitches."

Katie sang and giggled, dangling her hands in front of her face.

"Jesus, look at her. They're not going to let us on this bus," Frog groaned, and slumped his shoulders in misery. The icy cold breeze hit him and he shivered, his teeth chattering loudly.

"I can't believe you didn't bring a jacket, Frog. It's January in San Francisco. What were you thinking?" Moonbeam asked.. The bus drew closer. Moonbeam held on to Katie and steadied her.

"Katie, we have to get on the bus. It's coming now. You can't sing. Do you hear me? If you do, they're not going to let us on." Moonbeam took hold of her shoulders and, trying to stop her mid-song, shook her gently.

"Don't sing," Katie repeated in a daze. To Moonbeam's delight her friend stopped just as the bus pulled over at the curb.

This bus was nearly empty. Besides an old drunk man and two middle-aged women sitting in the very front, they had their pick of seats. Purposely, Frog led them to the very back bench, where he and Moonbeam sat with Katie between them. When the bus pulled away from the curb and Katie started dancing her hands in front of her face, both Frog and Moonbeam pulled an arm down into their laps. When Katie tried to pull away, Moonbeam leaned in closely and started whispering in her ear.

"That's it, Katie girl, just sit like that and be nice and quiet." And Katie was, for a while.

First light red. Frog sighed.

"Now, finish telling me the story," he said to Moonbeam.

"Dylan and Joey's ex-girlfriends were at the party," she said softly.

"Are you fucking kidding me? Why did we go?"

"We didn't *know* they were going to be there. Do you think Katie and I are stupid?"

Frog bit his tongue.

"According to Dylan and Joey, the girls were supposed to be in LA and that's why they invited us, the snakes!" Moonbeam shook her head, still shocked by the much anticipated evening that had turned into such a disaster.

Second light red.

"Why are the road signs trying to hit us?" Katie screamed. She pulled both of her hands away from Frog and Moonbeam and slid onto the floor.

"Fuck!" Frog muttered. In the front of the bus he could hear the two women gasp and then one of them uttered "animals" under her breath.

"What the hell is going on back there?" the bus driver, a heavy, balding man with a cigarette dangling from his lips called back to them.

"Nothing, our friend's not feeling well. We're just trying to get her home. She's quiet now, she'll be fine," Frog responded, as he and Moonbeam hauled Katie back up on the seat beside them, again each holding one of her hands in their laps, although tighter this time.

"Well, she better be. This is a respectable bus. If she can't sit quietly, then you'll have to get your hippie asses off," the driver said grumpily.

"Yes, sir. We have just a few more stops and then we're getting off," Frog responded in his most diplomatic tone.

"Damn dirty hippies. Of *course* you're getting off at Clayton Street, that's where all the zoo animals get off." The bus driver glanced in the back mirror so he could watch their reactions. Frog and Moonbeam, used to the occasional mocking by the establishment, ignored him.

Third light red.

"So let me get this straight," Frog said to Moonbeam. His eyes turned to the front of the bus where he could see the next stop looming in the distance. "Dylan and Joey's ex-girlfriends gave Katie a beer and she drank it?"

The bus stopped at the next location and the two elderly women got off.

"We didn't know they were their exes at first, Frog. We thought they were groovy chicks, welcoming us to the party," Moonbeam said, watching the two women walk down the street. Then she turned and looked at Frog blankly.

"And when you found out who they were, Katie continued to drink the beer the welcoming committee supplied her?" he asked.

Moonbeam rolled her hazel colored eyes. "Yes, something like that."

None too soon, the bus pulled over at their stop and Frog and Moonbeam helped Katie to her feet.

"We're here, honey. We're getting off the bus now. We're almost home." They started to walk with her but when she stumbled, Frog put his arm beneath hers and half carried her down the three steps that led to the sidewalk. Once they were out of the bus the driver shut the door quickly and pulled away from the curb.

"Asshole," Frog said, to nobody in particular.

"Come on, Katie Cat, just a block. You can flop with us tonight. Everything will be better in the morning, you'll see." Moonbeam smiled and took her friend's hand.

"Let's go, I'm freezing." Frog took a few steps and then turned around abruptly when Katie screamed.

"We can't go that way, can't you see them?"

"Katie, there's nothing there, honey. It's all in your mind. Those biker chicks put something in your beer. We're going to get you home and you'll feel better," Moonbeam said, trying to reason with her.

"All those eyes staring at us. How can you tell me there's nothing there?" Katie asked, her own eyes wild and her hair blowing into her face.

Frog thought she looked like a character out of a horror movie. The image of Norman Bates snapped into his mind and he shook the disturbing picture away.

"Katie, there aren't any eyes looking at us. Listen to me. Those biker girls slipped something into your beer. Do you understand? They drugged you and now you're on a bad trip." *Bad trip.* Moonbeam shook her head. Living in the Haight, she had seen many bad trips, some life threatening.

"We can't walk that way, they'll get us."

"Oh for fuck sake," Frog said. "Now what?"

"You might have to carry her," Moonbeam said as she wrapped her long sweater around her body and retied the brown leather belt.

"Carry her? Oh no, Frog doesn't carry people," he said, his hands held up in front of his face, peace like.

"He does if he wants to get home. How else are we going to get her there?"

"Katie, if we can't go that way, which way can we walk. Is there a safe route?" he asked, leaning his freezing body against her warm one.

"We can't go anywhere. They're all around us,." she whispered fearfully. Her body tensed and she opened her mouth to scream, but Frog placed his hand over her lips and stopped her.

"Shhh," he uttered as he held her body in front of his. "It's okay, Frog is going to carry you." He regretted his words immediately. Glancing at Moonbeam, hoping that she would stop him, Frog braced himself and threw the young hippie girl over his shoulder. *One block; how tough can this be?* He placed one foot in front of the other and made his way down Ashbury, a block away from their Page Street Victorian.

Chapter 6

Joey and Dylan stood in the front yard watching as Katie and Moonbeam disappeared around the corner of 22nd Street.

Big Jim, Skinner, and a handful of other Angels stood behind them laughing.

"The little mercenaries failed," Big Jim repeated for the twentieth time and when he did, the bikers on the lawn broke out laughing again.

"Fuck off!" Joey finally yelled. Which made the audience laugh even harder.

"Where are they? I'm going to kill those fucking bitches," Dylan announced loudly, ignoring the laughter. He stormed into the crowded house, pushing through the bodies angrily as he made his way to the kitchen.

"Where's Eva and Ruby?" he asked a young prospect, who was leaning on the counter next to the beer keg.

"I think they're in the backyard," the young man said, pointing to the door and what lay beyond.

Dylan flung the door wide open. He stepped onto the crowded porch, made his way to the banister, and stood searching the yard for the two she-vipers. As he stared into the crowd, Joey stepped behind him and put a hand on his shoulder.

"What are you planning on doing?" he asked, readying himself for the drama he knew was about to take place.

"For one, I'm going to call them on their shit. Two, I'll figure out as I'm completing step one." Dylan started down the wooden staircase.

Eva and Ruby were standing next to two other leather-clad women and they were openly laughing. Dylan was relatively sure that somewhere in the conversation his name had popped up.

"Clever," he said, and then he started to clap. "Here's to the biggest bitches at the party."

"Fuck you, Dylan. We didn't do anything wrong. You're the one that told your new little flower child girlfriend to leave. Eva and I were being nice," Ruby said with a sneer.

"Nice? Is that right?"

"Sure, we even got her a beer," Eva said, and then she and Ruby cracked up laughing.

"You got her a beer?" Joey asked, stepping next to Dylan and crossing his arms in front of his muscular chest.

"Yeah, we did. We were really nice, considering we got back from LA early and found out that your new old ladies were at the party. Actually, we were too fucking nice," Ruby said, glaring at Dylan and taking a defiant step forward.

"Hey, if you want to fight with them, why don't you go someplace else?" said a husky redhead named Bernice, who was sucking on the last of her cigarette butt. "Me and Sandy here are trying to have a good time and you're invading our space."

"Yeah!" announced Sandy, her mousy brown haired stick figure of a friend.

"See? You're a drag, Dylan, and you're bringing everyone down. Why don't you take your greasy friend here and blow away?" Ruby said. She lit a cigarette and offered the pack to Bernice, who quickly snatched a smoke and shoved it into her plump pink lips.

"Who did you come here with? Which members brought either of you?" Joey asked, his eyes flipping between the two women. "You aren't here with anyone and you sure as fuck aren't here with us, so get the fuck out of our clubhouse!" Joey yelled and pointed at the wooden staircase.

Instantaneously, the backyard became deathly silent. All eyes turned towards them, watching the heated scene play out.

"You heard me! Get your slutty asses out of here and don't come back. The rules are simple; you must be here as a guest of one of the members, or you can't be here at all. Now, as far as I know, you aren't here with anyone and you sure as fuck aren't members."

"We're friends of the club!" Ruby exclaimed arrogantly.

"Not when you're fucking with the members you aren't. Get out both of you, or I swear to God, I will haul your asses to the front door and throw you out!" Dylan shouted.

"Anyone here that wants to vouch for these two snakes better step forward now," Dylan said, stepping towards the two women. "Otherwise, I'm throwing their bitch asses out."

Eva and Ruby, hoping for some help from the crowd, glanced around disappointedly when the yard remained silent. When Bernice opened her mouth to speak, Dylan stepped forward and pointed a tanned finger into her pale white face.

"I'm talking to the members. Are there any members who object to me throwing these two cows out?" Dylan asked, turning to look at his brothers. Nobody spoke.

"Okay, both of you out!" Joey said, uncrossing his arms and stepping towards them.

"Fuck you, Joey!" Eva said smugly, and then she turned her back on him and started to walk away.

"Oh no you don't." Dylan turned her so that she was facing him.

"Fucking let go, Dylan!"

"Sure, when you agree to leave. Otherwise I'm going to carry you out. Either way, you're going." He gripped her upper arm so he could escort her to the staircase.

"Try it," Eva said.

"What?" he asked, thrown off guard by her defiance.

"You heard me. You want us gone so Goddamned bad, then remove us!" she said loudly, so that everyone in the yard could hear.

Dylan snatched Eva around her waist without hesitation and with one arm, lifted her off of the floor and walked with her through the backyard. When Joey saw what he was doing, he picked Ruby in the same manner and followed.

"Put me down, you fucking asshole!" Ruby screamed.

Joey dropped her immediately. Not expecting that, she fell to the ground. The crowd laughed and her face turned bright red, matching her leather outfit.

"Sure I'll let you go. Dylan, you drop your baggage too."

Ruby was ready to be dropped, so she landed on her feet and moved away from Dylan quickly.

"Now, both of you walk out on your own. That way Joey and I don't have to embarrass you further by carrying your asses and tossing both of you out the front door."

Ruby scrambled to her feet and glared at the man who had once been her significant other.

"Sure we'll go. Come on, Eva." Eva, who was still staying clear of Dylan, moved to her friend's side quickly. Without another word, the two girls walked up the staircase and into the kitchen. They stopped for several seconds, long enough to announce to the crowd that they were being thrown out. When nobody responded, the two leather-clad women walked slowly towards the front door of the clubhouse.

Before leaving, however, Ruby turned, blocking Eva's exit, and faced the two men.

"Go!" Dylan yelled. He opened the door himself and shoved Ruby out onto the porch.

"Sure, we'll go. But don't think this is over, Dylan, not by a long shot. You can't just throw us away like this. I can't speak for Eva, but I swear I'll get even," she snorted out so emotionally that she unintentionally spat in the biker's face.

Eva, who had stood inside the door watching until Joey shoved her outside along with her friend, walked over and put an arm around Ruby's shoulders.

"That's right, Joey. You remember what Ruby just said. This ain't over by a long shot."

Dylan kicked the door shut with his boot, slamming it in the two girls' faces.

"Hell hath no fury like a woman scorned."

"What?" Dylan turned abruptly and faced Sal, who was standing behind him smiling.

"Hell hath no fury like a woman scorned," Sal repeated. "While many attribute the quote to William Shakespeare, it actually comes from a play called *The Mourning Bride*, which William Congreve wrote in the late sixteen hundreds. I believe the complete quote is "Heaven has no rage like love to hatred turned; nor hell a fury like a woman scorned.' I think the meaning's plain. Those two aren't going to forget the insult anytime soon. Watch your backs for a while, my friends."

"Thanks for the history lesson, but we'll be fine, Sal," Joey said matter-of-factly. He headed towards the kitchen and the well-deserved beer waiting for him.

"Hmmm, not so sure about that. Those two can be really ugly. Have you ever seen them in a fight? If you had, you wouldn't say that. I know they're only bitches but the word 'cat fight' doesn't even begin to cover it," Sal responded as he followed the two bikers into the kitchen. "When are you going to see your cute hippie girlfriends again?"

"Never. You heard what they said, they never want to see us again," Joey said.

"But you aren't going to take that as a final answer. Everyone here saw how the two of you adored your little fairy princesses. You're going to see them again."

"What do you want, Sal?" Joey finally asked the senior member of the MC.

"Want? Now, why would I want anything from you? We're all brothers here, mate. We help each other out whenever we can." Sal smiled, which pulled his dark leathery skin taught across his angular face.

"Look man, we saw you talking with Frog. Frog and our two guests came together. Which means you followed us into the kitchen for a reason. Let's not play games, Sal. What do you want?" Dylan asked. He filled his red plastic cup with beer out of the iced keg and turned so he could stare at his fellow Angel.

"How well do you know Frog?" Sal asked in a low, raspy voice that sounded more like a whisper.

"Not well. We've dealt with him on some business in the Haight a few times. He's not our good buddy, if that's what you want to know."

"But you know him well enough to follow up on something for Dave and me, don't you?" Sal asked.

"A business proposition, no doubt," Joey said.

"No doubt." Sal smiled.

"Why don't you come out to the garage? Dave and I would like to talk to you for a few minutes."

***

When Frog put Katie over his shoulder he was hoping for cooperation from the tripped out girl, but he didn't really expect it. The night they'd had was bad, and he didn't expect his luck to change. Surprisingly, everything was going well until Frog picked up his pace, that's when Katie complained.

"Put me down! What's wrong with you people? I told you we can't walk this way!" she yelled.

"Actually, you told us we couldn't go in any direction. You wanted us to stay put, but those of us without a coat were reluctant. Of course, there are some of us that would like to go to bed too. All in all, the sidewalk is a bit hard to sleep on for Frog's liking. I'm pampered, I like my bed, that's why your request was denied, and Frog agreed to carry you," Frog said as he continued down Clayton.

"Katie Cat, close your eyes, there's nothing scary, honey. Frog is carrying you home because you've been drugged. Anything you're seeing isn't real. Just shut your eyes and nothing can hurt you. We're almost home. When we get there, you can go to sleep, and tomorrow this will all be over."

Katie was not convinced. From her viewpoint, the sidewalk was going up and down, twisting this way and that, until finally it morphed into a slithering psychedelic snake that tried to bite her face. She screamed, Frog jumped.

"Fuck, man!" Frog yelled, nearly tripping over his own feet.

"Relax and shut your eyes, baby!" Moonbeam repeated to the whimpering hippie girl wiggling on Frog's shoulder and trying to get down.

"That's it! I can't carry her any further." Frog slipped Katie off his shoulder and tried desperately to balance her on her wobbly feet.

"Now what?" Moonbeam asked.

"Now we sit with her until she's calm, because I can't carry her while she's trying to get down and she's screaming."

A dizzy Katie collapsed on the concrete. Despite Frog's and Moonbeam's efforts to catch her, she hit the ground hard. She stayed there with eyes wide open, staring at her surroundings, unaware of the fall she had just taken.

In Katie's mind, the serpent she had seen earlier continued to twist and turn. It was far away now, at the end of a long black tunnel. It didn't scare her anymore. What frightened her now was the inside of the tunnel where she was trapped. Everywhere she looked she saw red eyes staring at her, rodent eyes that terrified her.

"Rats," she said aloud. "There are rats and they're hungry," Katie sobbed. She crawled across the pavement on her hands and knees, heading for a black wall she saw in the distance. When she reached an obstacle, which in reality was a set of stairs leading to a house, she cowered. She pulled her body inwards and sat holding her knees, rocking back and forth. The red eyes didn't move, but they didn't go away either. They stared at her; she stared back and she shivered, knowing they would eventually attack her.

Moonbeam leaned beside her terrified friend and ran her hand though Katie's hair. "It's okay. Shut your eyes, honey." She placed her cold hand on Katie's cheek, leaned closer, and whispered in her ear. "Just shut your eyes. Frog and I are right here. We won't let anything happen to you. Trust us."

"But the rats are staring at me and they're everywhere! They're hungry, can't you tell?"

"Yes, but Frog and I are magical so you don't have to worry about them. We can take care of everything that's scaring you. All you have to do is shut your eyes and they'll be gone. Go ahead, honey, shut them for a second, you'll see."

Physically and mentally exhausted, Katie leaned on Moonbeam's shoulder, shut her eyes, and for several minutes remained silent.

"You're right, Moony, all the red eyes are gone. Someone must have fed them. All I see now are groovy colors dancing together."

"That's right, sweetie, just like I told you, Frog and I are magical. We used special fairy dust to get rid of all the bad and we replaced it with beautiful colors. Now there's nothing that can scare you. Just relax. Keep your eyes shut and watch the colors dancing; they're pretty aren't they?"

"Oh they are. They're lovely!"

Nobody moved and nobody spoke. Moonbeam held Katie and Frog stood protectively beside them. When Katie was quiet for what seemed like a long time, Moonbeam turned to Frog and asked, "Are you ready?"

"Not yet, she's quiet. Let her lay there for a few minutes before we try again," Frog said, finally sitting on the cold concrete beside the two hippie girls.

"Maybe we should tie her sweater around her eyes; blindfold her, so she won't see anything when I pick her up?" he suggested.

"No, I don't think we need to do that. She's calm. I think she's going to stay that way," Moonbeam said with a smile, still stroking Katie's hair.

"Then you're more optimistic than I am. It can't be that easy. Nothing tonight has been easy, and it won't get any better. Nightmares don't end that way and neither do horror movies."

"Katie, can you hear me? Frog is going to pick you up. We have to go home because we can't sleep here. Just keep your eyes shut and everything will be fine. All the monsters are gone, remember that. We took care of them with magical fairy dust. They can't come back."

Katie didn't answer. She continued to lean against Moonbeam's shoulder, eyes shut, resting peacefully.

"Well, I guess it's now or never," Frog said, rising to his feet. "Let's get this show on the road."

Frog took a deep breath, bent his knees, and lifted Katie once more over his shoulder. To his delight, she remained quiet. He graciously ignored the muscle strain and pushed forward.

"I think she's going to sleep," Moonbeam said all too soon. In the next instant, Katie was humming happily as she watched the colors dancing through her mind. "Well, maybe she's not sleeping, but she's definitely in the land of multicolored dreamland."

"We'll see. Don't say anything to jinx us. Just walk quietly and pray for a miracle," Frog said looking at Moonbeam, who nodded and followed him down the street.

***

When they finally reached home, Frog laid the now unconscious Katie on the couch. He stood, rubbing his lower back, and finally breathed a sigh of relief. This horrendous day was almost over. All he wanted to do was walk upstairs, fall into bed, and put the whole day behind him. He looked at his watch. 1:30a.m. He was just about to slip off to his room, happy that Katie had decided to "sleep it off," but Moonbeam's voice stopped him.

"Look at her, Froggy!"

Frog pushed the loose strands of his greasy hair out of his eyes and looked back at Katie, whose body had started to shake. Suddenly her eyes snapped open, she sat straight up and screamed.

"Fuck, she's going wake everyone in the house," Frog said. He sat next to her on the couch and tried to cover her mouth with his hand. Katie, continuing to scream, pulled away and tried to stand, but Moonbeam stopped her. The pixie-like girl got down on her knees, put her hands on Katie's face and gently turned her so that she could look into her friend's frightened eyes.

"Katie Cat, it's all right. We're home. You've been drugged, but everything is okay. Frog and I are here with you. Now you have to stop screaming, honey."

The lights snapped on, illuminating the living room. Standing by the switch was Ron Diebel, the man whose grandmother owned the house.

"What the fuck, man?" Ron asked, rubbing his bloodshot eyes.

Katie had stopped screaming, and was rubbing her arms as if she were trying to knock something off.

"She was drugged at the party we went to," Moonbeam explained as she sat on the floor holding her friend's hands still. Katie whimpered pitifully, unaware of what was going on around her.

"What's she on?" Ron asked. Without waiting for an answer, he approached Katie, leaned down, and stared into her extremely dilated eyes.

"We don't know what she's on; we think someone spiked her beer. My guess is acid, but I'm not sure."

"So you have no idea what they slipped her?" Ron asked, now showing some obvious concern. Moonbeam and Frog both shook their heads.

Katie used the distraction to pull her hands away from Moonbeam and started digging into her flesh with her fingernails. Before Moonbeam and Ron could stop her, she had several spots bleeding.

"No, Katie! You can't do that. You're hurting yourself," Moonbeam told her in a low, soothing voice.

"Can't you see the bugs on me?" Katie asked frantically. When she couldn't pull her arms loose from Ron's and Moonbeam's grasp, she started to cry. "Let me go. They're eating my skin!" she wailed.

"We need to get her into the bathroom and see if we can get her to puke the shit up. Then we can throw her into the shower. After that, we'll have to keep her awake. The best way to do that is to keep her walking. When did she finish this drink?" Ron asked.

"It's been at least an hour and a half," Moonbeam replied.

Ron's face had drained of color and his eyes were as wide as saucers. He was frightened. Last year he had seen a good friend die from an overdose. His concern scared Frog. He looked at Katie and noticed that her skin had a greenish tinge and the whites of her eyes were non-existent.

"He's right. She's fucking turning green," Frog said. He lifted the hippie girl again, this time taking her into the downstairs bathroom, where he waved for Moonbeam to go in first.

"Get the water going," he said as she passed him at the doorway.

"Warm or cold?"

"Lukewarm. Mostly cold," instructed Ron.

When Frog got Katie into the bathroom, Moonbeam had the shower going.

"Now, take her into the water," Ron told Frog.

"Me? You mean get in with her?" Frog asked, hesitating.

"Never mind, man. Give her to me." Ron wrapped his arms around Katie's body and entered the shower fully clothed, then lowered himself and Katie onto the white tiled floor.

"Frog, mix some salt and water and bring it to me. If we can get her to drink it, it will make her puke." Ron settled in the shower and positioned Katie so she was completely under the cold spray. She responded by flailing her arms wildly in the air, but Ron stopped her by wrapping his arms around her upper body. "It's okay, honey. No flying for you tonight."

Frog dashed into the kitchen, returning moments later with a red plastic cup of salt water.

"Katie, you're on a bad trip and we need to make you throw up," Ron told her.

"Stop, stop!" she yelled as she tried to stand and escape from the water. Ron held her close, speaking softly in her ear. "Katie, you've been drugged. You're on a real bad trip and you have to calm down. Lean against me; try to relax," he said soothingly. When she responded by leaning against his body, Ron loosened his grip. "Can you hear me?"

Katie nodded.

"Good girl. Now you need to cooperate. I need you to drink something. It's going to taste like shit, but it's going to make you puke and right now you need to do that."

Ron reached out of the shower and taking the cup, gently lifted it to Katie's lips, and coaxed her to drink. When she took the first sip, she pulled away coughing.

"I can't." She tried to push the cup away.

"Katie, you have to. Remember Barry Bog, my friend with the long blond hair? He used to party with us, you saw him a lot. Do you remember how he died? He died from an overdose, just like you're overdosing now. You have to drink this or we're going to have to take you to the hospital. Do you want to go to the hospital?"

When Katie didn't answer, he shook her.

"Do you want to go to the hospital?"

This time Katie shook her head. "No hospital."

"That's right. You don't want to go to the hospital because then the pigs get involved."

"No hospital, no pigs."

"Then I need you to drink this. Drink it fast and get it over with." Ron held the red cup to Katie's blue tinted lips and to his delight she finished the contents in seconds. With the salty water down, she coughed and started dry heaving.

Moonbeam picked up a psychedelic trash bucket and handed it to Ron.

"Turn the water off," he ordered. Frog did.

Katie vomited into the can repeatedly and Ron stroked her now sopping wet hair.

"That's it, girl. Get it all out," he replied several times.

When she was finished, they sat for several minutes while Ron rocked Katie in his arms. Finally he stood and dragged her to her feet.

"The worst part is over, honey," he told her. "Moonbeam, get her something dry to put on. Frog, hand me a towel."

Frog retrieved a tattered towel from a cupboard in the bathroom while Ron helped Katie out of the shower. He closed the lid on the toilet and sat her down. Meanwhile, Moonbeam returned with a floor length nightgown and Frog passed the towel to Ron. Several minutes later Katie was dry, dressed, and ready to leave the bathroom.

"Now we need to walk her, keep her moving. She's going to want to go to sleep but we can't let her," Ron said.

"For how long?" Frog asked, looking at his watch. 2:15a.m.

"To be on the safe side three hours at least. Then we'll check her. If her eyes are starting to look normal we can let her sleep, but right now the way she is...she can't go to sleep," Ron said, adamantly. "Why don't we take shifts?"

"Shifts? Walking her around?" Frog asked, knowing that he was never going to sleep, at least not this day.

"Yeah, man. No reason for all of us to be up with her. Shall I take the first shift?"

"No, I'll take first watch," Frog replied. "If I go to sleep, there's no way am I going to wake up in an hour."

"I'll stay up with you," Moonbeam offered. "I can't go to sleep and leave her this way."

"Okay, you two take first watch. Let me have an hour and a half and then wake me and I'll take over. If there are any changes for the worse, wake me immediately. I wasn't kidding. There were seven of us present that night and we let Barry Bog die. We should have taken him to the hospital, but we were scared to get the pigs involved. We thought that he would pull through, but he didn't. I wanted to take him for medical care but my friends and his friends talked me out of it. For the rest of my life I'll regret that decision, but one thing's for certain: it will never happen again, not on my watch. If you can't keep her awake, if she starts to change color, anything that indicates she's getting worse, then despite the consequences she goes to the hospital. Agreed?"

Frog and Moonbeam looked at each other, then they looked at Katie, who was sitting on the couch staring at her bare feet. Both nodded.

"Then I'm going to get some shuteye," Ron said, heading for the staircase. "You better get her up. Look at her. She's trying to shut her eyes." Ron then disappeared up the wooden staircase that led to his bedroom.

Chapter 7

Ruby and Eva were still livid about the situation when they reluctantly left the party. They walked down 22nd Street, turned left on 3rd and headed for the Dogpatch Saloon, which was located on the corner of 21st. There, they knew they would find friends. Someone who would listen to their sorrows, sympathize, and buy them a beer or two.

Both girls were in foul moods, especially Ruby, who was hell bent on revenge on the bikers who had thrown them out of the party.

The night was cold. The fog had rolled in from the San Francisco Bay and temperatures had dropped into the low forties. Ruby pulled her red leather jacket close to her body and rubbed her arms for warmth, but still she shivered.

When the girls arrived at the saloon their neatly teased hairdos were blown apart. The chilly January breeze whipped fiercely though the city, wrapping its icy fingers around their barely clad bodies. Eva, who had failed to bring a jacket, was unable to feel her fingers by the time they rounded the corner on 3rd and 21st. When she saw the saloon, she ran ahead of her friend and opened the door wide. The warmth from inside the bar drifted out, and Ruby smiled and rubbed her freezing hands when she felt it.

Even though it was well past midnight, the pub was crowded. Numerous people stood at the bar, others played pool at the two available tables, and still others sat talking and listening to the jukebox, which was currently playing an older Beatles tune over the monotone sound system.

When Ruby stepped into the saloon, Eva stood at the door trying to push her hair back into place.

"Let's head to the restroom," Ruby said. "Fucking wind destroyed my hair too."

Without a word, Eva led the way. The bathroom was vacant so the biker girls walked inside and positioned themselves in front of a large glass mirror. Using the shelf below it, Eva pulled her beauty supplies out of her purse and stacked them on the stainless steel shelf. Aqua net hairspray, a pink plastic teasing comb, a tube of lipstick, a Cover Girl compact, plus an assortment of eye makeup soon accumulated in front of her. Meanwhile, Ruby pulled her makeup out of her purse and added these to the collection.

"Can you believe this fucking night?" Ruby said, shoving a piece of Doublemint gum into her red stained lips.

Eva shook her head. She was concentrating on teasing her hair and spraying a thick layer of ultra-sticky Aqua Net on her henna colored concoction. "Fucking crazy shit," she responded eventually. "At least we got that little hippie bitch good."

Both of them laughed.

"Yeah, we sure did," Ruby added, snickering. "I wonder if the little flower child is tripping yet. What a stupid bitch, drinking a beer that we gave her. Too bad the other one didn't drink anything."

"How many tabs of acid did you slip her? Looked like a fucking lot," Eva asked, applying the last touches of black eyeliner.

"I was going to lace all ten tabs into the beer, but I was nice and only slipped her seven," Ruby said. She finished teasing her hair and sprayed it with a thick layer of Eva's Aqua Net.

"Only!" Eva laughed.

"Well, I didn't want to kill her," Ruby said, smiling sweetly, and trying to look angelic, which caused Eva to laugh even harder.

"You don't think seven tabs will kill her? Fuck, I've never done more than four myself, I can't even imagine seven." Eva rolled her eyes and shook her heavily lacquered head.

"Nah, seven won't kill her, but it will give her one hell of a trip." Ruby laughed again as she put her makeup back into her small black leather handbag.

"Better hope it doesn't kill her. That would be a real bummer. I'd have to visit you in the slammer." Eva sprayed her hair again and then piled her face paint back into her purse. "Ready?"

"Sure am," Ruby responded, and the two girls made their way into the bar.

The Dogpatch Saloon was a biker bar and generally was packed with Angels. Tonight however, there were none, since they were several blocks away attending the party that Ruby and Eva had been kicked out of. Tonight, the bar was filled with locals and another lower ranking MC who sometimes partied with the Angels.

The two girls approached the bar, hoping they would find someone they knew so they wouldn't have to buy their own drinks, and to their surprise they saw Terry Miller, the Angel who had been thrown out of the party for fighting. He was sitting motionless at the end of the old wooden bar. He stared into his beer, oblivious to the rest of his surroundings.

Ruby nudged her friend and gestured towards the lone Angel who, like them, was licking his war wounds.

"What do you know?" Ruby said. Although the comment was made mainly to herself, Eva nodded and smiled in reply.

The two women walked to the end of the bar where they slipped into stools beside Terry. Lost in his own thoughts, Terry didn't notice their arrival until Eva tapped him on the shoulder. Not expecting the intrusion he turned abruptly and nearly fell off the stool he was sitting on.

"What the fuck?" he grunted.

"What's up, tiger?" Ruby asked, batting her eyes attractively.

"Oh, hey," he replied happily, finally noticing the two biker girls who were sitting beside him.

"Hey, yourself, Cassius Clay. Buy a girl a drink?" Eva asked, while leaning on the bar, knowing that the position offered him an optimal view of her cleavage.

"They call him a different name now. I hear he takes offense to his birth name," Terry replied.

"You're right. Let's see, what does he call himself...?" Ruby said.

"Muhammad Ali," Eva answered.

"Yep, you're right, little lady. Now I'll buy you both a drink. Bartender, two for the beautiful ladies beside me," Terry called out.

A lean, thirty-something, balding bartender took their order and returned with two bottles of Coors, which he opened and poured into glasses.

"What are you doing here?" Terry asked. "Last time I saw you two, it looked like you were enjoying yourselves at the party."

"We were, until we got thrown out," Ruby said, pouting for Terry's benefit.

"Kicked out? You two? For what?" Terry asked, in a heavily intoxicated voice.

"Good question; that's what we wanted to know. Basically, we were thrown out for nothing."

"For nothing? They wouldn't throw you out for nothing. You must have done something."

"Okay, here's the reason. We were replaced. Our old men dumped us while we were in Los Angeles and when we got back, they had invited their new loves to the party," Eva said, as she wiped a non-existent tear from her heavily painted eyes.

"The club threw you out for that?" Terry drained the bottle. "Bartender, three more of the same, unless the ladies want something different." Both girls chugged their first drinks and happily accepted another bottle of the same brew.

"Dylan and Joey threw us out and the club didn't do anything to stop them, even though we did nothing to deserve it."

"So they threw you two out and kept their new old ladies at the party? Wow, that's fucked up!" Terry responded with a shake of his head.

"That's not the worst part," Ruby said. "Our replacements were asked to leave before us."

"They were kicked out too?"

"Yeah, by Dylan and Joey. They asked them to leave before us and there was a huge scene. Those hippie chicks freaked out."

"Hippie chicks? Really? Wow, I missed everything," Terry said, and then he whistled in amazement.

"Makes no sense," I know, Ruby said ruefully. "Why did they throw you out? Did they think you had started shit?"

"Who knows what they thought?" Eva cut in. "Truth is, we got thrown out for nothing and none of our so-called friends helped us. Now we got no ride home and we don't have warm clothes either, since we didn't think we were going to walk home."

"Geez, ladies, I'm real sorry," Terry said. "I would give you a ride if I had my car, but I don't. No way I can fit both of you on the back of my bike. I wish I could help you out though." He shook his head sadly. "It's not my business, but let me add my two cents worth. In my opinion, Dylan and Joey are fucking stupid to replace two foxy ladies like yourselves." Terry reached for his beer, finished it in one gulp, and ordered another.

Ruby leaned against his body and stroked his arm affectionately. "That's real nice of you to say, Terry ."

"I ain't just saying that, I mean it. Look at you both, beautiful women sent out in the cold to fend for yourselves, just ain't right." He took a swig off of his new beer. "I meant what I said before, I sure wish there was something that I could do to help."

Ruby moved her stool closer and leaned her head on his shoulder, batting her fake eyelashes seductively. Terry , who had no idea he was about to be woven into their plans, slipped his arm around her slim waist.

"You know, Terry , you might be able to help us out after all..." Ruby said, snuggling into his embrace.

"Anything for you, baby!" he said just before Ruby pressed her fat red lips against his.

***

Dylan and Joey followed Sal into the garage office, where they found Dave sitting at a desk, sipping a beer and smoking a joint.

"Hey, bro's, take a seat," he told his fellow bikers.

Dylan and Joey sat on the other side of the desk and Sal sat on a tan colored couch that was in the far corner. Before discussing business, Dave pulled several beers out of a mini fridge and passed them around.

"Did Sal tell you why we asked you here?" Dave asked the two men sitting nervously before him.

In the two plus years that Dylan and Joey had been in the club, they had never been invited into the office that Dave and Sal, two higher-ranking Angels, used.

"No, man, he didn't," Dylan replied.

"Then let me give you a brief summary. We would like to discuss business with you both. In all honesty, this has to do with your hippie girlfriends and their close friend, Frog," Dave said, with a politician's grin plastered on his weathered face.

"They aren't our girlfriends. Just some chicks we met in the park," Joey said.

"But you'll see them again, and they do have a tight relationship with Frog, right?" Dave asked.

"The short redhead is his roommate, the other one is her friend, and no, I doubt we'll be seeing them again. I'm surprised you didn't hear about the huge blowup we had with them tonight," Dylan answered, honestly. "The girls never want to see us again and at this point, at least for me, the feeling is mutual."

"Excuse me for asking, but you did invite us into this scene," Joey said. "What's the deal with the club and Frog? He's just your average street hustler, one of many. What could you possibly want with him?"

"Quite right, my man. We did invite you into this scene, so I'm going to answer that question. Frog is not quite average, actually. This hustler has connections to every part of the city, which, I understand, includes the business district."

"True enough. He gets around and people like him. What's that got to do with us?" Dylan asked hesitantly, knowing that between himself and Joey, they had asked more than enough questions for one night. Dave and Sal had a reputation in the club and as a lower ranking member you didn't want to cross them. This conversation, undoubtedly, was pushing the line.

Dave smiled an empty toothed grin and then leaned back in his padded chair. "As a trusted member of the MC, I'm going to let you in on some private information. You help us out and we'll cut you a generous deal."

"A deal?" Joey asked.

"Sal and I are investing in a new business project, but we need a trusted, honest hustler with connections all over the city if we're going to pull this off. We need someone flexible and able to mingle with diverse groups. From what we've observed, and from what we've been told, Frog is that perfect person." As soon as Dave finished talking, the politician smile was back in place.

"We saw you talking with Frog tonight, so what do you need from us? I know I'm taking liberties here, but what exactly is this business proposition that we're discussing?" Dylan said, leaning forward and resting his arms on the desk.

"How much do you know about the heroin trade?" Sal asked, smiling his toothless grin.

"I know musicians used to use the shit, like Billie Holiday and Ray Charles, so I figure it's a specialty drug. It's probably pretty expensive and it has bad side effects. I know that once you're hooked on the shit, you can't get off," Dylan said, and Joey nodded in agreement.

"You're thinking of refined heroin, processed, and yes more expensive than its crude cousin. What Sal and I are interested in is black tar heroin. There's less processing involved, it's just as potent, less expensive, and easier for us to get," Dave responded a little too cheerfully.

"Is this a club investment? " Joe asked. "Why isn't Big Jim sitting here discussing this?"

"Although Sal and I are willing to donate much of the profits to the club to help with the community services we support, this deal is a private matter. The MC is not involved. It's me, Sal, a handful of other bikers, you two, and your friend Frog if we can get him on board."

"I get it. Frog doesn't want to go along with this and that's where we come in. Am I right? You need mediators, the middlemen between you and Frog. You want us to pull Frog in and for that you're willing to give us a cut. Well, I for one am not interested." Dylan stood and walked towards the door.

"Now hold on a minute. Who said Frog wasn't interested? Frog is taking his time to think it over. You know the guy. He doesn't do anything spur of the moment. Frog thinks over all his business dealings, although we are fairly certain he will decide to do business with us. It would be a benefit if you could help him decide a little faster. Just discuss the numbers with him, get him excited, help him take the hook. That's all we're asking."

"No disrespect in anyway, Dave, it's just, we don't fit into this the way you think we do. Joey and I can't talk Frog into doing anything. We don't know the guy that well. As for the girls, sure they have connections to the guy, but we aren't going to see them again."

Sal raised his eyebrows in surprise. "Never?"

"Never!" Joey replied, shaking his head.

"If there's anything I learned tonight, it's to stay away from Eva and Ruby, and I learned to leave the hippies to the hippies," Dylan said.

"Man, maybe we should discuss the dough before you turn it down," Dave suggested.

"I don't see the point of that," Dylan said. "We already discussed the situation, at least on my end. Of course, I can't speak for Joey here."

"It's cool, man, I agree with everything you said," Joey replied. "The hippie girls are cute, and we like them, but they're more trouble than what they're worth."

"I don't know about that," Dave said, reaching for a pen and a piece of scratch paper. He wrote down an amount in bold letters and flashed the paper at the two bikers, who had already started to leave the garage. "What if we could guarantee this amount as base pay, with the understanding that in the following months, when this investment starts to really pay off, that amount will double? If that were the case, would you be interested? I bet with that amount of money in your pockets it would make those hippie girls more attractive and less of a problem." Dave smiled his politician smile.

Dylan glanced at the amount in shock. He turned and looked at Joey, whose mouth was hanging open. Joey let go of the door handle, turned, and nodded towards the table. He and Dylan walked back and sat down.

"Well for that amount," Dylan replied, "I love those hippie bitches."

"Me too!" Joey chimed in.

"I thought you might."

All four bikers broke into a laughing fit and clanked their beer bottles together in a toast.

***

"Come on, Katie, let's walk some more," Frog said, pulling her off the couch. Several minutes earlier, Moonbeam had placed her there so she could rest. Now, only five minutes later, the young hippie girl was falling asleep again.

For the last hour, Moonbeam and Frog had taken turns walking Katie around the lower level of the house. Several of the roommates had come home and upon seeing the commotion in the living room, had quickly scuttled off to bed.

"But I'm tired, Frog!" she said when, for the tenth time, he forced her to her feet.

"Believe me, Katie, we all are. There's nothing I'd love more than to go to bed, but for now, it's out of the question." Frog looked at his watch. 3:30 in the morning. In another half hour they could wake Ron and then get some sleep.

Frog shook his head, trying to keep himself awake. He took Katie by the hand and mechanically walked her around the room while Moonbeam, also exhausted by the night, sat on the couch and closed her eyes.

"Frog, I'm so tired. I don't want to walk anymore!" Katie protested. Frog ignored her.

"Katie girl, you got no choice, like I have no choice. We have to keep you moving, even if we have to crawl."

"Set me down on the carpet and I'll crawl," Katie said defiantly. She pulled her arms away from him and tried to sit on the floor.

"Oh no you don't." Frog gripped her by the upper arms and pulled her upright. "Keep walking."

"Come on, Frog. I'm okay, honestly. I know who I am, where I am, what the date is, and who the president is. Can't we just go to sleep now?" Katie asked, trying to push the hair out of her own eyes, but failing when Frog restricted her movements.

"Okay, I'll play along; answer your own questions," he said, stopping momentarily.

"I'm Katherine Stephanie Searfus, aka Katie Cat. I'm in San Francisco, the date is January 7th, 1967, and Lyndon B. Johnson is our president. There. Now can we stop walking and go to bed?"

"Nope, you were wrong. The date is January 8th," he said laughing.

"That's not fair, since we haven't been to bed yet!" She stomped her foot. Seconds later she was moving again, proceeding forward at Frog's insistence.

"Ron said to keep you moving until his turn to watch you, and that's what I'm going to do. Another twenty or thirty minutes then he can assess you and I can go to sleep, I hope."

"And me too?"

"No, I doubt that includes you. Here, let me look at you over here under the lamp." Frog escorted her to a pole lamp with a beaded lampshade that stood in the corner of the room. He angled her face so he could glance into her still much too dilated eyes. "Well, I can see some of the blue, but not enough for you to go to sleep, I'm afraid. How are you feeling, besides being tired? Do you want some more coffee?"

Apart from walking for the last hour, Katie had been repeatedly forced to drink cups of black coffee and water. The idea of drinking more of the bitter liquid made her cringe, and another glass of water was the last thing on her mind. When she walked, she could feel the liquid sloshing around in her stomach. She felt like she was drowning and had the constant need to pee.

"No more coffee and no more water. I have a headache, my stomach hurts, my head is still foggy, and colors are still running together, but I think the worst is over. I bet I could sleep and everything would be alright."

"No such chance," Ron said, suddenly appearing on the landing. He walked down the stairs wearing a pair of cutoffs. When he stepped barefoot on the bottom of the stairs, he stood and stared at her. "How are we doing?" Ron asked Frog, avoiding Katie, who was trying to answer his question.

"She said she's tired and that she's feeling alright, but look in her eyes, they still look heavily dilated to me."

Ron turned Katie's face into the light and nodded. "You're right, Frog. She's clearly not out of the woods yet."

"I'm fine," Katie protested. "Really I am."

"That's what Barry Bog said too. We put him to bed and the next morning I found him dead. Believe me, Katie; this is for your own good. You need to walk for at least another hour." Ron turned to Frog and asked, "When did you give her water last? Has she been drinking coffee?"

"No more water and no more coffee! I want to go to sleep," Katie announced loudly enough that Moonbeam, who had been close to falling asleep on the couch, sat upright and opened her eyes.

"What's happened?" she asked, startled.

"Nothing," Frog said. "Everything's the same, except Ron's up."

"I must have drifted off. I'm sorry, Frog. Is it my turn to walk her?"

"I'll take over," Ron said, placing a hand on Moonbeam's shoulder. "Why don't the two of you get some shuteye? I can handle Katie from here." He took hold of her wrist and headed across the room with her.

"I couldn't possibly leave her," said Moonbeam. "I just wouldn't feel right leaving her and going to bed. But if Frog wants to go to sleep, it's alright by me."

Frog, who had no intentions of staying up longer, smiled. "Then if you will excuse me, I'm going to bed." He turned the corner and headed up the long staircase.

"Good night, Frog. Thanks for everything you did tonight, or last night. I'm sorry it turned out to be such a drag," Moonbeam said in a timid, tired, voice.

"No problem," Frog replied, diplomatically lying.

***

Upstairs the house was quiet; too quiet. An eerie silence fell over the floor and for an instant Frog felt like someone was staring at him. Abruptly he turned, and finding nobody, he shook his head in amusement.

Now I'm hallucinating, he chuckled to himself. Several seconds later he tiptoed into his room, the last door at the end of the hall where the ancient floorboards squeaked if you didn't walk on them just right. Once inside, he flipped on the overhead light and an old crystal chandelier came to life.

Finally! Frog peeled off his clothes, turned off the light, and crawled into his cold bed.

Shivering and pulling himself into a ball to keep warm, he lay there dazed, thinking about his night. Images flashed through his exhausted mind: the T-shirts he should have made today and didn't; the bus ride in and out of the Dogpatch; the horrendous party—including the fights; the business offer he'd received; and most disturbing of all, the image of old Guthrie wandering the Haight, giving his morose prophecy. Seconds later, Frog fell into a deep sleep and drifted off someplace into the morning light.

Frog found himself in a large hallway that seemed to go on for miles. As far as his eyes could see, the crimson carpeting continued until it disappeared at a focal point. In the back of his mind, he remembered that the human eye could only see three miles away. Instinctively, he knew that the corridor in front and behind him was much longer than that.

On both sides of the hall a series of doors appeared, all three or four feet apart. They too went on as far as the eye could see. They were identical, a dark solid wood with a brass handle, and they were all closed. Knowing he was dreaming, he snagged the closest handle and finding it locked, moved on to the next door. Quickly he moved down the line, systematically searching for one that would open. Failing to find an open door, he stopped his hunt and sat comfortably on the carpet. There, he leaned against the wall intent on waiting until he woke up.

When he was relaxed and had given in to the odd dream, a door opened and an old woman in a maid's uniform stepped into the hall. She was oblivious to Frog, staring at her black shoes as she walked.

"Hey lady, wait," Frog called out, but when he didn't receive an answer, he scrambled to his feet and chased the gray haired woman down the hallway. "Hey lady, can you please tell me where I'm at?" Before he could reach her, she pulled out an antique key, shoved it into a door, and entered another room. Frog reached the door only seconds later and tugged on it in frustration when he found that it was locked.

"What the fuck?" he yelled, and banged on the door. When neither the maid nor anyone else answered, he walked down the line of doors beating on each of them. Behind him, he heard a lock disengage and again one of the identical doors burst open.

This time a man stepped into the hall, and Frog squinted so he could see his features. He thought he recognized the tall blond man and as the person came closer, he shuddered.

"Frog, my main man, long time no see!" the smiling figure called out, which caused Frog's jaw to drop open. He stood dumbfounded as the mysterious man approached.

"Hey dude, are you here for the party?" the longhaired hippie asked.

"Party?" Frog questioned. "Man, I'm just here because I'm dreaming."

"Temporarily, bro; just a premonition. Don't worry, you won't get it; you didn't get the last one. Best thing for you to do would be to stay here and save yourself a lot of misery. Just face your fate, like I have. Believe me, it's the easiest way, but you won't listen because you have to do things your own way. That's okay, Frog, because soon you'll be here permanently and we can party forever. Won't that be groovy?"

"*Barry*? You can't be here," Frog said to the man who was suddenly standing beside him.

"Of course it's me, man. Who else would it be? What a crazy question."

"Barry Bog?"

"In the flesh dude. Well, maybe in the spirit, right?" the young hippie laughed.

"But man, you can't be here. Don't get me wrong; it's groovy to see you but...I don't know how to tell you this so I'm just going to say it. Barry, bro, I'm sorry but you're dead."

Barry, upon hearing the news of his own demise, started to laugh. "Hey, bro, dig this. I got news for you too. You're just as dead as I am!"

"No, man, I'm not. I'm very much alive. I'm home in my room sleeping off this bummer night. You should have been there, bro, it was a bitch."

"Frog, dude, if you're not dead, man, what are you doing here? Look around, everyone is dead. If you're here, you're dead too!" Barry chuckled.

"Stop saying that, I told you I'm not dead! I'm here because I'm tripping on this dream," Frog replied, angry at the continued accusation.

"But what if you're not, Frog?"

"Not what?"

"Not dreaming. What if this is the real deal and everything else is the dream? What if you died a long time ago, just like I did? What if we've been dead for decades? Right now you're dreaming that you're back in the Haight, that you're alive, back in your bed. But what if that's the dream and this is the truth? Wouldn't that be a freak out?"

"Barry, man, quit saying that! I am alive. You're the one that's dead. You died six months ago from some fucking bummer of an overdose!"

"Okay, Frog, it's cool. Whatever you say, man. It's all groovy. Now, are you coming to this party or what?" Barry asked in amusement. "There's going to be a lot of people there that you haven't seen in a long time. It's a welcoming party for one of our mutual friends. You're going to be excited to see her! Maybe it will clear your mind; make you see things straight again."

"Sure, man. As long as I have to be in this stupid dream, I might as well go to a party."

As they walked down the hallway, Frog looked at the mysterious identical doors, wondering which held a welcoming party behind it.

"It's going to be so far out to see her after all these years. I'm so fucking excited, man. I love when we have newcomers, don't you? Never mind, dude, you don't have to answer that. I just remembered you're still trapped in the Haight-Ashbury dream and I don't want to go through that shit again. Don't worry man, as I said before, the party will wake you up. It will help you clear your thoughts; help you see what's up or, in our case, down. Just keep following me, Frog, I'll get us there," Barry said, walking down the red-carpeted hallway.

As they continued down the corridor, doors opened and closed. People who were dressed in century old clothing drifted through the hall. Frog peered into the doors when they opened and found that he was looking into rooms from a variety of eras. In one, an old man and woman sat on rocking chairs chewing tobacco and spitting into old rusty cans. They waved at the people in the hallway and when Frog passed, they smiled and waved at him too.

In another room, a crowd of people sat at a long table eating cake, white frosted wigs balanced on their white painted faces. A plump woman in a long gown sat sipping tea. She winked at Frog and he smiled back.

The room that interested Frog the most was the speakeasy. Inside, a multitude of guests dressed in costumes from the Roaring 20s drank bootlegged champagne and listened to Cab Calloway on an old wind up phonograph. Frog stalled at the doorway, watching the beautifully dressed flappers parade around the room, flirting with the impeccably tailor dressed men.

"Not here, Frog. This ain't our gig," Barry Bog said, tapping him on the shoulder "Our party's further down, follow me. We have to hurry or we're going to be late. You want to see her when she arrives don't you? Damn this fucking dream you're trapped in, Frog. It's really getting me down."

Barry walked further down what was now a crowded hallway.

Frog took one last look into the 1920's party and watched one specific girl in a red beaded gown turn and blow him a kiss. She tried to flag him inside, but Frog waved goodbye, turned, and continued following Barry down the plush red carpet towards "their" party.

More doors opened. The maid returned, following some Victorian dressed ladies. The women, who appeared way too snooty for Frog's liking, were sipping tea. One dropped a saucer on the ground and the gray haired maid quickly scooped it up. She pulled out a blue rag and cleaned the puddle of liquid that was left on the scarlet carpet.

Frog tried to pass her but the maid turned around and faced him. From the white apron that was tied around her waist, she pulled out a syringe and shook it in Frog's face. "Tea saucers aren't as bad as what I have to pick up after you, Frog. Take a long look and remember."

Trying to avoid the crazy woman and the hypodermic needle she held in her wrinkled hands, Frog ran through the crowd of oddly dressed people, trying desperately to catch up with Barry Bog.

When he was within arms' reach of Barry, another door opened. This time, a group of Japanese geishas emerged, blocking his way. He tried to get around them, but more doors burst open and Frog watched as a multitude of partygoers spilled into the already crowded hallway.

"Let's go, Frog! I told you we have to hurry or we're going to miss her arrival," Barry said anxiously, suddenly appearing at Frog's side. He tugged on Frog's tie dyed shirt, stretching the sleeve.

"Barry man, be cool. I'm coming; there's no need to drag me. I was just catching some of the vibes from these other parties. Did you see all of the costumes? They're out of sight man. Way groovy."

"Frog, don't you get it? We're going to be late. Snap out of that fucking dream, would you?" Barry yelled. He took a tight grip on Frog's arm and started forcibly dragging him down the hallway.

"Stop, Barry! Let go of my fucking arm. Forget it man, I don't want to go to your party anymore. I'm going to sit right here and wait until I wake up." Barry tightened his grip further, now his slender fingers were digging into Frog's arm. "Let go, Barry! I don't want to go with you," Frog snapped as he pulled his arm, trying to break Barry's grip.

"Frog, dude, we're going to be late! Let's go, we're getting close, just a few more doors."

"I don't fucking care. Let go of me! This is getting way too weird, man. I don't want to go to your fucking party anymore. I don't want any part of this shit. This dream is getting to be a real drag and so are you."

"That's what I've been telling you, Frog. Wake up!" Barry finally let him go. "Do what you want, man. I'm done with you. You figure it out for yourself," Barry said angrily. He walked into one of the identical doors and disappeared.

That's enough of this dream. I'm just going to sit here until I wake up.

Frog leaned against the wall, intent on watching the crowd in the hall until his nightmare was over. But when he turned, everyone was gone and once again the identical doors were closed. The only one left open was the door to the room where Barry's party was being held.

At first, he couldn't hear anything. The hall was completely quiet, but the sound of music drifted into the corridor and he found himself humming along with, 'I'm a Believer.' The music grew louder, and so did the voices behind the door. There was a crowd of people inside and some of the voices Frog recognized. With that knowledge, his curiosity was peaked, especially when a loud applause exploded and the partygoers started to cheer.

Frog rose to his feet and cautiously approached the mysterious doorway. He could see a crowd of people huddled around a lone figure. This somebody, a woman, according to Barry, was a person that he should know.

He stepped closer and studied the crowd. Barry was right, most of the people in the room Frog did know. They were all people from his past, and what bothered Frog the most was that these people, as Barry had pointed out, were all dead.

Frog saw faces he hadn't seen in years, family members that he had never met but instinctively knew. His grandparents were standing with what must have been their parents, and as he got closer to the door, the figures became clearer and they smiled. Frog recognized all of them! Especially the guest of honor, who suddenly turned around, faced him, and stared deeply into his eyes.

"Katie!"

"That's right, Frog, it's Katie Cat," said a voice from the dark corner.

Frog knew the voice. It disturbed him and he shivered. When the old man stepped out of the shadows and approached him, Frog took a step backwards.

"That's right, Frog, you better run, son. You see what happens when you ignore my warnings? Everyone dies, and you're to blame because you're the one who could have stopped it," Old Guthrie choked out in a raspy voice. He raised his dirty hand and pointed it into Frog's face. "You're the one to blame, Frog. You're the one who could have stopped it."

"No!" Frog screamed and backed into the hallway. "No! I'm not to blame, I'm not." Guthrie followed him. The old-timer didn't say another word, but he pursued Frog and backed him against one of the identical doors. Frog took a deep breath, intent on screaming, but the door he was leaning on opened and he fell into a sea of black nothingness.

Chapter 8

Annie flipped through her telephone looking for the number the hospital had refused to give out. It had been several years since she'd called Mark Rhodes' cell. She couldn't remember the reason she had the number to begin with, but now she was glad she did.

She stepped out of Highland Hospital, nervous but intent on making the call. She had never liked Mark. She remembered the first time she met him. The arrogant Stanford University student had come to San Francisco looking for Katie.

Annie's first impression was that he was a rude rich boy used to getting what he wanted, which at that time had been Katie. It was easy to see through his game, at least for everyone except Katie. She had blinders on.

Annie had always believed that Katie's younger brother's death had pushed Katie into the relationship. Before Richard died she wouldn't have even looked at the jerk, especially since her family was intent on shoving him down her throat whether she liked him or not.

In the early days, she and Katie had many conversations about Mark Rhodes, whom they both considered to be part of the establishment they were fighting against. That was until Richard was killed in 'Nam and Katie drifted back into the life her parents had planned for her. Which, unfortunately for her, included a handpicked husband.

Annie shook her head. Her memories of that era were vivid. Friends from the past flashed through her mind, and for several seconds she was overwhelmed by emotion. Using a Kleenex she pulled out of the pocket of her sweater, she dabbed her eyes for the millionth time today.

Taking a few minutes to compose herself, she postponed the call. She bought a cup of specialty coffee and a sugar cookie from the hospital refreshment kiosk. She chose a bench away from earshot and sat for a few minutes drinking the steaming hot brew and munching on the cookie.

Finally, finding her coffee much too hot to drink, she sat it on the bench beside her. The coffee sleeve caught her eye and she stared at it. It was just one of modern man's convenient innovations, another prop that made living in the present a little easier.

Before this innovation, coffee drinkers simply wrapped a few napkins around their hot cups and they were ready to go. But in the world of computers, cellphones, and disposable items, it was the little things in life that seemed important. At some point, humanity had forgotten what really mattered and she doubted if they would ever figure it out.

At one time her generation had thought they knew the answers, sure that, given the chance, they could make the world a better place. When her generation finally took over, that wasn't what happened. They failed. The world, the condition of the country, and the standard of living for all humanity had not improved. In her opinion, her generation had made things worse.

Annie shook her head, reminding herself that she couldn't drift into the past. What she had to do in the present was important. She couldn't allow a flood of emotions to detour that task.

She finished the cookie, gave her coffee another sip and, still finding it too hot, removed the lid and sat it next to her. She reached for her phone, hesitated briefly, and then pressed speed dial. Several seconds later, the phone clicked and a woman's voice came over the line.

"Hello?"

Annie, not expecting a woman to answer, paused before speaking.

"Is this the cellphone of Mark Rhodes?" she asked, thinking that she might have a wrong number or that the number had been changed.

"It is. May I ask who's calling?"

Thinking it might be Katherine's daughter, Annie smiled. "Angela, this is Annie Sullivan, your mother's friend. I haven't talked to you in many years. I'm so sorry about your mother's accident. Is your father home?"

"This is not Angela! I'm Mark's fiancée. What exactly do you want with my husband?" the irritated voice snapped.

Dumbstruck, Annie wasn't sure what to say. "I'm...I'm an old friend," she stammered. "Can you please tell him that I'm calling?"

"Possibly, but that depends on what you're calling about."

Annie blinked. This woman, who claimed to be Mark's wife, was more than she'd bargained for. Annie was prepared to deal with one idiot, but two of them? For several seconds, she said nothing. When she did speak she lowered her voice, authoritative-like and continued.

"I'm not clear who you are, but one way or another I *will* speak to Mark Rhodes. I can do that now, or I can do that at his place of business. It's entirely your choice. How about I make you a deal? If you put him on the phone now I won't tell him that you're screening his calls, but if I have to march down to his office and confront him face to face then he's going to know everything. As I said before, I've known Mark for a very long time, before you were born, I'd bet. The man I know wouldn't take kindly to his girlfriend screening his calls, but it's up to you."

Annie let t her words sink in. Then she repeated her question. "Can you tell Mark that I'm calling?"

The woman cleared her throat. Annie knew she had hit an exposed nerve.

"Just a minute. I'll get him."

Mark's phone was dropped on a hard surface. Annie pulled her phone away from her ear and waited patiently. Several minutes passed before a man's voice came over the line.

"This is Mark Rhodes. Can I help you?"

"I certainly hope so. Mark this is Annie Sullivan, Katie's friend from San Francisco. Do you remember me?"

"Yeah, her hippie friend, right? The short redhead, yep, I remember you."

"Mark, I'm at the hospital with Katie. The doctor asked me to contact you."

"Yeah, well she shouldn't have. I told the hospital last night that they could make the decisions. I've tried to get hold of the kids but they're out of the country on business. That's all I can do."

"Well, that's why I'm calling. I'd like to take guardianship of Katie. I'll make the medical choices, but I need you to sign the legal papers to authorize that."

"Take on guardianship? Sure, I'll sign whatever I need to, but I'm not spending any money on this. If there are legal fees, I'm not going to pay them. If you need lawyers involved then you'd better be ready to cough up some money for the expense."

Annie's anger rose. In the old days, when she believed in peace and love, she could choke down her emotions, try to rationalize with the person she was angry with, or at least try to understand their side of the story. Since peace and love hadn't worked, and she had taken on the position of asserting herself in life, it was hard to ignore an outright jerk. She drank some coffee and continued the speech she'd practiced before calling him.

"I'll pay the legal fees, that's not a problem. I'll find out from the hospital how this procedure works and then I'll call my attorney. I'll have the papers drawn up and assume the charges as long as you assure me that you'll sign them."

Annie watched an elderly couple walking across the hospital parking lot. They looked to be well into their eighties, walking hand in hand. How did some couples end up that way, old and happy together, and others like Katherine and the monster on the other end of the line ended up here, with one partner possibly dying and the other anxious to wash his hands of the problem? After thirty plus years of marriage, how could anyone be that cold, even if they were planning on remarrying and raising a new family?

"Yes, of course I'll sign the paperwork. I'll sign anything, as long as I don't have to make the decisions. I don't know why you're getting involved. Make it easy and let the hospital make the decisions. They're trained in this shit. I'm sure they want to keep her alive. I have really good insurance, and the payout from this little escapade will end up being quite high. Money talks. They'll keep her alive. It's in their best interest."

In the background, Annie could hear the she-monster's high-pitched voice complaining about Mark's insurance. She wanted to know how long a COBRA lasted after a divorce so they could wash their hands of Katherine forever. Annie pretended not to hear the conversation. She cleared her throat and drank another gulp of coffee.

To her surprise, Mark yelled at his pregnant soon-to-be wife. "Tiffany, leave the room! I'm having a conversation that doesn't involve you."

Annie heard a door slam and smiled, wondering if Tiffany was ready for the kind of husband Mark would undoubtedly become. She found herself hoping that the new Mrs. Rhodes would get everything that was coming to her.

"I have to do this, Mark. No, that's not true, I *want* to do this. I'll contact my attorney and when the paperwork is finished, I'll call you."

"No, don't call me. I'll text you with my attorney's information. Of course, before I can sign anything I want him to look it over. When the paperwork is complete, drop it off at his office. There's no need to contact me again unless she dies. If that happens text me and I'll let the children know."

The line went silent. Annie bit her lip, knowing that she was close to getting what she wanted. The satisfaction of telling Mark off wasn't worth the consequences. In the future she would have an opportunity to tell him what she thought of him. She would do it in public, at his office if possible, but that was further down the road. For now, she had to keep on his good side, regardless of how she felt about him.

"Thank you. Send me the information and I'll take care of it via our attorneys," Annie said, relieved at knowing she wouldn't have to make another uncomfortable call to this inhuman beast. "I'm going to get back to Katie's room now. I appreciate this."

"Good luck to you, Annie, I mean it," Mark said, and then the line went dead.

"Asshole!" she uttered, turning off her cellphone. She rose from the bench and headed back inside the hospital.

How on earth had her beautiful friend ended up with such a monster?

***

The lights flashed on and off. For brief seconds Katie was coherent and in the next she was dreaming.

During times of coherency, she found herself first in an ambulance, later in an emergency room. A young doctor asked her questions but she couldn't answer. She was aware when they rushed her into surgery. Flashes of the operating room were imbedded in her memory. But the dreamland she flashed in and out of was real too.

In one reality there was immense pain, old age, and eventual death, but in the other there was peace. Katie knew which reality she belonged to, which she should go back to, but the other was enticing.

The choice was made for her. Her body started to rattle as if she was in an earthquake and then she slipped into the darkness, into a cold that she had never felt before. Shadows engulfed her, twisting her this way and that. She fought against them, pulling away with all of her might and then, quite suddenly, they let go and she fell. She fell for a long time, all the while her arms flailing wildly in the air. She landed in an auditorium where she stood amongst old friends. They were having a celebration for her and she wanted to stay but she couldn't.

She was falling again, and this time when she landed her eyes snapped open and she sat straight up, surprised to be alive. She expected to be in intense pain, but despite a massive headache and incredible thirst, she was in reasonably good condition.

She realized she wasn't in a hospital, she was on a couch. A couch in a room that seemed very familiar yet, at the same time, wasn't. Reluctantly, she searched the room for clues, anything that would trigger her memory, telling her where she was. The stress was too much and she held her pounding head, swallowed a mouthful of bile and cringed.

"What the hell?"

Feeling dizzy, she shut her eyes and rubbed her temples for several minutes, running through the accident in her mind. She remembered going down the embankment and hitting the tree. She knew she had been in an ambulance and she remembered a slew of doctors surrounding her. Yet here she was sitting on a couch...somewhere familiar, a place she knew but couldn't recall.

A brown chenille bedspread covered the couch. There was a basic wooden coffee table, several antique lamps, one in the corner and another on an old table by a beveled window. The hardwood floor of the room was covered by an imitation Persian carpet.

The walls and even the ceilings were filled with posters; old bands like the Beatles, the Rolling Stones, Big Brother and the Holding Company, the Yardbirds, and even the Monkees. Some were drug related, promoting marijuana, mushrooms and LSD. Others were political, protesting the Vietnam War, even including a caricature of Lyndon B. Johnson dressed as John Wayne.

On the ceiling directly above her was a poster of Clint Eastwood draped in a poncho, cigar resting on his lip. A pose from *For a Few Dollars More*. She knew the film well. Beside it were several blacklight posters, psychedelic peace symbols, a hookah smoking caterpillar, and an assortment of twirling colorful designs.

The television, an old tube model from yesteryear, was in a wooden cabinet covered by stickers: STP; two local radio stations, KLIV and KFRC; Champion spark plugs; bare feet and peace symbols of various colors. Beside that was a flower painted guitar case that leaned against the wall. Everything in the room was familiar. She knew this house. She had been here many, many times, so why couldn't she remember whose house she was in?

Katie searched her memory. Where was she? Concentrating deeply, she pushed her much too long hair out of her eyes, but feeling ill and needing to pee, she tried to brush the odd experience out of her mind.

She opened her eyes and studied the room. Instinctively knowing there was a half bathroom at the bottom of the stairs, she rose from the couch and headed in that direction. To leave the parlor and enter an old-fashioned hallway, complete with a crystal chandelier, Katie had to push her way through a multicolor beaded curtain. On the other side of the beads was a small bathroom. She felt along the wall and finally located the small switch that was hidden behind an antique desk, flicked it on, and illuminated the bathroom. Katie took a deep breath and pushed the door open, walking into another room that she recognized.

The bathroom was small. A poster of the Cheshire cat hung on the inside of the door. On the far wall behind an old style toilet with a pull handled flush was a framed picture of Haight Street in the 1960s. Katie sat on the toilet facing a small pedestal basin from another era. She expected to be snapped out of this dream at any second and wake up in the hospital. When that didn't happen, she peed, dabbed herself with paper, and flushed the toilet, immediately knowing she had made a mistake.

The toilet was loud and she knew from experience that the sound of the pipes rattling echoed through the walls of the old house. Everyone upstairs would know she was awake. They would come looking for her and she would have to face this oddity head on. She shuddered again, wondering where she was, and whom she would be facing.

Katie approached the old fashioned basin, rinsed her hands, and washed her face. Cupping her hands, she drank from the faucet, which she knew wasn't healthy, but without a bottle of Alhambra handy, and being much too thirsty to care, she drank freely.

"Jesus! I feel like shit," she said, to herself. The accident flashed in her mind and she looked at her hands and legs for injuries. Finding none, except a large bruise on her right thigh, Katie swallowed, not believing what she was seeing. She went back to studying her hands; hands that were not hers. They were not her hands, but they were her rings, or had been her rings. Rings that she hadn't seen, let alone worn, for many years. One in particular, a silver heart with an amethyst stone, she remembered losing on her honeymoon with Mark. How was it possible that she was wearing these? Wearing them on hands that were much too young to be hers, but hands she remembered.

"My hair..." She ran her hands through it. This hair, not her hair, was halfway down her back. It was blonde, the color her hair used to be, and it was wavy. It was in a style she had worn when she was twenty, long and parted in the middle.

Katie swallowed hard. She sat back down on the toilet and shook her head, hoping the visions she was seeing would disappear. When they didn't she looked up at the mirror on the sidewall, her hands shaking. Terrified to look into the mirror she rose and walked several steps across the cold tiled floor. She faced the mirror, eyes diverted, and hesitated. At last she looked up, and what she saw caused her to collapse on the bathroom floor.

"No fucking way!" Seconds later there was a knock on the other side of the door.

"Katie, honey. Are you all right? I heard something fall. Do you need me to come in and help you?" a voice called from the other side of the door. A voice she recognized but couldn't place by name.

"Um...I'm okay, I just tripped. I'll be out in a few minutes," she said to the mysterious woman on the other side of the door.

"Okay, but considering the condition you were in last night, I'd feel a lot better if you'd unlock the door and let me in."

"No, I'm okay. Just give me a minute. I'll be out, honest."

"Okay, but, Katie, if you don't come out in the next five minutes, I'm waking one of the guys, and if I have to I'll have them force the door open."

"No, don't do that. Just give me a few minutes, please."

Katie heard the girl walking away from the bathroom and sighed in relief. Still sitting on the bathroom floor, she looked at her hands. Young hands with no wrinkles, without the characteristic age spots she had grown used to. She looked at her rings, her rings from another era, rings she had worn on her hands as a young adult. A wave of nausea came over her. She crawled to the toilet and vomited.

Seconds later, Katie wiped her mouth with the back of her hand and rose from the floor. She rinsed her mouth washed her face and then bravely looked in the mirror.

What she saw staring back was haunting. It was undeniably the image of herself, but it wasn't her *now*. It was her years and years ago. She leaned in for a closer look. Gone were the wrinkles under her eyes, the crow's feet, her laugh lines. Her skin was young again. Her hair was thick and long, reaching the middle of her back. Restored to its natural color, her wavy blonde hair didn't have a trace of gray.

"My God!" she said as she ran her youthful hand over her face. And then suddenly, she knew where she was. "I'm dead, I have to be."

Footsteps outside the door and then a knock. "That's it, Katie. Are you coming out or am I coming in?"

Katie's heart pounded and her hands shook. She felt cold and she shivered but found the nerve to answer. "Yes, I'm coming out now."

She took one last deep breath, turned the old brass knob, and stepped out of the bathroom.

***

Frog sat up in bed drenched in sweat and reached for his water glass. The clock on the dresser said it was 6:00a.m. Too early to get up, considering what time he went to bed, but after the nightmare he had just had, he couldn't go back to sleep. He got up, showered, dressed, and planned to leave the house before the rest of his roommates awakened.

Frog stepped on the right combination of floorboards so the floor wouldn't squeak and quietly headed down the stairs. He tiptoed across the living room floor and checked on Katie, who was still breathing and deeply asleep. He opened the closet, pulled out his canvas bag of trinkets, and walked out the front door.

When he stepped on the porch he looked at his watch: 6:45. The sun wouldn't be rising for at least another half hour, plenty of time to make it to the park before then. Today he would beat the crowds and hopefully make up for the loss of funds he suffered the day before.

He strolled along the mostly deserted street, enjoying the solitude. At this hour there were very few cars, the shops were closed, and he could even hear the birds singing in the trees. It wasn't often that one experienced quiet like this living in the Haight, and this morning Frog absorbed it. He needed all the good vibes he could get as he tried desperately to forget the day before, especially the night from hell he had awakened from.

About fifteen minutes into his walk, Frog stopped and stared towards the east, where the sun was just beginning to rise. Although the day was going to be cloudy, for a few minutes he could see a golden ray in the distance and he smiled.

Today will be better, he told himself. All the craziness of yesterday was behind him and he was going to do everything in his power to keep it that way. Just before hitting Golden Gate Park, Frog stopped at the I Thou Coffee Shop. He ordered a cup of coffee and a breakfast sandwich to go and sat at the counter while he waited for his order.

Frog faced the window and glanced towards Beulah Street. A memory flash took him back to yesterday morning, where all the weirdness had started, when he had found himself confronted by a prophesizing Guthrie. That thought then reminded him of his dream. Despite the mental control he was trying to use on himself, he couldn't stop reviewing the nightmare.

As he tried to rationalize everything that had taken place in the last twenty-four hours, he realized that it all had to do with Old Man Guthrie. First the warning and then the dream where Guthrie was accusing him of ...what? What had Guthrie accused him of? The memory upset him terribly. He could picture it clear as day, but for the life of him he couldn't remember what Guthrie said. Even though it had been frighteningly real and still made him shudder, he couldn't remember the accusation the old man had made.

Sandy, a middle aged waitress, approached the counter with a paper bag and a white Styrofoam cup.

"Here you are Frog, honey," the buxom blonde in a white skirt and a red-striped top said. "You're up early this morning. What's cooking, sweetie?"

Sandy reminded Frog of an aunt he had at home in Redding. She leaned in to inspect him.

"What is it, Frog? Are you feeling sick? You don't look so good. You have dark circles around your eyes the size of a baseball."

"I'm not surprised. I didn't get much sleep last night."

"Sorry to hear that. Come to think of it, I didn't sleep well last night either. There was a lot of activity coming from that convenience store on Schrader."

"Schrader? You mean Roman's Market? Do you live near there?"

Frog's curiosity was tweaked. What could have happened at the neighborhood market, and could this have something to do with yesterday?

"Yeah, I live across the street from the place. My kid and I have an apartment over there," Sandy said as she wiped the counter on the other side of Frog.

"What happened?"

"Hell if I know. It started around 4:00 a.m. The police started showing up, then an ambulance. When I left home, they had the place roped off."

Frog felt the color drain from his face and his hands started shaking. He knew that whatever had taken place at Roman's Market had something to do with yesterday.

"I have to go," he told Sandy, staring out the window towards the neighborhood market.

"Okay, honey, take it easy today okay? If you don't take care of yourself you're going to end up getting sick. You really don't look so good." She handed him his bill for $1.10.

Frog pulled his money out and paid his tab, leaving a fifteen-cent tip.

"Look there, another police car heading in that direction. I bet it's going to the market too. Something big must have happened over there," Sandy said, pointing out the window.

Frog watched the black and white Buick drive down the street and quickly put his wallet away.

"Thanks, Sandy, I'll see you later." Frog hurried out of the coffee shop and headed down Schrader Street, following the police car.

As Frog approached the market, two local street kids, Nate and Kerry Bug, ran towards him. Behind them several police cars and a coroner's van were double-parked. On the sidewalk, Mike, the owner, stood solemnly talking to a policeman and lighting a new cigarette from the one he pulled out of his mouth.

"Frog, dude, you're never going to guess what's happened, bro."

Frog stared at Nate and waited for an answer, saying nothing. Before Nate could talk however, Kerry Bug anxiously cut in.

"Guthrie's dead, Frog. He just died for no reason at all. Sometime in the early morning hours he started talking to himself, real crazy shit. Saying he was going to a party and he had to be ready."

"Are you sure he was talking about a party?" Frog asked, suddenly feeling ill. He put his hand on his forehead and a wave of dizziness came over him. He felt his legs turn to rubber and he started to go down, but Nate and Kerry caught him midstride.

"Hey, Frog, what's the matter, man? Are you tripping on something?" Nate asked as he and Terry helped Frog across the street towards a crowd of locals.

"No, I mean yes, I'm alright, and no I'm not tripping on anything. I'm just tired, probably dehydrated too. Yesterday was freaky. I didn't sleep well last night and I haven't eaten anything."

"I hear you, man. It's been a fucking freak show for us too!" Nate said.

When they reached the other side of the street, Mike, who had finished talking with the cop, approached them. He reached out, ready to shake hands with Frog, his other hand holding a smoldering cigarette that was quickly disappearing.

"Can you believe this, Frog?" Mike asked shaking his head. "Just yesterday he's missing and we're looking for him and now he's dead."

"What the fuck happened?"

"Last night around midnight Guthrie started acting really weird, pacing this way and that. He was real anxious, walking back and forth like a caged animal. The kids tried playing their guitars and trying to get him to smoke a doobie but he wouldn't. He stayed agitated, just pacing and mumbling to himself."

"About what?"

"Only thing we could get out of him was that he was going to be late for some party. A welcoming party, I think he called it."

"Are you sure he specifically said he was going to a 'welcoming party'?"

"Yeah, that part was plain as day, man," Nate, who had gradually worked his way into the conversation, replied. Mike turned and glared at him for the interruption but Nate ignored him. "Said he had a party to go to and he didn't want to be late because all his friends were going to be there. I think he mentioned a dude's name too, but I was too stoned to remember."

Kerry Bug brushed her dirty brown hair out of her chocolate colored eyes. "I remember. His name was—"

"Now just hang on!" Mike snapped and pointed a finger at her and at Nate. "This is a private conversation between me and Frog. Let me finish telling him my story before the two of you bombard him with confusing comments!" Mike cleared his throat and continued speaking, his eyes searching the two hippie youths, daring them to interrupt. "As I was saying... when he didn't calm down I brought out some food and a beer. He sat down right there, where he's still lying. He ate his meal, drank the beer, then he fell asleep. Next thing I know, the kids are screaming for me to come outside. When I did, old Guthrie was dead."

"Did you try CPR?" Frog asked.

"Of course. Do you think we're a bunch of idiots? He was gone, Frog, completely gone. Nothing could have brought him back. His skin was already blue. But that's not the strange part. When the pigs got here, he was holding something in his hand; something they've been taking pictures of for the past hour."

"What was it?" Frog asked, his heart racing in his chest.

"We don't know yet. Cops are supposed to show us when they're done. Told us to stand over here and wait for them to finish, and that's what we're doing."

"Looks like they're walking over here now," Frog said, nervously. The conversation came to a complete stop and the group waited for the two police officers to approach them.

"Good morning. I've been told that you're the group that found the deceased?" the taller of the two cops asked.

"That's right, Officer Jolson, I own the market," Mike said after reading the man's nametag. "Old Guthrie's been living here for the past five years. The kids and I tried to watch out for him."

"How much do you know about Mr. Guthrie? We can't seem to find an ID in his belongings. Do you have an idea of how we can contact the family?"

Mike shook his head. "That man never talked, Officer. Seriously, *never* talked, until yesterday, and nothing he said made any sense. All we know about him is what we heard in the neighborhood. The locals call him Guthrie. I have no idea why, and I don't even know if that's his real name," Mike answered truthfully.

"Do you recognize this?" the officer asked, pulling a plastic bag out of a sack he was holding. "This was found in Mr. Guthrie's hand. Any idea what it belongs to?"

Inside the protective plastic bag was an old-fashioned door key, a turn of the century antique that seemed to be in perfect condition.

Mike looked closer at the relic and shook his head. 'Never seen that before, Officer. I have no idea where it came from."

Frog stared at the key in the plastic bag and felt himself break out in a cold sweat. He recognized the key. It was identical to the one the maid used to unlock the doors in the long hallway. Frog's head swam; he shut his eyes and tried to steady himself.

What the fuck is going on?

Officer Jolson, noticing the odd reaction, stared at Frog suspiciously. "What's the matter, son? Have you seen this key before?" the cop asked.

"Yes, Officer, I've seen that key before," Frog said in a shaky voice. "I saw it in a dream."

"Is that so? You hippie boys are real sensitive that way aren't you?" Jolson said. He walked over to his partner, Dan Tuttle, according to the officer's nametag. "You hear that, Dan? Hippie boy here recognizes the key. Says he saw it in a *dream*. What do you think about that?" Both cops looked at Frog and laughed.

"You know what I think about that hippie boy, Matt? I think he's done way too many drugs," the second cop replied, and they walked away laughing. On the other side of the yard, the medics picked up the bagged body of Old Guthrie and placed it into the coroner's van.

Frog watched as they drove away.

Chapter 9

Katie walked out of the bathroom on wobbly legs, expecting at any moment to pop out of this reality and back into her own. When that didn't happen she stood staring at the girl in front of her.

"You look awful! How are you feeling?" Moonbeam asked concernedly.

Katie couldn't answer. She couldn't will herself to move and her head was spinning. For the second time her legs went out from under her and she landed on the floor.

"Katie!" Moonbeam shrieked, ran to her side and knelt beside her on the hard wooden floor.

"I'm going to wake Frog and we're taking you to the hospital," Moonbeam said, inspecting Katie closely.

"I wonder what the hell those bitches gave you. I thought it was only acid but who knows?"

Bitches? Katie asked herself. What was Annie talking about? *Annie?* No, this young girl wasn't Annie. Annie was in her sixties, and this girl wasn't past her early 20s. She would become Annie, but right now she called herself something else. As for acid, sure Katie had taken acid in the 60s, but that was a very long time ago. She certainly wasn't taking LSD at her age.

Katie tried hard to focus on the conversation but it was over her head, and what was the point? At any minute she was going to pop out of here anyway. She was much too tired and sick to question anything. Especially when the answer was plain; she was either dreaming or she was dead. There was no in-between.

Moonbeam helped Katie to her feet, and together they walked back to the couch where Katie was placed to rest. In the meantime, Moonbeam ran up the stairs and called out names that Katie recognized. She lay on the couch and closed her eyes, willing herself to wake. Despite her best efforts she remained in this dreamland.

Several minutes passed before Moonbeam returned, only this time she wasn't alone. Now she was accompanied by a medium sized young man with straight brown hair; a man Katie recognized but couldn't name.

"Katie, let me look at you. Moony, would you get her a glass of water please?"

Moonbeam scurried into the kitchen and the young man placed a hand under Katie's shoulder and helped her into a sitting position.

"Moonbeam said you've fallen down a couple of times. She's convinced that we need to bundle you up and whisk you off to St. Mary's. Me, I'm not so sure we should do that. I figure if you were going to die you would have done it by now."

"I already did," Katie blurted out, surprised at the sound of her own voice, which seemed to be higher pitched that what she was used to.

"Already did what?"

"I've already died. I don't think they're going to be able to do anything for me at the hospital. It would just be a waste of time."

"Exactly! You've already been through the worst. That's what I told Moonbeam. You're going to be fine. You need some water, maybe some food, and then you need to go back to sleep. Sleep all day if you need to. After what you went through last night, you'll probably sleep all day. By tomorrow, you'll be fine. Rest up for the weekend because it's going to be a busy one."

Katie was confused. Whoever this person was, he wasn't making any sense, but then again, none of this made sense. She started to open her mouth, intent on telling him her situation and then closed it. There really wasn't a point to saying anything. None of this was real and she wouldn't be here long enough to explain. All she needed to do was to relax and wait it out. Sooner or later she would move on.

"Here's the water, Ron," Moonbeam said, returning from the kitchen.

"Drink this, Katie, you need it. The last thing you want to do is to end up dehydrated. You threw up a lot last night so you need liquids." He handed the glass to Katie, who took it with shaky hands.

"Is it bottled?"

"Bottled?" Ron asked, laughing. "It's water honey, not beer."

Katie didn't argue. She'd already drunk tap water in the bathroom. Another glass wasn't going to kill her, especially if she was already dead.

"That's a girl, drink it up. How about something to eat? Some soup? I think we have some chicken noodle in the kitchen."

"No. Water is enough. I don't think I could eat anything; my stomach is queasy." The thought of food was repulsive. She felt bile rise up the back of her throat and swallowed a mouthful of water to wash it down. Last thing she wanted now was to eat. After all, this was just a dream. The water she was drinking was just an illusion.

"Understood. Just drink the water. If you get dehydrated then we will have to take you to the hospital. Go upstairs and sleep in Moonbeam's room. I don't think you're ready to go home yet, do you?"

Katie shook her head, finished her water, and handed the glass back. She rested her head on the back of the couch and closed her eyes.

"You're sure she's okay, Ron?" Moonbeam asked her roommate.

"Yep. Just hung over. She needs to sleep. Let's help her up to your room. By the way, did you find Frog?"

"No, he's not in the house and I didn't see him in the yard either. This is strange. It's not like Frog to be out this early. Not when he was up so late last night. Something's wrong, I can feel it."

"Another premonition, Moony? Rest assured, Frog wanted to get an early start this morning and Katie is on a bad drug-over. Normal hippie shit in the Haight and nothing for you to worry about. Let's get her upstairs so she can sleep this off."

They each took an arm and led Katie up the staircase and into Moonbeam's bedroom. Katie, who was exhausted, didn't argue. She simply followed them up the stairs and cooperatively lay on the bed.

After getting Katie settled, Moonbeam and Ron left the room. Relieved to finally be by herself, Katie laid on the bed and shut her eyes. Her head throbbed and for the life of her, she couldn't remember ever having a worse headache.

She was beyond rationalizing. All she wanted to do was sleep. Before leaving the room, Moonbeam had shut the blinds. Now the room was reasonably dark, light enough to see the interior but dark enough to block out direct sunlight.

She tried to glance at her surroundings but the effort made her head hurt worse, and she finally gave up. After all, none of this was real. She wouldn't be here when she woke up because this was just a dream.

Images flashed through her mind: the accident, her children, Mark, who had just walked out on her. She reminded herself of her present her life, or lack of one, and then she opened her eyes long enough to see a peace and love mobile rotating above her head.

She tried to think of the names of the people she had encountered today. Although it pained her, she couldn't stop herself from reviewing the oddity. Annie was Moonbeam again, the vibrant young girl she remembered, not the seasoned older woman that she knew so well. The man helping her downstairs, whose name she could now recall, was Ron Diebel. He owned the house. The other person, the one Moonbeam couldn't find, was called Frog.

Katie remembered him. He was a tall, skinny kid with wavy brown hair that reached midway down his back. He always kept it in a neat ponytail and he was always clean. Even though he fancied himself to be a diplomat, Katie had always thought of him as being cocky. He and Moonbeam had been tight, but Katie had always felt differently towards Frog. He was someone she had tried to avoid, a person with whom she could never see eye to eye. As a result, she had never gotten to know him personally, only through Annie. Something had happened to him but she couldn't exactly remember what that was.

"What the fuck is happening?" she asked out loud, trying to understand. She wanted something, anything that might make sense of the madness, but there were no answers. Nothing but the obvious, that she was either in the hospital, high on massive drugs, or she was dead.

Downstairs, she heard the front door slam. A discussion was taking place in the kitchen. She could hear the echo of voices and then quite suddenly she fell into a dreamless sleep.

***

"A dream, Frog?" Mike, the storeowner, asked.

"Yeah, I saw the key in a freaky dream."

"Frog, you're getting just as crazy as the street kids. What the hell are you on?"

"Sadly, I'm on nothing. That's the worst part of all of this. Weird shit is happening to me and I can't even blame it on good drugs."

"Jesus Christ, Frog. I've had enough of this supernatural bullshit. I have a store to run and I can't be bothered by any more of this." Mike turned abruptly and walked away.

Frog was going to say something in his own defense until he realized he didn't have one, so rather than embarrassing himself further, he kept his mouth shut and stared at the ground.

"I believe you, Frog," said Kerry Bug. "I have dreams that come true all the time. My grandmother used to say it was a family gift. She had it too, but of course my mother didn't believe it. According to her we were wackos. But she's a major square and nobody listens to her."

"Thanks for the vote of confidence," Frog replied. He started back towards Haight Street.

"Frog, wait!" Kerry Bug called after him. "Don't you want to know the name?"

Frog stopped dead in his tracks and turned towards her. "What name?"

"The name Old Guthrie was calling out. I told you, I remember the name. Do you want to know it or not?"

"Tell me."

"The name was Barry Bog. I remember because I have a brother named Barry and we used to live by a bog."

Frog's mouth dropped open. Despite the cool, overcast day, he felt his body break out in a cold sweat. Before he knew what he was doing he had hold of Terry's shoulders and was shaking her.

"What else did he say?"

"Stop it, Frog! Mike's right, man, if you're not careful you're going to lose it. You want to end up like Guthrie?" Nate said, pulling Terry out of Frog's grasp. "Keep in mind, bro, his spot next to the store is vacant. Pull yourself together, man."

"I'm sorry. I don't know what's got into me. Terry please tell me everything you remember." He took a few steps back and crossed his arms in front of him.

"Just like I told you, he said he was going to a party where he was going to see his old friends. It seemed like he was waiting for someone, walking back and forth for at least an hour. Jimmy Rat tried smoking a doobie with him but Old Guthrie would have none of it. Just kept mumbling to himself. Most of what he was saying was incoherent, like he'd forgotten how to talk. When we could understand him he was talking about the party, fretting that he was going to be late and calling out to some cat named Barry Bog. Mike brought him out some supper and he calmed down. Next time I looked at him he was asleep. That's it, really. When Nate woke up he walked behind the store to pee and found him. He came back screaming that Guthrie was gray and he thought he was dead."

"He *was* dead," Nate added, shaking his head.

"And the key that he was holding? What can you tell me about that?"

"I never saw it before. I didn't even know he was holding it until the pigs got here. One of them called out that there was something in his hand. That's when they started taking pictures."

"And you know the rest, you were here," Terry said.

"What the fuck is happening to me?"

"You have a sixth sense, Frog. Yesterday you had a prophesy from a dying man. Last night you had a dream that tied all this craziness together. Now you need to figure out what it means. Believe in yourself man, you're beautiful."

Terry and Nate, finished with the conversation, walked back towards the store holding hands and singing.

Sixth sense my ass. If I'm psychic why hasn't this shit happened to me before? Because it's bullshit that's why! I'm losing my mind. My perfect business mind is going mad.

Confused and depressed, he walked down Schrader towards Haight. He looked at his watch. It was only 7:30a.m, plenty of time to hit the park, walk up Stanyon, and then down Haight. There were early bird tourists already showing up and as he reminded himself, yesterday had been a loss. Today he needed to make up for it, but something inside wouldn't let him work. He walked to Golden Gate Park and sat on the lawn, thinking about the last twenty-four hours and how much had taken place in one day.

He ate his now cold breakfast sandwich and drank the lukewarm coffee. All the while he sat inactive, watching the cars pass by.

"Hey, Frog. I've never seen you just sitting around before. What's happening, man? Are you taking a day off?"

Frog turned and faced Don Austin, one of his roommates, who was walking towards him.

"Man, to tell you the truth, I don't know what I'm doing. Right now I'm contemplating. Planning my next move."

"Contemplating? That's not like you at all, man. You're a go-getter. Sitting and thinking about shit? That ain't your bag. Does this have anything to do with the scene in the living room last night?"

Don sat beside Frog and pulled a joint out of his multi colored bag. "This is what you need man. This shit's great! It will fix you right up."

Don lit the hand rolled delicacy, took a deep toke and passed it to Frog , who accepted it and inhaled deeply.

"You're talking about Katie's overdose? Surprisingly this has nothing to do with that. My problems are way stranger than that, bro."

"Oh I get it, spiritual. Far out, man. You're contemplating God, yeah, that shit is really a mind blower. I tried it myself but it messed with my self-worth and I had to give it up. It was giving me stomachaches."

Frog looked at Don. This was the first time that the strung out hippie had ever made sense, but he was right. He *was* contemplating the spiritual and it was giving him more than just a stomachache.

"Hey, that Katie chick was really blown out last night, man. What's her bag?"

Frog, who was still thinking about his own problems, shook his head and cleared his thoughts. "Yeah, she was. What you witnessed was the result of a night from Hell my friend. The Hells Angels had a party in the Dogpatch. Moonbeam and Katie conned me into taking them."

"Wow man, the Hells Angels? You're one brave cat, Frog. I wouldn't want to party with those crazy fuckers."

"No you wouldn't! It's the last time I'll ever do anything that stupid again."

For several minutes they sat in silence, smoking the rest of the joint and watching the neighborhood come alive around them. Small groups of hippie girls sat closely on the lawn making daisy headbands and necklaces.

Across the street a group of mimes were already performing and the shop owners were opening up. Sunday was a busy place in the Haight, and this day was just beginning.

"So dude, what happened to that Katie chick? You didn't tell me. Was she dropping acid with the Angels?"

Don's question surprised Frog, pulling him out of a daydream and bringing him back into reality.

"Yeah she did, but it was unintentional. The biker dudes they went there to party with had their ex-girlfriends show up. The chicks weren't too happy to share their men with our two little hippie girls, so they slipped Katie a spiked drink. Partway home she flipped out. What you saw was us purging her of her drug-induced demons. It was a miserable night, and it didn't end until early this morning."

"Wow man, that's a bummer. I've had nights like that too; really screws with your biorhythms."

"Yeah, you could say that again." Frog took a gulp of his cold coffee, made a face, and then poured the rest on the lawn beside him.

"So why are you goofing off here instead of selling? There's a good-sized crowd out there already. Isn't Sunday one of your best days?"

"Yes, it's one of my best days." Frog sighed. "You're right, Don. There's no point in me sitting here feeling sorry for myself. I need to give up the spiritual quest and get my ass back to work."

"That's right, man, you do. Get out there and face the world head on. It's all beautiful, man."

Frog rose and smiled for the first time today. He took a deep breath and filled his lungs with crisp morning air.

"Thanks, bro, I need to get to work. You helped a lot. I'll see you at home later. I'm fixing vegetarian meatloaf for dinner tonight. Don't be too late. It dries up if it sits too long."

"Groovy man! I'll be there. Peace."

"Frog flashed a peace sign, organized his canvas bag so he could get his macramé jewelry samples out and started walking toward the street. He was determined to start over. After all, old Guthrie was dead, so he couldn't give any more cryptic messages and dreams were just that, dreams.

***

By noon, Frog had sold all of his trinkets. He was glad that he had connected with Don in the park. Today was a great selling day and he might have missed out.

Determined to head home and replenish his merchandise, Frog drifted down Haight, occasionally stopping to talk to friends. When he got to the Psychedelic Shop, he saw Jay inside leaning on the counter. Jay looked up from his book and seeing Frog, beckoned him inside.

"Hey, Frog. I've been hearing some heavy rumors about you."

"Oh yeah, what about?"

"Word on the street is that you're a psychic. A natural guru who received a prophesy from a dying man. Is that a new business ploy or are you losing it, dude?"

Frog felt his stomach churn. Word got around the Haight quickly, but he didn't expect it to get around this quickly. A rumor like this, especially when it was true, could ruin his business image. Frog said nothing, his mind reeling for the perfect answer, something that would make him seem mystical, but in complete control. Something that would stop people from thinking he was nuts.

Frog shrugged his shoulders and laughed nervously, hoping he could play this off correctly. "Wow, that was fast. Tell me what you know and then I'll fill in the blanks." Frog's philosophy was to never tell more than you're asked, and if at all possible, allow your opponent to answer the questions for you.

"Couple of street kids came in here about an hour ago."

"Let me guess, a skinny tall kid with greasy blond hair and an acne scared face. He was with a cute hippie girl with long brown hair. They were dirty and their bare feet were dirty enough to make your floor black."

"Okay, yeah you guessed it. Nate and Kerry Bug were here. All they could talk about was you. They said you talked to Old Guthrie yesterday. I guess that's the first time the old man had spoken in over five years. Then he up and died last night. Freaky part is, at the same time of his death you have a dream about a key. A key that ends up in the old man's hand."

"Really? Is that all they told you?"

"Isn't that enough? You know Terry claims to be a witch; said her grandmother was one too. Anyway, according to her, an event like you experienced can't be a coincidence. It's a premonition. She's convinced that you're having a religious breakthrough. So let me ask you again, is this a new business plan or are you losing your mind?"

"Ha, ha, very funny, am I losing my mind. Very good." Frog laughed. He walked over to a rack of posters and started flipping through them, intentionally diverting his attention to something other than the conversation. "Is it bad to have a reputation as a soothsayer, Jay? I think it makes me mystical, and mystical is sexy to chicks."

"Is that so? Okay, what's your next move? Are you going to become a Hare Krishna? Fucking shave your head, invest in a tambourine, wrap a toga around yourself, and dance down the street?" Jay sat on a wooden stool and lit a cigarette. "Soothsayer my ass, what's the real story? There's got to be a moneymaking scheme in there someplace. I know you too well to think you've had a spiritual experience."

"Now, if I were on the verge of a brilliant business scheme do you think I would discuss it with you before I came out with it? Dude, just trust me, it's groovy."

"Yeah? Well I hope that's the case. A heads up though, by tonight everyone in the Haight will think you're a new age guru. If that's what you're hoping for, congrats man, you've accomplished your goal. If it's some freaky story that you wish you could blow off, then I'm sorry for the publicity."

A couple of young tourists walked into the shop looking to buy a pipe. Jay drifted away, showing them items from a locked glass cabinet. More customers walked in and soon the store was too busy for Frog to take up space. He waved to Jay and walked out, glad for the reprieve.

Great, now how am I going to integrate the occult into my merchandise?

Frog walked towards Clayton, the idea of selling tarot cards, mystic crystals, and crystal balls roaming about his mind. He smiled, knowing that he could turn this event into a business adventure after all. It would open up a new source of income and save his reputation.

He walked up the yellow steps and entered the house. He could hear talking in the kitchen. Hoping to avoid his roommates, who undoubtedly would want to catch him up on last night's events, he tried to sneak up the stairs. He almost made it too, but Moonbeam walked into the living room and they came face to face.

"What's with you, Frog? I was looking for you this morning. Since when do you start working before the sun comes up?"

"I had to make up for lost funds. As you might recall I didn't sell much yesterday. I got out early hoping to make some of that up. Why were you looking for me, did something else happen?"

"Nothing dramatic. Katie woke up and fell down a few times. I thought I might have to take her to the hospital."

"And you were going to drag me along? Hmm, I'm sorry I went out early, that could have been fun."

"Be serious, Frog!"

"I was being serious. Never mind, how is Katie? Did you end up taking her to the hospital?"

"No, Ron checked her and said she was fine, that all she needed was to sleep it off. She's upstairs in my room right now."

"Well there you have it. If Ron says she's fine, then I'm sure she is. The whole horrid experience is over. When she finally comes out of the pit, I'm sure she'll be her own annoying self again. Now if you'll excuse me, I came home to replenish my merchandise and then I'm going out on the streets again."

Frog walked up several stairs before Moonbeam called to him.

"I have a bad feeling about all of this. There's something wrong here, I can feel it."

Frog stopped, leaned over the banister and looked at her. He had a crooked grin on his face and when he spoke, his cocky attitude was meant to cover up his nervousness. Moony always had special "feelings" and they always scared him, especially when so many times she was spot on.

"And yesterday, you said we were taking a turn for the better; that we were in a time of change. Do you remember that prediction? The one you made in the kitchen before we left for the Dogpatch? So which is it, Moony, are we in a time of change that's getting better or are things changing for the worse? You're the fortuneteller so why don't you fill me in?"

"That's true, Frog, my charts yesterday indicated that we were in a time of change, a time of new opportunities. I know it doesn't seem like I'm right, but I do believe this is a turning point."

"A turning point? Great, it's been a real high so far. Anyway, I'd love to stay and chat but business calls."

Frog walked up the stairs avoiding the squeaky floorboards. He loaded up on a handful of tie-dyed T-shirts and the rest of his macramé jewelry. After they were neatly loaded into his canvas bag, he walked down the stairs, surprised to find Moonbeam waiting for him at the bottom.

"Frog, has anything happened? Something odd that you're not telling me?"

Moonbeam's question sent a shiver through his body. He had to admit that Moonbeam had a knack for reading him and it was eerie. If there were real psychics, she would undoubtedly be one.

"Nothing unusual. I'm just working like every other day. I think your imagination is getting the best of you. Maybe you need a nap. As for me, I'm groovy baby."

Frog walked down the rest of the stairs smiling when he passed Moonbeam and, before she could utter another word, he walked out the front door.

Chapter 10

Richard Terrance Searfus graduated from Antioch High School in June of 1966. Now, seven months later, he felt lost. He'd never been much for schooling, but coming from a wealthy, highly educated family, he didn't have a choice when his father pulled strings to get him into Berkeley.

His father, Al Searfus, was a self-made millionaire by the time he was thirty-five. As a result of his success, he expected the same from everyone, especially his children. This had made Richard's eighteen years of life very difficult.

Richard tried the college scene and had given it his best shot. He had even gone to private tutors twice a week, hoping they could help, and even then, after hours and hours of study, he had barely passed his classes. It had been three weeks since finals, and Christmas break was finally over. His classes started in two days and then the pressure would begin again.

He walked down Telegraph Avenue, heading for the Marines recruitment office, running through his decision again, and he decided that he was doing the right thing. This was the only way out. He could still make his parents proud by becoming an officer someday, and this would give him a legitimate reason to get away. Vietnam was the place to be, fighting for his country against the evil Viet Kong. Yes, a very good reason to escape school.

Unlike his sister Katie, who had taken off last year following a huge blowup with their parents, Richard wanted his escape to be family approved. He knew his father would be furious that he dropped out of school and enlisted, but the old man would get over it. After all, Al's brother was a Lieutenant Commander and his father had retired as a Brigadier General, so how much could he complain? Given the chance, Richard could work his way up the military ladder, just as his family had done before him. This was a good move. It would get his parents off his back and it would set him up for a lifetime career in the military; a career that both he and his father could be proud of.

Smiling at that thought, he arrived at the recruitment office. Sitting outside on the bench as promised was his father's assistant and his recent good friend, Mark Rhodes.

Mark was a student at Stanford, majoring in business. He had one semester left before graduating. When that happened he would move up the business ladder. He was a go-getter. A young twenty-three year old who was going places in Al Searfus' firm. Richard knew how much his father valued the young man. He knew that secretly his father wished that he were just like Mark, and that was another reason he was leaving. He would let his father have his perfect protégé now that he had found him and it would take the pressure off Richard. In a way, Mark Rhodes was taking a thorn out of his side, and for that reason they were friends and he was grateful.

"Hey, there you are, bud. I thought you might have changed your mind. Actually, I was hoping you had. Are you sure about this, Rich? It's not too late, you can change your mind."

"Look, man, I thought we weren't going to do this. We went over this shit on the phone remember? I gave you all my reasons for wanting to enlist and you did your best to try to talk me out of it. You're off the hook, bro. Now you're here to support me, right?"

"Right. I'm sorry, but as your friend I have to make sure you've thought of all the angles and that you know what you're getting yourself into. It's not like the US is in a time of peace."

"Stop right there, Mark. Yeah, I know what I'm getting myself into and I know that more than likely, I'll do a tour in Vietnam. It's okay, man. My uncle fought in both World War Two and the Korean conflict. My grandfather served during the Great War. Military duty is in my blood. I'm a smart guy. I'm not trying to get myself killed. I'll be fine, you'll see."

From inside, the recruitment officers watched their discussion. Three men were staring out the window and the unwanted attention was making Richard nervous.

"Great, now we have an audience. Let's go, Mark. There isn't anything you can say to talk me out of this, so let's just go inside."

Richard walked into the warm, inviting office. He scanned the posters on the wall that depicted how good life could be in the Marines.

Richard walked to the first table, where Lt. Brian Boyd stood and shook his hand.

"My name is Richard Searfus, I have an appointment."

"Yes indeed young man, welcome. I'm Lt. Boyd and I'll be running you through this process. I'll try to make it as painless as possible, okay?" the Lieutenant chuckled. "I see you've already taken your AGCT (Army General Classification Test) and, according to the results, you scored well into the 140s. That score gives you a lot of room for advancement in the Marines. It should be easy for you to move up in ranks. If you want to qualify for schooling, and eventual officer training, that's not going to be a problem either. All we need from you now is for you to fill out these forms and to pass the physical."

"When will I take the physical?" Richard asked.

"As soon as you finish filling out the remainder of your enlistment paperwork. Dr. Knowles is in the back room waiting for you."

Mark picked up a pen and handed it to his friend. "Knock yourself out, Ricky."

"That's exactly what I'm going to do, my friend, watch me."

Richard took the stack of paperwork the officer handed him and started filling out endless copies.

***

Forty-five minutes later Richard was done with his physical. He had the copies of his recruitment papers in his hand, along with his first assignment. In three weeks' time, on February 2, 1967, he would be sent east to North Carolina where he would be completing twelve weeks of basic training.

When he and Mark walked out of the recruitment center, Richard was numb. The great decision that he thought he was making didn't seem as glamorous now that he was faced with the reality. He belonged to the United States Marine Corps, an honorable club that he was determined to be a part of, even if he was frightened of the consequences.

As Mark had already pointed out, the United States was not at peace. That meant that eventually he would be sent to the Asian conflict in Vietnam to do a tour of duty. He knew he would make a great soldier— that was going to be the easy part. The hard part was going to be telling his parents about his decision and waiting those few weeks before deployment. What kept him strong was the knowledge that in three weeks all his problems would be solved because he would be far away from his over-controlling father.

"Okay soldier boy, now what?" Mark asked when they left the office.

"Now we get something to eat. Then you go back to work and I pretend to go back to school."

"Okay, but I'm buying. Seeing how you're going to be risking your life for our country, it's the least I can do."

Both young men walked silently into a small diner. They sat at the counter and studied the menu.

"When are you going to tell him?" Mark asked.

"I don't know. I wish I could tell you that I'm going to do it tonight, but you know how my father is. Everything depends on his mood. In the meantime, you can't let on that you know anything about this. If he finds out from you..."

"Are you crazy? I'm never going to mention this. As far as I'm concerned this event never took place, because I was never here. I'll keep your secret and you keep mine. If he knew that I took his only son down to the recruitment office and allowed him to sign up for the Marines, your dad would hate me, not to mention your sister, who already hates me. No don't worry about me, I'm not going to say a word to anybody."

"Good, let's keep it that way," Richard said just as the waitress arrived at the counter. Both men gave their orders and waited for their drinks to arrive before continuing the conversation.

"Speaking of your sister..." Mark said and then cleared his throat. "Have you heard from her lately? How does she like San Francisco?"

"Katie? No, I haven't spoken to her in over a month. As far as I know, she's still into the peace and love thing, if that's what you wanted to know."

"How long do you think that will last?"

Richard shrugged his shoulders. "You never can tell with Katie. She's a free soul, follows a different drummer than the rest of us."

"Yeah, I gathered that. She's pretty cute though. Too bad she hates me."

"She doesn't hate you, bro. She hates what you stand for."

"Is there a difference?"

"Sure there is. Katie is trying to change the world. She's under the impression that society is bad for people. She sees government as the epitome of evil. It's nothing against you personally. She just hates the world that you choose to be a part of."

"Right, well she's what, twenty? How long can that phase last? I mean at some point she's going to come home and be a normal person again. Every generation does the same thing. Maybe our generation is a little more radical, but eventually they'll fall into line too."

"Ahh...I don't know about that. Katie is a different breed. Hey, why are you asking so many questions about her? Do you have a thing for my sister?"

Mark's face flushed and he turned away just as the waitress returned with their food. Two orders of cheeseburgers were swiftly placed in front of them, and their Cokes were refilled. When the waitress stepped away, Mark tried to change the subject.

"North Carolina... I wonder what the winter is going to be like there?"

"Oh no you don't. I asked you a question. Do you have a thing for Katie?"

"I don't know, man. I hardly know her, but I wouldn't mind getting to know her a little better if that answers your question. She's really pretty and deserves a better life than living like a Bohemian in San Francisco."

"You want my advice? Forget about Katie. You're a good guy, Mark, and I like you. I know my parents like you too, but you're not for Katie and she's not for you. You need a corporate wife, someone who isn't going to mind living in your shadow. That somebody isn't Katie. And Katie, she needs someone who is going to be accepting of all her craziness. She will never be what she isn't and you could never accept what she really is. Sure she's pretty, but the two of you would make each other miserable."

"You can't say that. People change."

"Not true. Problems happen when one person thinks they can change another. The truth is, nobody really changes. You are what you will always be. And if you think that's not the case then you'll end up sadly disappointed."

"Hey man, you're what, eighteen years old? What makes you an expert on relationships?" Mark asked before biting into his burger.

"I'm not claiming to be anything. I just know that people don't change, not really. Deep down inside they are always who they were meant to be and you and Katie, you're meant to go in different directions."

Mark said nothing. He looked at Richard blankly and then finished his lunch quietly. When the waitress finally removed their plates, he glanced at his watch and shook his head.

"Will you look at that, it's nearly 1:00. I need to get back to the office and you need to get back to pretending you're a student," Mark said, rising to his feet and pulling his wallet out of his pocket.

"Hey man, I hope it's cool what I said about you and Katie earlier? I didn't mean it in a bad way. I was just pointing out what I see as the obvious. I want happiness for both of you, that's all."

Mark slapped Richard on the shoulder and smiled. "Hey, it's cool. It's not like I've been purposely scamming on your sister or anything. I was just stating my opinion and you were stating yours." Mark left the money on the counter next to the bill and they walked out of the restaurant smiling.

"Okay man, well, I'm going to head off. I told them at the office that I had a doctor's appointment, so they're probably wondering where I am right now. Good luck on breaking the news to your folks. Let me know how it goes."

"Thanks, Mark, for coming with me and for giving me the confidence to do this."

"Oh no, I didn't tell you to do this, that was *your* decision and *your* decision only. You're not going to pin this one on me." Mark waved goodbye to his friend and walked across the street to where his red Porsche was waiting.

***

Mark entered Highway 580 and joined the bumper-to-bumper traffic. This day had been a complete success and he couldn't have asked for more, but traffic was an annoyance that always ruined his mood and today was no exception.

He changed the radio to a local talk show and turned up the volume so he could hear Paul Harvey and tried to relax. As an added bonus he reminded himself of how successful he was going to be.

It was so easy to encourage Richard Searfus to enlist in the Marines. *As easy as pie.* He burst out laughing. An eighteen-year old kid was so easy to manipulate, just like molding clay. All he had to do was strike up a friendship and then occasionally drop a word or two about the positive aspects of enlisting in the Marines.

Of course, it hadn't started out as the Marines, but as he learned more about Richard's family and their ties to the Marine Corps, it was easy pickings. Mark occasionally brought up how much he respected the military. Sometimes he spoke about the men in his own family who had served and, as he learned more about Richard's uncle and grandfather, everything fell into line.

Hell, he even had the stupid kid believing that he had tried to talk him out of going. Never in his wildest dreams did Richard realize that Mark was the person who put the idea in his head to begin with.

It was a perfect plan; get rid of the boss' kid, the kid who was supposed to take over the firm when he came of age. Richard had signed up for six years, intent on making a career out of the Marines. By the time he got out of the service, if he ever did, he would be twenty-four years old. Within that time, Mark would be able to weasel himself in with the family. If he played his cards right, when Richard got out of the Marines, he would already be second in charge and well on his way to taking over the company.

Richard was wrong about Katie too. People did change and he was a perfect example. He had grown up in a family of losers. His father had inherited a fortune, which he had gone through before hitting forty. When Mark had come of age, the family was nearly destitute. Through his own genius he had saved himself and prevented his parents from going bankrupt, which would have tarnished the Rhodes name. A name that spoke of money even if, for the time being, they didn't have any.

Knowing that showing wealth attracted wealth, Mark Rhodes was living paycheck to paycheck just like everyone else in America. The difference was he had something to show for his poverty.

When Mark went home to his apartment that he couldn't afford in the car that he was renting, he thanked his student loans for keeping him afloat. That, and the second mortgage that had been taken out on the family mansion in Atherton was all the money the Rhodes family had left.

He had one more semester at Stanford; one more large debt that he would have to pay off, and then he would be on his way. Mark was made to be wealthy. It was in his heritage, in his blood. He wasn't going to be a failure like his father. He would succeed, and he would do anything to get there.

What Richard didn't understand was that Mark wasn't that person. What he was had developed from his need to survive. People did change. Situations in life changed them.

Richard's family was wealthy, the kind of family Mark felt he should have been born into. Al Searfus was a financial genius and his brokerage firm was worth millions. Mark was charismatic; when he wanted to he could turn on the charm. He knew that Al thought of him as a son already and now, with Richard shipped off to the military, he would become even more valuable to the old man.

The daughter was cute and she was young. She would come home after she had enough of smoking pot and disrespecting her father. When she did, Mark would make his move. Until then, he would check on her now and then, show her how much he cared while working his charms on her. Eventually, she too would be putty in his hands, just like every other girl he had ever known. If his plan worked as well as he hoped it would, he would be family and the Searfus fortune would be his legacy.

***

She was shocked, and now that her head didn't ache her mind was reeling. *What the hell is happening?* The urgent need to pee and a desperate thirst made her decide to focus on her own needs.

"Moonbeam," or Annie, was tucked under the covers fast asleep when Katie rose from the bed and headed for the bathroom.

She tiptoed to the door and gently tugged on the knob until the door opened. She paused and stared at the hall, a place she knew well. The bathroom was the second door on the left, and then she remembered something else; there was a pattern to the floor, a specific place where you had to place your feet to stop the floor from creaking. This creaking was a sound that echoed through the dark, eerie hallway and ricocheted through the walls. Katie smiled at the memory and tried to remember the pattern.

Several steps into the hallway she gave up and scurried across the hardwood floor hoping for the best but not surprised when she hit the wrong floorboard and the sound crept up around her.

Holding her breath so she wouldn't make any additional noise, she entered the bathroom and flicked on the overhead light. The room was just as she remembered. How could this be? She ran her hand across the top of the claw foot bathtub to see if it was real. When she felt the cold enamel beneath her hand, a shiver ran up her back.

Katie peed and then nervously approached the basin, where an antique mirror hung on the back wall. She washed her hands and face and then glanced at a younger version of herself in the reflection.

"My God, what has happened?" she asked aloud as she studied her wrinkle free twenty-year-old face in the mirror.

"I'm dead. That's the answer, I'm dead. I died and I came back to...Annie's house in the Haight?" It didn't make sense, but *nothing* made sense, and if she were dead why would it?"

Katie dried her face on a towel, cupped her hands, and drank from the sink, then she rinsed her mouth out, ran her fingers through her much too long hair, and stepped out of the bathroom.

The dark hall looked menacing, especially after being in a well lit room and then returning to the blackness. Katie headed back to the bedroom, intent on going back to sleep, still hoping that she might wake up back in her own time. She entered the bedroom and found Moonbeam sitting up waiting for her.

"Hey, you're up! How are you feeling?"

"Dazed and confused," Katie answered honestly.

"Yeah, I bet. It's been a rough couple of days that's for sure. What do you remember?" Annie asked her.

What did she remember? How was she supposed to answer this question? Should she tell her anything?

"I don't know what I remember. Can you fill me in and I'll add to the conversation as we go along?"

"Okay, let me figure out where to start." Annie took a few seconds, thinking before she finally replied. In the meantime Katie sat back on the bed and pulled herself under the covers.

"Two days ago, we went to Dylan and Joey's party. Do you remember that?"

That one threw her for a loop. She barely remembered those names. Vaguely, in a distant portion of her mind she did remember a party, although after all these years the details were sketchy.

"Well, I sort of remember that, sure. Yeah, I remember, go on..." Digging into the hard drive of her mind, she tried to place a face to the names and surprisingly was able to do so. Dylan and Joey had been bikers. For about a minute they had been an important part of hers and Annie's young lives.

"We went to their party and it was a disaster that continued to get worse. Don't you remember Ruby and Eva, the ex-girlfriends that asked if we lived in the park?"

Katie nodded. In reality she didn't have any idea what Annie was talking about. She remembered the party, fighting with the boys and then...what? Something had happened that night. Annie was right.

"When they got you a refill on your beer, they slipped you a shitload of acid. You've been strung out on that shit for two days."

Is that what Annie thought? That they had just come from a party that took place forty odd years ago? She didn't know how to respond.

"Two days?" she finally replied.

"Yes, two days! You woke up yesterday, do you remember that? You were on the couch in the parlor."

That she did remember. It was her last hallucination. She had awakened on the couch, used the bathroom, and saw herself in the mirror.

"Yes I do. I remember that. Was that yesterday?"

"Yep, honey it sure was. You had me real worried. You had *all* of us really worried."

"Yeah, I'm kind of worried too," Katie answered, deep in thought.

"Silly, you don't have to be. Not now. It's all over, and we learned a valuable lesson right?"

"Right," Katie said, even though she had no idea what the lesson had been. She was still processing, trying to make sense out of something, anything.

"We're awake now. I'm sure you've had enough sleep, so why don't we get an early start?"

An early start? What on earth was this girl talking about? An early start doing what? What was the date? Or better yet, what year did Annie think it was?

"Umm sure, but I don't think I want to go out in a nightgown."

"Well of course not. Hey, sorry it's a little short on you but we had to throw you in the shower and your clothes were sopping wet. I hung them up so they would dry.

Moonbeam jumped out of the bed and drew open the blinds, which made Katie squint. She retrieved Katie's white gauze dress and undergarments and handed them to her.

"That's what you came over in, honey. If you want we can go by your pad, check in with your roomie, and you can get cleaned up. I mean, you can take a shower here too, but you know what I mean."

"Yeah, I know what you mean." Her pad? Where the hell was her pad? This was Annie's place and she had a pad, only she didn't remember where. She'd had various rooms in the Haight, which one was she living in then?

"Yeah that sounds good. We can go there. Hey, how far from here would you say that is?"

"What?" Moonbeam turned and looked at her.

"You know, walking wise. I'm just figuring, I haven't really eaten in two days and walking a long distance and all, you know? So how far away is that do you think?"

"Oh, honey. I didn't even think of how hungry you must be, how rude of me. Do you want to see what we have here, maybe walk down to the I Thou Café? Or I could get Ron to drive us, I don't think he's left for work yet."

"I think that would be real good. If he doesn't mind can we get him to drive us to my pad?" she asked, still trying to remember which location they were talking about.

"Yeah sure. He's probably downstairs." Moonbeam changed her clothes, ran her hand through her hair, and skipped to the door. "Get changed and come down. I'll grab us something to eat on the way to your place."

Moonbeam rushed through the door leaving a very confused Katie inside.

Chapter 11

Moonbeam walked down the stairs deep in thought. It had been a weird couple of days, and today had started off strange too. The whole universe was out of whack. Nothing was the same. Thinking back on her astrological chart, she remembered only vague interpretations. There were changes coming, and they were large, but she had read them as positive, and this was far from positive.

Katie had scared the life out of her. Moonbeam had seen many bad trips but she never got used to them, and each scared her more, especially when the victim was her best friend. Even though she knew him and she had partied with him frequently, Moonbeam hadn't been there when Barry Bog died, and for that she was thankful. On that particular day, she had been at the Fillmore grooving to the Yardbirds and Country Joe and the Fish. If she had been home, she would have been at that fateful function along with all the rest of her friends.

When Katie woke yesterday, she seemed as if she was still trapped in an acid trip. Although Ron checked her and said she was fine, Moonbeam had her doubts. Katie had seemed lost, as if she were hallucinating. She didn't know where she was, and she was freaking out. When they took her upstairs she had fallen to sleep quickly and she had stayed asleep. Moonbeam sneaked into the room several times to check on her, just to make sure she was still breathing, and despite the interruptions, Katie hadn't woken. Not until this morning.

Today, Katie was trying hard to appear normal but Moonbeam could sense the tension. Katie couldn't answer a direct question, and she wouldn't look into Moonbeam's eyes when she spoke. Something else was different too. Something that Moonbeam could feel, and not just with Katie, it was around all of them. The vibes were disturbing Moonbeam. It wasn't just Katie who was affected, it was all of them. Her thoughts drifted to Frog, because he was behaving strangely too.

Frog was a private person. He kept to himself, or at least he tried. Moonbeam was one of the only people Frog opened up to; with her he revealed his true self, but with everyone else he was acting. It had taken her a year to gain his trust, but she had a way of getting people to like her, and Frog was no different, it had just taken her a little longer. What she needed was to corner him, force him to tell her what was wrong.

The last few days were exhausting. She had been so emotionally charged over Katie's overdose that she had neglected to check on Frog. Something had been wrong with him before the party. She remembered how he had acted on the bus heading to the Dogpatch and how he had nearly passed out at the bus stop. She had questioned him at the time but, of course, he brushed the incident off. But now, when she was trying to piece information together, she realized that Frog was already acting strange before they reached the party. And then there was his behavior yesterday. He was up at the crack of dawn and left the house; that wasn't like him. Then he had stayed out all day and all night. She had heard him creep in way past midnight, another oddity for her entrepreneur friend, who always had business on his mind. Did this have anything to do with the bikers and the deal they were offering him? That "opportunity", as Frog had called it, worried her too.

The next time she saw Frog, he was taking precedence, no matter what else was going on. She was determined to get to the bottom of his problems. He needed her, she could sense that, and she wasn't going to let his stubbornness stop her.

Katie smelled the coffee brewing and when she walked through the beaded curtains she found Ron sitting at the kitchen table, cup in hand.

"Wow, Moonbeam, you're up early. Are you after a worm?" he asked, smiling.

"Yeah, something like that. Katie and I are heading downtown to see if we can get some work done today. She's still a bit shaky though. You think you could give us a ride to her place? It's a long walk to Cole if you're recovering from a bad trip."

"Sure, I'll drive you. Just let me drink this and then we'll head out. How is she? I'm guessing better, if she's heading home."

"I guess."

"You guess? What's that supposed to mean?"

"I guess she's alright. She's different though, very strange. Is that normal after a bad trip?"

"Normal? I don't know, I've never been on a bad drug trip, just witnessed a lot of them. I guess it's normal. After all she was knocked out for a day and she was pretty fucked up, so yeah, it's probably normal."

"You don't think she's wrecked her chromosomes or anything do you? What if she's burned out part of her brain?"

Ron laughed and drained the rest of his coffee. "Okay, I get what you're saying. No, I don't think she's brain dead if that's what you're asking. As far as changing her chromosomes, that's a bunch of bullshit lies dished out by the Man. Here's the problem, Katie's been through hell. We have no idea what she was given or how much. What we do know is that she was really fucked up. That means they gave her a hell of a lot. Could she have some short-term memory loss? Sure that's possible, and it's probably normal too, but destroyed brain sections and chromosome malformations? Bullshit. Just give her a few days to pull it together. I'm sure by Saturday she'll be her old groovy self."

"If she's not?"

"Not what?"

"What if she's not her old groovy self by Saturday? What if there's something permanently wrong with her?"

"Moony, don't you think you're jumping to conclusions? Look, your imagination is running away with you, so just mellow out. You're getting uptight over nothing. Believe me, everything is cool. She threw up all the bad stuff, don't you remember? Just give her some time. You want some coffee?" Ron asked, just as a bewildered looking Katie entered the kitchen.

"Well, if it isn't the lady in question. And how is our little acid queen this lovely morning?" Ron asked.

"Katie and I don't drink coffee," Moonbeam answered, taking bread from the counter and pulling peanut butter out of the fridge.

"Actually, I wouldn't mind a cup of coffee. As to how I am? Now that would be a real tale but I don't think I'm there yet, so we'll have to wait on that one." Katie, who had thrown on the white gauze dress, sat on a chair and pulled her hair into a high ponytail.

"See?" Moonbeam said, staring at Ron, who had poured a mug of the brown brew for Katie. In a whisper only he could hear she said, "I told you so" and circled her temple with a pointed index finger.

Ron shook his head and placed the mug in front of Katie who gladly accepted the cup and gulped down the remains quickly, while Moonbeam watched in disbelief.

"When did you start drinking coffee?" Moonbeam asked.

"Oh, I don't know, today I guess, and I kind of like the stuff so I'm pretty sure I'll continue. In fact, can I have another cup?"

This time it was Ron who flashed a mystified glance in Moonbeam's direction and she nodded.

"Well, if you groovy chicks are ready, we'll split?" said a smiling Ron.

Moonbeam wrapped the two peanut butter sandwiches in napkins, put the knife in the sink, and the jar back in the refrigerator then nodded in agreement.

Katie finished her coffee, rinsed the cup in the sink, and followed Ron and Moonbeam out the front door.

***

Katie shivered and pulled her gray sweater around her body, glad that she had brought one forty-some odd years ago when she had left for a party. The inside of the car was cold and the windows were fogged up. Ron sat for several minutes letting the car warm up. When the bus was ready to go, he turned on the heat and drove out of the driveway, heading towards Clayton.

"Okay, Katie, I know that I've been to your place once before, but you're going to have to give me directions," Ron said.

Katie swallowed hard. Directions? Where did she live? In which of her three San Francisco apartments was she living in during this time, their time, whatever year this was?

"Umm yeah, sure. Do you need directions from here?" she asked, fishing for information and hoping that Ron would provide some.

"Well, I know you live someplace down Cole, but I don't know where the apartment is. So once we get there, just point the place out."

A good clue; she lived on Cole, so that eliminated the room she had lived in off of Fulton. Now she had two choices: the house she had lived in when she first arrived in Haight, or the place she had shared with Robin.

Once they turned onto Haight, Katie was mesmerized. It was like driving through a page in history, her history. It was early so the street wasn't crowded yet, but the people she saw and the shops that were getting ready to open were all from a past era, one she had lived in a long time ago.

They drove down Haight, passing the familiar shops and restaurants she remembered from her past. Katie was entranced. In front of the Psychedelic Shop a crowd was already forming. As she recalled, that was the local hangout where she had spent many hours in her youth. To her astonishment, she recognized some of the faces and that made her smile.

Moonbeam handed her a peanut butter sandwich. She nibbled at a corner while her mind focused on the hippies, real hippies whose day, like her own, had just begun.

"This is amazing," she said aloud, to nobody in particular.

"What, honey?" Moonbeam asked.

"Oh, just how early everyone gets started; even in the rain, it's amazing."

Moonbeam looked at Ron, who nodded and looked away.

The van heated quickly and Katie started sweating . She loosened her sweater and attributed the heat to a hot flash but then remembered that she probably didn't have those yet, at least not in this twenty-year old body.

"Ron, dude, can you turn the heater off? Man, are you trying to cook us?" Moonbeam asked. Katie started to laugh and once she started, she couldn't stop.

This ludicrous situation, her nerves that had been shot since the accident, the situation with Mark and Tiffany, the loss of her inheritance— everything that had been holding her down gave way like a dam bursting open, and she laughed hysterically.

"Katie, what is it? What's wrong with you?" Moonbeam asked with concern.

Ron, who had already turned onto Cole Street and parked halfway down the block turned and looked at her.

"Okay, Katie, where's your place?"

Instead of answering, the question made her laugh harder. "Good question. Where do I live?"

"Oh for fuck's sake. Where does she live, Moony? I have to get to work."

"This is fine; she lives across the street, kitty corner. We can walk from here, no sweat, man."

Moonbeam pushed at the back of the seat. "Come on, Katie, get out."

Katie, still laughing, obliged. She stepped out of the van and opened the door of the VW bus so Moonbeam could follow. She pulled herself together long enough to thank Ron for the ride. Moonbeam took her hand and together they walked across the street towards a split-level Victorian house.

Katie looked at the house and she remembered living here. This was the place she had shared with Robin. Her apartment was on the third floor of the building. It was a nice place that she was fortunate to find. She would have stayed there too, if it hadn't have been for Robin.

Katie's mind reeled back to a dark haired beauty who had the self-esteem of a doorknob and the loyalty of a jackrabbit. Now this would make her dream even more interesting! Knowing what she knew now about Robin and the two of them sharing an apartment, now that would be one great confrontation. This dream was getting funnier by the minute.

She chuckled, trying desperately to hold herself together, while her mind went through an imaginary scene she was anxious to share with Robin.

Finally, Moonbeam turned on her. "What is wrong with you?"

Katie smiled and ran a hand over her friend's freckled cheek. "Oh, Moony, how I've missed these times, you have no idea."

"Stop!" Moonbeam snapped and pushed her hand off of her face. "I want to know what the hell is going on. What is wrong with you?" Moonbeam asked as they entered the doorway of the old beige house where Katie had lived over forty years ago.

"I don't know," Katie answered.

"Well you better try to explain. Something is wrong, I can feel it. And don't tell me that you don't know what it is because you do. It seems to be your very own private joke at the moment but it's not going to stay that way. You're going to tell me everything because sooner or later you're going to need my help and given the way you are acting, it's going to be a lot sooner than you think."

"The way I'm acting?"

"Yes, the way you're acting. You don't exactly seem sane you know."

Katie shrugged. There was nothing Moonbeam could do to help her. The minute she told her what was happening Moonbeam would make calls and then she would end up where? She hadn't got used to being here yet, she certainly wasn't willing to go somewhere else, someplace worse, unless perhaps that someplace was back to her own time.

"Do you have your key, or is Robin home?"

Her key? Where would that be? Katie opened her psychedelic purse and starting frantically digging through it. In the meantime, Moonbeam knocked on the door and a tall, dark haired girl opened it almost immediately.

"There you are, Katie. You had me so worried. Where have you been?" Robin asked, and again Katie started to laugh.

This situation was a crack up. Here was Robin a two faced liar, ex-friend telling her how worried she was about her. This was hysterical. What the hell was the year? She mentally tried to work out when exactly she had roomed with Robin.

"Worried?" Katie chuckled until Moonbeam answered the question for her.

"We went to a party on Saturday night and we've been recovering at my place."

"Is she alright?" Robin asked.

"Oh hell yeah. Better than you can imagine," Katie replied, still laughing.

Robin shot an odd look her way, picked up her purse, and started to walk out the door.

"I wish I could stay and help, but I have to be at the university for a ten o'clock class. I'll be home early tonight and we can talk." She said looking sincere. The older, cynical Katie burst out laughing again.

"Oh boy, Robin. I can't wait for that talk. Have a good time at the university," she said sarcastically as her puzzled roommate walked out the door.

"That's it, Katie. What is going *on*? We aren't leaving here until I get a proper answer!" Moonbeam snapped.

"Then you'd better sit down, baby, because we're going to be here for a long time."

***

Frog's head ached. He groaned and opened an eye to the morning daylight streaming through his window. He sat up in bed and pulled his long, stringy hair out of his eyes.

What the hell had happened? Yesterday was a fog. It took several minutes before he could remember anything. When his memory returned he held his face in his hands and painfully went over the details. He had gone home and replenished his stock and then he had left abruptly, intent on rescuing his reputation. He had gone back towards Golden Gate Park, selling his trinkets along the way. When he came to the Psychedelic Shop, several of his friends were standing out front smoking a joint.

Naturally, he had joined them and he was enjoying himself for the first time in days until Washboard Dad asked him to read his palm, and the rest of the group started laughing. Of course, he had laughed along with them, pretended to play along with the prank. He looked into each of their palms and made up a comical story, but the incident had disturbed him greatly.

He knew then that he was going to need Moonbeam's help. He had to incorporate the occult into his gig. It was the only way to save his reputation. Needing Moonbeam was never a good thing, and with that disturbing thought and the crushing weight of the nightmare he'd been living in, he proceeded to drink the rest of the day away. His goal had been to forget everything, if only for a little while.

He bought a bottle of cheap vodka and he sat in the Panhandle along with some newcomers, and together they finished the whole thing. When his newfound friends had wandered off to find sleeping quarters for the night, he headed to Pal Malls, the local dive bar, where he continued 'partying' until it closed.

He remembered walking home singing and falling on the stairs while trying to get to his room. He had missed the "silent" floorboards and the squealing echo of his mistake had run up the walls. He shut himself in his room and passed out fully clothed on top of his bed.

Now he was paying the price. The vodka had helped him forget. For a short time he had been old Frog, carefree, joking, and happy, but a horrendous hangover had caught up with him. He cringed at the memory of the past few days, debating whether he wanted to get up at all. Part of him wanted to fall back into bed and return to his dreamland where the walls of his world weren't crumbling in. For a few blissful hours he had forgotten his problems and he had been happy. And for that, his current hangover was worth it.

He sat on the edge of the bed and stared out the window. If he were lucky he wouldn't run into Moonbeam this morning. Avoiding her indefinitely, however, was out of the question.

Moonbeam was a natural born sleuth. She could smell a story a mile away and once she got her teeth into a good mystery, she wasn't going to let go. If he asked for her help he would be opening a door. In exchange, she would want something, and in this case, that would be the truth. Frog shuddered at the thought. How could he tell her the truth? He couldn't let her know that he was losing his mind. Moonbeam was persistent, though, and she would hunt him down for sure, and he would be powerless.

For reasons that baffled him, she had a way of getting him to open up. She was the most unusual person he had ever met, and because of that, or in spite of it, he found her charming. The bikers were right, she was a cute little hippie pixie and she frightened him.

Frog rubbed his bloodshot eyes, intent on getting out of bed, the idea of which at the moment was overwhelming. First things first, he decided. He took the aspirin bottle from the bedside table and dry swallowed two of the bitter tablets. Then he rose to his feet and changed his shirt.

Sifting through his clothes on his floor, he found his shoes, two mismatched socks and a clean pair of underwear. Before leaving his room, he pulled the comforter over his pillow in a weak attempt at making the bed and pulled his hair into a ponytail.

He opened his door cautiously and stuck his head into the hall to look around, relieved to find the upstairs empty. He left his room quietly and stepped on the familiar pattern of floorboards to reach the bathroom quietly.

Twenty minutes later, and much cleaner, he stepped into the hallway and made his way downstairs. Nobody was home. If he wanted to, he could get out of the house unnoticed. *And then what?* he asked himself. His merchandise was depleted. His T-shirts were far from finished and he had multiple tasks that he needed to attend to. His business was falling apart, he had nothing left to sell, and all he could think about was escaping from the house so that no one would see him. What in the hell was wrong with him? He had to pull himself together or everything he had worked so hard for would fall apart. In just two days he had gone from professional business entrepreneur to crazy person. How was that possible?

The phone rang, startling Frog, and he jumped.

Jesus Christ. Look at me. I'm pathetic.

After the third ring he answered the call.

"Hi, is Frog around?" the voice asked.

"Yeah, this is Frog."

"Frog, my man, this is Sal from the MC I'm calling about our business proposal. Have you given any thought to what we discussed on Saturday?"

Frog was caught off guard. He had forgotten completely about the talk he had with Dave and Sal. He was supposed to get back to them in a day or two. Had it really been that long?

"Hey, Sal. Sure I have. Man, I've been thinking about it a lot," he lied.

"Good, good and have you made a decision yet?"

"Not quite. You know how I am. I have to give a lot of thought to my business dealings, but I'm real close to a decision."

"Excellent. Can you meet with us tomorrow?"

Frog hesitated. His business was falling apart. Obviously his new "cracker box" reputation hadn't reached the bikers yet, or they wouldn't be following up with him. Frog swallowed and made an impulsive decision. This could be his one and only saving grace. If he could pull this job off with his usual business style, his reputation might still be salvageable.

"Sure, we could meet tomorrow. Where and when?"

He wasn't used to making hasty decisions, and he had done that by bypassing his strictest rule: never make a decision off the top of your head.

"Let's meet in a neutral location. How about the old diner on Van Ness about 2:00? We can call it a late lunch."

"Sure thing, man, I can be there."

"Then Dave and I will see you at two o'clock tomorrow," confirmed the biker, and then disconnected the call.

Frog held the receiver for a long time. What had he done? This wasn't like him. He'd had no intentions of following through with the deal, but everything had changed. Now he was looking at preserving his sanity along with his reputation. If working with some bikers for a short time could restore what he was losing, then so be it.

The rogue biker had spoken of a new kind of drug, something that would eventually hit the Haight District with or without his help. This venture could make a lot of money and it could restore his credibility, whether he incorporated the occult into his gig or not. Why shouldn't he be on top of an opportunity? It wouldn't really be wrong. He wasn't going to force anyone to try it. All he was going to do was make it available in case they wanted to.

He put the phone back in its cradle and leaned against the wall, breathing heavily. He had to pull himself together. He couldn't attend any meeting until he had his cool business manner back.

I gotta do my shit. I have to get rid of this craziness and tend to my merchandise. I can't afford to be like this. I have jewelry to make and T-shirts to dye.

Today was a financial loss. He couldn't sell what he didn't have. One day without stock was a problem but two or three? There were other hustlers on the street anxious to take Frog's clientele. He couldn't allow that to happen.

Today, like it or not, he had to focus on work. He couldn't run forever. He was acting strangely, and that behavior was just feeding the rumors. If he continued on his current path, his street credibility would be gone and he would be shunned.

He shut his eyes and breathed in deeply as his mind tried to rationalize the situation. This, he realized, was one of the turning points in his life. On the one hand, he could leave the house and hide from the world, adding to the rumor that he just wasn't right in the head. Or, he could pull himself together, march into the kitchen and start a batch of dye for his shirts. He could move ahead as usual, replenish his merchandise, pull off a big job for the bikers, and move back on top where he was meant to be.

With that thought, Frog opened his eyes. He straightened the band in his ponytail and swallowed hard. He forced himself to walk into the kitchen and once there, he washed his face and then sat a pot of water on the old fashioned stove to boil. He sat down at the claw foot table and waited while his fingers drummed nervously on the old oak tabletop.

Chapter 12

Big Jim Bonham sat in the club's office working out the MC's monthly expenses. The party on Saturday had cost more than expected, which only added to his frustration.

He was glad they had held the party in the Dogpatch rather than at the house on Ashbury, which would have been an open invitation for a police raid. That house was always a problem because of the club's reputation. Having a house in the middle of the psychedelic scene was a bad idea. Particularly bad was the location, which happened to be across the street from the Grateful Dead's house, a local rock band who lived close to the cross streets of the Haight-Ashbury District.

This area received a lot of foot traffic from groupies, tourists, and hippie kids looking to party. It was the kind of place where the establishment watched everything because the neighborhood was becoming the center of the youth counterculture.

Although the M.C. still officially occupied the house—a constant complaint of Jim's since he wanted the MC to get rid of it—the Angels' major place of operation had been relocated to the Dogpatch.

The Dogpatch was an old area of San Francisco where fewer locals resided. It was a place well out of the limelight of ordinary San Francisco life. The newly established clubhouse and business offices were now located on a quiet street that dead-ended at an industrial lot. In this location, they were away from everyone; no tourists, no hippies, and best of all, no media. This move had been a first step in changing public opinion, which at the moment involved removing the club from the constant eye of the media.

The Dogpatch was an industrial area which took its name from the dog packs that used to run wild back in the late 1800s, once an area filled with slaughterhouses and a source of food for wild dog packs. It was a port to the 'Frisco Bay, and an area that had remained a quiet spot despite the crazy environment which was now San Francisco.

At first, the neighborhood was concerned over the bikers' relocation, but as crime in the industrial district declined and locals felt safer than they had in years, the MC was welcomed into the community. This positive rapport with the district had an uplifting effect on the members, who now felt a sense of belonging to the neighborhood. And that in itself was the First Skulls' number one objective. They wanted the club that they loved to give back to the city and the community they also loved. The First Skulls wanted the Angels to be visible in the community, to help the unfortunate, and to be known for their community outreach. No longer typecast as the rebel bikers that were feared, but a respected part of the San Francisco community.

The truth was that the Angels were among the first to help during an emergency. All they wanted was acknowledgement for the volunteer work that the biker community provided. They knew they weren't a perfect model, but as one of their officers often said, "If you want to know anything about America, look at the club. It's a reflection of America on all levels: High idealism and elimination."

Thus said, the club was a reflection of the country that had created it. Currently, that nation was being torn apart by a war that meant nothing to the average American. But despite their shortcomings, and Jim had to agree the Angels had many, they were also an active part of the community they lived in and they took care of their own. For that and the many donations and contributions the club made, all they really wanted was to be able to drive down the streets of their city without seeing fear in the eyes of their fellow San Franciscans. It wasn't too much to ask for, the respect for the good they did.

With America's lost youth swarming into the city, they had a chance to clear their name, at least a little, since they were never going to be seen as guardian angels. But perhaps by assisting the radical Diggers, who believed that everything should be free or on a barter system, they could reduce the negative impression that the masses held against them.

Jim had been appointed President of the club last February, and although it had almost been a year, he was far from organized. Things were improving but they weren't even close to being finished. When he had taken over the club it was a disorganized mess.

The First Skulls were a commission of veteran Angels, recently appointed by the chapter's officers. These elite members, many of whom had been founders in the club, pooled their forces together in deciding what would be best for the San Francisco Angels. Their findings were referred to the officers, and it was up to them to make the final decision, Democracy at its best.

From their combined efforts the club, as well as the First Skulls, was determined to bring the MC into a new age. An age where the good they did outweighed the reputation they had acquired as outlaw bikers, which unfortunately meant putting some distance between themselves and several other local chapters, who didn't share in their image as reformed bikers. This was the plight the San Francisco chapter had to endure if they were going to change their image, and as a group that's what they had decided to do.

Jim was been born in San Francisco. He had spent the early part of his life in North Beach, attending Abraham Lincoln High School. Upon graduation, he joined the military. As a member of the 2nd infantry division, he had seen a lot of action in 1952, when he did a tour of duty in the Korean Conflict.

War was a life-changing experience that was unlike anything else known to man. Conflict opened a window into the darkest crevices of a man's soul, an evil so deep that once witnessed it could never be forgotten. The war had changed him in ways he couldn't imagine. When he came back he was damaged and broken. He felt empty and lost, and he found that rejoining society was a lot harder than he had anticipated.

The truth was, he didn't belong in the world he came back to and to compensate for that, he had found the bottle. That was before he had become an Angel. For Jim, being a member of the Hells Angels had saved his life. He owed everything to the club because they had picked him up at his worst. They had made him a part of a brotherhood and he was proud of that.

Like Jim, many of the club's members were veterans. They had the same problems, coming back and mixing with a society that they no longer fit into. These men understood his pain, and together they had built new lives for themselves that centered on the MC Among their fellow vets, they had found the camaraderie that life as a civilian was missing.

Like the rest of the club's members, Jim lived and breathed the Angels. He was a man who cared about the community, a patriot, despite the present state of turmoil that was threatening to tear his country apart. He knew that his brothers felt the same. Like the hippies, they objected to the establishment, but for different reasons. The Angels wanted to do their part in changing the world, but they were trapped in a subculture where their reputation kept them in a social prison. And as their motto said, "When we do right nobody remembers, when we do wrong nobody forgets."

The media was responsible for that, the newsroom journalists with their exaggerated stories. Every time the club turned around, relaxed, thought they were safe from criticism, the media would attack again. Many times they were accused of crimes they had nothing to do with.

With all the bad press, it was impossible to do anything without being noticed. In general, it was becoming impossible to wear their colors without being harassed, judged, or watched by "The Man".

Jim was no fool. He knew the men in his club were tough, some more than others. Most members had criminal records, and many were card-carrying felons. But there were reasons for their indiscretions. They, like Jim, had once been among society's lost. But America had a long memory and a selective one. As a result, they were all seen in the same light. If you were an Angel then you were a walking advertisement for a specific stereotype, one that an individual assumed as soon as he donned his colors.

For the most part, they were law abiding citizens who just wanted to run their own gig in peace. In the eyes of society they were something more, something violent, because all the good they did was overlooked by the media, who preferred to portray them as a gang of dangerous criminals.

The newly appointed members of the First Skulls wanted to turn that image around even if they were the first to admit that the club's name had been tied to some pretty shady business deals. But that was the case with any club. No single organization could control the private affairs of their members. Even the Masons found themselves tied into bad dealings from time to time. Jim knew of Masons who had been sent to jail for scams, but their crimes didn't impact the group in the same way as it did with the Angels.

What the public refused to acknowledge, was that the club was separate from the affairs of their members. If a small percentage of bikers were associated with a crime, it was immediately pinned on the MC, even if those bikers weren't affiliated with the Hells Angels. The result had been a tarnished name that was becoming impossible to crawl out from under and that tainted the members of the club, especially the new order.

To counter the media's attack, the MC had chosen spokesmen from their more educated members. These men challenged the media by diplomatically defending the club's image. On the other end, even though they would probably never receive recognition for their positive contributions, the Angels submerged themselves into community activism, following the ethical values that, in their eyes, made them part of the biker community.

Throughout the year the bikers performed hundreds of small acts of community service, which of course the media never reported. They held an annual toy drive, helped feed the needy on Thanksgiving Day, organized and participated in cleanup projects or paid for improvements in San Francisco's parks, and helped others on the highways. Whether they got credit for their deeds or not, the members knew that their chapter played an important role in the city.

Their wish was to convey to America that they were a club, only a club, not an organized crime syndicate. They were simply men who cared deeply about their MC, each other, and the community they lived in, and that was the First Skulls' focus; to turn the club's image around, at least amongst the people they lived with.

In the meantime the club needed money. There were upcoming events on the calendar and Jim was going over the finances when Skinner walked up to the opened office door.

"You wanted to see me, boss?" he asked, sticking his head inside the room.

"Skinner, come in. Please shut the door behind you."

Skinner entered, shut the door quietly, and worked his way through the room by walking around several large boxes that stood in his way. He finally made his way to a spare chair next to Jim's desk and sat.

"Skinner, what do you think of the First Skulls' objective, our plans to move the club forward?" Jim asked.

"Objective?"

"The plan for the MC. How we are moving forward as a group?" Big Jim said.

"Sure, man. Everyone knows. We're getting involved, being seen more and helping people."

"Right, and you agree with that?"

"Sure, we all believe it's good. We unanimously approved the charter that the First Skulls drew up didn't we? That was months ago. Why are you asking me this now? Are you doubting my commitment to the club?" Skinner moved his chair closer to the desk and leaned forward, waiting for an answer.

"No, I don't doubt your commitment, and if I made it seem that way then I'm sorry, man. I'm not trying to put anyone on the spot. I'm calling all of my officers in so I can talk to them one on one. I'm asking each to define their commitment to the club and to the direction the new order wants to take us into. "I know we have always kept a standoffish position in the past, out of sight out of mind philosophy, and this is a one hundred eighty degree turnaround from that. But it's a turning point in San Francisco's history, and in the history of this country. It should be a turning point in our history too. "At least that's the belief of the members of the First Skulls, and that's why the charter was drawn up and agreed upon last year. And yes, we have been succeeding in getting involved in city activities and we've done a damn good job of it. But it's time to expand on that.

"We've decided that this is the time when the city needs us the most. They are under a constant bombardment of youths who are entering the Haight-Ashbury scene. This is the time for us to reach out and help. There is an abundance of kids living on the street. They're hungry, dirty, and ill. Some are strung out on drugs and many are underage. The Diggers are there, right in the mix of things, helping the newcomers find a place to stay and feeding the hungry. The Hells Angels are going to be there beside them, man. Making a name for ourselves outside the one the media's hung on us. We can create our own image if people see us involved. They won't believe what the media says about us. If they get to know us as their neighbors, as people helping them build a better place to live, then they won't look at us as a band of criminals. They'll see us for what we really are, and they'll know that we care about the people in this city. Then it won't matter how the media wants to portray us because the people we've helped will know the truth.

"The club's notoriety is tearing it apart. We're persecuted by the fuzz and we can't go anywhere without be heckled. Soon it will be impossible for us to wear our colors without attracting the attention of security. Sure, we're bikers first and foremost, but allowing ourselves to be smeared across the media as monsters and killers, well it just ain't working. For the good of the club, things have to change, and that means continuously tightening our belts. Playing it clean, clearing up our shortcomings by working the good guy image until The Man backs off, because let's be honest, the good guy act is farfetched. But it's the right move to make right now while issues are heating up in the city.

"It's a difficult transformation. It would be easier to dump all that we're doing and let the media continue to hype up our image, but in the long run that publicity will ruin us. It's only a matter of time. That's why we're here,

Skinner. I've been asked by the other members of the First Skulls to check our officers' commitment to the plan. Either we're all in, or this clean up act isn't going to work and we might as well get rid of the charter now."

"I'm hip, bro, I get what you're saying, and I'm backing you all the way, which is another reason why I don't understand any of this," Skinner said.

"We aren't sure that all our members are on the same page. There have been disturbing rumors and if they're true, they could tarnish what we're working towards and put us into a hole we can never dig ourselves out of."

"What do you mean?" Skinner asked. "Everyone is on the same page, boss. At least everyone that I know."

"I wish I could believe that, but I don't. What I do believe in is the First Skulls and the conservative direction they want to move this club into, but I'm not a fool. I know there are members who have their own ideas, their own agendas on what we should and shouldn't be doing. More specifically, there are personal business ventures that haven't been disclosed to the MC Business ventures that we would not condone. An individual's choice of how they make their bread is important to the club, but not if they are dealing in areas that are going to reflect negatively on the Angels. As our rules clearly state, nobody puts themselves above the best interests of the club."

"This conversation is leading to something big, Jim. Why don't we discuss what's really on your mind?" Skinner bluntly replied.

Big Jim took a deep breath, laced his fingers together behind his head, and leaned into the leather chair.

"Very well, let's do that," he replied and then he paused, deep in thought. For several seconds the room grew quiet. "If you knew of a member who was selling, or planning to sell, illegal contraband without the club's knowledge, would you inform us of their activities, or would your loyalty to your brothers prevent you from doing that?"

There it was, the bag was out on the table and Skinner swallowed hard. He knew what was coming next. He'd been through this scene before with the former president, and he hated being put into a position where he was cornered into making a choice.

"Man, are you asking me if I would rat on my brothers?"

"If their actions were detrimental to the club, yes, that's what I'm asking."

"Jim, my loyalty, of course, is to the club first and foremost, but my brothers are my brothers, man, you know that. I need a clear picture of what we're discussing here, if you want my honest opinion."

"In the beginning of the changeover, the First Skulls asked each member to disclose their business dealings and to keep them as legit as possible, excluding themselves from anything that could be truly detrimental to the club. But there are rumors. We've heard that there are members who are heavily involved in businesses that they are hiding from the MC What those specifics are, we can only guess, but we are trying to find out. So I am conducting damage control before the damage happens. I can't do that unless I have the full cooperation of my members, especially my officers. Let me be blunt. Do you know of anyone who is involved in any type of business that goes against the ethics of this club? And if you did, would you keep that information to yourself, protecting your brother, or would you protect your club? What do you think is right?"

"Wow, that's quite a question, man," Skinner said, shaking his head in disbelief and laughing nervously. "Okay, I'll give you an honest answer, man. I guess it would depend on the situation. Who the member was and what the offense was. If I felt it was powerful enough to threaten the wellbeing of the club, then I would talk to them personally. See where they're at, what they're thinking. If that didn't work and I truly felt they were making a bad judgment call, something that could injure the club, then I'd tell someone...probably not you though, I'd tell a fellow officer, I'd get their opinion, see if we could fix the problem. If that didn't work, then we would decide whether or not to come to you. If it were that crucial, something that could draw the club into a real bad space, then yeah, man, you would eventually know about it.

That's the God's honest Jim. You asked for the truth. I love this club and I love my brothers, but I gotta follow my heart, my conscience, and in my opinion that would be the right way to take care of it."

Jim said nothing. He sat in his chair for several minutes, thinking.

The room grew uncomfortably quiet. Skinner, who had been sitting forward for the whole conversation finally leaned back and tried to relax in the chair. He wiped his sweaty forehead with his bare arm and waited nervously for the president's answer.

Finally, Big Jim broke the silence. He leaned forward and spoke in a raspy voice. "I respect that answer, I really do. You're honest and I like that. I believe what you told me and to be truthful, I would do the same thing. I understand your loyalty to your brothers and to the club and that's why I'm asking you to follow your conscience. Remember what we're trying to build here, what's on the line if anything goes wrong. Just keep your eyes open and think about this conversation."

"I'll do that, boss, I promise," Skinner replied.

There was a knock on the door.

"Enter," Big Jim called. Bobby McClellan, another officer in the MC walked in the door and nodded to Skinner.

"I hope I'm not intruding here," he said.

"No not at all. Come in, man, I think my meeting is over," Skinner said, rising from the chair and walking towards the door. He stopped in the middle of the room, looked at the boxes closely and then shrugged.

"Hey, boss, what's with the boxes? Are you moving stuff in, or moving it out?"

"Neither. We're getting ready for the Human Be-In. It's charity stuff mostly: clothes, toys, blankets, coats, donations from the members and the public."

"Oh right. 'The Gathering of the Tribes' this Saturday in Golden Gate Park, Polo Fields," Skinner said, quoting the recent *San Francisco Oracle*, where he'd seen the advertisement on the front cover.

"Yeah that's right. Bowen said he'd have some jobs for us, so try to be early if you can. Gig starts at 1:00 so we're meeting here at 11:30, if you're interested in riding over with us. If not, we'll meet you at the sound truck."

"Okay, Jim, sounds like a plan. I guess it's time for me to split so you two can have your one-on-one." Skinner walked into the hall and shut the office door behind him.

***

Skinner walked out of Big Jim's office confused. He wasn't sure what he expected from the meeting, but he was shocked. The idea of choosing between his brothers and his club was unfathomable. How was that even a possibility?

He understood Jim's side, but Jim wasn't considering the other side. They were brothers, equal in the eyes of the club. They had always had their independent dealings, and those dealings had always been accepted—no questions asked. They were Hells Angels after all, not Boy Scouts. Now, all of that was changing. The club was becoming a real entity, achieving a reputation that was promoted by the media. The term "Hells Angels" had been personalized to a point where it had taken on human qualities and a human spirit.

Skinner agreed with the First Skulls' plan to give back to the community that you lived in, and the times, these times, they were crazy. Every day more kids arrived in San Francisco. They expected utopia and what they found was a cold climate, making it unpleasant to sleep outside. He wanted to be involved, looking out for his city through his club, but he believed in personal freedom too, and that placed him in an awkward position.

Off the top of his head he didn't know of any illegal business dealings because, quite frankly, he never asked questions. Were there dealings? Sure, some of the guys had dealings outside the club making bread where they could, they were bikers after all. What the specifics of those dealings were, he didn't know, had never cared to know, and therefore had never asked.

The other night, Dave and Sal had met with Frog, the hippie kid, over business. They were always conducting business, everyone knew that. They used the old garage outside the clubhouse, and it was no secret to anyone that on top of club business they were conducting their own thing too, but he had never asked, and he had never cared, until now. Big Jim's words ran through his head. Did he know something that was detrimental to the club?

Skinner saw himself as a fair, nonjudgmental guy. In his mind, the club and its members were one and the same. He had never tried to separate the two, and he didn't know if he could. After his talk with Jim, he felt insecure, and he hated feeling that way. He knew that he was going to have to work this out in his mind, second guess his decisions and ask himself questions that he didn't really want answered.

Skinner walked down the clubhouse steps, mounted his chromed '57 flathead Harley and, without looking back, drove down Tennessee and made a right hand turn onto 22nd Street.

Chapter 13

After Robin left, the two friends sat in the apartment staring at each other in silence. Moonbeam refused to budge without a full explanation and Katie had to rationalize the situation; weighing the truth against a good story—if she could come up with one.

"A dream? That's the reason you're acting so strange?" Moonbeam asked sarcastically.

"Not just a dream, Moony, a premonition about the future. I know what's going to happen."

"Of course you do, and all of this came from a drug overdose on Saturday night?"

On the one hand, she could tell the truth; come clean, be committed to a mental hospital. But on the other hand, maybe there was a way she could still save the situation. At least temporarily, long enough for her to get back to her miserable present, because she couldn't stay here forever.

Knowing that Moonbeam, aka Annie, had been a new wave guru back in the day— a tarot reader, astrology protégé, and a proclaimed Pagan practicing the Wiccan faith—she decided to explain the situation as a premonition. Perhaps Moonbeam would believe that, but time travel? There was no way she could pull that one off.

"Yeah, an internal trip into the corners of my own mind. It opened something inside me, something surreal. I saw the future."

"I see. And what did the stars tell you?"

"The stars? That's your gig, Moony, you're the spiritualist. All I can tell you is I've seen the future. Believe it or not, it's the truth."

"All of this enlightenment from an overdose?"

"No, not an overdose, a near death experience. You hear stories all the time about drowning victims being brought back after they saw the other side. A person's heart stops beating and they're pulled back just in the nick of time. Sometimes, those people have powers. They can see the future, or they can see spirits, maybe even talk to the dead."

Moonbeam didn't respond, she just stared at Katie. Finally she shook her head and crossed her arms in front of her.

"Man, I don't know. I really don't know what to say. You're going to have to prove this to me, Katie, it's a hard cracker to swallow."

"That's easy. I can prove it. Ask me something."

"About what?"

"About anything in the future. Go ahead, ask me."

"When will the war end?"

"Well, what's the date today?" Katie asked, hoping for the most crucial bit of information that she presently lacked.

"Hmm, let's see, the Be-In is this Saturday and that's on the fourteenth. Today is Tuesday, that would make today January 10th. Go ahead I gave you the date, now you tell me when the war will end?"

January 10th and the Be-In was this Saturday the 14th of January. *What year?*

"1967?" Katie guessed, hoping that she'd picked correctly so she wouldn't appear too crazy.

"Of course it's 1967. It just turned '67 ten days ago. When did you think it was?" Moonbeam asked, suspiciously.

"Obviously I thought it was '67. After all, several days of 1967 have been a blank to me. If I thought it was still '66 could you really blame me?"

"No, I suppose not. That's true," Moonbeam answered. "But you're stalling now. When does the war end? I'm curious to hear your answer."

"The Vietnam war ends in 1975. I don't know the exact date but I know we pull the last of our troops out then," Katie answered, hoping that Moonbeam's reaction would be positive.

"1975? Eight years from now?"

"Yeah, and we haven't even gone through the worst of it yet. We have another year before they start drafting."

"Drafting?"

"Yes, they do it with a lottery system. Every birthdate is entered into a bowl and they draw from that. They draw until every date has been assigned a number in chronological order. Those at the top of the list are the first to go."

"I'll have to take your word for it since we can't prove any of it. Not until 1975, and that's a long time to wait. You'll have to tell me something closer, something that's going to happen sooner to prove this to me."

"Alright, let me think about it. It's January 10th, 1967. The Be-In is this Saturday."

Katie thought hard. Forty-five years was a long time and it took several minutes before she could remember the day. What had taken place at the Be-In? She needed information that would prove to Annie she was telling the truth.

"Okay, there's going to be between twenty and thirty thousand people that attend. The media won't be able to tell for sure because the city will be so crowded and ill prepared for the event. The media coverage is going to be extensive and because of that, it's going to draw thousands of kids from all over the nation. They are going to flock to San Francisco and by summer, this place will be a zoo."

"No way, man. No way will that amount of people show up for a hippie event in the park," Moonbeam said, shaking her head and laughing.

"Then Sunday you'll have your proof," Katie said, stubbornly defending her predications. But, in the back of her mind she knew she wouldn't be here long enough to prove anything. By then, unfortunately, she would be back to the hell she had created for herself, forty-five years in the future.

"Fine, we'll talk about that on Sunday, after it happens. For now, tell me something else. What's going to happen at the Human Be-In? If you can see into the future, then tell me something specific. Something more than how many people are going to show up."

"Let me think for a minute." Katie leaned her head on the back of the couch and shut her eyes. Several minutes later, she sat upright.

"I know! Timothy Leary is going to make a famous speech, one that's going to send the psychedelic scene into a tailspin. He's going to announce to a crowd of over twenty thousand that what they need to do is to turn on, tune in, and drop out."

Moonbeam stared at her blankly, and Katie smiled. She knew that her friend was starting to believe, or at least she was questioning the situation. Katie knew that look on Annie's face well. She was deep in thought. Katie had hit a nerve by pulling Moonbeam's belief system into play, now her head was reeling.

"I think what he means is that we're taking life too seriously. If you do that, he predicts that your nervous system will break down and that will affect your internal organs. You know the scenario, how stress destroys the body? He thinks that by turning inwards, you can cure yourself. It's supposed to cut down or eliminate stress related illness, which if you think about it, most illness *are* stress related. Anyway, he claims that you can achieve all of that through the LSD experience, which he explains is spiritual. But don't take his words too seriously. I mean, the guy ends up dying from prostate cancer in his seventies, so the whole LSD trip thing doesn't seem to work for him. Oh, and how can I forget about the parachute? In the middle of the event a guy is going to drop right into the middle of Polo Field. Nobody is going to get his name, probably because they are too stoned, so nobody will ever know who this dude is."

"Katie, you're scaring me now. This isn't a game? Do you actually believe what you're telling me?" Moonbeam asked.

"That's what I'm telling you, Moony. I know what's going to happen in the future. You'll see on Saturday, and then you'll believe me."

"I don't want to talk about this anymore. You're creeping me out."

"Okay let's not talk about it anymore... until Saturday. What is this job we're supposed to be doing? Shouldn't we get to it?"

Katie had run through the assortment of jobs that she and Annie had kept while living in the Haight. There were many, since a daily accountable job didn't fit into their lifestyle. They worked irregularly. Sometimes they sold flower necklaces for money or trade. Sometimes Moonbeam would throw a blanket down on the lawn in Golden Gate Park and she would read the tarot for passersby. Katie would assist her by collecting money or items in trade.

Then there were community events. Sometimes they worked those, even though they were mainly paid in pot. Looking back, she tried to remember the Human Be-In, what had they done that day? The only thing she could remember was being stoned out of her mind.

"You can't remember what we're doing? You can tell me the future, but you can't tell me what we're doing today. Is that what you're saying?" Moonbeam asked.

Katie said nothing. After all, there was nothing she could say. Moonbeam had one upped her. She didn't have an answer.

"Now you're really scaring me!" Moonbeam exclaimed.

"I'm sorry. I don't know what we're supposed to do today and I don't have an explanation. So please, can you just tell me so we can get on with it?" Katie asked.

"We have to load up for Saturday. We're helping to dispense Owsley's new batch of White Lightning, and I hear this time it's in pill form."

Owsley? The name ran through her mind and then quite suddenly she realized who Moonbeam was referring to, and why she could barely remember the Human Be-In.

Owsley Stanley was a chemist from Berkeley. He was famous for his wide variety of homemade LSD. Now she knew what she and Moonbeam had done during the event, and why that day was so foggy in her memory. They had been among the group that passed out free samples of Owsley's newest batch. Five pills per person, until the heavy canvas bags they carried were empty.

"Oh that! Now I remember."

Moonbeam looked at her, obviously considering the validity of Katie's answer.

"Well I do remember. Owsley's going to drop the load off with the Diggers and we have to pick up our portion from their drop-off center. Then we have to organize our stash so it's easy to dispense," Katie said.

"Okay, you remember, that's groovy, but it sure took you a while. Let's split, man, we can go over all this craziness later. Right now I need to do something that feels normal," Moonbeam replied.

"Agreed," Katie said, relieved to have the conversation behind her.

Moonbeam rose from the couch and headed towards the door. "Do you have everything you need?"

"Well, I don't know. What do I need?" Katie asked.

"Your bag, your keys, a jacket? You tell me. Do you need to get anything or are we ready to split?"

Katie looked in her bag found her door key with her familiar flowered key chain and smiled. Her purse was a trip through nostalgia. Next to her key chain was a psychedelic thick cotton bag that she used as a wallet. She remembered stitching the bag herself along with Moonbeam.

"Well? Are you ready?" Annie asked, shaking Katie out of her daydream.

"I'm good, I have everything I need."

***

The Diggers were named after a group of radicals, who in 1646 took control over the common land at Saint George's Hill in Surrey England, protesting the high prices of food.

The Diggers in San Francisco were a left wing group of radicals who sought to create a mini-society free from money and capitalism. They visualized a society free from private property and all forms of buying and selling.

The Diggers of 1967 provided a free food service in the Panhandle of Golden Gate Park in Haight-Ashbury every day at 4 p.m., generally feeding over two hundred people. They opened stores, simply giving away their stock, provided free food, medical care, transport, and temporary housing. They also organized free music concerts and works of political art.

Today, Katie and Moonbeam were walking to Waller Street, where they would find the drop-off center to pick up their stash. Then they would sort hundreds of pills into packages of five for easy dispensing. On Saturday, they would walk through the crowds of thousands, giving out free samples of Owsley's newest batch of LSD until their bags were empty. And for that, they would be paid with as much acid as they wanted, plus a quarter ounce of Acapulco gold.

Waller Street was a five-minute walk. During the short hike the girls remained quiet, both lost in their private thoughts. For Katie, the silent walk was a much needed rest, which she used to gather her jumbled thoughts. She had expected to pop out of this dream well before now. If Moony's calculations were right, she had been in this twenty year-old body for three days. Three days. How was that possible? Since then, her head had cleared. The headaches and dizzy spells were long gone, yet here she remained, back in the center of Haight Asbury in 1967.

There were several possibilities, Katie concluded. The first was the most obvious. All of this was a hallucination. She was in the hospital, most likely in a coma waiting to die. Which brought up the second possibility—she was already dead. In which case everyone around her was also dead, yet none of them seemed to know it. For everyone except for her, it was January of 1967. Which left the last possibility and the most farfetched, perhaps she was really back in time. Either way it didn't matter, she didn't have a lot of choices. All she could do was wait until this dream ended and she went back to the present. Or not.

They arrived at the drop-off center, and Katie was tired of thinking. She was glad to have something else to occupy her mind. A normal Victorian house was the designated drop-off center. That location could and would change as needed. By tomorrow it could be located at the other end of Haight Street, and that was why the word of mouth was so important in Haight-Ashbury.

The girls worked their way through the crowded hallway and entered the house. A skinny, longhaired Hispanic kid dressed in jeans and a multicolored poncho approached them. He was smoking a cigarette, which was barely hanging from his chapped lips, and he was carrying a clipboard.

"Hey, Moonbeam and Katie, what are you here to work on today?" he asked while he searched his list for their names.

"We're Owsley's medication dispensers, Henry," Moonbeam said, smiling brightly.

"Yes you are," Henry said. He crossed their names off the volunteer list.

"Jake man, hand them their bags."

Jake, a shorter version of Henry, walked over and handed each girl a bland colored canvas bag that was filled with samples.

"This is the Bear's new stash. White Lightning he's calling it. There are five pills per person maximum, for as long as they last. Once you've given them all out, you're done. Bowen says you can keep the bags," Henry said with a chuckle. "However you want to dispense them is fine. Watch for the fuzz though. Since October when this shit was made illegal they've been all over Owsley's ass. So don't be too obvious. We don't want any of our volunteers being plagued by the media so they end up on camera. Any questions?" Henry asked. When Moonbeam and Katie shook their heads he smiled.

"Good. Then you can find a clear spot to organize your samples or you can take them with you and do that on your own time. Basically, do your own thing, baby," Henry said while nodding his goodbyes. Then he stepped away to help the new batch of volunteers.

"Alright, what do you want to do, organize them here or elsewhere?" Katie asked, trying to remember what they had done the first time around.

"Let's do it here, get it over with," Moonbeam said. "Besides, I'd like to stay 'normal' for as long as we can." She headed towards a large roll of butcher paper. "Katie cat, find us a spot at one of the tables and I'll get some paper off the roll so we can wrap our samples."

Katie changed direction and wandered over to a row of tables where a slew of volunteers sat working on projects.

She maneuvered her healthy twenty-year old body through the crowd and plopped herself down on the wooden bench just as Annie arrived carrying a handful of rolled paper.

"Good spot. Now let's get this shit rolled and remember, baby, no digging into the samples before Saturday." Moonbeam laughed. She pulled a pair of scissors out of her boho bag and started snipping white x3" squares of paper that would later be folded into small envelopes.

Before digging into her own bag to find her of scissors, which despite the forty plus year time span, she was sure she had, Katie looked around and was mesmerized by her surroundings.

She was sitting in a house on Waller Street in Haight-Ashbury. It was January 1967, just before the Human Be-In, and she was sitting with a bunch of hippies rolling LSD pills into small packages so she could pass them out at a hippie gathering.

How could this be happening?

Three days ago she was sixty-six years old. Her world was crashing in and she was trying to end her life. Now she was twenty. Yet here she was, sitting in the middle of her own history.

Katie scanned the faces of the people around her, some she recognized, but she couldn't name. Others she knew, and their names came flashing back. Two were former friends who were now dead. Not in 1967, but in her own time, where she really belonged.

One of these people sat across from her, a blond kid named Donny. He would die in 1970 after a motorcycle crash. At the next table sat a girl called Trisha. She would drown at a party in the 1980's. But now, in January of 1967, they both sat folding small envelopes and stuffing them with lysergic acid diethylamide.

"Are you okay?" Moonbeam asked when she took a break from cutting squares and noticed that Katie hadn't started.

"Oh yeah, I'm good; just getting my scissors out." She dug into the nostalgic bag and produced a pair of pointed scissors.

Katie avoided Moonbeam's questioning eyes, took some paper roll and cut her own 3x3" squares. She worked quietly, trying to act normal, but she was still marveling at the situation.

She knew that being here was only temporary. Nobody went back in time— it wasn't a human possibility. But as long as she was here, wherever here was, she vowed to enjoy it, all of it, starting with her young body. Her arthritis was gone, her knee pain was gone, she was whole again, and whether that was real or imagined, it was still a miracle.

The room was cool. She pulled her gray sweater over her shoulders and caught a whiff of patchouli oil, making her smile. That fragrance had been her favorite. She had worn it every day when she was young. This period had been the best in her life. It was the only time when she had ever truly been free, and whether it was a dream or a hallucination, she was going to get the most out of the experience.

Most of the people around her were focused on their samples or what they were constructing for the Be-In. Discussion was minimal, and Katie found herself quickly absorbed into folding and stuffing miniature envelopes.

***

Frog walked into the diner at 1:45. As predicted, he was the first to arrive. The lunch crowd had thinned out, and only a few stragglers remained. He chose a table in the back and ordered a cup of coffee. There, he waited patiently while nursing his fragile nerves.

Yesterday had been difficult, but Frog had finished a batch of T-shirts and some love beads, successfully replenishing his merchandise. All the while, his mind had been focused on this meeting, specifically what repercussions he would face for his rash decision.

Just as he was finishing his second cup of coffee the door swung open and Sal and Dave entered the diner. When they spotted him, Frog stood and waited for the two bikers to walk towards him.

"Frog, my main man," Sal said, shaking his hand. Both bikers sat at the table across from a very nervous Frog.

The waitress arrived and minutes later walked away with their orders.

"I loved this place when I was a kid. I used to come here with my parents for breakfast. That was a long time ago," Sal remarked. "How about you, Frog, are you a local boy?"

"I'm a Californian, but I'm not from the Bay Area. I grew up in Redding. I'm a transplant, arrived here last year."

"When are you moving back?" Sal asked with a laugh.

"Never, man. This is my home now," Frog said assertively, feeling his body start to relax.

Dave, who had been sitting quietly through the casual chitchat, leaned forward and in a low scratchy voice said, "No more beating around the fucking bush. What is it, Frog, man? Are you in or are you out?"

"Are we going to discuss this here?" Frog asked, looking around nervously.

"Look around, man, we're the only customers here and the waitress is in the back room. There's no problem, dude, calm down." Dave pulled a pack of cigarettes out of his pocket, took an ashtray off of the table next to theirs and lit up.

"Dave! Fucking chill, bro, give Frog some air. At least let him finish his lunch before you verbally attack him."

"Sorry, Frog. I don't mean to be abrasive, but I have a short attention span. We're sitting here cutting the crap and all I can ask myself is whether this is a waste of my time. So, let's be frank. Do we have business to discuss or is this just lunch?" Dave asked, taking a long drag off his Marlboro.

This time, Sal remained quiet, waiting for Frog's answer.

"Yeah," Frog said in a low nervous voice. "We have business to discuss."

Once he'd answered Dave's question, there was a part of him that wanted to take the words back, run out of the diner, and never look back. He bit his tongue and said nothing. In the meantime, their meals arrived from the kitchen and the table became quiet.

The waitress placed their food in front of them, delivered condiments, refilled coffee and Cokes, and once again disappeared into the kitchen.

When she was gone, Sal pulled an envelope out of his pocket and sat it in front of Frog.

Reactively, Frog jumped back and stared at the package as if he expected it to bite him.

"Man, don't look so startled, it's just the directions to the place where you're going to pick up the product."

Frog tried to smile, to play his nervousness down. He looked around the diner to see if anyone was watching them, and finding the place still empty, he swallowed and held the envelope.

"Here's how this works. The first time, you give the stuff away free. We provide you with small individual packages. All you got to do is spread the word to a selected few, and then give the samples away. After that, sit back and let the rest happen."

"Just let it happen?"

"Yep, the stuff is so fucking good and in such high demand it will sell itself, man. You just give it away and then personal orders will start coming in. When that happens you contact us and we provide you with the next batch, which by the way ain't free," Sal chuckled.

"And that's it, man? That's all I got to do? No hoofing it, no trying to talk people into trying it? None of that?" Frog asked, knowing the answer already but wanting to double-check so there would be no misunderstandings.

"That's it, Frog. It's a new product and you happen to have it available, that's all. You need to get the word out to the right people while keeping this on the lowdown. We want to attract customers but we don't want the wrong people catching wind of it either. You dig? This needs to be a balancing act on your end, Frog. But shit, you're good at that, right? It's second nature. That's why we chose you. So just do what you do best, keep it cool, keep it balanced with the rest of your shit, don't sample your own product, and other than that, just sit back and collect the bread when it starts pouring in," Sal said, much too cheerfully.

"And if I get caught, I don't know you, right?"

"That's right, man, you don't know us. And one more thing, Frog, this deal is between us, not the MC You know what I'm saying?"

"Yeah man, it means the only bikers I talk to about this are you and Dave."

"You're absolutely right, Frog. You know, we're going to get along famously, I can already tell. This is going to be a very successful business venture. Now, all you have to do is build your clientele. When you have more business than you can handle, we'll expand. For now we just want to move this along slowly, make sure everything runs smoothly. You dig, man?"

Sal finished off the rest of his burger and washed it down with a gulp of his Coke.

"Sure, man. I know what you mean," Frog answered. "We do business in private and we're the only ones who know about it."

"Then we're set, and we're just in time for Saturday's event, right?"

"Sure, man, just in time for Saturday's event," Frog said apprehensively.

"Well enough of that topic. What do you think of our new Governor?"

"New governor?" Frog asked, his mind trying to transition into the new topic.

"Yeah, Mr. Ronald Reagan. He took office last Friday, you must know that. I know hippies are out of touch, but you don't live under a cabbage, man."

"Yeah, I'm in touch, bro. I mean, I know we have a new governor. I just wasn't thinking about politics."

"Well, now that you know we're talking politics, what do you think of him?" Dave asked.

"I don't know man, I don't follow politics. To me he's just another governor. He won't keep his promises either," Frog said, looking directly at Dave.

Dave shook his head and laughed. "That's right, you have your own society in the Haight, don't you? One that's based on *love*?" Dave said, overemphasizing the word "love", so that it sounded elongated. *Loooooouvvveeee.*

Frog, who wasn't sure where this discussion was going, was wary of answering. Since he'd been put on the spot and he wasn't feeling like himself these days, he finally snapped.

"Yeah, Dave we do. That's why we don't keep up on current events, apart from war news and the government's tactics to protect the American youth from the evils of drugs. The rest of it, who the politicians are, what they promise, the lies they tell, we aren't really involved with any of that bullshit. To us it's all a meaningless game that never gets anyone anywhere."

Frog wasn't sure why he had voiced his honest opinion. Normally he would have kept his mouth diplomatically shut, but he wasn't normal these days. Shocked at his own answer, he waited to see how his opinion would be accepted by the bikers whose members, although part of the counterculture themselves, were more inclined to feelings of patriotism.

Even though their own affiliation with the government was one of tension and occasional clashes, on occasion they had a tendency to defend the American way of life, which was one of the main reasons mixing Angels and hippies together was a bad idea. Once hippies opened that political floodgate and gave their radical viewpoints on the way things should be, harassment would follow, and that was where the Angels and the flower children always clashed.

Frog sat waiting for that floodgate to open and he braced himself for the political backlash that would ultimately follow. He was surprised to find that both bikers were amused by his answer and instead of getting angry, they started to laugh. Frog, who still felt one step behind his business partners, laughed too.

"You got guts kid, I like that," Dave said as he rose from the table. "Hey honey, we need our check," he called into the back room, searching for the waitress who had chosen to stay clear of the dining room while they had their little talk.

She emerged smiling and handed the bill to Dave.

Frog rose from the table and reached for his money pouch that he wore around his neck.

"Never mind, man, I got this," Dave said. He paid the bill, including a sizeable tip for the waitress. "You just take care of your shit, you hear me, Frog?" he said with a wink, and then he and Sal walked out of the diner.

Chapter 14

On October 6, 1966, California passed a law banning the use of LSD. The Human Be-In (Pow-Wow or Gathering of the Tribes) was planned as a direct response to that new law.

January 14, 1967 had been chosen by an astrologer as the best date to hold the event. And for added success, several new age gurus had blessed Polo Fields. Scheduled to start at 1:00 p.m. and run for four hours, this gathering would mark the beginning of what would be called the Summer of Love.

Despite weather reports predicting rain, the day was bright and sunny, even though the rest of the week had been raining. So in the minds of the hippies, the advice of the astrologer and the blessing from the clergy had worked. What started out as a hippie event, directed at getting the Bay Area's tribes together as a coalition against the new law, became the turning point in Haight-Ashbury's history. After today, the innocence of the Haight-Ashbury District would be gone forever.

***

Katie opened one eye and then, reluctantly, the other. Every morning when she woke her heart would begin to pound and, frightful to find she was back in the present, she would go through the same nervous ritual. First she would look at her hands to see if they were still young, and when she saw her old familiar rings and wrinkle free smooth skin she would relax and give thanks to whichever deity was listening.

During the week she had been here, she had learned to take one moment at a time, enjoying each to the fullest. At night she went to sleep fearful, knowing that when she woke next, the odds were against her. At some point in this beautiful dream she had to return to her future. As a result, when she woke each morning still in the past she became overwhelmed with happiness.

Today was special. Today was the Human Be-In! As the week progressed she had wondered if she would still be here to relive it. And now that the day had arrived, Katie was ecstatic.

The last few days had whirled by. She had spent the time reconnecting with her past, surprised to find that her memories from that time period were slowly resurfacing.

She had spent her days and nights reacquainting herself with old faces. She walked up and down the Haight visiting her old stomping grounds, including shops like Mnasidika, House of Richard, and the Phoenix. She loved hanging out in front of the Psychedelic Shop, smoking grass with friends from the past, and reliving the excitement of her youth.

She had finally stopped herself from focusing on when she would return to the present and concentrated on having fun in 1967. Every night she hoped against reason that she would be able to awaken again in the past, and when she woke this morning she deemed it a miracle.

When she had first arrived, she worried about looking forward to the next day. As if the mere thought of planning for the future would automatically transport her back to 2014 When that didn't happen, she gradually allowed herself to hope that, at least for a while, she would be staying. Since she had nothing to go back to, she would gladly stay here indefinitely but she knew she had to return to the present eventually. Nobody got a second chance, right?

The clock on her nightstand said it was 9:30 a.m. She had two hours to get ready. She was meeting Moonbeam at 11:30 on the corner of Stanyon and Waller. The Be-In didn't officially start until 1:00, but she knew people would drift in early, especially anyone from outside the city who had to drive in from other areas.

Katie rolled out of bed amazed at the amount of energy her young body had and the resilience she possessed at being able to spring back from almost sleepless nights. Not to mention that returning to 120 pounds was a rush in itself. Before heading to the bathroom, she gathered her clothing and wandered into the hall where she found the bathroom occupied.

During the week she had been here, she had avoided Robin. She knew that coming face to face with her nemesis was inevitable, but she was trying to put it off for as long as possible. Which, as it turned out, had been a good idea. It had given her time to weigh the situation. She didn't like Robin. How could she when her first impulse had been to hit her? But she knew that wouldn't be right. How could she punch a person for crimes she hadn't yet committed?

She decided that Robin could be useful. After all, she knew what Robin's game was and that information put her at an advantage, considering the prize was the biggest joke of all. Katie had decided that if she were still here, she would do everything possible to see that Robin won that worthless prize this time around and that knowledge made her laugh every time she thought of her roommate.

Now, unless she wanted to scurry out of the apartment without a shower, that meeting was going to take place. Katie placed her folded clothes on the sofa and drifted over to the window. The street outside was already buzzing. She watched a cluster of hippie groups drifting down Cole, migrating towards Golden Gate Park.

Katie heard the lock disengage and seconds later stifled a laugh when Robin walked out of the bathroom wrapped in a towel.

"Oh, Katie, it's good to see you this morning. How are you feeling?" She towel dried her hair while treading towards her bedroom.

"I'm groovy, how about you?" Katie asked with a chuckle, not being able to control herself.

"I'm fine, just fine," Robin said. "I'm getting ready for my classes." Robin opened her bedroom door and disappeared inside. Katie, glad to have the confrontation out of the way, collected her pile of clothing and headed into the steam filled bathroom.

When she came out with her long hair dripping, she had expected Robin to be gone. So when she walked past the living room and caught sight of her roommate, Katie was startled and she let out a gasp.

"Katie, I only have a few minutes but I think we should talk. Is there some reason why you are treating me oddly? I feel as though you have been avoiding me and I'd really like to know why."

Katie wrapped her hair in a large towel and, still in a bathrobe, sat on the couch smiling. How do you tell your roommate who, for all intents and purposes hasn't done anything against you, why you don't like her? How do you explain that in several weeks' time, your future husband would come knocking on the door and that she and he would start a relationship that would last on and off for twenty some odd years, despite his marriage. She didn't know what to say so she sat there silently.

"Katie, please, I want to know what's wrong."

"Robin, nothing's wrong. I know you'll think that I'm lying but I'm going to tell you the truth. In a few weeks a man called Mark Rhodes is going to come around looking for me. When he arrives, baby, he is all yours. You keep him away from me and we're good. You have my blessing, no contest, end of subject." Katie rose from the couch and headed over to the window for another peek outside.

"What are you talking about?" Robin asked, shaking her head in bewilderment.

"I know it doesn't make sense now, but it will, you'll see. Have a good day at the university. Everything is cool between us now so don't worry. I have to get dressed. I have a hippie event to attend and I gotta tell you, I'm anxious to get started."

"Katie, I don't understand any of this. I don't know any Mark."

"No, not yet. In a couple of weeks, maybe less, he's going to come knocking on our door and you're going to know immediately that it's him. When that happens, if you want to talk more, I'll be available," Katie said, disappearing into the bedroom and locking the door behind her.

When she emerged twenty minutes later, clothed and made up to look like her usual fairy self, Robin was gone. She glanced at Felix the Cat, a black and white clock with a movable pendulum tail that swung back and forth. It was 10:30. The phone rang.

Katie, who was used to the sound of cell phones going off at all hours of the day in all sorts of locations, froze. This phone didn't have caller ID, so she would have no way of knowing who was on the other end and that caused a shiver to crawl up her spine.

At first she debated whether to answer it or not, but in the end, deciding that it was probably someone for Robin, she picked up the receiver.

"Hello?"

The voice on the other end left her speechless. She plopped herself on the couch so she wouldn't fall over.

"Katie?" the voice repeated and she felt her eyes water.

"Richard?" she finally said, in a low voice choked with emotion.

"Yeah, it's me. Why do you sound so weird? Are you on something?" he asked suspiciously.

"At 10:30 in the morning?"

"Well I don't know what time you hippie people get started," he laughed and Katie, who was in total shock, laughed with him.

"Richard, it's good to hear your voice. How are you?" She wiped warm tears off her face, smearing the yellow daisies she had painted on her cheeks.

"Now I know something's wrong. You just talked to me last week. So what's with the weirdo act? Is there something you're trying to keep from me?"

"Hey, who's the older sibling here, smart ass?"

"Listen, Katie, I called for a reason this time, not just to shoot the breeze, and I don't think you're going to care much for what I have to tell you." The line became quiet.

Katie's mind shifted, searching her memory for what he was going to spring on her, and before he had time to utter a word she remembered. Her heart skipped a beat.

"Oh no, Richard, no," she said, pulling the phone away from her face so he couldn't hear her sobbing.

"Hey, I haven't told you anything yet," he said, and then without pause he sprang it on her. "I've enlisted in the Marine Corps, Katie, and I'm leaving in two weeks."

The phone went silent. It was January of 1967; Richard would leave on February 6th. He would be back for a week in August, and by the end of October he would be dead.

"Richard, why did you do this?" she asked, although her question wasn't fully understood. What she meant was how could he allow himself to get pulled into a war that would become an American embarrassment, and how could he end up losing his life over nothing?

"Come on, Katie. Try not to be a bummer," he pleaded.

"Have you told...Dad yet?" she asked, feeling awkward. She was having a conversation with her eighteen-year old brother who had been dead for forty-five years. They were talking about their father, a man who had been dead for fifteen.

Katie knew the outcome, she knew exactly how this one played out, and she felt hopeless. She knew that she wasn't going to be able to convince Richard of anything, at least not now. How could she?

If she talked about a premonition he wouldn't believe her. If she told him the truth, that she was from the future, he would be convinced that she was on drugs. There was no winning. The only possibility of stopping his death was to stay in the past long enough to prevent it.

"Yeah, I t-told him last night," Richard stammered, and his words brought her back to the present. She swallowed, biting her tongue so she didn't have a chance to blurt out the truth. *There is plenty of time for that,* she told herself. After all, she knew the date of his death, and she knew the specifics. She had eight months to come up with a reasonable story, something that might prevent the inevitable if, of course, she was still here.

"He wasn't happy but how much could he say, since Granddad and Uncle Thomas were both in the military? He's not talking to me, but it will blow over. Mom was too blitzed out of her mind to understand. I think it will take a few days to catch on. She needs the time to sober up first."

"Listen, promise me that I'll see you before you leave, okay?" Katie said, knowing that the first time around she didn't get a chance to do that.

"Sure," he promised, although he sounded insincere.

"I mean it, Richard. I want to see you before you leave. If you can't make it here then I'll come there and I'll find you."

"And chance a meeting with Mom and Dad? Fat chance of that happening." Richard's words unexpectedly made her cringe. She was sixty-six years old, sure at the moment she was trapped in her twenty-year old body, but she wasn't a child. Even now after all these years, the mention of his name still haunted her. How could the man still have this much power over her?

"I would if I had to," Katie said, doubting her own words.

"You're going to wander over to Antioch and chance a meeting with Mom and Dad if I don't come to 'Frisco before I leave. Is that what you're telling me?"

"Yep. Can you dig it?"

"No, actually I can't," Richard laughed. "Look, Katie, I'll do what I can to see you before I leave, I promise." The line was silent for what seemed like ages. Then, "I gotta go, sis. I have things to do but I'll call you soon." He hung up the phone.

For several minutes Katie sat on the couch clutching the receiver, crying and reminiscing. If only she could stay long enough to prevent her brother from dying she vowed that she would sell her soul to the Devil.

***

Around 11:30, Katie arrived at the designated spot and found Moonbeam already waiting. The park and surrounding streets were filling up quickly and the stores were already busy.

On the outskirts of the event, small arts and crafts booths were popping up. The whole area was buzzing with excitement as people stumbled about their businesses preparing for the event.

Moonbeam and Katie, both carrying their canvas sample bags crisscrossed over their shoulders, smiled and hugged each other.

"Are you ready for this, Katie Cat? It's going to be groovy!" Moonbeam gushed.

"Am I ever. You can't possibly imagine how ready I am," Katie chimed, her eyes sweeping over the crowd and the attractions around her.

"Hey, you want to snag some of the samples now?" Moonbeam asked with a giggle.

That's what they had done the first time around, sampled the samples, and then they had sampled more samples so that the whole day passed in a fog. *Not this time,* she told herself. She had things to prove to Moonbeam, things that were important, and to do that she needed Moonbeam to be coherent. She wasn't sure how she would do it exactly, but she knew she had to keep Moonbeam's attention focused on the events of the day.

"Nah man, it's way too early for that. Let's just get some breakfast and a cup of coffee."

Moonbeam looked at her oddly. "Coffee, really?" she asked, confused.

"Okay, not necessarily coffee but something to eat and drink. We have a long day ahead of us, we should take things slow."

"Slow?" Moonbeam asked, her blue eyes studying Katie suspiciously.

"Yeah, slow. Remember our talk several days ago? You asked me not to bring the subject up until Saturday. Well honey, it's Saturday. It's time to talk. Let's grab some food, take it across the street to Polo Fields, and before we officially start giving out samples, let's talk about the events that are going to happen. For that I need you focused and sober. Promise me, Moony, no sampling, not today. You can smoke as much grass as you can get your hands on, but I'm asking you, please, don't use any of the samples."

Moonbeam sighed and rolled her eyes. Although visibly disappointed, she finally agreed and nodded her head.

"Alright, fine. You're right. I promise, I won't use any of the samples, at least not today."

"Thank you, Moony. I know it's a real bummer, but I really need you to focus on today's events. It's the only way you're going to believe me." Katie hugged the small redheaded pixie beside her.

"It's cool. But what are we going to talk about?" Moonbeam asked with a pout. "I thought we already had that talk. I'm supposed to notice Timothy Leary's speech, where he's going to mention tuning out. Then I'm supposed to notice a parachute, which drops into Polo Fields. I can do that on samples."

"No, you can't. No possible way. You promised."

"Yeah okay, I promised, no samples, I got it," Moonbeam said disappointedly.

"Hey, what about that snack? The park's starting to fill up, and I think we should get a move on things," Katie said when she saw a mass of hippies heading into Golden Gate Park. "Let's just get a hotdog at that vendor's stand then we can walk over."

The two hippie girls walked across Stanyon towards a hotdog vendor who had just set up on the corner.

Lunches in hand, they drifted into the park following a horde of others. When they arrived at Polo Fields, a large grassed-in stadium, the girls quietly ate their hotdogs and sipped on a shared can of Pepsi. Katie smiled at the archaic can, especially the pull-tab removable top, which Moonbeam slid into the opening of the can, an act that would eventually (in the early 1980's) lead to safer tops.

When they were finished and had disposed of their trash, the two girls sat on the lawn waiting for the beginning of the festival. According to Moonbeam's leather strapped watch, it was 12:30. They had a half hour to smoke a joint and relax before their shift as "Owsley's sample girls" began.

Moonbeam pulled a pre-rolled joint out of her bag and lit it. Katie watched the smoke drift upwards, blending with the rest of the marijuana smoke filled air, so that the aroma of pot was overwhelming. Katie, amazed at the phenomenon, studied the clouded space that surrounded them.

"I'm worried about Frog," Moonbeam suddenly blurted out. "He's avoiding me, that's not like him. I just don't get it."

Katie, who had been focused on the miracle of being in 1967, hadn't given much thought to what was taking place around her. Now, she stopped what she was doing and gave Moonbeam her full attention.

"What do you mean?"

"Look, I know you don't dig Frog. There's friction between the two of you. But as your mutual friend I'm starting to think that whatever your thing is, it's somehow related to his. Neither of you are acting normal. Frog is just... *absent,* and I don't only mean missing, I mean mentally not there too. And you, well you sure are different. Both of my best friends acting strange at the same time. That's got to be connected somehow."

Katie searched her memory banks, the spots that had eroded from loss of use. What had happened to Frog? She knew that he had disappeared, but when exactly had that taken place?

What she did remember was minimal. During that era she had been egocentric as all youth tended to be. She was having a good time. She was out of her dominating father's house and she was free. It was before all the bad things occurred, when she still believed her life could be good.

Frog was a sarcastic, arrogant young hustler in his early twenties. He was just shy of six feet tall with a slim build, long, wavy brown hair halfway down his back, and he was always clean-shaven. This was in contrast to his otherwise sloppy hippie attire, which consisted of tie-dyed shirts and Levis. He had been a close friend of Moonbeam's but Katie had merely tolerated him. The truth was, she had never really liked Frog and the feeling was mutual.

As a result, she had taken little interest in him, generally only putting up with him when she had to. She should have paid more attention to his disappearance. She should have been a better friend to Moonbeam during that time period. Now, looking at the worried expression on Annie's face, she sighed, disappointed in the younger version of herself. Frog obviously had been more important to Moonbeam than she had realized.

"What do you mean?" she repeated.

"I think he's gotten himself into something scary. I don't know all the specifics because I can't find him to ask him. Look, I know you aren't fond of Frog and I know you don't really care about his world, but I'm real worried about him. And by the way, I'm really worried about you too."

"What do you mean he's acting weird?" Katie asked, purposely avoiding the comment about herself. "How is he different?"

"It started at the party on Saturday. No, that's not true, it started on the bus before we even got to the party. Don't you remember the way he was acting?"

Of course she didn't remember. That was forty-five years ago.

"Remind me," Katie said, leaning forward and resting a comforting hand on Annie's shoulder.

"It started when we got on the bus heading to the Dogpatch. He was acting strange, like he might pass out, like he was on something. That was the beginning. Something happened that night before we left for the party. Whatever it was, that's what he's not telling me."

Katie took a hit on the joint that they were passing between them. "Go on..." she said.

"When we were at the party, he had a talk with two of the Hells Angels. Sal and Dave pulled him into the garage and he was there for over an hour. According to Frog, they offered him a business proposition."

"What kind of business?"

"I don't know, he wouldn't tell me. He did let on that he wasn't interested. I thought that was the end of it, but now he's doing this disappearing act. He's up and out of the house before I am and he sneaks in long after I'm in bed. He knows my schedule. I know he's staying away on purpose. He's avoiding me and I can't find out why until I find him." Moonbeam sounded despondent.

"Wow," Katie said, running over the details in her mind. "I don't know what to say."

"There isn't anything to say. That's all the information I know," Moonbeam said sadly, staring at her already dusty moccasins. "Don't worry about it, I'm sure everything will turn out fine." Moonbeam rose to her feet and dusted off the back of her multicolored hippie skirt. "I guess it's about time to get started right?"

Just then, there was a tap on a microphone and a wave of people climbed onto the upraised stage. They started tapping at the equipment and pulling on wires. Moonbeam took one last drag on the roach, dropped it on the ground, and stepped on it.

Yeah, I guess it's about that time," Katie announced, rising to her feet.

"Now just remember, the stage is on the west side of the park and the Diggers' table is on the east. When you're out of pills I'll meet you by the Diggers Free Frame of Reference. That's where they're giving out the turkey sandwiches."

"Okay. Make sure you stay within speaker range while you're wandering. I'm not sure what time Leary takes the stage but try to stay close enough so you can hear him. As for the parachute, no matter where you're standing in Polo Fields you'll see him." Katie grasped Annie's hand and gave her a squeeze for good luck.

"Which side are you taking?" Moonbeam asked.

Katie pointed behind them, towards the east. "I'll go that way. I want to keep you close to the stage."

Moonbeam nodded and they both drifted off in separate directions.

***

Katie wandered through the crowd studying everyone around her. When the first speaker started broadcasting she handed out individually wrapped samples of Owsley's latest batch of homemade goodness. He had donated ten thousand hits of White Lightning to the Diggers for this event.

"Samples!" she called out, amazed at her own daring. After all, there had only been a handful of police officers there that day. Because they were understaffed, the SFPD concentrated on crowd control only. The hippies were left to their own devices, which meant ingesting and smoking anything they liked.

"Fuck yeah, man, I'll try a sample," said a young, bare chested hippie who scratched at his lice infested hair.

She stepped back when she noticed a white nit falling from his matted greasy hair. "Here," she said, handing him one of the paper envelopes.

"Can I get a second one?" the young man said, using the sample package to scratch his head. "I need one for my girlfriend." He smiled with a nearly toothless grin, stepping forward and holding out a filthy hand.

Katie dropped a second package into his hand, taking extra care not to touch him.

"Outta sight, thanks." He flashed the peace sign, which she immediately reciprocated.

Wishing she had hand sanitizer, which was only just being invented, she watched stunned as the skinny kid walked over to an equally skinny girl, and started kissing her.

"Yuk!" Katie said out loud.

"Is that what you think of me now?" a voice said from behind her. Katie turned and saw a face from her past. It took her a few seconds to recognize the young biker. When she did she was surprised to find her heart beating faster.

"Dylan," she said almost absently when his name popped into her head.

She could barely remember the young Hells Angel who stood before her, but he had been important for a minute in her young life. That was before tragedy and the realities that came with it started seeping in.

"Well, I know I'm not supposed to be very happy with you," Katie said.

"Look, I'm sorry, I really am. I had no idea that Eva and Ruby were going to show up at that party. I told you they were in Los Angeles. They weren't supposed to be back for another week. Do you really think I would sabotage a new thing by being that stupid?"

"Well, you are male," Katie said, searching through the rusty edges of her mind, trying to remember a night forty-five years ago.

"Come on, baby, don't be like that." He made an attempt to touch her arm but she pulled away.

"Don't! You're not going to get off that easily. You kicked us out, told us to go home," Katie said, vaguely remembering the night.

"No, actually Moonbeam asked if the two of you should leave and Joey and I agreed with her. If she wouldn't have asked we wouldn't have thought of asking you to leave." Dylan frowned. For several minutes he stood staring at her.

He had truly been a beauty, Katie noticed as he stood leaning against a tree, head down kicking at the dust around his boots in nervousness. He was stocky, about six feet tall, and had sandy brown shoulder length hair that was blowing in the breeze. Katie couldn't help but smile. She had never gotten the chance to know this young man. What could have developed into something more simply didn't. The clubhouse party had put an end to him and Joey. They had come around a few times looking for her and Moonbeam but the girls were stubborn. When they said they were done they had meant it. Now she stood with sixty-six years of wisdom behind her. Stubbornness was a waste of time, literally. If she had let go of hers back in 1967, where would this relationship have gone?

"See, you can't be mad at me, you're smiling." He reached out and brushed a lock of hair back from her eyes.

"I love your hippie dresses. You look like an elf or a fairy every time I see you."

He smiled, and she couldn't resist smiling back.

"Oh no you don't. Charm isn't going to get you out of this. Do you know what your old ladies did?"

Dylan stood silently, waiting for an answer.

"They drugged my beer," she said with an edge of anger.

"What?" Dylan's face became harsh. He had no idea what Eva and Ruby had done. What he'd tried to avoid by suggesting that the hippie girls leave the party had happened anyway. Despite his best efforts to divert Eva and Ruby's revenge, he had failed. Now that he realized the extent of their treachery, Dylan's face softened. A look of concern washed over his features.

"Those fucking bitches. What did they spike your drink with?"

"Hell, I'm not even sure. But my friends tell me I was flying for a couple of days. Ron had to purge me, if you know what I mean."

"Katie, I had no idea. I swear to you, neither did Joey, he would have told me. This is the first I've heard of it. I'm so sorry they did that to you and Moonbeam." His face filled with sincerity. Dylan might have been an Angel but he wore his emotions on his sleeve. Katie liked him.

She didn't remember meeting Dylan on the day of the Human Be-In, but she didn't remember much about that day, period. She wasn't sure if this conversation had taken place before, but if it did, it didn't take place the way it was happening now.

Dylan leaned over and kissed her. She felt a burst of electricity that she had never felt with Mark. She could have stood here forever but much too soon he pulled away.

"Listen, I got something important to do. I wish I could spend the whole day handing out LSD samples with you, but I have to meet with someone. I'll be back though. I mean maybe not today, since it might be hard to find you in this crowd, but I'll be around," he said. Then he turned, and without looking back, walked towards the west side of the park. Katie watched him and felt her heart melting.

Chapter 15

When Dylan walked away, Katie felt silly. Here she was thinking about a young man when she was close to retirement age. *Penniless retirement,* she reminded herself. The very thought of she and Dylan was ludicrous. She shook her head to rid herself of her crazy ideas and then let her mind drift elsewhere, to the discussion she had with Annie. Forty-five years was a long time. She had been another person then. A child.

Her depth of thought was broken when a handful of teens ran towards her for samples. One of the girls was topless, painted like a flower, twirling around and singing.

There are four of us," said an Asian girl, who looked to be about seventeen.

"Three of you," Katie corrected.

"No, there are four of us," the girl repeated, pointing out the members of her group. "Me, Tom, Allison and Rosy." Rosy was the strung out dancer who was happily staring at the sky and laughing.

"Wrong again," Katie countered. "There's you, Tom and Allison. Rosy has had enough."

Katie selected three individually wrapped packages and dropped them into their hands. "You don't want Rosy there to OD. It would ruin your day. By the way, you better get some water into her and keep her from dehydrating."

Feeling a presence behind her, Katie turned and found a pair of identically painted mimes staring at her. They went through a silent, well-acted skit of an acid trip, and Katie laughed and clapped her hands. She gave them both a sample package of White Lightning and they drifted away play-acting into the crowd.

Katie, who had taken the uphill route, was standing at the edge of Polo Fields looking down on the crowded event. A feeling of euphoria wrapped its arms around her and she smiled. Standing there for several minutes she was mesmerized as she watched the crowd. This was a historical miracle. She was reliving the event in mind-blowing realism. She asked herself again how something like this was possible, and the idea that she was dead popped once more into her head.

If she were dead, the idea of spending eternity here appealed to her. Who would have thought that her idea of heaven would turn out to be the Summer of Love?

Katie finished her nostalgic moment, and feeling the heaviness of her ugly canvas bag, wandered downhill.

"Excuse me, miss," someone said and then tapped her on the shoulder. She turned and came face to face with her aged counterpart. A woman around her real age stood smiling at her, and as much as Katie tried to act normal, the incident was disturbing, as if she were looking at a glimpse of herself from two angles. She swallowed nervously, trying to keep her cool.

"Do you think it would be safe if me and my companion tried some? You know, at our age and all?" the hip older woman asked, pointing to her companion, an aged man who was standing under a tree next to a group of hippie kids.

"Hmm, are you sure you want to do this?" Katie asked, slipping from being creeped-out into drug advice counselor. After all, she had enough experience, plus forty-five years. Who better to give advice?

The hip grandma, who identified herself as Iris, nodded and laughed nervously.

"We've discussed this. They say it can open your consciousness, an event that pulls you closer to the divine," Iris uttered, almost whispering as if she were conducting a secret service mission instead of scoring free samples of LSD.

"Sure, it's safe but don't down the whole package. Start slow, one or two pills maximum, save the rest for later." Katie pulled the samples out of her bag and handed them to Iris.

"Thank you, honey," Iris said, flashing Katie the peace sign before wandering into the park.

Katie headed into the multitude of swaying bodies below. She heard a tap on the archaic sound system, which had been going on and off all day, and then she heard the introduction of Timothy Leary. She stopped and watched the acid guru and his team of advisors enter the stage and address the audience.

Katie was too far from the stage to see his features, though she was close enough to hear the broadcast. She continued to hand out samples to the hippies around her, staying within listening distance of the stage.

The bag's weight on her shoulder became noticeably lighter the more samples she handed out. She attempted to hand one to a well-dressed black man who looked to be in his mid to late twenties.

"No thanks," he answered. His clothing, and the sound of his voice made her really look at him, and she quickly realized who the man was, forgetting all about Timothy Leary's speech.

"Huey P. Newton," she said without thinking.

Huey's eyes squinted, studying her suspiciously. "Do I know you?" the infamous cofounder of the Oakland Black Panthers asked.

The newly formed group was yet unknown. It would be three months before their notoriety would grow and they would be recognizable everywhere in the Bay Area. At this time, on Jan 14, 1967, only a select few recognized the uniforms (black beret, blue shirt, black pants and black dress shoes) as those belonging to the militant group.

"No, you don't know me, but I know who you are. Your group is doing great community service across the bridge. Word travels fast." She smiled and flashed the peace sign. "It's groovy that you're feeding the schoolchildren free breakfasts and that you're helping the elderly and protecting your streets."

Huey's suspicions fell away and he smiled too. "You gotta help your own," he said.

"You sure do. Okay then, no samples for you, but have a good day anyway," Katie said, debating whether to give him a few words of warning but deciding against it.

In 1989, Newton would be shot and killed in Oakland by a rival group member. After leaving a crackhouse he would be confronted by Tyrone Robinson. Ironically, the murder would occur in the same neighborhood where, twenty years earlier, Newton, as minister of defense for the Black Panthers, organized social programs that helped destitute African Americans.

Newton's last words as he faced his killer would be, "You can kill my body but you can't kill my soul. My soul will live forever." And then Tyrone Robinson would shoot him twice, directly in the face.

When the Black Panthers walked off, her focus shifted back to Leary's speech as his words drifted towards her.

"So what you've got to do is tune out, tune in, and drop out," he announced to a crowd of twenty thousand people. *"By dropping out I mean, drop out of high school, drop out of college and drop out of graduate school."*

There, now Annie would know she was telling the truth, provided she had heard the announcement.

Katie felt a bit smug as she walked through the crowd handing out her dwindling supply of acid.

Drawing closer to the stage, Katie was surprised when a scruffy hippie girl came walking up laughing at something the man behind her had said.

"Five please," the bubbly girl said, smiling a classic grin. Katie immediately knew who she was.

"Janis," she said, startled.

"Yeah, do I know you?"

"Not officially. I live in the Haight and I've seen you in some of the stores and on the streets. I've heard Big Brother and the Holding Company play a few times too. You guys are fantastic," Katie said, wanting to add more to the conversation but knowing that if she did, she would be crossing a line into weirdness. She couldn't walk around prophesizing to people. As much as she wanted to warn them, there was a fine line between crazy and eccentric that she didn't want to cross.

"Wow man, that's groovy. What's your name?" Janis asked, brushing her unruly wavy brown hair out of her face.

"I'm Katie." She extended her hand, which Janis promptly shook.

"Well, Katie, next time you see me stop and say hi. I'll remember you, I promise. Maybe we can have a drink together," Janis said, sounding sincere. Janis Joplin was known to love her fans and she loved to be recognized.

"I will," Katie said, handing Janis five small packages of LSD.

The talented blues singer walked away, and Katie's heart bled for the tragic loss of the little rock star from Port Arthur, Texas.

In just three years, Janis Joplin's multitalented life would be extinguished, debatably dying from either an ultra-strong batch of heroin (since eight people would die that weekend from the same supplier's batch) or the combination of strong heroin and alcohol together. Her autopsy would say that she died of acute heroin-morphine intoxication due to an injection of an overdose. But she would also be legally drunk at the time, and the combination would take her life on October 4, 1970.

Katie headed towards the stage. Three quarters of her samples were gone. With the remainder, she decided to hit up the rock bands. *Why not try to meet the musicians?* Katie told herself while she watched the Grateful Dead take the stage.

"This is so fucking cool," she said out loud to herself, glad to experience the event sober. The first time around she couldn't remember anything that had happened.

For several peaceful moments she stood feeling the sunshine on her face and enjoying the happiness around her. She looked across the field where, about one hundred feet away, Frog stood. He too was carrying an ugly canvas bag.

She weaved through the crowd, sleuthlike, so Frog wouldn't see her and split. She stepped behind him, contemplating her next move, when surprisingly he turned and faced her.

"Groovy meeting you here," he said with a nod of his head as he attempted to walk past her.

"Wait," Katie called after him.

"I'm busy, Katie. I'm working."

"I know, but I have to talk to you. It's important."

"I highly doubt that. How could you have anything important to say to me?" he asked sarcastically.

"What if I know that you're going through a weird head trip? It's something you're keeping to yourself. You wish you could share it, get it off your chest, but you know it's just too strange to tell anybody?"

"What are you fucking talking about?" Frog said laughing, but there was something in that laugh hat told her she had hit a nerve.

"You know exactly what I mean. And the reason that I know, is because I have a weird secret too and I'm thinking they're connected."

"Katie, I don't want to be rude, but I'm not interested in having this discussion with you." He turned to walk away.

"I've seen the future, Frog. I know what's going to happen. Let me prove it to you. Within the next half hour a plane is going to fly over Polo Fields and a parachute is going to drop out. There's going to be a lot of speculation as to who he is, but no one's ever going to know for sure. And that's not all. At the end of today's festivities at approximately 5:00, one of the organizers will blow a Viking horn, a signal to the tribes that the event is over."

"You're a mental case, Katie. I always thought there was something wrong with you. Now I know it's true."

"You're going to disappear, Frog. You can go ahead and think that I'm crazy if you want to, but it's going to happen, in the summer towards the end, I think. No one will find a single trace of you. You're here one day and then you're gone the next. No links, no clues, nothing. You're just gone."

Frog didn't move. He stood frozen, drained of color while he let her words sink in.

Katie was getting through now, she could feel it.

"Here's what I know. All your weirdness started before we went to the Angels' party and when we got on that bus, your trip had already begun. That trip is not going to stop until you dissolve into thin air." She snapped her fingers for emphasis, and Frog flinched.

A crowd had assembled for samples and Katie handed them out while Frog stood staring, vacantly waiting. When she was free, he approached her.

"When is this skydiver supposed to arrive?" he asked straight-faced and pale.

"It will happen during the Grateful Dead's set. I can't tell you which song, because I don't remem—I don't know, but it will happen before they leave the stage."

Then, as if it were part of a movie, a small private plane flew over Polo Fields. Halfway across, a parachute emerged from the plane. The crowd went wild. The event was announced on the primitive sound system by one of the Dead. Frog suddenly felt dizzy and sat on the lawn, watching, speechless, as the skydiver hit the ground, disconnected his parachute, gathered it together and then, almost magically, disappeared into the crowd.

"How did you say you knew all of this?" Frog asked, visibly shaken.

"I've seen the future," she replied, moving away momentarily to hand out the rest of her samples. When she returned she sat on the lawn and Frog sat beside her, so close that their legs were touching.

"No more games, Katie. Not on either end, okay?" He cleared his throat and nervously adjusted his ponytail. "How did you know all of this? How did you supposedly see the future?" he asked with curiosity in his voice, rather than the sarcastic tone he generally reserved for her.

"Frog, how much honesty can I give you in one day? How much more can you rationally absorb before you're overloaded? Because I'm not sure how much more I can deliver. I have a story, a long one. It's complicated and it's scary. It makes no sense, but it's factual. I'll share it with you, but I won't do it here. And before I can tell you anything more, you have to level with me. What's your bag, Frog? What secrets are you hiding? Our situations are intertwined, I know they are. It's time to share. Why have you been acting so strange?"

Frog didn't say anything. He sat looking at the crowd, thinking. Finally, reluctantly, he spoke.

"You're right, it started the night of the party; on that morning to be exact. I had gone out on my usual travels. I had some leads on fresh veggies, a barter trade. On that particular day the traveling market happened to be off of Beulah. I had to pass the old neighborhood market, Romans. Do you know the place?"

Katie ran through forty-five years of dust in her circuits before arriving at a picture of an old mom and pop store on the corner of Cole and Beulah. She nodded. "Yes, I remember the place."

"Do you remember the old homeless guy, Guthrie? He lived in the back of the market. He was an old-timer, kind of a mascot to Mike, the owner, and the teenyboppers who looked out for him. He was a mute. He's never spoken a word in all the time we've known him. "

Katie searched her memory banks and this time came up empty. "No, sorry. I don't think I remember him."

"On the day of the party he wandered away from the market. For five years Guthrie lived in that area and he never left. But on that day, he went missing. I looked for him and then, after running my deals, I found him. He was standing on a street, blocks away, zoned out of his mind, like he was in a trance. Then he did something he hadn't done in five years; he spoke. He actually spoke to me, Katie, directly to me. He walked straight up into my face and he pointed his dirty finger and then he told me that "this time I could get it right, but I had to believe." Believe in what, man? It doesn't make any fucking sense."

"This happened on the day of the party?"

"Yeah, but that's not all. Guthrie returned to the market acting normal like nothing had happened. Of course he didn't talk to anybody. The next morning they found him dead."

"Dead?"

"Yep, dead. He delivers a cryptic fucking message directly to me, which makes no sense and then he dies. How fucking eerie is that?" Frog asked, diverting his eyes from Katie's.

"This time around you can get it right, but you have to believe..." Katie repeated.

"Yep, does that mean anything to you?"

"Actually, it means a lot. Too much, and that's really scary." She rubbed her eyes.

The sound of a Viking horn rang through the park, marking the end of the Human Be-In.

"It's getting cold, I think it's time to go. I'm supposed to meet Moonbeam at the Diggers' table on the east side of Polo Fields. Why don't you come with me?"

"Hey, you can't just take off. You tell me that Guthrie's message makes sense and then you split? That ain't cool, Katie."

"I know, but I can't explain it now. Moonbeam is waiting. You might as well come with me since you can't avoid her forever."

"Who's avoiding her?" Frog said innocently.

"Oh come off it, Frog. She's not stupid. You know she has a thing for you right?" When Katie saw his expression, she shook her head. "No, you don't. You mean you never suspected? Wow, Frog, you are young and naive. Didn't you ever see the clues? She talks about you all the time, she's home every day around the time she knows you'll be cooking. How could it not be obvious?"

"Ahh...things like asking me to drag her across the city to a biker party to see one of the Angels?"

"Okay, I can see how that might send mixed messages, but it's not like you've ever shown any signs of reciprocating her feelings either. Have you ever made it clear that you like her?" Katie asked bluntly.

"Who said I like her?"

"Right, okay, strike that, never mind. You have to face her sometime and when you do you have to tell her the truth. Why not do that now? Come with me, Frog. She's already there waiting."

"I'll go but not just to tell Moony the truth. I'll come because you're going to tell me everything you know. It goes both ways. I want to know everything and in return, I'll spill my guts. Deal?"

"Deal."

***

Below that arch the radical anarchist group served "Diggers' stew" daily. This free meal was provided in the Panhandle at 4:00 p.m. In order to get a bowl full of hot stew and a tin of bread (bread baked in a can so that it was shaped like a large mushroom), all you had to do was to show up with a bowl. You didn't have to be a hippie to partake either. All you had to be was hungry, and then walk under the Free Frame of Reference and chow down.

Today, the familiar arch was standing over a set of tables where Peter Berg, Emmett Grogan and Peter Cohen (who would eventually take the surname of Coyote and costar in a very popular movie called *E.T.*) were passing out the last of the turkey sandwiches while other volunteers cleaned up.

Moonbeam was standing under a large eucalyptus tree, her multicolored hippie skirt blowing in the wind. When she saw Frog and Katie walking towards her, her mouth dropped open in shock.

"Wow, normally it would be groovy to see the two of you walking together, but something tells me this is more than just bonding." Moonbeam crossed her arms in front of her and nervously chewed on a thumbnail.

"Depends on your definition of groovy," Katie answered. "If you mean groovy like let's go take samples and party, then perhaps not. But if you mean groovy like the three of us have a problem which we've identified and can hopefully solve, then you're in luck." Katie was trying to sound upbeat and optimistic even though she wasn't.

"We need to talk, but we can't do it here," Frog said, glancing around at the dispersing crowd.

"My place is closest but there's a chance we might run into Robin, so I don't think it's such a good idea," Katie said.

"What is it between you two?" Moonbeam asked. "I thought you liked her?"

"Geez, that's a long story. I don't have time to tell it right now, but I promise to fill you in later."

"Let's take the bus down Haight, if we can catch one," Frog suggested. "Our place is best, and if all the roommates are home we can go to my room."

"Nah, your room's a sty, Frog," said Moonbeam. "We can meet in mine."

"Okay, your room, my room, the living room, it doesn't matter. The point is we have a lot to discuss so let's go somewhere," Frog said, his natural leadership qualities kicking in.

***

"This here is Sal's boy," she announced to a room full of bikers sitting around a table.

"Hang on, Mickey, I'll get your package. Don't be shy, come in," said the stout, bearded man who opened the door.

"Go on in, sweetie," prompted the black woman. Frog stepped into the room and she left, shutting the door behind her.

"Sit down, Mickey, we want to talk to you."

"Sure, but my name's not Mickey," Frog politely responded.

"Oh yeah it is. Anytime we have dealings together your name is Mickey. You understand?"

Frog, who sat on an overstuffed chair, swallowed.

"Your name is Mickey and my name is Toto you got that?" "Toto" asked with a crooked smile on his pudgy pink face.

Frog nodded.

"Good. That's Tom Thumb," Toto said, gesturing towards a young man dressed in leather gear that nodded in response. "Over here we have Bugs," a blond biker thug in his late twenties glanced at Frog fiercely. "And Daffy," Toto said, pointing to a small, thin man who was also dressed in leather and sitting on a wooden chair in the corner of the room.

"In this room we are all unpatched and we are known only by the name our contact gave us. Do you dig what I'm saying?"

"Oh yeah, I get it," Frog, aka Mickey, said to the assembled group of men.

"When you post an order you take it to your connection. He contacts his contact and that person sends you here. When you are directed to come here, you will knock on Valentine's door and she will escort you here where one of us will greet you. You'll come in and chitchat for a few minutes to make it look like a real visit. In and out shit makes our gig look real shady, you understand. We'll shoot the breeze, you'll pick up your supply, maybe we'll smoke a joint or two," Toto said. He pulled one out of a pocket on his patchless leather vest.

He lit the joint, took a hit, and then promptly handed it to "Mickey."

Frog, cautious of the uncomfortable situation, accepted the smoke and, concentrating on staying calm, took a long hit before passing it to Daffy.

"You see, we're like a family," Toto said, sitting back and smiling.

"Now you understand this batch is free, right?" the man they called Bugs said, leaning forward to stare at Frog.

"That's what my connection said," Frog answered.

"You're a smart guy, Mickey. You're going to do well, and you catch on real fast. I like that," Bugs replied, nodding to Toto who now sat at the end of the small room smoking a cigarette.

"You'll be able to find your clientele easily. Valentine is going to be back any minute. She'll fill you in on the rules, then you'll be on your way, my new friend." As expected, there was a knock on the door, and Tom Thumb opened it.

"All done?" Valentine asked as she entered the apartment smiling.

"Yep, we're all done," Toto replied, standing up. He took an envelope out of his back pocket, handed it to Mickey and slapped him on the back.

"Good luck, Mickey, we'll see you real soon I'm sure."

"Let's go, Mickey," Valentine said in a gentle voice and Frog, glad to have this meeting behind him, happily followed her down the long hallway, down the dark staircase and into a small room on the first landing. The room was nearly bare except for a couch, a table, and two chairs. Valentine locked the door behind them and gestured for Frog to sit down.

"You know how to choose your clients, honey?" She lit up a cigarette and puffed on it. A ring of smoke rose above her head, encircling it like a halo. "You want one?" she asked, offering him the pack.

"No thanks, they aren't my thing."

She sucked on her quickly decreasing cigarette. "Baby, all you need is that one lucky strand of players. Word of mouth is a beautiful thing."

"Yes, I understand, but how do I find that right strand?"

"You'll see. All you gotta do is open your eyes. Your customers are the ones who look hungry for the drug. Their bodies are emaciated, ravished, they're generally skinny people with pale skin, lousy teeth, and they look strung out. They look like they "need" the medication you're offering."

"Right," Frog answered, a picture of an Auschwitz victim flashing in his head.

"Now we're gonna go over some rules. They're real easy, honey, just plain logic. Use your head and you'll be fine. Number one, don't ever sample your own stash. The last thing you want to do is to get hung up on this shit. Second, don't let your friends know that you're selling horse. You gotta be discreet, smooth. Don't let the fuzz get you, because you're looking at some heavy time for peddling heroin. Third, and the most obvious but the hardest to achieve, is to remain anonymous. Disconnect yourself from your private life; keep the two completely separate. The better you are at that, the better you'll be at surviving the game. You don't want anybody to know your real name.

"Your name is Mickey when you're here. If I were you I would chose a different name for the streets. Don't leave links or roads that lead back to yourself. The more twists and turns you create, the better you are at this. Be smart, use your head. Don't lead anyone back to us. If you see any of us outside of this building, you don't know us. And lastly, the most important rule of all is to keep your mouth shut. Other than that, fuck you and have a nice day." Valentine burst out laughing.

"That's it?"

"That's it besides protecting yourself, man. Never, ever tell anyone for any reason about any of this. If you cross that line, Mickey, then you're putting yourself in a very dangerous position. I can't emphasize how dangerous these men can be. You're playing with the big dogs now. You do something stupid and nobody will ever hear from you again. You'll just vanish."

***

When Frog left with the envelope of samples, he was shaking. He knew then that he had made a serious mistake. He should have thought this over. He was way out of his league on this one.

It was 11:30 a.m. and people would be showing up at the park. It was time to go to work. Despite his fear, Frog caught a bus, which took him up Fillmore and dropped him off at Haight. There he caught a second bus, which took him to Golden Gate Park. From the bus stop he walked to Polo Fields but he was dazed, watching the faces around him as if he were shopping for victims.

He finally arrived at the "Gathering of the Tribes" and sat on the lawn. He was nervous, shaking, and he felt sick to his stomach. This was a bad idea. He knew it was but he also knew there would be no way to get out of it, not now. This had gone way too far to stop.

When his head cleared enough to work, Frog walked around Golden Gate Park trying to conduct his own "regular" business, but he felt lost. He knew he couldn't put it off forever. He would have to conduct Sal and Dave's business because soon they would check on him. Before that meeting, he had to get rid of some of the samples.

A couple of potential customers caught his eye. Lying close to a tree was a couple who looked the way Valentine had described. They were dirty, vacant, thin, and obviously tuned on to something more than grass and free acid.

He approached them smiling, but they didn't seem to notice until he was nearly on top of them. The man put his hand up to shield the sun from his eyes and let out a weak "Hey, man."

"I'm sorry to bother you, brother, but do you and your old lady want some free samples of horse?"

"What's that, man?" the woman said, sitting up.

"Horse, heroin."

"You say you're giving it away?" said the chick, who looked to be well into her thirties, but was probably much younger.

"Yeah, I'm giving it away. Do you want a sample?" Frog looked around nervously to see if they were being overheard. Satisfied that nobody was listening, he stepped closer.

"Really man? That's outta sight. Fuck yeah we want some. We've been sitting here hurting for a fix with no supplier in sight and up you walk," the man said. "You're an angel in disguise man, a fucking angel."

Frog cautiously pulled two small wrapped packages out of his bag and handed each of them a sample.

"You're groovy, man. How can we find you again? Our regular dealer is a junkie. He's always running low on merchandise because he uses his own shit. It's a real fucking bummer, man. We got friends too, dude. We got a lot of connections that are with the same shit dealer. They're always hurting for a fix."

Frog sat on the ground beside the couple. "You live around here?"

"We live across the Bay, in Oakland. All our friends live there too. We're close enough to make the trip over and we sure would be glad to have a regular supplier again. My name is Arthur and this is Grace." The two strung out hippies extended their hands in introduction. Frog grasped each and introduced himself as Darryl.

"If you're interested in scoring more, I make a sweep of the park every Wednesday at 3:00. Meet me here in Polo Fields under this tree."

"Groovy, man, we'll be here this Wednesday. We'll pack the car with friends and make the drive over," Arthur said, showing a yellowed smile with missing teeth.

"Then I'll see you Wednesday," Frog said, rising from the lawn and brushing off the back of his Levis. "Peace out brother," he added, drifting off into the crowd to search for more junkies to introduce his samples to.

***

Two hours, and ten samples of smack later, Frog arrived at the meeting spot. He was surprised to see Joey and Dylan approaching him from the trees.

"Looks like the party's getting bigger," Frog said under his breath. "I was expecting Sal and Dave."

"Yeah, well, we're their support group," Joey said, laughing.

Dylan, knowing that the comment had made Frog even more uncomfortable, glared at him, silently willing the biker to shut up.

"Look, here's the thing, Frog. Sal and Dave asked us to check on you, to make sure you're doing okay. You know, no second thoughts, no doubts. I guess they figured coming from us it would seem less intimidating," Dylan said calmly.

Frog remained silent, staring at them.

"Well what is it, Frog? Are you okay or are you second guessing your decision?" Joey asked.

"I don't know, man. I mean things are going great. I got the samples this morning and I've already made a strong connection..."

"But...?" Dylan asked.

"But it's new and it doesn't feel natural, all this sneaking around. I've sold drugs before, man, but this time it's different it just feels...wrong."

"Sure, man, we know this is new, we're walking into dangerous territory. It's unfamiliar and that's why it feels wrong. As the business grows we'll get into a groove and then it won't feel so bad. You're good at what you do, Frog, and that's why they chose you. Just believe in yourself and it's all going to be beautiful," Joey said soothingly, almost in a whisper.

Just believe... The words flashed the image of old Guthrie into Frog's mind and an icy cold shiver ran up his spine. He bit his tongue and looked down at his shoes to cover up his nervousness, waiting until Dylan broke the silence.

"It's all good, Frog, man. Just relax. If you have any problems, questions or concerns, Joey and I will be around. We're on your side, brother, remember that. Think of us as your friends, man, your comrades in the trenches. Let us help with whatever we can. You're not alone in this, you can just hit up a different audience than we can."

Frog felt slightly relieved.

"You know how to get a hold of us if you need to. You have our home numbers. Call us there, not at the clubhouse. The Angels aren't involved in this, and we don't want to tweak their suspicions. If you have to leave a message, leave it with Chuck at the Dogpatch Saloon. We run into him daily."

"Gotcha."

"Okay, man, great job so far. Just hang in there. It will get easier as time goes by." Joey slapped Frog's back in support.

The men nodded, said their goodbyes and then Dylan and Joey walked off. Before disappearing into the park however, Dylan turned around and called back, "Hey, Frog! Put in a good word for us with your roommate and her friend Katie. We want them to forgive us."

"Good luck with that!" Frog yelled back, and for the first time in days, he smiled genuinely.

Chapter 16

Terry pulled his '57 Chevy pickup next to the curb and Eva opened the door.

"Look, maybe this isn't such a good idea," Terry said for the tenth time.

"Honey, you agreed to help us. You know how badly Dylan and Joey treated Ruby and me, and how they humiliated us in front of everyone at the party. Baby, nobody is getting hurt. It's just a much-deserved payback. A little fun to get even with them."

"Yeah I know, babe, but they're my brothers. If they found out, if *anyone* found out that I was involved, it would mean my neck." He looked around nervously and pulled his Raiders cap further down on his forehead.

"You aren't doing anything except dropping Ruby and me off at the park. You don't know what we're doing so therefore you aren't involved."

"Correction, I'm the one who's dropping you next to their bikes, not the park. And I was stupid enough to tell you where the bikes were parked in the first place. Now you're leaving my truck with a box of something and I'm supposed to meet you in two hours on the other side of the Panhandle. What does that say to me? It says I'm fucking involved."

"Not really," Ruby, the third occupant of the truck, chimed in. "It only makes you partially involved. For all you know we could have cake and ice cream and we're going to surprise them. Don't take this personal, honey. You're just dropping off your girlfriend and her friend at the Human Be-In, that's all. So drop us off already and get on out of here!"

"It's 12:30 now. We'll be on the corner of Willard and Fulton at 2:30," Eva said. She and Ruby got out of the truck and slammed the door. "Pick us up there, drive us home, and then return to your buddies. It's as simple as that."

Shaking his head in defeat, Terry pulled back into traffic and slowly made his way down Fell Street.

***

As promised, Dylan's and Joey's Harleys were parked on the corner next to a slew of other bikes. They were on a deserted side street away from the activities in the park. The biker chicks in their leather garb looked the part amongst the bikes.

"Perfect. They couldn't have parked in a better spot if they'd tried. You see, this is meant to happen, Eva, luck is on our side," Ruby chirped.

"It sure is. It's about time we got even with those pigs. I bet there are a lot of chicks out there cheering us on right now," Eva replied. She sat the box of supplies on the curb next to the bikes. "Dumping us and then replacing us with those fucking hippie chicks! What nerve, throwing us out of the party like they did. Those fuckers deserve everything that they're getting." Eva opened the box. "We don't want to get anything on the other bikes so I'm going to pour the paint into a cup first and then dump it over just their bikes. All you need to do is keep your eyes peeled and make sure no one sees what I'm doing. If you have to, hold up my jacket, make it look like I'm taking a pee and you're covering me." Ruby nodded in agreement.

Eva opened the gallon can of oil based high gloss paint. "I'm going to do this fast," Eva said. She cut the feathered pillowcase open with her knife and glanced around furtively. Seeing no one, she poured a thick layer of egg colored paint over Dylan's custom blue paint job and leather seats. When she was finished with Dylan's, she did the same to Joey's red bike, then dumped the last of the paint over the handlebars and front lights.

"Car coming," Ruby whispered and very calmly lifted the leather jacket to shield the damage inflicted on the two bikes. When the car had passed, Eva took a handful of feathers out of the pillow and spread them evenly over the wet paint. Ruby took her own handful and within minutes both bikes were covered with a layer of goose down that was held in place by thick, oily paint.

"That's beautiful. I wish I had a camera," Ruby laughed.

"Don't be stupid. You can't have a picture of something like that, it would be evidence. Just take a picture with your mind and let's get the fuck out of here before somebody sees us.

Satisfied with their "artwork," they threw the empty paint can and the box into a dumpster behind an apartment complex. Laughing uncontrollably, they walked towards the Panhandle.

What they didn't see was the house across the street, where someone stood in an upstairs window watching the whole incident.

***

After leaving Frog, Dylan and Joey headed towards the stage. On the right-hand side was the sound truck, where the Angels had been asked to protect the equipment. The sound system at the event had been a problem from the beginning of the day. Totally inadequate for the amount of people that showed up, and with aged, peeling wires, the sound constantly cut in and out.

Early in the afternoon the cables had either broken or were intentionally cut, and they had to be replaced. As a result, Michael Bowen (chief editor of the *San Francisco Oracle* and the producer of the show) asked the Angels to guard the sound truck.

It was here that Dylan and Joey headed with their own business interests complete. They were ready to volunteer the rest of the day for whatever the Angels had in store for them.

"Put a good word in with the hippie girls? What the fuck, Dylan?" said a laughing Joey.

"Hey we're supposed to make good with them, right?" Dylan asked. "At least that's what Sal and Dave asked us to do. They thought it would help by getting us closer to Frog, remember?"

"I remember, but it's not going to work. Those girls fucking hate us, man."

"Maybe, but I just saw Katie before I met up with you."

"No kidding? And how did that turn out?"

"Not as bad as you might think. Sure, she's pissed, but I think she'll get over it."

"Was Moonbeam with her?" Joey asked casually, trying not to sound too interested.

"No man, they're Owsley's sample chicks. They split up to hand out their supplies. I only saw Katie but she sure looked cute. It's going to be fun getting back into her good graces. That chick is going to bring some man a whole lot of trouble but you know what? The more I see of her the more I think she's worth it." Dylan fired up another joint.

"Yeah, and maybe she's not worth it."

"Hey man, you said it yourself, those hippie chicks are adorable. They look like little pixies. You can't tell me you don't feel the same way. I've seen the way you look at Moonbeam."

"Yeah they are adorable, but women like that have been causing misery for men like us since the beginning of time," Joey said.

They made their way to the group of Angels who were standing next to the sound truck. Freddy was sitting on the top of the truck staring at the sky. Miles, Phil, Sal, and Skinner were standing in a group smoking a doobie, and the rest of the Angels were at the front of the truck playing with children.

"What's up, fellas?" Joey asked the group, one of which immediately handed him a smoke.

"Quite a lot actually," said Miles, one of the veteran angels. "I think you'll be surprised at how much we have going on here. Crazy shit too. Check this out. We're the fucking babysitters can you dig it?"

"Babysitting?" Dylan asked with a puzzled look on his face.

"Yep, taking care of lost kids and others whose parents are too fucking wasted to take care of them. Big Jim and McClellan are off handing out clothes and supplies to the needy," Miles informed them. "They're probably over at the Diggers' tables, and we're guarding the cables. It's hard work but somebody's got to do it."

"What about him?" Joey asked, nodding towards the sound truck where Freddy stared silently skyward.

"Oh Freddy? He had some free samples, man. Just leave him, he's happy up there. Skinner tried to get him down a couple of times but it's not worth it, he's flying."

"Well we're reporting for duty. What do you need us to do?" Dylan asked Skinner, the next in charge.

"Hey man, before you go anywhere, update me on our situation," Sal said. "Is everything cool?"

Dylan glanced at Skinner and from the corner of his eye caught a strange look that washed over the biker's face.

Dylan realized Skinner was suspicious and Skinner caught the vibe, which put Dylan into an awkward situation. He swallowed hard and stared at the ground.

"Man, I know what I'll have the two of you do," Skinner said. "Joey, can you go over to the stage and check with Mike Bowens to see how the sound system is working? Dylan, you come with me. Let's take a walk to the Diggers' tables so we can check on Jim and McClellan and see if they need any help."

Before either man could respond, Skinner was walking east away from Polo Fields and Dylan hurried to catch up.

They were partway across the field before Skinner spoke. Dylan knew it was coming and he prepared himself for the questions that he knew would follow. When Skinner finally addressed him, the older biker stopped abruptly, turned, and stared into Dylan's eyes.

"You and Joey are the new age in the MC, the next generation who will eventually run things, provided you stick around that long. My generation, we've been around for a while. We served under the originals, the toughest bunch of guys you can imagine." Skinner laughed, remembering the startup of the club. "In those days we were truly free, man. Just one of the many clubs built by men coming back from the war. Nobody really paid any attention to us. We were as free as the birds, flying down the highway without being heckled. All that freedom ended when that fucking Hollywood movie came out. Brando and Lee Marvin broke that scene wide open. After *The*

Wild Ones, the biker world has never been the same again and all that publicity has taken its toll.

"You know what I mean, man. When we're representing our colors people see us as something more. Don't tell me you haven't taken your colors off to fit in someplace; we all have. This club is never going to be thought of as the fucking Diggers, man. I mean, look at us. We don't exactly look like model citizens, nor do any of us want to. All we really want to do is to wear our colors and ride in peace.

"I know this goody-goody shit the First Skulls are pushing seems like a bit much. But if we don't do something to change our image away from a bunch of thugs and ex-cons our reputation will run us into the ground. If we keep going in the direction we are now, the time will come when we'll have to meet in secret, like the fucking KKK. Then there won't be any colors to worry about."

"Why are you telling me this?" Dylan managed.

"You know what I'm talking about, and I'm not going to ask for any specifics. All I'm asking is that you think about what I've said. My job is to protect this MC but I shouldn't have to police it. Our members should be able to police themselves. Right now all our members should be double-checking themselves, making sure that their personal lives won't impact the club in a negative way. You and Joey are the new men on the totem pole and I know what it's like to be one of the young-uns. You're just starting out and you want to impress the older, more established members. They know that and they can use it to their own advantage. Just be careful. You need to really think about what you're walking into. I don't think I need to say anything more." Skinner finished his speech just as they reached The Free Frame of Reference.

The line to the Diggers' table for free sandwiches was long. McClellan and Jim were hidden behind it, surrounded by boxes and several scruffy hippie youths who were searching for jackets.

When Dylan and Skinner walked up, Jim nodded. McClellan was helping two hippie girls find a suitable coat.

"Great timing. Dylan, can you help out the Diggers? They're being swamped," Jim requested.

"Umm...sure," Dylan replied with trepidation. He walked towards the back of the tables knowing that he was going to be the first Angel in history to invade their private space. Nervously, and consciously aware of his colors, he stepped into the makeshift booth.

"Fuck yeah, another set of arms to help! Over there, bro, wash your hands in the bucket. All the sandwiches are premade so all you have to do is hand them out."

Dylan washed his hands and walked back to the tables where a stack of sandwiches awaited him.

"Groovy man, thanks for the help," said a tall, thin, blond hippie who introduced himself as Peter Cohen. "Just find an open spot and start handing them out. Peace, brother."

Dylan took a tray of sandwiches, found a free spot at the table and then alongside the two Diggers started handing out turkey sandwiches to the hungry. For the first hour the job was interesting. Although infrequently, Dylan had been to the Haight, but he had never seen this many hippies in the same place before. The sight was overwhelming. If this was only a small selection of the counterculture, then what must the whole scene look like?

The baby boomers were coming of age; every manufacturing company in the United States knew that. There was big money to be made off their generation because there were so many of them. How could the government not understand that? When you had this many people making noise, demanding changes, how long could you rationally hold them off? True, they were only kids, or at best young adults, but they came in great numbers. This counterculture— which the Angels considered themselves part of—was just maturing. Their time was yet to come and they weren't about to back down.

When the crowds had died down and the multitude of sandwiches had been given away, Peter and a man named Emmett asked Dylan to share a smoke. The three men climbed the hill behind the tables and sat overlooking the park. Emmett pulled a small glass pipe out of his jacket and filled it with Mary Jane.

"Maui Wowie," he said proudly and lit the magical content with a red Bic lighter.

"Thanks, Dylan, man, you saved us. We should have had more of us working the front lines, but who would have expected this many people at a hippie event?" said a tired Peter.

"How long have you been an Angel, man?" Emmett asked with his thick New Jersey accent as he packed another bowl of weed.

"Patched a little under a year. Before that I was a prospect for a year and before that I was a hangaround. It's a long process, really. How about you man, how long you both been Diggers?" Dylan took a hit off the pipe and then handed it to Peter.

"Now that's a complicated question," laughed Emmett. "Officially two years, but our true beginnings go back before that. We were, for the most part, still are, a troop of traveling actors slash activists. We both belonged to the San Francisco Mime Troop. Maybe you've seen them preform in the Panhandle?" Dylan shook his head. "We left that organization a while ago and became full time Diggers. Well, at least I did," Emmett replied and gave Peter a wink.

"Hey, I know why you look so familiar. Peter, aren't you a ridealong?" Dylan asked.

"No man, not really. I'm just friends with some of the Angels. I'm building a chopper right now in my buddy's garage. You probably know him. His name is Peter Knoll?"

Dylan nodded at the familiar name. "Yeah sure, I know him."

"Change of topic, but did you have one of the turkey sandwiches, Dylan?" Emmett asked.

"Me? No, man I didn't. Why?"

"Ahh... that's too bad." Emmett laughed.

"We used the remainder of Owsley's White Lightning in some of the turkey," Peter said. He dumped the ash out of the pipe and lit a cigarette to replace it.

"For real?" Dylan asked. The two Diggers laughed and he laughed along with them.

***

Chocolate George was the first to find the ruined bikes. Having had too much to drink he had decided to walk off his buzz, and with that thought he had decided to check on the bikes.

When he rounded the corner on Fell he thought he was seeing things and rubbed his eyes. *Man, I've really had too much booze this time.* He stared at what looked like two large white birds perched among the motorcycles. He took off at a trot, keeping his eyes on the fuzzy large birds that he thought perhaps were ostriches.

Confused and out of breath, he arrived under the patch of eucalyptus trees where hours before they had parked. He stopped to study the ostriches but was quick to determine that the two white "birds" were a pair of feather-covered motorcycles.

"Holy shit!"

He checked his own bike, thankful to find that it was parked safely a full car's distance away, right where he left it. He would have to use the process of elimination to figure out whose bikes they were since the Harleys were beyond recognition.

"Not Terry's, his bike is parked next to mine," he muttered to himself. Not Melvin's or Freddy's. Not Sal's or Dave's or Phil's. Who else had ridden in with them this morning? And then it hit him. It was the two newbies, Joey's and Dylan's rides.

"Fuck! Fuck!" he said repeatedly as he circled the two bikes shaking his head at the destruction. The gas tanks and the seats were covered in paint, the engine and the gearshift was nearly unrecognizable because of the amount of feathers that were plastered across them. Since the bikes had sat in the sun all day and the new paint job was done early, the horrendous mixture was dry. George could tell hours and hours of work would be needed to strip the bikes down and get all the shit off the frames and the motor. All that, and obviously a new paint job would be needed.

Unsure of his next move, George sat on the curb and stared at the feathered monstrosities. "Who the fuck would do this?" he muttered to his still drunken self.

"Shame about dem bikes," an old black woman called from a garage across the street. "Damn shame." She shook her gray head in disgust. "Beautiful machines like dem too. I doubt dey gonna run a'gin."

Chocolate George rose from the curb, and walked across the street to speak to the woman. "Hey lady, did you happen to see anything?"

"Miss Emma Hill din't see not'n. That's why she lives in this neighborhood peacefully with dem hippies." She added a few grunts here and there to let him know what she thought about the hippies who were invading her neighborhood.

"What if I gave Miss Emma Hill five dollars? Then would she remember something?" He reached towards his back pocket where he kept his wallet.

"For five bucks Miss Emma's blind." A few more grunts and a sly nod of her head got the point across.

"Okay lady, ten."

"Fifteen might help Miss Emma see the light." She crossed her arms in front of her chest defiantly.

"Fifteen? Damn lady, you better have a full story for that kind of dough." He handed her three five-dollar bills and she shoved the money into her ample bra.

"Ohh...I do, hun. You ain't gonna be dis'pointed. You'll be getting yo money's worth fo'sho. 'Bout 12:30 I was cleaning my upstairs when I saw two girls standing in the middle of dem fine mo'sickles. Dey had a box with dem and dey laid it on da curb, jus 'bout where you was sitting. Dat's when they opened a can of paint and started decoratin' doze two bikes. Only dem two was real careful not to get it on any of da udder bikes." Miss Emma shook her head, adding, "Say, I sure hope needer one of dem is yourns."

"Thankfully not, but they do belong to a couple of my brothers. What did these two broads look like?"

"Yo kind, biker gals. Dey was dressed in black ledder. One a tall redhead, the udder was short with real dark hair. Dey had their hair all teased up an dey was painted like dolls." She added a final grunt. "Dat's all Miss Emma knows." She waddled back into her garage and shut the door behind her.

"Fucking Eva and Ruby," George said as his mind drifted back to the party where Dylan and Joey had thrown the two psycho bitches out. "Fuck man, I gotta warn them. They'll go crazy if they see this shit."

George started retracing his footsteps, heading back into the park where he'd last seen the rest of the Angels.

By the time Chocolate George reached the sound truck the sun was just beginning to set. He looked at his watch. It was 4:30 p.m. There was a half hour left of this gig and then it would be time to leave. He had to warn Dylan and Joey before they found the bikes themselves, at least to give them time to cool down before they saw the mess.

"Hey, George. Where you been, man?" Phil asked when he saw George walking up to the truck.

"I took a walk to check on the bikes. Hey man, you seen Dylan and Joey?"

"Yep, they're with Terry and Skinner. They're giving the last of the lost little kids away. Up in front, next to the colorful bus." Phil pointed in that direction.

George nodded, lit a cigarette, and headed in that direction, contemplating on how he would tell them. A guy had to be subtle when he gave his brothers news like this. He had to break it to them gently in some nice way. For the life of him, he couldn't figure out a way to candy coat this.

When he neared the psychedelic bus, owned by some ultra-strange hippies who called themselves the Merry Pranksters, George saw Joey. He was standing with Terry and Dave shooting the breeze. In front of them was a makeshift corral, which was constructed by any materials that seemed to be handy: chairs, a detached door, several boxes, and a nightstand. This material was used to contain two small boys who at the moment were contently playing with several motorcycle-chained belts.

As George joined his brothers a Viking horn sounded in the distance, echoing through Golden Gate Park.

"What the fuck?" Dave asked.

"It's five o'clock, the Be-In is finished, that's the signal," George relayed.

"Oh, right."

"Listen man, you seen Dylan?" George asked, trying to act calm. If he had to tell the story then he was only going to tell it once. Even if he wanted to blurt the information out now and get it half over with.

"He'll be back soon, man. He was helping the Diggers," Joey said. "Hey, think it's time to get Freddy off the bus yet?" he asked the group.

"Nah, let's wait till the last of the kids get picked up. No reason to stir the shit now," Skinner replied. A thin hippie girl with matted brown hair stepped up to the makeshift corral.

"That one there with the brown hair, he's mine," she said. Beside her was presumably the boy's father, a balding man in his late twenties who appeared to be a bit green around the gills. "I guess we had a little too many free samples," the girl said, wiping the back of her hand across her mouth. "Bobby," she called out and the three-year old child, recognizing her voice, shot straight up and ran towards her.

"Mommy!"

"Hey, you're okay to take him, right?" Dave asked, shooting a crooked grin at the father, who still seemed to be in a vacant trance.

"Sure, we're not driving, mister. We're flopping in one of the houses for the night." The woman lifted her son over the corral.

"You mean one of the flophouses?"

"Sure, we've stayed in a few of them. We've been here close to a month now." She wiped her son's runny nose on the sleeve of her filthy blue dress.

"Aren't you scared? I mean, you never know who's staying in those places, and you have a little kid. Are you okay having him around people you don't know, people that are using an assortment of drugs?" Dave asked.

"What's your bag, man? I appreciate you watching Bobby, but I don't need anyone telling me how to raise my kid. I had enough preaching when I lived at home, that's why I left."

Dylan walked up then, and having heard the conversation he addressed Bobby's mother. "That's true, but since you have a family now, we could find you someplace safer, more permanent."

"Who, the Angels?"

"No not us, but the Diggers will. That's what they do; they find homes for newcomers, feed the hungry, give away free clothing. I'm sure some of the flophouses have been great, but wouldn't you rather have a place to call your own?" Dylan asked and the teen mother nodded.

"Where do I find these Diggers?" she asked.

"In the opposite direction. They have a few tables set up where they've been giving out free food. You might have noticed them earlier in the day?" Dylan said.

"Thanks for everything. I'm Cherry, and this here is Buck," she said, pointing at her ozone flying husband, "and you already know Bobby." She set her son on the ground, took his hand and Buck's and then led them east in the direction of the Diggers' table.

"Man that shit breaks my heart," Dylan said.

"Look at you, man. You spend one afternoon with those fucking do-gooders and now you're talking just like one of them," Joey said laughingly.

Behind them a mother was picking up a little boy called Max, the last of the children. She was a local in the neighborhood who had been working at one of the craft booths. When they were gone, Chocolate George tried to make his move, ready to spill his guts, but before he could reach Dylan and Joey, Terry stepped out in front of him, blocking his path.

"Hey man, what's your hurry? You look like you've been running in a race."

"Dude, I'm on a mission. I have to talk to Dylan and Joey. It's important."

Terry felt his heart skip a beat, fearing that in some way he was involved in the news George had to deliver.

"Anything I can help you with?" Terry asked, hoping to intercept the inevitable.

"Well, you're going to be involved eventually, like it or not, but I have to talk to them first," George said as he walked away. "Don't worry, you'll know what's going on soon enough."

When he broke away from Terry, Dylan and Joey were missing. The rest of the group stood together in a pack talking but the two newest bikers were missing.

"Hey what happened to Dylan and Joey?" he asked, and Skinner pointed towards the trees.

"They went that way."

"Fuck man!" Chocolate George turned around and starting walking up the hill towards a grove of birch trees.

***

Dylan had been disturbed by his discussion with Skinner. It had come as a total surprise. The insinuations that Skinner made had hit a nerve. Now he was second-guessing his part in all of this. The business he and Joey were promoting was an opportunity to make a lot of cash. He knew that it was an outside job when he had taken it, but he had never thought that what they were doing was so blatantly obvious to the club. Now he was confused, and he needed Joey's advice before moving forward, which was why he had pulled him away from the group on the premise of a smoke.

The two bikers quietly headed uphill towards a patch of birch trees. They sat overlooking Polo Fields and Dylan lit up a joint, took a hit, and passed it to Joey.

"Look man, Skinner is onto us."

"What are you talking about?" Joey asked, taking a large hit on the joint, which made him start coughing.

"When he walked me over to the Diggers' table he gave me this whole fucking pep talk that centered on undisclosed business deals that 'jeopardized the longevity of the club'."

"What is that supposed to mean? Fucking speak English!"

"It means he knows that we're involved in something that's against the club."

"You mean the shit with Sal and Dave? That has nothing to do with the MC."

"Not directly, but if we got caught up in something that brought negative publicity to the Angels, then yeah it is."

"Dude, calm down. When did you start to get a conscience, man? Hell, I've known you since seventh grade and I've never seen you get soft on me like this. Fuck, we even held up that convenience store together when we were seventeen, remember that? It didn't bother you."

"You think I look back on that now and I'm proud? Fuck no! Come on, Joey, it's been a long time since we were kids. Granted, we were lucky back then, but that was then and this is now. We're grown men and we're talking about the Hells Angels."

"Okay, point taken. What do you think we should do? Talk to Sal and Dave?" Joey suggested, sucking on last of the roach and dropping the brown paper on the ground.

"Yeah, I think we should mention it to them."

"Fine, then we'll mention it, but in the meantime you need to mellow out, dude. Dave and Sal have been members for a long time. You think they're doing this behind the club's back? And even if they are, they know what they're doing. They aren't stupid. They aren't about to do anything that's going to hurt the Angels. We're safe with them. This is an opportunity for us to make a lot of bread without doing a lot of work. We aren't peddling the junk."

"No, we're overseeing the pushers...eventually there will be more of them to keep an eye on. Think about it, Joey. If the peddlers get caught, who do you think is going to take the rap? It sure as fuck isn't going to be Sal or Dave, so why do you think they put us in overseer positions?"

"Oh, you're talking all big ass now. So tell me, Mr. Big Shot, where were you when we decided to do this? It's done, Dylan. We're involved. Are you suggesting we try to pull out?"

"No, I'm not stupid either, and we can't just pull out even if I wanted to. We have to see this through. But yeah, Sal and Dave need to be told about my talk with Skinner. Fuck, *they* need to deal with this shit, that's why they're making the big money in this deal."

"Then we're in agreement," Joey said. "Stop fretting. We'll turn the problem over to Sal and Dave and they'll handle it. Hey, who is that walking up the hill towards us?"

"It's Chocolate George. I wonder what he wants."

"Fuck, you boys are hard to find. I've been searching for the two of you everywhere," George puffed out in between gasps for air.

"Well, you found us. What's up?"

"Man, I wish I was up here with good news but truth is I ain't. I got something to tell the both of you and it's not going to be pleasant."

"Okay, get on with it," Dylan said. "What do you have to tell us?"

"I took a walk to check on the bikes and yours have been doused in paint and covered in feathers."

"What the fuck? Who the fuck did that?" Joey screamed.

"The paint is dry too, so I'm figuring it must have happened early in the day."

"Our bikes are fucking *what*?" Dylan screeched.

"They're trashed, dudes, totally trashed. Paint has been poured into the engine, all over the tanks, your seats, even the handle bars and the gears. They're covered in a thick layer of paint and some kind of feathers."

Joey and Dylan looked at each other red faced and took off, charging down the hill towards the other Angels. Chocolate George, who had yet to finish his story, casually walked down behind them.

***

As a precautionary measure Terry, whose place was in walking distance, had left the park and picked up his Chevy. The intent was to drive Dylan and Joey to the bikes, giving them time to cool down, and then tow the bikes to Arnold's garage, the MC's private mechanic, in the hopes that he might be able to salvage the engines. So, by the time Dylan and Joey reached their motorcycles they were less explosive.

Terry parked his truck behind the cluster of bikes. Dylan and Joey hopped out and dragged themselves towards the mess that had once been their rides. When they reached the dead machines, they both sat on the blacktop next to their bikes.

"Fuck man! Who could have done this?" Dylan asked, his voice cracking with emotion.

"And why our rides, man? What the fuck!" Joey yelled.

Chocolate George pushed himself through the other bikers and sat next to Dylan and Joey on the pavement. "It was your former old ladies. The chicks you threw out of the party. They did this."

"How do you know that?" Joey asked. He had removed his Buck knife from his pocket and was trying to scratch the dried paint off his gas tank.

"The old lady across the street, she saw them. Said it was two biker chicks dressed in black leather. Said one was a tall redhead and the other a short brunette. Takes all the guess work out of this, don't it?"

"Those fucking cunt bitches!" Joey screamed. "I'm going to fucking kill them."

"No man, you aren't! We're going to do this the right way. We're going to call the police and have the bitches arrested. They can spend a few days in county thinking about their actions and then when the bitches get out they can pay for the damage they caused to the bikes," Big Jim said.

"We call the cops?" Terry asked, shocked and sickened at the suggestion.

"Hell yeah, and why shouldn't we? Any other citizen would. Let's see what happens if we try to go through the legal channels. That's why the bitches pulled this in the first place. You think it entered their minds for a second that we would call in the police? Fuck no. They expected us to handle it, and since we all know them, and some of us have dated them, they figured they'd get off easy. All this talk of doing good deeds, well fuck, man, that's what we were doing! We have a thousand plus eyewitnesses that can point to our events today. So we report two vandalized bikes, plus the culprits, since we know who did the damage. Shit, we even have a woman who can identify them so why the fuck not? Let's see what happens if for once we go through the proper channels."

Marvin, a tall stocky Angel wearing a German helmet with an Iron Cross painted on the back nodded in agreement. "Wow, man, that's heavy."

"How do you want to play this, man?" Skinner asked, looking at the bikes again and shaking his head in disgust.

"Don't touch the bikes yet, leave them here," Big Jim said. "Let the police see the damage and take a report. Terry, you and George go across the street to the gas station and call the pigs. Anyone who has anything on them that they shouldn't had better ditch it or split now." Jim pulled Dylan and Joey away from their damaged bikes.

"Let's go, man, why are you fucking stalling?" Chocolate George asked as he headed towards the pay phone. "Fuck, you're slow, man."

"What do you think is going to happen?" Terry asked.

"How the fuck should I know? I don't think I've ever called the cops before. You want to do it?"

"No man, I'm not talking about the phone call. I'm talking about the whole situation. What do you think is going to happen?"

"I think Ruby and Eva fucked themselves good, that's what I think. And I don't think they acted alone either."

"What do you mean?" Terry asked, feeling his heart beating harder in his chest and hoping that George couldn't hear it.

"I mean, how did they know where the bikes were parked? They weren't with us when we arrived so what did they do? Did they follow us? No man, I'm careful about shit like that. I don't remember any cars following us, and I would have noticed. We used a lot of side streets coming here. If they'd been following us I would have noticed. That means that they 'coincidently' found the bikes. Just out of the blue, walking to the Be-In and *poof*, there they are. Highly fucking unlikely, I'm not buying it. Look where we parked, on a side street away from the main event. What are the odds that they just happened upon our hogs? No man! And if that didn't happen then it means they had help. Someone who knew where we parked because they saw us this morning." George reached for change in his pocket and then remembered the $15 he had paid out for information.

"Fuck, I forgot to get my money back. Terry, you got some bread?"

Terry fidgeted through his vest pocket and came out with a few dimes, which he handed to George. "What happened to your money?"

"I had to pay our eyewitness to get the information. She was a real gutsy old woman that one, a real bitch. I liked her." George entered the phone booth, dropped a dime into the slot, and in the next second was dialing the number to the police station.

In the meantime, Terry was standing outside of the booth listening to the call. Secretly, he felt ill. He remembered his conversation with the girls this morning. He knew they were going to do something to the bikes, but he never expected this. He would never have thought that they were stupid enough to ruin two Harleys. *Now what?* He asked himself. Were they going to be arrested? And if that happened, what was going to happen to him? He should have known better, he should have insisted on knowing what they had in the box. Sure, Eva was a good lay, but he should have been smarter than this!

He should try to warn them, sneak away from the group and make a private call. But that would draw attention to himself and he didn't want that. He hoped beyond reason that the girls would not implicate him in the crime, but he wasn't secure believing that. If they could take some of the blame off of themselves, they weren't going to just walk into jail without a fight, were they?

George finished the call and walked out of the booth. "All done, brother. Let's go back and wait for the pigs. This will be a different experience. I wonder if any of us are going to end up in cuffs?" George asked, laughing as they crossed the street heading back to the pack of Angels who stood waiting.

Chapter 17

Going home sounded easy, but in reality the huge dispersing crowd made it nearly impossible. Catching a bus, as they quickly discovered, was out of the question. They were forced to walk home along the heavily populated sidewalk.

For a long time they walked in silence, each lost in their own thoughts. When they were nearly home Moonbeam walked close to Katie, joined arms with her and whispered. "You were right about Leary's speech and the skydiver. I can't understand it, but you were right. I've been trying to find a logical way to understand this, but I can't. Despite all of that, I want you to know that I believe you. I don't know how it's possible, but somehow it is. You have seen the future."

"Yes, I have."

"But how?" Moonbeam asked, her voice becoming louder so that now Frog could hear the conversation.

"I don't know. You're the spiritual one, the practicing Wiccan, you tell me. Seriously, you've been reading cards and palms and charting astrological graphs since you were fifteen, so you explain it to me. I don't have any idea how it's possible. It's just happening, that's all I can say, except that everything, including Frog's bag, started the day of the party."

Frog nodded in agreement. He stepped closer to the girls, looking around to see if they were being overheard and, satisfied that they were speaking privately said, "That day is the key to all of this. Some unexplained metaphysical trip that sucked us in. Now we're stuck in a vacuum and we can't get out."

The group turned left on Page Street and several houses later headed up the staircase to the yellow Victorian where Frog and Moonbeam lived.

As expected, the house was crowded. All the normal lights had been extinguished, and a series of blacklights illuminated the posters on the walls, making them glow in vibrant colors. All the roommates were home and they all had guests. The party had started at the park and it wouldn't be finishing until daybreak. This celebration had just begun.

When Frog, Katie and Moonbeam entered, they were quickly invited to join the party. The first person to greet them was Ron Diebel. He walked over and slapped Frog on the back, handing him a joint. "Hey, Frog how goes it? Bet you made a fortune out there today in that crowd, or were you working?"

"Semi working. I did okay," Frog said, and then he drifted over to a table that was filled with random snacks.

"Well, Miss Katie, how are we feeling these days?" Ron asked, taking a long drag off the doobie before handing it to her.

"I'm much better than I was last Saturday. By the way, thanks for the help, it's a bit embarrassing to talk about, if you know what I mean."

"You're welcome, Lady Kate." He bowed. "As far as being embarrassed, don't be. I'm just glad that you're here walking around enjoying yourself. The alternative would have been a real bummer. I've already been down that trip and it fucking sucked. Look at it this way, now I can honestly say that I've shared a shower with you." He laughed and moved closer.

Kate studied the young hippie who was obviously making a move on her. While the glowing hookah-smoking caterpillar grinned from the wall behind them in all its psychedelic glory, Ron kissed her.

Katie was shocked. She had no idea that Ron liked her that way, but here he was blatantly flirting. Why hadn't she picked up on that before? Had he made a pass at her the first time around? He may have, and she may have been too wasted to remember. Perhaps he had and she had rejected him.

She had always liked Ron. He had been kind and she had thought that he had "dreamy" good looks, resembling a shaggy James Dean. She had even mentioned it to Moonbeam several times, but she had never acted on the attraction.

At the time, back in the real 1967, Ron had seemed so much older, so untouchable. When you're twenty, twenty-eight seems ancient. Knowing what she knew now blew all those former beliefs out the window. In reality, anything was possible. No wonder Ron had been in such a hurry to help her the night of the party. She stood tongue-tied, staring into his eyes, and didn't know how to respond.

As a sixty-six year old woman, she had come to accept her life for what it was. She was at the end of the journey and she had made a lot of mistakes, way too many to count. Her life decisions had led her into a routine, where she was waiting out her days in slow moving misery. Some people she knew were happy. People like Annie who, despite two failed marriages, had made something out of her own life. Annie's life, except for being lonely, was the exception to the rule. Most people hit old age and then realized that they had wasted their lives.

Up until last week, her days of turning men's heads had been long gone. Now she was twenty years old again. Her future was yet to be formed and anything was possible.

Ron made a move to put his arm around her shoulder and Katie, enjoying the attention, didn't resist.

"Listen, Katie, would you be interested in having dinner with me some night?"

Before she could answer, Frog was by her side. "Listen, Katie, we didn't come here to socialize. We have important things to discuss, remember?"

"Yeah, okay," Katie said absently, ignoring Frog's interruption and staring into Ron's dreamy blue eyes.

"Katie," Frog persisted. "I'm sorry, Ron, I'm not trying to be a dick but I really need to talk to her. I promise I'll return her in one piece, man."

"What's your hurry?" Katie asked Frog. After many years of spending her evenings alone, Katie was enjoying every minute of 1967, and right now that included a party.

"It's cool, go talk to him. I'll be here when you're done. Otherwise he'll just bug the shit out of you until you give in," Ron chuckled.

"That's right. That's exactly what I'll do," Frog replied, and Katie reluctantly followed him towards the staircase.

"Wait!" Frog halted. "Where the hell is Moonbeam?"

Katie glanced through the crowd looking for her tiny friend but Moonbeam wasn't in the living room. Frog held Katie's hand and together they searched the parlor before heading towards the kitchen. Once through the beaded curtain, they saw Moonbeam sitting on the floor listening to a scruffy hippie play a guitar. The man, who was bent over the guitar in such a way that Katie couldn't see his face, was leaning against the far wall. He was surrounded by a group of women who, like Moonbeam, sat mesmerized at his feet.

The song he was playing, obviously his own composition, sounded vaguely familiar and Katie found herself listening to the lyrics while she tried to identify him.

"Sorry for interrupting your gig, man, but I need to talk with one of your fans. Moony?" Frog gestured for her to come with him.

"What's your bag, man? She's enjoying herself," the dark haired guitarist said without missing a chord. The girls sitting next to him nodded in agreement.

"That's cool and all, and no disrespect, but I need to talk to her. It's really important, man. I just need to borrow her for a little while," Frog said, using his diplomacy tactics.

"Baby, you want to go with him?" the hippie asked.

"Yeah, actually I have to talk to both of them but I loved your music. It was beautiful and it was groovy to see you here. I'm sure I'll see all of you around since you're locals now." Moonbeam rose from the floor, further obscuring Katie's view of the small musician.

"That's groovy, baby. You come over anytime. You know where we live, right down Cole. We're in a basement apartment." The hippie resumed strumming the same tune; still so familiar to Katie but she just couldn't place it.

"Sure, I know where your pad is, it's only a few doors down from my friend's apartment. She lives on Cole too," Moonbeam said, turning with the intent of introducing her new friends to her old ones.

Katie stepped forward so she could join the discussion.

"This is my friend Katie; she's your neighbor. Katie this is Charlie, Susan and Mary. They live about three doors down from you. And you already met my roommate Frog. Moonbeam stepped back and Katie was finally able to catch a clear glimpse of the man's face. She gasped, stepping back so quickly that she backed into the refrigerator, causing it to rattle.

"Jesus fucking Christ!" she said, bringing her hand to her mouth.

"Katie, what's wrong?" Moonbeam asked.

"Hey, sister, what's your trip?" Charlie Manson asked her.

Katie's mind unraveled. Her body shook and she tried desperately to pull herself together but it was hard to do when she was standing in front of the devil himself and two of his famous disciples, Susan Atkins and Mary Brunner.

"I-I'm s-sorry," she stammered, searching for a reasonable explanation, something beyond the truth, which she couldn't blurt out without sounding crazy.

"Hey, baby, do I scare you for some reason?" Manson asked, and the girls beside him giggled.

"I'm so sorry, it's not you. For a minute you looked like someone I use to know. He was a good friend and he died in Vietnam," she lied. "For a few seconds I thought you were him and quite frankly, it scared the shit out of me." Katie gasped for air, willing her pounding heart to calm.

"Groovy, you thought I was a ghost?"

"Fuck, yes I did."

"Wow, that's heavy, man," Susan said. Losing interest in the conversation, she took a seat on the floor and strummed Charlie's guitar.

"That song you were playing, what is it?" Katie asked.

"You like that one? I call it 'Cease to Exist,'" he said, smiling at the compliment he thought he'd received.

This song, Charles Manson and the "family" would record in September of 1967. It would appear on an album entitled, "Lie: Love and Terror Cult." Later, the Beach Boys would record the 'Cease to Exist' song; it would be renamed 'Never Learn Not to Love' and Dennis Wilson would claim to have written it. It would be released in 1969 on the Beach Boys' 20/20 album. By that time, Charlie Manson would be unable to sue for stolen material.

"Moonbeam, honey, you come over anytime and bring your pretty friend Katie with you. And, Frog, my man you're invited too," Charlie said. His small group resumed their previous positions and Charles Manson resumed playing his guitar and singing.

"What is it?" Moonbeam asked when they walked away. "You don't have a friend who died in Vietnam that I know of. Why did you react that way?"

Katie took a deep breath and tried to think of an explanation. For several long minutes she said nothing. How could she answer that question? The truth was too farfetched for anyone to believe, and it would lead to a long discussion they didn't need to have, at least not yet. She watched Charles Manson's group and her mind went through the grisly details. In just three years Manson's face would be one of the most recognizable in the nation, maybe even the world.

Manson would lead a group of fanatical young hippies into committing multiple murders. In 1967, he had just been released from prison, a career criminal who asked not to be paroled at all. Despite his own objections he was released into mainstream San Francisco, drifting into the Haight-Ashbury scene, and was able to use the love and peace generation to his own advantage.

It was here that he would begin collecting his "family" and the two women sitting with him were his first converts. Because Manson portrayed himself as a new age guru, it was easy for him to practice simple brainwashing techniques on his followers, most of whom weren't even old enough to legally drink.

By 1969 he would move his "family" to the desert outside of Los Angeles. On the night of August 8-9, in Benedict Canyon, Susan Atkins, along with Patricia Krenwinkle, Charles "Tex" Watson, and Linda Kasabian (whose testimony against the others would send them to prison for life), would be sent out by Charles Manson to start an Armageddon race war. Their target was the home of the beautiful and very pregnant starlet Sharon Tate. On that night Sharon, along with her unborn son and three of her friends— Jay Sebring, Wojeciech Frykowski, and Abigail Folgers— would die at the hands of these radical psychopaths.

Now it was 1967 and Charles Manson, as well as the eventual murderer Susan Atkins, were sitting in Moonbeam's kitchen. The other girl with them, Mary Brunner, would be the eventual mother to one of Manson's sons. Although she would not commit murder herself she would be present during one of them, and she would be in and out of prison for multiple crimes including credit card theft.

Yet here they were, singing and enjoying themselves at Ron's party, before the catalogue of horrors ever began.

Katie's stomach churned. How many lives would she save if she poisoned Charles Manson tonight? Forensics in 1967 would be primitive; perhaps his death could be written off as an overdose, she told herself. If he died tonight the girls beside him would be free and the rest of the would-be 'family' would never be organized. Along with the murdered victims, the young killers might have a chance at life too.

How many innocent lives would she be saving if she just added antifreeze to one of his drinks? Then she remembered that they were in San Francisco and didn't need antifreeze, so dismissed the idea.

"Katie!" Moonbeam said, and the interruption snatched her mind away from poisonous drinks and back into the present of 1967.

"Yes?"

"Why did you react that way? Are you tripping?" Moonbeam repeated and stared at Katie.

"Not now, Moonbeam, let's go upstairs," Frog said, gently grabbing both of their arms and leading them to the stairwell.

Moonbeam's room was neat, but it was also cold. She shut the windows and the blinds, wrapped a blanket around her shoulders and gestured for the group to sit down.

"It will warm up in a few minutes. I left my windows open because it was so nice this morning I thought I would air the place out." She shivered and handed a blanket to both Katie and Frog off of a pile she kept on a wicker chair. She took a seat on the bed and looked at Katie. "What just happened downstairs? Those people in the kitchen are friends of Chet's, he's the one that invited them. I've seen the one girl before, Susan something. She used to live in a house with Mike. Now she lives on Cole with Charlie and his old lady. They seem to be really hip people, why did you freak out?"

"Stay away from them, Moony, they aren't good people at all. They're very, very bad people and they're going to commit horrendous crimes."

Moonbeam looked at Katie and shook her head. "How do you *know* that? And how exactly did you know about Leary's speech and the parachute?" Moonbeam asked, glancing between her two shivering friends.

Frog looked at Katie, waiting for her response.

"I don't know how to start this conversation. It's going to sound crazy because it is, and I don't have an explanation. All I can tell you is what's happening to me. And when I do that, you're both going to think that I'm certifiably insane."

"Oh, we already think that, Katie. That isn't news at all," Frog sneered. "Quit stalling and get on with it."

"On the day of the party, far from here and now, I was in a car accident."

"What?" Moonbeam asked. "No you weren't! I was with you the whole day. You told me that you had a premonition about the future!"

"Yes, but there's a whole lot more to the story."

"Moonbeam, let her talk. Stop asking questions and let's hear her out, and then you can ask anything you want," Frog said.

"On the day of the party I had a car accident, a very bad one. It was raining and I purposely drove my car off the road. The next morning I expected to wake up in the hospital or not at all. I woke up here, on the couch in this house." Katie paused and swallowed.

"But...?" Frog prompted.

"But the accident took place forty-five years from now."

"What?" Moonbeam and Frog chorused in unison.

"Okay, now I have a question," Frog said, shaking his head in disbelief. "You're telling us that you...you traveled back in time?"

"Yes. That's exactly what I'm saying. I know how crazy it sounds, but it's the God's honest truth."

"So forty-five years in the future, on the anniversary of the Hells Angels' party, you deliberately drove off a road? And when you woke up you were on the couch in the living room recovering from an overdose?" Moonbeam asked, readjusting the blanket so that she could move closer to Katie.

"Yes. Last week I was sixty-six years old. It was January 8th, 2014. I was driving my car through the hills, hoping that I would get in an accident and I did. I remember going down an incline and hitting a tree. I remember bits and pieces of the ambulance and the emergency room. When I woke next it was January 9, 1967 and I was lying on the couch. Forty-five years were gone. Now I'm sitting here with sixty-six years of experience and I'm only twenty years old."

"Fucking hell!" Frog said, unwrapping himself from the blanket and standing up. "I don't think I'm buying this. This is way too fucking farfetched for me." He paced the small room, back and forth.

"Okay, if you don't believe me then *you* explain today. Explain how I knew about Leary's speech and about the parachute jumper?"

"Maybe you know Michael Bowen or someone else at the *Oracle*. They could have filled you in."

"And they knew exactly what Leary's speech was supposed to be?" Katie asked sarcastically.

"Yeah, maybe he turned in a script and let them know prior to the event."

"Then how do I know about you? Specifically the head trip that you're on right now?"

"You guessed."

"I see. Am I also guessing when I tell you that you're going to disappear? Do you want to take the chance that I'm wrong?" Katie asked, unwrapping herself from the green blanket.

"Wait a minute," Moonbeam interrupted. "Did you say that Frog disappears?"

"That's right, he just disappears. One day he's here and the next day he's gone, not a fucking trace of him."

"Jesus, Frog, what if she's right? She's been right about everything else she predicted. And don't tell me she knows anyone at the *Oracle,* that's bullshit and you know it. She knows, Frog, no matter how you try to disguise the truth, she *knows*."

"Why don't you tell her about Roman's Market and old Guthrie? Tell her your whole story and then let her decide," Katie said stubbornly, crossing her arms in front of her.

Frog hesitated, as if he had forgotten the incident all together. His eyebrows squinted together as he replayed the image in his mind and he frowned. "The day of the party I had a weird experience and that situation led into a series of others. The truth is that my world has become a pretty strange place."

"Go on," Moonbeam urged.

"I had forgotten about the party in the Dogpatch and I had made other plans for that day. When you caught me in the kitchen I was off guard. I had promised to take you to the party so I shifted my schedule around, but I was already fucked up by then. Earlier in the day I had been shopping. You know, one of Dustin's throwdown farmers' markets. This one was off Beulah, and to get there I had to pass Old Roman's Market. That's when it got weird.

"Old Guthrie, the homeless man that lives out back next to the building, was gone. I don't know if you know of him but he's this old-timer that never moves from that spot, not for over five years. Mike and the street kids feed him and watch over him, but for the most part he sticks to the side wall next to the market twenty-four hours a day and never talks. No one has heard him say a word, ever." Frog cleared his throat. "On that particular day, Guthrie was gone, they couldn't find him anywhere. It was very strange and got even stranger when I ran into him after shopping. He was waiting on a corner, like he knew I was going to pass that way. He stepped right up to me, pointed in my eyes and told me 'I could get it right this time if I believed.' Then he went back to the market and he stayed there, mute as always. Except, dig this, he died that night or early the next morning."

"Which makes sense because of my situation," Katie injected. "You can get it right this time...this time, which means this has happened before and that time it turned out bad. Now you have a chance to get it right, but you have to believe. Look at yourself, Frog. Earlier today you were shaking. Now you're trying to find a reason to logically explain all of this. You aren't even close to believing, so how do you expect to get it right this time?" Katie asked bluntly.

Frog stared at the floor and then mechanically, as if he were stuck back in dreamland, started to speak. "I-I had a dream that night, after the party. I was in a hallway. For as far as I could see in either direction there was nothing but doors. It was a giant hotel that went on forever. But all the doors were locked. Periodically they would open either from the inside, or a maid would open them with an old fashioned key. Each room opened to a different time period. Behind one of the doors it was the roaring twenties. And behind another door it was our party. The reason I found that party is because Barry Bog saw me in the hall and he took me. I tried to tell him that he was dead, but he laughed, told me that I was too." Pausing briefly, he coughed and rubbed at his eyes and then, still staring at the ground, continued.

"When I stepped into that room, at first I was surprised, and then when I really looked around it scared me. Everyone at the party was someone from my past and every one of them was dead. We were there to welcome a new member. Someone who was just arriving, and this was her welcoming party and everyone, except for me, was excited. I waited because I wanted to see who that mystery woman was. When she arrived and I saw her face, I knew I had to get out of that room. The person I saw, the new arrival who joined the group of people who were already dead was you, Katie. The experience freaked me out so bad that I went back out to the hallway, hoping to wake up, but I didn't. Not before seeing Old Guthrie one more time. He was there, in that room, with the rest of the dead and he stepped into my face again and delivered the same cryptic message. The next thing I knew I was falling through the doorway and it led me back into my own bed where I woke up shaking and drenched in sweat.

"Later that morning I walked down Beulah, heading for the market. I guess I was curious after my dream. I had this crazy idea of confronting Guthrie. I was going to try to get him to talk to tell me. When I got closer to the store I saw the yellow tape and I saw the police out in the front of the market. I knew right then before I saw anything else, I already knew. Guthrie was dead.

"Somewhere in the early morning hours the street kids found him dead in his regular spot. But here's the real weird bit: not only was he dead, but he was holding an exact replica of the key in my dream." Frog stopped talking, again rubbing at his eyes.

"Then maybe I *am* dead. Maybe all of us are," Katie said, her voice cracking.

"No way! I haven't been around before. I am twenty years old and this is 1967. At least to me it is," Moony said, shaking her head.

"Well, I'm twenty-three and to me it's also 1967, but I have to say in that dream I really started to wonder if Barry Bog was right, that I was dead along with everyone else. And Katie, she had just died, that's why she was there. She's why they were holding the party in the first place. She probably came right after her car accident. Maybe none of this is real and we really are dead?"

"Stop it! Both of you, we are not dead. This is 1967," Moonbeam insisted. "The two of you are just fucked up."

"Well you were still alive when I crashed in 2014, so I would agree you probably are still alive but Frog and me, we're both goners." Katie drew an imaginary knife across her throat for emphasis.

"What good is it going to do to think that way?" Moony asked.

"How *should* we be thinking? You're the spiritual one, you tell us. Now you've heard both parts of the story what do you think is going on?" Frog asked, still pacing nervously across the floor.

"I don't know what to think of this. I really don't. I mean, how can time travel possibly exist? I know this is the Twentieth Century but we aren't that advanced."

"We aren't that advanced in 2014 either, in case anyone was wondering."

"2014? Really, Katie, is that where you believe you've come from?"

"Believe? I *know* that's when I come from. Haven't I proven that to both of you yet?"

"You haven't proven anything, Katie. Sure, you knew about Leary's speech and you knew about the parachute. That doesn't mean that you come from forty-five years in the future. I'm not sure what it means but it doesn't mean that," Frog said.

"Then ask me anything you want. I already told Moonbeam the Vietnam War ends in 1975. Next year, not that you're going to be around to see it, Frog, but the U.S. will start a lottery draft system, and 1968 will be a terrible year in this war. Lyndon B. Johnson won't run for a second term; the U.S. will elect Richard Millhouse Nixon and he's going to make everything worse.

"You want to know something more personal perhaps? Annie, you're going to marry twice. The first one is a podiatrist, the second an artist. You won't truly be happy with either one, so you'll end up relying on yourself to get by. After Frog disappears you stop everything metaphysical, throw your cards away, and you never plot another chart again.

"In 2014 you live in the mountains on a half-acre of land, you have a dog and two cats. You're a journalist, you work in the city for a paper and basically, I believe you're happy. Until January 2014 that is. I can't tell you what's happening in your life now because I'm not there."

"Katie, stop! I don't want to hear any of this!" Moonbeam yelled.

"Then how am I supposed to prove anything to either of you?"

"I'll ask some questions. First, what can you tell me about this?" Frog pulled a folded piece of paper out of his back pocket and laid it on the bed.

Katie snatched up the yellow flyer and stared at it. Music, Love and Flowers. It was an advertisement for the Monterey Pop Festival. This was an event that would put the Bay Area's local bands on the national charts. The three-day, outdoor concert was the first of its kind and a turning point in the San Francisco music scene.

"Wow, the Monterey Pop Festival? Where did you get this?"

"Some chick was passing them out at the Be-In. From your reaction I'm guessing you know something about the concert?"

"Yeah I do," Katie said, still studying the flyer.

"Well?" Frog prodded. "The flyer doesn't tell the date because they haven't decided on it yet. It doesn't name any of the bands because they are still being decided on. Tell me about this event, Katie, or won't I be around long enough to see it?"

"Yes, you'll still be around by then. You don't disappear until the end of summer, late August early September, I think."

"Well, at least I have a little bit of time left," Frog said snarkily.

"This is not funny, Frog. This is serious," Moonbeam snapped.

"Don't you think I know that? After all I'm the one that's supposed to disappear and yeah, I'm concerned."

"Well you should be! You heard her. I'm the one that's going to marry the podiatrist and live a long life, but according to Katie you're on your way out and you shouldn't be thinking of that as a joke." Moonbeam looked at him closely. "What are you involved in, Frog? What exactly is your business with the Hells Angels?"

"I'm not conducting business with the Angels," he said quite honestly. His business was with the unpatched bikers, the ones he met up with in a condemned apartment complex, the ones who knew him as Mickey fucking Mouse. Frog shook the disturbing thought away.

"Well, you're doing something stupid; something that's going to get you fucking killed. I bet you already know what that something is."

"This is getting us nowhere!" Frog yelled. "Katie, please tell me about the flyer," he said in a calmer voice after clearing his throat.

"The flyer? Are you fucking serious, Frog?" Moonbeam screeched. "With everything else that's going on, you want to know about a stupid flyer that's advertising a concert six months from now?"

"Yeah I do, because it's a starting point. It's something to discuss, something more important than this. Does anyone have a better idea? Because, this worthless bickering is getting us nowhere."

"No. I don't have a better idea," Moonbeam sighed. "Go ahead, Katie, tell us about the concert."

"It's an important one, one of the most important rock concerts of the 1960s. It launches a lot of our San Francisco bands into superstardom."

"When is it held?" Frog asked.

"It's held in the middle of June, 1967. If you show me a calendar I can tell you the exact date. It's a three-day concert and it's held outdoors. In fact, it's the first outdoor concert of its kind. It's a predecessor to Woodstock, the greatest rock concert of all time."

"Wood what?" Frog asked. "Aren't you getting off topic?"

"Yeah, sorry. Woodstock is a ways off. But if I'm still here in 1969, you can bet your ass I'm going since I missed it the first time."

Moonbeam pulled a kitten calendar off the wall and handed it to Katie, who quickly flipped through the pages until she came to June, represented by a Himalayan kitten laying comfortably in a window sill basking in the sun.

"There," Katie said, pointing at the third weekend in June. The concert is on June 16, 17 and18."

"Are you sure that's the date?" Frog asked.

"Positive. As far as bands go, there a lot of them playing since it's a three-day gig. The ones I can remember off the top of my head without looking at the Internet: Jefferson Airplane, Simon and Garfunkel, Janis Joplin with Big Brother and the Holding Company, The Mamas and the Papas, The Who, Otis Redding, the Grateful Dead, The Animals, Steve Miller Band, The Byrds, Buffalo Springfield...The Rolling Stones can't perform but Brian Jones attends the concert and he introduces The Jimi Hendrix Experience. Ironically, they both end up in the 27 Club. Wait, that's not true, there are three of them at the concert who end up in the 27 Club, Jimi Hendrix, Brian Jones and Janis Joplin. They all die from drug overdoses, although there is a conspiracy surrounding Brian Jones' death, so maybe he was murdered."

"Katie, you're drifting off topic again," Frog reminded her.

Moonbeam jumped in. "What is the 27 Club, and what the hell is the Internet?"

"Let's see, you want to know more about the concert... The Beatles refuse to play, claiming their music is too complicated to replicate live. The Beach Boys screw up royally by booking a spot and then cancelling at the last minute, a move that wrecks their popularity indefinitely and gives them a bad reputation. And yes, the 27 Club. It's a post-mortem "club" for musical artists that die at the age of 27. As far as the Internet goes, it's too complicated to explain right now. Is that enough information, Frog?"

"Yes, that's enough information."

"Oh wait, I almost forgot, Jimi Hendrix sets his guitar on fire with lighter fluid," Katie added.

"He sets his guitar on fire?" Frog asked.

"He sure does. He squirts lighter fluid on it and burns it onstage."

"Fucking crazy! I want to see that," Frog replied. "Glad I'm I'll still here for the concert."

"Now what?" Katie asked, looking between the two hippies who stared back at her.

"Now we need to figure out what to do with the information. We already know that Frog disappears in late August. That gives us time to stop it from happening," Moonbeam said. "We have an advantage, don't you see? Instead of sitting here feeling helpless and sorry for ourselves we need to focus on how to change this. We have eight months to use this information so that we can stop it from happening."

"Can we stop my brother from dying in Vietnam too?"

"Richard dies in Vietnam? But he's not even in the military!" Moonbeam said, shaking her head.

"Yes he is. I heard from him this morning. He enlisted. He joined the Marines last week and he leaves at the beginning of February. He comes back once in August, before Frog disappears. In late October he dies in combat," Katie said, her voice cracking.

"Jesus, Katie, I'm sorry," Moonbeam said. "But honey, it hasn't happened yet, so we can stop it. Maybe that's what all of this is about, setting things right. Fixing whatever went wrong the first time. The two of you obviously have a mission and me, I guess I'm just along for the ride."

"I don't believe that. You're here for a reason too," Frog said. "If we're going to accept all of this as fact then we can't negate any of it. That means the three of us, for reasons unknown, are in this together. The powers that be have made sure of it, which means there are no coincidences. That's what Guthrie meant when he told me to believe. He wanted me to accept everything at face value instead of brushing it under the carpet. If we put all of this together into one interconnected story, it points to some type of divine intervention."

"Meaning?" Moonbeam asked.

"Meaning why don't you study that astrological chart again. See if you can pick up anything else. I know I never believed in that shit, but hell, I never believed in premonitions or time traveling or second chances either and now look at me. As I said before, it's a start. It's not going to provide us with all of the answers but at least it might tell us something."

Chapter 18

When Katie entered the small diner, Richard was already there, sitting at a back table facing the door. He rose when he saw Katie and smiled.

For Katie, it was a moment of nostalgia and shock. The sight of her brother, who had been dead for forty-five years, made her shake. She could barely cross the room without bursting into tears. When the two embraced, her control disintegrated and she started to cry.

"Hey, what the hell? It hasn't been *that* long since you've seen me. What's with the weirdo act? Come to think of it, you were pretty strange on the phone too. What gives?" Richard asked suspiciously.

Katie broke the embrace and sat at the small table using a napkin to dry her eyes. "I'm sorry, Richard, but you joining the military? It's a choice that's shocked me and I feel awful about it. I really wish you hadn't done that."

"Come on, Katie, it's not the end of the world. It will be good for me, better than college."

"Vietnam?"

"Not necessarily. There are lots of other places I can be deployed, Germany for instance, back east or even to the Pacific. This doesn't mean I'm going to end up in 'Nam. And if I do, well then I'll deal with it."

"You'll deal with it?" Katie echoed.

A middle-aged waitress arrived at their table to take their orders. After this brief interruption Richard went on.

"Katie, please don't turn this visit into a bummer! I've already had enough crap from Mom and Dad."

"Yeah, I can imagine," she said, thinking of her parents. They would have been in their late forties in 1967. It was a memory she was having a hard time picturing in her head. When she thought of her parents, she saw a nasty, shriveled up old man and a drunken seventy-year old woman. She found the idea that her parents were alive, living across the Bay, and younger than her real age, very disturbing.

"Are they accepting this?" she asked, already knowing the answer.

"Well they have to, don't they? After all, I'm leaving the day after tomorrow."

The waitress returned with their food. After placing their selections in front of them and refilling water and soda glasses, she retreated once again into the privacy of the kitchen.

"Dad is acting civil and I think Mom has come out of her drunken stupor enough to realize that I'm leaving. What else can I ask?" he said, then he dug into his meal.

"Your first stop is North Carolina?" she asked, taking a bite of her BLT. It was remarkable how much better food tasted, everything— vegetables, meat, even packaged meat. She cringed when she thought of the crap she was forced to eat in the future and wondered what impact it had on her medical problems.

"Yes. The first twelve weeks are boot camp. When that's over, I'll find out what my real destination is." He poured a significant amount of ketchup on his French fries. "Change of subject, Sis, but Mark Rhodes has been asking about you. I wouldn't be surprised if he shows up in 'Frisco one of these days looking for you."

The mention of her soon to be ex-husband's name sent a shockwave through Katie's spine. She dropped her sandwich and stared at her brother, instantly losing her appetite. "When did you see that dirt bag?"

"A couple of weeks ago. He's not such a bad guy, Katie. The truth is, you don't even know him."

Katie laughed derisively. "*That's* an understatement," she said, shaking her head. "Believe me, Richard, I know him. He's out for Mark and only Mark. He's selfish and he'll do anything underhanded to eliminate his competition. He's a bad guy and I'm sure he sees you as a competitor for Father's attention. He's bad news. You shouldn't have anything to do with him. If he asks about me again, tell him to go fuck himself." She giggled, thinking of the impact the response would have on her sleazebag husband. How his face would flush and puff up with anger. That thought made her laugh again and then she couldn't stop smiling.

"Katie, that's an awful thing to say," Richard snapped.

"I know. Isn't it wicked?" She asked, still chuckling. "Richard, if you knew him like I do, you would find it funny too."

"You don't know him though, Katie, and he's...well, kind of a friend."

"A friend? Are you fucking kidding me? That's like keeping a pet crocodile and sleeping with it for Christ's sake. Trust me, he's a piece of shit. For your own good, don't have anything more to do with him. He better not show up in 'Frisco if he knows what's good for him. I have friends in the Hells Angels."

"Okay change of topic again," Richard said, and then the ultimate whammy she'd been waiting for. "You should check in on Mom and Dad once in a while, Katie. I know you don't like to deal with their shit, but they are our parents and deep down they really do want what's best for us. With me away, well, it would just be a nice thing to do."

This was a typical response from Richard. He had always stuck up for their parents, and no matter what the situation he had an excuse for them. At the time it had driven her crazy, now she remembered why. Their different points of view in regards to their parents had always kept them apart. It was the reason they had never been close and it was one of the reasons she had gone home guilt ridden after Richard's death in 'Nam.

Sadness combined with that guilt and an intense feeling of loss had caused her to cash in her beliefs and go home. When she married the family's choice as her husband, it was a tribute to Richard. She knew that her brother would have agreed with the union and it was that knowledge, combined with survivor guilt, that had pushed her into the marriage.

Even now, forty-five years of experience hadn't stopped the conversation about their parents from raising her blood pressure. The very thought of them and the control they had over her younger brother had always infuriated her.

"Richard, do you really believe they want what's best for you or do you think they want what's best for them?" she asked earnestly. "You must know them better than that. You're old enough by now to realize the truth. They don't do anything that isn't going to benefit them, ever. Not even for their children."

"Perhaps this isn't such a great topic either," Richard said ruefully. "Maybe there just isn't a topic that we can communicate on."

"Perhaps not."

Katie was at a loss for words. What could she say to an eighteen-year old kid brother she barely remembered? So far she wasn't doing very well. She wasn't here with the intention of driving another stake between them, and she feared that's where the conversation was heading.

"Listen, Richard, we aren't going to agree on Mom and Dad, we both know that. As far as Mark Rhodes goes, now you know how I feel about him. In reality, though, none of this is important. The only thing that's important to me right now is you. You being safe, getting through basic training and then coming home safely. You write to me while you're there, okay?"

"Of course I will."

"They'll send you home on leave in August. I mean, more than likely they will. I expect to see a lot of you during that two-week period. I'll hold my tongue or we will just talk about the weather," she told him, sounding melancholy.

"When they send me home on vacation I'll flop with you in 'Frisco. Spend a few days playing hippie, how about that?" he asked, laughing now that the conversation had become lighter.

"I would love that," Katie said. The first time around she saw him once during those two weeks. She couldn't remember if she was too busy or if he was, and decided it was probably a combination of both.

During that one visit they had argued and then he had gone to Vietnam and never returned. This time she vowed it would be different. This time she would find a way to spend more time with him, and she would keep her mouth shut.

"Katie, I'll write to you every week. When I'm home on my break I'll spend half of it with you, and I'll be careful. Just don't start preaching. I'm a man now and I know that what I'm doing is right for me."

Katie nodded and bit her tongue. There was so much she *wanted* to say, yet nothing she *could* say. She had time, she told herself, providing she stayed here. When Richard got home in August she would have a plan, something— anything— that might give him a chance at survival.

They finished their meal in silence and then walked through some shops in downtown Berkeley, reminiscing about their childhood for several hours. When they finally separated, Katie caught the bus back to San Francisco. On the ride home the sun was heading down in the western horizon. She spent the trip back to 'Frisco marveling at the miracle that was1967.

***

It had been two months since Katherine Rhodes' accident. Within that time Annie had become her legal guardian, agreeing to two surgeries; one to pin Katie's broken pelvis and the other to insert stents into her skull to drain off extra fluid.

Annie had moved into a temporary apartment close to the hospital, and she had finally contacted Katherine's children. Although concerned, they were unable to come home and left Annie fully in charge of their mother's welfare.

Katie had been diagnosed with severe traumatic brain injury. The impact of the car accident caused brain impairments that couldn't yet be determined. Not until she came out of the coma would they know the true extent of her injuries.

Today, Annie sat in Dr. Stevenson's office along with Dr. Thorne, the specialist in neurology at Highland Hospital.

"Here are her recent CT scans," Dr. Thorne explained. "We were hoping that the stents would have done a better job with drainage and we've given them enough time. Now we need to step up treatment."

"Which means?" Annie asked.

"We want to open her up again and preform a hemicraniectomy. This is the only way to relieve the massive brain swelling before it leads to an increase in intracranial pressure. If that occurs, it could result in an enlarged area of brain damage. In the long run, the increased cranial pressure will prevent blood from flowing into the afflicted area, resulting in a rapid progression towards brain death.

"Because of that risk, the only thing we can do is to relieve the cranial pressure through a hemicraniectomy. Releasing that pressure might pull her out of the coma."

"And the odds of success?"

"Ms. Sullivan, there aren't percentage chances when we're discussing brain surgery, not in the way you're thinking. Without the surgery her chances of survival are very slim. With the surgery, she's got a shot at recovering. I know it's not the odds you're looking for, but it's the best we can expect given the circumstances. She's alive; that's a miracle in itself. This surgery might give her a chance at something more."

"I see," Annie said, studying the CT scan on the wall monitor. "When are you thinking of doing this?"

"This afternoon. The faster we move, the better her chance at recovering."

"Today? And what is a hemicrany...? Whatever you just said."

"We will temporarily remove a portion of her skull. If the swelling is bad enough it might mean removing up to a half or even more it. This will allow the expanding brain to extend beyond the confinements of the skull, basically stopping the swelling from causing further elevations in brain pressure and preventing further damage.

"During the surgery we remove part of the skull and we freeze it until the swelling in the brain has been resolved. When the swelling goes down, and the brain is recovering from its trauma, then we suture the removed portion of skull back into place."

"My God! That sounds complicated. And you say she's going into surgery today?" She stared at the clock on the wall.

"That's right, Ms. Sullivan, the sooner the better."

"Where do I sign?" she asked after a deep sigh. Dr. Thorne handed her the consent forms and a pen, watching emotionlessly while Annie mechanically signed them.

"Doctor, one more question before I go," Annie said. "If, I mean *when*, Katie comes out of the coma, will she be able to walk again?"

"Not without further surgeries, I'm afraid. And even then the odds aren't great. I'm not an orthopedic surgeon, mind you. They would be able to tell you more. From what I've seen of the x-rays, her pelvis was severely shattered. It's going to take a lot of work to overcome that injury. But it's much too soon to have this conversation and I'm not the doctor to discuss it with." He rose from his chair and escorted Annie to the door.

***

Annie hated calling Mark Rhodes. Every time she did it was drudgery. In fact, she wasn't sure why she even bothered. It wasn't as if he cared what happened to Katie.

After giving the situation considerable thought, she realized that she kept him updated for other reasons, reasons of her own. As long as she had control over Katie she wasn't going to allow Mark and his baby's mama peace of mind. She knew her weekly updates caused a division in their relationship and that, quite simply, was the reason she made the calls.

She knew that Tiffany the bimbo checked Mark's phone and she loved using that knowledge to her advantage. When she made her calls she could picture the monster bride's face exploding in anger. She loved that thought! Age really did have its benefits. Tiffany was way out of her league in the manipulation department.

Annie loved knowing that her calls disturbed the new couple's world, it made her smile and sometimes it brightened her whole day. Not today. Today things were different. This was no ordinary torture call. This call was going to do more than just rock their whole world.

She tapped Mark's number on her phone's screen, hoping for once that she would get his voicemail so she wouldn't have to talk to him. Deep down inside she knew that wasn't going to happen. Mark wanted to talk to her. He had even left her a message. Apparently, his insurance company was questioning more of the expenses.

Mark had always had a big mouth and when Annie called he spent a lot of time updating her on his problems. His main concern understandably was out-of-pocket expenses. With his baby coming, and Katie's medical bills climbing, he was worried. Now that he had given away his custodial rights so that Annie could make all the necessary decisions for his wife, he was beginning to complain to her about money.

Of course, normally, she loved to hear his complaints in some sick, twisted way. But today, when she knew what her friend was about to go through the last thing she wanted to do was to hear Mark complain about his life.

The phone rang twice.

"Annie?"

"That's right."

"Please tell me you have some good news for a change, like they're moving her into a rest home."

"Really? Would that be good news?" she asked, and without waiting for a response she announced her reason for calling. "Katie's going in for surgery at 3:00 today."

"*Another* surgery?"

Annie was sure he saw dollar signs flash in front of his eyes.

"Yes, Mark, another surgery. This time they'll be cutting away part of her skull, to relieve the pressure. This will give her brain time to heal and that could help pull her out of the coma."

"Maybe."

"What?"

"Maybe pull her out of the coma. I'm just guessing the surgery doesn't have a one hundred percent recovery rate," Mark snapped.

For the past two months they had been playing civil with each other. Now that balance was teetering.

"What exactly are you saying, Mark? That you'd rather I just cut the cords?" She was still trying to maintain an inkling of control instead of completely going off on him.

"No, of course not. I didn't say that, Annie. Don't jump to conclusions."

"Then what did you mean?"

"Look, she's been in a coma for two months. Have you ever seen people when they awaken after a few months of being in a coma? Even if she comes out of it, she's never going to be normal, is she?"

Annie was too stunned to speak.

"You've probably seen those shows on how much rehab they require just to be able to do basic tasks."

"Sounds expensive," Annie said, playing Devil's advocate.

"Doesn't it though? If we were talking about a sure fix, then of course I would be all for it, but realistically what are the chances of a full recovery?"

"Probably pretty slim," Annie said. She felt the vibes lighten. Mark believed she was listening to his reasoning and that she understood. His tone changed. He became almost friendly.

"As it is, we're talking about low chances. If, and that's a big *if*, she comes out of the coma what is she going to be, a vegetable? Do you think she wants that? Hell, would you?" he asked. "And yes, the expenses too. I have great insurance, but this, as well as Tiffany's pregnancy, well you can see what I'm getting at."

"Yes, I think I do." Annie grasped the steering wheel of the car so tightly that her knuckles turned white, trying hard to keep the anger out of her voice.

"I'm glad we're talking, Annie. I always knew you were a woman of reason," Mark said, sounding like a politician.

"You were able to get Tracy on your insurance? That's wonderful."

"What do you mean?" Mark asked. "And her name is Tiffany."

"Well considering your divorce was stopped through the courts because of 'special circumstances', with Katie still listed as your lawful wife, how were you able to work that out?" she asked in a sickeningly friendly voice.

"I had to list Tiffany as a domestic partner and it cost me a shitload in lawyer's fees. Fortunately, they were able to find a clause that exempts the one legal partner rule. I'm not sure how they did it, but if it works then I'm all for it," Mark said smugly.

"Poor Tiffany. This must be affecting her terribly. How far is she away from delivery?" Annie asked, even though she had already marked the date down on her calendar.

"Two weeks. I'm hoping that she has an easy delivery too. Tiffany doesn't know it, but because Katie is listed as primary spouse on the policy that limits the amount of money we can spend on the baby's delivery, which of course puts me in a spot."

"Yeah, Mark, I can see it your way. As President of Rhodes Investment Company, at least you were able to pull strings so that your two spouses could be insured, provided nobody asks questions. But now you've reached a limit where the insurance company is starting to question your expenses and they're kicking back charges so that you have to pay some of them.

"I can see how it would be a real inconvenience to put out funds that, in your opinion, are going to waste. As you pointed out, Katie's full recovery is a long shot. Hell, coming out of this coma, that's nearly impossible. Here you are with a pregnant fiancée waiting in the wings, biting your ear off because she's moody and jealous of Katie's continual presence. It puts you in a real shitty spot actually," Annie said, biding her time, wanting to get as much information out of Mark as she possibly could.

"Damn, you're good. You hit the nail on the head. I want to make something perfectly clear, though. If I were sure that Katie would make a full recovery from this surgery, then of course, despite the cost I would be all for it. But as you said, the chances are minimal."

"I see your side, Mark, I really do. And crazy as it is, I actually have a feasible solution to all of your problems. Although you won't like what I'm about to tell you, in reality it's a solution to everything. "

"Go ahead, I'm listening."

Annie could hear a change in his voice. He was readying himself for battle, expecting her to blast him. She took a deep breath and in a calm voice said, "You take Katie's father's company and you sell Katie's half. Then you use that money to fund whatever Katie's needs are going to be in the future. You know, things like specialized rehab for instance, stuff the insurance company's not going to pay for. Then you take your half, which is plenty of income to support your new family, and everyone wins. When the insurance issues clear up, probably after the bills are paid, then your divorce can be finalized and you and Tiffany can get married. That way, everyone is taken care of. As I recall, Al Searfus left a sizable estate along with the company, so I'm sure there's enough to go around."

"Annie, it didn't exactly work out that way."

"What do you mean?"

"When Katie's health deteriorated and she wasn't able to make business decisions any longer, she signed the company over to me."

"Really? Isn't that interesting. And when exactly did this take place? I don't remember Katie telling me anything about it."

"Well, you haven't exactly been around for the past five years have you? You lived out of state, Washington wasn't it?"

"Yes, that's right. But Katie and I still talked and we sent emails." Inside, Annie's blood was boiling and she wanted to scream at Mark, but outside her voice remained calm. This was a perk of being a good journalist, a skill that she used often in her profession.

"You weren't actually around, though. You didn't see her mood swings, the depression. You can't say how her mental state was because you weren't there."

"What are you getting at?" Annie asked flatly.

"Just that Katie doesn't own half of the company," he replied, keeping his own voice surprisingly civil.

"Then it's a good thing she's still your legal wife."

"Temporarily."

"I've got to hand it to you, Mark. You did pretty damn well for a poor little rich boy, who, as I recall, lied to Katie about coming from money—or had your family lost it all?— I can't remember. How convenient that you wormed you way into a family with two heirs and you, no blood relation at all, ended up with everything."

"This conversation is over, Annie," Mark said, anger finally entering his voice.

"No, I don't think so. You can hang up if you want, but my next actions would come as a surprise. I'd rather tell you about them personally. I don't like secrets and backstabbing, but if you don't want to hear them, suit yourself," she said, preparing to hang up the phone.

"Wait." Mark sighed. "Look, there's no reason for us to argue. We should be working together, at least until I can remove you as guardian and replace myself since, as you pointed, out I am still her legal husband. Until that happens, nothing's changed. There's no reason to argue. Katie obviously is going into surgery so let's see how the surgery turns out before we go any further."

"So you'd like guardianship returned would you? You signed legal documents, Mark, drawn up by my private attorney, a good one I might add. I don't think it's going to be that simple to get out of a binding legal contract. You go ahead and try, though. In the meantime, maybe I should do some investigative work of my own to see what kind of legal papers Katie signed and while I'm at it, I'm going to check into Rhodes Investment Company finances too. As you might expect, as a journalist, I have a lot of resources at my fingertips."

"Is that a threat?"

"Hell no. I'm not stupid enough to make a threat. I'm telling you my intentions so there are no secrets between us. I have to tell you that you have my curiosity tweaked. How can a man who comes from basically nothing, since his own family was bankrupt, end up eliminating both of the true heirs in the family and wind up with everything?"

"Eliminate? Now wait a minute! I haven't eliminated anyone. I resent that statement."

"Not true. You're attempting to eliminate Katie right now, and as for Richard, who the fuck knows what part you played in that?"

"Richard died a long time ago. You can't say I had anything to do with that."

"I don't know that. I'm a journalist, Mark, my mind works differently. I tend to classify my memories like I organize my stories. That way I'm always looking for an angle. It seems to me that you were real chummy with Richard about the time he enlisted. You're a sneaky character, Mark. Maybe you had a hand in that. Maybe you became his best buddy and then you gave him a shove. It must be pretty easy to manipulate an eighteen year old kid."

"That spoiled brat? Why would I want to do that?"

"Because he stood in your way. He was the heir to a lot of money. With Richard out of the way, let's just say it put you in a good position."

"You can't say that! I had nothing to do with Richard's death. The stupid kid enlisted in the Marines for fuck's sake. It was during Vietnam. What the hell was he thinking? I tried to talk him out of going, as did everyone else who knew him. He just wouldn't listen."

"Yeah, I bet you tried real hard."

"Do you think I wanted Richard dead?"

"No, but I think you wanted him out of the way. Richard's death was just a bonus. If he had come back you would have figured out another way to weasel your way in. Maybe you would have convinced the old man that you were the son he never had. Don't tell me you didn't think of that approach."

"You're insane, Annie. I'm questioning your mental stability. And to think that you have custodial rights to my sick wife."

"Yeah, you would love to be able to push that button. You go right ahead and question me. You do anything you want; I'm not scared of you. Katie will have her surgery and I, as her custodial guardian, have the right to question her finances. Now everything is up front, Mark. We both know where each other stands. I guess the next time I talk to you it will be through attorneys. Goodbye, Mark." Before he had time to respond, Annie disconnected the call.

***

In January and February the weather in San Francisco was wet and cold. It rained almost daily until the middle of March, when the days finally cleared. Despite the weather, which could change within a day's notice, every day was an unexpected party. Katie loved everything about being back in 1967.

She and Moonbeam made money in a multitude of ways. Sometimes they helped in some of the shops on Haight. When the weather was nice, Moony would throw a blanket down in Golden Gate Park, the Panhandle, or sometimes Fisherman's Wharf. There she would read the tarot and palms for the tourists and Katie would advertise for clients.

At other times they worked at the local clubs like the Avalon, the Fillmore and the Matrix. Every day was different, exciting, a new adventure. Nothing was routine, and nothing was ever boring. If they were working, they were having fun. If they walked down Haight, they could find a party in front of the Psychedelic Shop. And beginning in March, when the sky cleared, there were free concerts in the Panhandle.

On those days all it took was for two pickups trucks to back into each other, creating an instant stage. Someone would hook up amplifiers and then bands like the Grateful Dead, Quick Silver and the Messenger Service, Moby Grape and others, would step on the makeshift stage and start grooving. Life in Haight-Ashbury was good. Katie had forgotten how good, and now, every day she was reminded and she appreciated her youth far more this time around.

As the Diggers had feared, the "Be-In" had brought unwanted attention to the good thing the real hippies had created. Now they were being invaded by America's lost children. The problems in the district were beginning to multiply. The hippies watched their world start to crumble, while the merchants relished the opportunity to make money as Haight-Ashbury's reputation brought hundreds of tourists to the once impoverished neighborhood. As for Katie, she knew from history that nothing could stop the avalanche of publicity that was about to hit the area.

The Haight-Ashbury District of love and peace would reach its height in a matter of months and then gradually it would fall apart. Recreational drugs like weed, LSD, and magic mushrooms would be replaced by shooting speed or heroin, long-term highs but highly addictive drugs. By 1968, the area would be infested with crime and junkies. The original founders of the hippie movement would leave San Francisco, many heading for communes in Marin County. By 1969, The Altamont Free Concert would bring a permanent end to the psychedelic era.

But that was later, yet to come. Right now, the Summer of Love was approaching. This was an event that would take San Francisco on a tour of psychedelics. Over the next few months Haight-Ashbury would become the center of the youth culture for the world. The San Francisco sound in music was about to explode as local bands became overnight sensations and the Summer of 1967, an event that would change the world forever, was about to take place. For Katie, having experienced it once before, this was an unbelievable dream come true.

She had stopped worrying about popping back into the future at any second. Every day she woke in a twenty year old, energetic, healthy body— no more morning pains, no arthritis, hemorrhoids, or fatigue. No, she was sharing the best time of her life, a second time, with her best friend.

Around them, world events repeated themselves. In early February 25,000 troops were sent to the Cambodian border. This mass migration would lead to Operation Rolling Thunder, further pulling the US into the Vietnam conflict.

Stalin's daughter, Svetlana Alliuyeva, defected to the US through the embassy in New Delhi. A stupid move, Katie explained to her friends, since Svetlana's grown children would disown her over the decision and she would never be happy in the United States. Eventually, she would return to the Soviet Union to make peace with her family.

Look magazine published their article about the 'generation gap', a term coined by John Poppy, and as March rolled in like a lion, Johnson announced his plan for the 'lottery' draft, another validation to Katie's predictions of the future.

Most interesting of all was the Banana scam, which exploded when the *Berkeley Barb* published an article in their March issue. They reported that bananas contained Bananadine, an ingredient which, when dried and smoked, created a high similar to marijuana. The original hoax was designed to raise questions about the ethics of making psychoactive drugs illegal: *"What if the common banana contained psychoactive properties? How would the government react?"* The propaganda, along with a song by Donovan entitled 'Mellow Yellow', had stoners everywhere drying banana peels and smoking them.

The months sped by, and the problems they shared continued to engulf them. Even though every day was a party, in the back of Katie's mind she remembered what was at stake. As the days progressed and 'those' times approached, her mind was busy constructing plans in the hopes of changing the future for her brother and for Frog.

Katie's friends had a different way of relating to her now that her predictions continued to come true. With each validation, Frog became closer. He asked questions about the future, he talked to her extensively about business investments he could make if he were around to see them, and he probed her mind hoping to release some memory, no matter how small, which might give them another clue to his disappearance. But try as he might, Katie's memories of Frog in 'her' 1967, were vague. She had remembered nothing more and because of that, Frog's mystery continued to elude all of them.

Although she and Frog spent hours together going over possible plans and their scenarios, for the most part, life had become as normal as it could be under the strange circumstances.

While Frog became closer, Annie became distant. She spent her spare time studying astrological charts, going over one theory or another as she questioned the reasons why this was happening.

During the day, when they were working together, Katie tried to act as normal as possible. Whereas Frog would ask questions, curious to know about the future, Moony would ask none. She preferred to remain blind to her own path. In fact, she had forbidden Katie from telling her anything about her life.

Out of respect for her friend's wishes, when they were together, Katie kept her judgments and her knowledge to herself. Unless Annie specifically asked her a question, which was extremely rare, she tried to act like her twenty-year old self, which was a difficult thing to do when you were mentally pushing 65.

If she recognized someone on the street and a flash of that person's future popped in her head she refrained from speaking. She had her goals, things she wanted to change, and the rest she had to let go. It was difficult to realize and then accept that she couldn't change the world. No matter how much she wanted to, she couldn't warn everyone about their futures.

She was aware of the "butterfly effect" and "temporal paradox" courtesy of her Hollywood education. She knew that she couldn't change everything in the past without changing the present. It was that knowledge that kept her focused on the few things she really wanted to change. Still, she found it difficult to know the outcome to so many issues and then keep them all to herself.

***

One evening when Katie and Frog were sitting in the living room watching *Hogan's Heroes*, Moonbeam excitedly burst into the room with a bundle of charts in her hands.

"I've got it!" she announced. "I think I finally understand the whole sky pattern the night this started .

That chart I drew was filled with conjunctions and oppositions. Those distracted me from the real culprit, the real oddity in all of this. Look here," she said, producing one of the charts and dropping the others on the wooden coffee table. She pointed to a new addition to her previous drawing. At the center, in red ink, was a kind of circular pattern.

"That's a T-square in astrology. You see how it forms an isosceles triangle? That's what I left out of the last chart. It was stupid of me because it was as plain as day. I missed it because I put too much emphasis into the rest of the chart. You see, a configuration of aspects is formed when two points of a horoscope are in opposition to each other and in quadrature to a third planet. This configuration gives certain obstacles and the necessity to overcome them. You need strong, vigorous, ambitious aspirations to act, and you have to act, or the situation will become out of control very quickly. The T-square indicates an immediate crisis situation.

"In the T-square the opposition is connected with attitudes and the square to actions. It's a dynamic configuration that creates strength, as long as you find all the possible problems before acting. But it's forceful, clumsy, aggressive, creating emptiness in the other hemisphere. This void is what causes problems with self-assurance, making the recipient feel discontent with destiny.

"Here's the good part, for us," she said, clearing her throat. "If we aren't hung up on self-assurance issues, then we can solve very complicated problems, through strong-willed pressure."

Frog shook his head in confusion and turned to Katie. "What the fuck did she just say?"

"Beats me," Katie responded blankly, staring at Moony.

"What are you talking about?" they said, in unison.

"Oh, I'm sorry." Moonbeam laughed. "I forget you aren't hip with the metaphysical lingo. What it means is that the sky that night was right for change. Remember my first chart? That's what I told you. What I missed was how dramatic that change was going to be and that it could go either way, positive or negative.

"Everything depends on our will to act, and how fast we're able to do that depends on how quickly and fully we understand all the problems. This is a dangerous combination in astrology because it causes a feeling of weakness when in reality the individual is strong, but they're filled with crippling doubt.

"We're going to have to work very hard to overcome our individual feelings of inferiority. If we fall into that trap, then we're going to achieve nothing. And here's the bigger problem; no matter how many times you prove to us that you know what you're talking about, Katie, deep down Frog and I will always have doubt, and it's that doubt that will block us from believing everything we need to."

"What are you talking about? I didn't say I didn't believe her," Frog said. "She's proven to me that she knows about the future. Hell, she can tell me the end of the TV shows we watch together. These are new shows too, just filmed maybe a week or two before airing. How can she know the ending of new shows unless she's telling the truth?"

"Easily, you just answered it, Frog. You said she knows about the future, you didn't say time travel, because deep down you still have a problem believing something that farfetched. And that's okay because I do too. It's human nature. How can anyone possibly fully believe that another person is here from the future? There will always be doubt. We have to expect that, and it's an obstacle we need to fight against.

"I know Katie shares the future with both of us, more you Frog, since I'd rather not know my outcome. Point is, we believe her predictions but you have to admit there's still a part of you that doesn't believe the time travel idea."

"Okay, I guess so, maybe," he said, deep in thought.

"And that goes right back to Guthrie's prediction," Moonbeam said. "You can change things if you believe. We're still hung up on believing."

"Right, and the chart of stars told you all of that? How world shattering. Which part of that is news to any of us?"

"It has to do with everything. My bet is that the same star pattern appeared in the sky on January 8, 2014. The same pattern allowed Katie to fall back into 1967. Was it some freak occurrence, or was it divine intervention?"

"Wait," Frog said, "you just said you don't believe in time travel, now you're contradicting yourself. This conversation is going nowhere. I'm going back to watching *Hogan's Heroes*." He turned his attention towards to the television.

"Don't bother, Frog, I'll tell you what happens," said Katie. "During the next camp inspection Hogan gets rid of Sergeant Franks by messing the camp up and throwing dirty clothes everywhere. Then Sergeant Frank's uniform comes unglued when his body temperature reaches ninety degrees. That happens in front of the visiting German General. As a result, the army takes Franks away. I think they arrest him."

"Oh nice one, Katie, thanks again. I fucking hate that. I told you before stop ruining the shows for me or we aren't watching them together anymore! You're getting to be a bummer, man."

"Both of you stop!" Moonbeam yelled. "I'm talking and I intend to finish what I'm saying!"

Apart from the television, the parlor became quiet instantly. Moonbeam turned the console TV off and then stood in front of it with her arms crossed defiantly.

"Okay, Moony," Frog said, mad over having his television show ruined and now turned off all together, "you have our attention now. Spill the beans but get to the point since so far you've said nothing of value."

"Don't you see what's happening?" she asked. "We're starting to argue." That's the point of all of this. Fate is working against us! It's going to be hard to change anything if we don't get 'us' together first."

"Let me try to understand this, Moony," Katie said interrupting her friend. "You're saying that the reason I fell back into 1967 is because the star pattern was the same in 2014?"

"Yes, that's part of the reason. I think the other part was due to forces outside of our control, I mean fate, the gods and goddesses, whatever you believe in. We are meant to change things, which is not going to be easy because the forces of the universe are working against us. For every step forward, we need to expect to take several backwards."

"And that's because of this unique freaky star pattern," Frog mumbled under his breath.

"Yes, it's because the stars are against us but it's more than just that; it's the possibility of creating a paradox in time. Time doesn't want to be changed, it's going to be fighting us all the way. And we have to keep the ultimate goal in mind because the more we change the present the more we alter the future. Every action we make permanently changes the world that Katie knows in the future.

"I'll tell you what, Moony, for someone who never wants to talk to us about the situation, preferring to act normal like nothing out of the ordinary is taking place, you sure are wordy tonight," Frog said sarcastically.

"I couldn't talk about it until now. I had to redo my chart, make sure I was right this time. You asked me to use my talents to understand this, Frog; well, that's what I've done. Here I am trying to tell you what I know to be fact and you're on a downer because of a television show."

"Moonbeam, don't worry about him. I think I'm starting to understand what you're getting at." Katie said, getting off of the floor so she could move closer to Moony. "You're saying that I'm here to fix things but there are contingencies to that, one being the universe itself that will be trying to stop us. Which means we better have several plans available anticipating failures. Because all of these forces are against us, we have to know everything that we're facing no matter how small the situation seems to be. We can't have any surprises, meaning," Katie looked significantly at Frog, "we have to disclose everything to each other."

"Oh come off it. I've already told you everything about my involvement with the Hells Angels. I don't know why we keep coming back to this."

"I hope so, Frog. I really do, because if you aren't being honest with us then you could end up sabotaging everything," Moony said, and Katie nodded in agreement.

"We want to believe you, Frog, but there are so many discrepancies. Like where are you when you disappear and we can't find you?" Moonbeam asked him. "You seem to spend a lot of hours in a place called 'nowhere'."

"Okay, now I'm really done with this conversation." Frog rose from the couch and headed for the door. "If I can't watch television in my own home without being interrupted or without somebody telling me the end of the episode, then I might as well go to the Psychedelic Shop and smoke my frustrations away." He zipped his sweatshirt and walked out the door into the night.

Chapter 19

Terry had spent every day of the last four month in a constant state of fear. He was terrified that the Hells Angels would finally find Ruby and Eva.

After the fiasco with the painted bikes, the girls had split, probably back to LA, leaving a guilt ridden Terry to face his brothers.

The Los Angeles Hells Angels had kept their eyes open, but as of yet there had been no sign of them. It was only a matter of time before they were found though, since the police had a warrant to arrest them and the Angels were watching and waiting.

To make matters worse for Terry, Chocolate George had convinced the club that the girls had an accomplice, someone who had led them to the bikes. As a result, everyone studied each other, knowing that there were only eight guys who had ridden in together that morning.

Terry and Freddy had loaned both Dylan and Joey a bike to ride, although neither looked like much, and certainly weren't what they were used to. The bikes ran and they kept the two Angels mobile. Their ruined bikes were still at Milton's garage, stripped into pieces. The paint and feathers had finally been cleaned off and now the bikes were being rebuilt.

The last few months had been mind-bending. Some nights Terry lay awake trying to figure a way out. When he did sleep, his dreams were troubled. His guilt kept him in a state of turmoil. Once, he woke screaming, thinking that he had a knife to his throat only to find that it was his bed sheets wrapped around his neck.

Sooner or later, Eva and Ruby would be found and they would rat him out. He was sure of it. That meant possible jail time and the risk of being kicked out of the MC

Two months of pressure had caused him to lose weight. He couldn't eat when he was constantly watching his back and that was the reason why Terry was here at Arnold's garage tonight. He would rather face his demons head on than continue to deceive his brothers, or go into hiding. He knew he had it coming and he knew he deserved it. The sooner it happened, the better off he would be.

Terry prided himself on being a man of his word. In his eyes, a man who couldn't keep his promises wasn't a man at all. So along with the guilt he already felt and the knowledge that he had turned on his brothers, whether willingly or not, it had all become too much for him to bear. Even the bike he intended to give to Dylan hadn't cleared his conscience. There was only one way to do that.

Terry got to the garage just a little before closing. He sat in the parking lot across the street and watched, waiting until the regular employees left. Today was Tuesday. It was the night Arnold let Dylan and Joey stay late, unaccompanied, to work on their bikes.

Before leaving home he called Skinner at the clubhouse and asked him to come to the garage. If Terry was going to come clean, he wanted to do it the right way. This meant having an officer present for his own protection and because it was official club business.

When Skinner's familiar Indian motorcycle pulled into the lot, Terry got out of his truck and met him halfway up the walkway. They clasped hands in greeting.

"Hey, man, what the fuck are we doing here?" Skinner asked, glancing around the empty lot.

"I got news and it ain't good. I got something to tell Dylan and Joey and I need you present when I do it," Terry said with a troubled sigh.

"Dylan and Joey?" Skinner asked and then immediately swallowed, knowing what was about to happen.

"Yep." Terry pulled on the unlocked door and entered the hallway.

Inside, the office was dark but the garage in the back was brightly lit, music from a local radio station playing in the background. A song finished and the DJ came on the air:

"This is Bobby Ocean at KFRC in San Francisco. It's March 28th and it's 7:30 p.m. It's going to be a mild night with temperatures currently in the mid 50's. That last song was a new release from our very own Jefferson Airplane. That was 'White Rabbit' off the 'Surrealistic Pillow' album, which I'm happy to report is quickly rising in the charts. Here's another cut off that album, this one's entitled, 'Somebody to Love'."

Skinner walked into the garage and shivered. "Fucking hell this place is cold! How can you stand it?"

Dylan and Joey sat on two metal folding chairs working on pieces of their bikes.

Joey looked up from the greasy parts he held in his hands. "Skinner, Terry. What the fuck are you guys doing here?"

"Man, I got something to tell you," Terry said, his voice wavery in his nervousness. "I've done something stupid, something I'm ashamed of, and I knew it was wrong when I did it, but I did it anyway. Worse of all, I did it for pussy, plain and simple. It's the oldest fucking reason for deceit in history and I fell into it."

"What are you talking about, man?" Dylan asked. He stood up, wiping his hands on a cloth.

"Eva and Ruby," Terry said nervously. "I'm the one who showed them where the bikes were parked."

"You fucking did *what*?" Joey said. He jumped to his feet and rushed towards Terry, only to be stopped by Skinner.

"Stop, man. Let's hear him out."

"I've heard enough, I'm going to fucking kill him!" Joey screamed, trying to pull away from Skinner. Before he got a chance, Dylan walked around the two bikers and punched Terry in the face, breaking his nose. Terry flew backwards and hit the pavement hard. He lay bleeding for several seconds before finally sitting upright, holding his dripping nose.

"Great, you stupid idiot. Why don't you fucking kill him before he has a chance to talk to us!" Skinner screamed, red faced. "Now back the fuck away from him, that's an order."

Dylan raised both hands above his head and took three steps backwards.

"Okay, man, it's cool. He can talk. I'm done. Temporarily" "But he better make it fast or I'm going to pound his fucking head into the floor!" Joey added, shaking in anger.

"Okay, man, you got the floor. What's this shit about?" Skinner asked, throwing Terry a grease rag out of a clean stack Arnold kept in the corner.

Terry took the rag and held it to his nose, wiping the blood away from his face so he could talk. "Evan and Ruby....they hooked up with me the night of the party. After I got kicked out for fighting with Abel, I went to the corner bar."

"The Dogpatch Saloon?" Skinner asked.

"That's right. I walked there. I thought it would help me cool off, you know what I mean? When your blood is still boiling right after a fight? I was there about forty-five minutes and had a pretty good buzz going. That's when Eva and Ruby walked in. They were fucking pissed off because they'd been 86'd from the party. They were yelling and swearing, looking real cute in their short little leather getups. I bought them a few drinks, Eva and I got friendly. Next thing I knew she had spent the next few days at my place, in bed. It was mind-blowing. Dylan, you know what she's like in bed. A few days of that shit and she had me brainwashed." Terry stopped talking long enough to dispose of the now fully red rag and replace it with a clean one.

"Brainwashed my ass you motherfucking trader piece of shit. When I get my hands on you, I'll show you fucking brainwashed!" Joey yelled and took a few steps towards him before Dylan held his arm out to stop him.

"Wait man, I want to hear the whole fucking pathetic story. I want to know how stupid the little shit is before we kill him. When we've heard him out and we're ready to tear him apart you'll get your turn first. I promise," Dylan said calmly with an evil grin on his face.

"Go on, man. I don't know how much longer I can hold them back," Skinner said.

"I felt sorry for them. I knew what it was like to get thrown out of the party, we had a common bond. It was stupid, I know that now, but they're foxy and I was..."

"Brainwashed," Skinner said.

"Yeah that's right, brainwashed." Terry swiped his hand across his face. "The day of the Be-In they asked me for a favor. They said they wanted to know where the bikes were. I should have asked more questions, I shouldn't have trusted them, but I did. I never thought they were going to ruin your rides, man. I thought they might leave you a note or a sign, but never in a million years did I imagine that they would fuck up your rides. I swear to God I didn't. If I would have known that's what they were going to do I would have never been involved. That's the God's honest truth. I know it's not an excuse for my actions but that's what happened. I got sucked in and when I realized what they had done it was too late.

"I feel like the scum of the earth and that's why I had to tell you the truth. I know I got it coming. I'm okay with that. I'm a fucking idiot and I deserve it. That's all I got to say. Now the two of you can pound on me."

Terry was still sitting on the floor covered in his own blood.

"There's a protocol for this shit and we're going to follow it," Skinner said. "We can settle this ourselves, here and now or we can take it to the head table. Dylan, Joey, it's up to you. How do you want to proceed with this? How far do you want to take this?"

"I'm good with finishing it here," Joey said, cracking his knuckles.

"This is a patch decision, you understand?" Skinner asked. "I want you to understand what you're agreeing to. If you feel strong enough about his disloyalty then we can put him up for a hearing and let the club decide if he should be thrown out and de-patched."

"No need for that," Dylan said. "I think we can take care of it ourselves."

"Then let's go over the rules. Three hits apiece, nothing below the waist, no kicking or using your feet. Plus, his nose is already busted so you can't hit him there," Skinner said. "Everything is a go until I stop the fight. When I say it's over then it's immediate. You got it?"

Joey nodded, and then Dylan.

"Okay, Joey, I guess you're on, man. Dylan said you could go first."

Skinner and Dylan stepped closer to the wall. Joey walked up to the injured biker and offered him a hand. "Here, man, let me help you up."

Terry hesitated, still sitting on the floor.

"Come on, man. I ain't going to hit a man that's sitting on the ground," Joey said.

Terry grasped his hand and struggled to his feet, dropping the bloodied rags.

Joey unzipped his leather jacket and threw it over a stool, then took a step towards his blood-covered opponent.

"Look, man, I appreciate the fact that you told us yourself. If I'd found out behind your back you'd be a dead man. I mean that. Seeing how you got the guts to come here face to face, I respect that. But you're one stupid motherfucker letting yourself get used by those sleazy sluts." Joey threw a punch, hitting Terry in the eye and sending him backwards a few steps. "You said it yourself, man, you got this coming."

Terry wobbled but he didn't fall. It took him a few seconds to steady himself but when he did he stood emotionless, ready for the next blow.

"Leading those fucking skanks to our bikes, man? How fucking stupid can you get?" Joey asked.

"I know, man. I know."

Joey took another swing, this time burying his fist deep into Terry's ribcage. Terry buckled over in pain, holding his side. He stood several seconds and then spat a congealed crimson glob on the cement floor next to his boots.

"One more, man," Joey said, waiting for Terry to rise and steady himself. When he did, Joey hit him in the ribs again, same location, but this time something cracked. Terry fell to the floor panting, holding his ribs and rocking back and forth in pain.

"You doing okay, Terry?" Skinner asked.

"Yeah, I'm okay." Terry scrambled to his feet, slouched over holding his ribs and watching as Dylan unzipped his jacket and approached him.

Dylan swung fast, smashing Terry in the mouth and sending him stumbling over. Terry hit the garage floor and this time he didn't get up. He remained on his back bleeding and gasping.

"Fight's over," Skinner said as he approached them. "Sorry, Dylan. You don't get that extra shot but I think he's had enough."

"Agreed. I was going to stop anyway. Seeing how you told us yourself, Terry, we're cool."

Dylan helped Skinner sit Terry upright against the wall and handed him a handful of clean grease rags.

"You okay, Terry?" Skinner asked again. Terry nodded and dabbed at his bloodied mouth and nose. "Punishment is paid by your brothers, but now you have to face the wrath of the club. You went against our bylaws and against your own brothers, man. We can't have that. Dylan and Joey are gracious. They've released you and allowed you to keep your patch. That's generous man, damn generous. I hope you realize that."

"I do man, I do. I'm so sorry, guys. I know that I owe you big time. The club is my life and not taking my patch away means everything," Terry managed to say between coughing up chunks of blood.

"The matter is closed after tonight, but you got to pay the piper, brother. Terry and Dylan's bikes are out of action, now, so is yours. The club is confiscating your ride and you know we have the right to do that. You need to sign the title over to the club."

Terry nodded. "At least I've still got my truck."

"You got another problem, son. You need a bike to be a member and you only have a few months to fulfill that requirement."

"Yeah I know. I got another bike, man. The one I loaned to Dylan. Once his bike is repaired, I'll use that. Sorry, Dylan I was going to give it to you, but under the circumstances I'm going to need it back."

"That's cool, man. Our bikes should be running within a few days and then you can have yours back."

"Then as far as the club in concerned, this matter is closed. Agreed?" The men nodded. "Good, then nothing leaves this room, it's over. Terry, the title and the bike need to be delivered by Friday. I would say tomorrow but I think you're going to need a few days before you can ride. You going to be able to get yourself home okay, or should I call somebody to help you?" Skinner asked.

"My truck's outside. I'm sure I can make it two miles home."

Skinner helped Terry to his feet.

"Then I'll follow you to make sure you get home alright," Skinner said patting the injured biker on the back. "Let's go, brother, I think you've had enough for one day."

The two men walked down the hall towards the front door, with "Break on Through to the Other Side" squealing from the transistor radio in the workroom.

*****

The Wednesday after The Be-In he had five customers waiting for him in Golden Gate Park, and the Wednesday after that, he had twenty. Now he had a multitude of customers all over the district, and sometimes he delivered to other parts of the city.

Frog had even gotten used to being "Mickey" and picking up his supplies from the abandoned apartment house in the Fillmore, but in the back of his mind he knew that what he was doing was wrong. If Katie was right and he was going to disappear, then it would have something to do with dealing heroin.

He hadn't lied to the girls, not really. His business *wasn't* with the Angels. True, he was dealing with some of the members, but the MC wasn't involved, only the unpatched bikers.

Frog wanted to tell the girls the truth and he knew they were trying to watch over him, but of course that was out of the question. His dealer authorities had made it clear. He knew the outcome if he opened his mouth. He was no dummy, and knew that the men he was working for could do away with him anytime they wanted. All he had to do was become a liability and he would be gone in a minute.

Frog wanted out, but he had to find the right opportunity to get out. Regarding his own demise in late summer, he had plans. If he wasn't in 'Frisco then he couldn't disappear. When he had enough money saved he would leave, maybe take Moonbeam and Katie with him. Either way, by August he would be long gone, far away from the San Francisco Bay Area. First, though, he had to finish things here. One of which was trying to find out who was going to try to dispose of him. In the meantime he was going to continue raking in a shitload of dough.

Valentine had told him the rules and how to survive the game. Number one on the list was to be discreet, and he had been. In fact, he had been extra careful, watching everything he did, creating twists and turns so that nobody could follow his tracks.

His customers on the street knew him as Darryl, and he met them in Golden Gate Park on Wednesdays and the Panhandle on Thursdays. The rest of the week Frog took care of his own business, slim as that had become, and in between all of that, he delivered smack once a week to Oakland.

The Oakland run was an added responsibility, something Sal had dropped in his lap. Frog would meet him at a location, which changed weekly. He would pick up a van, which also changed weekly, and then he would drive it across the bay. Once in Oakland he handed the vehicle over to a second party, then he would hitchhike back to 'Frisco, and some time the next week he would do it all over again. This small weekly trip paid him an additional $500 in his pocket. All he had to do was drive the truck, hand it over, and keep his mouth shut.

As Sal and Dave had promised, the money was rolling in and Frog had an abundance of it. As a result, he found himself spending less time on his own gig and delaying his escape as more and more bread fell his way. It was now the end of March; he had five months of safety until the end of summer. He figured between now and then he might as well stockpile a fortune. That way, when he left San Francisco he would be able to easily start someplace new.

Tonight, Frog walked down Haight Street shivering. The wind was blowing hard and the cold air coming off the San Francisco Bay was bitter. He pulled a pair of knitted gloves out of his pocket and covered his numb fingers.

Despite the weather, there was a small group in front of the Psychedelic Shop. That was always a given. If you lived in the Haight and you wanted to find a place to party, no matter what time of day it was, you could always find what you were looking for in front of the Psychedelic Shop.

Tonight, four hippies stood outside the store, smoking weed with one of the owners. They were huddling against the wall of the building trying to stay out of the freezing wind.

When Frog stepped in front of the store he squeezed his way into the doorway, where two other guys were already standing, Jay, one of the owners, and a cat everyone knew as Crazy Eddy.

"Hey, man, I haven't seen you in a while. Where you been?" Jay asked.

"I've been around, man," Frog said, reaching in his pocket for a joint.

Jay snatched the joint from Frog's hand and lit it. "Not much. I used to see you selling to the tourists every day out on the main streets. You're not out there anymore, brother, you're off somewhere else doing God knows what."

"Man, you're in here working all the time, what do you know?"

"I know when I'm right," Jay said taking a long hit on the joint before passing it to Crazy Eddy, a stout hippie who chuckled like a squirrel and nodded his head.

"He knows when's he's right, Frog. I'm out there all the time and I never see you anymore, not the way you used to hustle. What gives, brother?" Crazy said, and then turned to stare at Frog, the multiple sets of love beads around his neck banging against each other and causing him to rattle.

"Nothing gives. You're both full of shit. I'm around. I just got a lot of business outside the district now that's all."

"Is that right? Business outside the Haight, how about that?" Crazy said, laughing like a rodent and shaking his love beads.

"Hey, Frog, some cat was in here asking about you a few days ago."

"Yeah? Who?"

"Damned if I know. I've never seen him before. Strange dude, didn't seem like someone you'd associate with."

"Why's that?"

"This dude was in a suit man, a slick suit too, expensive. He got out of a fancy car. Some foreign ride, classy, black. Like I said, he didn't seem like someone you'd know."

Frog thought through a long list of acquaintances and he didn't know anyone who fit the description that Jay had given him.

"I don't think I know him."

"He didn't really know you either, man. It was a strange scene. Dude looked like an Italian gangster. Fucking dead ringer for Al Capone. Anyways, he left you something dude. Come inside I'll give it to you." Jay took one last hit on the roach then dropped it into the dirt next to his feet.

Jay pushed on the glass door and a string of bells rang when he and Frog walked inside. He walked behind the main counter, bent down, and he pulled out a plain white envelope.

"He left me a letter?" Frog questioned. "Did he know my name?"

"No man, he didn't know your name, but he described you to a T. Said you were about 5'10", wavy brown hair that reached halfway down your back that you wore in a tail. He said you wore tie dyed T-shirts and that you're clean-shaven. He knew you were a popular fellow in the Haight, said you were a street peddler and that he knew you hung out here at the shop."

"That could be a lot of people. Half the men in the Haight fit that description. How do you know he was looking for me?"

"Hey man, it's you. He knew your real name. He called you Darryl. I'm guessing that's what your mamma named you?"

Frog felt his stomach lurch and quite suddenly felt sick. If a slick gangster type was in Jay's shop looking for 'Darryl' this couldn't possibly be good.

"No man that's not my name. My name is Curtis Redmond."

"Here," Jay said handing him the envelope. "If this isn't meant for you then throw it away. I don't know anyone else that fits the description and I'm not going to spend a lot of time on this."

Frog took the envelope and Jay headed towards the door. "Come on, man, let's go be social," he said, prompting Frog towards the front door.

Frog shoved the envelope in his jacket pocket, fighting the urge to tear it open immediately. He knew it was for him; there was only one Darryl that he knew, his alter ego the drug dealer, the one he thought was sharp enough never to get caught.

Frog stayed and partied with his friends for about forty-five minutes, long enough that his departure didn't seem sudden or suspicious. As soon as he felt he could dip out without causing a scene, he politely excused himself.

Shaking nervously, he walked across the street, entered the Pal Mall bar and ordered a dark beer and a love burger. When his nerves had settled and his hands were no longer shaking, he took the white envelope out of his pocket and sat it on the counter in front of him. He stared at it, turning it over several times before finally tearing it open.

Inside he found a sheet of lined binder paper with a handwritten note. He took a long swig off his beer before moving closer to a dim table lamp where he could read the letter.

Hello there Darryl, Frog, or is it Curtis?

You thought you were so clever and look how quickly I found you. Here's a drug peddling lesson:

Know whose territory you're walking into. Ask questions if you don't know what area you're selling in, and don't assume that San Francisco is up for grabs, because it isn't.

Admit that you're playing way out of your league and get out while you're still alive.

If you disregard my advice and decide to stay in the game, then you're going to have to get a hell of a lot smarter than you are now.

This is your one warning. The next time I'll see you at home. I'm sure I won't have any problems finding it either.

Stay out of the Broadway/Little Italy area. Tell your bosses whom they're playing with.

The Family

Frog dropped the letter in front of him and swallowed hard. His first reaction was to burn it but he knew that would be a mistake. He refolded it, put it back in the envelope and stuck it in his jacket pocket. This was something that Sal and Dave needed to see, and perhaps it would be his ticket out of the business.

Frog finished his love burger, his mind reeling with ideas. In the end he decided to go home. He would see Sal and Dave in the morning, and with any luck he would be able to bow out of this whole deal.

He wasn't sure who "The Family" was, but he had a pretty good idea, and he wasn't about to find out for sure. Somebody important was on to them. Surely the bikers would know it was time to get out and the whole ordeal would be over.

Frog smiled happily, sure that he was free from the drug-dealing ordeal. He ordered another beer and for the first time in a long time he finished his dinner in peace, thinking that his problems were over. Little did he know they were just beginning.

Chapter 20

The Avalon Ballroom was on the corner of Sutter and Van Ness in a neighborhood known as Polk Gulch. The Victorian building was built in 1911 and was originally the Colin Traver Academy of Dance.

In 1967, it was one of three spots within the city of San Francisco to hear live concerts, the other two being the Fillmore and the Matrix. Robert Cohen and Chet Helms' production company, The Family Dog, owned the ballroom. Chet just happened to be the manager of Big Brother and the Holding Company, a local band he founded. In 1966 Helms hitchhiked to Texas and back to bring the band a singer he knew from the University of Texas. Her name was Janis Joplin.

Tonight, Ron Diebel, Moonbeam, and an ecstatic Katie were attending a concert at the Ballroom. Katie had bought the tickets several weeks earlier and now that the day had arrived she was on cloud nine. Not only was she going to experience the nostalgia of the music firsthand, she was equipped with a large purse and the tools necessary to confiscate some of the most beautiful artwork of the time; The Avalon's famous psychedelic band posters.

"I'm still shocked that you wanted to see this show," Ron said, chewing on a slice of beef jerky he bought at the Texaco station near their house.

The truth was, Katie had missed most of the shows, apart from the free concerts in the park. She had either been too busy doing her own thing or she was conserving money. In her 1967 she had been proud. Every month her parents had sent her a check in the mail, their control money. Katie had habitually sent it back unopened, but not this time.

The last check she had received and the one before that she had simply deposited in the bank. She knew it was a bribe, but what the hell? The way Katie saw things, she wasn't going to get an inheritance no matter how things turned out, so why not use the money while she could? It was stupid to send it back. Eventually they would cut her off, but as long as they were willing to foot the bill for her vacation in 1967, let them.

Last time around she had worried about money constantly but she wasn't about to do that again. Now Katie had bread. Why deny herself anything? If she was going to be given the chance to do it all again, then she was going to do it in style.

This time she would do everything she had missed the first time, and that meant attending every concert and hippie event that she could. Thanks to her parents' blood money, she could afford it.

That's why Katie had bought two tickets to the concert tonight. Moony didn't have pocket money for a ticket and Katie wasn't going alone so she splurged and spent an extra $2.50 to bring her friend with her. When Ron found out they were going, he happily bought his own ticket and graciously offered to chaperone the girls to the event.

Ron parked his VW bus several blocks away and the three got out. They wrapped jackets and scarves around their bodies to protect themselves from the wind and then set out towards the Avalon.

"I didn't think you liked concerts," Ron said finishing off his beef jerky and shoving his hands in his pockets to keep them warm.

"Of course I like concerts, who doesn't?" Katie answered.

"Well I've never known either of you to attend one before."

"Do you go to all the concerts, Ron?" Moony asked.

"As many as I can. The 'Frisco sound is unlike anything else in the country, it has a style that's just waiting to take off. It's just a matter of time before some of these bands get that one big break. The right person will hear them and then bands like the Grateful Dead, Jefferson Airplane, and Big Brother and the Holding company will set the scene on fire."

The line around the Avalon was already forming when they arrived. Even though it was only 7:30 and the show didn't officially start until 9:00 o'clock, there were two dozen kids waiting in line.

The three found the end and, with the rest of the sheep, stood in line.

"What time is it now?" Katie asked.

"It's 7:45, they should let us in around 8:15, maybe 8:00 o'clock if we're lucky," Ron answered. "Hey, Katie, what are you doing?"

Katie was facing the wall staring at an Avalon poster. It was advertising a future concert featuring the Doors and Country Joe and the Fish. Without answering, she dug deep in her bag and found her fingernail clippers. Opening it to the metal file, she started to work on the industrial staples that held the poster down as the crowd around her stared.

"Katie?" Moony asked, tapping her on the shoulder.

"I have to have this poster," she mumbled, pulling the second staple out of the wall.

"Why?" Ron asked.

"Are you kidding? Do you know how famous the Doors are going to be? The original poster from the event is going to be worth a fortune." She removed the poster from the wall happily.

"How can you say that? Sure, they're popular now, but in ten years someone better will come along and your poster isn't going to be worth shit." Ron laughed heartily. "That's how the world works. I think you misunderstood what I said. I meant some of our local bands would become big. The Doors aren't even a local band. They're from Los Angeles."

"Sure I know that, but they're a California band and they're great. Plus, I love the design of this poster, it's groovy," Katie said, having realized her mistake and now making excuses to cover her original statement.

She rolled the poster up, used a hair tie to band it, and then very gently shoved her newfound treasure into her large boho bag.

The Avalon's posters were extraordinary. They advertised each upcoming event in psychedelic brilliance. Haight artists Wes Wilson, Rick Griffin, Stanley Mouse, Alton Kelly, and Victor Moscoso created some of the greatest posters of the time. In 2014 the original prints, in outstanding condition, could be worth several thousand dollars.

Several of these artists also designed posters for Bill Graham's Fillmore, but unlike the Avalon, where Chet Helms granted them autonomy in deciding the artwork for the posters, the Fillmore's advertisements just didn't measure up.

The Avalon's posters were beyond the norm; colorful, psychedelic, and beautifully designed. Eventually, the posters became famous for their elaborate artwork and the hippies, who used them as decorations in their homes, snapped them up.

There was a loud bang and the front doors to the Avalon swung open. At a snail's pace, the line inched forward.

"We're in luck," Ron said, looking at his watch. "They're letting us in ten minutes early."

"Hooray, I'm freezing," Moonbeam said, blowing air on her hands in a futile attempt to warm them.

Several minutes later they were standing at the open door where their tickets were examined, torn in half and handed back to them.

"I suppose you're going to save that too?" Ron asked curiously.

Katie looked at her ticket stub and smiled. "What a great idea, thanks." She tucked another keepsake into her overflowing bag.

"Let's head for the left side of the stage," Ron suggested. "It's closer to the exit doors and the refreshment stand." Ron led the girls forward through the quickly forming crowd. "This looks like a good location," he said, stopping about twenty feet from the stage. "Not close enough to get shoved around and deafened by the speakers, but close enough to see. Now, who wants something to drink or eat?"

"I could use a Coke," Katie said. "I'm so thirsty."

"Me too, man," Moony piped up. "But Katie and I can share one. Well, we can all share one if you want."

"Coke? Hell no, I'm having a beer but I'll grab a large Coke for the two of you."

Both girls nodded and he headed towards the refreshment booth.

"The Doors?" Moony asked.

"Yeah, The Doors. In a few years they're going to be hella famous. Oh and by the way, Jim Morrison ends up in the 27 Club too."

"The 27 Club? You mean that post mortem musician group you were talking about?"

"There's going to be a lot of them that die at twenty-seven, drug overdoses; mostly heroin, I think."

"I don't want to hear any more of this," Moonbeam replied, swallowing uneasily.

"Yeah I'm surprised you asked me in the first place. Anyway, you should totally nab some of the posters too. If you take real good care of them, in forty years you'll be glad you have them."

"Right, I'll consider that, but I'm not going to start right now. I don't want to carry a dumb poster around with me all night. What about the ticket stub, why are you keeping that? You can't tell me that a half torn ticket is going to be worth something someday."

"An original torn ticket from the Avalon for an early Big Brother and the Holding
Company concert. Are you kidding? In 2014 , there's no telling how much something like that could go for on eBay."

"EBay?"

"Yeah, eBay. Sorry it has to do with the Internet, and once again I don't have the time to explain it."

Ron returned holding two large drinks. "Here," he said, handing one of the cups to Katie, while taking a sip off his own.

"Great, thanks," Katie responded, gulping down some of the soda before handing the cup to Moony.

"Hey you know what would be great?" Moonbeam said, pulling something out of her bag. "I still have some of those free samples of White Lightning, the LSD tabs from the Be-In. Let's take them?"

"Far out," Ron said. "Why the hell not? It's Friday, we're young, and I don't have to get up for work tomorrow."

"There are five pills inside," Moonbeam said. "I don't think you want to take that many, they're pretty strong. My suggestion, don't take more than two or three at a time. Here," she said, trying to hand Katie one of the small envelopes.

"No, I'm cool, I don't want any, thanks."

"Why not, Katie? You need to lighten up, live a little. You're always on a downer these days. You're twenty years old you're supposed to enjoy yourself. Let your hair down, groove a little." Moonbeam pouted and tried again to hand the packet to Katie.

This time Katie took the package and stuck it in the pocket of her jacket. "For later," she said, taking another large drink off the soda while watching both Moonbeam and Ron swallow the white tablets.

The lights dimmed and the psychedelic light show began. An overhead projector displayed a complex mixture of interlinking colors that danced across the screen and illuminated the walls.

In 1967, most hippie concerts included a psychedelic light show; swirling colors supplemented with slides and film, and often accompanied with ultraviolet lights that made the Day-Glo painted posters in the walls explode in fluorescent brilliance. Many included a liquid oil overhead where the operator mixed colored oil and water on a flat glass surface and projected light through the colored mixture. This, accompanied by a flashing strobe light and whatever drugs the audience might have consumed, worked together to create a hypnotic alpha wave of rhythm. Family Dog Productions created some of the best light shows of the times.

After a brief introduction, the opening band, a local group called the Charlatans, stepped on stage. Dressed in a combination of western and hippie gear, they opened with a song Katie remembered. "Walkin'," blared over the oversized speakers and the kids in the room danced to the music. By the third song, "Jack of Diamonds," Moonbeam and Ron were beginning to feel the effect of the LSD. Katie could tell by the way they were swaying with the music.

When the fourth and final song came on, and everyone in the Avalon started singing, *"We're not on the same trip,"* Katie decided to explore. It was time to make a break from the group and search for more posters.

After telling Moony and Ron of her intent, neither of whom seemed to hear her, she walked away in search of more trophies.

***

When Katie walked away, Moonbeam barely noticed. The effects of the White Lightning were just beginning to take hold and she was moving her body, grooving to the music. Beside her, Ron was swaying rhythmically, also feeling the effect of the LSD.

When the first band ended and the overhead lights came on, the crowd stopped moving, most covering their eyes from the brightness. The hippies gradually sat on the floor, including Moonbeam and Ron.

"You know Katie's changed," Ron said.

"That's an understatement," Moony replied under her breath.

"She really seems so much older, so mature. Have you noticed?"

"Who wouldn't?"

"Then you have noticed. So why the sudden change, what's her bag? Enlighten me."

"What do you mean?"

"Come off it, Moony. Something's going on and you know what it is. Spit it out girl, what's the deal?"

"There is no deal. That overdose changed her that's all. I told you that two months ago, you just didn't listen. She hasn't been the same since."

"As a matter of fact, neither have you or Frog. All three of you are different."

Moonbeam laughed, but she didn't deny it. How could she? They *had* all changed. They were different people, but Katie most of all.

"Look, whatever it is, I wish you'd tell me. I bet I could help. I know a lot of people, contacts if you need them."

"Contacts? What do you think is going on, Ron? Whatever your idea is, I guarantee you, it's wrong."

"Then why don't you tell me what is going on?" He was trying to trick her into answering. Ron was smart; he worked in the "scientific field", which amounted to secrecy and a lot of bread. Moonbeam had always suspected that he had connections with Owsley Stanley. Everyone thought so but no one asked and he never told.

"I know what you're trying to do, Ron. Fess up. Katie walks off and you try to pick my brain. You figure the combination of LSD and pot will open me up, get me talking, but it's not going to work," she said in a singsong voice.

"You know I really dig her, right?"

"What's that got to do with anything?"

"Are you kidding? It has to do with everything. If she's involved in something heavy, something that I can help with, then I want to."

"How come you've known her for a year and I've never heard anything about this before? You never came across as really digging her. In fact, if memory serves me correctly you used to complain that when she and I got together the giggling drove you crazy. Why the sudden change?"

"Not true, I always thought she was beautiful. I even told you so. I was just waiting for her to grow up, mature a little. Over the past few months, I have to say that she's done just that. She's grown up, and I like what I see."

Moonbeam stared at Ron's handsome face. He had money too, and a house in Haight Asbury, not a bad catch. Katie could do a lot worse. Like the dork that worked for her father, the one that was always snooping around 'Frisco looking for her.

"Ron, I'd like to tell you I really would, but you have to understand I can't. I think you're groovy. You'd be real good for Katie, but what's going on is her thing, you dig? I can't tell you. If she wants your help, then she's got to tell you herself. What kind of friend would I be if I talked about her shit behind her back? No man. If you want to know something about Katie or Frog then you're going to have to ask them yourself."

Ron nodded and took another drink of his beer.

"I dig that." He nodded, solemnly. "Your loyalty to Katie won't let you tell me. That's admirable. I respect that. Thanks for confirming that something is wrong and for giving me the impression that I might be helpful. I will talk to Katie. Could you do me one tiny favor though?"

"What's that?"

"Could you let her know that I'm a good guy and that I could be helpful in whatever situation she's involved in? Maybe coax her to tell me, so I'm not going to hit a brick wall?"

Moonbeam's concentration was impaired by the effect of the LSD, which had intensified over the course of the conversation. Still, she was fairly sure she would remember, so she nodded her head vigorously.

"Sure, Ron, I can do that."

The lights dimmed and she jumped to her feet. Blue Cheer walked onto the stage and the audience pushed forward applauding. Their first song, "Summertime Blues" started playing and Moony hopped up and down with excitement. In the next few minutes she gave herself over to the LSD experience as she watched the walls swirling and the colors exploding around her.

Ron, who had taken considerably less of the hallucinogenic substance, stood contentedly waiting for Katie's return. He had learned something useful tonight. Maybe he hadn't learned everything he'd set out to, but he knew that

Katie was involved in something bad and that knowledge made her even more desirable to the part-time chemist.

***

When she came close to the back wall it was easy to tell that she wasn't the only poster thief in the room; there were several blatantly blank spaces staring back at her.

"The bastards," she mumbled, walking closer to the wall where a poster advertising tonight's event hung.

"Ahh, here we go." She sifted through her bag for several seconds, pulled out her fingernail clippers. She opened them and started digging at the staples that were holding the poster to the wall.

She couldn't help but laugh. In 2014 she could never have brought the "potential weapon" into the building. Metal detectors would have gone off and the clippers would have been confiscated at the door. But in 1967, an age still partially shaded in innocence, anything was possible.

Before she could remove the second staple, the band ended and the overhead lights came on.

"Shit," she said and then slithered down the wall beneath the poster of Big Brother and the Holding Company.

Too self-conscious to remove the poster with the lights on, she sat on the hard linoleum floor intending to sit and wait. Across the room she saw Moony and Ron briefly until they, along with the rest of the room, sat on the floor.

Katie gazed at the room full of young bodies and she was suddenly overwhelmed with nostalgic amazement.

This is fucking awesome! she told herself for the millionth time. Here were her peers, young people dressed in granny dresses, crocheted ponchos and vests, wire-framed glasses, bell-bottoms adorned with patches and embroidery. She saw a few Nehru jackets, some fringed suede vests, girls with flower painted faces and men with long hair and sideburns, and everyone – including herself— was wearing several strands of colorful love beads.

How was this possible? She pinched herself hard on the forearm and flinched at the pain. Then, watching the area swell into a red raised patch that would undoubtedly bruise, she decided again that she wasn't dead. Dead people didn't feel pain and they certainly didn't bruise.

Katie's attention was drawn to the open doorway as a group of winged skull vested men walked into the Hall. The Hells Angels had arrived. Ten or twelve members strolled into the concert hall. Katie stared at two of them, Dylan and Joey, bikers she and Moonbeam didn't want to see.

When they walked past, Katie dropped her head into her lap, hiding. The last thing she wanted to do was to run into Dylan. She hadn't seen him since The Human Be-In where, despite his vow to "see her around" he hadn't even tried to find her.

"The slime bag," she said quietly to herself.

It made sense though. She should have known the bikers would be here. She should have expected their presence. After all, Big Brother was the Hells Angels cover band and Gus, a so-called former Angel, if there was such a thing, managed Blue Cheer.

When the lights dimmed and the show started, Katie lifted her head, peeking through spread fingers to see where the bikers were. To her delight, they had disappeared into the crowd of a few hundred bodies that were rising from the floor.

Anxious to catch a glimpse of the next band, the horde of spectators moved closer when Blue Cheer, dressed in jeans, vests, and psychedelic shirts took the stage.

Blue Cheer was a local Haight-Ashbury band that played a kind of psychedelic blues-rock. They were named after a street brand of LSD promoted by the infamous chemist Owsley Stanley. In the late 60's they were the epitome of the San Francisco psychedelic sound. Jim Morrison called them "the single most powerful band that he had ever seen."

Later they would be credited as the pioneers of heavy metal. And one of their songs, which they now opened their set with, was a rendition of "Summer Time Blues." This cover song would lead to the creation of a new genre of music, popularly known as punk rock.

The crowd moved closer to the stage, giving Katie the room she needed to take her poster. She rose and faced her treasure. She took one last look around just to make sure that nobody was watching and then, biting nervously on her bottom lip, started picking at the remaining industrial staples. When she had taken the third staple out, a familiar clacking laugh behind her made her turn abruptly.

"I thought I recognized you. Katie, right? You were the Owsley acid chick at the Be-In? See, I told you I'd remember you the next time we met. What's with the poster kleptomaniac shit?" the woman's raspy voice asked.

Katie stood perfectly still, semi-shocked. For the second time, she was standing face to face with Janis Joplin, and this time the singer remembered her name.

Janis was wearing dark slacks, a white long sleeve flowered shirt, and a brown crocheted poncho. Around her neck she wore several strands of love beads, around her right wrist an assortment of bracelets, and on her left what looked like a fresh tattoo.

"You look beautiful," Katie said without thinking and Janis laughed.

"Thanks, man. You look good too. Seriously, what gives with the posters? Although I have to say you have good taste in bands." She pointed at the poster of Big Brother and the Holding Company.

"I have great taste in bands, not just good. Only the best posters for me," she joked. "But seriously, they're going to be collector's items someday and in the meantime, I'm going to use them as far out wall decorations."

"Them? You mean there are more? And here I thought it was just my band that you wanted."

"Sure them, as many as I can get my hands on. But of course yours will always be the best of the bunch," Katie said warmly. "Especially if you give me the honor of signing it."

Janis laughed, took the permanent marker Katie produced from her oversized bag and, using the wall behind her as a table, signed "To Katie, Love Janis."

"Wow, thanks. This is absolutely the grooviest thing I've ever been given. I will always value this." Katie blew on the wet ink and then, when she was sure it was dry, rolled it into a tube and added it to the growing collection in her bag.

Janis walked over to another poster on the wall, advertising Moby Grape, and studied the artwork.

"I've never thought about the posters much but now that you mention it, the ones from the Avalon are pretty groovy, so yeah, I bet they'd look good on a wall." She flashed her famous grin.

"So, Katie, besides stealing posters off walls and passing out free samples of LSD at hippie events, what else do you do?"

"Tonight? I'm just here watching the concert with friends, no samples. They're up closer to the stage and I drifted away to..."

"Steal posters," the girls said in unison, laughing.

"Man, it's way too fucking loud in here. Do you want to step outside? I was heading out there for a smoke and some fresh air when I saw you. Why don't you come with me? Seems to me I promised you a drink."

"Sure!" Katie said without hesitation. After all, who wouldn't want to share a drink with *Janis Joplin?*

"Far out, man. Let's go," Janis said, heading for the exit. She shoved the steel bar handled door and it swung open. The night was cold. They stepped into the side alley between two buildings. The icy wind coming off the San Francisco Bay wrapped around their legs and they shivered. They both pulled their clothing tightly around their bodies.

Before shutting the door, Janis kicked a large rock in front of the door to prop it open. Then she sat on one of the cement stairs and pulled a pack of cigs out of her purse, followed by a half pint of Southern Comfort.

Katie sat on a lower step beside her and watched Janis uncap the bottle and take a long swig. She handed the container to Katie and offered her a cigarette. When Katie passed on the cigarette Janis shrugged her shoulders, lit her own smoke and drew in a long hit of tobacco.

Katie held the bottle for a second, considered the germ factor but quickly decided it was worth it and took a sip.

"No way man, if you're going to drink with Janis then you're going to take a real drink baby." She pushed the bottle back towards Katie.

With Janis's prompting, Katie took a big gulp off the bottle and then flinched and wiped her hand across her mouth.

"Fuck, that's strong," she said.

Janis laughed at her. "Amateur drinker, I love it." Janis clapped her hands. "Baby, you got a lot to learn about drinking. Now, watch a pro in action." She swigged down a good portion of the brew without making a face.

"You got a new tattoo?" Katie asked pointing towards Janis' left wrist, which was covered with Vaseline, Saran wrap and tape.

"Yeah man, I got it this afternoon, isn't it groovy? It's a Florentine bracelet, an exact replica of a piece of jewelry I own. I brought the bracelet to this guy named Lyle Tuttle. He's like a tattoo genius or something. Anyway, he free handed the design on my arm and went to town on it. He has this hip shop over on Seventh Street if you're interested."

"Perhaps," Katie said.

She took Janis' hand within her own and studied the tattoo closely. She had seen pictures of the artwork but always in black and white. The few color photos that existed left a lot to the imagination. Which was why, in the future, there was an ongoing debate as to what the color combination actually was. Truth was, nobody would really know for sure, but Katie was about to change all of that.

"It's beautiful," she said, studying the colors through the flimsy sheet of plastic. "What color is it?" she asked, trying to solve the forty-five year old mystery.

"There are three colors actually. I know you can't see them out here, it's too dark." Janis tore the plastic wrap and tape off of her arm. "I can take this shit off now, it's been a few hours. I'll wash it with soap before I go on stage; sure as shit don't need an infection." She stared at the design. "It's outlined in black, the three flowers are red, and the rest is dark green. Hey, I got a second one too." She said, laughing.

"You did?"

"I wanted to be decorated, you know what I mean? Sometimes you just have to be different. Hurt like a motherfucker though. I almost didn't have the second one put on." Janis took another chug off the Southern Comfort.

"The artist cat, Lyle, he had me take a break. He led me to this back room and gave me a beer." She chuckled. "I probably sat there twenty minutes before I let him start the second one. You want to know where the other one is?"

Katie knew what and where the other tattoo was. It was a small red heart on Janis' left breast. Both pieces had been done by one of the most famous tattoo artists of the 1960s. Lyle Tuttle would go on to tattoo other celebrities like Peter Fonda, Cher, and Paul Stanley, all within in the city of San Francisco.

"I got a small red heart on my left tit," Janis said, and then she laughed. "I would show it to you, but it's covered up with all this clothing and I don't want to start peeling off layers now, it's too fucking cold out here."

"Are those your only tattoos?" Katie asked, knowing that the singer had a third, a small flower on the outside of her right heel. (A fact noted on Janis's autopsy report in October of 1970.)

"Nah, I have another one. It's a homemade tattoo on my right foot, a flower. A friend of mine put it there when I was at the University of Texas." Janis finishing off the last of the bottle and then stuck the empty container in her purse. "What about you, Katie, any tattoos?"

"Not yet. I'll have two but that won't happen for a few more years." She was starting to feel the effects of the Southern Comfort and watched Janis pull a second container out of her purse.

"Not yet? What's that supposed to mean?"

"It means I'll have two tattoos. One will be a dragonfly on my right shoulder and the other a butterfly on my left ankle. I don't have either of them yet, but I will."

Janis laughed. "Man you're really not used to drinking, are you? Hell man, I feel like I'm corrupting you."

Katie realized her mistake and shook her head, clearing her train of thought. "You're right, I don't drink much." She laughed. "As far as corrupting me, believe me, that happened a long time ago. At this point in my life very little would surprise me."

"Man, you're talking like you're seventy years old and you're what, twenty?"

"Yeah I'm twenty pushing sixty-seven." Katie laughed again. "What I meant to say was that I don't have any tattoos, but I plan to have several."

She thought of the artistic bodywork she would have done at the end of the1990's.

"Dragonflies are cool, man. You should check out this Tuttle guy, his work is outstanding. This dude is going to be famous someday."

"No doubt," Katie said, thinking of the possibility of having an original Lyle Tuttle tattoo of her own.

"So, Katie, where are you from? How did you end up in Haight-Ashbury?" Janis asked. She passed the new bottle of Southern Comfort to Katie, who rolled her eyes before accepting the bottle and taking another large swig.

"You're going to have me shitfaced by the time I go back to my friends," Katie laughed. "I'm a local from Antioch, a city across the Bay. I'm here because this is a groovy place with groovy people."

"It's the best place in the world," Janis chimed. "Fucking way better than Shit Hole, Texas. At least here you can be yourself and nobody is going to judge you."

"True enough," Katie agreed. "San Francisco is a crazy place."

Janis lit another cigarette. "You have family in Antioch?"

"Yes, my parents and a kid brother who just signed up for the Marine Corps."

"Signed up for the military? Man, that's a bummer."

"Yes it is. I wish he wouldn't have done that but what are you going to do?"

"I know what you mean. Everybody's got to do their own thing. Too bad his thing is the military. Fortunately my brother Michael is only fourteen so I don't have to worry about that, unless this shit war lasts that long. I have an eighteen year old sister too, but I don't think Laura is thinking of going into the Army anytime soon." Janis smiled then, thinking of her younger siblings smiling. "So tell me about Katie. What do you do?"

Katie hesitated. What part of her crazy world could she share with Janis Joplin?

"Come on, man, the question's not a hard one. What do you do? What's Katie's thing?"

"I do the basic I guess. I work when I can, here and there. Sometimes I work in the shops. Little stuff, I'm not looking for anything steady. I have a friend that's a spiritualist. She reads the tarot and palms, I help her out sometimes."

"Well that's groovy, maybe she can read my fortune sometime."

Katie bit her lip, knowing that she herself could tell the ill-fated singer her future, but doubting that Janis would want hear about her outcome, at least not yet.

"That's cool for your friend, baby, but what about you? I mean who are you, Katie? Who are you really?" Janis asked. She passed the bottle and stomped her cigarette butt out on the concrete.

"I don't know how to answer that. I don't know what I am. I'm just trying to have fun and be young I guess."

"That's all groovy, you should be doing all of that, but that's not who you are. Who are you really? Deep inside here." Janis tapped Katie on the chest, just above her heart.

"I understand what you mean, but I don't think I have an answer for you. I don't think I know who I am," Katie said, reaching for the now half empty bottle.

"Wow, man. You have to know who you are. You really need to figure that shit out. Take me for example. I'm a blues singer inside. It's not just what I do, it's who I am. You dig it? How I think, how I react to the world around me, it's what makes me feel. What makes you feel, Katie? What makes you who you are?"

Katie watched Janis finish off the last drops from the bottle.

"I don't know," Katie answered, stunned. Nobody had ever asked her that question. The truth was, she didn't know who she was. She had been a housewife and a mother; she had belonged to the country club; but who she really was, she had no idea. That was her problem and it always had been.

"Don't trip ,Katie, you're young, you'll figure it out. The big problem would be if you hit thirty and you still don't know who you are. Now honey, that would be a real fucking tragedy. That's what happens to the squares. They live in their tract homes, follow the rules of society, and they do what the establishment tells them to. At the end of the day they don't know who they fucking are. They don't feel anything so they never have a chance to live. Don't let yourself end up like that man, that's not living."

Katie didn't say anything. She had already let that exact thing happen. She had done exactly what had been expected of her and as Janis had predicted, she had never fully lived. *Not this time around,* she vowed. This time she would know who and what she was. This time she would follow her dreams instead of her parents' visions, which had taken her nowhere.

Katie pulled a joint out of her sweater and lit it. She took a large toke filling her lungs with the green herbal remedy and passed the smoke to Janis.

"I don't usually smoke pot, it takes away my other highs, but I'll make an exception." Janis took a hit off the joint. "So, about your posters, baby, I bet I can hook you up. Unless, of course, you like pulling them off the walls yourself." Janis laughed and handed the smoke back. "I have some connections around here you know? I bet I can pull a few strings and come up with some future show posters, maybe some old ones too, if there are any floating around. What do you say about that?"

"Oh hell yeah. I would love that."

"Then consider it done."

Janis put the second empty bottle into her purse and rose from the steps. "Shit what time is it?" she asked and Katie shook her head. "I'm pretty sure break time is over. They'll be searching for me pretty soon. I have to get back and I bet your friends are starting to wonder about you too."

"Yes they probably are."

Janis kicked the rock away and entered the building, and Katie followed.

"It was groovy sitting with you. We'll do it again sometime after I find you a case of posters. By then maybe you'll be able to answer that question and tell me who you are."

"Thanks for everything, Janis. The drink, the talk, but most of all for remembering me."

"It's cool, baby, I'll see you on the flip side. Enjoy the concert." Janis turned and walked away.

Katie stood by the door and watched until the one and only Janis Joplin disappeared from her view.

When Janis was gone, Katie walked through the auditorium trying to warm her freezing limbs by rubbing her arms. She was wasted, she knew that, and she tried to keep her wits about her and walk straight.

Blue Cheer had just finished their set and Katie wove through the crowd looking for her friends. When she finally located them, they were indeed beginning to worry about her.

"Ahhh, there you are. Katie, honey, where have you been? By now you should have enough band posters to cover your apartment and our whole house," Ron said in a slightly drug-induced voice.

"Not quite. I only got one, but it's real special."

"All that time and you only got one poster?"

"Yep, but it's autographed," she said in between hiccups.

"Katie Cat, you been drinking?" Moonbeam asked.

"Oh fuck yeah," she answered, happily.

"What did you end up doing?" Moonbeam asked.

The overhead lights turned on and the crowd drifted away from the stage. Katie and her friends sat on the cold linoleum floor.

"You're never going to believe this, but I was outside with Janis Joplin. We drank a pint of Southern Comfort," Katie said excitedly.

"The chick singer from Big Brother and the Holding Company?" Ron asked and Katie nodded. "I didn't know you knew Janis Joplin."

"Well I met her at the Be-In when I gave her some free samples. She told me she'd remember me and that we'd have a drink together, and that's what happened. She saw me peeling her band's poster off the wall and invited me outside for a drink."

"To a bar?" Moony asked, still swaying even though she was sitting on the floor.

"No not a bar, out back. There's an alley between the Avalon and the next building. That's where we sat. She had a cigarette, we shared a joint, and drank some Southern Comfort."

"Outta sight, Katie," Moonbeam giggled.

"How many tabs of acid did she take, Ron? Although look who's talking, since I just polished off a half pint of liquor," Katie said.

"She took three tabs, I took two. She weighs a lot less, and it seems to have affected her more than me."

"Obviously."

The third band's equipment was being set up. Hippies were beginning to move closer to the stage, getting ready for the headline band.

"Come on, let's move up closer to the stage. I want to see this band." Katie pulled Moonbeam to her feet, then led the small group further to the left where they had a clear view of the stage.

She stopped. "This is the spot."

She turned towards Ron and smiled just as the lights in the room switched off and the light show, once again, began.

The men in the band, Sam Andrew, James Gurley, Peter Albin and Dave Gertz, took the stage. For several seconds they played an instrumental introduction and then Janis Joplin took the stage, and the crowd went wild.

Flashing her famous grin she sang "Down on Me."

Janis's loud voice blared through the hall, and Moonbeam, along with many of the hippies in the room, danced happily. Katie stood perfectly still, mesmerized by the experience. Ron moved closer to her side and slipped his arm around her slim waist. Katie smiled and leaned against his body, fresh tears drifting down her cheeks.

"Are you okay?" Ron whispered.

"I'm perfect," Katie said. "I'm absolutely perfect."

Ron wiped the tears off her face and Katie leaned her head against his shoulder and shut her eyes. She stayed there several minutes just feeling the moment. When she finally opened her eyes she was startled to find Dylan standing right in front of her.

Chapter 21

"You were right, he came looking for you."

Katie opened one eye and stared at her roommate, who had intruded in her space and was now trying to awaken her.

"What time is it?" she asked, shielding her eyes from the light in the hall.

"It's 3:30," Robin answered.

"In the morning?"

"Yes, of course it's morning."

"And one more time, why are you waking me?" Katie pulled herself into a sitting position.

"You were right, he came looking for you."

"And it's important to wake me and tell me this because...?"

"Well, don't you want to know who I'm talking about?"

"Oh, I know who you're talking about. I'm just wondering why I need to know this at 3:30 in the morning?"

"Because he's going to be back. He came into the city and he's spending the night at the Travelodge. He's planning on being here early in the morning to see you."

"Is he here now?"

"Of course not. It's 3:30 in the morning. Why would he be here now?" Robin asked, shaking her head in confusion.

"I know this has to make sense somehow, so let's start over. Why are you waking me?" Katie asked, turning on her bedside lamp.

"I had class today, well yesterday now. Thursday is my crazy long day. My first class was at 7:30, so I was out the door really early. I was home about 2:00, but I had to leave again at 6:30 to head back for a 7:30 lab. Anyway, I was studying in the living room and just after 3:00—I know what time it was because *Dark Shadows* had just come on—someone knocked at the door. It was he, all fancy dressed, short business haircut and all. I told him you weren't home and that I didn't know what time you would be back, but he was persistent. He wanted to sit and wait for you. I guess he has this idea that you're trying to avoid him so he's trying to hit you up at odd times, hoping he'll catch you.

"I told him he couldn't wait, that I had to leave to go to class and that I wasn't comfortable letting him into our pad and then leaving. I don't think he believed me because he sat out there in his fancy red sports car for a long time staring at the building. I don't know what time he left. It was before I left for class though, because I didn't see him when I was driving to school. If I were guessing I'd say he sat across the street for over an hour just waiting and watching for you.

"He told me he's on vacation from work so he's staying here in San Francisco, just so he can find you."

"And once again, why are we discussing this at 3:30 in the morning?" Katie asked, shaking her head.

"Because he's going to be here early, silly. He's going to sit outside all day until he sees you. I didn't want you to go into an ambush. I know you don't want to see him but now it looks like you're going to have to. I don't think the guy's going to give up until he's seen you."

"Let me guess, you just got home from a date and felt the need to tell me this before you crashed?"

"Yes, exactly. I didn't want to write a note for Christ's sake. This is the kind of message that you should give a friend in person."

"I see." Katie shut off the light and slipped under the covers. "Now you've delivered the important news I can go back to sleep, right?"

"Well sure, but what are you going to do? I have an early class tomorrow. I'm not going to feel good about leaving you at home knowing that you don't want to see this guy and that he's out there stalking you."

Who would have ever known that Robin was sensitive? This was a different side to the girl, something Katie hadn't seen the first time they had roomed together back in the real '67. That time they had only been roommates for a few weeks before she had moved out.

"Thanks for your concern, and for the warning, but I'll be fine. Don't worry about me. I can take care of myself. I'll make a phone call in the morning and have Frog come over. Then together we'll confront Mark Rhodes and hopefully get rid of him for good."

"Are you sure? I mean, the guy seems kind of creepy. Why don't you come with me in the morning? You can have breakfast in the cafeteria and when I get off school we can go shopping at Stonetown Shopping Centre?"

Katie's eyes snapped open and she sat up again, looking at her roommate. "Really, you didn't find him the least bit attractive?"

"Are you kidding? The guy won't leave you alone and he tells me he's going to sit outside our apartment and wait for you. How could you ever think I would find him attractive? He's creepy," Robin said, heading for the door.

"Robin, I'm serious. You don't find him attractive at all? Not the blond hair, or the fancy red car, or the job that bought him that car?"

Robin stopped at the door and stared at Katie, shaking her head. "I had a guy stalking me once, it was freaky. I was in high school and my parents were really worried. It took a long time before I got rid of him. Believe me, anyone who's willing to do that to you...well, I don't want any part of that person. That's a weirdo with a capitol 'W'. So how about it? I'll wake you at 6:30 and you can come with me? Please say yes, we'll have a groovy time together."

"Thanks for the tempting offer, but I think it would be best if I stayed here and dealt with him. You said it yourself he's not going to go away until he sees me. Why postpone the inevitable?"

"Because he's a weirdo! I really wish you would change your mind. Call Frog from the school and have him meet you here. That way you don't run the risk of meeting the creep while you're by yourself," Robin said with a worried look on her face.

"I'm going to be fine. Believe me, the sooner I deal with him the better. We don't want him hanging around 'Frisco for a week do we? That would be worse."

"I hope you know what you're doing. This whole situation worries me." Robin walked into the hall and closed the bedroom door behind her.

Katie pulled the covers over her head and smiled. This was a good sign. If Robin wasn't attracted to Mark this time around, then it showed that events could be changed. If that were the case then there was hope for Richard, Frog, and perhaps even Janis Joplin.

***

"Fucking idiot."

She rolled out of bed, trying to ignore the incessant knocking.

Oh no, this was *not* going to happen the way it did before. Mark would not have the upper hand, not this time. In her 1967, Mark had come to the door too. That time she did not have Robin's warning. Mark had knocked on her door, pushed his way in, and insisted on talking to her. That time she had no other choice, she had to sit and listen to his ranting, but it wasn't going to happen this time. If he tried to push his way in she would have him arrested, but better than that she wasn't going to give him the opportunity.

She sat in the living room listening to the pounding and trying to figure out a plan that would undermine Mark Rhodes.

"Katie, I know you're in there and I'm not going to go away until you talk to me!" he yelled through the locked door. "I saw you come in last night and I know you haven't left the apartment. You're probably sitting on the couch right now and you can hear me, so why don't you open the door? I'm here to help you."

"Help me right into a nursing home," Katie mumbled to herself.

Katie heard a door open. One of her neighbors had walked into the hall.

"What in the hell are you doing? There's no one home, stop pounding on the door like an imbecile, my kids are sleeping!" the woman yelled.

"I'm trying to get a hold of my friend. I'm worried that something might have happened to her," Mark said in his best diplomatic voice.

"Then go to the manager. Mrs. Ellis lives downstairs in apartment number one. If you're that concerned, she has an emergency key to the apartment. Just quit beating on the door. I have a baby and a three year old. If you wake either of them I'm going to come out here and box your ears in. You got it?"

"Mrs. Ellis, you say? Apartment one?"

"That's what I said."

Her neighbor promptly went back in her apartment. Katie heard the door close, then

there were footsteps going down the stairs as Mark trampled down in search of the manager.

Great! Now the manager would come and try to open her door. No doubt Mark would come up with a fictional story to get himself inside.

"Shit."

She pulled on a pair of torn and faded 501's and an oversized T-shirt.

No way is that son of a bitch getting in here, she thought, preparing to leave the apartment. At least if she confronted him outside there would be witnesses, unlike the last time when he shoved himself inside. Before leaving, she dialed Moonbeam's pad, hoping against odds that one of the roommates would pick up.

When you need a cell phone, where the hell are they? Twenty-five years in the future, that's where!

The phone rang on the other end of the line. Three rings and then a voice.

"Hello?"

"Good morning. I'm trying to reach Frog or Moonbeam. Are either of them home?"

"Katie?" a man asked. Ron had answered the call. Katie hesitated, not sure if that was a good thing or a bad one. Did she really want to draw Ron into her drama?

"What's wrong, Katie?"

In the end desperation won out, and she found herself rattling off at the mouth. "Ron, I'm sorry, I didn't recognize your voice. Yes, it's Katie. I know it's a lot to ask but could you come and get me? This creep that works for my father is here. He's trying to see me and I don't want to talk to him."

"I'll be right there." The line went dead immediately. She could hear noises on the stairs. Two sets of feet this time. As she had suspected, the landlady had bought Mark's story, hook, line, and sinker.

She could hear them in the hallway. Mrs. Ellis had her large key ring, jangling and clanking together.

"I hope everything is alright. Such a nice girl," Mrs. Ellis said.

"Yes she is. I sure appreciate you opening the door for me. You know how these hippies are, anything could have happened," Mark said.

It's now or never, Katie told herself. If she had to face Mark Rhodes then she would do it in the hall, no way was she giving him access to her apartment.

She snatched a jacket off the coat rack and hurriedly put it on, retrieved her purse, made sure she had her keys, and then took hold of the door handle just as the keys were inserted into the lock. She took a deep breath for courage and then opened the door. She stepped into the hall, shutting the door quickly behind her and locking it.

"Oh there you are, honey, thank goodness. Your friend here was very worried about you," Mrs. Ellis said in relief when she saw Katie.

"I bet 'my friend' was," Katie said. She smiled at her landlady. "As you can see, I'm just fine. And as a matter of fact, I'm just heading out the door. I must have been in the shower, I bet that's why I didn't hear him knocking."

"Oh dear, I'm so glad that you're okay," Mrs. Ellis said with sincerity.

"Katie, you had me so frightened. I thought, well, never mind what I thought, I sure am glad that I was wrong," Mark said, in his clean-cut boy next door style that made him sound like Dobie Gillis.

"Well, as you both can see, I'm just fine but I have an appointment and I'm running late." She walked down the staircase followed by the manager and her once future husband.

Without saying another word Katie walked to the sidewalk and stopped, intent on waiting for Ron, who she hoped would be there in a matter of minutes.

"Katie, where are you going?" Mark called to her.

"I'm leaving. What does it look like I'm doing?"

"But I just got here. I was hoping that we could talk, you know catch up on things," Mark said in his charismatic fashion that was meant to win her over.

"Sorry, Mark, no can do. Too bad you made the trip all the way out here for nothing. Next time, try calling first."

"I did call. I have called a lot, but you never seem to be home, or at least that's what your roommate tells me."

"And you haven't taken that as a hint?"

She stared at him. A young Mark Rhodes, what a sight. He was dressed in tight fitting black slacks, a red sports jacket and a thin black tie. For the day and age, he was in GQ fashion, impeccable as always.

Gone were the crow's feet and the thinning gray hair. Here he was in all his youth and glory, reminding her of a young Robert Redford once again. After everything he had done to her, all he had taken from her life, after knowing him for the phony womanizer that he truly was, Katie would be lying if she said he wasn't attractive, and that thought made her cringe.

"Here's the thing, Mark. I'm not interested. I don't want to be your friend and I certainly don't want to be anything more. In fact, we don't have anything in common and I don't want to hang out with you. I don't want to be mean, but you're wasting your time here. Please go home. We have nothing to talk about. Now, I have things to do and I'm sure you do too, so have a good day." She turned away to watch for Ron's van.

"Listen, Katie, I know you probably think your parents sent me here to talk some sense into you, but that's not the case. I came on my own. I wanted to see you, to talk to you, so please hear me out."

"What exactly do you want?" she asked, already knowing the answer, since money had always been his incentive.

"All I want is an hour of your time. We can sit in your apartment or we can go to get coffee. Whatever you prefer." He was still trying to sound like he was charming, even though Katie knew him for what he really was.

"Why? You and I have nothing to talk about. We come from different worlds. Which reminds me, I need to get back to my world and yours is across the bay. Good luck crossing the bridge. Goodbye, Mark." She spotted Ron's VW bus turning onto Cole Street.

"I've come all the way here and you can't spare an hour of your time to talk to me? You don't even know me, Katie, how can you pass judgment on me so easily? That's not the hippie way of peace, love and understanding," he said, trying to sound like the gentleman Katie knew he wasn't.

"All the way here, huh? What is that, a twenty-minute drive? And you drove it all by yourself? High-five." She chuckled to herself, since in 1967 the meaning would be lost in translation.

"High what?" he asked, confused, which made the comment that much funnier. "Katie, I'm staying all week."

"Don't." She walked towards Ron's bus, which had parked next to the curb.

"What do you mean? Why are you so hostile? I don't get it."

"Oh my God, Mark, if only I could tell you all the reasons, but I don't have that much time."

Ron stepped out of the bus and started towards them.

"Katie, I have to see you. Just choose a time and a place and I'll be there. I'm only asking for an hour of your time." Mark glanced towards Ron, who towered over him by at least four inches.

"Hey, man, is there a problem here?" Ron asked.

"No, there's no problem. Katie and are old friends. I'm just trying to talk to her, that's all," Mark said.

"That's funny, man, that's not what I heard. She called my house and asked me to come over because your fucking ass was harassing her."

Ron walked over to Mark and shoved him backwards. Mark stumbled but caught himself before falling. He raised his hands in a non-threatening manner and in his best diplomatic voice started making excuses for himself.

"Listen, man, I don't know anything about a phone call. All I know is that I came here this morning to talk to her, nothing more. You don't have to come at me all aggressive. I don't want any trouble. If Katie tells me to go then I will."

Ron cracked his knuckles, took a glance at Katie, and then stared at Mark.

"Mark, you need to leave," Katie said. "Go back to Antioch and don't come here again. I'm not interested, you understand? Now please, just leave me alone." She walked into Ron's embrace.

"Fine. If that's the way you want it, Katie, I'll leave. But know this, you're making a big mistake."

"What the fuck is that supposed to mean, man, are you threatening her?" Ron said, gently pushing Katie to the side so he could walk closer to Mark.

"No, it wasn't a threat. I meant it just like I said it. Katie, you're making a mistake. But according to your father you seem to make them all the time, which is obvious by the way you're living."

"What's wrong with the way she's living, you square motherfucker?"

Several passersby gathered on the sidewalk watching as the heated conversation took a turn for the worse. Suddenly, Ron pushed Mark again, and this time the dapper young man fell backwards.

"Let me make this clear. Katie called me to come here because of your freak ass. She's not going to have to do that again because you're going to take yourself back to Squareville and you're going to fucking stay there. The next time you show yourself on this side of the bay I'll deal with you. You understand that, you stupid bastard? Stay away from her, period." Ron put his arm protectively around Katie and led her to the van.

Mark got up off of the sidewalk and brushed off his expensive clothes. "What are you fucking staring at?" he yelled at the small crowd of hippies who quickly dispersed.

Ron drove away, watching Mark in his rearview mirror. He laughed hard when he saw the clean cut Stanford graduate give him the finger.

***

Mark was humiliated and that made him very angry. He had been bullied as a child and he had learned early that the way to deal with bullies was to get even.

He slunk across the street and slithered into his red Porsche, deliberately avoiding the stares of the few people who were still standing on the sidewalk. He could tell that his face was crimson, and he hated that too. Nobody humiliated Mark Rhodes and got away with it. *Nobody.* Especially a hippie slut and her longhaired boyfriend.

Mark took a few deep breaths before pulling onto the roadway. He thought about following the van but realized that would be a mistake. So rather than following Katie to her next destination and confronting the hippie freak she was with, he drove back to the Travelodge steaming.

I'm not going to let that hippie bitch get away with this.

Mark had always gotten what he wanted in life. He'd worked hard to achieve everything that should have come to him at birth. Although he was proud of his accomplishments, he resented the reasons behind them. His father and his grandfather, who together had lost most of the family's fortune, embarrassed him.

They had nearly ruined the Rhodes name, a very old name that had always been associated with money, but Mark, in his few years of leading the family, had nearly restored it. He didn't have the money that he felt he was due but he was working towards that dream and like everything else he touched, it too would turn golden.

Al Searfus was a shallow, arrogant man, but his family had money and his ancestors were respected for their accomplishments. The Searfus name, like the Rhodes name, was old; their money went back to the railroads and the Gold Rush where their predecessors had made a fortune.

Al's firm was a multimillion dollar a year corporation and he needed a successful right-hand man to succeed him. The old man had hoped it would be his son, but now that Richard was in the Marines that succession was in question. There was always the chance that Richard might return and have a change of heart, decide to become a businessman and take over the firm, but that was doubtful, and if Mark had anything to say about it, it would never happen.

That left Mark in a great position but it wasn't the position he really wanted to be in. He didn't want to take over as CEO. What he really wanted was to own the company for himself. That meant marrying the owner's daughter or somehow convincing the old man to adopt him. Realistically, adoption was a long shot. But if he could become Al's son in law then that would seal his future.

Not only would his children come from two very distinctive families, they would be born into the future that purebloods were entitled to. With his bloodline and a wife from the Searfus family he could open a lot of doors for himself, perhaps even political if he decided to pursue his dream that far.

Katie was a great catch and she and her father's reputation could take him far in life. She was pretty, she came from good stock, and she had money. In Mark's eyes, she was perfect for him. All he had to do was clean her up, take her home, and her parents would help him by pushing her into the marriage.

He wasn't about to give up on her yet. Mark always got what he wanted. Right now what he wanted was Katie, and nothing was going to stop him from that, especially some long haired hippie boyfriend.

He wasn't sure what Katie had against him. Sure, he stood for the establishment she fought against, but today she had been rude and ruthless. He had never done anything against her, nothing that should have resulted in such hostility. That should have confused him, but it didn't. Her comments had infuriated him and that was why he would enjoy getting even with both her and the longhaired freak she was sleeping with.

None of that mattered though, not yet. What mattered was he needed to find a way to charm the boss's daughter. He would bring her back from the pits of hippiedom and transplant her back into a life of normalcy. In so doing, he would establish a place for himself in the family and after that, he would be in like Flynn.

Mark laughed, remembering his favorite James Coburn movie and suddenly felt empowered by comparing himself to the secret agent.

She was a stupid little hippie girl, a spoiled rotten rich brat. How hard could it be to win her over? All he needed was the right scam, something that made him seem important. If he looked like a hero then she would be all over him. With his good looks and warm personality how hard could that be?

Suddenly feeling quite smug with himself, humiliation forgotten, Mark returned to the Travelodge. He turned on the television and began to plan his next move. He wondered if he could cry on Katherine's roommate's shoulder.

Robin was a pretty little number. She could take his mind off the miserable little hippie princess. Maybe he could confide in her, bring her into the picture as a confidant. Women loved that role. All he needed to do was to get in good with the roommate, and with the right encouragement she could be a real asset to his plan.

Before heading into the bathroom for a shower, Mark picked up the phone and took a deep breath. For a few seconds he hesitated and then he finally dialed the number he had memorized. After the third ring a woman's voice picked up.

"Hello?"

"Is this Robin?" he asked, trying to sound heartbroken. "I know it's a long shot but is Katie there?" He could tell she recognized his voice.

"No she's not."

"Listen I want to apologize for my actions. I didn't mean to come off as some psycho, I'm actually a really nice guy. I don't know what I'm doing wrong and I don't understand her behavior towards me. I'm just trying to help her and the family. You see, they don't agree with her living in San Francisco as a hippie. I came out here hoping to talk some sense into her. I guess I really thought she would listen to me and I'd be able to take her home.

"I really care about Katie and her family and I hate having to go home in defeat. What am I going to tell her parents? I wanted so much to bring them good news about their daughter but they will be so disappointed with how this turned out. I don't like to judge people, but that boyfriend didn't seem like someone who is advancing her life. I'm worried and you, as her friend, must be concerned about her wellbeing. That's why I'm coming to you. You see, Robin, you're my last hope. Maybe you can talk to her for me. I know it's a lot to ask, but would you have dinner with me tonight? If she won't hear me out then maybe you will, and you can pass my message along," Mark said in his best sad voice.

"Mr. Rhodes, Katie has asked you to leave her alone. I don't know her reasons but I know she's serious. She warned me about you. She said you would be calling and coming around. She said when you did that I was to tell you she didn't want anything to do with you. Now why would she do that? She didn't say anything about her family, only about you.

"She's fine, and you don't have to worry about her. And since I don't see any reason for me to get involved any more than I already am, I'm going to have to decline your offer for dinner. Please, Mr. Rhodes, just go home and leave her alone."

The line disconnected.

Mark banged the receiver on the desk and yelled.

This isn't happening to me! I always get what I want!

Then he made a vow. He would marry Katie Searfus no matter what he had to do to get her and then he would pay her back for this day by making her life miserable.

***

"So who's the clown?" Ron asked as he drove towards his home.

"His name is Mark Rhodes. He's an overachiever who works for my father. According to my dad he's the boy wonder. He would have been a perfect son but since that didn't happen he's my parents' choice as the perfect husband. If they could marry me to him tomorrow they would. But fortunately for me, they aren't going to get the chance."

She breathed a sigh of relief.

Ron chuckled. "I take it he's not your first choice for a husband?"

"Oh hell no. The pretty boy bitch makes me want to gag."

"You say the strangest things. It's like you're from another world."

"I am," Katie said. "The problem with Mark is he's not going to take no for an answer. He's going to show up again; it's only a matter of time."

"And when he does I'll be here waiting for him, just like I promised. The next time he pokes his nose in where he's not wanted, I'm going to flatten it. If he comes back here snooping around after you, then he's going to get his ass beat."

"He's smooth. He'll find a way to get around that."

"Sounds like we're talking about a bloodhound instead of a square from your parents' world."

"We are. I mean, he is a bloodhound. He fixes his sights on something and he will pursue it to the end of the world. He's cutthroat and dishonest so there's no telling what he might do."

The last time around she hadn't rejected him. She had fallen into his trap and done exactly as he and her parents had wanted. This time she was not going to end up with him, nor did she have any plans of ending up with her family's money. That life came with a price she was unwilling to pay.

All she wanted was to try and do things differently, which meant stopping her brother's death in Vietnam, and Frog's disappearance. Beyond those responsibilities she was free, and this time everything would end up differently.

Mark Rhodes was going to be a problem. Money was his motivator and her father was the king. Marrying Katie held a huge advantage for him and getting rid of him wasn't going to be that easy. Which meant she didn't know what the slimebag was capable of.

After a few moments of silence, Ron reached over and covered Katie's hand with his own.

"I'm not going to let anything happen to you and neither will Frog or Moony. You have a lot of friends in the Haight and none of us are going to stand by and let you be harassed by this creep. So don't worry, all right? I'll handle it."

Katie nodded, but inside she knew it was going to take more than just a few hippies working together to get rid of Mark.

"How about some breakfast? What do you say we stop and get something to eat?" Ron asked.

"Sure. I could use some coffee right about now." Next thing she knew, they had parked in front of the I Thou Café and were inside ordering breakfast.

"Thanks for coming and getting me, Ron. I really appreciate the help."

"My pleasure, Lady Katherine. Chivalry is not dead, at least not when I'm around." He bowed his head, making Katie laugh.

"Did you know Chet is moving out of the house?" Ron asked.

"No, I didn't know that. Where is he moving to?"

"He's going to a commune in Marin County. Apparently some pioneer deal where they're going to grow their own food and stuff." Ron sipped from his cup of coffee. "Point is, Katie, we're going to have a room open and...well maybe it would be a good idea if you moved in."

"What?" She hadn't seen this one coming.

"It would be a practical move, think about it. If pretty boy crossed the bay then he'd have to come to my house to see you. I'd say that would be a deterrent wouldn't you?"

"Wow, I don't know. I'd have to think about it, you know, talk it over with Robin since she'll be left without a roommate."

"If Robin cares about you, she'll understand. Truth is, this creep probably unnerves her too, and she doesn't want him hanging around. What better way to get rid of him? I'm sure Moony and Frog would be happy to have you there. So it would be a win-win situation all around."

"Let me think about it, okay? I appreciate the offer and I just might take you up on it, but I have to consider a few angles before I make that decision."

"Of course, I understand. You clear up some loose ends and then come and live with us. We'll protect you," he said, just as the food arrived.

For several minutes the two were quiet. They sat at the table eating their meals and glancing out the window.

"Listen, Katie. I've noticed that something is up with you and Frog. I know it's none of my business but if you want to talk, I'd be happy to listen."

He had caught her off guard twice today. Ron was full of surprises. How had she missed out on him the first time around?

"I don't know what you mean," she said.

"Come on, Katie, something's up. You know it is and so do I. I'd like to help you anyway I can and I mean that sincerely."

"I know you do. It's just..." *Just what?*, she asked herself. What could she possibly say to Ron that would make any sense at all? Yet here she was trying anyway, even though she knew any kind of explanation would sound ridiculous. "It's just that my situation is crazy unique. It's impossible for me to explain it to you and if I did you would probably change your mind about everything."

"Are you a hit man for the mafia?"

"No."

"A spy sent here by the Russian KGB?"

"Of course not." She laughed.

"Have you killed someone?"

"No. Nothing like that."

"Then what could be so bad that it would make me change my mind about you?" Ron stared at her, waiting for an answer.

"It isn't bad, it's unique...it's odd."

"Ahhh, I get it. You're really an alien from outer space."

"Actually that's a lot closer to the truth."

"Well whatever it is, I'm offering my help. When you trust me enough to tell me then you'll find that I can be a real groovy friend, or perhaps even a little more than that," Ron said, and then turned his attention back to his meal, while Katie sat quietly and stared out the window.

Chapter 22

Frog walked into the storefront on Seventh Street. A strand of bells hanging on the door jingled. Sal, Dave, Dylan, and Joey looked up.

"Hey, man." Frog nodded to the room full of bikers. "The sign out front says motorcycle parts but I don't see any, only the hogs in the back. I suppose you're parting them out?"

"Very funny. The parts are ordered, Froggy. We haven't officially opened the doors yet. Which reminds me, Einstein, lock the door behind you," Sal said.

"Frog."

"What?"

"My name's Frog."

"Yeah, whatever. Just lock the door behind you, Frog boy."

Frog turned the lock on the door, made sure the closed sign appeared in the window and followed the rest of the men into the back room.

"Everyone find a seat. We have things to talk about," Dave said, sliding behind an oversized desk. "First on the agenda, the Skinner problem. I know he's been asking too many questions and there are members sitting in this room who believe he's had them followed."

Dylan and Joey nodded.

"Sal and I believe the best way to deal with all our problems is the place we're sitting in now; a legit business. This shop will ease tensions." Dave handed out beers from an old relic resembling a refrigerator located in the corner behind his desk. "It should put us in good standing with the club and anyone else who's snooping around because of our sudden wealth."

"So we've completely moved out of the garage at the clubhouse?" Dylan asked. "Won't that look suspicious?"

"No, we haven't moved out of the garage. You're right, that would look suspicious. For that reason Sal and I are running all club business from that location. Anything else will be done here, which offers us several benefits. One, we have a legit business to explain funds, which is important to show the club and the IRS. And two, it will hopefully put to rest any suspicions Skinner is hanging on to," Dave said, sucking on his beer.

"I don't know, Skinner's a problem man, he's still on our backs. I'm constantly looking over my shoulder," Dylan groused. "I feel like he's watching everything we do. He knows things are going on. Not just suspects, he fucking knows!"

"That's right, man, I feel the same fucking way. He's on to us and it's only a matter of time until he goes to Big Jim with his suspicions. This place, we'll it's fucking too little too fucking late," Joey added.

"Maybe it's time to cut him in," Dave ventured. "There's enough money floating around, and it might solve our problems in a diplomatic way. What the fuck? We'll cut him in as a silent partner. All he's got to do is to sit back and collect a bundle. How the hell can he say no to that? One way or another, Sal and I will take care of him, so just mellow out all of you. Stop the fucking paranoia, kick back, and enjoy the bread that's coming in. Sal and I have this shit covered." Dave lit a doobie.

"I don't know, Dave. Skinner doesn't strike me as the kind of guy who can be bought off," Joey said, reaching for the joint. "You know what I mean? He's on a vigilante trip of some kind to save the club."

"Vigilante trip, my ass. Everyone's got a price. Everyone!" Dave said, banging his hand on the desk.

Joey passed the deteriorating roach to Dylan.

"I don't know, man, we'll see. But I'd be damn surprised if money is going to sway him."

"I agree," Dylan said, thinking back to the encounter he had with Skinner at the Be-In.

"I don't see him cashing in. In fact, I'd be surprised if he hasn't already mentioned his suspicions to someone else in the club."

"Look, until Sal and I tell you it's time to worry, don't. As I already said we got this shit taken care of. The matter is closed." Dave turned to Frog. "Let's see the note."

Frog produced the envelope and laid it on the desk in front of Dave, who quickly snatched it up. He read it, frowned, and passed it to Sal.

"Okay and what have we learned from this, Frog?"

"Hmm, that the Mafia is on to us? I just figure Little Italy and it being signed by 'the Family', well it's kind of obvious, right?"

"That's not what I mean. What did *you* learn from it?"

"That I'm way too fucking easy to find!" Frog said, visibly unnerved.

"Good lesson. Hope you take it to heart, hippie boy. If you're too accessible, you're only a bullet away from not being around anymore!" Sal glared at him with piercing black eyes.

Frog nodded and swallowed hard. It was a lesson all right, and one that scared the shit out of him. Sal pointing out the obvious added another stir to the already boiling pot.

"For the time being, we stay out of the Broadway area. Only for the time being, mind you. We need time to build our alliances and ourselves before we confront gangsters. That's why we've had a change of plans," Dave said. He drank the last of his beer and reached for another. "Oakland," he said, looking at Frog.

"We're already driving into Oakland, man. I drive that route once a week. I pick up a van, pass it off in Oakland, and then I leave." Frog leaned forward and grabbed his untouched beer off of Dave's desk. Out of nervousness, he finished it in one long chug.

"Sure, we have our foot... no strike that, we have one toe in the door. It's time to put a whole leg into the operation."

"What?" Frog asked, rising to his feet. He knew instinctively that this latest scheme involved him and right now, all he wanted was out.

"You, my pal, are going to pick up your regular load tomorrow. You're going to drive it into Oakland only this time, you're not going to pass off the van."

"I'm not?" Frog's hands shook and he put them in his lap to steady them.

"No man, you're not. We're going to give you an address and you're going to drive the van there."

"An address?" Frog echoed. The idea of running home and hiding in Redding entered his mind but he shook it away.

"Yeah, man, an address. Would you fucking concentrate and stop asking so many questions?" Sal said, raising his voice.

"You're going to take the van there. You'll knock on the garage door and someone will open it," Dave said, ignoring Sal's interruption.

"Someone?"

Sal glared at Frog and he bit his lip to stop talking.

"Yeah, a middleman working for us. He's going to take the van, and he's going to hand you a bag of dough. You're going to take a second van to a second garage and you're going to knock on their door. You get the picture?"

Frog felt sick to his stomach. "And how many of these Oakland deliveries will I be making?"

"Just the two for now, but later on, who knows?"

"I see," asked a shaking Frog. "And when will the new deliveries begin?"

"Tomorrow, man. Isn't that your regular delivery day?" Sal asked with a crooked grin on his greasy face.

Dave handed Frog an envelope. "Everything you need to know is inside. When you finish reading it, burn it."

"Dylan and Joey," Sal said, pointing at the two bikers, "your job is timing, you understand me? You make sure everything is ready and waiting when Frog gets there. Frog drops a van off and then receives a bag and a key to the next van. He pulls in and then he pulls out. There are no mistakes. It's swift and on time, you both understand?"

"Come on, man. Have we ever made mistakes?" Joey asked.

"Mistakes are not the issue, Joey. We're talking about delays. If the question was 'have you and Dylan had delays', then the answer would be yes. Over the last few months you have had several delays."

"Not our fault, man, and everything came out perfect in the end. You admitted that."

"Those times you were lucky. This is a new venture. Delays are unacceptable because they are mistakes. If we have delays that means Frog has to wait. Anytime Frog has to wait, that adds an unnecessary risk to the operation. We want everything smooth. No risks, just in and out, quick and efficient. I want him to get the first van easily and get across the Bay Bridge. He'll meet with our first customer, pick up the second van, meet with the second customer. There, he picks up a third vehicle and he heads back across the bay. The whole operation should take only an hour."

"Right man, we got it," Joey insisted.

"Frog, you pick up the first vehicle at exactly three o'clock, you understand?" Sal asked.

Frog nodded.

"That puts you in between traffic. At 3:00 the roads won't be completely bare and by 4:00, they won't be packed."

"Why doesn't he head over the bay between 11:30-1:00 o'clock?" Joe asked. "There wouldn't be anyone on the road. Then we could get him in and out faster."

"No, man. We want enough traffic on the road that it provides a cover but not so much as it causes an inconvenience. That's why three o'clock is perfect. Which means if everyone does their part and the timing is right, this will be a breeze." Dave smiled and nodded his head in excitement.

"This is going to put another seven hundred bucks a week in everyone's pocket, maybe even more. In the meantime, we stay out of the Italians' way. That's a problem for another day, end of that topic."

"Any word on the skanks that ruined your bikes?" Dave asked, lighting a cigarette.

"Nah, not yet," Joey replied. "Eva has family in Tijuana. The Los Angeles chapter thinks they're hiding south of the border. I can't imagine they'll stay there long since neither of them speaks Spanish. We figure the girls are going to camp out, wait until everything seems to die down and then come back to the States."

"That's a fucking bummer about your rides," Frog said.

"Yeah, it sure is. How long has it been now, two months?" Sal said.

"A little over I think," Dylan responded. "Anyway, they have to surface sometime. I doubt they're planning on spending their miserable lives south of the border, and when they come back, the police and the club will be waiting for them."

"Dumb ass chicks! What about the loser guy they played? What's happened to him?" Dave asked.

"We're square with him. Worked out our differences, so we're all cool now."

"Fuck, man, I would have killed him."

"Nah, Terry's a good guy, he's just not too bright and he got played. It's not his fault. He's not the first guy to fall victim to a piece of ass. It's Ruby and Eva who got it coming. Eventually, they'll get theirs. All we have to do is sit back and wait."

"Are your bikes running again?" Frog asked.

"Yep, see for yourself, they're right out there." Joey nodded his head towards the back door. "They aren't perfect, but they're nearly there. Mechanically, they're in tiptop shape. Now it's basic cosmetics. They're primed and have secondhand seats, but they're coming along. Next cut we get we'll be able to finish them off and they'll be way better than they were before."

"Are we all good here?" Dave asked, glancing from one man to another. When each nodded, he hopped to his feet. "Very well, I'd say we're done." Dave stood. "We have a truck arriving soon with Harley parts. If you need me or Sal you've all got the number to the garage" he said, opening the door and walking into the front of the shop.

Dylan, Joey, and Frog looked at each other, rose from their seats and followed Sal out the door. Before they could say another word they were ushered out onto the sidewalk and Sal shut the door behind them.

"Fuck. Were we just thrown out?" Joey asked, scratching his head.

"I think the word would be 'dismissed'," Frog corrected. He straightened his ponytail and walked away.

When he had taken several steps, Dylan called after him. "Hey man, what's with Katie and that Ron dude? You know the guy that owns the house you're living in?"

Frog laughed. With everything else that was going on, the stupid biker was still asking about a chick.

"How would I know what's going on between them? I mind my own business."

"I saw them the Friday before last at a concert at the Avalon. Looks as if they've gotten pretty friendly."

"I don't know about that, man. Katie moved in last week, I can tell you that. I guess some weirdo who works with her father was coming around and bugging her. Ron suggested she move in and...well, now she's a roommate. Apart from that, I don't think there's anything going on between them."

This was true. Frog knew that Ron was really into Katie, but so far the relationship had moved slowly. He was sure that was Katie's idea, because Ron by now would do anything for the girl. It seemed as though the more standoffish Katie was, the more Ron wanted her, but up until now nothing had gone on, as far as he knew.

"Is she living with him?" Dylan asked.

"No, man. They aren't 'living together'. She's renting a room, the same as everyone else who lives in the house."

"Yeah? So they aren't together?"

"No, man, not in the way you're thinking." Frog walked away and then stopped and turned around. "Hey man, let's leave it that way. I mean, I know you dig her and all, but she doesn't need any part of this shit."

Dylan nodded. He agreed wholeheartedly. Katie deserved better than him, he knew that. It was the main reason he had stayed away from her. The truth was, he almost had her out of his mind. Almost! That was before he saw her arm in arm with Ron at the concert. Seeing her that way had crushed him.

Katie was too good for him, much too good. That's why he decided then and there that the best thing he could for her was to let Ron have her. After all, the guy had money (rumor had it he worked for Owsley), he had a house, and a fancy job. The cat was going places...places that Dylan wasn't.

Yeah, he would let Ron have her. It would be the best thing he could do for Katie. All he needed to do was to never see her again. If he never saw her again then he could let her go with ease.

***

Today was the first day of his new assignment, another foot deeper into a situation that he was sure would lead to his demise.

And why aren't I ready to get out yet?

"Four months," he told himself. Four more months before the end of August, which meant that today, he was safe. He still had time before the end of summer, and he promised himself that between now and then he would find a way to get out of this mess. In the back of his mind, however, a little voice told him that all he was doing was digging himself a bigger hole to crawl out of.

But it was April, he reminded himself. Only April. He left the bathroom, dressed in a hurry, and walked out the front door ready to face the new day.

His first stop was an address on Fell, where he would pick up the first van and head across the Bay Bridge on a brand new adventure.

Frog caught the bus on Clayton and headed west towards Golden Gate Park. His destination was a house across the Panhandle, close to Jefferson Airplane's estate. A short bus ride and a deep breathing yoga technique Frog had learned from his ex-girlfriend helped settle his nerves. By the time he left the bus and walked to the location, his confidence had been restored.

As instructed, he walked to the side of the house, carefully checking his surrounds. When he was sure nobody was watching he knocked on the door. Two knocks and a scrape of his knuckles, several seconds later the door opened.

"Hey, Frog man, you ready for something new?" Joey asked.

"Honestly?"

"Come on, man, it's all cool. Dylan and me, we got everything timed perfectly. No way can anything go wrong. Come in, smoke some Mary Jane and let it energize your psyche."

"Nah, man, I think I need to do this sober, at least the first time around," Frog said, breathing deeply and trying to keep his calm.

"Dude, don't be a drag. Lighten up. It's not the end of the world."

"Not until the end of August," Frog said.

"What, man?"

"Never mind. It's all good, man. I'm ready. Let's just get it over with, okay?"

"Okay, Frog, if that's the way you want it. No sweat, brother. The van's right there, inconspicuous don't you think?" Joey pointed to a plain gray van. No insignia; nothing distinct that anyone would notice. It was something that would easily blend with its surroundings.

"Nice," Frog said, nodding in approval. *So far so good.*

"See man, we got it set up so there's nothing to worry about. It's all going to turn out golden, you'll see," Dylan said, handing him the key to the first van.

Frog climbed behind the wheel. He dropped the window and turned the key in the ignition. The engine was strong and sounded dependable. He breathed a sigh of relief. Perhaps this day would go easily after all and he had nothing to worry about.

"Have a safe trip, man. You should be there and back within an hour to an hour and a half. When you get back to this side of the bay you call us at Dave and Sal's garage. Use a payphone and remember where it is so you don't use the same one next time," Joey instructed, smacking the side of the Chevy.

"Gotcha man."

Dylan opened the garage door. Frog gave him the peace sign and the plain gray van headed out of the garage. As soon as the van pulled onto the roadway the garage door shut.

Frog glanced around nervously, searching for anyone who might be watching, and again seeing nobody he turned at the end of Fell and made his way towards the Bay Bridge.

As predicted, the roads were busy but not crowded. There were just enough vehicles that the plain gray van blended in. Frog had even dressed the part. Workman clothes, no jewelry, and a black baseball cap with his hair tucked neatly inside. Plain, so that he too could blend into the surroundings.

The trip into Oakland was uneventful, in no way an indicator of things to come.

Stop one was a place in East Oakland known as the San Antonio Housing Projects, drab, dirt colored apartments piled on top of each other. Everyone he saw was dark skinned and he suddenly felt very out of place.

He pulled into a parking lot behind the complex and a black kid around thirteen years old banged on the truck's door.

Frog opened the window slightly.

"Hey, man, pull up there behind that brown van." The kid pointed to a truck across the parking lot.

"Back there in the corner?" Frog asked. The kid nodded and walked in the same direction. Frog dutifully parked behind the brown van and braced himself, not knowing what he'd be facing next. He took a deep breath, pulled the key out of the ignition, and stepped out of the truck.

"Man, I can't believe they'd send some stupid white motherfucker to do this job." another kid said, stepping out from the shadows. He walked into the sunlight and tossed a key towards Frog.

"Here you go, man."

"You're my tradeoff?" Frog asked, looking around nervously.

"Nah, man, I work for your tradeoff. He's a shy guy, doesn't like to show his face much. You leave this van with me and you take the brown one. Then I turn the gray one over to my boss."

"Your boss sends kids to do his work?" Frog asked.

The black kid shrugged his shoulders. "Hey man, I just do as I'm told. You got the key to the next van. What you waiting for, white boy? Hand over the key to the gray van and take your cracker ass outta here." The kid shoved one hand into the pocket of his dirty blue jeans and the other into Frog's face.

"For one, I was told I'd be exchanging funds and I don't see that happening. Besides that, I'm not cool leaving the van with a kid."

"What you mean? I ain't no fucking kid, man. I'm a hustler, you stupid white motherfucker." The kid lifted the bottom of his shirt, revealing a gun that was casually tucked inside the waistband of his Levis.

The first kid arrived at the van then and stared at his cohort. "What's wrong man? Why ain't he gone?"

"Dunno man, he's some jive motherfucker that don't wanna turn over the van to 'kids' and he's crying about bread."

"What the fuck man?" the kid asked, stepping closer to Frog's face.

"I was told I would pass off the van and I would collect some dough."

"And?" the second kid asked, stepping forward again and pulling his shirt up.

"What are you doing man? Fucking move back, Milton. Shit man, Calvin would flip if he knew you were flashing a piece. You'd better step back and let me handle this."

The first youth, a bit taller than Milton but the same age stepped forward. "Sorry man, Milton's jumpy. He's new at this, you know what I mean?" The kid extended his hand. "My name's Felix and I represent Calvin. You'll eventually meet him but not at first. First step, he sends in cats like Milton and me. We do his grunt work while he's off doing his upper management shit."

Meanwhile a pissed off Milton leaned against the beige cement wall glaring at them both.

"I got that, but come on, man, you have to admit this seems a bit...unorthodox."

"Un-what-the-fuck? Look, man, I'm sorry it was set up this way. You were obviously misinformed, but this is the deal. If you want to complain then you need to take that shit over the bridge. I understand what you're saying. Sure you're handing off the merchandise to what looks like kids, but you don't know shit. When you leave here ask around, man. You tell them you handed off the van to Felix the Cat and then you see what they say. They'll set you straight, man, so that the next time we won't have to go through this shit."

"Next time?"

"If you make it that far, man. Like I said, Calvin's shy. You won't meet him for a while so you might as well accept what's fact. For the time being, you'll be doing business with me and Milton."

"Wow. I don't know about this," Frog said, handing Felix the key to the gray van.

"I feel you, man, but it's cool. You'll see." Felix smiled a white Cheshire Cat grin. "Now just get yourself in the brown van and go to your next stop."

"That's just it, man. I'm supposed to collect a van here, money, and my next instructions," Frog said, walking towards the brown van.

"Dude, I don't know what to say about the dough except that Calvin ain't money shy. I never get to handle bread man, never. The van's right in front of you and here's your next location..." Felix pulled a folded piece of binder paper out of his jacket pocket. He handed it to Frog and then tipped his head, gesturing towards the driveway, which made his dark Afro bounce almost comically. "Make sure you destroy that."

"I will."

"Then split, man, you've already wasted enough time." Felix the Cat turned his attention to Milton and chastised him loud enough for Frog to hear as he powered up the van.

He looked at the West Oakland address, crumpled the piece of paper, and dropped it in his lap.

West Oakland was close to the Bay Bridge. All he had to do was hit the next location, where hopefully he would get to get paid, and then he was only a hop away from home.

The next drop was on 16th and Adeline Street, somewhere close to DeFremery Park. It was an easy location to get into, and because of its closeness to the bridge it was easy to get out of too. Frog felt a burst of optimism and smiled. Perhaps this nightmare had an ending after all.

Unlike the gray van that had seemed mechanically sound, the brown van was not well. It sputtered and coughed, the transmission was off and it nearly died several times at stoplights. Frog started sweating.

What would I do if the van broke down?

Frog rounded the corner onto Peralta Avenue and headed North towards 16th Street. He had to slam on his brakes when a dark figure entered the roadway.

"Fuck!" he said as the van came to a complete stop and he hit his head on the dashboard. When he looked up, a black man was slapping the window.

"Open the door. That's my van. What you doing with my van, white boy?" he yelled, hitting the window repeatedly.

"You get your white fucking ass outta my truck, you hear!" he screamed, and several people on the sidewalk turned to stare at the spectacle.

Unable to think of a better plan, Frog drove off quickly. He made sure the man was long gone before finally slowing down.

"No fucking way, man, stolen cars? I'm not fucking doing this again!" Frog said aloud in the empty van. He wiped dripping sweat off of his brow with the back of his hand. "Jesus Christ, Jesus Christ, now what?"

The voice in the back of his head told him to dump the van and get his still living ass out of Oakland.

Rather than heeding his own advice, he made a U-turn, intending to double back up Adeline Street so he could hit the residence from the opposite end. Then he'd get rid of the fucking stolen van, collect his bread, and make his way back to normalcy on the other side of the bay.

The address was at a run of the mill, normal looking house. Nothing distinctive, nothing out of the ordinary, just a small place shaded by a variety of large trees that hung over the property.

He pulled into the long driveway and parked as far away from the street as he could. He hoped that the owner of the van was nowhere in sight. After several quiet minutes he got out and found himself standing on shaking legs.

"There you are, young man," a voice called from the side of the yard. "It took you long enough. I thought you were on a strict time limit?"

Frog turned and faced a middle-aged biracial man who was approaching. Besides his obvious African heritage he had reddish-blonde hair and pale yellow skin that made him look more like a cartoon character than a real person.

"Did you have complications?" the man asked, sounding very well spoken.

"Yeah, you might say that," Frog said, accepting the man's leathery outstretched hand.

"My name's Oscar," the cartoon character said.

"Darryl," Frog said, using his street name as he'd been instructed. "Look, man, the whole trip has been fucking weird," Frog said. "First I was asked to hand the gray van off to a couple of kids. One was a little smart ass with a gun and the other..." Frog thought of the tough young youth and laughed. "Well he was a good little talker, I'll give him that."

"Oh, you met Calvin's brat pack. They give you their names?"

"Yeah, the sharpshooter was Milton. The other one, the one who saved my balls, called himself Felix."

"Ahhh, Felix the Cat Mitchell, sharp kid, Calvin uses him a lot. He's priming the boy. He gets them young and loyal and then he raises them up the ladder himself." Oscar laughed and lit a cigar.

"I was told that I was supposed to drop off two vans and I'd be picking up greenbacks. Am I supposed to collect the bread from you?"

"From *me*?" The man laughed and his oversized belly shook. "Hell, boy, they don't let me touch money, I'm just an old man. All I know is that you are to park the van here, hand me the key and then take your ass back to the other side of the bay. I expect someone will be in touch with your higher-ups soon enough. Now how about that key, boy?" Oscar asked through a puff on his cigar.

Frog shook his head and his ill-fitting baseball cap fell to the ground. "This whole thing is off balance. I'm supposed to pick up a ride here, another van or a car. Something that I'm supposed to drive back to 'Frisco."

"Well you don't see another vehicle here, do you boy? Nobody told me you'd be picking up another vehicle."

"And did you know this van is stolen?" Frog asked, still holding tight to the key.

"Stolen? No, I think you're mistaken," Oscar said, only this time he wasn't laughing and the perpetual smile had left his face.

"Yeah man, stolen. On the way over here I had some fool run in front of the van. Fucking scared the shit out of me, I thought I was going to hit him." Frog touched the knot that had formed on his forehead from head-butting the dashboard.

"The cat was screaming and yelling, man, beating on the van and trying to get me to come out. Dude's just a block from here, maybe two." Frog glanced around suspiciously.

"Probably some delirious junkie. You know how that is, it happens."

"No man, I don't think so. This guy was serious. I bet that's his van. Watch out for him. He's probably walking the streets right now looking for it." After several moments of silence Frog retrieved his baseball cap from the dust.

"Now what?"

Oscar's smile was back on his cartoon face. "What do you mean?"

"I mean what am I supposed to do, man? How am I supposed to get back? Do you just expect me to cut out or what?"

Oscar shrugged his shoulders.

Frog counted to ten, reminding himself to stay calm. He put his black baseball cap into his back pocket and crossed his arms in front of him defensively. "Look, man..." he started calmly, but was interrupted when the house phone started ringing. Oscar excused himself and moments later returned, smiling from ear to ear.

"Good thing you're still here, boy. That was Calvin. He says someone will meet you at DeFremery Park so you're to head over there right away."

"That's a big park, man, what part?" He had started to sweat again he could feel it trickle down the back of his neck.

"They'll be watching for you. They'll find you, don't you worry. Now get going, boy, you've wasted enough time." Oscar pointed in the direction Frog needed to walk.

"Wait a minute, man. The dude who owns the van is that way!" Frog said shaking his head.

"Now you're not in the van. He's not going to remember your face, so start walking. Besides that, all white boys look the same."

Frog sighed. He didn't like this. This shit was supposed to be organized down to the minute, that's what Dave had promised. Joey and Dylan had been in charge and obviously they had failed. If he ever made it back to San Francisco in one piece he was going to deal with them.

Frog walked toward the park in a daze. He was locked in his daydream, scolding the two bikers he held responsible for this disaster when a group of men approached from the right. When he caught sight of them in his peripheral vision, Frog jumped backwards and nearly fell over.

"Dat's him. He da one fo sho. He was drivin' my van I tell ya."

Frog stared at the man who obviously recognized him. "What?" Frog gasped, turning to face four black men, three of whom were impeccably dressed in black berets, blue shirts, black pants and very shiny black shoes.

Frog shuddered. This militant group even carried weapons blatantly exposed to the public. His heart pounded against his ribcage.

"That so, white boy? You know something about Duane's van?" one of the uniform clad men asked.

Frog wanted to disappear. This was bad and he knew it.

"No, man. I'm j-just out walking," Frog stammered.

"Out walking? How is a white boy hippie just out walking right here in Oakland?" the spokesman for the bereted group asked.

Frog's brain flipped rapidly through short circuits trying desperately to come up with a reasonable explanation. "Look, I don't know anything about a van. I'm just out for a walk. I've never seen DeFremery Park and I thought I'd compare it to Golden Gate Park, that's all. I didn't think it would be a problem." Frog suddenly felt very small next to the militant group members who towered above him.

"Well Duane here says he saw you driving his van. See, his ride has been gone for several days and then today, he sees this white boy in workman's clothes driving it. Right here in West Oakland, imagine that. You see we don't get too many white boys fitting that description around here. Fancy seeing two of them in the same day. Bit suspicious don't you think?"

Before Frog could answer another black man in a fancy tweed suit walked up to the group. "There you are, Michael. When you didn't come back I began to worry about you. May I help you gentlemen?" he said to the uniformed men. "I'm Calvin McCleary. Michael here has been doing some work on my home, remodeling," Calvin said with a friendly smile.

"That so? Well, Duane here thinks he saw your workman driving a van that was stolen from his house two days ago."

"Well, I assure you Michael wasn't driving. He's been at my place all day working up until about fifteen minutes ago when he went off to take a smoke break. When he didn't return I realized he didn't know the neighborhood and I thought I had better come out here looking for him. I guess it was a good idea." Calvin laughed. "Come on, Bobby, this guy's not who you're looking for." Calvin placed his hand on Frog's shoulder and gently pushed him several paces forward.

"Yeah he is. I'm telling you, that's the guy. He's the motherfucker that was driving my van. I'd know his face anywhere." Duane took an impulsive swing that missed Frog by several inches.

A beret clad man pulled Duane backwards and the leader of the group, the one they called Bobby, responded.

"Look, Duane, if Calvin says it ain't him then it ain't him, man. Mr. McCleary isn't going to cover up for someone who stole your ride. You know that."

"I assure you, Duane, Michael here did not steal your van." Calvin pulled out a wad of cash and started counting bills. "I've seen that brown van of yours, and it's not worth more than two hundred dollars. But take this. Get yourself something better." Calvin handed him four crisp one hundred dollar bills.

"Thanks, Mr. McCleary." Duane pocketed the dough and walked off with a smile on his face.

"And for your magnificent group," Calvin said, handing over another five one hundred-dollar bills. "That should be enough for a ton of pancake mix. It should feed a lot of school kids. The neighborhood sure appreciates what you're doing. Keep up the good work, men."

Calvin nudged Frog a little further up the road in an attempt to get him moving.

Bobby smiled, pocketed the cash and nodded at Calvin. "Always a pleasure, Mr. McCleary." Before leaving he stopped in front of Frog and stared at him for a few seconds. "Michael, I'll remember you, man. As I said before there aren't too many cats that fit your description around these parts." Bobby turned and walked away, followed by two identically dressed soldiers.

Calvin glared at Frog. "This has turned into a nightmare." "How on earth did it get so out of control? This is not inconspicuous." He talked like he was scolding a child.

"Look, man, you're the one who wanted me to hoof it to the park. I tried to tell your man Oscar that it wasn't a good idea. How was I supposed to know that the van was stolen? That's on your people, man." Frog immediately regretted both the statement and the tone in his voice.

"What exactly are you implying?" Calvin asked dangerously.

"Nothing, man. It's just I was told what to do and everything on this side of the bay turned out to be, well, not what I'd been told to do. I mean, handing a van full of ...handing that over to kids. Driving in a stolen van and not just a stolen van, one that was taken from this very neighborhood. Then I get to the address and what? I was told transportation would be there, that I would be handling cash and that it was an in and out operation. No disrespect, but that's not what happened."

"You've been misguided, Darryl. That is what they call you isn't it?"

Frog nodded.

"Well it's perfectly obvious that someone made a mistake and now you've been recognized. Do you know who the group just interrogating you was?" Calvin asked.

Frog shook his head.

"The man I just paid off, his name is Bobby Seale. He's a Black Panther, a group he created to protect the streets of West Oakland. They try to control crime, keep kids off the streets and drugs out of the city of Oakland. This is their neighborhood and everyone who lives here sees them as heroes. Those are the men who now know your face and this is your first trip to Oakland. I'd call that a streak of real bad luck."

They stopped on the edge of the park next to a black car. Frog assumed it was Calvin's because inside waiting was a driver.

"I'm going to tell you how this works, son. Handing cash over to you, well that's just not going to happen. You go back to San Francisco and you tell your people that I'll be in touch. You understand?" .

Frog, who by now just wanted to get out of Oakland alive and back on his side of the bay, nodded. The last thing he needed was thousands of dollars to carry around in a city that was obviously against him.

"Good, then we understand each other perfectly. I'll give you a ride to the bus stop closest to the Bay Bridge. Then you'll go home from there." Calvin handed Frog a $5 bill.

"What's that for?"

"It's enough for a bus ride and a hotdog. I think there's a vendor close by. That will get you over the bridge and from there it's up to you."

Calvin's driver pulled over at the curb next to the bus station and let Frog out. It was 6:00 p.m.. He had been in Oakland a lot longer than planned and his so-called adventure was far from over.

He wasn't sure whose mistake this was but he was intent on finding out. This was the last time he would run a mission like this, especially when he was going to end up at a bus station in Oakland at nightfall.

Calvin's Lincoln Continental pulled out into traffic and Frog crossed the street. As promised, there was a hotdog stand on the other side and $5 was enough for several dogs, some chips, and a large coke.

Frog's stomach growled and he was preparing himself to dig into the warm meal when he felt a hand grab the back of his jacket. Someone pulled him to the side of the street. He whirled around and found two young black men in their early to mid-twenties staring at him.

"So you're Darryl, huh? The mysterious smack dealer who's been stealing our clients?"

Frog felt his stomach lurch. He tried to make a run for it but was stopped instantly when the same man pinned him against a signpost. Frog looked towards the bus stop hoping to find help, but was disappointed to see a young black couple purposely looking in the other direction.

"Who's Darryl?" he said.

"Nice try, white boy, real nice try. But you see, we've been looking for you for quite some time. Imagine our surprise when we found you were on our side of the bay." The second man pulled a switchblade out of his back pocket and started swinging it around.

"We need to talk to you Darryl. There, across the street in the empty lot. Get going."

The switchblade found its way to the small of Frog's back and with little choice he found himself walking forwards.

Frog prayed for a passing car or bus, anything to give him a chance to escape. As they crossed the street and entered the empty lot, he knew that help would not arrive. It was April, he reminded himself. Only April. He vowed he would come out of this alive.

The taller of the two men led Frog to the very back of the now pitch black lot and the pair stopped walking.

One of the men pulled a gun out of the back of his pants. "So you're Darryl, just a simple white hippie boy. Imagine that, Ricky. This is the motherfucking dealer who's been stealing our business for the last few months. Look at the weak ass motherfucker, he's shaking."

"Stealing your b-business?" Frog asked. He still hoped against reason that he might be able to talk his way out of this.

"All those refugees who have been coming across the bay every Wednesday and meeting you in Golden Gate Park. Did you ever wonder who they used to buy their drugs from before your happy ass showed up?" He pointed the gun at Frog. "Well, Ricky and I are those guys. Should we tell you how much money you've stolen from us or do you want to guess?"

"Since I'm not Darryl and I'm not real good at guessing, perhaps you better tell me," Frog mumbled.

"Shut up." Ricky punched Frog in the face. "Do you think this is a fucking joke? We know who you are, so stop playing us for fools."

Frog spat out blood and shook his head. *This*, he told himself, *is no fucking joke. This is way too fucking real.*

"You're costing us a thousand dollars a week, you hippie freak," Ricky said. "That amount of money is getting larger all the time, but it's going to stop, ya hear?" He pressed the switchblade into Frog's throat.

Frog could feel the blade slip beneath his skin and the blood trickled down his neck.

"You got any money on you?" Ricky asked, not waiting for a response. He searched through Frog's pockets for a wallet. When he didn't find one he hit Frog in the back of the head and he collapsed on his knees.

"Empty your fucking pockets."

Frog pulled out his front pockets and from his back produced the five dollar bill that Calvin had given him. Ricky snatched the money up, shoved it in his own back pocket and then swung the switchblade around.

"That's it man, that's all you got in your pockets? Here you are taking away our business and all you got on you is five dollars?" the taller black man asked, laughing.

"I told you, I'm not Darryl," he managed to choke out before Ricky punched him again and sent him flying backwards. His nose broke, he dabbed the blood with the sleeve of his jacket and tried to get to his feet before Ricky kicked him backwards.

"Sit down you pale faced motherfucker, you ain't going nowhere."

Frog complied. He sat in the dirt.

"You aren't going to show up in Golden Gate Park on Wednesday you understand?"

Frog nodded.

"If you do we'll hunt your cracker ass down and the next time we find you we will kill you."

Frog nodded and then the beating continued. He was continually pulled to his feet and punched until, exhausted and bleeding, he finally passed out in the dirt.

Several minutes later his attackers walked across the street to the hot dog vendor, where they spent five dollars on a few hotdogs, some chips and a large cherry cola.

Chapter 23

Frog woke in a ditch, lying face down in the dirt. When he was able to raise his head he spit out a mixture of dirt and blood, which missed the ground and rolled down his chin.

"Hey man, get up. You have to help me. I can't get you out of here by myself," a voice said.

Frog's vision cleared and he studied the face that stared back at him. He knew this person. It was the kid from the first drop; the kid in the parking lot who had tried to help him.

"Man, listen to me," Felix said, shaking Frog's arm. "Everyone on this side of the bay is looking for you. You know what time it is?" the teen hustler asked.

"No man." Frog pulled himself into a sitting position and felt for his wristwatch, which was gone. Everything in his body ached. He spit out another mouthful of muddy blood, this time successfully hitting the ground.

"It's past midnight, man. You're people on the other side of the bay have been crazy looking for your white ass. They got everyone trying to find you. How did you manage to get yourself thrown in a ditch man?" Felix asked, helping Frog to his feet.

Frog stood for several seconds evaluating his wounds. Cracked ribs, that was a given, a broken nose maybe, and an eye that was completely swollen shut. Beyond that, he was alive.

"You okay?" the kid asked.

"I'll survive," he said, wiping his bloodied face with the sleeve of his jacket. "How did you find me?"

"It wasn't difficult, man. I knew your second stop and from there I figured you'd head for the bus stop. When you wasn't there I started walking around the area looking for you and then poof, there you are right down the side of a cliff. Man, and you called me a kid. Here you are a grown motherfucking man and you can't get your ass in and out of Oakland even once before you get your shit fucked up."

"Okay, Felix the Cat, point made."

"Now we gotta get you outta this ditch and across the bay so you can check in before something ugly starts between your motorcycle friends and my connections."

It took several minutes for Felix to get Frog up the incline. When they made it to the side of the road Felix stopped, pointed to a car parked next to the bus stop, and whistled. The black '62 Impala slowly made a U-turn and headed towards them. When the car reached them, Felix opened the door.

"Get in, man, what are you waiting for?"

Frog hesitated. "I don't know, man," he mumbled.

Felix laughed. "Now you're scared? *Now* man? Don't you think it's too late for that? Come on, man, that's Marco, he's on our side. Get in."

"What's our side?"

"Man, I don't know. Our side is the good guys. Come on get in."

"I don't think there are any good guys."

"Man, who the fuck cares? Okay we're the guys who are going to save your ass and take you across the bay, so get in the car. Look man, do you have another choice? I don't think you can walk across the bridge can you?"

Reluctantly, Frog climbed into the back seat of the car and Marco, a youth who didn't look old enough to be driving, pulled away from the curb. They headed west, over the Bay Bridge.

Frog breathed a sigh of relief and rested his pounding head against the back of the seat, hoping that this nightmare was nearly over.

"They worked you over good," Felix said, studying Frog's face.

"Yeah, it feels that way."

"Man, you're going to be fucking sore tomorrow," the kid said, whistling.

"I'm fucking sore now."

"We're going to drive you to the first public place we find on the other side of the bridge and drop you off there. Fisherman's Wharf would be my choice, unless you have objections to being let off there?" Marco, the mysterious driver said, pulling a black fedora down over his eyes.

Frog studied his features in the rear view mirror and decided positively that Marco was too young to be driving.

"Sure, that would be fine." He hoped the kid knew what he was doing.

The rest of the trip was silent. As promised, Marco pulled over in front of a blues bar on Bay Street. Frog covered his battered head with the hood of his jacket and prepared to jump out of the car, but stopped at the last minute and turned back.

"Thanks, Felix. I'm sorry I called you a kid before. I won't make that mistake again."

"You don't have to thank me, I'll be getting paid good bread for finding you. It makes Felix the Cat look real good too." The young black kid smiled. "Get going, white boy, I'll catch you later." Felix said with a flick of his head that rattled his Afro.

"Be careful," Marco said and before he drove off he handed Frog a $10 bill. "Just in case you have to take a taxi, man. After all of this you deserve to get home." Frog nodded his thanks and flashed the boy-men a peace sign as they drove off into the night.

***

Frog held his injured ribs. He walked to a phone booth between the blues club and a dive bar. Short of breath and ribs aching, he worked himself inside.

Sitting on a small metal bench, he barely breathed to ease his aches and pains. He pulled some change out of his shoe and reached for a greasy receiver. He dropped a dime into the box, dialed a number, and waited.

"Hello?" Dave answered.

"Man, it's me," Frog managed to choke out between gasps for air.

"Jesus Christ, Frog. Are you all right? Where are you?"

In the background Frog could hear several other voices asking the same thing.

"I've been better, but I'm still alive. I'm at the Wharf," he said, "on the corner of Bay and Taylor."

"Wait there, man. We're coming to get you."

"Wait, Dave. There's a blues club about three buildings in. I'll be there at the bar."

Frog eased his injured body out of the phone booth and walked the short distance to the club, where the door stood open. He entered the bar and looked at the clock on the wall. 1:15 a.m. Despite the late hour he was surprised to find the bar moderately busy.

He walked into the bathroom, used the facilities, and washed his swollen face. He studied his wounds in the mirror and tried to make himself look respectable. After washing the dried blood off of his face, he turned his shirt inside out, straightened his ponytail and, finding himself passable, pulled his hood up over his head to hide his battered face. He took a deep breath for courage and reentered the main room.

He took a seat at the bar next to the wall, which made it easier to hide his damaged face. A burly bartender arrived and stared at him briefly before taking his order of a shot of Wild Turkey and a Budweiser. He sat quietly, waiting. Now that the initial shock had worn off, he reviewed the last few horrendous hours.

What the fuck just happened?

This was supposed to have been organized. There were supposed to be three vans and he was supposed to pick up money. How did the plan fall apart, or had there ever been a plan in the first place? This was Joey and Dylan's fault he decided. He wondered if he had been deliberately set up.

Frog ordered another shot of bourbon and washed down his rage. Moments later four Hells Angels walked in the door surveying their surroundings. It didn't take long before they spotted him sitting in the corner and approached.

When the Angels walked through the door the bar population turned, and suddenly Frog felt as if everyone inside the bar recognized him. His face flushed and he diverted his gaze in shame.

"Ready to go, man?" Dave asked.

Frog held his ribs and laughed. "Am I ready to go? Did you just ask me that, man? Fuck yeah, I'm ready to go." Frog hopped off his stool, cringed with pain, and followed the bikers out of the bar.

Next to the curb sat Terry's '57 Chevy, minus Terry. Alongside that, three hogs. That meant he was riding back to the garage with either Dave or Sal. An icy chill ran through his body and he shivered. Was this a premonition? Or was he just paranoid? It didn't matter. Frog hopped into the side seat of the truck and watched Dave enter the driver's side and start the engine. Without saying another word, Dave put the Chevy into drive and headed back to the garage.

***

The ride back was uneventful. Despite Frog's earlier fears, he had not been murdered. In fact, the drive back was peaceful. Dave said nothing. They sat in silence and for the first time in many hours, Frog relaxed.

The noise the tires made on the roadway calmed him. He sat deeply into the cushioned seat and closed his one good eye. While Dave drove in silence, Frog used a visualization technique. With his psychic inner eye he concentrated on his wounds, directing a piercing blue light above them. He held the vision in place until the warm ray of healing entered his body and took his pain away.

By the time they reached the garage, Frog was nearly asleep. Dave nudged him on the shoulder and gestured towards the building.

"We're here, champ. Let's go inside and talk." Obediently, Frog followed.

He sat in an overstuffed chair next to Dave's desk where the biker handed him two bottles, one aspirin the other a beer. Seconds later, three hogs pulled up next to the shop and the other bikers joined them.

"So what the fuck?" Frog asked after swallowing four tablets and finishing half of his beer.

"We were hoping you could tell us that," Dylan said, lighting a joint and handing the smoke to Frog, who drew in deeply hoping for herbal relief.

"Me man? You want *me* to tell you? Fuck, man, everything you were supposed to have planned went wrong. Everything. Then you ask me why? Fuck you." Frog shook his head in disgust.

"Frog, tell us everything that happened," Sal demanded, glaring at him.

"Fuck you too. I've put up with too much today to give a damn. If anyone wants me dead then do it now and put me out of my misery."

"What are you talking about, Frog? Do we need to take you to the hospital?" Dave asked.

Frog laughed, holding his ribs tightly. "You've been with me nearly an hour and you ask me that now? No man, I don't think I need a fucking doctor, but thanks for finally asking." Frog finished his beer and leaned his head on the table. Suddenly he sat upright and stared at Dave. "You want to know what happened? Okay I'll fucking tell you what happened. I got the first van to the designated area where a couple of kids met me."

"Kids?" Dylan asked.

"Yeah man, kids. Thirteen, maybe fourteen but I doubt it. They expected me to leave the van with them, no money, nothing. They gave me a key to a second van and shuffled me off. The second van, that fucker was stolen. Its owner saw me driving and chased me down the road."

"*What*?" Joey asked.

"Stolen man, the fucking thing was stolen and from that very neighborhood too. I got this black man chasing my ass down the street and I'm trying to find an address that's within walking distance. I had to take off, reverse my route, and backtrack to find this pad. I get there, at the second drop, and this old fool tells me I don't have a ride back to 'Frisco. Then he sends me hiking, *literally*, to the park, right back in the direction of the owner of the stolen van, and fuck yeah, the guy sees me and he recognizes me. He brings this fucking posse, some militant group who call themselves the Black Panthers. They're discussing burning me at the stake and then the motherfucker who I guess organized this fiasco finally shows up. He saves me, temporarily, until the next group got hold of me.

"This Calvin cat hands me five dollars and leaves me at the bus stop. Mind you, the sun is already down and he fucking takes off without a glance to see if I make it across the street, which by the way I didn't."

"You didn't make it across the street?" Dylan asked.

"No man. I didn't even make it across the fucking street before these two black thugs grab me, drag me into a deserted lot, and work the fucking shit out of me. Which, by the way is because 'Darryl' has taken their clients away. Oh yeah, I'm talking about my drop on Wednesdays. The business I do in the park, well those junkies are his former customers. I guess I don't have to tell you that he and his partner aren't too happy about our new expanding business into Oakland." Frog stopped talking and laid his head back on the desk. "I feel dizzy and sick," he mumbled.

"Concussion most likely," Sal said matter-of-factly.

Frog raised his head and stared back at Sal until the biker finally looked away.

"Here," Dave said, throwing a paper bag at Frog which almost hit him in his already damaged face.

"What the fuck is that?"

"It's your cut, slugger. Despite everything else, you got the job done. You took item A to location two and you took item B to location three. If it wasn't for your own stupidity everything would have been perfect."

"Are you fucking kidding me?" Frog asked incredulously.

"Look in the bag, kid."

When he did, Frog saw the additional money inside and his good eye widened.

"Pain and suffering. Mr. McCleary sends his apologies. He takes full responsibility for the stolen van incident. Said you're a brave young man. He thought you stood up for yourself surprisingly well under the circumstances."

"He what?"

"If it hadn't been for your own stupidity, I repeat, this would have been a complete success," Dave said.

"My what? You're blaming this on *me*?"

"Blaming what, Frog? Nothing went wrong on our end. The first van was perfect, Dylan's pick. The second, which by the way was waiting for you as promised when you arrived, that one was on Calvin's people. Which of course accounts for the sizable bonus. Apart from the incident caused by the stolen van the mission went spot on. The second van was delivered and you got out of Oakland. Anything else that took place was self-inflicted."

"Self-inflicted? Are you serious? I didn't have transportation back to 'Frisco, was that spot on?"

"A minor adjustment for next time. That was a miscommunication between Calvin's league and my own, both believing the other was providing it. Now corrected. Dylan will be handling that end of the operation."

"Is that so? Well I sure feel better, since Dylan was so outstanding in this operation," Frog said. He tried to stand up but stopped when a ripple of pain ran through his ribcage.

"Hey man, you're the one who got yourself recognized in Oakland. We..." Dylan said pointing to himself first then Joey, Dave, Sal, "...had nothing to do with that. Someone on that side of the bay recognized you from your 'Frisco business. They turned you into the dealers who worked your stupid ass over.

The question is how did they recognize you, Darryl? You've obviously been blowing your end of the operation. Shit, you can't even figure out a way to get yourself out of Oakland. Gee, I don't know Frog, how about walking to a fast food joint with a phone booth and waiting there for a ride? There's a hard one to figure out."

"Oh yeah? Why don't you try my end of the operation, Dylan? It makes more sense for you to drive into Oakland," Frog said, pointing an accusing finger at the biker.

"Right on, bright boy. Let's send me, a 'Frisco Angel, into the Oakland Charter's territory. How long do you think it would be before one of their members recognized me? Wouldn't Sonny Barger's people love that? Unlike you, I think before blindly walking my ass into shit."

"That's enough!" Dave yelled and banged his fist on the table. "This topic is over. Do you understand? As far as I'm concerned, from a business perspective this run was successful, we all got paid. "You," he said, pointing at Frog, "will be smarter next time, won't you, Darryl?"

"Next time, man?" Frog screeched, coughing into the already stained sleeve of his jacket.

"Next time!" Dave repeated. "This wasn't bad for a first run, all things considered. Next time everyone will be smarter. The van mix-up has been straightened out, the contacts have been established, and I think we all agree Frog won't be accepting bread on the job. It's much safer that way. Next time it really will be an in and out operation, no complications."

"And my Wednesday gig? What about that man?" Frog asked. "I was told not to show my face in Golden Gate Park again, and right now, I don't have much of a face left."

"This Wednesday we'll give you the day off. Dylan and Joey will take your spot and by next week you'll resume your regular responsibilities, only this time with a larger cut of pay."

"More dough?"

"Yeah. And as I said, besides your own problems, which finally caught up with you—the one Dylan and Joey will take care of this Wednesday— you actually proved yourself today, kid," Sal said, his dark eyes sparkling.

"You made it into Oakland, you got yourself out of a possible arrest or worse, you had your ass kicked but you still come back smelling like a rose, hippie boy, a fucking stinking rose."

***

Dave drove Frog home. When he pulled in front of the yellow Victorian, the sun was just coming over the horizon.

Dave opened the driver's side of Terry's truck. "Can you make it inside by yourself?"

"Yeah, after all the shit I've been through in the last twenty-four hours, I can walk twenty feet into the house and then up a flight of stairs, no problem." Frog started to laugh but stopped when a jolt of pain cut through him.

"Okay, man. Take a few days to heal and then give me a call at the garage. I'll give you your next assignment."

"My next what, man?" Frog asked in surprised.

"Not now, Frog, we'll discuss it later. Go heal, man. It's the best thing you can do for all of us."

Frog wanted to scream that he was done, that under no circumstances would he ever be involved again. He wanted to say a lot, enough to get himself out of this mess so that he could leave and go back to Redding, but he couldn't say anything. He squeezed the bag of money inside his jacket and pictured all that cash. Then a voice somewhere inside told him that it was only April...

***

Frog walked the short distance to his pad and disappeared inside, closing and locking the door behind him. The house was dark and quiet, and for that Frog was thankful.

He staggered into the kitchen, got some ice out of the freezer, and put the cubes into a plastic bag for an ice pack. He drank an endless amount of water from the spigot, washed his face in the flow, and headed upstairs to his bedroom. All he wanted was to change his bloody clothes and hop into bed with the ice pack.

Using the correct floorboards to avoid the creaks that could wake anyone in the house, Frog slipped into his room. He dropped the ice pack on his bed and peeled off his blood-soiled shirt.

"There you are, I've been so worried," Moonbeam's voice said from out of nowhere.

A startled Frog pulled the semi-clean T-shirt over his head and with one eye open, the other sealed firmly shut, stared at the hippie girl who was invading his space.

"My God, Frog! What happened to you?" she screeched, and the high-pitched shrill made Frog flinch.

"Fuck, don't do that." He sat on his bed, holding his head in his hands and rocked himself. "Please don't do that."

He maneuvered his injured body onto the bed. Half on, half off, he let out a loud sigh and lay there quietly.

Moony stood motionless, watching Frog lay his broken body on the bed. She bit her tongue so she wouldn't make a sound. When he was quiet, she tiptoed over to the bed and stared at him.

"Say something, Moon, but don't ask me how this happened or I'll have to throw you out."

"What can I do to help?"

"Very gently, please help me get the rest of my body on the bed."

"How? I don't want to hurt you more."

"This leg," Frog pointed to his left leg, "just help me by lifting it up a little. That way I can pull myself onto the bed a little further."

Moonbeam bent at the knees, gently picked up Frog's left leg, and worked with him until he was able to get fully onto the bed.

At first he lay trembling, the pain wrapping around him like a black cloak, and gradually he relaxed and opened his one good eye.

Moonbeam sat on the floor at the edge of his bed staring at him, her hazel cat shaped eyes blinking rapidly.

"You're not going to cry, right?" Frog asked.

"No, if I cry you'll throw me out."

Frog tried to smile but recoiled in pain. "Can you find that ice pack and put it on my eye?"

Moonbeam wrestled through a pile of clothing, searching for the ice pack. When she found it, she lowered it onto Frog's bulging black eye.

"Look, Moon, if you're going to stay in here then crawl up on the other side of the bed and sit down. You're making me nervous hovering above me."

"I'm not sure how to do that without hurting you."

"Just don't touch any part of my body and I should be okay."

Moonbeam pulled her long hippie skirt up to her ankles and made her way around his body. She sat on the other side of the bed and then leaned against a clothes covered headboard.

"For someone so little, you walk like an elephant," Frog said, taking her hand in his own and feeling her fingers curl around his.

For several seconds they sat absorbing warmth through the palms of each other's hands, feeling a sense of contentment.

After a while, Frog said, "Moony, I can't tell you okay? For your own safety I can't tell you anything. I know what you're thinking, that Katie is right. Hell, I'm thinking that myself. I know what the problem is, I really do, and I swear to you I'll be long gone from 'Frisco before the end of August."

"What does that have to do with anything?" Moonbeam whispered.

"It has to do with everything. I'm supposed to disappear at the end of summer remember? This is April."

"I see. You believe you're immortal until then?"

"Well...yeah, I guess I do, kinda sort of."

"Like there's an invisible cape that's going to protect you?"

"Sounds insane, doesn't it?"

"Sounds like you think you're Underdog."

Frog smiled a painful smile.

"What are you going to do, Frog?"

"I'm not sure, but I don't plan on disappearing if that's what you're asking me."

"Aren't you? You're already heading down that road."

Frog didn't answer. He didn't have to. He knew the answer, he just wasn't ready to admit it to himself.

"I don't want to see this happen," Moonbeam said sadly.

"I know."

"Do you? Do you really know?"

Frog nodded. He reached up and touched her face just as a tear ran down her cheek, smearing a yellow painted daisy.

"I do know. I really do, but I'll be out of 'Frisco long before anything can happen to me."

"What if Katie's timetable is wrong? What if you take more risks this time because you think you're invincible?"

"Katie hasn't been wrong once," he said, more for his own benefit than Moonbeam's.

"Because she can tell you what happens in the episodes of the shows you watch together? I repeat, what if you're taking more risks this time because you think you're safe until summer? Don't you think that might be giving you a false sense of security? One you wouldn't have without Katie's involvement? That has to have a different effect on all of this."

Frog hadn't considered that aspect, but discrediting it immediately, he shook his head. "So you believe her now? Wholeheartedly, no doubts?" Frog asked.

"Yes, I believe her wholeheartedly. I don't know how I can, but I do. I've seen enough to know that she's the real deal. Don't you?"

Frog shrugged his shoulders, cringed, and then nodded.

"Frog, we're being offered a second chance here. Just like my astrological chart predicted. The world has turned unexpectedly and there's a gap. It's not supposed to be there and it's going to close itself quickly, but until it does we have a groovy opportunity. If we don't grab onto this with both hands it's going to slip through our fingers and there won't be anything we can do about it, ever. If we miss out on this then we have only ourselves to blame because we knew it was coming."

Deep down Frog knew she was right, but he rationalized the situation. The time of his demise was still set for the end of August, which meant no matter how you cut the sandwich, for now, he was safe.

"Frog, it's going to happen. It will. Some things just can't be changed. Maybe this is one of them."

"Hush," Frog said, tightening his grip on her hand.

"It will, Frog. I can feel it. Despite our best efforts it's still going to happen and there's nothing we can do about it, because some things can't be changed."

"Don't talk like that, Moony. You're wrong, okay? It's going to turn out all right."

"It won't, and I don't want to stand by and watch without being able to change anything."

"What is it you want?" he whispered.

"I want to leave. You and I. Let's just pick up and head to that commune, the place where Chet is living. Let's go there next week. For a while let's just live off the land, really be hippies. What do you say, Frog?" Moonbeam squeezed his hand. "You and me, maybe Katie too. It will get her away from that freak that works for her father. Let's go north to Marin County. Please say yes, Frog, please? Just walk away from whatever it is that you're doing. I won't even ask what it is. Just come away with me."

Moonbeam slid down on the bed, laying her head on a mound of clothing that she thought was another pillow. Her eyes stared deeply into Frog's and then suddenly filled with tears.

"Please, Frog, don't make me watch you disappear."

Frog put one finger over her lips. "Hush." He ran his hand through her auburn hair. "You have beautiful hair you know. Well, not just beautiful hair, *you* are beautiful. The most beautiful girl that I know. You're smart, and talented, and a bit off center, but I love that about you. If I could end up with you then the world would be wonderful. I want that. Whether it's in a commune in Marin, a cabin in Redding, or a tent outside Santa Cruz, it makes no difference to me."

Moonbeam smiled and moved closer to Frog.

"But I have things I have to finish first and you've got to give me that chance, Moony. Give me two months, just two months and then we'll go anywhere you want, I promise. I'll even follow you to the moon if that's how you want it. But I need those two months." He cuddled beside her, kissed her on the top of the head. Moonbeam started to rise but Frog stopped her. "No just lay there just like that and cuddle with me. Just for a little while." He closed his one good eye and drifted off to sleep.

Chapter 24

The phone rang, startling Katie and she jumped. Who was on the other end? Should she answer it? These were questions that went through her mind every time she heard the familiar ringing. The uncertainty of who was on the other end of a phone call was something she couldn't get used to. Caller ID, voicemail, and handheld computers were a lot to give up.

The phone rang again and she stepped nervously towards it. Dates flashed through her mind. Who could be calling? Was it for Robin? It was mid-April, and it could be Richard calling to tell her he was out of boot camp. She picked up the receiver.

"Hello?"

"Oh hello, darling. It's Mother. It's so hard to reach you, Katherine, I've been trying for days."

Katie gasped. Her mother had been dead for fifteen years and yet here she was on the telephone.

"Hi, M-mom." A cold, dark shiver ran through her body. All of these years later, with everything that had taken place between then and now, speaking to her mother still brought back feelings of inadequacy.

"Is Richard okay?" she asked, knowing full well that in April of 1967 he was still in North Carolina.

"Oh yes, dear. As far as I know he's fine. He's just getting out of boot camp you know. He'll be getting his assignment soon. He's hoping to go to Germany."

Hope as he might, that wasn't going to be the case. It wouldn't be long now before they received word of his deployment to Vietnam.

"I guess you're wondering why I'm calling," her mother said with a sigh.

There was a silence, her mother expecting a comment from Katie that didn't come.

"We have a cocktail party next month on the twentieth. I'm calling to invite you, Katherine."

"Oh, I see. Well, I have plans that night so I won't be able to make it. But thanks so much for the offer."

"No, dear, you'll be there."

"I'm sorry?"

"I said you'll be there. Unless, of course, you want that monthly check I've been sending to stop?"

Here it was, the control that Daddy's money always brought. Everything that came from the Searfus household came with a huge price tag.

"Oh..." Katie said, silently gathering her thoughts.

Was she ready to tell Patricia Searfus to stuff it or...?

"Katherine, are you still there?"

"Yes I'm here."

Her parents' money was keeping her psychedelic trip going. With it she could afford the life she wanted to live this time around. That money meant attending any concert she wanted, especially the Monterey Pop Festival, which was coming in June. Without those funds there was no way she would be able to afford that, which was why she had missed the event the first time around. This time she had the bread and she had Ron to drive her. Thanks to that monthly check she could enjoy the event to the fullest, all three days of it. Wasn't that worth a shitty cocktail party?

"Okay, Mother. I'll come, but I'm going to bring a guest."

"A guest?"

"Yes, a guest. Everyone else who gets invited to your parties gets to bring a guest. Doesn't that mean that I get to bring one too?" she asked. "The person I bring will be respectable, I promise."

"You know Mark will be there... and you know how he feels about you," Patricia whispered into the phone like it was the family's dirty little secret.

"Mark is the reason I'm bringing a guest, Mother. He freaks me out. I don't like to be around him, which is why I don't really want to come. But for the sake of family, I'll come as long as I can bring a guest."

"Is this going to be an embarrassment, Katherine? Is this your way of getting back at the family?"

"Not at all. Why would you think that? This is my way of keeping Mark Rhodes away from me, that's all. If he comes around me, which the stalker will do if I'm alone, then we're going to have a scene. I'd like to avoid all that and the only way I can do that is by bringing a friend. Frankly, Mother, I don't like Mark. In fact, I'd go so far as to say that I can't stand him."

"I don't see why. He's a good-looking young man who is going places in your father's company. He'd be perfect for you."

"That's like saying arsenic is a vitamin. No, Mother, Mark Rhodes is *not* perfect for me. He's a creepy stalker. Did you know he came to San Francisco looking for me a few weeks ago?"

"He might have mentioned something about it to your father," Patricia answered.

"Well, I'm in the process of moving because of that."

"Moving?"

"Yes, Mother, moving. In fact, I'm already living at my new address. I'm just here to pick up the last of my stuff and my mail."

"You moved and you didn't tell us?"

"No, not exactly. I would have called you eventually," Katie lied. She had had no intentions of ever calling her parents. Until this minute they were the furthest things from her mind.

"Katherine, this is very disturbing."

"No, it's not disturbing. I was going to call and tell you that I'd moved. I've just been busy finding a place and boxing stuff up. Like I said, I'm moving because of Mark's surprise visit to 'Frisco. I don't want him to know where I live and I don't want him to have my new phone number. Which is why I'll come to the party only if I can bring a guest."

"And the guest won't cause any embarrassment? This party will be filled with a lot of important people. If something were to happen..."

"Nothing will happen. I'll bring Ron. He's got a degree and a good job, he'll fit."

"The hippie with the long hair? The one who assaulted Mark?"

"So, Mark did share his sob story with you, I see. There's nothing wrong with Ron, and by the way, all hippies have long hair."

"No, Katherine, not him. That would be adding fuel to a fire! You can bring a guest, but it can't be Ron. If you show up with him, your monthly check will be cut off. Do you understand?"

"I got it, crystal clear. No Ron and no problems. I'll bring Frog. He's just a groovy friend."

"Does he have a real name?"

"Sure. I don't know what it is, but I'll find out before the party."

"And I suppose he has long hair too?"

"Mother, they all have long hair, they're hippies."

"Hmmm. Very well, Katherine. You can bring this Frog character, but he can't be introduced with that name, and his hair needs to be...contained."

"He'll have a real name and he'll look respectable."

"Your view of respectable."

"How about a cross between the two?"

"Not too outrageous?"

"Nope, not too outrageous," Katie agreed.

***

"I have today ordered to Vietnam the Air Mobile Division and certain other forces, which will raise our fighting strength from 75,000 to 125,000 men almost immediately. Additional forces will be needed later, and they will be sent as requested. This will make it necessary to increase our active fighting forces by raising the monthly draft call from 17,000 over a period of time to 35,000 per month, and for us to step up our campaign for voluntary enlistments." (Lyndon B. Johnson address to the nation. July 28, 1965.)

In 1965 200,000 American soldiers arrived in South Vietnam. In 1966 that number doubled to 400,000 and by 1967, there were nearly 500,000 American servicemen stationed in Vietnam.

On the home front, Martin Luther King, Jr. denounced America's role in Vietnam, calling it, "a war of the poor." (April 4, 1967) He protested the deployment of American troops and accused Lyndon B. Johnson of leading unlimited violence against the country of Vietnam and its people.

This speech was planned to coincide with the MOBE's (The National Mobilization Committee to end the war) spring protest, where Dr. King and his wife were scheduled to give speeches; Martin Luther King in New York City and Coretta Scott King at the Kezar Stadium in San Francisco.

The march on the West Coast, originally scheduled to run from Marina Green to the Army Presidio and up the north end of town, was changed. The protest organizers wanted the hippies involved so the route was relocated, and the procession would go through the Panhandle and wind up at Kezar Stadium in Golden Gate Park.

In honor of the week-long event, Haight-Ashbury began a series of events beginning on April 9th. These included a non-judged art show, a free poetry reading, and rock concert in the Panhandle, six fundraising concerts, and at the very end of the week, a huge protest march.

Meanwhile, life in the Haight was changing. As publicity spread across the nation increasing the hippies' notoriety, the peaceful district of love was about to be invaded by the world.

Every day, more people flocked into the city. The streets filled, and the homeless problem that the Diggers had worked so hard to combat, intensified. Underaged teens organized into small clusters that took to sleeping in doorways.

On Wednesday, April 5th, Gray Line tours organized a Haight-Ashbury line. Tourists were driven through the neighborhood to gawk at the new youth movement as if they were animals in the zoo. Cameras flashed, squares pointed. The tour was an unwanted attention giver; an invasion into the private world of the counterculture.

Hippies started to carry mirrors so they could flash the buses. The idea being, when the tourists tried to invade their privacy the mirrors would provide them with a reflection of themselves.

On Saturday, April 8th, the tour's third trip through Haight-Asbury, an unidentified hippie entered the bus. He declared the passengers free and explained that the bus had been taken over by the Diggers. Then he directed the bus driver to go to the Grateful Dead's house at 715 Ashbury and then to the Diggers' office at All Saints. Before leaving he graciously handed out avocados to everyone.

Henceforth, the Grateful Dead's house was added to the Gray Line's itinerary.

On April 11th, the Gray Line bus was pelted with tomatoes as it drove though the Haight-Ashbury District. The tour would officially end one month later on May 15, 1967 due to the animosity imposed by the hippies.

On the day of the Spring Mobilization march, which was held during San Francisco's proclaimed National servicemen's week, Moonbeam and Katie joined the progression of protesters on the corner of Fillmore and Fell. Katie, reluctant to go at all, since she knew how the Vietnam game would play out, finally agreed to march from the halfway point, and Moonbeam, who didn't really want to walk the full 6.3 miles up and then back, agreed.

The day was cold. It was sunny, but the temperature was low and frigid winds bombarded them. By the time they reached the destination point they were beginning to warm up. Katie removed her knitted gloves and shoved them into the pocket of her jacket. She had done this march before. Last time, Moonbeam had convinced her to do the whole walk. They had gotten up early, and by way of bus and hitchhiking, had made it to the Embarcadero at the 10:00 a.m. meeting time.

From the Ferry Building they had walked the whole distance up Market onto Fell and through the Panhandle. They had been drugged on something. "Flying," they had made it to Golden Gate Park, where they fell asleep on the lawn. Hours later, groggy and freezing, they woke disoriented.

This time around Katie had her gloves, an extra warm jacket, and her worldly sixty-six years of experience. She wasn't about to get loaded and end up passing out in the park. And she knew now, after living in the past for four months, that history, at least *her* history, wasn't set in stone. She had already changed things, although minor, which proved she had free will. That opened up a whole world of possible outcomes, starting with today.

"Let's go, baby, why are we standing here?" Moonbeam asked.

"Because this is the beginning of the protest. Wouldn't you rather be somewhere in the middle?" Katie asked. This Annie was impulsive, so much different than what her friend would become.

Present day Annie was educated, steadfast, her whole life led by logic. This girl, this child Annie beside her, was so innocent. Had Katie truly been that way once, so trusting and naive? She studied the twenty-year old girl beside her and wondered where her own child self had gone now that she had replaced her.

"Just chill and enjoy the scenery," Katie said, scouting her surroundings.

"You're right. If we just stand here then we're going to get cold again, so let's split."

"What?" Katie's attention flashed back to Moonbeam.

"You said it yourself, we'll chill if we stand here very long, so what are we supposed to do?"

"Look, if we march now we'll be among the first to arrive at Kezar Stadium, then we're going to have to sit there and wait for everyone else," Katie said. "Do you want to do that?"

"No, but you said if we stand here we'll get chilled."

"Never mind. Let's walk back to Fillmore, get a cup of something warm, and then return. Then we won't get cold."

Moonbeam nodded and they turned back in the direction they had come.

"So what's up with Frog?" Katie asked. Two days ago, Frog had isolated himself in his room where he was supposedly nursing some mysterious illness.

"He's sick. What else can I tell you?"

"I bet quite a lot if you wanted to." Moonbeam stared at Katie. "It's perfectly obvious Frog's involved in something bad. Do you think I haven't noticed? So, what's really wrong with him?"

"He's beat to shit, Katie. Cracked ribs a broken nose, cuts, scrapes and bruises everywhere. I don't know any more than that. He said he couldn't tell me anything or I'd be in danger."

"I see."

"It's going to happen, Katie. It's a bummer, but it's going to happen and we're not going to be able to do anything to stop it because some things just can't be changed."

"That's not true. Things can change; I've changed them. I'm living differently this time, Moony. Last time, I never moved into your house, I never got close to Ron and I never spoke to Frog except when I had to. By this time Mark was sleeping with Robin, but this time around she insists that she can't stand him. It's not the way it was before. Things are different."

"Small things, yeah, but what about big shit?" Moonbeam said. "You don't know about that because none of them have been changed yet. Sure, you've made different choices small things. Now you have the impression that everything can be changed. What if you're wrong? What if that doesn't include the big things? The stuff that really matters like Richard's death and Frog's disappearance? You don't know if they can be changed, we haven't tried. You dig what I'm saying?"

"Big events? Like marrying Mark Rhodes?"

"You marry him?" Moonbeam laughed hysterically.

"Last time around I did. This time there's not a chance of that happening, not a chance."

"I don't know, Katie. You've diverted the psycho square temporarily but you said it yourself, he'll be back. You could still end up being his old lady," Moonbeam chuckled.

"See, I knew you would react this way. That's why I didn't tell you about marrying him before."

"I'm sorry, it's just funny. You and him, him and you. I bet that worked out really groovy."

"It didn't, which is why it's not happening again, not this time."

"Imagine you marrying that? Mrs. Katherine Rhodes from Squaresville, USA with a square house, a square dog, and square kids. That's outta sight, man. Way to go, Katie!" Moony howled with laugher.

"Yeah, very funny, it's a riot believe me. I lived it. But you're changing the subject. You're not giving up on Frog are you? Because it sounds like you're saying Frog's beat up, he won't tell you anything, so there isn't anything you can do. Is that what you're saying?"

"Man, I don't know what I'm saying," Moonbeam answered just as they arrived at a small coffee shop a few feet off Fillmore.

A hot chocolate and a cup of coffee later they wandered back towards the protest, sipping on steaming cups of warmth. They passed a group of street kids who looked to be fourteen at best, and dumped a few coins into a hat they had thrown out on the sidewalk.

"What do you mean you don't know?" Katie asked, returning to the conversation. "I thought we were set on this thing. That we would work together so that we could stop it from happening. Now you're telling me you don't know? I don't get it? What gives, Moony?"

"Look, here's the thing," Moony said. She bit the side of her lip and stepped closer. "Frog's got this crazy idea that he's immune to everything until the end of August. He's on this superhero trip and it's fucking with his head. He's involved with some underground business shit, and I think he's working with the Hells Angels, despite what he's told us."

"I'm sure he is. That doesn't surprise me at all."

"Man, if he comes home that fucked over, then what kind of bummer shit is he involved in? It scares me, Katie, really scares me. I don't think he's going to make it until the end of summer...not the way things are going. This cape of protection bullshit he's tripping on, it's going to get him killed. He'll be dead long before the end of August.

"He's not packing yet, I checked. But he will, you watch. After the way he came home two days ago, he'll be carrying a gun soon. And despite everything falling apart, he isn't anywhere close to getting out, so he must be making a ton of bread."

"That doesn't mean that we can't stop it, Moony. It just means that we have to get started now. We can't rely on my timeline. If he's as deeply involved as it sounds then we have to do something now."

"And get ourselves killed in the process?" Moony asked. "If you're right and everything can be changed, then doesn't that mean that we can die in this mess too?"

Katie hadn't considered that possibility. The idea that she and Moony were going to fix everything was so imbedded in her mind that she had never considered another outcome.

Last time, she and Moony had stayed out of Frog's business and he disappeared. If this time they were involved, wasn't it possible that they too could succumb to Frog's ending? Katie swallowed hard. "I hadn't thought of that," she said. "Then let's split. Let's take him away somewhere."

"I tried that. I tried to get him to go to the commune where Chet moved, but he wasn't interested."

"Frog wasn't interested in going away with you?"

"No, he said he'd go anywhere with me, but he needed two months to take care of shit here first."

"Two months, after the Monterey Pop Festival. Then we'll leave. We'll pack up and drag Frog off someplace safe."

"And if he doesn't make it until June? You said things aren't set in stone, Katie. If that's true then he can disappear any time, can't he?"

"Then we'll have to find a way to intervene."

"How are we going to do that? Besides following him, and I don't think that's a good idea."

"No. We aren't going to follow him, that would be suicide. I'm not sure what we're going to do, but I'll think of something. Something that's safe and doesn't get any of us killed. For now, let's just plan on leaving after the pop festival. We can go to that commune if you want. And in the meantime, I'll figure out what Frog is involved in and how we can get him out of it."

***

The excitement of the crowd was overwhelming. Katie and Moonbeam jumped into the parade following a tall hippie with hair down to his waist. He carried a sign which read "Johnson's War". Katie laughed at the patched "S," which, omitted the first time around, had been added on with an additional sheet of paper.

Beside them a group carrying a short banner read, "Berkeley Students' Association" chanted and the crowd, including Moonbeam and Katie, joined in with them.

"Hell no, we won't go! Hell no, we won't go!" The street echoed with the chant.

From the corner of her eye, Katie caught Moonbeam popping something into her mouth, which she proceeded to wash down with the last of her hot cocoa. Moments later, Moony slipped something into her ungloved hand. A confused Katie stared at the two red beans in her palm.

That was it. Now she remembered what she and Moony had been loaded on; red beans, a form of Indian peyote.

She thought of her child self again, wondering where that part of her had gone. She and Moonbeam had experimented with nearly everything in their day, but one of their worst experiments had been peyote.

Moonbeam had already consumed her two berries. That meant she had about an hour before she would start to feel the hallucinogenic effects. She would fly for a while, happily trip out on her surroundings, and then she would get sick to her stomach and eventually fall asleep. That was how this red bean experience would play out.

Moonbeam watched Katie while she pretended to drop the peyote into her mouth and swallow it. She smiled contentedly and inconspicuously dropped the red beans on the roadway. *Not this time.*

It had been difficult on Katie. She tried to play a role whenever she and Moonbeam were alone and oftentimes she failed. It was easy to return to a twenty-year old body, but to act twenty again when mentally you weren't, that was difficult. She caught herself acting like Annie's mother much too often and when she did, Moonbeam would fly into a rage.

All Moonbeam wanted was to be twenty. She wanted her world to be normal and when Katie reminded her that it wasn't, it brought drama. For that reason, Katie pretended to be a person who no longer existed.

The damage was already done. Moonbeam had eaten the berries so she couldn't take that back. She could tell Moonbeam what the next few hours would entail but that wouldn't help either, so she pretended to go along with Moonbeam, knowing in several hours she would be dealing with a very sick friend.

The body warmth the crowd emanated allowed the girls to remove their jackets. When they passed Divisadero Street the crowd got thicker as latecomers joined the procession. Along with chanting, several protest songs were sung simultaneously: "We Shall Overcome" and "Universal Soldier". Katie and Moonbeam were caught between the two melodies and felt as if they were bouncing between the two groups.

A woman waved an upside down American flag above the crowd. The girls dropped back several paces when the flag flapped against the tops of their heads.

The City of San Francisco had three hundred and fifty police officers stationed along the protest route and some servicemen standing on the side of the march dressed in full riot gear. Among their numbers were motorcycle police and even cops on horseback. As best as Katie could remember, the protest had been peaceful, and given the stationary position of the officers, they didn't have much to do except supervise the large crowd that would number between 62,000-67,000 before the day's end.

Katie marveled at the diversity of the crowd. Young people marching with the very old and families marching with their children. Several paces ahead a man held the hands of his identical twin daughters. The two blonde children, who looked to be about six years old, were draped in American flags and they marched along the street diligently.

Student groups, young Republicans, black militants, the elderly, wounded veterans in wheelchairs, all races and ages united in one goal, to end the war in Vietnam.

Somewhere in the crowd a bullhorn rang out. The announcer repeatedly told the protestors that the US government needed to get out of Vietnam. And then their counterparts appeared, protesting beside them. Clean cut squares holding signs that warned the world against the evils of communism and the domino effect. They praised LBJ's Great Society philosophy.

Helicopters circled the crowd, police, radio, and television stations searching for a story. More signs passed by: "I'd rather save my ass than Johnson's face", "Are you bombing with me Jesus?", "Johnson is a war criminal."

The enthusiasm was addictive. The more energy displayed, the more outrageous the event became. Some protesters joined hands and weaved in and out of the crowd building a human chain. Katie felt her hand clutched up in Moonbeam's and the two swirled through the protestors.

Their path was blocked and the chain was broken when the LBJ supporters clashed with several members of the Berkeley Students' Association. Words were thrown and the full riot gear assembly stepped in. Within seconds the main disruptors were swept up neatly and effectively by the police, who grabbed each offender and between two officers dragged them backwards towards a side street where a police van sat waiting.

With peace restored, what was left of the two groups drifted away from each other and the protestors moved forward again. The police reassembled quietly on the sidewalk. Below them the pungent odor of marijuana drifted freely. Without a word the officers ignored the blatant use of drugs, sending a clear message through the crowd: "Let's do this peacefully, so everyone gets through the day."

When they turned onto Stanton Street the crowd parted unexpectedly and for a few seconds Katie caught a glimpse of a line of Hells Angels. Almost instantly the crowd grew thicker and swallowed them up. Protestors were pushed against each other as the progression, now wall-to-wall, made its way toward Golden Gate Park.

Moonbeam and Katie were steered by the crowd towards the opening of the park on the corner of Waller and Stanyon. There they came to the main entrance, which would lead the flowing mass towards Kezar Stadium.

The two girls pushed their way to the side of the road where they stood watching the endless flow of bodies. Katie had experienced this before, but back then she had taken it for granted. This time, through the eyes of a sixty-six year old woman, it seemed magical. She marveled at the number of the people, how organized and peaceful an event this size could be. She felt a sudden sense of pride for the generation she was a part of. They had stood up and they had tried to change the world for the better. Somewhere along the years they had failed, but unlike the youth in her present, 2014, they had given it a hell of a try.

Inside the mouth of the park where the roadway forked, the majority of the crowd headed left, where a steady procession of bodies weaved their way towards the rally at the stadium. On the other side of the fork in the road, military personnel stood alongside police officers. Several young hippie girls carrying baskets of daisies were handing them out to the passersby, including the officers and soldiers beside them. Several men on duty refused a flower but the majority accepted graciously and smiled at the young barefoot girls who followed the crowd towards the stadium.

Katie nudged Moonbeam and pointed at the sky above the parking lot where a lone parachute opened and a skydiver drifted to the ground.

"Look, I wonder if it's the same guy from the Be-In?" Katie asked, watching the parachute until it landed in the parking lot.

"The trees are melting into pretty pink faces," Moonbeam announced happily, pointing at several large pines in front of them.

Katie turned and looked at her. Moony's pupils were heavily dilated. It had been forty-five minutes since she had taken the peyote and this was only the beginning.

"Can you see them, Katie Cat?" she slurred.

"I sure can, Moony. They're groovy aren't they?" Katie said, playing along.

"Baby, they're outta sight, dripping pink fluffy faces."

"Right on, Moony. They're something, that's for sure." Katie wondered how long it would be before her friend became physically ill.

The crowd lightened between the bodies Katie could see the other side of the pathway.

Underneath a sign reading, "Burn Draft Cards Here" stood Ron and a very battered looking Frog.

"What the hell?" Katie uttered. "Moony, let's go. Frog and Ron are on the other side."

"Beneath the pink faces?"

"Yes, exactly, underneath the pretty pink faces. Come on." She coaxed Moonbeam off the incline and back onto the pathway where they linked arms.

"Come on, honey. We just need to pass through the crowd," Katie said, steering them across an ocean of bodies that parted and let them pass through. "Ron!" she yelled when they emerged on the other side of the human tunnel.

Ron turned and smiled, immediately recognizing them. "Katie, baby. Imagine finding each other in the middle of all this. How groovy is that?"

"And beneath the pretty pink faces too," Moonbeam said, flapping her arms excitedly and reaching for something that wasn't there. When she caught one of the imaginary floating objects she giggled and turned to show her invisible prize to Katie.

"Look, Katie, look!" she beamed. "Isn't it the cutest?"

Katie pretended to pet the invisible treasure, which pleased Moonbeam to no end. Still giggling, Moonbeam jumped up and down and then spun while still holding on to her invisible friend. When she stopped to rest, Ron smiled at her and he too pretended to pet her "friend."

"What's she on?" he asked Katie quietly.

"I'm on love, man," Moonbeam announced.

"Yep, that and peyote," Katie said.

"Love, baby, I'm on love." Moonbeam started spinning again. Frog, who finally noticed their arrival, walked over to greet them, and stopped her bizarre behavior by slipping his arms around her small body.

"Hey there, Froggy." She looked up at him and then breaking the hug, she put her hands together and displayed her invisible friend.

"Very nice," Frog said, patting the tops of her hands.

"Careful, Froggy, you'll smash him," Moony said, stepping back with a scowl on her face.

Frog tried to smile, but stopped when a bolt of pain shot through his battered face.

Katie shook her head. "You look like shit, Frog."

"Doesn't he though? I got tired of him hiding in his room, so I dragged his lazy ass out of bed and brought him here," Ron said with a smirk. "Imagine my surprise when I saw his Frankenstein mug. And he tried to say he was sick for the past two days. Now he says he got into a bar fight."

"I did," Frog snapped.

"Like hell you did. I'm not buying it." Ron stared at him and Frog diverted his eyes. "Now he has this crazy idea about burning his draft card."

"Perfectly logical idea, actually. There isn't a point to me having a draft card." He looked straight at Katie.

Katie glanced at Ron and the look on his face made her shudder. *He knows.* In the next second the look of acknowledgement was gone and he smiled, patting Frog on the back.

"It's cool, Frog. If you want to burn the fucking thing then you go do it, man. You got to do your own thing, brother. If that's your bag, stop fucking talking about it and go and do it."

"Right on, man." Frog reached into his front pocket and pulled out a leather wallet. He opened it and removed a folded document. Shaking the piece of paper loose, he put his wallet back in his pocket and pulled out a Zippo. He held the draft card in one hand, the lighter in the other and looked around at the small crowd of spectators who had assembled in front of them. "I'm going to do it, man. I'm going to fucking burn it."

The small audience cheered, drawing even more viewers. Within seconds, two other young men joined him holding identical documents.

"Far out man, me too," said a tall hippie with a leather headband and a fringed vest. When he approached the burn station his multitude of love beads shook and rattled together.

"Me too," said a clean-cut kid who told them he had just arrived from Wisconsin.

The three huddled together and at the count of three simultaneously lit their lighters and shoved the detested documents into the flames. The bystanders went wild, exciting a larger crowd who stopped to watch the action.

When the cards were fully ablaze the men dropped them on the ground. A woman holding an American flag appeared and threw it into the flames. It caught fire quickly and the group jumped back, cheering. They stood and watched the growing flames with excitement dancing in their eyes.

Two policemen appeared beside them. They too watched the flames peacefully but did nothing to stop the incident. Within minutes the flag had burned itself into ashes and the crowd dispersed and headed towards the rally.

Katie turned to check on Moonbeam, and was startled to find that her friend was no longer beside her.

"Oh shit. Moonbeam," she called out and when she received no response, she headed off to hunt for the missing girl.

"Moony? Moony!"

"What's wrong, Katie?" Ron asked.

"Moony's gone."

"She can't be. She was just here a moment ago," Ron said, glancing around. "Well, she couldn't have gotten far, not in the strung out condition she's in."

"She's here," they heard Frog call out from behind some bushes. Rounding the corner, they found her on all fours vomiting into the dirt.

"Oh ,Moony..." Katie dropped to her knees and embraced her friend.

"I don't feel good," Moonbeam gurgled. She pulled away from her own vomit and laid herself out on the lawn.

"No man, no. Don't sleep there." Frog crouched down beside her and tried to lift her to her feet, wrapping his arms around her shivering body. "Don't sleep here, Moony. I'll take you home, baby. Just hang in there, I'll get you home safely." He turned to face Ron and Katie, holding on to a sleepy

Moonbeam. "I'm taking her home, dudes. Stay here and have fun. Don't worry, I've got this. I want to go home anyway, this whole scene is getting to be a drag." Without another word he half carried Moonbeam towards the exit of Golden Gate Park.

***

Katie watched Frog and Annie disappear in the crowd. When she turned back around, she caught Ron staring at her.

"Are you cool with this?" he asked.

"This?"

"With Frog taking her home. I mean, you're okay with him taking care of her and all?"

"Yeah, I guess so. I mean, Frog's not in the best of shape, is he?"

Ron smiled. "He's been better," he admitted.

"Do you think they'll make it back to the pad, or should we help them?"

"They'll be fine. Frog will take it slow. He wants to be her hero, so yeah, they'll be fine." Ron chuckled. "So you want to head towards the stadium and join the rally?"

"Nah, I got a better idea. Come with me." She turned and headed away from the crowd.

"A better idea?" Ron said mischievously, wrapping his arms around her.

"No, not that," Katie said, playfully pushing him away. "Let's go to Kezar Field. I have a feeling the show will be better on that side of the park."

"Is that so?"

"Yeah, I got a tip that the Diggers might be arranging a free rock concert."

The rock concert would be brief, but if they hurried they would be able to watch all of it before the police broke it up. The event was not planned. It was thrown together by the Diggers in retaliation for the political theme of the rally, which consisted of boring speeches by pacifists and unions seeking solidarity. The way the Diggers saw it, it was an organized bill set on telling the crowd how they should think and feel. Fearful that the venue would push the hippies away from the peace movement, the Diggers quickly organized their own rally.

Together with Country Joe and the Fish they would cut the chain leading to Kezar Field, pull in Joe McDonald's flatbed truck, and within minutes hook up a series of amps and speakers. The concert would last between twenty and thirty minutes, but it would draw the crowd away from the boredom of the political realm in which they were trapped.

Katie looked at Ron's watch. They would have plenty of time to make it to the field before the start of the bootlegged concert, something she was excited to see.

Ron slipped his hand into Katie's, wrapping his fingers around her own, and they walked along the wooded path.

"I know I might be overstepping my boundaries, and I know it isn't any of my business but I'm worried about Frog, and I'm worried about you. I'm pretty sure that whatever Frog's involved in, somehow you are too," Ron said, without looking up from his feet.

Katie's body tensed. *He knows,* she thought again. "If you're asking me about his recent beating, I don't know anything about that."

"I'll bet you know more than you're saying."

Katie said nothing.

"You're different, Katie, very different; like night and day. Four months ago you were a child. Cute, don't get me wrong, but you were an annoying child. You and Moonbeam used to get together, and the two of you would drive me crazy giggling and carrying on. I used to look at you and wonder what you would be like if you were grown up, and then overnight, it happened." He raised her hand he was holding, "This Katie is not that Katie. I don't know what that means or how it's possible but I know it's the truth. Nobody changes that drastically that fast unless ... now that's the part I haven't figured out yet, but I'm working on it."

Katie played dumb. "What are you talking about?"

Ron stopped walking and turned to looked at her. "If you want to we can go on pretending that a drug overdose changed you. That some chemical compound invaded your brain and just like that," Ron snapped his fingers, "you were turned into a grown up woman, but I'm not stupid. I see what's going on, even if I don't understand it."

Katie's mind went blank. What could she possibly say? What excuse could she give? She looked at the ground and said nothing.

"I see Frog on a downward spiral," Ron continued, "and I see you knowing way too much about everything that's going on."

"I really don't understand what you're getting at."

"No, you're hoping that I don't know too much because you don't want to let me in on whatever this is. But I know that you, Frog, and Moony have an understanding, something that belongs only to the three of you. When you look at each other it's like you're all in your own private world. And then there are the random comments. Little slips of the tongue that all three of you make. It's enough to tell me that some pretty strange things are going on. Word has it that you know about the future, that you can even predict the ending of television shows that have never been aired before, which has me wondering if you're the soothsayer instead of Moonbeam."

Katie tried to think of something to say in her own defense, but couldn't come up with anything. Ron was smart. He worked in the science field. His work involved watching, gathering data, and then coming up with a hypothesis. She realized that was what he was doing now, and little by little he was getting closer to the truth.

"Ron, I..."

Ron put a finger over her lips. "Hush." He kissed her gently. "Not now. We'll talk later. For now I just want you to know that it's all right. Whatever it is, you can tell me. You see, this Katie? The one that's standing beside me? I really dig her. This Katie, the mature woman with a mind of her own, I think she's what I've been looking for, for a long time. So whatever brought you to me, it doesn't matter." He stared deeply into her eyes for a moment, then kissed her again. Hand in hand, they resumed walking towards Kezar field.

"Well, look at that, I guess you were right. It looks like a couple of the Diggers are cutting the chain on the fence," Ron remarked, pointing at a small group of men huddled next to what looked to be Peter Berg and Emmett Grogan, operating on the large metal gate.

The two ran excitedly and when they reached the bottom of the hill the gate was wide open and a blue pickup truck was pulling onto the field. Their exhilaration ended when a black sedan pulled up next to the curb and a man got out. Recognizing the person, Ron muttered a curse and excused himself. For several minutes he talked with the man and then returned to where Katie was standing.

"Work calls, honey. I'm sorry, I have to split," he said sadly.

Katie looked at the expensive car and at the man who had come looking for Ron.

"How did he find you?"

"Lucky break on his part I guess. I'm really sorry, baby, but I have to go." He kissed her goodbye. "You go watch your concert and enjoy yourself. I'll catch you at home later." He walked to the car, got inside, and the car sped away.

Katie stood for several minutes watching until the car disappeared into traffic. Rumor had it that Owsley Stanley was looking for a new cookhouse. His last batch of White Lightning LSD, which was processed back in December, was running low. He couldn't go back to his place in Berkeley because the cops were watching him, so he and his associates were actively looking for a new work place. Something inside told Katie that Owsley had just found that spot, and that's where Ron was off to.

Her head spun. There were so many recent developments. Frog's impending catastrophe, Ron's suspicions. *What's next?*

Country Joe and the Fish broke the monotony as they started the Fish Cheer. "Give me an F..." sounded over the makeshift P.A. system. "Give me an I..." Katie's thoughts of doom were interrupted and she smiled brightly, skip-walking towards the gathering.

"Give me an S, give me an H, what's that spell?" Joe McDonald's voice yelled out. "What's that spell?"

Country Joe and the Fish were local Haight-Ashbury musicians notably known as a political protest band because of their heavy involvement in the peace movement.

The group's name came from communist politics. Joseph Stalin, who ruled the Soviet Union from 1928 until his death in 1953, was commonly referred to as "Country Joe." The "Fish" portion of their name was taken from a Chairman Mao speech where the former Red China leader said that the true revolutionary "moves through the peasantry as the fish moves through water."

From their early beginnings in Berkeley through their psychedelic period in Haight-Ashbury, their appearance at the Monterey Pop Festival, and their future performance at Woodstock, Country Joe and the Fish were there for the whole ride, the full psychedelic experience, and through the peace movement that followed. But now it was 1967, they were all in their twenties, and today Katie was going to enjoy herself listening to them perform.

***

Katie entered the field just as the Fish cheer ended and "I Feel Like I'm Fixing to Die" started:

> *"Well, come on all of you big strong men,*
> *Uncle Sam needs your help again.*
> *He's got himself in a terrible jam*
> *Way down yonder in Vietnam.*
> *So put down your books and pick up a gun,*
> *We're gonna have a whole lotta fun."*

Katie headed towards an area on the lawn and sat on an incline, where she watched a crowd of people start showing up.

> *"And it's one, two, three,*
> *What are we fighting for?*
> *Don't ask me I don't give a damn,*
> *The next stop is Vietnam."*

It was surprising how quickly the flow of protestors, escaping from the boredom and the freezing temperatures of the rally, showed up. When the band finished their second song and started their third, an untitled protest song, the field was filling up quickly. A group of hippies sat beside Katie and nodded their heads in greeting. Seconds later they had a joint going around the group and Katie joined in when a redheaded girl with freckles handed her the smoke.

"Groovy coming across this scene," the girl said, gesturing towards the stage. "We were freezing back there and the rally thing, man what a drag." She offered her hand. "I'm Paula, but some people call me Gretchen."

"Nice to meet you Paula Gretchen, I'm Katie."

Katie took a hit off the joint and passed it to a hippie with sand colored hair fastened into a loose and frazzled ponytail.

"I'm Mike," he said smiling. "We're here from La Honda."

"Yeah? Are you heading back tonight?" Katie asked.

"Nah, we have friends that have a house on Ashbury and we're going to stay there for the night," Gretchen told her. "We have an old bus that we traveled in. Hey, maybe you've heard of it, we call it 'Further'."

Katie looked at the group, really looked at them. She had indeed heard of the bus named Further. It belonged to a famous group formed around Ken Kesey, the author of *One Flew Over the Cuckoo's Nest*. His friends, who called themselves the Merry Pranksters and whose personal motto was to "never trust a prankster," spent the summer of 1964, and a similar trip in 1966, conducting what they called "electric Kool-Aid acid tests."

In a psychedelic painted school bus, they drove from La Honda, California to the World's Fair in New York City, promoting the use of LSD. Their bus named "Further" was the stated goal of the Merry Pranksters. Going 'further' referred to the only obtainable way to expand one's own perceptions of reality, through the use of LSD.

And so the group traveled across the United States giving out free LSD to anyone who was willing to try it. (LSD became illegal on 6/6/66)

As for the house they were staying in tonight, the one Gretchen described as being on Ashbury? Katie was relatively sure that the address was 715 Ashbury, locally known as the house of the Grateful Dead.

"Hey, Gretchen, Mike, Katie. Page, my brother how goes it?"

At the mention of her name Katie spun around and found Dylan standing behind her.

"Dylan. Far out man, how goes it?" one of the Pranksters said, jumping to his feet and embracing Dylan and the Angel beside him, Chocolate George.

"Good seeing you here," Page Browning said, smiling at Dylan. Page was a member of the Pranksters and at one time a candidate for the Hells Angels, and he happily greeted the bikers.

"You too, man," said Dylan, pulling an herbal smoke out of his vest pocket.

"What brings you to the city?" Chocolate George asked, flopping on the lawn beside Gretchen and giving her a hug.

"The protest, baby. We came to add to the numbers, man, show our support for the cause," Mike answered.

"Did you come in your crazy psychedelic bus?" Chocolate George asked. He reached for the joint that Dylan handed him.

"Yeah, man, we sure did. She's parked over at Buena Vista Park. The rest of our crew are at the Dead's house partying. The wimps cut out saying they were cold." Mike laughed and putt an arm around Gretchen. "What you see here are the real troopers."

"Right on, man." George sucked in deeply on a hit of weed and then handed the smoke to Katie.

"Hey, baby, I remember you," George said to her. "You're one of the hippie chicks Dylan and Joey brought to the clubhouse party."

Katie nodded, embarrassed.

"That's groovy, baby, and here the two of you are together again," George said, smiling at Dylan.

Mike shivered. "Fucking cold in Kezar Stadium," he commented.

"Boring as shit too," Gretchen added.

"Yeah, boring as shit too," Mike agreed. "I would like to have heard Coretta Scott King talk, but I couldn't sit through the rest of that bullshit while freezing too. You dig?"

"Were the stands filled?" Dylan asked.

"In the beginning, but the crowd left quickly. When we left it was only half full. Not much of a crowd for Mrs. King but...you know 'Frisco weather."

The sound of a siren could be heard and moments later two squad cars pulled outside the gate to the field. Officers left their cars and headed towards the stage, where Joe McDonald and the rest of the band were still desperately continuing to play despite the advancing posse.

The oxen lie beside the road their bodies baked in mud
And fat flies chew out their eyes then bathe themselves in blood
And super heroes fill the skies, tally sheets in hand
Yes, keeping score in times of war takes a superman
The junk crawls past hidden death its cargo shakes inside
And soldier children hold their breath and kill them as they hide
And those who took so long to learn the subtle ways of death
Lie and bleed in paddy mud with questions on their breath
And we send prayers and praises.

(Joe McDonald, written in 1967)

"Oh man, fucking party's over," George grumbled, and along with the rest of the Pranksters stood up.

"Here comes the man," Page said, shaking his head in disgust.

Plugs were pulled and the band, along with several of the Diggers, started talking to the cavalry.

"Wow, man, that's a bummer. Nice while it lasted though," Gretchen said, rubbing her arms against her body for warmth. "Cold as shit anyway, so I guess it's time to split."

Below them, cops on horseback arrived and herded the crowd towards the exit.

"All good parties come to an end," Mike said, waving his goodbyes as he and the rest of the Pranksters headed out of the field.

"Hey, it was nice to meet you, Katie. Stay groovy," Gretchen said, flashing a peace sign before walking off with the rest of the Pranksters.

"Time to leave," a cop on horseback said as he started up the incline. "This is a private area that's been unlawfully occupied. It's time for you lot to get out."

"We're going, officer, not a problem, man," George said amiably. He, Dylan, and Katie walked towards the gate.

Meanwhile, while Country Joe and the Fish gathered their equipment, Peter Berg and Emmett Grogan talked to the officers.

"Think they're going to be arrested?" George asked.

"Nah, they'll find a way to talk themselves out of it," Dylan said. "They always do. Let's go before they start heckling us."

Although he hadn't said a word to Katie other than a brief greeting, Dylan slipped his hand into hers and escorted her through the metal gate that led out of Kezar Field.

"Now what?" Chocolate George asked.

"I don't know, man," Dylan answered.

"Then I guess I'm going to split, man. I'll head to the clubhouse or maybe the Dogpatch Saloon. You want to come?"

"No man. I think I'm going to hang out here for a while."

"Okay, man." George clasped Dylan's hand. "Katie baby, nice to see you again."

"You too, George," she replied.

Chocolate George was the hippies' favorite Hells Angel. He was loved for his humor and admired for his friendliness and kindness in the Haight. George, who had earned his name because of his fondness for chocolate milk, was a regular face among the counterculture where he appeared often and always with a smile on his face.

When George was gone, Dylan turned and looked at Katie. "You cold?"

"A bit."

"Do you think you could handle a motorcycle ride?"

"A ride? Now? Are you serious?"

"Dead serious," he said, staring intently into her eyes.

"Where would we go?"

What was it about Dylan that made her feel weak in the knees? *You're a sixty-six year old woman, you should know better!* Katie silently scolded herself.

"Have you ever crossed the Golden Gate Bridge at night on a Harley?" he asked, smiling sweetly as he ran his hand sensually across her face.

"No, I can't say I have."

"Would you like to? I have an extra jacket and a helmet in my side bags that should keep you warm."

"You know what?" Katie said, looking up at him. "I think I would like that ride very much."

Dylan kissed her on the forehead. "Then let's go, pretty lady."

Chapter 25

The lights on the Golden Gate Bridge whizzed by. Katie decided there was nothing better in the world than to be young and riding on the back of a Harley. Her return trip to 1967 taught her an important lesson— live every moment to the fullest— and right now that moment was electrifying.

Her hair tied back in a long golden braid and wearing Dylan's German helmet and an extra thick jacket, Katie felt as if she was on top of the world. Dylan occasionally lowered his hand to give her leg a reassuring squeeze, and despite her advanced age, Katie found the act endearing.

The ride ended much too quickly when Dylan reached the other side of the bridge. He exited Highway 101 and headed south into the hills of Golden Gate National Forest. He parked his Harley on a ridge overlooking the San Francisco Bay.

"God, it's so beautiful here," Katie said, getting off the bike and removing the helmet. She walked close to the edge of the hill for a better look at the bay and stood there, admiring the lights of San Francisco.

"I agree. The place is groovy, especially at night. I sit here, watch the bay and think, or sometimes I try not to think," Dylan said with a laugh.

"It's wonderful." Katie started to sit on a patch of wild grass and Dylan stopped her.

"Wait! You don't want to get wet." He pulled a red and black checkered blanket out of his saddlebag and handed it to her.

"Oh, I get it. This is where you bring all your girls. This is your makeout point?"

"Hardly. The chicks I hang out with don't need romance to put out. You saw Eva," Dylan laughed.

"Right, don't remind me."

"This is where I bring someone I admire, someone I want to get to know."

Katie spread the blanket out across the hillside. She sat, pulled her knees up to her chest, and wrapped her arms around them. "And how many chicks have you done this with?"

Dylan sat beside her. "Just this one." He smiled a most magnificent smile that made Katie blush.

She turned her reddened face away and stared at the skyline. "San Francisco is the most beautiful city in the world."

"Because you've seen so many cities to judge it against?" Dylan asked.

"I've seen enough to know that San Francisco is special."

"I think it's special too."

"Were you raised here?" Katie asked.

"Here about. I spent some time in Richmond and Oakland. But yeah, I'm a local boy."

"You spent time in Richmond and Oakland?"

"Yeah, that sounded bad, didn't it? I meant that I lived there shortly when I was a kid. I did a couple of stays in foster care. I tend to think of foster care as doing time, you dig?" He lit a joint and took a healthy toke.

"Yeah, I bet that's how it feels. I'm sorry you went through that."

"Don't be. I learned a lot from the experience and I met Joey. I consider him my brother, so something good came out of it." He handed the smoke to

Katie. "Besides, my life with my mother was worse, so foster care was almost a vacation. My mom would show up occasionally, dried out from alcohol, and she'd try to play parent. When it got to be too much for her, she'd start drinking and then she'd split again. Six months to a year later she'd be back and we would start the whole game again. Each time she disappeared I got better at dodging social services. The first two times I tried staying in the apartment on my own, thinking I could run things." Dylan shook his head and laughed. "Stupid kid. As soon as bills went unpaid, social services caught up with me. Those were the times I lived in Richmond and Oakland. The third time she split on me I was 15, and I was done with the system. No fucking way was I going back into foster care, so I split.

"By then I'd met Joey. He was 17 and he wanted out of the system too. We bought a couple of crap bikes, fixed them up, and went on the road. Eventually that road led us back to San Francisco. "

"And your mother?"

"Who knows? Who cares? She's probably someplace sucking on a bottle of gin. I hope the old bag chokes on it."

Dylan lit another joint, inhaled deeply, and stared at the bay.

"Your father?"

"Nonexistent. I suppose I have one, I mean everyone does right? I have Joey and I have the club, they're my family." He reached over and pushed the loose strands of hair out of Katie's eyes.

"Where did you and Joey go when you left?" she asked.

Dylan laughed and handed her the herb. "Man, those were some crazy days," he said, remembering. "First we went to Santa Cruz to check out surfer babes. We stayed there a few weeks and then we moved on to Los Angeles. From there we just kicked around going wherever we ended up. Of course, it depended on how the bikes were working. Which, by the way wasn't often, piece of shit Yamahas. Anyway, along the way we joined a few bike clubs and eventually ended up back in the city as Hells Angels."

"How old are you?"

"I'm twenty-four going on fifty."

"I beat you, I'm twenty going on sixty-seven," Katie said and they both laughed.

"Okay, enough about me. What's Katie's story?"

"My story?" She laughed, thinking of her unusual situation and what Dylan would think if she told him the truth. "Let's see, the condensed version; rich child who was attention deprived grows up dissatisfied with her parents' world. Knowing that they worship the establishment and all that it stands for such as money, greed and power, which they wash down with plenty of alcohol, daughter ditches out. She becomes a flower child and moves to San Francisco looking for a groovy way of life."

"Did she find it?"

"Yeah, she did."

"Spoiled little rich girl, huh?"

"I said rich, not spoiled, and I'm disinherited in case you've got any ideas."

Dylan laughed. "Disinherited because you're a hippie?"

"No, disinherited because I refuse to play the game that would lead to all that bread."

Dylan stared at her.

"Well, say something." She nudged him.

"I can't. I don't know what it's like to grow up with money, so I'm finding it hard to relate. But unhappiness, now that's a topic I understand fully, so if you tell me you were unhappy I can dig it."

"Unhappiness doesn't even begin to cover it," Katie said, thinking back over sixty-six pitiful years. "I know it's hard to understand. From the outside it looks like I was born into luxury, a dream life, but that's not how it works. When you have wealthy parents you might as well be invisible. When you are visible then you'd better fit into a perfect role that makes them look good. You have to have perfect manners, know your place, and know when to keep your mouth shut. And most important of all, obey your parents without asking questions.

"Suffice it to say that I don't fit into that perfect child mold, I never did. And you know what? I'm not even going to try. It's a sick way to live. I'd rather be disinherited than to live in that world." Katie almost added the word "again," but stopped herself.

Dylan's hand squeezed hers reassuringly and she looked at him, really looked at him.

"Who are you, Dylan? Who are you really?" she asked, and then she laughed, thinking of Janis Joplin who had asked her the identical question.

"Who am I really?" He repeated. "Hmm, that's a hard one. What do you mean? Are we talking professionally, morally, or just in general?"

"I think it means, who were you born to be?"

"You think that's what it means? You're not sure?"

"No, not really. I had a chick ask me that recently. I'm still trying to figure out what it means and what my answer is. But the question gets you thinking, doesn't it?"

"You are an odd one, Katie. Exceptionally pretty but odd." He touched her nose with the tip of his index finger.

"I'm just a hippie."

"Is that your answer to the great philosophical question? If it is, then my answer's easy. I'm a biker."

"No, you're a Hells Angel."

"Same difference."

"No it's not, and you don't believe that either. If you did then you wouldn't be one."

"Touché. Do you want to analyze me?"

"No thanks. I can't even analyze myself."

Dylan kissed her and she kissed him back. The kiss turned into more than just one, and after several minutes Dylan tried to lower their bodies onto the blanket.

Disturbed by the euphoric feeling that stirred within, Katie pulled away and sat up, suddenly embarrassed. *Imagine, at my age, kissing a twenty-four year old kid? How despicable.*

"Problem?" Dylan asked.

"No. Yes. I don't know. Jesus." Katie laughed. "This is so complicated," she said, running her hands through her hair.

"Ron?"

"So much more than that." She crossed her legs Indian style. "Despite what you think, Ron and I...we haven't... I mean, we aren't...." And then she stopped herself, wondering why it mattered to her that Dylan knew the truth. She looked at him. "I wish I could tell you everything. For some crazy reason I really wish that I could."

Dylan pulled a toothpick out of his vest pocket, shoved it into his mouth, and chewed on it. He lay down on the blanket and stared at the sky. He was quiet for a long time, thinking. Then he rolled over, propped himself up on one elbow, and stared at her.

"I know what it means," he said.

"What?"

"Your question, I know what it means. Who would you be if there were no outside influences; if you grew up in a perfect environment that didn't color your view on life? If that were the case and you were allowed to develop in a bubble, who would you be?"

"And you have an answer?"

"Yeah, I think I do." Dylan sat up. "Deep down, I'm smart. If I'd been allowed to become that person, then I would be doing some type of normal shit. Maybe I would have gone to school, become an architect, designed some far out building. Something crazy, like a fucking pyramid right in the middle of San Francisco." He laughed. "Yeah man, that would be something, it would sure blow some fucking minds. Imagine me, a Hells Angel and an architect."

Katie stared at him, wondering who the architect had been who had actually designed the pyramid building in San Francisco. All she knew was that construction would start in 1972.

"Do you think that's a strange idea for a building?" he asked, noticing the unusual smile that came across her face.

"No, I think it's an absolutely brilliant idea for a building."

"Yeah, I'd be an architect, I'd have a house and a car."

"A wife, a dog, and two and a half kids," Katie added.

"Yeah, something like that. But none of that is for real, baby, because the world has colored both of our lives and everyone else who's in it." He pointed across the bay. "Who you become is a combination of things. It's where you're born, what color your skin is, what sex you are, what religion you're born into, whether you're rich or poor, tall or short, healthy or ill, all of that changes who you become."

"Only if you let it. If you wanted to go to school, Dylan, then you would be going."

"Are you so sure about that?"

"Yes, I can answer that with sincerity. Motivation is a powerful tool. People do amazing things when they have it. If you really wanted to be an architect then you would find a way to be one. You would fill out grant applications, work two jobs, and take out student loans, anything in order to go to school. You want to be an architect but you don't want to be one that bad."

Dylan smiled. "True enough."

"So in a perfect world you would be an architect?"

"Yeah, it's possible. I think about it sometimes. I know that's crazy but I look at some of the old buildings and houses in the city and then I think about my own designs. Not ordinary stuff, mind-bending buildings. They would be different, my own thing, you dig?"

Katie nodded.

"But...that's not the case is it?" he asked. "Despite who I could be, I'm not. I live life on the edge, and I like it that way. I don't have any plans to change that part of me."

"Then you're a daredevil. Whether you're on a bike, or you're designing unusual buildings, you want to be noticed as different. That makes you a daredevil, so that's what you were born to be."

Dylan nodded. "Yeah, I think you might be right. I suppose either way I grew up I would still have that wild streak in me, so it's fair to say I was born a daredevil. What about you, baby? Since we have me all figured out?"

"Me, I'm complicated. I've been trying to think of an answer for days and I'm still nowhere close. But I'm going to find one. Before this year is over I'm going to answer that question. I vow that by the end of 1967, I, Katie Searfus, will know who I was born to be." She took a long toke on the dwindling joint.

"Fair enough. Are you cold?" Dylan asked. She nodded and he slipped his arms around her. Katie leaned comfortably against his body.

"When I was a little kid I used to stare at the stars. I thought they were past generations looking down on us, watching over us, you dig? I'd look up at all those stars and I'd think that was my grandparents and my great grandparents all the way back, watching over me, making sure I was doing what I was supposed to be doing and protecting me."

"I used to stare at them and wish I could go there. Anywhere to get out of my parents' house."

"That bad?" Dylan asked. In his opinion, anyone who grew up with money was automatically happy.

"Money doesn't mean happiness, Dylan. Of course, being dirt poor doesn't mean happiness either, so I guess what I mean to say is 'things are rough all over, whether you're on the west side or on the east side.'" Katie smiled, pleased with her quote from S.E. Hinton's *The Outsiders*, which in 1967 had just been released.

Dylan stared at her. Obviously he hadn't read the book.

"It doesn't matter if you're rich or poor. Everyone has problems. They may not be the same, but they're still problems. Nobody lives in perfect peace and harmony."

"Maybe, but people with money are a lot closer to it," Dylan countered. "You have choices with money. In poverty you don't even have those."

"That's not true. My father is a CEO in his own company. An arrogant, opinionated, all around bad guy who will do anything, including stab a best friend in the back to get ahead. He's had affairs with every secretary he's ever had and multiple women in between. He's locked into that lifestyle. Do you think he still has choices? Not anymore; he's a slave to the establishment he helped build. All that bread, you probably think he's happy, but he isn't, he's miserable.

My mother? She's a corporate wife. She pretends to be something special, turning her nose up at others, but beneath the act she's miserable too. She has the golf course, or should I say, the bar at the country club. She has her bridge partners, her volunteer work. She drinks socially, privately, or for no reason at all. Not to mention her illicit affairs to get back at my father. They are a dysfunctional mess. I couldn't wait to get out of that house and I have no intentions of ever going back. And I'm never going to live like them," Katie said, thinking of her own failed marriage and how she had indeed become her mother.

"Do you have siblings?" Dylan asked.

"I have a younger brother. He plays the establishment gig better than I do. Only now he's signed himself up for the military."

"Yikes."

"Yikes is right. He's just getting out of boot camp and he'll be deployed to Vietnam soon."

"Wow, babe, that's heavy."

"Yeah, very heavy."

Katie wanted to tell him the truth, that her brother would be dead by the end of October, shot in the back of the head, but again she bit her tongue.

"You don't have siblings?" Katie asked.

"I bet I do, somewhere out there but where, who the fuck knows? As far as children of my mother, fortunately I am the only one. I wouldn't wish that bitch on anyone."

"Oh."

"As you said, foxy lady, things are rough all over."

Katie stared at him. His light brown hair was neatly trimmed, although his bangs fell into his eyes occasionally, which just added to an aura of mystery. His eyes, normally a light blue, appeared black in the moonlight. He was handsome. It had been several days since he'd shaved, preferring the midnight shadow look that made him appear tough, but with a shave and the right clothing he could look classy and impressive.

"Hey, I know it's a lot to ask, but I have this party to go to and I need an escort."

"A hippie party?"

"Unfortunately not. It's a cocktail party in Antioch. My parents are throwing it."

At first Dylan said nothing, he just stared at her and then he started to laugh. "You're kidding right?"

"I wish I was."

"You want me, a Hells Angel, to take you to some rich ass party in Antioch? Let me guess it's with doctors, lawyers, and Indian chiefs?"

"Not as exciting as that I'm afraid. These guests are businessmen and their corporate wives, perhaps a few mistresses here and there."

"I think a hippie party sounds better."

"I think so too."

"Why are you going? Fake the flu or something if you don't want to go."

"I can't. It's hard to explain, but I've been getting these monthly checks from my mother."

"Because you're disinherited?"

"Well not yet, but I'm working towards it. In the meantime, I might as well get as much bread as I can before they shut off the faucet. You dig?"

Dylan shook his head. "Okay, I'm lost. Let's try this again."

Katie took a deep breath, choosing her next words carefully. "It's like this. I can live in the Haight with money or without money. I'll survive either way. But right now, if my mother is still willing to fork out the bucks then why not go with the groove, baby?"

"Okay, but...?"

"But... those monthly checks stop if I choose to have the flu on the night of the party. My parents and their friends are bad news, but for one night, faced with the alternative, I can stand them."

"I see. So they still own you?"

"Until the stakes get too high, which they will."

"And then you'll cave in, give up your hippie ways and go home. You'll rejoin that establishment, marry a business executive, and have WASP babies."

"Not this time," Katie said, staring deeply into Dylan's dark eyes, trying to show dire sincerity.

"Okay, I believe you, but where do you draw the line?"

"When their demands begin to infringe on my lifestyle. Once that happens, I'll be a hippie living off the land in Marin County. When I'm living there I won't need her bread. They can burn that shit for all I care; in fact, I wish they would."

"I don't believe you mean that," Dylan said with a Cheshire Cat grin.

Katie smiled. How do you explain to a twenty-four year old man that you've lived with money, albeit unhappily, all your life, and that this time around you wanted to try it the other way around?

"There isn't any way for me to explain how strongly I feel about this, except to say that I guarantee it."

"You're right, I don't think you can explain it to me."

"So how about it?"

"What, the party? Are you fucking serious?" he asked. "Why isn't Ron taking you? And besides all that, why do you need an escort at all? This is your parents' house, are you scared to go there alone?"

"Hmm, where to begin? My father has a young Robert Redford look-alike executive working for him. My parents seem to think that he would be the perfect husband. I think he is a manipulator and an opportunist. When he looks at me all he sees is money and power. The clown came to the city a few weeks ago and made a big scene at my apartment complex. I called Ron and he met me there. When Mark kept rapping at me with all his bullshit, Ron confronted him."

"Ron confronted Mark the executive?"

Katie nodded. "Since Mark works for my father and my dad accepts him as a surrogate son, that confrontation caused quite a stir in the family. For that reason, Ron can't go anywhere near the party."

"I see, because Mark the executive will be there?"

"That's right."

"I'm assuming that pretty boy Mark is an annoyance to you."

"More like a stalker. As I said, he sees me as his opportunity into my father's company and he's not about to take no for an answer. He's the reason I moved into Ron's house. I couldn't stay where I was because he knew where I lived. I had to move. I figured he might be scared of Ron and Frog, which might make him stay away from me. That's how I ended up living at Moonbeam's pad."

Dylan smiled and ran his hand across Katie's jawline and then over her full lips. "You need a bodyguard, somebody tough, so you decided on an undercover Hells Angel. What better way to get revenge on your parents while protecting yourself from Mark the executive?"

"Yeah, that's what I need, and on top of all that you're pretty cute too."

Dylan smiled. "Well, if Ron might scare this stalker asshole then he better be fucking terrified of me because I'm not going to play games with pretty boy. He comes to 'Frisco again to bother you, then me and a few of my boys are going to pay him a visit."

Katie smiled, imagining Mark's face if three or four Hells Angels showed up to "talk" to him.

"Does that mean you'll come with me?" she asked hopefully.

"Sure, I don't know why I'm doing this, but yeah I'll go with you to the fucking party." He shook his head in disbelief. "Man, the things I'll do for a beautiful hippie chick."

"Oh thank you, Dylan!" Katie said. She flung her arms around his neck and hugged him tightly. His arms slid up her back and for a few moments they stood heart to heart, holding each other. "Although you might not want to go with me after you hear what I have to say next." She pulled away from his warm body and swallowed nervously, trying to draw enough courage to breach the next topic. The real reason she had agreed to take this ride with Dylan. "I have something I need to talk to you about..."

"Why did that sound bad?" Dylan asked. When she didn't answer he stood and stared out across the bay. "I see, it sounded bad because it is. Okay, you've got my attention now, baby, what's your question?"

Katie rose to her feet and moved close to him, wanting to see his face clearly. "I want to talk to you about Frog. I know that you're involved in some kind of business deal together."

She didn't need light to see the shocked expression on his face. That look told her everything she needed to know. Dylan was involved, even the moonlight couldn't hide his guilt.

"What about Frog?" he asked, trying to act surprised.

"Look, I'm not going to play games or beat around the bush."

"You're not? Isn't that what you've been doing? You accepted this ride, we've been discussing topics that men and women discuss when they're...anyway, now I find out that you're here with me because you want to talk to me about Frog. I'd call that leading me on, wouldn't you?"

Katie knew this game oh so well. Mark used that tactic; it was called "I'll turn the subject on to the questioner so that the original topic is overlooked." A twenty-four year old man, no matter how street smart he might be, couldn't possibly play the game as well as Mark Rhodes. Dylan was out of his league on this one.

Ignoring the remark completely, Katie continued. "As I was saying, I'm not sure how to start this conversation so I'll begin by telling you what I know. I know the night of the Angel's party Frog met with two of your guys. The same guys who now own a garage over on Seventh Street where you and Joey just happen to be working. I've seen Frog go into that shop several times," she lied, playing on a bluff, "and I'm fairly sure he doesn't own a Harley. That means your shop is involved with much more than selling motorcycle parts. If I were guessing, considering the year and what drugs are moving in and out of the Haight, then I'd say we're talking about heroin." She waited several seconds to let the topic sink in and when Dylan didn't respond, she went on. "Have you seen Frog recently? I bet you have."

Dylan was bothered by what she was saying and she could tell that her hunch was heading her in the right direction.

"Moonbeam described his condition as being 'beat to shit.' I'd say he was bludgeoned deliberately doing a job that you know about. The reason that you know about that job is because you and Joey are both in on it."

"Why are you telling me this?" he asked. "How do you expect me to respond?"

"I guess I don't care how you respond. I'm not here for your story and I'm not here for excuses or for graphic details. To be honest, I don't want to know about any of it. I'm here for Frog. I know that he, you, and Joey are involved in something stupid that will have him dead before the end of summer. I'm here to ask if you know what you're doing? I think you're a better person than you think you are. I'd bet inside you know how dangerous this is and you know that it's wrong."

"Wrong? You're calling my actions wrong? All of these accusations are coming from an entitled little rich girl. What do you know about right and wrong?"

"Look, I'm not here to judge anybody, even though right now you probably think that I am. I already told you I don't want to know the specifics, but I'm not stupid either. I'm here as a concerned friend. You see, Frog will be dead by the end of summer and I'm sorry to tell you this, but so will you," she lied, twisting him into her plans.

"What?" Dylan's mind was blown by the twisted turn the conversation had taken.

"I have dreams, premonitions really. My grandmother used to call it 'the shining'" Katie said, paraphrasing from Stephen King's book, another phrase she plagiarized from the future.

Dylan stared at her and crossed his arms in front of his chest, all hostility gone now, his face calm and blank. "What are you talking about?"

"I had a premonition. I saw you and Frog die."

"Are you telling me that all of this, this whole conversation that we've been having, is about a premonition? And you're here to warm me about it?"

Katie nodded, and felt a slight twinge of guilt over the story she was weaving together.

"Okay, you're a hippie, why not? It comes with the territory, right? I'm all ears, pretty lady, go on." Dylan returned to the blanket and sat back down.

Katie's head churned as she fished for information. *What would Melinda Gordon, Sylvia Brown or John Edwards say?* Then she decided to start at the beginning.

"Ever since I was a little girl I've had 'dreams,'" she said.

"Dreams?" Dylan asked with a disbelieving smirk on his handsome face.

"Yes, dreams."

"Did I tell you that you're exceptionally pretty but that I think you're odd?" he asked, his face softening.

"Yes, I think you did mention that." Katie smiled, pleased that her fabricated story was sucking him in. "I have realistic dreams that come true. Scary stuff would happen when I was growing up and I'd know about it before it took place. Things like auto accidents, deaths in the family, breaking news events. I even dreamt that Kennedy was going to die days before it happened. I know you're doubting what I'm saying, everyone does at first."

"Everyone doubts your premonitions? I can't imagine why," he said, laughing until she glared at him. "I'm sorry, go on. I won't interrupt again and I won't make jokes, I promise." He used a hand gesture suggesting that he was zipping his mouth shut.

"At the end of April, Mohammad Ali is going to be drafted. He'll refuse to go and the boxing commission will take his championship belt away. Not just the belt, the title and everything that goes with it. They'll try to put him in jail and they'll even try to stop him from ever professionally boxing again."

"Mohammad Ali? You mean the black boxer that used to be Cassius Clay?"

"That's right. He'll refuse to fight in a war that white men started, saying that he won't kill people of color who have never done anything against him."

"And you dreamt this?"

"That's right," she said, nodding her head. "When it comes true then you'll believe me. After that happens, what I'm going to tell you next will mean much more. Right now you're a disbeliever and that's alright, but listen carefully to what I have to say because come May, I guarantee, you'll be thinking about it a lot."

"Ready," he said with a touch of amusement on his face.

"In my dream, you and Frog are beaten to death. A lot of men are involved. They throw your battered remains into a shallow grave and then they cover you up with dirt. You and Frog disappear and your remains are never found. Come the end of August, you and Frog will enter a forest somewhere and you'll never come out."

She could tell she hit a nerve. The disbelief fell from his face, replaced by a blank stare. "And this happens at the end of August?" The cocky amusement was gone from his voice.

"In my dream it happens at the end of August but sometimes my dreams are off and they happen earlier than I predict. So I'd say it can happen anytime from now until the end of August. What I know for sure is that come September, neither you nor Frog will be alive to see it."

"This is a dream?"

"No, it's a premonition, and you're going to find out that my predictions come true."

"Okay that's eerie. So, what's the moral of the story?"

"The moral? If you need a moral then I guess I can come up with a few clichés, including crime doesn't pay, or karma's a bitch. Any way you cut the mustard, Dylan, your days are numbered."

Dylan wanted to laugh. He wanted to show her that he was tough, that her metaphysical bullshit didn't bother him, but she'd hit a raw nerve and he started to shiver. Suddenly the color drained from his face and he swallowed hard. He put his hands in his lap to stop them from shaking.

"Wow, man," he said with a shake of his head. "Wow, what a trip." He stood and started to pace.

"What is it?"

"You man, you and your dream. This whole fucking thing. Katie, I have dreams too. Maybe not as realistic as what you're describing, but I've had certain recurring dreams my whole life." He sat on the blanket, took both of her hands in his own and turned her so she was facing him. "The worst is that I'm lying in a hole and someone's lying beside me. I know the person is dead because I can smell them, and I know that I am dying too. I'm in a forest, the sun is high, and I know I should be hot but I'm freezing. Flies are landing on my face and I can't move to swat them away. Then someone above starts to throw dirt into the hole and I can't do anything to stop it. I wake when my grave is half full, drenched in sweat and gasping for air. When I have that dream I can't go back to sleep because it feels so fucking real."

"Jesus," Katie said aloud. *Have I accidently hit upon the truth?* That was how it sounded. She felt the hair on the back of her neck stand on end and she shuddered.

"I've had that dream for as long as I can remember," Dylan said. Suddenly freezing, he wrapped his arms around his body for warmth. "Even as a little kid I used to dream that I was being buried alive."

Katie put her hand on his shoulder. Not only would Frog die at the end of summer, she knew now that Dylan would turn up missing too.

"And your other dream?" she asked. "You said there were two."

"The other one is just as vivid, and it's recurring too."

He hesitated, shoving the hair out of his eyes, then he pulled another joint out of his pocket and lit it.

"I wake in this hallway that's filled with doors. The doors open and close and people dressed in period clothing walk in and out; weird shit like flappers, soldiers, musicians, even political figures. There's this ugly fucking hag bitch with no teeth. She's in this maid uniform and she carries around this old fashioned key ring that she uses to lock and unlock the doors.

"Whenever she can she corners people and ridicules them. She'll force them against a wall and then breath in their face till they puke." He shivered, remembering. "There's always a party going on and everyone is happy, except for the maid. I know instinctively that everyone there is dead, including me." Dylan's eyes seemed to focus far away, staring at a memory.

A vivid picture of the hall flashed in Katie's mind and she knew beyond a shadow of a doubt that she had been there too.

"There's a girl somewhere in all those hallways," Dylan continued. "I don't know who she is because I can never see her face clearly, but I feel this intense love for her. We are never together because our souls just pass each other by, but we touch just barely, enough for me to feel her flesh but never close enough so that I can actually see her. When I do catch her shadow or I feel her presence there's this feeling that comes over me. It's so powerful that I can remember it when I wake the next morning. I know it sounds ridiculous but I grieve the next day because I can still feel her touch and I want her so badly even though she doesn't really exist."

Katie was paralyzed. A bitter wind whipped across her body numbing her limbs, and she couldn't move. What had started with a hunch and a plan of deception had turned on her. She was the one who was surprised. She had no idea that Dylan was involved in any of this. She had bluffed her way along hoping to get information out of him, but she had never expected this. Everything she learned in the early morning hours of April 16th would haunt her for a long time to come but now, numbed by the cold and filled with exhaustion, she couldn't feel anything except astonishment.

"When I was little, I used to think that someday I would meet my mystery love, that our paths would mystically cross because we were destined to be together. I think that's the reason I got through my fucked up childhood as well as I did, because I always knew that she was out there, and that it was only a matter of time before I bumped into her," Dylan said. "That knowledge somehow made everything else seem all right. As I got older, I thought differently. Like maybe I'm not supposed to ever meet her, that this is a punishment. I know she's out there somewhere, that she's mine, but circumstances being what they are, we can't ever be together. That's one harsh punishment right? This twisted part of me believes just that. I'd even go so far as to say that we've had several lifetimes together just like this one. Always coming close to each other, close enough so that I can feel her but never close enough to meet.

"I bet at some point I even bump into her you know? Like she lives on the same street and we pass each other in the grocery store all the time, that kind of close. I believe she's always around the next corner but that I'm never fast enough to catch up with her. Think of it, an eternity of lives always coming close to the woman that I love but never being allowed to be with her.

"That's what I feel the day after I have that dream. Like once again she was there and she slipped right through my fingers."

Katie shivered. Who would have thought that Dylan was metaphysical? A tough biker, a romantic, and a spiritualist as well, no wonder she found him attractive.

He pointed east where the sun was just popping up. "Look." Dylan put his arm around Katie and she leaned against his body. For the next few minutes they sat watching the sunrise over the San Francisco Bay, awed by its beauty.

"You ready to go home, honey?" Dylan asked. He glanced at his wristwatch and laughed. "I have to be at work in two hours."

"I had no idea that we've been talking that long."

"I'll tell you what, this is a first. I stayed out all night with a beautiful chick and all we did was talk," Dylan said. He chuckled. "Who would ever believe that? Let's go, baby."

He jumped to his feet and helped Katie up. She folded the blanket and they walked back to Dylan's bike hand in hand. He put the blanket away, handed Katie the German helmet, and before starting the bike he turned and face her.

"There's something about you, Katie, something very different. It's crazy but I feel like my soul was just touched by my mystery woman, only this time, I actually got to see her face." He kissed her then.

Chapter 26

The Vietnam War was a result of centuries of foreign domination. First China ruled ancient Vietnam, and then in the 1800s, France took control and established French Indochina.

In the Twentieth Century, nationalist movements emerged, demanding more self-government for the Vietnamese and less control by France. The most popular of these was led by Ho Chi Minh, the communist George Washington of his people who was credited with driving the French out of the country.

Fighting between Ho Chi Minh's forces and the French ended in 1954, after a humiliating defeat at Dien Bien Phu, which pushed the French into a peace settlement.

When France pulled out, the Geneva Accords of 1954 declared a cease-fire and divided Vietnam into two parts: North Vietnam (under Ho and his communist forces) and South Vietnam (under Bao Dai). The dividing line was set at the 17th parallel and was surrounded by a demilitarized zone, or DMZ.

The northern Vietnamese seeking a united country had no intention of following through with the peaceful conditions. What ensued instead was a civil war, which turned into an international conflict.

In 1955 when the country was officially divided, the people had a three hundred day period to choose a side and relocate. During this "free period," most Catholics went south and the communists went north.

About one hundred thousand communist Viet Minh guerrillas, who had been fighting the French in the south, relocated to the north. They operated against the South Vietnamese government much as they had against the French, murdering landlords and village officials, collecting taxes from the peasants, and recruiting new soldiers.

Obviously the new force couldn't be called Viet Minh, because the vast majority of Vietnamese regarded the Viet Minh as the army that had liberated their country from the French. So a new name was chosen, Viet Cong, meaning Vietnamese Communist.

These former southern guerrillas were retrained and then sent down the jungle route that would become famous as the Ho Chi Minh Trail; ten thousand miles of secret roadway that carried men and war supplies south. This "trail", was actually a series of roads, footpaths, and waterways that when combined wove from North Vietnam through Laos and Cambodia all the way into the RVN (Republic of Vietnam.)

The United States got involved in an advisory capacity. By 1961, fifteen hundred American advisors were in the country teaching the South Vietnamese how to fight against the Viet Cong.

Because of US involvement, China, who saw the Americans as "imperialist, capitalist aggressors", sent in troops and advisors to "protect the people." The Soviet Union, who couldn't allow themselves to be outdone by amateur socialists from China, sent in troops and advisors too.

What resulted was the North Vietnamese Army (NVA), or as they were also called, the People's Army of Vietnam (PAVN), allied with the Viet Cong, or as they were sometimes called, The National Front for the Liberation of South Vietnam (NFL). Their cause was supported by China and the USSR (The Union of Soviet Socialist Republics).

On the opposite side of the war was the Army of the Republic of Vietnam, (the ARVN) or South Vietnam, aided by the United States, UK, Australia, and South Korea. Essentially, the civil war became a war between socialism and capitalism, a playing field for the Cold War.

What complicated matters more for South Vietnam's cause was the high percentage of South Vietnamese who supported the Viet Cong. Because of civilian loyalty to the other side, US soldiers could never be sure who was fighting with or against them.

The Cold War played a major role in Vietnam politics. US policy at the time believed in the domino theory, that the fall of North Vietnam to communism could trigger all of Southeast Asia to fall, setting off a communist chain reaction.

Within a year of the Geneva Accords, the United States offered support to the unpopular South Vietnamese leader Ngo Dinh Diem, a fanatical Catholic anti-communist politician with a poor record on human rights. Although Diem was unpopular with the Vietnamese people, who thought of him as corrupt and brutal, he was still backed by the United States. In fact, Ngo Dinh Diem was so disliked by his own people that on November 2, 1963 the South Vietnamese Army allegedly overthrew his rule and murdered him.

President Lyndon B. Johnson deployed the first American troops into Vietnam on February 9, 1965. A US Marine Corps Hawk air defense missile battalion was sent to Da Nang to provide protection for a key US airbase.

Military aid between the RVN, led by Nguyen Van Thieu and the United States, would continue until America was deeply involved in the conflict. When the United States finally pulled out in1973, the civil war would continue for another two years. It ended in 1975, when the North Vietnamese Army defeated the South and united the country under communistic rule.

***

His first month in Vietnam had been a real eye opener. As a "greenie", he'd been told that he had a sixty percent chance of dying during the first six months of combat. If he could make it to the six-month deadline, then his chances of getting through his thirteen-month tour of duty improved. But at the rate he was going, Richard knew he'd be lucky to make it through the next few days.

He had arrived at the Da Nang Airport in South Vietnam on April 12th, 1967. After a twenty-two hour flight on Pan Am Airlines, Richard and his fellow Marines arrived exhausted, dirty and disoriented.

When he walked off the plane the tropical heat and humidity hit him in the face like a brick wall. He'd heard that Vietnam was hot, but he had never expected humidity to this degree. Almost immediately his flesh became damp, and by the time he and the other "newbie" Marines were loaded onto a helicopter to be flown into Da Nang base 80 miles to the north, his shirt was wet through and sticking to his body.

When they arrived at Da Nang base, Richard and four other men were loaded on a bus to transport them to their new home, Camp Carroll.

The bus was military issue. Plain green seats like you'd find on a school bus, and regrettably, no air-conditioning. The bus didn't even have windows. In their place was a layer of chicken wire spread across the openings. This, they were told, was protection against hand grenades, which could be tossed into the moving bus by anyone, including civilian women and children.

After a twenty-minute bus ride through a country devastated by an ongoing civil war, Richard arrived at what would be his new home, Camp Carroll.

Camp Carroll was an artillery base located five miles from the town of Cam Lo. The camp was named in honor of Captain J.J. Carroll, the commanding officer of Kilo Company 3rd Battalion 4th Marines, who was killed during Operation Prairie by friendly tank fire.

Camp Carroll was commissioned on October 5, 1966, and on November 10, it was equipped with heavy artillery guns. These weapons included the M-107 and the 175 mm guns, the most powerful artillery guns that the American forces possessed.

Richard had been assigned to the 2nd Battalion 9th Marine troop known as "Hell in a Helmet." His troop's mission was to locate, close in, and destroy the enemy by fire and maneuver or repel the enemy's assault with fire and close combat.

The 2/9 was a proud unit first established in 1917 during the First World War. It was reactivated in 1942 shortly after the attack on Pearl Harbor and then again in 1965 for the Vietnam Conflict.

The 2nd Battalion 9th Marines were ordered to Vietnam on July 4, 1965. During their first year, they took part in forty-five battalion-sized, and several company-sized operations. During the next four years, they operated in or around Da Nang, Hue, Phu Bai, Dong Ha, Camp Carroll, Cam Lo, Con Thien, Than Cam Son, Quanq Tri, Cua Viet, Vandergrift Combat Base and Khe Sanh.

For its actions in Vietnam, 2nd Battalion 9th Marines were awarded a third Presidential Unit Citation, a bronze star in lieu of second award of the National Defense Service Medal, the Vietnam Service Medal with two silver stars, and Vietnam Cross of Gallantry with Palm.

In August of 1969, they left Vietnam and returned to Okinawa. Its role in the Southeast Asian Conflict ended with the recapture of the Mayaquez and the landing on Koh Tang Island in May 1975. Camp Carroll would be surrendered to the North Vietnamese Army on April 2, 1972.

The 9th Marines distinguished themselves wherever they fought. They set precedents that Marines and units throughout Vietnam would emulate, precedents in protecting Vietnamese rice crops, in fighting the Viet Cong, and in heavy fighting with the North Vietnamese Army in and near the DMZ.

The troop had a high mortality rate because of its location at Camp Carroll, where their mission, to watch over the camp, specifically protecting it against the North Vietnamese who had taken occupation of the DMZ, was extremely dangerous.

As an elite club, membership was earned, not given. This meant that making friends wasn't easy. Seasoned soldiers, knowing the odds against "newbies", were slow to accept the new additions that were thought of as replacements for casualties, with a high probability of becoming a casualty themselves.

Watching new soldiers die had taught the men of 2/9 to close themselves off emotionally, becoming professionally cold to the new arrivals.

To be fully accepted as a full member of "Hell in a Helmet," a man had to prove himself by either staying alive a full six months, or by distinguishing himself in battle. Until then, the newbies were left to their own devices, causing them to create a bond between themselves, which excluded them from the rest of the company.

Rich's first month in 'Nam consisted of getting used to the place, basically learning the essentials of staying alive. This meant learning what to do and what not to do, regulating one's own malaria regiment, learning the camp schedule, getting over jet lag, and allowing the body to get used to the heat, torrential rain, bugs, and flavorless food.

There had been several small skirmishes during Richard's first month, but essentially it had been calm, too calm. Job rotation, patrol duty, latrine duty, and other humdrum assignments became his daily life; boring but essentially safe. That silence gave the newbies a false sense of security even though they, and everyone else, could feel a storm brewing.

Against the Geneva Accord, the North Vietnamese Army built numerous artillery positions, camps, supply sites, and other well-protected military installations within the DMZ. These sites conducted frequent attacks on the American soldiers, who were able to shoot back in self-defense but were not allowed to pursue their attackers into the DMZ.

In the spring of 1967, just before Richard's arrival, the North Vietnamese Army conducted major operations from Khe Sanh, the district capital of Hurong Hoa District in the Quang Tri Province.

The increased hostile activity in northern Quang Tri had finally gotten the attention of Washington. On May 18th, 1967 they approved a raid into the DMZ, which would begin at dawn. This mission, a combined effort by the Army of South Vietnam and the US Marines, would be conducted as four simultaneous but separate operations. The attacks where known as: Operation Lam Son 54, Operation Beau Charger, and Operation Hickory/Operation Belt Tight.

On that day, H Regiment was awakened before dawn and ordered into the DMZ along with many other troops stationed at Camp Carroll. For Richard and the other four greenies who'd arrived with him, their virgin mission had just begun.

Now, two days later, these same newbies, all under the age of twenty-one, were crouched in a foxhole. Fresh to combat they stayed low, completely silent, and prayed for their lives.

To Richard's left was Clyde Owens, a farm boy from Ohio. Owens had been raised around guns, making him the most experienced shot in the foxhole. At the age of twenty, he was also the oldest of the five soldiers. Beside him sat four terrified "city boys", recently trained in weapons during their twelve week course in boot camp. All five had only been in Vietnam for a little over a month and the M16s at their sides still felt awkward.

On Richard's right, Tom Lewis, a tall, spindly city boy from Chicago sat crying, a stream of mud smeared on his sunburned face.

Across from Richard was Edwin Torres from New York City, and next to him, Jesse Rodriguez from Austin, Texas.

"Incoming!" Owens screamed, and the five young men pulled their bodies down as debris fell into the hole surrounding them.

Lewis sniffled and rubbed his dirt stained face. Rodriguez said a few Hail Mary's, Owens called the VC "a bunch of fucking bastards", Torres added a few descriptive words of his own, and Richard laid face up staring at the jungle and hating it.

In the two days he'd spent stuck in a foxhole, Richard had learned several valuable lessons. One, the North Vietnamese were able fighters, well trained, and fearless in battle; two, they appeared to be gifted in strategic planning; and three, they were fighting for their own country. Adding emotions to the pot was something the US soldiers couldn't imitate.

If you took the average U.S. soldier, all they wanted to do was to stay alive and go back home. The Vietnamese *were* home. They were fighting for their families, their past, present and future. That made them fearless opponents.

Richard swallowed and looked at his watch. It had been forty-eight hours since they were stranded. Within that time there had been troop movement, Richard was sure of that. What he wasn't sure of was whether they were still sitting on their own side's territory. Despite their uncertainty they sat waiting, conserving what little they had left: two ready pouches each and enough water to last another day. By tomorrow afternoon they would have to make a decision.

Richard tried to remember why he didn't want to stay in college. Right now, that life didn't look as bad as he had thought. He wished that he were sitting in a class instead of a foxhole. He shut his eyes and for several seconds tried to imagine it.

Owens studied the compass on his knife, turning it in several directions. "I'm telling you we should get out of this fucking hole, head south back the way we came."

"No man! They were south before all this shelling started. Since then there's been so much troop movement, there's no telling where the 2/9 is, or any other US troops for that matter." Torres shook his head adamantly. "I'm not fucking going anywhere."

"But chances are—" Rodriguez began.

"Chances are if we step out of this hole we're going to get our fucking heads blown off," Torres cut in.

"But if we're in enemy territory, staying here isn't going to help us," Rodriguez argued.

"If man, *if*. If you want to make a run for it dude, you go right ahead. Me, I'm staying put."

"So we're just going to sit here until we die? Or they catch us?" Rodriguez asked. He wiped his face with the backside of his hand and spread a layer of mud across his face. He was sweating heavily, they all were.

"Both of you calm the fuck down," Richard intervened. "This isn't helping anyone! Before Lt. Franco disappeared, he knew where we were. We're in the same spot, man, give or take a few feet. They'll send men out to search for us, all we have to do is wait. Be patient, man. With this fucking shelling going on nobody is going to be searching for us, not yet. We have enough food and water for the rest of today. As soon as this shit calms down they'll find us, you'll see."

"And when we run out of supplies and they still haven't come for us? What then?" Lewis asked wiping his tear stained face.

"If we run out and we can't hold on any longer, then we'll make a decision. When we do we'll make it as a group, we're all in this together," Richard snapped.

"They haven't sent anyone because they think we're fucking dead. They know the Lieutenant is dead so they assume we are too. I'd bet nobody knows we're out here," Torres said.

"So basically, we're fucked," Rodriguez said. Artillery fire shot across the sky and the men ducked.

"That's right, man. That's exactly what I'm saying. So stop fucking complaining and be glad that we're still alive," Richard said with an authority he didn't know he possessed.

Two days ago Lt. Franco had gathered the radio operator, Phil Gorman, along with the five greenies, and they had headed north away from the 2/9. Their mission was simple: head south and rendezvous with F Company, who were just entering the conflict.

Lt. Franco would talk with their troop leader, brief him on current troop movement and locations, and then they would return to their own company. It was meant as a simple excursion, a good training opportunity for the newest of the men, a chance to get them away from the conflict.

Richard sat remembering the trip and trying to understand where they had gone wrong. At first, the walk through the jungle terrain was easy despite the high humidity, mosquitoes, and dirt, but halfway to their target unexpected artillery fire exploded and the men were forced to hit the ground.

"What the fuck? There's no troop stationed in this area," Lt. Franco had complained. He turned to the radio operator. "Gorman, get on the radio and find out what the hell is going on."

That's when their horrendous adventure started.

Gorman fiddled with the radio as another wave of explosives detonated somewhere to their left sending shrapnel and debris into the bushes where they were hiding.

"Fucking gook bastards," Lt. Franco snarled, surveying their surroundings. Noticing a string of large boulders thirty feet away he began to crawl. "On your stomachs, men," he called back and they followed.

Richard remembered crawling for all he was worth. In front of him Rodriguez was kicking back a steady flow of rocks and dirt, which made its way into his nose and mouth. He sneezed, rubbed at his dribbling nose, and continued crawling without losing pace with the others.

In what seemed to be hours, but was merely a matter of minutes, they arrived at the boulders and threw themselves behind the protection of the rocks, panting heavily.

"Gorman, Gorman. Where the hell is Gorman?"

Owens pointed towards the spot they had just vacated. There, lying in the brush, was the still body of the radio operator.

"I don't think he made it, sir," Owens responded as Lewis started to sob.

"Jesus Christ, Gorman." The Lt. turned towards the new soldiers. "Wait here," he told them and then he crawled back to where Gorman lay unmoving in the dirt.

Richard and Owens peeked between two large boulders, silently watching their commanding officer crawl away from the group. He spent several seconds examining Gorman's much too still form, shook his head, took hold of the radio and made his way back to the rest of the troop.

"Shrapnel got him. One in the jugular," the Lieutenant informed them. "The radio's been chewed up something awful. I'm not sure if I can get it working." The Lieutenant fiddled with the thing, which was just as unresponsive as Gorman.

They heard gunfire close by but moving in the opposite direction. The men sighed in relief.

"Fucking broken piece of shit. If Gorman were here he could get it working..." The Lieutenant had tried to act cool but Richard and the other men could tell he was terrified. He too was a newbie; he'd only been at Camp Carroll for two months and this was his first scouting expedition too.

"Listen!" he told the men. "I think there's an American patrol up this hill maybe a mile or two ahead. I'm going to try to make it there. You men stay here behind these boulders. I'll be back."

"You're going alone?" Torres asked, pulling himself into a semi-sitting position.

The Lieutenant nodded. "No point in all of us going. With any luck I'll be back within the hour and we'll have this shit all sorted out."

"But sir..."

Owens had tried to reason with the inexperienced officer, who in his opinion was making a mistake by leaving the group.

"That's an order, Private."

"Yes, sir," Owens said, turning away.

Within seconds of Lt. Franco's departure there was an explosion from above in the same direction.

"Oh fuck, oh fuck," Rodriguez sniveled. "He's dead man, he's dead. They killed him and we're next."

Lewis wept.

"No man, I don't think so. I think we're stuck between two hostile groups and neither of them knows that we're here," Owens reasoned.

More artillery exploded, this time from somewhere up the hill. "Owens is right. I think we've wandered into the middle of two groups who are firing on each other," Richard agreed.

"Now what, man?" Torres asked.

"Now we get out of the fucking way and we let them have their battle." Owens pointed to a raised dirt area under a series of large over grown trees. "There! We go there and we dig in. We're sitting ducks here. If whoever is up there decides to fire down then we're fucked."

"You're the country boy, Owens. If you say we're better protected down there, then I believe you. What are we waiting for? Let's go men, head out," Richard said, and then leading the group, he found himself flat in the dirt crawling once again, this time down an incline.

Despite the overhead rumble of shelling, all five men made it safely to the trees next to a dirt mound.

"If someone comes looking for us or the lieutenant happens to come back then we'll be able to see him from here," Owens added, dropped his pack, and pulled out a trowel. The other men followed suit, and an hour later they had a decent foxhole where the group pooled their resources and started rationing water.

Now, forty-eight hours later they were still hidden in that foxhole. Above them, a heavy artillery match took place and all they could do was sit and pray that their own side would find them.

This morning they had finished off the last of their water supply. Richard knew it was only a matter of time before they'd be forced to make a difficult decision and he knew that it would come down to him and Owens to enforce it.

"I've heard that Vietnamese prisoner of war camps are brutal. They torture soldiers, even peel their fingernails off," Rodriguez said.

"Would you fucking shut up?" Torres yelled.

"Fuck you, you Puerto Rican *pendejo*."

Torres made a grab for him and Owens blocked it.

"No, man. We aren't going to start fighting amongst ourselves. Stop, both of you." The two men sat back on their heels and nodded in agreement.

"Rodriguez, quit with the negative shit, man. It's not helping anyone. Just sit back and be cool. We've made it this far, we can wait a little longer," Owens said, patting him on the back reassuringly.

Subdued, Rodriguez leaned against the dirt wall and started praying.

Meanwhile, Owens made his way across the other men and flopped next to Richard.

"It's up to you and me, Searfus. We're going to have to figure a way out of this fucking mess."

"I know," Richard said, looking at the mud that had accumulated around his feet.

"I thought the shelling would stop, you know, they'd move on, start shooting in another direction but...well, it's not looking that way. I don't want the other men to know, but the shelling is getting closer."

"I know," Richard repeated.

"Shall we flip for it?" Owens asked and then chuckled.

"Flip for what, man, command?"

"Nah, I think you and I are in command man. I was talking about directions. Shall we flip a coin to decide which direction we head in?"

Richard smiled and shook his head.

"You're the country boy, I think you'll come up with something more sophisticated than that."

"Yeah, but that doesn't mean it's more reliable. Fuck, I wish I had a shot of tequila right now, or a doobie. Shit man, both sound so good." Owens smacked his lips. "Okay, man, this is how I see it. Lt. Franco got his ass turned around. All of this has to be his mistake. The dude was new himself, that's why they sent him on this little expedition in the first place. The guy seemed like an idiot to me, don't you think the officers thought he was an idiot too? Guy was from where, fucking Detroit? What the hell does he know about jungle warfare? If he were any damn good at his job he'd be back there with the real officers. Nope, they sent him out here to get rid of him."

"What about Gorman?"

"Who knows about that dude? We didn't really get to know him did we? Maybe he was an idiot too. Okay, consider this. Franco fucked up big. The only thing we can be sure of is the direction we came from. We have to head south, Searfus, we don't have another choice."

Mortar and artillery fire exploded. Owens was right it was getting closer. When the dust settled, Torres started to cough.

"What the hell are you two Nancy boys whispering about?" he asked, spitting out mud.

"Is it time to make a decision?" Rodriguez asked hopefully, his voice cracking in fear.

Another round of shelling exploded above their heads, this time much too close. It was obvious things were about to get much worse.

Lewis curled into a ball and Rodriguez finally cracked under the pressure. He screamed and crawled around the foxhole mumbling something incoherent. When the shelling finally ended, his eyes went wild and he tried to scramble out of the hole. In one hop he was at the top trying to run when another round of artillery burst out. Terrified, Rodriguez hit the ground and Torres pulled him back into the hole by his left ankle.

Rodriguez tried to fight him off but the other men jumped in and between the four they were able to pin him to the dirt floor. Unable to move he started to scream.

"Shut up and stay down, you stupid motherfucker! What are you trying to do, you dumb bastard? You want to climb out there and get yourself killed?" Torres screamed through clenched teeth.

"I gotta get out of here, man. I gotta get out, I can't breathe." He screamed and fought against their hold, and then he started to hyperventilate.

"Calm down man, breathe. Breathe brother, deep breaths," Torres repeated. "You have to get this shit under control, man. Shut your eyes."

"Listen," Richard said soothingly, "we're all going to get out of here, okay? We're all leaving just as soon as you get this shit under control. We can't take you anywhere like this, man. You understand me? We need to leave, we all know that, but we can't do it until you're breathing normally. If you're freaking out like this then you'll get us all killed."

"But I gotta get out of here," Rodriguez repeated.

"That's right, and we're all going to do that just as soon as you calm down."

"Right. Okay man, I'm trying." He closed his eyes. After several seconds of heavy breathing, he was able to sit unassisted. Propped against the back of the foxhole he turned his attention to Owens.

"Listen," Owens started. Lewis leaned in closer and nudged Richard's arm. "You tell them, brother."

"We're heading out," Richard announced, clearing his throat. "The only thing we can be sure of is that we came from that direction and it's that direction we're going," he said, pointing towards the cluster of trees they had originally stepped through.

"That's where Gorman's at," Rodriguez said nervously. "That's where they... they killed him."

"No, that's where shrapnel killed him. I'm talking beyond that, back in the lowland, where there's enough trees and brush coverage to protect us. We'll just take our time and slowly work ourselves back in that direction. If we have to, then we'll find another place to dig in, but we can't stay here." Richard was trying hard to make himself sound confident.

"Well we can't go up, that's where Franco got blasted," Torres said. "I'd rather not go forward, and down, that's the direction we're being shelled from so...yeah let's go south." Torres gathered his belongings.

"No man, wait," Owens said. "We're packing light. We're already out of water and food; there's a bunch of shit in this pack that we don't fucking need, we're going to leave it."

For the next few minutes the men lightened their loads, leaving behind anything that they didn't find essential to immediate survival. When they were ready, Richard nodded at each of the soldiers, waited for a break in the shelling, and then hit the ground and crawled through the underbrush, heading towards the decomposing corpse of Lance Corporal Gorman.

Without hesitation he passed the body and continued on into the thick trees and brush. After another twenty feet, he stopped and waited for the rest of the men.

Owens rose to his feet and brushed himself off. He pointed towards a cluster of strangler fig trees. "That direction. We keep those trees to our left and we keep going."

Gunfire exploded and the men jumped, but when they realized it was far away they resumed walking into the jungle.

"You lead, man, I'll take the rear," Owens said.

Richard swallowed hard, nodded, and held his weapon. Carefully, he led the group into the thick of the forest with Torres only steps behind him.

"Fucking ticks, man," Rodriquez said, picking at a black spot on his arm.

"Leave 'em, man. You want to break one of those fucking things off and have half of it stuck inside?" Lewis asked.

"Where the hell are we?" Torres said. "I swear we never walked this far before and we were never in the jungle this long."

"You're right, we weren't." Owens checked the compass on his knife to make sure they were heading in the right direction. "We're running parallel to where we were but there's more coverage here, it's safer."

"I don't know, man, I don't think in this case more coverage is necessarily safer. We're not in Ohio, Owens," Torres said, shaking his head.

"Honestly, man, trust me. This way is longer but it's safer, and I'm sure we're heading in the right direction."

"How do you know?"

"I know how to track, man. My dad was a hunter, a good one too. He taught me everything he knew and his dad taught him everything he knew. This I can tell you with certainty, I can get us back from where we came, unless something unexpected happens."

"It will," Rodriguez said, still picking at the ticks that had embedded themselves in his arm.

"Fucking, Rodriguez, man. You make everything worse." Torres turned to look at him. When he did, North Vietnamese soldiers dressed in camouflage popped out of nowhere.

What happened next took place in slow motion. One second Rodriguez was looking at Torres, his mouth open about to speak, and in the next a bullet entered his right temple. Rodriguez was thrown sideways as his head ripped open. Thick crimson brain matter, along with blood and bone splinters, splattered across Torres's face.

"Fuck!" he screamed, and jumped backwards wiping at the blood in his eyes. Temporarily blind to his attackers, he hit the ground and rolled into a bushy area beside him.

Richard reacted first. Without hesitation a switch went off in his head and he went on autopilot. He felt as if he were outside his own body, watching someone who looked like him raise the M16 rife at his side and opened fire on the North Vietnamese soldiers.

The closest man was the first to go down. He reached for his midsection, then fell to his knees uttering something in Vietnamese. Behind him one of the remaining soldiers got off a random shot that missed its target.

Richard continued to spray their bodies with bullets until his clip emptied. Then he stood watching while Owens and Lewis took up the slack and unloaded their weapons into the remaining dying men.

"Fuck man," Owens let out as he and Richard pulled Torres to his feet.

"Let's go, man. That way." Owens pointed and they scrambled through the underbrush in a frantic attempt to get out of the jungle.

At first Richard thought they were being followed, but gradually he realized that the loud thumping he heard was the pounding of his own heart. They ran for what seemed like hours and finally stopped where the grass was tall. Here, the men collapsed under a cluster of trees.

They lay there trying to catch their breath, their weapons poised, all eyes watching, waiting for pursuers that didn't come. When they were sure they were safe and the adrenaline started to wear off, Richard dry heaved.

"That was some fast fucking shooting, Searfus," Owens said, slapping him on the back. "You're entitled, man, you go ahead and puke your guts out. You just saved our fucking asses."

While Richard emptied his stomach in the red clay soil, Torres wiped the last of the blood and brain matter out of his eyes and Owens studied his compass, turning it around slowly.

"I think we're close. Lewis, crawl up that hill and have a look around would you, man?"

Lewis, who was no longer crying, scrambled up the hill. When he arrived at the top and scanned the area, he started to laugh.

"Man I can't fucking believe it!" he screamed. "We're found, we're actually found!"

The rest of the men climbed up the hill on all fours and when they reached the top, they too started cheering.

"I don't know who the fuck is down there man, but they're definitely American," Lewis called out. For several emotional seconds they stood happily staring down on a troop of American soldiers.

Richard and Owens were the first down the hill. Halfway there, a group of soldiers noticed them and by the time they made it to the camp, there was a small crowd forming.

"Where the hell did you men come from?" a tall man wearing Sergeant stripes asked.

Owens saluted. "We were lost sir, but now we're found."

"Lost? Where the hell is the rest of your troop? Identify yourselves soldiers."

"We're with H Company 2nd battalion 9th Marines, sir. We were on a private mission with Lt. Franco. We were supposed to meet up with F Company but ended up in between two hostile groups shooting at each other. Lt. Franco went up the hill thinking there were American troops and he never returned. That was three days ago, sir."

"Three days ago? Jesus H. Christ. Come with me."

He led the men to a makeshift tent where several officers sat drinking out of paper cups.

"Captain Shefland, Major Harmon, I'm sorry to interrupt, sirs, but we just found some lost men that wandered out of the jungle."

"What did you say, Sergeant Nielson? Lost men?" the Major asked, rising to his feet.

"That's right sir, lost men. They said they were with Lieutenant Franco and that he left trying to find help three days ago and never returned."

"Where are these men, Sergeant? Bring them in," the Captain said.

Sergeant Nielson flagged the four soldiers inside. The very haggard men walked in and for several seconds the officers studied them. Finally Captain Shefland approached.

"You said you're with the 2/9?" The four green soldiers nodded. "What are your names, soldiers?"

Owens saluted and introduced himself first; the other three men did likewise. When they were finished Owens stepped forward and asked for permission to speak.

"Sir, we started out three days ago with Lt. Franco and radio dispatcher Lance Corporal Gorman. Our mission was to meet with F Troop 2/9 when they were just entering the battle but we never got the chance. About halfway there we wandered into crossfire and Lance Corporal Gorman was killed and the radio was destroyed. Lt. Franco thought American troops were above us. He left to get help and he never returned. We held out as long as we could hoping he'd come back, but our water ran out this morning and we had to make a choice."

"That was three days ago, private?"

"Yes sir, that's right. On our way here we walked in the thickest part of the jungle hoping it would camouflage us. But we ran into the NVA and I'm sorry to say that Private Jesse Rodriguez was killed."

"What? You met up with the North Vietnamese Army?"

"Yes sir, about five miles from here in an area surrounded by Banyan trees. We were walking there hoping for optimal coverage when five or six NVA popped up in front of us. One of them shot Private Rodriguez in the head, sir. We wouldn't be here if it wasn't for Private Searfus. When the first man jumped up Searfus shot him without hesitation, giving us enough time to plug the rest and escape."

"You engaged in gunfire with the North Vietnamese Army and you killed them and then escaped?" the captain repeated confused by the story, which in his opinion was getting better by the minute.

"That's right, Captain."

"How many battles have you men been in?" the Major asked.

"This was our first, sir."

"Your first? And you're all privates?"

"That's correct, sir."

"Well, I'll be goddamned." The Major started to laugh. "Your first mission and you lose your commanding officer, manage to take out five or six gooks, and then you return to talk about it!" He laughed heartily. "Sergeant, get H Company 2/9 on the radio, tell them we found their missing boys and that we'll be bringing them home shortly. In the meantime, let's get these boys a beer. I think they deserve one."

**

Corporal Hodges sat in the enlisted men's bar at Camp Carroll alongside Clemmings and Clark.

Since it was Buddha's birthday, a ceasefire was in place. Some of the soldiers, those who had been in the thickest of the fighting, had been rotated out, which was why they were partying and waiting to greet the returning greenies of the 2/9.

Since it was Buddha's birthday, a ceasefire was in place. Some of the soldiers, those who had been in the thickest of the fighting, had been rotated out, which was why they were partying and waiting to greet the returning greenies of the 2/9.

Clemmings snapped open another can of Beer 33 (*ba moui ba*) and in one fast gulp, finished the can.

"Imagine, their first day and their first mission out. The LT who was supposed to lead them fucks up and they end up in crossfire. He walks towards enemy lines and gets himself blown up and they spend the next seventy-two hours out there alone in the jungle without leadership. Fucking Gooks ambush them, and they manage to take all of them out. Then they just *happen* to wander into the 2/26 Marine Division. That's just fucking unbelievable." Clemmings laughed. "True members of H Company 2/9. I tell you, man, there's just something fucking wonderful about us; even our fucking greenies rock."

" I told you Franco was a clueless fuck, but how do you screw up that bad? Imagine turning the map around like that," Hodges shook his head and polished off own can of Beer 33.

"Inept training, that's how. They take a guy with a degree, make him an officer, and send him here. Boot camp and a quick course on how to lead men aren't going to cut it here. But what the fuck do they care? Plenty more young college educated men where they come from, a dime a dozen." Clark smacked his lips after finishing his beer.

"Hey, man, I heard a jeep, I think they might be here."

The three men jumped to their feet and scrambled for the door.

Outside, four privates hopped out of a dust covered jeep, which as quickly as they exited, sped off in the opposite direction.

" I'm sure glad to be back here," Torres said gratefully. "Never thought I'd hear myself say that."

"All I want is a shower and a cot," Lewis said as he shambled along dragging his feet exhaustedly.

From across the perimeter someone whistled and the four men turned.

"Hey fresh meat, where the fuck you going?" Clemmings yelled.

Richard and the other privates stared at each other. Never before had Clemmings and his group so much as looked in their direction, let alone speak to them unless they absolutely had to.

Richard looked perplexed. "Are you talking to us?"

"No, I'm talking to the girls behind you dumbasses. Get your green asses over here and have a drink with the rest of Hell in a Helmet."

Leery of the attention they were suddenly awarded, the soldiers hesitated, then crept towards the open door of the enlisted men's club.

Richard was the first inside and was surprised when Clemmings and the others slapped him on the back in admiration.

"Way to go, Clipper John, we heard you did some mighty fine shooting out there. Wiped out a small troop of NVA."

"My name's Richard Searfus. It wasn't a troop, just five or six guys."

The seasoned soldiers laughed.

"You hear that, Clark?" Clemmings said. "It was just five or six guys. I told you the 2/9 rocks, even our greenies."

Clark passed out warm beer to the newcomers and pointed them towards a table. "Have a seat, men."

The four men reluctantly sat, overwhelmed and suspicious of the attention they were receiving. Once seated, they popped their warm cans of beer open and drank greedily.

"Now, let me get this straight…" Clark said . "You spent three days out there completely turned around, you lost your commander first thing, and your radio operator plus the radio, yet you still managed to find your way back and you took out five or six of the bad guys along the way?" He whistled. "Smooth shit." He drained his beer, smashing the can on his head and throwing it into a growing pile of empties in the middle of the floor.

"Let me guess. You, country boy," Hodges said pointing at Owens, "you're the homing pigeon. You're the one that got everyone back. And you…" he said, looking at Richard, "you're Clipper John. When you were needed, you clipped all them motherfuckers. Torres, you're the bull, you just keep on going, brother, pushing forward no matter what happens. And you…" He stopped and smiled at Lewis. "You've been on the down low, undercover, secret agent. All this time making everyone think you were a pussycat when underneath it all you're a fucking lion." Hodges slapped Lewis on the back, nearly knocking him off his seat.

Clemmings raised his beer can in a toast. "Here's to the new additions to Hell in a Helmet."

"Here's to Buddha's birthday and a ceasefire for a day," Clark said.

"Drink up men, because tomorrow we'll be back in the trenches," Hodges added, and then everyone lifted their cans.

Chapter 27

Katie waited by the front window nervously twisting her hands. It had been fifteen years since she'd seen her mother and eighteen since she'd seen her father. She wished she could feel positive about this reunion, but she didn't. There was just too much bad blood between them. She had made the mistake of following their wishes the last time around, and this time she vowed she would never give in to their demands. And their demands were plenty. They had been wrong in all their advice. The direction they had steered her towards had ruined her life, plain and simple, and it wasn't going to happen again.

Katie went through her closet for days deciding what to wear, knowing that whatever she decided on would undoubtedly result in ridicule from her mother. After much thought, she decided on modified hippie attire, determined to be herself without offending others. She wore a plain black boho skirt and a light pink blouse with small flowers. She pinned her hair up, applied light, tasteful make-up, including pale lipstick, which was fashionable in 1967.

Fortunately, Ron had gone out for the evening with friends. Katie hadn't told him about the party and a part of her felt guilty. Over the past few weeks they had spent a lot of time together. He was getting serious about Katie and she wasn't sure how she felt about him. Ron was adorable, good looking, kind, and generous. Katie was flattered. There had always been a part of her that had secretly longed for a relationship with him but back then he had never seemed interested. Katie knew now that she had been too immature for him.

Now, everything had changed. She wasn't a little girl anymore. She had a lifetime of experience behind her and that experience made her reluctant to enter a relationship with Ron. The problem was she could easily picture a future with him, and that possibility terrified her. They had not been intimate but they'd come close. After that incident she had limited their alone time, trying only to be with him in the presence of others.

And then there was the elusive Dylan, famous for his disappearing acts. She hadn't seen him since the ride to Sausalito. She wasn't sure that he'd really show up tonight, although he had called last week to get directions. A part of her hoped he would stand her up, giving her an excuse not to go to the party. With the jitters she felt now she would gladly be disinherited given a choice. There was another part of her, however, that knew he would show up. When Dylan made a promise he was true to his word.

An old blue pickup pulled in front of the house, and the driver jumped out, heading up the pathway. Seconds later the doorbell rang and Katie hurried to answer it.

She opened the door to a stranger. If she hadn't known it was Dylan she would have never recognized him. Not only had she never seen him without his colors, specifically his death skull leather vest, but also she had never seen him fully shaven either. His hair was neatly combed back, rather than hanging loose in the wild shabby look he preferred.

He wore dark trousers, a white shirt, a sports jacket and a narrow black tie. Katie was shocked, hesitated briefly and then swung the door open so the biker could enter the hallway.

"Wow!" was all she could say. This was a very different image of Dylan.

"I was going to say the same about you," Dylan said, appraising her appreciatively.

"No motorcycle?"

"Did you really think I'd show up on my bike to drive you to this upscale party?"

"No, but I didn't expect you to show up looking like this either."

"I figured at least we could start out on the right foot." Dylan was a charmer. Her mother would love him. "And speaking of setting off on the wrong foot, where is Ron the boyfriend this evening?" Dylan asked, glancing around the house.

"He's not my boyfriend."

Dylan raised his eyebrows questioningly.

"Well, he's not. Not officially anyways, and he's out with friends."

"How convenient. Does he know about our date or are we sneaking around behind his back?"

"Are you ready? We really should be going," Katie said, evading his question. She reached for a long black sweater she'd hung over the back of a chair.

Dylan took hold of her hand and turned her to face him.

"Does Ron know about our date?" he said again, staring at her intently.

"No. He doesn't know," Katie said with a twinge of guilt.

Dylan dropped her hand and without another word led Katie out the door.

The first part of their trip was quiet. Obviously disturbed, Dylan was locked in his own thoughts and Katie sat bracing herself for the nostalgic meeting she was dreading. Ten minutes into their drive, she cleared her throat and broke the silence.

"I didn't know you owned a truck."

"I don't, I borrowed it. You didn't really think I'd pick you up on a bike did you?"

"I didn't know what to expect. I guess I didn't really expect you to show up at all."

"That's not true. You knew I'd show up."

"No I didn't."

Dylan glanced at her with that beautiful grin and she averted her eyes.

"I haven't seen you in weeks. How would I know if you were going to show up or not?" she asked, looking at her sandaled feet.

"Because I made a promise and you know full well that I keep my word."

"I don't even know you."

"Well you seem to be keeping track of the amount of time we spend together. You know that you haven't seen me in weeks so I guess that means you've missed me."

Katie didn't look up, knowing that grin was back on his face. *Why does Dylan make me nervous?* Every time she saw him he had this effect on her. He was intimidating and cocky but she found herself drawn to him.

"Why would I miss someone who's inconsistent? You say one thing and you do another. You're good with your words, Dylan, but you obviously have too much on your plate."

"Ahh, I get it now. You don't see enough of me. So noted."

"You're smug," Katie snapped, suddenly annoyed with the conversation.

"And you're beautiful. I keep forgetting how much."

For several minutes there was a feeling of unease between them and then Katie spoke.

"Whose truck is this? It looks well taken care of."

"It's Terry's, a guy in the club. He keeps it in mint condition. This and what used to be his bike."

Katie looked at him questioningly.

"Don't ask, it's a long story."

"Speaking of bikes, what exactly happened to yours and Joey's? Frog said they were destroyed."

"They were. Eva and Ruby fucked them up good, poured latex paint all over them and then covered them with feathers. It took us weeks to strip them down, clean them off, and rebuild them."

"That's awful! Why would they do something that evil?"

"It was retaliation for having them thrown out of the party."

"What party?"

"The one you and Moonbeam were at. After the two of you left we threw them out. Actually carried them to the front door and tossed them on the stoop. That's why they fucked our bikes up."

"That's terrible. What's happened to Eva and Ruby?"

"Nothing, yet. They went MIA. Both the police and the club are looking for them. There's a rumor that they ran off to Mexico, I guess Eva has family there."

"I'm so sorry. They were such beautiful bikes."

"They still are. Now they're better than ever. We put a lot of work into them."

"I can't believe that Eva and Ruby got away with that."

"They didn't. They'll show up, it's only a matter of time. Nobody can hide in T.J. forever, especially when they can't speak the language."

"And what's going to happen when they do show up? What then?"

"They're going to need to pay for the damages. I'm not sure about the specifics yet but Joey and I will figure it out when the time comes." Dylan glanced over at her. "Listen, we're getting close, you better give me directions from here."

Katie swallowed hard; they were indeed getting close. She could feel her heart start to pound and her hands tremble.

"Take the next exit turn to the left and keep going for about three miles. Then turn left on Fernley and follow that into the foothills. When we get close I'll point the house out."

Dylan took the exit and followed Katie's directions heading into the mountains.

"Fernley," he announced when he turned onto the street. "Now what?"

"It's the third house on the right, 727, the one with all the cars parked in front."

Dylan found a parking space across the street and turned off the engine and the lights. Katie felt sick to her stomach.

"Listen, about my family," she said, stopping Dylan from opening the door. "When Mom drinks socially she's been known to flirt with my dates, so beware."

"Oh yeah?" Dylan laughed. "What does she look like?"

"It's not funny, wait till you find yourself cornered."

"Sounds exciting."

Katie glared at him. "My father is arrogant and his friends are too. They will probably try to embarrass you. But worst of all Mark Rhodes will be there, expect him to be ultra obnoxious."

"Katie it's all right, believe me, baby, I can handle myself and take care of you at the same time. You have nothing to worry about. Everything will go smoothly, I promise."

"I wish I could believe you, but you don't know these people. They're ruthless, cruel, and underhanded. Their lives revolve around money and how they fit in with high society. They can be awful."

"All people are ruthless, baby, and everyone can be awful. I've been around the worst humanity has to offer. Believe me when I tell you that this will be a cakewalk. True, I don't know these people, but I know what awful people are like. Trust me, I've got this one covered. You ready to go, pretty lady?"

Katie stared at the front door and closed her eyes, trying to imagine the interior of the house as it was back in 1967; rattan chairs, flowered paisley drapes; an assortment of small elf figurines that her mother collected.

She opened her eyes turned and looked at Dylan. "I guess I'm as ready as I'm going to be."

"It's going to be that bad?"

"Worse than you can imagine."

Katie swallowed hard and reached for the handle but Dylan stopped her.

"Just one thing before we go." He reached over and pushed loose strands of blonde hair out of her eyes. "I missed you too." And then he kissed her.

***

"There you are, dear, I'm so glad you could make it." Patricia Searfus stepped onto the front stoop and embraced her daughter. The smell of Chanel No. 5 suddenly surrounded Katie, and an expected nostalgia washed over her.

"Hello, Mother," Katie said, pulling away from the embrace.

"And who is this handsome chap? Is this your Frog?" her mother asked and in an instant the nostalgic moment was over, replaced by the reality of where she was.

"Mother, this is Dylan. Dylan, this is my mother, Patricia Searfus."

Her mother looked like an older version of Katie, or a younger version of Katie's 66-year old image. Her blonde hair was elegantly styled into a classic 60's bouffant. Her clothing was always the latest style. Tonight she wore a pink-laced empire cut dress. Below the lace, light pink taffeta and on top a dark pink cummerbund with a back tied bow, and of course, her 2-inch pumps that were dyed the exact same color of her dress. At 43 her mother was the image of perfection and she knew it.

"Well, aren't you a darling?" Pat slurred, hugging Dylan a little too tightly.

Dylan glanced at Katie and she nodded, remembering why she had moved to San Francisco.

"Come in, come in," Pat said, backing away from the entrance so the couple could walk inside.

Katie entered the house and stared through a sea of gray cigarette smoke that hovered just below the ceiling like clouds. The house was just as she had remembered it. Green shag carpets, yellow, green and orange flowered wallpaper with matching paisley drapes, a green couch and gaudy modern artwork that covered the walls. Stuff that looked like it had been thrown on the canvas by a blindfolded artist and probably had been.

In the background Herb Alpert and the Tijuana Brass played "In a Spanish Town." Katie remembered her parents' contemporary walnut cabinet console phono with record changer and an AM/FM radio. She was there when her parents had bought it. At the time it had cost a small fortune at three hundred and fifty dollars. Katie wondered what had happened to the classic piece of furniture and for the life of her she couldn't remember.

The view from the large oversized windows caught Katie's eye, and she took in the beautiful lights of the city twinkling below them. It had been a long time since she had stood at those windows. Now that she was older she could appreciate what she had formerly taken for granted, and she purposely steered Dylan towards the windows wanting to relive the beauty of her childhood.

Several feet from the window she stopped when a man blocked their path. Katie turned to see Burt Anderson, her parents' next-door neighbor, grotesquely stuffed into a Nehru collared shirt, trying to look hip but failing miserably. Burt was Katie's introduction into a dirty old man. When she turned sixteen he had been the first to pinch her ass. Looking back on it, she should have decked him.

"Well, well, look who the cat drug in. I was wondering if you would show up and here you are," he said, and then moving fast, embraced her before she could stop him and plastered a wet ashtray smelling kiss on her forehead.

"Yes, here I am all the way from San Francisco." She stepped back and wiped at her face with the sleeve of her black sweater. "This is my boyfriend, Dylan," she announced, and the biker looked at her in surprise.

"Nice to meet you, Dylan. I've known Katie since she was this big." Burt said holding his hand about three feet from the floor. "Boy, she was an active little kid."

Just then a tall, solemn faced man stepped up beside Burt. Katie's heart dropped into her stomach. Dressed in a fancy silk shirt and expensive black slacks stood her 45-year-old father. This of course was Al Searfus in his prime.

Katie breathed in deeply, trying unsuccessfully to will her body not to tremble; even her teeth started to rattle.

"Well, Katherine you did show up after all. So, who's your escort?" Al asked with a sneer in his voice while stirring his martini and running his eyes up and down Dylan's obviously cheaper clothing.

Katie felt Dylan slide his hand into hers, intertwine their fingers, and he squeezed her hand reassuringly. She smiled.

"Dylan, this is my father Al. Dad this is Dylan."

Reluctantly her father shook Dylan's hand.

"So, Dylan from San Francisco, do you have a last name?"

Dylan laughed, attempt at intimidation noted. "Sure do, name's Dylan Taylor."

Al studied him, his distaste displayed plainly on his face as he ran his eyes over Dylan's clothing again, sizing him up. "And what do you do, Dylan Taylor?" Al's voice held that sarcastic tone that Katie remembered so well. He was trying to demean her date.

"I'm an entrepreneur like yourself, sir," Dylan said confidently. "Right now I'm the co-owner of a garage on 7th Street in the city. We design and build custom motorcycles and we repair bikes too."

"Oh I see, you're a mechanic," Al said, raising his martini and taking a generous drink.

"No, I think you misunderstood, Mr. Searfus. I'm not a mechanic. I build custom bikes from scratch. I tend to think of myself as an engineer, an artist. A custom bike, if you are not aware, Mr. Searfus, is not a cheap item." Dylan smiled his Cheshire grin and for several seconds Al Searfus was speechless.

He wasn't used to being corrected and the blatant act had shocked him. He stared at Dylan blinking rapidly and then he nodded. Dylan was a tougher opponent than he had anticipated.

"Custom built motorcycles, you say?" Al repeated.

"Yes sir, that's right." Dylan was pleased with himself. He had one-upped the great Al Searfus and he knew it. Katie looked proud.

"Well look who it is," a fat woman with fake read hair and blue eye shadow called out. "Excuse me boys, excuse me, let me through." Doris tried to squeeze her large body into a small space by shoving the men out of the way. "Little Katie, my goodness." She embraced Katie and smothered her with repeated kisses to the forehead. Meanwhile, Burt and Al made a quick getaway, anxious to avoid a conversation with Pat Searfus' good friend.

"Hi, Aunt Doris," Katie said, trying to back away from her. Doris was quick to hug her again and squeeze her into an overly tight embrace. Then she reached past Katie and twisted one of Dylan's cheeks. "Where did she find you, honey?" Aunt Doris asked sweetly, her breath smelling of bourbon, garlic, and Certs wintergreen breath mints.

"She found me in Golden Gate Park, or rather, I found her there."

"Golden Gate Park. Oh that's right, Katie is one of those beatniks isn't she?" Doris asked in a voice loud enough to draw attention from the whole room. Several couples stopped and stared. Katie felt her face grow crimson.

"A beatnik you say?" Dylan said with a wink in Katie's direction. "Hmm, I'm not sure if I'd call her that, but I would call her adorable."

"Oh aren't you a charmer," Aunt Doris gushed.

Aunt Doris's eyes were diverted to the center of the room where a man, Doris' equally large spouse, was attempting to dance the tango with Pat.

"Oh no, no, you're doing it wrong, Arthur," she called out. "Hang on, let me help you." Doris disappeared into the party on a mission to teach dance classes, much to both Katie's and Dylan's relief.

"Now what, baby?" Dylan asked.

"Now we get a drink. It's going to be a long evening and I can't possibly do this sober." Katie took his hand and headed for the makeshift bar.

She made a Manhattan for herself, got a beer for Dylan, and they casually drifted into a corner where they could observe the room without being interrupted.

"So what's Aunt Doris's bag?" Dylan asked.

"Ahh, her. She's not really my aunt, she's Mother's best friend. One of the most obnoxious women I've ever met. Thank God she went off to do the tango." Katie rolled her eyes and Dylan laughed.

"You weren't kidding, this place is already a trip." He looked around the room and for several minutes they stood silently observing the extravagant partygoers.

As Katie had said, they were all about show. Expensive cars parked outside, designer clothing, beautiful jewelry, and a house in the hills that the average person would die for. These people were about wealth, they lived it and they breathed it. They were the upper crust of the establishment; those the hippies were fighting against. These people could even work the government since official bribes where never far from the equation.

"We're in a sea of vultures that are just waiting to pounce on us when we dare to come out of this corner," Katie remarked and Dylan laughed.

"We're just standing here to give you a break. You don't have to worry about me but you're so nervous I don't know how we're going to get you through the night." He smiled. "So where is this stalker jerk you were telling me about?"

"He's not here yet, unless he's in the back yard."

"Maybe he won't show up," Dylan said.

"Oh, no such luck, he'll be here. I'm sure my parents told him that I was coming so the asshole will definitely show."

"Okay, and when he does, what do you expect to happen?"

"Nothing at first, then he'll start drinking. Booze makes Mark cocky and he'll approach us. When he does he'll work on degrading you. He's sly, at first you won't even know that the conversation is leading into a bummer topic until he stings you. That's when he makes you look stupid."

"Sting me? Make me look stupid? I don't think so, honey." Dylan started to laugh.

"It's not funny, Dylan. He's awful."

"I doubt it. He just thinks he's awful. Hotshot smartass rich boy doesn't know shit. I got this, baby, you have nothing to worry about." He stepped closer and ran his hand along her cheek. "Trust me, baby. It will all work out fine, I promise. "

The front door opened and Katie flinched, her mouth suddenly cotton dry. He was here. Dylan turned and saw a clean-cut blond man resembling Robert Redford enter the room. He was dressed in a tweed sports coat and looked smooth like a New York model. His eyes flashed across the room and he immediately focused on Katie. Dylan knew him without needing to be told. He studied the Stanford student, sizing him up.

The first thing that Mark did was walk to the bar where he fixed himself a drink. Then he made his way around the room jovially, mingling with the other guests while constantly scanning the room for Katie.

"You look nervous as shit. He knows he's getting to you," Dylan remarked. "Look at me, let's give this dork something to stare at." When Katie turned, Dylan kissed her. It was a perfect kiss that made her forget momentarily that it was all for show.

As quickly as it happened, it ended and Katie pulled away, watching Dylan's face brighten with his magnetic grin. Across the room, a red-faced Mark Rhodes stood fuming. Katie smiled.

"Stay with me, baby. Don't worry, just stay cool and let me do what I do best."

Mark, now on his second or third drink, made his way across the room. Dylan led Katie out of the corner explaining, "We don't want him to think he has an advantage because he's cornered us."

Katie put her hand into Dylan's and intertwined their fingers. He looked at her and winked.

"Well, hello there, Katie. I suppose it's time to break the ice." Mark said, stepping up to them. "How are you? Who's your friend?"

"Boyfriend," Dylan corrected, offering his hand. "The name's Dylan Taylor."

"Mark Rhodes," the young Robert Redford look-a-like responded. He was cool; Katie had seen him this way many times. Mark was ready; he was setting himself up for the kill.

"Where's the other boyfriend?" Mark asked. "The hippie that assaulted me at your apartment complex?"

"Ron is not my boyfriend, he's just a friend." She paused. "Dylan is my boyfriend." She chose not to comment on the assault jab Mark had made against Ron, not taking the bait.

"Oh, really? Could have fooled me. I take it you replaced him, Dylan. I don't know if you met the other guy, but he was explosive. But then maybe he's the real boyfriend and you're just here because she was told not to bring him," Mark said and shrugged his shoulders.

Dylan laughed, insult detected. Mark wasn't nearly as clever as he thought he was.

"And what do you do, Katie's present boyfriend?" Mark asked, running his index finger around the crystal martini glass so it whistled.

"I design and build custom motorcycles. I'm co-owner of a shop in the city."

"Custom bikes, hmm..." Mark sipped his drink. "How about you, Katie? What are you doing with your life these days?"

"I'm doing the same thing as I was the last time you saw me, Mark. No changes in my life."

"I see," he responded. "So you're still trying to 'find yourself'."

"Something like that," she said lightly, wanting to add much more, but biting her tongue. *Every dog has its day, and today is not that day.*

"What about you, Mark, what do *you* do?" Dylan asked, finishing his beer.

"I'm an executive in the finance department at Katie's father's firm," Mark crowed.

Dylan nodded, unimpressed. Katie could tell Mark was annoyed with the biker's response. *Now it will start,* she told herself.

"I suppose your bike shop's not large enough for executives?"

Dylan laughed at the jibe. "You obviously have no knowledge of what a custom bike shop is. I bet you'd be surprised at the income that we pull in. But no, we don't have any executives in charge of operations. We really don't need employees who can't do anything but delegate. We have all our ends covered." Dylan put his arm around Katie's shoulders. "If you'll excuse us, Mark, I'm going to get Katie and me another drink," he said, setting up their escape.

"Oh, certainly. I'll entertain Katie until you get back," Mark said smugly.

"Entertain her? Thanks, but no need to do that, she's coming with me." Dylan took her hand and steered her towards the drink bar. Mark looked on in shock, not believing that he had just been dismissed.

"You know he's not done with you, right?" Katie said while Dylan refilled her glass.

"What makes you think that I'm done with him?" Dylan winked.

"He's going to think you're scared of him now; that you're easy prey." She said in a warning.

"Good. That's what I want him to think."

Katie heard her name and turned to find herself face to face with her mother.

"Oh, Katie dear, I really wish you could have worn something more appropriate," Pat said, touching Katie's skirt and making the *tsk, tsk* sound. "Don't you have any of the pretty dresses I bought you last year? You should have worn one of them."

"I couldn't, I gave them all to the secondhand store," Katie said, unable to help herself. "I traded them for these." She grinned at the look of shock that came over her mother's face.

"I think she looks positively radiant," Dylan said, but Pat ignored him.

"Have you heard from Richard?" she asked.

"Actually I have," Katie answered. "He wrote me when he arrived at Camp Carroll."

"Pity he got sent to that awful place. Your Uncle Thomas assured me he'd get him out of Vietnam as quickly as possible."

Her uncle wouldn't be able to do that, just like John McCain's father, an Admiral, wasn't going to be able to get his own son out of a P.O.W. camp. Richard would remain in 'Nam until the end of October when he would die.

"I do hope things between you and Mark aren't going badly. I saw the two of you talking to him." Pat smiled sheepishly. She had always been nosey, Katie remembered.

"My goal is to just stay clear of him, but I promise, Mother, I'll be civil."

"Go easy on him, Katie. He really is quite hung up on you and he's taking your rejection badly."

Yeah, real hung up on taking over the family's business and fortune, she thought but refrained from saying aloud.

"No insult intended, Dylan dear," Pat said coyly.

"None taken, Mrs. Searfus." Dylan smiled back sweetly.

"Well I should mingle with my guests now. Katie, you should do the same." Noticing that some of the guests were looking at her and her daughter, Pat hugged Katie. This time the act felt suffocating. The things her mother did for show.

When Pat moved away, Dylan took Katie's hand and they moved across the room as far as they could get from the phony crowd who appeared sweet to their friends' faces but were secretly talking behind their backs.

"Mrs. Robinson, er, I mean your mother, hasn't cornered me yet," Dylan said.

Katie laughed. "She's not drunk enough yet. Just you wait though, it will happen."

"Promises, promises." His blue eyes twinkled and Katie felt her heart skip a beat.

"Oh look, Katie, here comes my good friend Mark." Dylan laughed. "I guess he finished another drink and he's ready for round two."

Katie swallowed and stopped herself from putting her foot out to trip her future ex-husband. She reached out for Dylan's arm instead and he kissed the top of her head.

"Katie, as you know your parents' twenty-fifth anniversary is coming up, and I was wondering if you wanted to collaborate with me to put something together for them."

The offer was so unexpected that Katie just stared at him, trying to understand what he was talking about. When she finally got it she started to laugh.

"I'm sorry, did I say something funny?" Mark asked.

"Everything you say is funny, Mark. I wish I could explain why, but I just can't." She shook her head thinking of the many arguments that they had had. Knowing now how Mark fought passive aggressively put her at an advantage.

"It's their anniversary, Mark, if they want a party they can throw one. If you want to throw a party for them you go right ahead. As for me, I'm not interested."

"That's cold, Katie."

She bit her tongue. There were so many things that she wanted to say but if she opened that gate she wouldn't be able to close it and now was not the time. She was here to put in one night, just one night so her monthly funds could continue. A fight with Mark Rhodes wasn't worth as much as it would cost her.

"Look, man, she said she wasn't interested so just leave it alone," Dylan responded in her defense.

"What are you, her answering box?" Mark asked.

Dylan laughed and Mark's face reddened.

"Look, funny man, I've known Katie for a long time. You need to keep your nose out of this," Mark said arrogantly, which made Dylan laugh even harder.

"Is this cat for real?" Dylan said, still laughing as he nudged Katie with his elbow.

"I'm afraid so."

"Unfucking real," Dylan said. He seemed unable to stop laughing.

"You want to tell me what's so funny? Why you think this is such a big fucking joke?" Mark snapped.

"Stop it, Mark," Katie said. "People are starting to stare."

"You think I care?"

"Considering where you work and the people you are surrounded by, I think you should care. If you make a scene, just imagine how foolish you'll look to your own crowd. They'll be talking about you for days, weeks, maybe even years. But then again why should I care? You go right ahead and make a spectacle out of yourself."

"Fine," Mark said in a lower voice. "I'll let you and your illiterate boyfriend get back to whatever you were doing. Don't worry about your parents, Katie, I'll take care of them while you're 'finding yourself'." Mark was drunk but he was an expert at hiding it.

"Let's go, Dylan," she said, tugging on the biker's sleeve.

"Wait a second, honey, illiterate?"

"That's right."

"Man, I'm not illiterate."

"Really? I suppose you're in college?" Mark asked as Katie continued trying to pull Dylan away.

"Nope, I've already graduated."

"You're a college graduate?" Mark asked in disbelief.

"That's right."

"You must mean a community college," Mark said smugly.

"No, a university," Dylan corrected.

"Okay then, college grad, enlighten me. Where did you go to school?" Mark's sarcasm was back, he was sure he'd found an area where he could embarrass Dylan.

"You a college grad?" Dylan asked.

"Not yet, but I will be. I have two semesters left. Oh, and I'm in Stanford," he gloated.

"Hmm, my university is just as big and just as well known."

"I'll bet." Mark chuckled.

"Oh, it is."

"Okay, you have my curiosity tweaked. Where did you go to school, Dylan?"

"Tell you what, I'll show you the tattoo of my university."

"You have your university tattooed on your body?"

"That's right. If you want to see it I'll show it to you."

"Okay, let's see it." Mark chuckled again.

"I can't show you here, bud, we'll have to go out in the yard. You don't really expect me to show you a tattoo right here do you?"

"I suppose not. Tattoos aren't really that clever are they?" Mark had hit his element and he was going to play this lead to the end.

"You want to see it or not?" Dylan asked, dangling the hook.

"Yes, I'm going to have to see it now or I'm going to ponder the mystery forever."

"Well we wouldn't want you to do that, would we, Mark?"

Katie pulled on Dylan's sleeve one last time and he turned to look at her. This look was unlike any she had ever seen on his face. She dropped her arm and stepped back. This undoubtedly was what Dylan did best.

"If you want to see it we have to go out back, someplace private, you dig? As you pointed out, tattoos aren't really that clever so I'm not going to pull my shirt up in here."

"Okay." Mark nodded.

Dylan started towards the back door and Mark followed, ready to attack his prey. Katie walked silently behind them, not sure if she was invited to the event or not.

The Searfus backyard was large. Towards the side fence there was a grove of trees that created a private spot where Katie and Richard used to hide and smoke pot. This was the location where Mark steered Dylan.

"Okay, college boy, you have a nice sheltered area with no witnesses so let's see it."

Mark laughed, so did Dylan.

"Okay. Let me show you where I went to school, Mark, and then you can tell me if you think my school is as well-known as yours."

"Deal," Mark said. He was ready for a show, and his eyes gleamed evilly.

Dylan took his jacket off and handed it to Katie. He removed his tie and his white button down shirt. Then he turned around. Dylan's back was adorned with the winged death skull of the Hells Angels. In red lettering above the artwork was the name of his "university". According to the tattoo he had become a member in February of 1966.

Katie turned just in time to see Mark's face drain of color. His hand started to shake so hard that most of the martini in his glass spilled over the edge. He took several steps backwards and his mouth dropped open.

Meanwhile, Dylan had turned around and was in the process of dressing.

"So, Mark, do you think my school is as famous as yours?"

Mark sputtered, cleared his throat in an attempt to pull himself together, and then finally he answered.

"Yes. Yes I do," he mumbled.

"I thought you would. I think we're known worldwide, and our insignia— or in this case let's call it our mascot— is well known too. Membership was a long process," Dylan said finishing the last few buttons on his shirt. "First I had to be a hangaround that lasted a year, my freshman year. Next, I got promoted to prospect. My sophomore and my junior year were the hardest. In case you don't know, a prospect gets all the nasty jobs, the grunt work, cleaning up all the messes. It kind of sucked, but I hung in there. In February of last year, my senior year, I got patched. I graduated into full membership of the Hells Angels, a big accomplishment, I'm sure you'll agree."

"Yes, of course," was all Mark was able to say. Katie could tell he was itching to get away but he didn't know how to do it without offending Dylan.

"In my four years with the Angels, I've seen some out of this world shit. When I was a prospect I saw this guy get his tongue pulled out of his mouth. Right out of his fucking mouth, man, can you imagine that?" Dylan reknotted his tie and took his jacket from Katie. "One of those situations where the guy just didn't know how to keep his mouth shut, you know what I mean? He was warned but I guess he didn't take us seriously." Dylan whistled. "Man, it was an eye opener, you can't imagine all the blood, but I hear he took us seriously after that. So you see, Mark, I've had a full street education much like the business or finance degree that you're working on."

Mark stood, mouth agape, listening and nodding his head in nervous agreement.

"Great thing about my university is that all the alumni watch each other's backs. You mess with one of us, you mess with all of us. And then you take our girlfriends, like Katie here, well my university has her back too. Do you understand what I'm getting at?" Dylan stepped closer to Mark and stared into his large, terrified eyes.

Mark gulped.

"I think Katie's made it crystal clear that she doesn't want to plan a party with you and I think it's pretty clear that your little trip to 'Frisco several months back wasn't appreciated." Dylan clapped Mark on the back and the unexpected physical contact made Mark visibly start. "Man to man, friend to friend, I'm going to ask you nicely to stay away from her. Can you do that, Mark?" Dylan smiled, but it didn't reach his eyes.

"I-I," Mark stuttered. He shut his mouth and his eyes for a few tense seconds before answering. "Yes, I can do that," he said, his eyes nervously flashing between Katie's and Dylan's.

"Smart move, my friend. You see, I knew you were a reasonable kind of guy." Dylan turned to Katie. "Ready to go inside, honey?"

Katie nodded, relieved that Mark's lesson was over and there had been no bloodshed.

"I think Katie is getting cold so we're going to step back inside but it's been great chatting with you, Mark."

"G-g-good talking to you too, Dylan," Mark managed to choke out.

Dylan put his arm around Katie and rubbed her shoulders, then he kissed her on the forehead and led her into the house, leaving Mark Rhodes alone outside to catch his breath.

The house, still clouded over with smoke, smelled musty. Katie purposely left the door open and watched as the smoke drifted outside as if a vacuum was sucking it up. She looked at the clock in the kitchen. It was 9:00 p.m.; they had only been here for an hour. Katie sighed.

The stereo finished playing "Casino Royale" then the automatic record changer dropped the next LP on the turntable and Frank Sinatra's voice filled the room.

"You okay?" Dylan asked. "I hope my little show wasn't too much for you?"

"I thought you were brilliant. Oh my God, Mark's face, it was phenomenal."

"Good, I couldn't think of another way to deal with the idiot without making a scene. Hopefully I've made an impact on him. How long do you think it will be before your parents know you're dating a Hells Angel?"

"As long as it takes Mark to stop himself from shaking, devise another plan in his sick head, and then attack from the sidelines."

"You're kidding, right?"

Katie stared at him.

"Man, that guy is stupid."

"He's arrogant and he's determined, not stupid," Katie said. "He'll put some passive-aggressive plan together. I can't imagine him giving up without an underhanded fight."

Dylan shook his head and laughed. "Man, I'm going to enjoy another round with him."

"It won't happen for a while."

"You want another drink?" Dylan asked.

"I'd rather smoke a doobie."

"To the backyard then?" he asked as Frank and Nancy went into their duet, 'Something Stupid'. "To your private little corner?"

"You mean the spot where I taught my kid brother how to smoke pot?" She giggled.

"Yeah, that's the place."

They weaved between the partygoers heading for the open back door but were stopped by Katie's mother before they could reach it.

"Where are the two of you going?" Pat asked, much drunker than the last time they'd talked to her.

"To the backyard for a cigarette, I need some fresh air," Dylan responded.

"That's a wonderful idea," Pat slurred, staggering a bit. "I could use a ciggy and some fresh air myself."

Pat wrapped her arms around one of Dylan's and then she handed her glass to Katie.

"Be a sweetie, honey, and get your mother another gin and tonic." Before Katie could say a word, Pat was wandering into the backyard with her pretend boyfriend.

"That bitch," Katie muttered.   She walked towards the makeshift bar in search of gin and tonic.

***

Pat hung onto Dylan's arm as they strolled into the yard. The backyard was empty. Pat had Dylan all to herself.

Halfway down the sidewalk, she pulled a Benson & Hedges 100 and a Bic lighter out of a small cigarette purse and offered one of the smokes to Dylan. He declined.

"So how long have you and my Katie been dating?" she asked. As manners dictated, Dylan took the lighter and lit her cigarette then handed it back politely.

"A few months," he lied.

"I thought she was going out with that hippie boy Ron, when did that end?"

"I have no idea. You should probably ask your daughter that question."

Pat held the front of Dylan's shirt and moved her body in closer. "Katie is a lost soul right now, she's trying to find her roots. She's young and she's smart so I have no doubt that she'll give up all of this hippie nonsense and eventually come home and do what's right."

"Maybe, but maybe not," Dylan said stepping backwards, which freed him from Pat's grasp. "She's the daughter of a new age, Mrs. Searfus, and she's determined to do her own thing."

"Well of course she's thinking that way. As you said, this is the age, the Aquarian age, am I right?"

Dylan nodded. Pat leaned in and whispered in his ear. "You know, you really are adorable. I can understand why my daughter finds you attractive. I wouldn't mind a turn with you myself but as for Katie, I hope you realize that you're not in her league."   Pat finished by rubbing her hand against Dylan's chest seductively.

"I see, I'm all wrong for Katie, but Mark Rhodes is right, and you'd like to get rid of me?"

"It's not just you, honey, it's anyone who isn't in the same caliber as Katie. Don't take this wrong, Dylan, but Katie has blood, breeding, and an important name behind her. She has an obligation to carry that line on, and of course that means she needs to marry a man that's socially and economically her equal. I don't think that group includes you."

She tried to kiss Dylan's neck but he stopped her. "Mrs. Searfus, I think you're a beautiful woman, you look so much like Katie that it's tempting, but it's Katie that I want, not you. As for breeding and blood and all of that high society shit, I don't think she's interested in any of that. Maybe I'm wrong and later those things will be important to her, who knows? I can't say, but I can tell you this, she will never end up with Mark Rhodes. But since you seem to be so interested in him and you look so much like Katie, perhaps he'd be interested in you instead."   Dylan's jab took its toll.   Pat, surprised, stopped what she was doing and stepped backwards to stare at him.

Katie walked into the backyard and noticed the mischievous smile on Dylan's face and the shocked expression on her mother's.   She knew immediately that something dramatic had just taken place. She walked up to her mother, handed her the gin and tonic, and smiled sweetly.

"Is everything alright, Mother? You look flustered?"

"I'm just fine, dear.   But it's getting cold out here and I really should get back inside." She smashed the cigarette butt under one of her pink pumps, excused herself, and made a beeline for the back door.

"Why do I feel as if my mother was just put in her place?" Katie asked.

"Because she was. You ready for that joint, baby?" He led her to the private corner of the yard where he pulled out a nicely sized doobie and lit it. Breathing deeply, he closed his eyes savoring the herb and then handed the smoke to Katie.

"Mark should leave you alone now, I think," he said.

Katie accepted the joint and then started to laugh. "You should have seen his face when he saw your back, I thought he was going to pee his pants."

"I can imagine. He still looked fucking shocked when I turned around," he joked. "You still think he's got the balls to bother you?"

"Not for a while, but I can't imagine him just going away. He'll lick his wounds and come up with another plan, but eventually he'll show up again. He's hungry for power in my dad's firm. He wants to eventually take over the company and what better way to do that than through me?"

"I don't know, Katie, I don't think he has the balls to come to San Francisco. I would really be surprised if he shows up."

"No, he won't show up there. Whatever he plans, it will be something underhanded. Something to get us back. Revenge is Mark's thing, his main bag. He's not done with anyone yet, I'm sure of it."

"What a fucking idiot!" Dylan passed the joint back to her. "Hey, you weren't kidding about your mother coming on to me."

"I told you it would happen. She's always trying to bed younger men." Katie laughed thinking of the many times her mother had hit on her dates.

"Yeah it was a trip that's for sure, but here's the thing, while she was hitting on me she took the opportunity to put me down. That was the strangest part. How do you come on to someone expecting them to go for it, while you're dropping insults? I just don't get it." Dylan laughed even harder. "Man, your family is a trip. Talk about all fucked up."

"You were warned. So spill the beans, what happened with my mother? I want to hear all about it."

"Basically, she told me that I'm not good enough for you. You're going through a wild stage right now but you're going to eventually come to your senses and come home. I guess that includes matrimony with Mark. I simply told her that I wasn't interested in her, that I was only interested in you, and that since she thinks Mark is such a catch and you don't, perhaps she should try for him instead."

Katie burst out laughing. "You didn't!"

"I most certainly did. Man, she was shocked. I don't think anyone's ever suggested that possibility to her before."

"I wish I could have seen her face. Jesus that must have been funny as hell." Katie hit the last of the roach, dropping a small piece of paper into the garden.

"I don't think she'll approach me again."

"I doubt it."

"So your brother's in the Army?" Dylan asked.

"The Marine Corps," Katie corrected.

"And he enlisted?"

"That's right. Eighteen years old and he decided the military would be better than college." She thought of her brother, who at this moment was stationed in one of the most violent areas of the war-torn country.

"Wow, man, what a bummer. What possessed him to do that?"

"He wanted to get away from my father's influence. Figured he would make a big name for himself in the military so my parents would be proud of him. He's young and stupid."

Dylan nodded. "I hope it turns out alright."

"It won't. He's in a company that's well decorated, that means they see a lot of action. Believe me he won't make it home alive."

"Another premonition?"

She nodded sadly.

"Listen, about all of that, I have to admit that shit freaked me out. When the news about Mohammad Ali hit...let's just say it was a trip that I've been trying to get over ever since. You predicted all of it Katie, how is that possible? How could you know exactly what would happen? What's the real story?"

"I told you the real story, Dylan. I've had premonitions my whole life, I don't know why."

"Maybe, but how do you explain the other oddities about you?"

She stared at him tongue tied, wondering what he sensed.

"You have this look in your eyes, like you're a very old soul. Like you have wisdom beyond your years. Why is that, Katie?"

"I guess I'm a very old soul."

"And then there's this weird circle of knowledge between you, Frog and Moonbeam. The three of you share a very private secret, something you're reluctant to let me in on.

Katie said nothing, she just looked at him.

"The real reason you haven't heard from me since the ride to Sausalito is because that whole scene creeped me out. Your premonition about my death, I haven't been able to get that out of my mind. I tried, but when the Mohammad Ali news broke...just as you said, our conversation that night took on a whole new meaning. I thought if I just stayed away from you then everything would be okay, you dig? But that's not the case because during that time, I still couldn't get you out of my mind."

"You predicted your death in your own reoccurring dreams, Dylan," Katie said. "All I did was confirm it. You can't fix things by ignoring them."

"Then how do we fix this, Katie?"

She shrugged. "I'm working on that."

"Then there's this weird thing between you and me. Don't tell me you don't feel it too. We're drawn to each other and it's more than attraction, it's like a magnet, as if we belong together. Can you tell me why?"

"I don't know, but if we're being honest then I admit, I feel it too."

Their eyes locked.

"I'd say the evening's about over, baby, what do you say? Do you want to blow this joint?"

"Fuck yes. I've had enough for one evening."

She led Dylan to the side yard, unhooked a wooden gate, and they escaped unnoticed.

Nobody saw them when they snuck through the front yard, finally arriving safely at Terry's '57 Chevy. Dylan unlocked her door and she climbed into the bench style seat. Seconds later he unlocked his own door and got in beside her. He put the key into the ignition and they left Fernley Street and for the first time today, Katie felt her body relax.

"So now what, Katie? What happens next?"

"I wish I knew the answer to that, Dylan."

"That's just it, I think you do know the answer."

"I guess we go back to San Fran and return to the way things were?" she suggested.

"Really, is that it? We just go back to the way things were before?"

"I don't know how to answer that because I'm not sure what happens next. Maybe you should tell me?"

"Me, tell you?"

"You and Frog disappear, Dylan. It will happen just as Mohammad Ali lost his title. How I know what I know is irrelevant, it doesn't change anything. You and Frog are involved in something that's going to cause both of you to lose your lives. I can only do so much on my end with the limited information that I have. I told you what I know. You have until August, if you're lucky, to correct your mistakes." Katie sighed deeply. "It's your turn to run with the ball Dylan, and don't tell me that you don't know what I'm talking about. It's time for you to confront Frog about your concerns. You need to be honest with each other or neither of you will survive."

Dylan pulled the truck over in a quiet residential area. He turned the ignition off and stared at her as she continued her speech.

"You can avoid me all you want. You can avoid Frog too, but it's not going to get you anywhere. This is for real, Dylan, this is playing for keeps. The big question is what are you going to do about the information I've given you?"

Dylan was visibly shaken. Katie had hit that raw nerve that would hopefully ignite a fire under his lazy ass. If she couldn't get Frog motivated to do something, then perhaps she might break through to Dylan.

He stared out the front windshield and said nothing, his eyes distant, thinking. When he turned to face her, all seriousness was gone and the jovial biker had returned.

He moved closer and put his arms around her. She relaxed against his chest and they just held each other, listening to heartbeats.

"Listen, I really enjoyed being your knight in shining armor tonight, it felt good."

"You were great, by the way. I couldn't have asked for more from a pretend boyfriend."

"I wasn't pretending." He smiled at her. "You know I'm not good for you, right?" he asked, still holding her in his arms.

"At this moment nobody is good for me, not you, not Ron, nobody. I need to work things out by myself before I can think about a relationship with anyone."

"As much as I hate to admit this, I have to be honest. When you are ready, Ron is a better choice for you, Katie. He has a job, money, and a house. Frog thinks he's a great guy, and I'll take his word for that. He can offer you a future, literally speaking. One that even if I manage to make it through August, I can't. Not the kind of future you deserve anyway."

"Hush," Katie said. "Don't say anything, don't ruin the moment." She kissed him then, and for a long time they stayed locked in each other's arms.

Chapter 28

The beginning of June brought a feeling of optimism Katie's way, and she had begun to believe that anything was possible. After all, if she could return to 1967 and stay here for six months, that was a sign. Maybe she was here for a reason, to change things that should never have happened.

She knew she couldn't save the world, of course it wasn't possible, but if she could stop Richard from dying and prevent Frog and Dylan from disappearing, that would be a miracle.

One June afternoon, Katie had the windows open and a fresh breeze blowing through the house. She was downstairs cleaning and the rest of the roommates were out, one of those rare occasions when she had the place all to herself.

The local radio station, KFRC, was playing the top ten song countdown and she was working on the battered coffee table, trying to remove something that looked like a melted Jolly Rancher with a butter knife.

The doorbell rang. At first she thought it was part of the radio show, barely noticing the noise as she continued to chip at the hard candy that seemed to be permanently stuck to the table.

When the bell rang again, she realized that someone was at the door. She put the knife down and headed towards the banging, believing the visitor would be a kid selling magazine subscriptions or a Hare Krishna delivering religious paperwork. When she opened the door and saw Janis Joplin standing on the porch, she was stunned.

"Hi, baby, I hope you don't mind me crashing your pad like this unexpected and all. I asked around, and people on the street told me that you lived here. Anyway, I come bearing gifts." In her arms, she carried a box that obviously contained concert posters.

"Of course I don't mind. Please come on in." Katie opened the door and the blues singer entered the front parlor of the yellow Victorian house.

"Groovy place you have, Katie, it's really outta sight. I love these old houses don't you?" Janis asked without expecting an answer.

Katie led her guest into the sitting room where Janis plopped down on the old sofa. She started to lay the box on the coffee table but stopped. She squinted and then stared at the gooey substance that was stuck to the table and at the butter knife beside it.

"Yuk. What the fuck is that?" She asked nodding her head towards the clump of crud Katie had been trying to scrape off.

"Man, I don't know. I think it's a Jolly Rancher, but it's stuck to the wood like a bitch and now it's just a melted blob, so who knows?"

"Like a bitch huh? Fucking bummer for the table, man." She laid the box on the couch beside her.

"How are your tattoos?" Katie asked. "Did they heal up okay?"

"Oh yeah, baby, they're groovy, both of them, see?" Janis offered her left arm for inspection.

Katie smiled at the Florentine bracelet tattoo, which had indeed healed well. "It looks great!"

"Yeah, man, I think so too." Janis rubbed at the tattoo and grinned. "Never mind that, look what I brought you." She undid the string bindings around the box and lifted out the top Avalon Ballroom poster.

"The first one is undoubtedly the best and the most important," she said, flaunting a Big Brother and the Holding Company concert poster, which advertised a date in the near future.

Katie studied the beautiful artwork and the signatures of every member of the band. When she noticed that it was personally addressed to her, Katie's eyes watered. She had never in all of her sixty-six years been given a gift like the one Janis held in her hands.

"Hey, come on, man, don't lose it yet. That's not the only thing in this box, baby. You have to check out the rest of this shit and then you can lose it." She laughed that wonderful Janis Joplin laugh.

Janis held up a past dated, beautifully illustrated poster of Country Joe and the Fish, which had also been autographed personally to Katie. The other posters in the box included one signed by Mad River, another by the members of Moby Grape, and the very last, a signed poster of a future show that would be given by the Grateful Dead.

"My God. This is the best gift that I've ever received." Tears of joy rolled freely down her face.

Katie crossed the room, knelt beside Janis, and hugged her, a spectacular moment that she would never forget. "Thank you so much, I'm speechless."

"Right on, man, I'm so glad I made you this happy." Her face glowed with satisfaction and in that moment Katie made a critical decision.

If she was truly sent back to fix what had gone wrong, that must include Janis Joplin. She couldn't let this beautiful person walk into what awaited her without a warning. She owed Janis the same chance she was giving Frog and Dylan. The one she intended to give to her own brother. Maybe she was meant to save Janis too, the young inspirational hippie who was only weeks away from superstardom?

"Janis, have you ever had your tarot cards read?" Katie asked, grasping at straws.

"No, man, I haven't."

"Can I read them for you?" Katie asked.

She had never officially read cards, but she had watched Moonbeam do it plenty of times, so many that she was sure she could do it herself. What she didn't know she could fake. After all, she already knew Janis Joplin's future.

"I don't know, man. Besides, I thought you said it was your roommate who did all that spiritual stuff?"

"Sure, but she trained me. I can read cards just as well as she can."

Janis's blue eyes pulled together in thought, and several rows of lines ran across her forehead. In an instant the lines were gone, her face softened, and she started to laugh.

"I don't know, man, what if you give me some fucking horrible news? That would be too much, it would fucking creep me out."

"I guess, but what if you learned something really important from the cards? Something that you wouldn't have known if you didn't have them read?"

"That's true, I guess, but wow, baby, I don't know." She swallowed and scratched the side of her head. Then she nodded. "Sure, I guess so. I mean, why not? Let's fucking do it."

Katie smiled and prayed to the powers that be that she could come up with a story that would influence the future decisions of Janis Joplin. She ran up the stairs taking them two at a time and entered Moonbeam's bedroom.

She took Moonbeam's canvas tie dyed boho bag containing her tarot cards and other fortunetelling essentials. She apologized in advance to the powers that be for using cards that didn't belong to her. Any self-respecting fortuneteller would never use someone else's deck, especially without permission. Since she might be given the opportunity to save Janis Joplin's life she was sure the Gods and the Goddesses, along with Moonbeam, would forgive her.

She went downstairs and took a clean sheet out of the closet. Using Moonbeam's deck was one thing, but if she got Jolly Rancher crud stuck to the cards, that would be another.

When she returned to the sitting room, Janis was staring at a few of the posters.

"You know, this artwork is really outta sight. I never thought about it until that night we were outside rapping but since then, I've really checked out a lot of these dudes' work and yeah, these cats are fucking talented." She laughed her raspy laugh. "Get this, I even scammed a few of the posters for myself, man. Can you believe that? I actually have them hanging in my pad. That's crazy shit, right?" She shook her head. "They're really hip, you know, all those psychedelic lines intersecting. Have you ever stared at that shit when you're on an acid trip?" Janis twisted her hands in a variation of interchangeable ways, meant to indicate the patterns of distortion caused by an LSD trip.

Katie remembered "her" 1967, when she had done just that. What she found crazy now, was that she had been able to influence Janis enough that the free loving hippie had put Avalon posters on the walls of her own pad. She only hoped that she was just as successful in forewarning her about choices that would lead to the tragic end of her promising young life.

Katie spread the clean flowered bed sheet over the coffee table, removed a white candle from Moonbeam's bag, lit it, and placed it alongside a clear white crystal on the table. She opened the hand carved wooden box, pulled out the deck, and unwrapped the blue silk scarf that covered them.

"You ready?" Katie asked.

"I don't know, baby, I'm a bit nervous." She hesitated for a few seconds before nodding her head. "Okay, man, I'm ready, let's do this. I just hope it's not a bummer trip. That would really fucking stink, all this nervousness for a bad trip."

There are multiple ways to read the tarot and good readers have their own technique, which includes their own system of placing and reading the cards. Katie was forced to use the only method she knew, a variation of the Celtic cross, which Moonbeam had devised for her readings.

"What's your zodiac sign, Janis?" she asked, knowing full well that Janis was a Capricorn.

"I was born January 19, 1943. I'm a Capricorn."

Katie flipped through the deck looking for the one card she would use to represent Janis Joplin, the Queen of Pentacles. She found it near the bottom of the deck and pulled it out, then handed it to Janis.

"This card represents you in the reading. Study it until you feel a familiarity with it." Janis reached for the card and stared at the Queen of Pentacles.

While she became 'familiar' with the card, Katie shuffled the rest of the deck, her mind flashing over the many readings she had watched Moonbeam perform. *How am I going to do this?* she asked herself. Would the deck work with her or against her?

She breathed deeply, trying to tune into the vibes that surrounded her. Those vibes, Moonbeam had explained, would let her know when to stop shuffling the cards. When they did, she held the deck still and waited.

There were several ways she could play this. One, tell Janis everything. Let her know upfront that she was going to die, then point out the bad decision that would take her life.

No, that wouldn't work. That was impulsive, immature. It could backfire and make her look like a lunatic. She chose option two: *Always leave the audience wanting more.* She would have to pull Janis in slowly, just as she had done with Moonbeam, Frog, and Dylan. Before Janis would believe, she would have to see for herself that Katie was the real deal.

This reading had to blow her mind in a positive way, and Katie could do that easily since everything she was about to tell Janis would come true. Once that happened, she would be a believer and she would come to Katie for another reading. In the next reading Katie would warn her; let her know everything that was coming, but not yet. After all, Janis was just about to enter her three-year career high, a beautiful time. It would be easy to predict the next few months. Katie rubbed her hands together. *You can do this.*

Janis laid the Queen of Pentacles on the table. "Hey man, what's with the groovy crystal?" Janis asked, pointing at the oblong rock that sat next to the white candle.

"It brings positive energy to the reading, good vibes, you dig?" Katie said and then cleared her throat, her voice taking on a spiritual quality. "I'm going to hand you the deck now, I want you to hold it and concentrate on a question."

Janis took the deck in both hands and held it close to her body. For several seconds she closed her eyes. When she was finished she stared at Katie, her eyes blinking rapidly.

"Now place the deck down in front of you," Katie instructed. "Are you right or left handed?" she asked, already knowing the answer.

"Right."

"Then with your left hand divide the deck into three piles."

"Any way I want?"

"The way you feel they should be split."

When she finished, Katie asked her to rotate the middle stack and then place the divided deck back into one.

"Now hand me the cards." She took them in both hands, closed her eyes and said a blessing to the Gods and Goddesses of all religions. When she was finished, she tapped the deck three times for luck and then she smiled at Janis.

She dealt the cards, laying them face down on the table, the first one placed on top of the Queen of Pentacles. Then moving clockwise she built a circle of four cards that surrounded it. From there, Katie placed another four cards up the left hand side of the circle and finished with three cards across the top, for a total of twelve cards.

"Are you ready?" she asked. Janis, biting on one of her fingernails, nodded.

"Do you want to tell me your question? I can read it either way, but it helps if I have an idea of what I'm working with."

"Just a general question, man. You know, what will be happening in my life."

"Okay, here we go..." Katie took a deep breath. "This is what crosses you," she said, turning over the first card; the one she had placed on the top of the Queen of Pentacles. "The Six of Wands. The beginning of a new journey, a new start." Katie pointed at the card that showed a youth sitting on a horse and six staves raised in celebration.

Her hand moved to the left of the circle and hovered above the next card. "This is your past." She flipped it over. "The Seven of Wands reversed. In the past you had to fight against many opponents and a lot of criticism."

"Ain't that the fucking truth," Janis said, "you don't even know, man."

"This next card is also your past, but it's more recent. The Seven of Cups means change of views and beliefs tainted with melancholy feelings from the past, childhood memories, and thoughts of home and family."

Janis smiled when she thought of her family.

"Your near future," Katie said flipping the next card, the Eight of Wands. "Your journey continues, everything moves together perfectly, just like a dream."

"That's outta sight, baby."

Katie moved her hand to the next card, the last one in the circle. "If time remains the same without any shifts or waves, because sometimes there are changes that interrupt what's supposed to happen, then this is one of your outcome cards." She flipped over the Six of Pentacles, and smiled. Despite her original plan, fake it till you make it, this was turning out better than she could have imagined. So far she had yet to fake anything, the cards were cooperating with her completely. "Material wealth is coming your way." Katie smiled.

"Wow, man, so far so good." Janis laughed and rubbed her hands together. "But, half the cards are still left, so the bad shit is coming, watch."

Katie started on the bottom row of unturned cards. "This is the environment and how it affects you, Four of Swords. You're recovering from past unhappiness, learning to believe in yourself again."

Janis nodded in acknowledgement.

Katie flipped the next card. "This is the card of strength. You gain strength from where you live, the people you surround yourself with. They're helping you recover from the criticism and self-doubt you learned before."

"True, man, Texas was a fucking bummer and San Francisco people are real, you dig?" Janis asked, and Katie nodded. It was true the hippies of 1967 were gentle, loving souls, their world a peaceful place. That would all change by the end of the Summer of Love. By then, the influx of newcomers would change the dynamics and the original hippies would start to move out.

"This card represents either your hopes or your fears, depending on the card. Nine of Cups reversed, this is your fear. You're waiting for all your dreams to fall apart like a house of cards. You're filled with doubt. You try to believe in yourself but sometimes you find it hard to do."

"I know, man," Janis agreed. "I hate doing that too, but I can't help it."

"Are you ready for the three outcome cards?" Katie asked, pointing to the remaining unturned cards.

"I guess." Janis swallowed hard, leaned forward on the edge of the couch, and stared at the cards.

Katie flipped the first card across the top of the circle. "The Three of Discs. Continued money and wealth." She immediately turned the second card. "The Wheel of Fortune. The world continues to turn in your favor, anything is possible." Katie paused before flipping over the final card.

"And..." she turned it, "The World. It means you're not far from all of your dreams coming true."

"Wow, man, really? Fucking crazy reading." Janis was happy and laughing now.

Katie was happy too. Her tarot reading abilities came through with flying colors. Moonbeam was a pretty good teacher after all.

"What are you doing now?" Janis asked

"I'm studying the cards, making sure I didn't miss anything. I'm looking for combinations; things that imply karma or how many other people are involved."

"And?" Janis prompted.

"Your reading isn't karmic but it does show that your music will affect a lot of people."

"That's good, right? I mean the whole reading, man, it's all good right?"

"Yeah, it's all groovy, but one more thing before we're finished." Katie reached for Moonbeam's canvas bag and pulled out an embroidered sack. "These are runes," she explained. "They're rocks painted with the Viking alphabet the Nordic soothsayers used thousands of years ago. Put your left hand into the bag and chose one of the rocks. Don't wiggle your hand around just pull it out straight in front of you and wait until I tell you what to do next."

Janis put her left hand into the bag and chose a rock. As instructed, she pulled her hand out straight and waited.

"Now turn your hand over so your fingers are facing up and then slowly open your hand."

Janis did as instructed.

"Mannaz, it's the rune of self. It means you need to think about yourself. Your world is about to go crazy. What you need to remember is that you need to take care of yourself. Don't take it for granted that you're young and healthy," Katie said, hoping for some acknowledgement from Janis, that she didn't get.

"What, man? I always take care of myself, baby. When I leave here I'm going to take care of myself real well. I'm going to band practice and I'm going to do some tequila shots with the guys. Cuervo man, nothing but the best for Janis."

She laughed and Katie shook her head. "You're on a beautiful journey, Janis, one that's going to keep spinning in your favor. You'll make a lot of money, gain a lot of material wealth, and the whole world will adore you."

"I'm going to be famous?"

"You're going to be very famous, and it's going to happen very quickly. After the Monterey Pop Festival, your world will never be the same. You won't be able to just walk down the street anymore because everyone will know you. Whatever you and Big Brother and the Holding Company do will turn to gold. You'll be a great success."

"Far out, man! That's fucking groovy, wait till I tell the guys in the band." Janis frowned. "But I don't know, man. I don't want to be a pessimist but I'll believe all of it when I see it. Hey, how long is a reading good for?"

"Three to six months," Katie answered. She had said enough, she didn't want to push the reading too heavily. "Before we finish do you want to blow out the candle and make a wish?" Katie asked.

Janis nodded, shut her eyes and concentrated for a few seconds, and then opened them and blew out the flame.

"Now the smoke will take your wish up to heaven."

"That was one groovy reading and I sure hope it all comes true, but you know how it is, man" Janis grinned and Katie smiled back knowingly.

Yes, she knew how it was. People had to see proof before they believed the supernatural. That was fine, she had time. It was only 1967. Janis would live another three years. All Katie had to do was wait, sit back, and watch as Janis's world exploded and she became a superstar overnight just as the tarot cards had predicted.

"There's something else I picked up on while I was reading your cards," Katie said. "There's going to be a documentary shot at the pop festival and your agent or somebody close to you is going to advise Big Brother against being filmed."

"How do you know about that?" Janis asked, startled, the smile melting from her face.

"Just something I picked up on while doing your reading," Katie repeated. "Anyway, it would be a mistake. You have to allow them to film you because that concert will make history. In forty-five years people will still be watching it, and you don't want to miss out on that."

"Oh come on, man, forty-five years?" Janis snickered, then got serious. "But seriously, how did you know about the documentary and the discussion that we've been having in the group?"

Katie just stared at her.

"Wow, man. That's fucking creepy." Janis was laughing again, making light of the situation.

"Yeah, it's a lot to hear and I'm really sorry if I creeped you out. You were so nice by bringing me those wonderful posters, I just wanted to repay you somehow."

"Sure, man, and you did. I appreciate the reading. It was phenomenal and I hope it all comes true. I mean, it's creepy, but it's cool too. But how you picked up on the documentary, that was weird stuff, baby. That made the hair on the back of my neck stand up." Janis rubbed at her neck.

"That's a sign that what I told you is the truth, but you'll see for yourself when it all starts to come true."

"Are you going to the Monterey Pop Festival?" Janis asked.

"Yes, I'm going all three days. Moonbeam and I are driving up in a van with a friend. If we can't find anywhere else to crash, we figure we can sleep in that."

She wondered how a three-day trip with Ron and Moonbeam was going to work out even as she said it.

"Groovy, baby. I'm glad to hear you're going. It's going to be a far out experience, you dig? All those bands together in an outside venue for the first time. Just out of sight, man."

Katie was looking forward to the concert that she had missed the first time around.

"Even Simon and Garfunkel are going to be there, right out of Hollywood. You heard they're doing all the music for a movie there, something about Mrs. Robinson," Janis said.

"Yes, I heard something about that. It will be a great film." Janis was referring to *The Graduate*, which would be released in December 1967. Katie couldn't even count how many times she had seen it.

"I guess I should go," Janis said, standing up from the couch. "The band is practicing and they're expecting me to show up. Imagine that." She snickered. "Hey, good luck getting the Jolly Rancher off the coffee table, I don't think the bed sheet is going to cut it."

"Oh hell, I forgot about that. You're right. Now I have to go back and try to scrape that shit off." Katie walked her guest to the door. "You don't think the roommates might miss the tablecloth?"

Janis laughed and shook her head. "No man, not even close."

"Thanks again for the visit and for the posters, Janis. That was a fabulous gift, it means a lot to me."

"Listen, Katie," Janis said, taking Katie's hands in her own, "the reading was groovy, baby, it really was. When you're at the festival come and have a drink with me."

"Janis, you're going to be so swarmed while you're there nobody will be able to get near you. In fact, nobody will ever be able to get near you again. You will be surrounded by security. It will be impossible for me to see you."

"Dream on, baby. Anyway, if you're right, and I'm flooded with popularity, I'll just tell security that Katie, my spiritualist, is going to visit me." She smiled. "I mean it, baby, stop by and see me."

And then, Janis Joplin was gone.

* * *

He had a meeting with Sal and Dave at 7:30, but Dylan had called last night asking to meet before the rest of the team showed. All the biker would tell him was that it was of major importance.

The call had been strange. Dylan acted oddly, and it had left Frog with a feeling of unease. As he walked towards the private meeting with Dylan his skin started to crawl. Something was wrong, he could sense it.

Since Frog's beating in Oakland, Joey and Dylan had taken over his Golden Gate Park gig. That was a huge relief. The Oakland thugs had shown up once or twice, but realizing that they were facing members of the Hells Angels, they backed off; at least temporarily.

Frog had taken on a new role in the organization; he was now the full time delivery boy. To him, that was worse than the small time sales he was making previously.

Now he was driving the van daily, carrying a loaded .45, along with a hidden shotgun and large amounts of heroin, but as promised, never cash. His deliveries stretched as far south as San Jose and as far north as Santa Rosa. Basically, he was all over map. Without question he would go anyplace that Dave and Sal sent him, and most times that included neighborhoods that he was much too white to be delivering into.

Frog wanted out desperately but he had dug himself into a hole so deep that he had no idea how to climb out of it, especially now when the dough was just pouring in. If he could get out safely he had enough bread to build a house in Marin County. If he could get out without fear of retribution, he and Moonbeam could start their own commune. If only there were a way... but as brilliant as he was he couldn't think of one. In the back of his mind he was fully aware that the deadline to his death was closing in, and so was the promise he had made to Moonbeam.

They were supposed to leave right after the Monterey Pop Festival. With that event less than two weeks away, she was busy planning their move. As far as she knew they were heading north into Marin County right after the three-day concert. Once there, they would move into the commune with their friend Chet. This was supposed to lead them into the good life where they would be truly free from the rules of the establishment. Frog had to admit that living off the land was an exciting possibility, and one that he would embrace happily if it weren't for his problems.

He had every intention of keeping that promise, but now that the time was drawing near he feared the truth, that he wasn't going to be allowed to get away that easily. It wasn't like he could just give a two-week notice. If he walked away from these people, they would find him. They would hunt him down like a dog and then there was no telling what would happen. He and Moonbeam would be easy targets.

When he turned the corner onto 7th he could see the front of the garage. It was still dark. If Dylan was inside he hadn't bothered to turn on any of the lights. Expecting to find the door locked, he was surprised when it opened easily.

He entered cautiously, and once inside finally started to relax. The lights in the back of the shop were burning brightly. Dylan was here.

He started down the partially lit hallway but after only a few steps, Dylan popped out from nowhere and Frog jumped.

"Fuck man, don't do that! You scared the shit out of me."

"Sorry, man, I didn't mean to. Just bad timing I guess."

"Right, well here I am, man. I'm only half awake but I'm here. So you want to tell me what's so important that we have to meet at this ungodly hour?"

"Sure, man, I'm going to explain everything. Let me get a couple of mugs and we'll go in the back and rap."

Dylan reached for two dull colored cups and then led Frog through the hallway and into the florescent-lit garage. Taking a red-checkered thermos off of a desk, Dylan filled two cups with black steaming coffee and handed one to Frog.

"Sorry, man, I drink it black; I hope that's okay with you."

"Sure, I drink it black too." Frog sat on a cold metal chair and blew on the steaming cup of coffee.

"Look, man, I know this seems weird and all me calling you and having you meet me here in the dark of morning all secret agent like, but, man, we really have to talk."

Frog sipped at the hot coffee, burned his tongue and flinched. "Talk about what?"

"Man, I don't even know where to start, so I guess I'll start with what we have in common: Katie.

"Katie?" Frog asked. His mind reeled. *What had she told Dylan?*

"Yeah man, her predictions, they involve both of us." Dylan sipped at his own cup of coffee, and sat on a chair next to Frog, waiting for his words sink in.

"Her predictions?"

"Yeah, her predictions, specifically the ones where we both die."

In that instant Frog understood, and the look on his face told Dylan that he got it.

"I'm not going to play games, man. I'm not Moonbeam and I'm not Katie. I want the truth when I ask you questions, you dig?" Dylan asked, staring into Frog's saucer like eyes. The hippie nodded.

"Do you know how we're supposed to die?" Dylan asked bluntly, starting with the most obvious question.

"No man, not exactly. I only know that *I'm* supposed to die. I didn't know that you were coming along for the ride."

"Well, surprise surprise, Frog boy, we die together somewhere out in the woods. We're buried in a hole side by side, only you're dead, and they bury me alive next to your rotting ass."

"Katie's prediction?" Frog asked, wondering why Katie hadn't updated him on the situation, which had obviously taken a turn for the worse.

"Partly her prediction, but the rest...I have dreams. I understand you have dreams too, Frog. So, in a nutshell, that's what we're going to rap about, you dig?"

"We're here to discuss dreams?"

"I already told you once, Frog, and I'm not going to say it again. I am not Moony, and I'm not Katie, and I'm not fucking playing with you. I want the truth. Tell me about your dreams, Frog, especially the ones that involve the endless hallway."

Frog started to shake visibly and sloshed some of his coffee over the top of the mug.

"H-how do you know about the hallway?"

"I've been there. I've seen the doors and the hag with the rotting teeth. I've seen the parties and the freaky celebrations because somebody 'new' is joining them. Tell me what you know, Frog, stop wasting our time."

"Alright, alright, sure. I've been to the hall several times. I know about the hag and the endless doors that open and close, and I've seen the famous people and the soldiers from old wars that walk around the hall. Yes, I've seen the weird celebrations. Is that what you wanted to know?"

"That's a beginning. When did all of this start?"

"It started before the party, man, the one at the clubhouse. It happened before that. There was this old dude in the neighborhood called Guthrie. He was a permanent fixture outside of Roman's Market, just a neighborhood bum. Anyway, this old dude was mute, he never left his doorway, but on the day of the party he left his spot, and he spoke to me. It was the first time in five years that the dude spoke, and he chose me. You know what he tells me?"

"What?"

"Well, the old cat puts his dirty finger in my face and then he starts to prophesize, he tells me I can get it right this time around. If I listen and I believe, I can still get it right. But that's not all, man. He went back to his doorway and that very same night he fucking died."

"He died?"

"He sure as hell did. That was also the first night that I ever dreamt about the hallway. I never saw it before that night, but since then I've seen it several times. Anyway, get this, man, because this is the real clincher of the story. When Guthrie was found, he was holding an old key in his hand. It was the antique key that unlocks all those doors in the hallway. The very same key the old hag carries around."

Dylan felt his stomach churn. He ran his hand through his shaggy hair and shook his head. "You know we're dead in that hallway right?"

"Yeah, man, that's what Barry Bog keeps telling me when I'm there."

"Barry Bog?"

"He was an old friend who died last year from an overdose. Whenever I dream that I'm in the hall he and Guthrie are both there with me. They try to warn me but..."

"But you don't listen," Dylan finishing for him. Frog nodded. "I've dreamt about that hallway my whole life, even as a kid. But I have another recurring dream, one that is worse than the hallway.

"In this dream I'm in a hole and someone is burying me. There's a dude beside me but he's already dead. I'm not sure if they're burying me alive on purpose or if it's a freak accident, although in the dream I feel as if the killer hates me more. I know who the other person in the hole beside me is. It's you, Frog, we die together. It happens someplace in the woods, someplace far away from everything. So far, that our bodies will never be found."

"That's what Katie said, that my body would never be found."

"Well according to my dream and her premonition, neither will mine."

The two men stared at each other.

"Have you told this to anyone else?" Frog asked.

"No man, the only other person I've talked to is Katie."

"Yeah, man, I don't know how much I can trust you. I mean, your loyalties lie elsewhere, you can't deny that."

Dylan opened the thermos and refilled the two coffee cups. "Man, have you been listening? You really do hear what you want to; no wonder Guthrie and Barry Bog's warnings mean nothing to you. We die *together*, Frog. Do you think that's a fucking joke? Because I don't."

"I don't know what I think. We have until August, did Katie tell you that?"

"August? Are you for fucking real man? This is June. Do you really want to wait another three months hoping that Katie gets the date right? She already told you man, she could be wrong on the timing; it can happen anytime!"

"Then what are we supposed to do, Dylan?" Frog asked sarcastically.

Dylan's fuse blew. Maybe it was the party at Katie's parents and the ridicule he had endured, maybe it was the frustration at believing what he didn't want to believe, or maybe it was the sudden distrust he felt towards everyone around him, but that response was the last stupid remark he was going to hear. In seconds he was off the metal chair. He snagged onto the front of Frog's jacket and jerked him to his feet. The metal chair beneath him fell and Dylan kicked it free as he pinned Frog against the wall.

"Look, you stupid fucking idiot. I have no intentions of being buried alive in a fucking hole and I'm thinking now that it's probably your smartass remarks that get us there. Since we die together I'm going to give you one more shot at this before I fucking kill you myself. Now are you ready to take this shit seriously?"

Frog tried to nod, but Dylan shook him.

"Are you ready to take this seriously?" Dylan repeated.

"Y-yes."

"Good!"

Dylan let go of the front of his jacket and Frog slumped down the wall.

"Okay, man, okay. No more bullshit. What do you think we should do?" Frog asked, pulling himself off the floor and retrieving his chair.

"Tell me the truth, you can't still be thinking about the cash?"

"I know it's stupid but it's so much bread. I want out, I really do, but I keep thinking that I have until August, and I can make a pile more by then."

"Poor Moonbeam. Man, you really are a stupid motherfucker. We aren't waiting until August, Frog, at least I'm not. I believe this shit. I believe the warnings that you seem to think are just a joke. Don't you have enough brains in your head to realize that you should be paranoid of everyone around you? Anyone can be involved in this, because the worst part of all of this is, we don't know who is trying to rub us out. It could be anyone, the club, some drug-crazed loony, the goons from Oakland who beat you senseless, anyone."

"The Italians from Broadway, the patchless bikers, the cats in the Fillmore we're competing with, the list is long, Dylan. Despite what you think I have thought about this, I just didn't know we were a double act then."

"Well, we are, man. We're in this fucking shit together. That means we have to blow this place and the sooner we split, the better."

"And do what, hide out forever?"

"Of course not. We hide out until we can figure this shit out, man. It's the only way to be free, Frog, really free from all of this fucking shit. We have to find out who is trying to have us killed."

"How are we going to do that?"

"I have connections. When we get to where we're going, I'll put out feelers."

"What about Moonbeam? What about your friends, the guy you ride with, Joey?"

"When it's safe we contact them. Once we know what's happening and who's behind this, then we come back. That's when we blow this whole fucking underground bullshit up. We come clean with the club and we let Big Jim and the First Skulls figure out the rest."

"Why can't we just do that now, save time?"

"For one, we don't know who is out to get us, and before I start snooping around I want to be well clear of 'Frisco."

"I see what you're saying, but I can't just walk out on Moonbeam, I can't just leave her behind without an explanation. See, I sort of have plans to split with her, right after the pop festival."

"It's too late for that, Frog, do you want to risk her safety? I have my own concerns about splitting on people I care about too, Katie and Joey mainly, but man that's what we got to do if we want to stay alive. We can't trust anyone right now, and we can't guarantee anyone's safety either, especially the people we care about the most. That means we go alone."

Frog nodded reluctantly. He stared into his coffee mug and then in one gulp finished the contents. "Okay man, I understand."

"Can you ride?"

"I rode dirt bikes as a kid. I had a Honda in Redding that I used in high school. It was my main source of transportation for a long time so yeah, I can ride, but I don't have a bike."

"That's an easy fix. I'll find you one man. It's not going to be a Harley, so don't get your hopes up, but I'll find you a decent ride. I'll get you one soon so you can practice and be ready for the big day. Not only that, we don't want you to stand out. We want everyone to be used to seeing you on a bike so that by the time you leave for the concert seeing you on a motorcycle is an everyday occurrence.

Then when we're in Monterey, we'll blow from there, just up and leave right in the middle of the gig. You understand?"

Frog nodded. He thought of the promise he had made to Moonbeam and the multiple lies he had told her over the last few months. This would be the end he was sure. She would never forgive him.

"Be ready, man. Have your stuff together in an easy pack that you can strap to the bike at a moment's notice, because that's how we're going to play this. At some point in the concert I'll give you the word and we split."

"Where to, man?"

"Oh no, man, I'm not going to tell anyone that, not even you. I have a location picked out, don't worry about that. You just be ready, okay?"

"Yeah I understand. I'll be ready."

Dylan slapped him on the back. "No hard feelings, man. I mean for knocking you into the wall and all. But let's be truthful, brother, it was about time somebody knocked some fucking sense into your empty skull."

"Yeah, you're right. It was the only way that I would listen," Frog admitted. "You had to do it, I dig."

"Hey, is anyone here yet?" a voice called from the front office.

"Our private party's over, Frog. Just remember what we talked about and be ready." Dylan raised his voice. "We're back here, Joey!" he yelled, and a moment later the second biker joined them.

***

The meeting started late. Dave didn't even arrive until quarter to eight, and when he did he was pissed off. This was not going to be a positive meeting. Dylan shook his head wondering how he had ever allowed himself to get involved in something like this.

"What the fuck?" Dylan whispered to Joey.

"Skinner, man, that's what this is about. That cat doesn't know when to fucking stop."

Dylan thought the Skinner situation had been solved ages ago, this was news to him.

"Let's get this fucking meeting going," Dave bellowed. He rolled a padded chair into the middle of the shop. The rest of the men each pulled a metal chair beside him.

"We have problems," he started. "Firstly, I've heard from the Italians in Broadway, they want a meeting. They said our little operation has become large enough that we might need their protection. That means they want money. This meeting is going to happen in July and they specifically asked that you be there Darryl."

Frog, AKA "Darryl", swallowed hard, remembering the note they had left for him at the Psychedelic Shop. A meeting with the Italians didn't sound like something he wanted to attend.

"Our next and our biggest problem is Skinner. I had a heart to heart with him yesterday and the outcome wasn't good. Our little scheme of buying him off is not going to work. I offered him a lot of dough too, and an ongoing interest in the business. Let's just say his loyalty towards the Angels is preventing him from accepting a large payoff. He wants us to come clean. He wants me to talk to Big Jim and admit that we're running a business behind the club's radar, one the Angels wouldn't condone. He made it clear that either we talk to Big Jim or he's going to take the situation to the First Skulls."

"Is he for real, man?" Joey asked.

"I'm afraid so."

"Now what?" Dylan asked, silently hoping that the end of this operation might be in sight.

"Now I take the issue to the unpatched bikers, that's what. This is beyond me; the higher ups are the ones who are going to decide Skinner's fate."

Dylan jumped to his feet. "Decide his fate, man?"

"That's right. Did you think this operation stopped here with us? That it's all on Sal and me? We work for others man, we all do. The line goes upwards, brother. This isn't a small operation, it's a new branch on a very old tree. Skinner stepped into something way over his fucking head. Now I've done what I can, and it's time to turn this over."

"Wait a minute, are we talking about rubbing out Skinner? Is that what this meeting is about? Because I for one don't think that's a great idea."

"It's not up to us, Dylan, take a fucking breath. You're not being asked to do anything. This isn't a democracy and this issue is not up for a vote. The decision on Skinner has nothing to do with us, do you understand?"

Dylan looked around, surprised to find that everyone else was taking the news emotionlessly, as if they were talking about dirty laundry instead of a man's life.

"Look, man," Dylan insisted, "I didn't sign on for murder. When I signed on, this was a beginning operation, a way to make quick bucks."

"And you did, man, you made fast bread and you spent it fast. Everyone in this room did the same. We all enjoyed the ups and the perks. Well every up has a downside, get used to it."

"Let me get this straight, we're turning over the fate of one of our Angel brothers to these unpatched bikers? And those cats are going to decide Skinner's fate? No man, I'm not in on that. If that's where this is going then sign me out. You can keep my interest in the shop, I don't want anything. I'm not getting involved in a fucking murder, Dave."

"Sit down, Dylan, and shut your fucking mouth," Sal said, jumping to his feet.

Dave put a hand on his shoulder and whispered, "Calm down, brother."

"Are you nuts, Dylan? Do you know who we're dealing with? There *is* no out, brother. What happens is we move up the ladder. Eventually we delegate to those below us. That's when you don't have to get your hands dirty anymore. This is business man, it's not personal. This is how business runs; the powers that be control the masses. Now, keep your mouth shut and your mind on your own business, and you'll be fine. You got it, hotshot?"

Dylan bit his tongue and leaned against the wall of the garage, arms crossed. If he wasn't sure about leaving before, he was now. This shit had gone much too far. There was only one way out: he and Frog would bail from the pop festival. Deadlines in the club prevented him from leaving sooner, the same deadlines that would keep him alive until the concert, but once his obligations to the Angels was met, he and Frog would be long gone.

"What about the Italians?" Frog reminded them, still fixated on the meeting he was going to have to attend, the one where he would be sitting in a room full of gangsters.

"The Italians?" Dave laughed. "You don't need to worry about them. Haven't you been listening? This operation goes way up the ladder, Frog. I told you there would be a time when we would confront them."

"Confront them with me there? Are you fucking serious?"

"Sure, man. You, me, and Sal. We go to the meeting and listen to their demands and then we take that information back to the unpatched bikers. They will handle it from there, just like they're going to handle the Skinner issue. Until then, everyone stay out of Little Italy. No selling in or near that area, no delivering in or near that area, don't even go to dinner on their turf, understood?"

Everyone nodded.

"That's it men, meeting's adjourned. It's time to get to work." Dave rolled the chair back to the desk he had taken it from. "Dylan, I want to see you in my office for a minute."

Dylan entered the room and shut the door behind him.

"Sit down, brother."

Dylan sat on a ripped upholstered chair.

"Skinner and I were hangarounds together. I've known him for nearly fifteen years. Don't think this decision is easy for me, Dylan. It's ripping me up inside, but I have to do what's right for business. I did everything I could to defuse this. I offered him more than I should have, but no amount of bread would buy him. We can't allow this to go any further. Do you have any idea what would happen if he went to the First Skulls? The repercussions would be huge." Dave sighed heavily. "The club stays out of this at all costs; remember the vow we took? Just step back, Dylan, do what you're getting paid to do. No more thoughts of leaving, no more outbursts like the one you had today. There's only so much I can control and from there it goes up the ladder of command. Be smart, use your head, and for your own sake keep your mouth shut. Now get the hell out of my office, I have work to do and so do you."

Joey stood outside Dave's office waiting for Dylan. "Are you fucking losing it?" he asked with a stern look on his dark face when Dylan walked out.

"Me? Are you for fucking real? Doesn't all of *this*," Dylan said, gesturing around the room, "scare you just a little? I mean this is the big time, brother, did you know we were signing up for this?"

"Do you hear yourself, man? Why are you internalizing this shit? We aren't making this much bread to do the thinking, Dylan, so fucking stop. Pull yourself together fast."

Dylan stared at the man he had known since childhood, the one he thought he knew so well. Right now, Joey seemed like a complete stranger and that impact struck him like a boulder.

"Sure thing, man. I fucking got it, all right? No thinking, no talking, my mistake."

"I hope you really believe that, man."

Joey's eyes were dark and menacing, something Dylan had never witnessed before.

"Listen, man, you ever dreamt of being buried alive?"

"What?"

"Being buried in a hole or being stuck in an endless hallway filled with doors?"

"Are you fucking nuts, Dylan? Now you're talking about dreams? Cool it, are we clear?"

"Crystal clear," Dylan said, shaking his shaggy hair and walking away.

"Hey, man, Frog is outside. He said he wanted to ask you something before he split!" Sal yelled across the garage.

Glad to pull himself away from the bad vibes he and Joey shared, Dylan headed for the front door. He found Frog smoking a joint outside.

"Hey, man, you need to be cool. I've met with these unpatched biker dudes, real fucking scary people. They're bad news, man. They won't think twice about plugging any of us, you dig?" Frog said.

Dylan nodded.

"We're leaving, man, just remember that. We're leaving and we can't tell anyone that we're going, because right now we don't know who we can trust," Frog said, repeating Dylan's earlier words.

"I know." Dylan thought of the confrontation he had just shared with the man he considered his own brother.

"I'll be ready. You give me the word and we're gone. Murder's not my bag either," Said Frog. He handed the joint to Dylan.

Chapter 29

Annie Sullivan sat at the window of her attorney's office staring over the San Francisco Bay.

Robin Crosby finished going through the growing stack of legal documents and closed the folder. She took her reading glasses off and rubbed her bloodshot eyes.

"We got him, Moony. Don't worry, just be patient."

Annie laughed. "It's been a long time since anyone's called me that."

Robin's smile broadened. The years seemed to melt away, and for several precious seconds Annie saw her as the girl she had once been, the young college student, Katie's roommate, and their lifelong friend.

Back in the '60's, Robin was busy going to school at San Francisco State. The truth was Annie and Katie barely saw her until she graduated, and they had never seriously partied with her, something that mattered heavily at the time.

Over the past forty-five years, the women remained in touch, growing even closer. Annie had also worked with Robin on several high profile cases, so they were familiar with each other's work.

When Robin heard about Katie's accident, she was anxious to take on the case. She remembered when Mark Rhodes had come to her and Katie's apartment all those years ago, how he had stalked the front of their house for several days looking for Katie, only to make romantic advances to her at the end of the day.

The first motion of business when Robin came on board was to legally defend the guardianship paperwork awarded by the courts. Mark had tried everything to negate the original terms of the contract, but he had been unsuccessful for the past five months.

"This court shit is exhausting, does it ever end?" Annie asked for the millionth time, not really expecting an answer.

"It's a long process. Think of it as playing a game of chess. We make small moves and Mark throws boulders. We make more small moves so we can cover our tracks and he spends bundles on legal fees. We let him beat on us and use up his money while we just stand back and wait. When he runs out of ammunition and he's tired, or when his funds dry up, then we go for the jugular. No worries, you should just sit back and enjoy this. I am. I love watching him scramble around trying to save his already worthless ass." Robin laughed in an evil lawyer like way, making Annie smile.

"Look at how much we've already accomplished. I know you think five months is a long time but in the corporate world of law, believe me, this shit can last for years," Robin said.

"God forbid. I wouldn't be able to stand the stress for years."

Annie shook her head, thinking of the tailspin life she had been living since the beginning of the legal battles. In a nutshell, it had been five months of playing cat and mouse with Mark. Robin wanted a slow kill, and as it had turned out, Mark was a worthy opponent. He was good at covering his tracks but Annie and Robin had access to avenues he couldn't even imagine.

Over Annie's thirty-six year career she had made close friends with some very influential people, specifically fellow reporters, big shot attorneys (like Robin), and several private detectives.

Robin brought another set of skills to the table. As a partner in an influential firm, she had a range of skilled attorneys at her fingertips and since many had dealt with Mark's dirty politics over the years, they were all just itching to bring down a corporation such as Rhodes' Investment Corporation.

So what had started as an act of friendship on Annie's part had turned into a full-fledged conspiracy to destroy Mark Rhodes, and thanks to the organizational skills of many, they had all their bases covered, someone watching Mark's movements, a team of accountants going through his financial records, all the way back to the year Al Searfus promoted him into a leadership role in the company.

Annie and Robin's case was moving forward perfectly. They were building momentum as a group and they were happy with their findings, but the slow pace drove Annie crazy. She understood that it was a waiting game revolving around Mark Rhodes' actions, but it was still a rollercoaster of emotions. Since she was a local journalist, the case had made it into the public eye, especially when Rhodes' legal team had gone after Annie's credibility as a journalist.

Focusing on her integrity as a reporter, they tried to say that she had compromised on stories, taken handouts and kickbacks, but their smear campaign had failed miserably. In the end, all they were able to prove was that she was an honest reporter and that had added to her popularity, pushing her into a recognized position as a first rate Bay Area journalist.

With the first battle lost, Mark's team tried to push the instability card, examining Annie's mental status for legal guardianship. They accused her of being an overstressed journalist with too many obligations on her plate. These obligations, they insinuated, made her a poor choice as the sole custodian of a critically ill patient. They tried to paint her as an old, withering journalist who was losing her marbles and suggested she should hang up her quilled pens.

With a set of small moves Robin had turned that argument around. Pointing out that Mark's excessive use of the term 'instability' had taken him far in life. After all, he had used the same diagnosis and the same incriminating argument to take control of Katherine Rhodes' company five years earlier. In the end Robin had left an impact on the court by showing that Mark Rhodes was a poor judge of instability if he thought an upstanding San Francisco journalist such as Annie Sullivan fit the mold.

Mark's lawyers had continued trying to play hardball, hitting below the knees, digging for any possible loopholes they could find to negate the legal contract that had been drawn up between Mark and Annie, but as of yet, they had been unsuccessful. Robin wanted to keep it that way.

"Rather than focusing on how far we have to go, you really need to think of what we've accomplished. It's not like Mark is living the high life," Robin laughed.

It was true; Mark was far from living the highlife. Robin had made sure of that. When she came on board she filed documents to freeze company assets pending legal scrutiny. That move limited Mark's spending, and now a man in need of cash, Mark's legal difficulties had just begun.

Tiffany's son was born in March, ironically sharing Katherine and Mark's daughter Angela's birthday. A memorable day, Annie was sure. Of course, due to an insurance fraud claim that arose from an unknown source, Tiffany had been forced to give birth at an HMO facility instead of the luxury hospital she would have preferred.

According to sources close to the couple, Tiffany and Mark's relationship was strained. Apparently the lack of a wedding ring, along with Tiffany's new limit on spending, plus watching big bucks being paid for Katie's care, and another bundle going into legal fees had taken its toll.

Tiffany had signed on for an easy life. By marrying an older man of means she had expected a plush lifestyle, a nice car, big house, plenty of spending cash, and a man who doted on her. Now, without a wedding ring or even a divorce date, strapped on cash, and stuck with a newborn, Tiffany's all-star life had turned sour. She was just 26 years old, beautiful, and now faced with an older man, his incapacitated, comatose wife (who he couldn't currently legally divorce), and debts that were piling up fast. The promise of a nanny to care for the infant had fallen through like the rest of Mark's promises, and now she saw herself as a woman trapped in a situation she had been tricked into.

There were numerous fights. Tiffany had learned the hard way that Mark did what Mark wanted and that crying and pleading did little in the way of changing his egotistical mind. Of course, Katie could have told her that long ago if she had asked.

Towards the end of May, Tiffany had walked out, taking her two-month old son and relocating to Washington State where her parents lived. That arrangement hadn't lasted long, and by the second week of June she was back in the house with Mark. How long that would last was anybody's guess, but Robin and Annie had taken bets on when she would leave for good.

What made the situation worse for Mark, if his situation *could* get any worse, was the realization that as his son grew older the infant looked more and more like Tiffany's ex-boyfriend rather than her husband to be. The obvious resemblance between the two was noticed by many, and was now common talk among the couples' inner circle of friends. So much so that Mark had insisted on a DNA test, and that's what had finally driven Tiffany out of the house.

Several weeks later, they were allegedly living together, awaiting the results of that genetic test. Robin was anxiously waiting also; because of her 'contacts' she could easily know the truth before the couple did.

Today's meeting was just protocol, going over files, making updates, clarifying future movements. All they concentrated on now was allowing Mark's attorneys to run the gambit fighting over the custodial rights of Katie. Robin wanted her opponent worn down before she filed her real paperwork: a breach of contract between Katherine Rhodes and her husband. That's when Robin would tear Mark's house of cards down one at a time until she made sure he owned nothing.

"It's all beautiful, Annie, it really is. It's like the gods are with us; as if everything is destined and falling into place the way it's supposed to be. Sometimes I feel as if the situation is correcting itself by mystical means."

Annie laughed. "Jesus, Robin, you sound so 'back in the day'. Katie and I were the hippies remember?"

"Yeah, but I didn't have time to be a hippie back then so I'm making up for it now."

Annie couldn't argue that. At sixty-five, Robin's life had taken on a Bohemian style that certainly made up for days gone by. She and her old man lived on several acres in Marin County. Her partner, a retired chemist, grew medicinal marijuana in a legalized grow coop that consisted of high tech engineering. Annie didn't understand the modern day terminology, remembering simpler days of dime bags filled with Colombian Gold.

Robin reached into the drawer on her desk and pulled out a blue studded rhinestone box and opened it.

"Ron's new batch, you really need to try this."

The joint looked professionally rolled, thinner than a cigarette, and the paper was see-through, as if it had been rolled in saran wrap. Annie shook her head. Robin had indeed changed.

"He says it's a hybrid mix between sativa and indicia but heavy on the sativa side. It's called Flying Dutchmen Thai-tanic. I say it makes my arthritis feel better and lessens my stress by creating positive vibes. Whatever you want to call it is up to you."

Robin lit the joint and inhaled deeply, shutting her eyes as she savored a hint of chocolate in the herb. "Just wonderful. What would I do without this stuff?" She passed the joint to Annie.

Annie, who once smoked only for enjoyment, had to admit that her occasional indulgence with Robin relieved aches and pains that were a daily reminder of her age. She drew on the joint and coughed, not used to the THC.

"A couple more months, Annie, and then we'll be in this kicking and scratching. I have him right where I want him."

"Yeah I know, it's just the whole ordeal, especially how long it all takes. Plus I'm still getting emails from Mark asking if we can settle this reasonably, which doesn't help."

"He's desperate. Sitting in that expensive house he can't afford, watching Tiffany rant and rave, looking at the kid that has brown eyes and skin too dark to be his, watching his funds being thrown into the best care for his comatose wife, one he can't legally divorce while he's fighting for custody."

"Honest, Robin, I am glad. I really want to see him get what he deserves it's just—"

"That it takes so long. I know," Robin interrupted. She finished the last of the smoke and disposed of the evidence. "Once he's exhausted all of his attempts at negating your contract then we start to play. That's when I hit him with my lawsuits. That's when the little balding weasel is going to piss his pants. That contract he signed with Katherine is full of holes, forcefully signed under duress due to fraudulent clauses and contract terms that could never be met. There is no possible way he has any claim to that company. He will *absolutely* lose ownership. Then we'll have other problems. Does the company ownership go to a comatose woman? Her custodial best friend? The two absent children who have yet to come forward?"

"Then what?" asked Annie.

"Another fight, but that could be years away so don't worry about it. Listen, Annie, are you taking care of yourself? I know this is a lot of stress, and you have Katie's medical concerns too."

"I'm alright. I'm only working part time, and Katie's care is ongoing so nothing really changes there. I stop by the hospital and visit with her three or four times a week. We talk about the past and I tell her about the present. Somewhere deep inside I feel as if she's listening and sometimes she even smiles. The doctors are hopeful; they said the surgery to reattach her skull went well. They expect improvement, but I guess where the brain is concerned that can take a long time. I don't know... I try to remain hopeful."

"Any word from her kids?"

"Nope, nothing."

"Better for your case."

"Yes, but it's not better for Katie."

"Annie, what are you doing for yourself? You know Ron and I worry about you."

"Yes, I know you do, but you don't need to. Really, I'm fine. I have some friends I see frequently."

"When are you going to move out of the city? You've been there long enough. Come back to Marin County, you can't stay in San Francisco forever."

"I know, but for now I'm content. I'm close to Katie, work, shopping; I know it's a rat race and I'm sure I'll get fed up with city life but for now it's working."

"Are you dating?"

"Please, Robin, really? I'm too old to date, and besides...well... I have my reasons."

"You are not too old to date. There are online sites, places to meet people that have the same interests you do. You could find someone fun, someone you can do things with. Take a chance, who knows what might happen?"

"No more chances like that, I don't need them and I don't want them."

"I know what you might want. Why don't you call him, Annie?"

Annie laughed hard and looked at her friend. This was a conversation they hadn't had in years.

"Now you're talking insanity. We aren't going to have this discussion Robin. The whole idea is silly." Annie rose from the chair and started gathering her belongings.

"Hey, what if I called him for you?"

"You really are crazy. What brought this up?"

"The metaphysical stuff, I really meant what I said. I feel like there are outside forces surrounding this situation. It's crazy I know, but I want to believe that it's true. That the powers that be have looked down on us and have decided to correct what shouldn't have happened in the first place."

"What does that have to do with me?"

"You know perfectly well what I'm getting at."

"All of that was a long time ago, Robin."

"And it's something that shouldn't have happened."

Annie's phone rang, ending the awkward conversation.

"Annie Sullivan," she answered when she didn't recognize the number. "Oh, hello, doctor, is everything alright?" Several seconds passed while Annie nodded. "Really? I wonder what that's about. I'm actually close by, let me come there." She ended the call. "Katie's having some unusual brain activity," she told Robin, "and earlier in the day she was moving her hands. I'm driving over to the hospital now to check on her. Thanks for everything, Robin. We've got him, I know, and I'll try to be patient. I'll call you in a few days and check in. Let me know if anything new turns up."

"I sure will, and let me know if this is a breakthrough for Katie."

Annie nodded and then walked out, shutting the door softly behind her.

Robin walked into the lobby to speak with the receptionist.

"Cindy, in the morning I want you to do some detective work."

"Sure, Robin, sounds exciting. What am I looking for?"

Robin took a piece of notepaper off of Cindy's desk and scribbled down a name. "I want you to find this person for me," she said, smiling from ear to ear.

"Sure thing, boss lady. I can't wait to get started."

***

Frog floated peacefully and then he started to fall. His eyes snapped open and he hit the ground.

"Fuck!" He rose to his feet and rubbed his butt. "Not here, man. Not again!"

Despite his protests, Frog stood in the hallway of endless doors. He turned when he heard keys rattling and there beside him was the haggard maid waddling down the hallway.

"No man, no!" he yelled, stomping his feet.

A door opened and Barry Bog walked out. He saw Frog, smiled, and walked towards him.

"Far out, man. You're back. That's outta sight, brother. Are you ready to party?" Barry asked ecstatically.

"No, Barry, I'm not ready to party. This isn't far out, this is a bummer, man. I don't want to be here. I want to be home in my bed where I'm lying next to this groovy beautiful chick."

"Ahh man, you're still on the Haight-Ashbury trip? That's a downer! Damn man, when are you going to be done with that shit? Look, brother, you want to be here otherwise you wouldn't be."

"That's not true, I *don't* want to be here. You don't know what you're talking about. This fucking place doesn't make any sense."

"No man, it's you. *You* don't make any sense. After everything you've witnessed and you're still not listening. Open your eyes, man."

"Where are we?" Frog asked, looking at the endless doors that spread out in all directions.

"You know where we are. Oh right, you're freaked out on the Haight-Ashbury time warp thing. This is the hallway of endless possibilities."

"The what? This place is making me crazy."

"It happens, man. All that traveling around, it disjoints you, man, makes you disoriented, you dig? Up is down and down is up."

"What the fuck, Barry?" Frog rubbed his temples.

Doors simultaneously opened and guests entered the hall: a businessman and a Las Vegas showgirl, a cowboy and a surgeon. The businessman noticed them.

"Excuse me gentlemen, when is the show supposed to start?"

"When they're ready, man, they're setting up now," Barry called back.

"Very well, we'll just get a drink and wait." The group walked halfway down the hall where they entered a room.

"Concert?" Frog asked.

"Yeah, the 27 Club is playing tonight. Stick around and check them out, you'll know plenty of the musicians."

"The 27 Club? I've never heard of them, man."

A door swung open. Jim Morrison walked out. He met a pretty flapper in the middle of the hall. The woman, whom he called Zelda, laughed and her white beaded gown shook, sending a cascade of reflections across the ceiling and walls.

"Man, I know him," Frog said, pointing at Jim Morrison. "He's in the Doors, they're an L.A. band who play in the Haight sometimes."

"They used to play in the Haight. Now he's in the 27 Club, they play here," Barry corrected.

"Who's the flapper chick?"

"Her, man? Pretty, isn't she? Her name is Zelda Fitzgerald. She's an artist, a dancer, and a writer. She married some cat named Scott. He wrote something called *The Great Gatsby*."

"F. Scott Fitzgerald?" Frog asked, glancing at the woman again as she made her way down the hall holding onto Morrison's arm.

"Yeah, man, something like that. The guy's around here somewhere, but he and Zelda don't see eye to eye, you dig?"

"Yeah, I dig."

Doors opened and closed. Occupants changed rooms, conversed briefly in the hall, and then disappeared into the room where the "show" was being held.

"Hey, man, that's Janis Joplin and Jimi Hendrix," Frog said when the pair entered the hallway.

"Yeah, man, they're in the 27 Club too. You really should stay for their show, they're outta this world." Barry laughed at his joke. "Outta this world, man, you get it?"

Frog did not.

Barry pulled a joint from his pocket and lit it. "Wait till you get a taste of this shit, Frog. It will help you remember, it will blow your fucking mind, man."

The maid appeared. She locked a door and opened another. With a toothless grin she smiled at Frog. She tapped the pocket of her apron, reminding him that inside she carried a hypodermic needle.

Frog turned away uncomfortably, but she pointed at him and started to laugh.

"Frog, I have some candy for you," she teased, removing the syringe from her apron pocket and wagging it in his face.

"Don't pay any attention to her, Frog. She's an evil bummer. She's here to torment us man, to remind us of our shortcomings and feed into our guilt." Barry took a quick puff on the joint then handed it to Frog.

Frog took a deep hit and coughed. "Fuck man, this shit is strong."

"I told you, man. Nothing but the best here, baby. Anything you want too."

Doors shook, plaster fell.

Frog jumped away from the wall. "What the fuck?"

"It's cool man, don't worry. That's just the war door, they're always blowing shit up. Crazy ass parties though, fucking wild. As I said, nothing but the best here."

Two doors opened, Vietnam and Civil War soldiers walked out. Some immediately walked down the hall heading towards the concert. Others stood conversing in the hall; confederates and union soldiers alongside Vietnam vets.

"Man, what *is* this place?" Frog asked again.

"I told you, man, this is the hallway of endless possibilities."

"Why are all these people here?"

"They're waiting for another chance, man. We're all waiting for another chance"

"But what am I doing here?"

"You man, you're already working on your second chance but you'll be back soon, because you're blowing it."

More doors opened. Albert Einstein, a robed Gandhi, and John F. Kennedy walked into the hall.

"Man, are they...?"

"Yeah man, that's Albert and Gandhi, they're with the President." Barry nodded his head. "Pretty cool cats, actually."

"They're waiting for a second chance?"

"That's right, man, especially them. Let me tell you, brother, it's not an easy thing to get either. You have to go through all kinds of bullshit. You have to prove you're more responsible, that you're able to learn from your mistakes, and then you have to send a petition upstairs. It's a real motherfucker, Frog." He shook his head. "Then, when you're finally approved, they make you wait for that one crack in time, man, and that takes a while, you dig?"

"The crack in time that lets you have a second chance?"

"That's right, man."

"What did you think this was about, son?" a voice behind them asked. Frog spun around and found old Guthrie standing behind him.

"Guthrie man, you're talking!"

Guthrie, holding a bottle of Thunderbird, smiled and took a swig. "Best fucking Thunderbird I ever tasted." He smacked his lips together. "Of course I'm talking, boy. I could always talk, there was just nothing to say down there." Guthrie offered the bottle to Frog, who declined.

"Man, you don't know what you're missing out on." Guthrie took another swig. Then he wiped his wine stained lips on his shirtsleeve and belched. "Frog, it's disturbing to find that you're still not taking any of this seriously." Guthrie passed the bottle of Thunderbird to Barry, who accepted it graciously and chugged a good portion of the brew.

"I told him he's blowing it, man, but he's not going to listen. You're wasting your breath," Barry said. "Let's ditch him, man. He's getting to be a bummer trip. I want to go to the concert and party."

"Good idea." Guthrie turned and they both started walking away.

"Hey, man, that's fucked up," Frog said. "You're going to leave me here in this fucking hallway?"

"You can come with us, but there's no point talking to you anymore, man," Barry said. "You're dense, you just don't get it."

"You want me to come with you and watch the 27 Club preform and if I don't you're just going to leave me here?"

"That's right, man. There's just no point in warning you again. People wait a long time for a second chance; you get one handed to you and you waste it. Watch, you'll be back soon complaining that it wasn't your fault, and when you are, you know what, man? Me and Guthrie we aren't going to listen to you."

"The only reason you were granted a second shot is because of Katie," Old Guthrie chimed in. "Your time period correlates with hers, so you were able to coattail on her trip. Otherwise your petition would have been rejected. Everyone upstairs knows that you're a waste of a good crack in time."

"Katie? What does she have to do with this?"

"Everything, man. This is her bag, not yours. You dig?"

"He doesn't, Barry, that's the problem. He doesn't dig, no comprende. You said it yourself, stop wasting your time, man, he's not going to get it and I'm ready to party. They have an endless supply of Thunderbird, best shit I ever tasted."

Doors opened and closed, the hallway grew crowded. Brian Jones appeared and started herding the stragglers towards the showroom.

"The concert's about to start my friends!" he yelled into the hall. "Let's go party." Everyone cheered then quickly moved towards the designated room.

"Hey, man, he's a Rolling Stone," Frog pointed out.

"He was. Look, Frog, forget about everything and join us. Don't go back, man, just give up. You're losing anyway. Come to the concert, and in no time at all your memory will come back," Barry advised. "A cat named Kurt Cobain is singing tonight. He's groovy, man, you'll dig him. He's a real kick ass performer. Then there's a new chick named Amy Winehouse. That girl has one fucking great voice. Janis and Jimi love her singing so she'll probably perform tonight too."

"This doesn't make any sense," Frog insisted. "Most of these people are musicians living in the Haight District. How can they be performing here?"

"They're all dead, Frog. *We're* all dead."

"No, Barry, I told you before, you're the one that's dead. You and Guthrie are, but me and Katie, Jimi Hendrix, Janis Joplin, Jim Morrison and Brian Jones—we're all alive."

"Except you're not," Guthrie replied.

"Yes we are, man," Frog insisted.

"He's not going to listen, brother, let's go." Barry walked off.

"It's not too late, Frog. Barry is frustrated with you but I believe you still have a shot. Better start using your head, son." Guthrie turned, ready to follow his hippie friend down the hallway.

"Wait, man."

Guthrie stopped and faced him.

"This is just a dream, right?"

"This is your second chance, Frog, don't you want it?" Guthrie asked and then walked away.

The music played, perfect acoustics as Jimi Hendrix's guitar wailed somewhere in the distance. Anyone left in the hall quickly entered the concert room, leaving Frog completely alone. He breathed a sigh of relief.

I'll just sit and wait until I wake up, he told himself, but before he could move, a door opened and the toothless old maid walked into the hall laughing.

"What's the matter, Frog? Did all your friends leave you?" She walked closer. Frog backed into the wall trying to get away from the hag but suddenly she was on him, just inches from his face. Frog winced and tried to push her away but she was stronger. She leaned against his body and her stench turned his stomach. Frog gagged.

"Get away from me you ugly fucking bitch!" he yelled, which made the hag laugh even harder.

"You can go back now, Frog. You can go back and pretend that all of this was only a bad dream. You're stupid, so of course that's what you're going to do. But just remember this, you'll be back real soon begging to try again. You're going to fail because you're a loser and you don't deserve another chance. You hear me, Frog? You don't deserve shit, you know it and I know it. Once your back here, I'm going to torment you for eternity."

Then she stepped back a few paces and pulled the needle out of her pocket. Before Frog could react, she flew at him with the syringe and plunged it deep into his forearm. Frog screamed.

"Go back, Frog. Go back and fail because you're worthless."

A door behind Frog opened and the maid maliciously pushed him through the opening. He felt himself falling again and screamed.

"What is it, Frog? Did you have a nightmare?"

Panting loudly, Frog opened his one good eye and found Moonbeam lying beside him.

"What the fuck is happening?"

"You're having a dream, baby, it's just a dream." She put her arm carefully around him.

"But it was so real."

"What happened?"

"I dreamed that I was stabbed with a needle."

"Hmm...it's just a dream, baby. Everything is fine, go back to sleep."

"Yeah, you're right. It was just a dream." Frog settled himself into a comfortable position.

Moonbeam snuggled against him and closed her eyes. Frog rubbed the swollen, bloody wound on his forearm.

Chapter 30

The month of June 1967 set off a whirlwind of change in the United States and around the world.

On June 1st, the Beatles released *Sgt. Pepper's Lonely Hearts Club Band,* and what followed was a month packed with action. On June 7th, The Haight-Ashbury Free Clinic was opened. Sick hippies would no longer have to go to the Diggers to see the once a week doctor; now they could receive daily medical treatment.

A series of race riots occurred in the United States: on June 2nd in Roxbury, Boston; on the 11th in Tampa Bay, Florida; on the 12th Cincinnati, Ohio; and on the 27th in Buffalo, New York.

On June 3rd, Aretha Franklin's ballad "Respect" reached number one on the charts, and on the 4th, *The Monkees* and *Mission Impossible* won Emmy awards for best television series. On the 14th, Paramount Pictures released *To Sir With Love*, and on June 20th, Muhammad Ali would be sentenced to five years in prison, a $10,000 fine, and he would be stripped of his heavyweight title and banned from fighting in the United States due to draft evasion. On June 17th, China would detonate its first hydrogen bomb and enter the Atomic Age.

The biggest changes of all would take place in the Middle East, where on June 5th, Israel attacked Egypt and began the Six Day War. By the 6th, Israel's troops occupied Gaza, by the 7th they captured the Wailing Wall in Eastern Jerusalem and the cities of Jericho and Bethlehem.

On June 8th, tragedy struck when the US warship *Liberty*, stationed in the Mediterranean Sea, was mistaken for an Arab troop ship and torpedoed. This mistake killed thirty-four American soldiers.

By June 9th, Israeli troops reached the Suez Canal, and on June 10th Israel, Syria, Jordan, and Egypt signed a UN ceasefire ending the conflict. On June 29th, the Israelis removed the barricades and for the first time in nearly twenty years, East and West Jerusalem were reunited.

All in all, Israel gained all of the Sinai Peninsula, the Gaza Strip, East Jerusalem, the West Bank, and the Golan Heights. This more than tripled the total land under control of Israel prior to the war.

Within this month of craziness a place called Monterey on the central coast of California would host the first high profile three-day pop festival. This quiet beach town would rock in the official start of the 'Summer of Love.'

The City of Monterey is located on the southern edge of Monterey Bay on Central California's Pacific Coast. It is nearly nine square miles and consists of sandy dunes, the historical home of John Steinbeck and the famous Cannery Row. It is one hundred and eighteen miles south of San Francisco, a two-hour drive down Highway 101.

The Monterey Pop Festival was held June 16, 17, and 18, 1967 at the Monterey County Fairgrounds. On that second week in June, the quiet beach city became the focus of the American youth counterculture.

***

It was the first real music festival and the predecessor to Woodstock. Its lineup included thirty-six very diverse acts, ranging from the soft rock of The Association and Simon and Garfunkel, to political activists Country Joe and the Fish and blues legend Otis Redding. It also featured the national debuts of the yet unknown The Who, Jimi Hendrix and Janis Joplin.

The pop festival was unique for many reasons: it was the first three-day rock concert held outdoors, and for the first time acts from different regions of the US came together. It was also the first time many of these bands had met in person, which was especially important to the California music scene. Before the pop festival, Bay Area and Los Angeles musicians regarded each other with skepticism and distrust. The Monterey Pop Festival ended that rivalry.

Music writer Rusty De Soto argues that pop music history tends to downplay the importance of Monterey in favor of the "bigger, higher-profile, more decadent" Woodstock Festival, held two years later. But, as he notes, *"Monterey Pop was a seminal event: it was the first real rock festival ever held, featuring debut performances of bands that would shape the history of rock and affect popular culture from that day forward."* The County Fairgrounds in Monterey, California ... had been home to folk, jazz and blues festivals for many years. But the weekend of June 16–18, 1967 was the first time it was used for rock performances.

***

Katie placed her small suitcase and sleeping bag into the overcrowded van. It was 9:15 a.m. If they stayed on schedule, they would be leaving in less than an hour.

This was the day she had been waiting for, the beginning of the Monterey Pop Festival. She should be excited but she wasn't. Instead, she had the feeling she was entering a critical point in her journey. She kept thinking about a movie she had seen on late night television. In the film, a young Gwyneth Paltrow had two distinctly different paths, one if she enters a sliding glass door and another if she doesn't. That was how Katie viewed her situation, with two separate possibilities depending on which way the tables turned.

The last few weeks she had felt different, as if she was teetering on the edge of a cliff. She sensed this concert would determine the outcome of everything. Nothing would be the same after it.

Moonbeam had been fluttering around like a butterfly for days, getting ready for her big move. After the festival on Sunday she and Frog were relocating, going north to Larkspur in Marin County where they would join Chet's commune. This would happily get Frog out of the city long before the August deadline, and Moonbeam believed that it was the end to all their problems.

Katie was tempted to go with them, and she promised Moonbeam that she would join them at a later date, but she couldn't leave yet. There were too many unfinished events. Until she had a chance to fix what had gone wrong she was stuck in San Francisco.

She had seen Dylan twice since the cocktail party, and both times they had discussed future events. He had wanted to know every scrap of information she could predict (remember), but she had nothing to offer. The first time around she hadn't gone to Monterey Pop, as she couldn't afford it. That time, her pride had kept her poor, but this time when she was allowing her mother to pay for the trip. She had a lot more options, and having money made the ride a hell of a lot easier.

Her meetings with Dylan were not dates, just one platonic friend talking to another. Although there were undeniable feelings between them they had agreed not to pursue an entanglement, knowing that the last thing either one of them needed was a romantic relationship.

The decision had set Katie free, and despite her feelings towards the rogue biker, she was glad. Dylan had his problems and they were many. She had her own issues to deal with. Together they would be a walking disaster.

Richard would live another four months. He would come home for two weeks in August and then he would go back to Vietnam and Katie would never see him again. During his visit she had to figure out a way to save her brother's life. She didn't need anything— or anyone— interfering with those plans.

At least Dylan, unlike Frog, was taking her predictions seriously. He wasn't willing to discuss his plans with her, but he assured her that he wasn't going to end up in a hole in the backwoods. Knowing that was enough to keep her going. All she wanted was to see him get out of the web he was caught in.

Katie was here to prevent a series of events from taking place. She wasn't here to throw the cards to the wind and run off with a Hells Angel. She was sixty-six years old for crying out loud, she knew that romantic love was for the young and foolish. Those feelings never lasted; she knew that. At the end of the day, she and Dylan had nothing in common.

He was leaving, she just didn't know when it would happen. Part of her believed that he was already gone, and if he wasn't, he would be soon. By the end of the three-day festival she was sure she would never see him again. As much as she believed that was a good thing, she couldn't deny that she was going to miss him.

The situation with Ron was different. She wasn't sure where that would lead. Ron was ever patient, older, and smart enough to imagine more than he'd been told, yet still not ask questions. He knew she had changed drastically, and he knew she had mysterious responsibilities. He watched her with knowing eyes, and sometimes she suspected that he knew everything.

Although at a standstill, their relationship was far from over. It was more on pause, waiting for Katie to fix the things she needed to. Although Ron claimed to be unaware of the events that were unfolding, there were times when he would make comments indicating that he was far from spectator status, and that's where they left the situation. Ron knew *something,* she just didn't know what, and they didn't discuss it.

Katie could picture a future with Ron. He was kind and even-tempered; theirs would be a relationship of maturity, unlike her marriage and unlike the impulsive lifestyle she would be living with someone like Dylan. Still, the feelings she wanted to feel for Ron just weren't there, even though she knew Ron would be the sensible choice, and this time around she was all about being sensible.

***

Moonbeam walked out of the yellow Victorian with another box of 'stuff' and shoved it into the back of the van.

"Well, that's the last of it," she announced.

"You know Ron hasn't even put his stuff in yet," Katie reminded her as she looked at the four large boxes that Moonbeam stacked in the back end of the bus.

"I know, but it's not that crowded is it?"

"It is if we end up sleeping in the van. You know you can leave most of that here and one of us will bring it to you. You're only going to be twenty minutes away from us, it's not like you're moving across the country."

"Yeah I know, but I've got this funny feeling that if I don't take it now I will never get the chance."

Katie shivered. So Moonbeam could feel the negative vibes too.

Ron walked out of the house. "Hey, I heard my name out here. What you hippie girls rapping about?"

Katie glanced at Moonbeam and said nothing.

"I packed some stuff into the van, Ron."

"I should hope so, we're going to be gone for three days."

He took his navy field bag and started to toss it into the van but stopped short. "Wow, Moony, you sure did pack stuff. What's all that?"

"Frog and I are leaving after the festival. I just want to be ready."

"Ready? This is kind of desperate, isn't it? I mean, we aren't going to hold your stuff for ransom. You can come and get the rest of it at any time. This is like...well, it's like you're not ever planning to come back." Ron looked at her, his smile fading.

"I need to find Frog, I want to say goodbye before he leaves," Moonbeam said, breaking the uncomfortable silence.

"Is he still insisting on riding that old Honda down there?" Ron asked.

"I'm afraid so. I don't know what it is about that old bike but he digs it."

"Yeah, he does. I never thought I'd see Frog riding a motorcycle," Ron chuckled. "He just doesn't seem like the type."

"I know, that's what I thought when he brought the old thing home but he proved both of us wrong. He loves it so much that he wants to drive the damn thing to Monterey. It seems like a cold ride, but that's his bag."

"Next, he'll get a Harley and he'll be trying to join the Angels," Ron joked.

"Nah, that would be a little hard to do from a commune in Larkspur."

"Speaking of Larkspur, how are you going to get there? You've got stuff and Frog has a motorcycle. That's not going to work."

"We were going to take Greyhound but now that Frog has the bike I guess I'm going to take the bus and he's going to meet me there."

"It would make more sense to drive back with us to 'Frisco, wait a few days, and then move," Ron said, "but what do I know?"

Moonbeam looked at him questioningly but didn't comment. She walked towards the back of the house in search of Frog.

"Are you ready to go?" Ron asked. Katie nodded. "Concert starts at 4:00, maybe they'll open the doors around 2:00. If we leave at 10:00 we'll get there a few hours early."

"You think that's enough time?" Katie asked.

"More than enough. We already have our tickets and we have assigned seats so we'll be fine." Ron pulled a smoke out of his breast pocket, lit it, puffed on it, then offered it to Katie. "Mary Jane?"

She took it from him and took a toke. "It would be a drag to get there late and have to deal with traffic."

"Yeah, that would be a real bummer." He cleared his throat. Ron stepped closer and took the joint back from Katie, taking a hard hit before handing it back. "Listen, I know I'm supposed to be in the dark as to what's going on here, but I'm going to take a wild guess and say that Moonbeam isn't returning to San Francisco ever."

"I don't know, Ron. Honestly, I'm just a spectator at this point. Your guess is as good as mine."

"I doubt that's true, but if it's all you're going to tell me then..." He threw his bag into the back of the bus and then started to rearrange the clutter. "What is it about this trip?" he asked after a tense moment. "It's supposed to be fun, exciting, the first huge rock concert ever, but looking at all of us you'd think we were going to a wake, solemn bunch of bastards all of us."

"Yeah, and I don't know why," Katie said. "I just have this feeling that we're at a turning point. Nothing will be the same when we return from Monterey.

"Is this a premonition, or is this from personal experience?"

"No, it's just a feeling, nothing more. I don't know what happens at the Monterey Pop Festival, Ron." Katie turned to look him straight in the eyes. "I didn't go the first time around."

Ron stared at her for several seconds, then he relit the joint that had gone out, took a toke and handed it to her. "You know, I want to believe that. It's really the only thing that makes sense."

Katie could tell that he had thought about this a lot.

"I mean, the way you know things, the way you became another person overnight. It's why you matured so quickly, why you don't giggle anymore. Moonbeam and Frog seem to be in on the gig so I'm assuming they know everything. What I can't figure out is why you won't let me in, even though you know that I've figured most of this shit out already." He tipped her chin upwards so she would look at him. "Katie, why are you so different?"

"Didn't I just tell you? I didn't go to the Pop Festival *the first time around*, Ron. I don't know what happens there. I don't know what Frog's bag is and I don't know why Moonbeam packed all of her stuff. I can tell you about the concert if you want to know. That Peter Townsend from the Who will smash his guitar on stage, that Jimi Hendrix will give the performance of his life and then burn his guitar at the end. I can tell you that it will threaten to rain on Sunday and we'll need jackets. I can tell you anything you want to know about the performance, but about any of us I'm in the dark. I didn't go to the pop festival the first time around," she repeated, shocking even herself for finally telling the truth.

"Time travel..." he said, more as a statement than a question.

"That's right, time travel. As crazy and absurd as that sounds, I've been here before in a different 1967. You wanted the truth, there it is. I know it's going to rattle your brain. It sure as hell rattled mine, but it's the God's honest truth."

"I suspected. I mean the possibility has run through my mind. The prediction excuse was convenient, but it doesn't explain the drastic overnight personality change."

"And now that you know?"

"Wow. I don't know. I guess I have to absorb this before I can answer that. Suspecting something and then finding out that it's true are two different things. I need time to think this over so I can come to terms with what you've told me."

"That's totally understandable. Take all the time you need."

"From what year?" he suddenly asked.

"What?"

"What year are you from?"

"I came here from January 2014."

"Forty-five years in the future?" he asked in astonishment.

"That's right. I was sixty-six years old and I drove off a cliff. When I woke I was on your couch. Everyone told me that I had been overdosed at some Hells Angels' party but that wasn't me, at least not me *now*. I remember that party and I remember being drugged, but that was forty-five years ago in my time. That's when the change was made. Young Katie overdosed at that party, and I took her place."

"That's some fucking story." Ron whistled. "Okay, tell me something that's going to happen; something that's not related to the concert."

"Okay. Next week Muhammad Ali will be sentenced to five years in jail for draft dodging. He'll never do the time, and he will be released on appeal. Eventually, he'll be granted his status as a conscientious objector due to religious beliefs. Sometime this weekend, China will detonate its first hydrogen bomb, joining the ranks of the Atomic Age. And now that the Six Day War has ended, Israel will reunify East and West Jerusalem. Is that enough? I can go through the whole summer if you want..."

"Well, I was thinking of next year's Super Bowl," he laughed. "No, that's plenty. Let me digest this. I don't need any more to think about."

Katie looked at her watch. "Man, its 9:50 already, where are those two? We really should get started."

"Katie," Ron said, and she turned to look at him. "You're the foxiest sixty-six year old woman that I've ever seen," he said with a broad smile on his handsome face.

***

Moonbeam walked out of the yellow Victorian with another box of 'stuff' and shoved it into the back of the van.

"Well, that's the last of it," she announced.

"You know Ron hasn't even put his stuff in yet," Katie reminded her as she looked at the four large boxes that Moonbeam stacked in the back end of the bus.

"I know, but it's not that crowded is it?"

"It is if we end up sleeping in the van. You know you can leave most of that here and one of us will bring it to you. You're only going to be twenty minutes away from us, it's not like you're moving across the country."

"Yeah I know, but I've got this funny feeling that if I don't take it now I will never get the chance."

Katie shivered. So Moonbeam could feel the negative vibes too.

Ron walked out of the house. "Hey, I heard my name out here. What you hippie girls rapping about?"

Katie glanced at Moonbeam and said nothing.

"I packed some stuff into the van, Ron."

"I should hope so, we're going to be gone for three days."

He took his navy field bag and started to toss it into the van but stopped short. "Wow, Moony, you sure did pack stuff. What's all that?"

"Frog and I are leaving after the festival. I just want to be ready."

"Ready? This is kind of desperate, isn't it? I mean, we aren't going to hold your stuff for ransom. You can come and get the rest of it at any time. This is like...well, it's like you're not ever planning to come back." Ron looked at her, his smile fading.

"I need to find Frog, I want to say goodbye before he leaves," Moonbeam said, breaking the uncomfortable silence.

"Is he still insisting on riding that old Honda down there?" Ron asked.

"I'm afraid so. I don't know what it is about that old bike but he digs it."

"Yeah, he does. I never thought I'd see Frog riding a motorcycle," Ron chuckled. "He just doesn't seem like the type."

"I know, that's what I thought when he brought the old thing home but he proved both of us wrong. He loves it so much that he wants to drive the damn thing to Monterey. It seems like a cold ride, but that's his bag."

"Next, he'll get a Harley and he'll be trying to join the Angels," Ron joked.

"Nah, that would be a little hard to do from a commune in Larkspur."

"Speaking of Larkspur, how are you going to get there? You've got stuff and Frog has a motorcycle. That's not going to work."

"We were going to take Greyhound but now that Frog has the bike I guess I'm going to take the bus and he's going to meet me there."

"It would make more sense to drive back with us to 'Frisco, wait a few days, and then move," Ron said, "but what do I know?"

Moonbeam looked at him questioningly but didn't comment. She walked towards the back of the house in search of Frog.

"Are you ready to go?" Ron asked. Katie nodded. "Concert starts at 4:00, maybe they'll open the doors around 2:00. If we leave at 10:00 we'll get there a few hours early."

"You think that's enough time?" Katie asked.

"More than enough. We already have our tickets and we have assigned seats so we'll be fine." Ron pulled a smoke out of his breast pocket, lit it, puffed on it, then offered it to Katie. "Mary Jane?"

She took it from him and took a toke. "It would be a drag to get there late and have to deal with traffic."

"Yeah, that would be a real bummer." He cleared his throat. Ron stepped closer and took the joint back from Katie, taking a hard hit before handing it back. "Listen, I know I'm supposed to be in the dark as to what's going on here, but I'm going to take a wild guess and say that Moonbeam isn't returning to San Francisco ever."

"I don't know, Ron. Honestly, I'm just a spectator at this point. Your guess is as good as mine."

"I doubt that's true, but if it's all you're going to tell me then..." He threw his bag into the back of the bus and then started to rearrange the clutter. "What is it about this trip?" he asked after a tense moment. "It's supposed to be fun, exciting, the first huge rock concert ever, but looking at all of us you'd think we were going to a wake, solemn bunch of bastards all of us."

"Yeah, and I don't know why," Katie said. "I just have this feeling that we're at a turning point. Nothing will be the same when we return from Monterey."

"Is this a premonition, or is this from personal experience?"

"No, it's just a feeling, nothing more. I don't know what happens at the Monterey Pop Festival, Ron." Katie turned to look him straight in the eyes. "I didn't go the first time around."

Ron stared at her for several seconds, then he relit the joint that had gone out, took a toke and handed it to her. "You know, I want to believe that. It's really the only thing that makes sense."

Katie could tell that he had thought about this a lot.

"I mean, the way you know things, the way you became another person overnight. It's why you matured so quickly, why you don't giggle anymore. Moonbeam and Frog seem to be in on the gig so I'm assuming they know everything. What I can't figure out is why you won't let me in, even though you know that I've figured most of this shit out already." He tipped her chin upwards so she would look at him. "Katie, why are you so different?"

"Didn't I just tell you? I didn't go to the Pop Festival *the first time around*, Ron. I don't know what happens there. I don't know what Frog's bag is and I don't know why Moonbeam packed all of her stuff. I can tell you about the concert if you want to know. That Peter Townsend from the Who will smash his guitar on stage, that Jimi Hendrix will give the performance of his life and then burn his guitar at the end. I can tell you that it will threaten to rain on Sunday and we'll need jackets. I can tell you anything you want to know about the performance, but about any of us I'm in the dark. I didn't go to the pop festival the first time around," she repeated, shocking even herself for finally telling the truth.

"Time travel..." he said, more as a statement than a question.

"That's right, time travel. As crazy and absurd as that sounds, I've been here before in a different 1967. You wanted the truth, there it is. I know it's going to rattle your brain. It sure as hell rattled mine, but it's the God's honest truth."

"I suspected. I mean the possibility has run through my mind. The prediction excuse was convenient, but it doesn't explain the drastic overnight personality change."

"And now that you know?"

"Wow. I don't know. I guess I have to absorb this before I can answer that. Suspecting something and then finding out that it's true are two different things. I need time to think this over so I can come to terms with what you've told me."

"That's totally understandable. Take all the time you need."

"From what year?" he suddenly asked.

"What?"

"What year are you from?"

"I came here from January 2014."

"Forty-five years in the future?" he asked in astonishment.

"That's right. I was sixty-six years old and I drove off a cliff. When I woke I was on your couch. Everyone told me that I had been overdosed at some Hells Angels' party but that wasn't me, at least not me *now*. I remember that party and I remember being drugged, but that was forty-five years ago in my time. That's when the change was made. Young Katie overdosed at that party, and I took her place."

"That's some fucking story." Ron whistled. "Okay, tell me something that's going to happen; something that's not related to the concert."

"Okay. Next week Muhammad Ali will be sentenced to five years in jail for draft dodging. He'll never do the time, and he will be released on appeal. Eventually, he'll be granted his status as a conscientious objector due to religious beliefs. Sometime this weekend, China will detonate its first hydrogen bomb, joining the ranks of the Atomic Age. And now that the Six Day War has ended, Israel will reunify East and West Jerusalem. Is that enough? I can go through the whole summer if you want..."

"Well, I was thinking of next year's Super Bowl," he laughed. "No, that's plenty. Let me digest this. I don't need any more to think about."

Katie looked at her watch. "Man, its 9:50 already, where are those two? We really should get started."

"Katie," Ron said, and she turned to look at him. "You're the foxiest sixty-six year old woman that I've ever seen," he said with a broad smile on his handsome face.

***

Moonbeam found Frog in the backyard rolling a blanket around his personal stuff. He started to fasten the bundle to the back of the Honda but stopped when he saw her walking towards him.

"Hey, there you are, babe," she called out.

"Yep, here I am." He looked up and smiled at her. He finished strapping his gear to the back of the bike with a red and blue bungee cord and then stood up.

Moonbeam bounced towards him and flung her tiny arms around his waist. Frog held her, shut his eyes, and savored the moment. He loved the feel of her long auburn hair against his body, and the way the smell of patchouli oil and flowers surrounded her. *Heaven,* he thought. Heaven that he would never know again after this weekend.

Frog kissed the top of her head and pulled her close for one more hug. In that moment he realized how much he was giving up and his eyes watered.

"Hey, what's up with that?" Moonbeam asked him.

"It's just an extra hug for the ride. Two hours without you, I'll miss you."

"Are you leaving soon?"

Frog looked at her, really looked at her. She was beautiful, like a little red-haired fairy out of a storybook. Her eyes sparkled and they were filled with trust. A sudden stab of guilt hit him and he turned to look at the bike.

"Yep, I'm just tightening my load. I don't want to ride alone so I'll follow the van, unless Ron wants to follow me."

"I don't think it will matter to him, either way will be fine. Are you sure you won't just come with us? You can leave the bike here and we can pick it up later," she asked again, hoping he had changed his mind.

"No, that would take all the fun out of the trip. I'm looking forward to the ride. It will be beautiful."

"Beautiful yes, but cold."

"Refreshing. I have a heavy jacket. I won't be cold, I'm from Redding, remember? It gets a lot colder there. This is nothing."

"Frog, why do I get the feeling that something's wrong?" Moonbeam asked, totally out of the blue.

Frog wasn't ready for the question. He flinched, and in that second Moonbeam was able to read his face and she knew. Her eyes flashed with knowledge and she looked away.

"There's nothing wrong, baby, I don't know what you mean," he said, trying to recover but failing miserably.

"Don't say any more, Frog. You don't have to." She turned to walk away.

"I love you." It was the first time he had told her that, but he had known it for months. "I love you and I will always want you. Remember that."

"What is this, Frog, a farewell?" She stepped back several paces and crossed her arms in front of her.

"Never. Not on my end."

"Then on my end? Are you expecting me to say goodbye?"

"Moony, I can't tell you anything. I'm sorry, it shouldn't be that way, it's my mistake. I should have never allowed my world to get so completely out of control, but I did. Now I'm just trying to clear my own mess. I want to be able to live just like we planned. I want that life on the commune more than anything, and if it were that easy I would be there in a second, but it's not. I'm in way over my head, baby. Just know that everything I do is in your best interest, even if you don't believe it."

Moonbeam's eyes watered. The yellow daisy painted on her face ran down her cheek. "And you can't tell me anything more?"

"Only that I love you and that I want a life with you," he answered, his own eyes watering.

"But that's not going to happen, is it, Frog?"

He remained silent.

"Is it?" she asked again louder, this time stomping her bare foot.

"I hope so," he answered honestly as he watched her march off towards the front yard.

Moonbeam walked around the house and stopped at the back of the van. She took one of boxes and started carrying it back into the house.

"Change of plans," she announced. "I'll come back to get my stuff."

Ron looked at Katie. "I told you, I don't know," she said, shaking her head.

Minutes later, when Moonbeam's belongings were back in the house, she returned to the bus sporting a freshly painted flower on her face and a large floppy hippie hat. Without saying another word she jumped into the back of the van.

Frog kick started his bike and it roared to life. Seconds later, he came down the driveway and pulled in front of the van.

"Ready?" he called out, and Ron gave him a thumbs up. "You want to follow me or the other way around?"

"I'll lead," Ron said. "It's easier for you to find me in traffic, the van's a lot larger than your bike. Plus I'm slower, this is a Volkswagen bus don't forget. If you lead I'll never keep up."

"Alright then. Lead on, brother."

Ron drove down Page Street, turned right onto Octavia, and then entered Highway 101 heading south.

***

Mark put the last of his belongings into his red Porsche. His business colleague and traveling partner Dennis Long was already seated on the passenger side adjusting the radio.

"I can't believe you're paying me to go to a rock concert," Dennis said, snapping his fingers to the tune on the radio.

"Shut up man, don't fucking say that to anybody."

Dennis spun around, looking up and down the street and then he started to laugh. "Look at that man, not a soul in sight."

"I don't care. Don't fucking talk about this, you understand?"

"Understand what? I don't even know what you're expecting me to do when we get there. Fifteen hundred bucks is a lot of bread man, it must be something big."

"Shut *up*. I told you, man, I'll explain on the way."

Mark jumped into the driver's seat and pulled his car onto the empty street, heading towards the 101 freeway entrance.

"Okay, man, so now we're on our way," Dennis said, still snapping his fingers to the Beatles version of 'Twist and Shout.'

"Shit, Dennis, give me a minute, would you? At least let me get on the freeway before you start yapping."

"Suit yourself, man, it's your bread. As long as I get paid as promised, I'm on board." Dennis shrugged his shoulders and pushed the button to change the station.

They drove several blocks in silence. Once Mark was on 101 he started to relax. He cracked his window and undid the first button on his white dress shirt and then he started to talk.

"Okay, man, now don't repeat any of this, you understand? Not even if you're joking, not even if it's just you and me with nobody else around. If you can't do that tell me now and I'll get somebody else."

"Whoa, I got it, slow down. I made one mistake on a completely empty street. Let's not beat this into the ground, brother. I'm hip; I'll shut my mouth. Have I said anything about the rest of the jobs you've had me do? No, I fucking haven't. If you didn't trust me I wouldn't be here, so take a deep breath."

"I have to make sure, man, because one mistake, even if it's small..."

"And what? What kind of shit are we getting involved in? I'm not doing jail time, man."

"Calm down. I'm trying to explain, just shut up and listen."

Dennis gestured zipping his mouth shut and then silently stared at Mark.

I don't want to have repeat this conversation, and I only want to tell it once," Mark said, swallowing hard.

"Okay, man, shoot. I'm all ears."

"There's this chick..." Mark said and Dennis laughed.

"Isn't it always about a chick?"

"Exactly. At least it always seems to be. So listen..."

Mark pulled a pack of Camel's out of his pocket. He extracted one cigarette without looking and shoved it into his mouth, took his silver Zippo out of the overflowing ashtray, and lit up.

"There's this chick..." he repeated. He paused, sucked in deeply on his cigarette and smiled. "I really dig her, man. I mean I *really* dig her, you get what I'm saying?"

"Sure, so what's the problem? Does she hate you or something?" Dennis asked, flipping the radio station. This time Simon and Garfunkel harmonized on 'The Sound of Silence.' "I love this song. I sure hope they sing it at the concert."

"Yes, actually. You hit it right on the head. She hates me."

"Really, man? Why? What did you do?"

"That's just it, I didn't do anything. She has no reason to dislike me except that I'm part of the establishment and I'm ambitious."

"That doesn't make sense. Chicks love money, and they love guys who are going to be rich."

"No, it doesn't make any sense. Here's the thing: she's a hippie chick living in Haight-Ashbury."

Dennis snorted. "This is a joke, right? There is no way somebody like you would be interested in, let alone settle, for a hippie chick that's strung out on LSD."

"Who said anything about LSD?"

"Man, you don't have to. If she's a hippie living in 'Frisco then she's strung out on the shit. They all are, that's why they're hippies. Not just that but hippie chicks stink. They don't take baths or use deodorant because they're drugged out on banana peels and other shit. They don't even wear makeup or fix their hair. They don't even fucking shave their legs or armpits man, they're nasty."

"They don't smoke banana peels, that was a hoax. Where have you been?"

"It doesn't matter, banana peels, weed, LSD, speed— they've tried it all. You can't be that into a hippie chick man, it doesn't suit you. You want somebody that can get you ahead in life, that's what you're looking for. You can't fool me, Rhodes, I know you too well."

"This hippie chick is special."

"Special how, man, is she rich?"

Mark shot him a glance and in an instant Dennis knew the answer; this hippie chick was loaded. He started to laugh. "Okay I get. Let's start over. There's this rich hippie chick that can take you places in life. You want her, but she can't stand you."

"Yeah, that pretty much explains the situation."

"Problem solved, get another rich chick. There are others out there."

"Not like this one. This one is the boss's daughter."

"Katherine Searfus? Jesus Christ, Rhodes, are you insane?"

"Do you know how much that little beauty is worth?"

"I don't care, man. If anything went wrong her dad would make a bad enemy."

"Nothing's going to go wrong."

"Scamming on the boss's daughter? And not just anybody's daughter, *Al Searfus'* daughter." Dennis whistled. "You got balls, man."

"Nothing's going to go wrong. I have this planned right down to the wire. Don't worry."

"That makes me feel so much better. We're going to be fucking around with Al Searfus' daughter, but I'm supposed to trust you."

"And you're going to be getting paid a lot of money. So as I said before, if you're not on board let me know so I can get somebody else.

"If you ask me, this is a lot of fucking trouble to go through for a chick."

"Well nobody's asking you, but since you're here for the long haul I'll try to explain. She's everything I want. She's beautiful, rich, and she can offer me entrance to the high society life I crave. Frankly, I want her, and you're going to help me get her."

"Okay, man. So what's the plan?"

"The plan is to get the girl to like me."

"And how are you going to do that, slugger? This is not just any hippie, this is the boss's daughter. She can have any man she wants. I've seen her at company picnics. She's pretty and she looks like a blonde doll."

"Yes she is, and yes, she can have anyone she wants. But after this weekend she's going to want me."

"How are we going to do that? With witchcraft or voodoo? Are we going to have to bite the heads off of chickens?"

"Chicks love a hero; I'm going to be her hero," Mark said, ignoring Dennis's comment. "You're going to play the bad guy and I'm going to save her."

Dennis didn't say anything. He squinted his eyes together and shook his head.

"You're going to be the boogieman, Dennis, and you're getting paid a lot of money to play the part. Not to mention you already got a free ticket to a three day rock concert."

"I'm not hurting a chick, man. Not for any amount."

"Relax, nobody is going to get hurt. This is just playacting. At some point in the concert we'll find her alone, and by then we'll have a structured plan that will be foolproof. You'll attack her and I'll come to her rescue just like a knight in shining armor. After that, the rest will be history."

Dennis stared at him. "I still don't know, man, this sounds stupid and dangerous."

"Does it still sound stupid and dangerous at two grand?"

Dennis laughed and Mark, confident that his colleague had just become his accomplice, laughed with him.

***

Dylan was running late. Generally that would have bothered him, but not today. Today was different, it was the day he was leaving.

Guilt stabbed at him. He wanted to tell Joey what was happening, but he knew that was impossible. Joey had changed into a person he didn't know. He was sold on being a heroin pusher.

Dylan turned on 16th Street and wondered how long it would be before he drove this path again, if ever. In his heart he wasn't ready to leave, but he knew he couldn't stay.

Never in his wildest dreams did he think he would be splitting 'Frisco with Frog the street hustler. He laughed in spite of himself, thinking of days gone by and remembering the old saying about hindsight being 20/20. It would be a long weekend. He wished he could leave now and avoid the hassle but he had his obligations to the club and he couldn't cut out on that.

He had tried to think of a way to stay, a way to solve this 'in house', but he didn't have enough time or enough information. Telling Big Jim that he had dreams and that his chick had premonitions wasn't going to cut it. The only sensible thing to do was to leave and deal with the problem from the outside, someplace safe, someplace where nobody would find them. Once there, he would get his head straight, figure out all the shit that was rattling through his mind. Then he would contact the club and he would spill his guts, but not now.

He had resigned himself to leaving, emotionally detached himself from the people he cared about. All that was left now was to complete this weekend and then he would be gone.

His thoughts frequently drifted to Katie. He tried not to think about her but he couldn't control his mind. He loved her; he couldn't pretend otherwise, and looking back now he realized that he had loved her since the first day he saw her in Golden Gate Park.

He had seen her twice since the horrendous cocktail party. Both times had been for practical reasons; he'd wanted to know anything she could tell him about her predictions, anything she might have missed or something she had remembered. Even if it was minimal, any kernel of information might be the difference between his living or not. In the end he had learned nothing new, and he had to admit that he didn't expect to. He wanted to see Katie, and that was the real reason he had sought out her council.

It was hard sitting in the same room with her and denying his feelings, but that's the way she wanted it and so he had agreed. After all, she *was* right. How could they pursue a romantic relationship? The idea was ludicrous. Still, he had the feeling that he almost had the girl in the hallway but one more time she was slipping though his fingers like she had done so many times before in his dreams.

When Dylan tuned the last corner he could see that the front of the clubhouse was packed with bikers. All eyes were on him as he rode down Tennessee and parked. Big Jim met him and the oversized biker tapped the face of his watch.

"You know what 9:30 looks like, Taylor."

"Yeah, I know. I'm sorry, man, I overslept."

"Well, you're in luck. Another two minutes and we would have left your sorry ass."

"Right, man, I dig. You should have left, I would have caught up."

"Well you're fortunate now you don't have to." Big Jim started his ride and pulled out slowly with a parade of bikers behind him.

In the confusion, a bike pulled beside Dylan and stopped. Joey smiled at him.

"Time problems, bro?"

"Something like that. What's up?"

"Did you check out the scene behind you?"

Dylan hadn't noticed anything. He glanced at the remaining bikers and then he saw Dave, Sal, and Skinner. They seemed to be locked in a hot debate.

"Something new?" Dylan asked, hopeful that the men had come to some type of agreement.

"I don't know, man, but by looking at their ugly mugs I'd say they're at a stalemate."

It was true the three men looked angry. Dylan couldn't hear any of the conversation but he was convinced there was no agreement, meaning the unpatched bikers would still get involved.

"Fuck man, now what?" Dylan asked.

"You already know what the score is, brother. The question is, are you cool now?"

Joey's dark eyes scanned his face and Dylan smiled.

"Hey, man, you know me, I'm always cool."

"I sure hope so, we come as a pair, remember? If you crack under pressure then you make both of us look bad, you dig?"

"Man, I thought we went through this shit the other day. Why the repeat convo?"

"Because I'm worried about you. You don't seem right, if you get my drift."

"I'm right as rain, man. Everything is groovy."

"There's a lot of money to be had here, Dylan, and very little risk. Don't fuck this up for us." He sped off, and seconds later Sal and Dave joined him.

Dylan waited several minutes, watching as a few stragglers set off, including Skinner. When the pack thinned he pulled his bike out from the curb and headed towards the freeway.

He was sullen, trying to understand how his world had changed so dramatically and so quickly. All he could come back to was that he had met Katie and the thought of her sent a pang of sadness through his already breaking heart.

Chapter 31

Terry looked at his watch. It was 9 a.m., perfect timing. He parked his old Chevy close to the football field at Monterey Peninsula College. This was one of several spots approved for camping during the music festival.

"Well man, this is it; our home away from home. We're here, buddy, nice and early just like we planned. We'll have the prospects set up camp when they get here and then we can fuck off for a while and find something to eat," Terry said. He shoved his sandy blond hair out of eyes and jumped out of the truck.

"Chilly man," Chocolate George said when he opened the door. He zipped up his leather jacket and sniffed the air. "It feels different than San Francisco... smells different too."

"That's ridiculous, man. It's cold here and it's cold in the city, they're both on the ocean so it's the same. I mean yeah, you got more trees here, but location wise it's the same shit."

"No man, it's different."

"You know what, George? If you say it's true then it must be."

They walked around for a few moments, stretching their legs, and another truck and a few bikes arrived.

"There they are now. We'll get them organized and then we'll split for a while."

The 'hangarounds' and prospects got to work quickly, unloading Terry's truck and a van. Soon, tents, chairs and camping gear were spread out everywhere.

One of the new arrivals, a prospect named Mike, walked towards them with a beer in one hand and a joint in the other.

"We're ready to set up, where do you want everything?" he asked.

Terry shrugged. "It's a football field, you'll figure it out I'm sure."

"I don't know, man. You want to be in the middle, near the bleachers close to one of the sides?" Mike asked.

"Who cares? This isn't a fucking Travelodge. Figure it out, Mikey," George said as he snagged the joint out of the prospect's hand.

"Right man, I'll let the crew decide." Leaving the joint for the two veteran bikers, he walked off to give directions to the rest of the men. Soon the Angel "wannabes" were setting up camp.

"Well what do you say, man?" George said to Terry. "You want to mosey into town and find a diner or something? I could sure go for a tall glass of chocolate milk."

"Sure, man, sounds good, but we have to keep it low key. Jim doesn't want Angels running around the town scaring people, you know what I mean?"

George laughed. "I never scare anybody." He sucked in on the joint and then passed it to Terry.

It was true, Chocolate George was everyone's favorite Angel, a popular guy in Haight-Ashbury, and was friends with all the hippies.

"Yeah, that's why I want to go now, before the others show up. You and me going for breakfast no sweat but if it were you, me, and twenty others, Big Jim would freak.

As with every place the Angels visited, Monterey was less than happy to receive them. In fact, the city of Monterey wasn't happy about the whole event. They had concerns over food and water, sanitation, and where to house the drug-crazed hippies. Due to these concerns, extra police officers were placed on duty so that their presence seemed to be everywhere.

As an added frustration, the idea of having several chapters of Hells Angels, along with thousands of flower children, made the event even more stressful for law enforcement. With the club's intent on cleaning up their image, this was a slap in the First Skulls' faces. They wanted the event to go smoothly and to do that, the club had been asked to stay away from the main part of town.

The First Skulls thought that if they didn't give authorities anything to be concerned about perhaps their reputation would mellow over time. At least that was the hope of Big Jim and his officers. Terry figured that they were Angels for a reason, and that their reputation, no matter what they did to change it, was always going to stay the same.

Despite the fear of law enforcement, the pop festival proved to be the first large-scale rock concert with no arrests, no injuries, no violence, and no deaths. It proved to be so peaceful that long before the festival was over, Monterey Police Chief Marinello felt confident enough to send half of his security force home. In an interview after the event the police chief said that in all his thirty-three years of service, he had never encountered such a huge crowd, and certainly never one so peaceful.

Terry and Chocolate George considered themselves to be the exception to the rule. After all, they were the ones who volunteered to leave 'Frisco at the crack of dawn to secure a spot at the football field. This, they felt, entitled them to a good breakfast and a relaxing few hours of touring the beach town, which was the reason they were anxious to take off before anyone else showed up.

"Hey, man," Terry called to Mike, who was erecting a tent. "We're going to split for a few hours. You think you can handle things here?"

"For sure, everything's under control," Mike said, opening another beer from the cooler.

"Speaking of beer, you might want to send somebody out on a beer run. We're going to have a lot of thirsty men when they get here. There's a place down on the corner. Nobody into town you understand?" Terry asked, and Mike nodded.

Mike pointed to a hangaround named Oliver and seconds later he and another hangaround went on a beverage run.

Terry closed his eyes and breathed in deeply. The air was crisp. He could smell the ocean and the pines. Although he would never admit it, Chocolate George was right, the air did feel different here. It was pure and clean, none of the smoke and pollution he was used to in the city. He told himself was going to be a fucking wonderful trip.

Terry and George jumped into his truck, pulled back onto Hwy 1, and five minutes later took the exit for downtown.

They found a breakfast diner easily and parked. Terry followed George towards the restaurant.

"Must be a good place, there's a lot of people here. What do you want to do, put our name in or go someplace else?" Terry asked.

"Let's put our name in. I'm ready for a good breakfast. Are you in a hurry to get back?"

"Fuck no. I'll put my name in." Terry headed towards the front door of the diner, amazed as always when the crowd, after seeing his colors, parted and moved out of his way. At the very front of the entrance was a podium where a teenaged girl stood with a clipboard in hand, taking names.

Terry approached and the girl immediately became nervous. When he got to the podium she was red faced and staring at the clipboard.

"I want to put my name in please," Terry said, then waited until the girl looked at him. "Terry, party of two. Anything, even the counter, would be fine."

Debbie, according to her nametag, swallowed nervously as she scribbled his name on the clipboard.

"I won't bite, honey, I'm only here for breakfast." Terry winked, which made the young girl smile.

When he got back to where George was standing, the biker seemed to be distracted, his eyes staring across the street at one of the small shops.

"What's up?" Terry asked, following George's gaze.

"Candy store, man. Now that you're back can you hold our place?"

"For candy? We're going to be drinking beer all weekend."

"Yeah, that's cool man. I like the two together, don't you?"

Ignoring the question, Terry gestured for George to cross the street and get his sugar fix. The scruffy looking biker trotted away excitedly. Terry turned to study the crowd: preppy college students, hip young executives, lawyers and accountants, a sailor, and what must be locals were all crammed together waiting for breakfast.

They were all going to the concert. Terry knew that because at Monterey Pop, it was about 'Music, Love and Flowers.' Nobody was black or white; the three-day concert was about the integration of music.

It was groovy, Terry realized, that all these people from very different walks of life could converge on a simple beach town for one weekend where everyone could connect and listen to music.

Caught in the beauty of the moment, Terry looked down the peaceful street, still grooving on flowers and love, and saw two girls who looked so familiar that they caught his eye. The women were dressed in hippie garb, and mesmerized him. He was sure he knew them.

The girls walked into several shops, making their way down the row of stores. One of them, a tall redhead, started to laugh, and the short brunette with her turned so that Terry was finally able to see her face. His eyes flashed with recognition and his jaw dropped open.

"Eva and Ruby," he said out loud, and before he knew what he was doing he was already following them.

The girls walked into a store specializing in hippie clothing and Terry followed. He watched while they shopped. Disguised as hippies, that was slick. He had to hand it to them. The club was looking for two biker chicks; they would never think that the girls had transformed themselves into hippies. They could have gone the whole festival without being spotted once, except that Terry happened to be in the right place at the right time.

Terry pondered his next move, but the temptation to reveal himself became overpowering and he finally succumbed. He moved behind them and, hiding behind a rack of clothing, jumped out and yelled, "Boo!"

The two girls jumped. Eva put her hand to her chest and let go a string of profanity. It was so out of character for the peaceful hippie part she was playing that everyone in the store turned to look at them.

"Terry, you fucking asshole you scared me to death!" Ruby pushed him.

"I should think so, depending on where you're at, who you are, and who's looking for you."

"Come on, Terry baby, be nice." Ruby raised her hand, trying to place it on his shoulder, but the biker moved back before she could touch him.

"Don't even fucking think about it. Do you know what I had to go through because of the two of you?"

"I can imagine, baby, and we're sorry. We realized that we made a mistake and it was wrong to bring you into it. It's just that we didn't intend for it to get so out of control," Ruby admitted.

"Meaning you didn't think you were going to get caught," Terry whispered since the patrons of the store continued to stare at them.

A saleswoman walked over and asked if she could help them, a cue to let them know that they needed to leave. Remembering Big Jim's command for a calm weekend, Terry pulled himself together quickly, apologized to the saleswoman, and led the two girls out of the store where they could speak privately.

"Listen, Terry baby, can we just keep this between us?" Eva asked with pleading eyes.

"Hell no! This time they would kill me. Here's what the two of you need to do. Leave right now, and I mean *right now,* before I get back to camp. When I get there I will tell the club that you're here and they will hunt your sorry slut asses down. I'm not doing anything for either one of you. You fucking wrecked Dylan's and Joey's rides and then you left me to take the blame. Fuck both of you."

He started to walk off but Ruby wrapped her hands around his upper arm. "Hang on, honey, didn't we have fun together?" Ruby asked coyly.

"Not that much fun. Not enough to take the beating I did."

"Look, Terry, nobody is going to know that we're here, and if they do find out they are never going to know that you spotted us first. All you have to do is keep quiet. We could have fun together all weekend, you, Eva, and me. If you know what I mean." She winked for emphasis.

Playing the sultry part, Eva licked her lips seductively and placed a hand around his other arm.

"Sure, Terry, anytime you want. We'll tell you where our tent is and you can sneak out of your camp late at night for a 'walk.' Think about it, both of us, all weekend long. All you have to do is keep quiet. Just let us enjoy the concert with the other thousands of people and on Sunday we'll be gone, no complications."

"That's right, Terry. No complications, baby. Just a weekend of music, love, and flowers," Ruby said, smacking her glossy lips together.

Terry pulled his arms away from both of them. "I mean it, you need to leave. I'm going to tell them that you're here."

"No baby, I don't think you will. I think you'd rather enjoy the weekend, have a few rendezvous with Eva and me, share in on the multitude of drugs we brought with us, and then on Sunday just drive away on your motorcycle."

"I will tell them," Terry insisted weakly, thinking of the possibility and staring at the two very attractive biker chicks in hippie disguise.

He remembered the day and night he had spent with Ruby and the kinky exploration they had enjoyed together. That held a powerful pull, and with the added promise of having Eva too, whose escapades he had heard about from several of the members, he couldn't help but have his body react to the fantasy of a ménage a trois.

Ruby pulled a piece of paper out of her canvas bag and drew a map of the outside of the fairgrounds.

"Our tent is here, Terry, on a long grassed area under several trees." She marked an X on the map and handed it to him. "That's where we'll be until the concert starts, and it's where we'll be every day after the concert. Come by anytime...come by a lot. Whatever you want, Terry...all you have to do is stop by." Ruby flashed her very white teeth and then she and Eva walked away.

Terry stared at the piece of paper. He told himself that he would hand the information over to the club as soon as he got back, but in the back of his head he couldn't help but imagine just one session with the girls. *What could it hurt?* he asked himself as he pocketed the map and walked back to the diner.

When he returned, George was standing on the sidewalk with a white paper bag, chewing on a piece of chocolate turtle.

"There you are, man. What the fuck? I asked you to hold our spot and you split. What's up with that?"

Terry's conscience told him to hand the map over to George. It's what he wanted to do, but despite his best intentions, he just couldn't do it. He told himself that he would hand the information to Dylan and Joey personally, but he wasn't sure he would be able to do that either. Feeling ashamed, he swallowed deeply, put on a fake smile and lied.

"I thought I saw an old friend, but when I caught up with the guy it wasn't him."

"That's a bummer." George pulled another chocolate out of his bag and plopped it into his mouth.

"Terry for two," the hostess called out, and the two men quietly walked into the diner.

***

Ron pulled the van into the fairground parking lot and seconds later Frog's bike pulled up beside him.

"I figure we'll park here, that way we can set up camp on the lawn, there." Ron stepped out of the VW. "The van can sleep two, we'll let the girls have that, and you and I can pitch a tent."

"That works," Frog said. He parked the old Honda as close to the van as he could, then he and Ron started to unload. They chose an area of lawn close to the bus and erected an old canvas tent.

Katie chuckled to herself. *I wish we had a modern day pop up.* She imagined the men's faces if she could pull one out of a bag right now.

Moonbeam had said little during the trip, and even though they had arrived, she was still sitting in the back of the bus.

Katie leaned over the back seat and slid the hippie hat off of Moonbeam's head. "Okay, the men are gone, so spill it, what's going on?"

"Officially, I can't tell you because I don't know."

"I see. So how about the unofficial version, can you tell me that?" Katie tried the floppy hat on and turned to gaze at herself in the rearview mirror.

"Sure, that I can tell you. As far as I know, the move to Marin County is off. Frog has plans that don't include me. I don't know what they are, but I know they're made, which means at some point he's going to split when I'm not around."

Katie's brain tried to wrap itself around this new piece of information. "What?"

"I said he's leaving. Not with me, not the way we planned. He's splitting without me."

"How do you know that, did he tell you?"

"No, not in so many words. He didn't have to, his eyes told me. It's what he didn't say that gave him away."

"Wow, that's a change of plans alright."

Katie handed the hat back and Moonbeam, who placed it on the seat beside her.

"Groovy hat, by the way. I love how you wrapped the love beads around it."

Moonbeam cracked a smile. "I like it too, I think it makes me look suave."

"Yes it does, very suave," Katie acknowledged. "So are you planning on getting out of the bus anytime soon? I hope you're not going to stay in here all three days?"

"What time is it?"

"12:30."

"So I have three and a half hours."

"No, not that long. They'll let us into the fairgrounds around three o'clock, which gives you two and a half."

"Well there you have it, that's what my plans are."

"Seriously? You're going to sit here that long?"

"Maybe. I haven't decided yet."

"Right. Well do you mind if I go and mingle a bit? I'll be back to check on you in a little bit, I promise."

"Sure, you go right ahead. It will give me some private moping time. Besides, I'm interested to see how Frog acts around you. Go party with them a bit and then come back with a report."

"Okay, I won't be long." Katie almost told her to call if she needed anything and then shook her head. It was taking a long time to get over the absence of cell phones.

When Katie arrived at the makeshift camp the men were still struggling to get the tent up. They had spread out chairs and set up an old metal card table. Metal, a sturdy material replaced by plastic in the modern day. This table would probably last another twenty years, unlike its modern day counterpart.

"Hey, baby, you ready for a beer?" Ron called out.

"Not yet, it's too early."

"Then can you bring me and Frog one? This is thirsty man work."

Ron was sweating. He and Frog had removed their shirts and tied bandanas around their heads.

"Two beers coming up." She reached into an old gray cooler, the kind that had a bottle opener on the side, and removed two Coors cans from the ice. She pulled the tabs off of both, then delivered the beers.

Although the tent appeared lopsided, it was sturdy enough to stop what they were doing long enough to drink a beer and spark a joint.

"What do you think?" Ron asked. He wrapped his arms around her and planted a kiss on the back of her head.

"I think it looks very manly."

Ron made a grunting noise, imitating a Neanderthal, and she laughed.

Frog remained silent, too silent. Her eyes met his and he looked away. The gesture wasn't lost on Ron who picked up on the action immediately.

"We have a few hours to eat and get buzzed," he said, taking a drag on a joint and passing it to Frog. "The Association comes on first, supposedly around four o'clock, but you know how that goes, starting times vary." "Hey, is Moony going to join us anytime soon?" Ron asked. "She's still deciding," Katie said, looking Frog's way.

Frog said nothing, just accepted the joint. He took a toke, another sip of his beer, and handed the joint back to Ron before walking off to fix the tent.

"Fun stuff going on?" Ron asked.

"So much fun, you won't believe it."

"Try me." "Well, for starters, she won't come out of the van because she doesn't want to see Frog."

"I see. Shall I go and talk to her? Maybe I can get her to come out."

"No, give her some alone time; she'll come out when she's ready. I'll go to check on her soon."

"This will be an exciting few hours with them arguing." Ron finished the smoke and disposed of the roach paper.

"I wouldn't exactly call it arguing, it's more like reacting to disappointment."

"Oh, I get. That's the reason she pulled the boxes out of the van. I guess we won't be looking for a new roommate after all."

Katie shook her head.

"Let's get this concert thing on the go. We can hand out the sandwiches and open a few bags of chips so we don't have to buy the expensive stuff inside. We'll get everyone fed and then worry about what plays out when it happens, agreed?"

"Sure, I can deliver food to Moony, update her on what's going on, and try to get her to come out," Katie offered.

"Good. I'll talk to Frog and see if I can get anything out of him."

"Good luck with that, Frog's not much on talking."

Katie thought of the many times she had tried to get through to the stubborn street hustler and shrugged. Frog just didn't seem to take anything seriously.

"Well, maybe one guy to another is a different story. Let me try." He opened a cooler filled with sandwiches, chose two and a bag of Lays Potato Chips, then wandered over to the tent which had started to look straighter.

Katie got two sandwiches, two Shasta Colas, and another bag of chips then headed for the open door of the van.

Moonbeam sat comfortably on the bench seat painting her fingernails a pale shade of orange, her floppy hat back on her head. "Hey," she said without looking up. "How goes it?"

"About the same as when I left you. Here, eat a sandwich. Ron doesn't want anyone to leave camp hungry."

"Groovy, I'm starved. What kind is it?" Moonbeam sat up happily and reached for the food.

"Peanut butter and jelly, I think."

"Far out, I love peanut butter and jelly." Moonbeam pulled on the plastic wrapper carefully so she wouldn't smudge her fingernails.

"Here's the update. Frog wouldn't even look at me, which means he's guilty as hell. Ron is going to talk to him and see if he can get any information out of him but realistically, we can't torture him so..."

Moonbeam laughed and took a bite of her sandwich. "He's leaving, Katie; all of his promises were lies. Regardless of everything we said to each other and the plans we made for a future together, he's leaving without me. There's nothing more to say."

"I see your side and I understand why you're mad. I would be furious too if I were you. But let's look at this situation another way. Frog is a guy, which makes his thinking a bit slow. In his eyes, he's protecting you from whatever it is that's after him."

"And what's that? Drug clientele? Bikers? Or just a blend of people associated with the heroin trade?"

"Exactly! That's why he's not taking you with him, silly. And under the circumstances, that's not such a bad idea."

Moonbeam's tears once again washed the flower off her cheek. All that remained was a yellow streak of paint.

"You're twenty years old, Annie. You do a lot with your life; you're well educated and you have a job in the media later. You're someone who can and does make a difference. You're the person you wanted to become. You've helped many people in your career and you've uncovered a lot of shit that needed to be told. You need to live, do you understand that?"

Moonbeam nodded.

"Then you can't be any more involved in this than you're supposed to be. Originally, this doesn't happen, none of it does. We didn't go to this concert, we stayed in San Francisco because we couldn't afford to come. The weekend of the festival you and I partied with some of the Diggers. They didn't go because they wanted the concert to be free, and they were against the publicity, scared that it would bring an end to the Haight District, and they were right. We're only here this time because we have my mother's money. Which reminds me, I told Ron the truth. Well, I confirmed his beliefs, because he had already figured most of our story out. Anyway, he knows. It was time to fess up."

"He knows? How is he reacting to the news?"

"Not really reacting at all, not yet anyway. I just told him before we left so he hasn't had much time to think about it."

"He needed to know." Moonbeam finished her lunch and disposed of the remains in a paper garbage sack.

"Yes, he did," Katie agreed.

"So are you ready to come out and join the world? You don't have to talk to Frog. There are plenty of other people setting up camps all over the fairgrounds, I'm sure you'll make a lot of new friends."

"Wait. Isn't there something else you can tell me about this weekend? Or something else you've remembered about Frog? Anything at all?"

"No, nothing. I've told you everything that I know. We never came to the concert so I have no idea what takes place here. If you want to know about the bands that play I can tell you tons, but about any of us I have no clue. I'm sorry, I wish there were something that I could remember but there isn't."

Moonbeam looked away and wiped at her tears with the sleeve of her sweater.

"You can't go with him, Moony, even if you want to, even if he were going to take you. You have to let him figure this out alone, that's the way it's supposed to be. He's been warned and he knows what's at stake. Now it's up to him. I know it's going to be hard, but you need to stay out of this and let him do his thing."

Katie took some Kleenex out of a box and wiped Moony's tears away. She wiped the rest of the wilting flower off of her friend's face and smiled. "It's going to be alright, Moony. Whatever happens we'll get through it together, that's how it's always been, whatever came down the pipeline you and I would handle it together. Now wipe your eyes, the parking lot is filling up fast and we have people to party with."

***

"Well the tent's straight now, man. That old thing was a bitch to set up."

"Yeah, it's a bummer to put up but it's a great tent. It really keeps the cold out even when it's raining."

Ron unwrapped his sandwich and took a bite, then opened a can of beer. "So man, what's going on?"

"What do you mean?"

"I mean Moony's refusing to get out of the van, you won't even look at Katie, you brought that old Honda up here instead of riding with us... it sounds to me like something's up." Ron opened the bag of chips and stuffed a handful into his mouth.

"Ron, I can't tell you much man, but here's the scene. I'm involved with some really bad people. If I don't split, I'm going to end up in a hole someplace."

"Wow. Is this something Katie remembers from her first '67 trip?" Ron asked, and noticing Frog's shocked reaction quickly added, "She told me, man, you don't have to pretend any more. She told me the truth, that she's from forty-five years in the future."

"And you believe her?" Frog asked, draining his beer.

"Don't you? Isn't that why everyone is acting so strange, because they believe her?"

"Yes, we believe her. She's proved it to us over and over again. It's odd, but she seems to be the real deal, I have no doubts about it."

"What did she tell you?"

"That I disappear at the end of August. But now that events have changed she said it could happen any time."

"So what's with this weekend, man?"

"It's getting close to summer and since Katie believes that it could happen now, I'm splitting before it does, you dig?"

"Who's after you?"

"Who knows man? The bigger question is who's *not* after me."

"Fuck, really?

Frog nodded.

"What are your plans?"

"I can't tell you any more than I told Moonbeam. I have to figure this shit out. If I don't clean this mess up then there's no future for me, whether it's one with Moony or without."

"So you're going to split sometime over the next three days?"

"I'm going to do what I have to do, but most of all I'm going to protect Moonbeam at all costs. Whatever happens to me, it happens to me alone. I don't want her getting hurt in any of this." Frog finished his sandwich and opened a fresh paper sack for a trash bin.

"I get your drift, man. You have to do what you feel is best. I'll make sure Moony's taken care of while you're gone, I promise. Is there anything else that I can do to help?"

"If you want to help, stay out of this, Ron. Make sure the girls stay out of it too. The people I'm dealing with are real nasty, you dig? You can't try to help me. I don't want to be responsible for anyone's safety. Please, just take care of the Katie and Moonbeam and let me do what I need to do."

Ron nodded and looked at his watch. "It's getting close to two o'clock. Let's get this camp finished shall we?" He rose from the card table. "They should be opening the doors in less than an hour. I want to work our way up to the front so we're among the first ticketholders to get in."

"Sounds like a plan, man." Frog also stood, and followed Ron over to the van to get the last of the camping gear.

***

Mark pulled into the parking lot at the Travelodge. It was just past one o'clock; they had several hours to rest before heading to the fairgrounds. The sign above the motel indicated there were no vacancies, but he had reserved his room long before the event.

Mark had overheard Katie and her Hells Angel boyfriend discussing the concert at the Searfus cocktail party. That's how he knew she would be here, and he wasn't going to miss the opportunity to be here too. Best of all, she was here with her lowlife hippie friends, including the one who had threatened him at Katie's apartment.

His plan, which of course was interlaced with revenge, was simple. He would end up with the girl but first he would have his fun. What that meant, he wasn't sure yet. Maybe he would pay Dennis an extra grand to rough her up a bit. If he couldn't persuade him to do it then maybe he could find someone else. As a last resort he could disguise himself and rough her up himself. Either way, she would pay for her initial rejection and the humiliation he suffered at her apartment in San Francisco. And she wasn't the only one who would pay, so would her hippie ex-boyfriend.

All he had to do was wait. The perfect opportunity would present itself. He had three days, and he was confident in his abilities. This was going to be one hell of a weekend and he couldn't wait to get started. As soon as he found Katie he would trail her and wait until she did something stupid. Once they got her away from her group, then the little hippie bitch would pay. Until then Mark was going to enjoy this adventure. After all, he was forking out a lot of his hard earned bread for this weekend.

"You're looking at a valuable item, Dennis," Mark chuckled, "a motel room in Monterey. Thousands are expected to be here but we are among the very few who have a room." Mark loved having something that nobody else had. It didn't matter if it was a motel room, expensive clothing, or a woman everyone else desired. As long as he could have the envy of others he was on cloud nine.

"One room though," Dennis said, snapping his gum loudly.

"Yeah, one large room with twin beds, asshole. I'm already paying for the trip, the tickets to the concert for three days, and I'm handing out two thousand bucks to you. We can stay in one fucking motel room, get over it."

"Fine by me man, I'm just saying…"

"Well, don't say anything."

Mark went into the motel lobby, surprised by the variety of people waiting inside. Barefoot hippies adorned with beads, an old couple trying to be hip, young college students, and a trio of young twenty-something's….all were represented.

The clerk behind the counter was wearing a tie dyed T-shirt and a string of colorful love beads. He looked to be in his early 30s, with thinning blond hair and a large button pinned to his left breast which read 'Music, Love and Flowers."

It took fifteen minutes to get the room key, much too long for Mark's liking. When he walked out of the office he was frustrated.

The parking lot was filled with the same people he had seen inside the lobby, and everyone was scurrying to get their bags and get to their room. Dennis had both suitcases out, along with a white ice chest, and was sitting on the lawn under a tree.

"Hey," he called out when Mark passed him by. "Figured I'd get everything out of the car and save some valuable drinking time."

"Right, well let's go." Mark rubbed his hands together in anticipation. "The room's on the bottom floor next to the pool."

"Outta sight, man."

The room consisted of two twin beds, a breakfast nook with a table and a modern hanging lamp, and because it was the 'deluxe' twin suite, they had a small refrigerator they could stack with beer.

"Nice," Dennis commented. He pulled several six-packs out of the Styrofoam ice chest. On the way from the chest to the fridge he pulled two cans off the stack and sat them on the Formica table. "Might as well get a few down us before we go." Dennis sat on a green kitchen chair. "What time is it?"

Mark opened a beer and took a long gulp. He looked at his watch. "1:20. We have plenty of time. We can drink a few cold ones here, get to the fairgrounds around 2:30-3:00, have a few more cold ones there, do a little investigative work, and then find our seats."

"And what about our actual business? When does that take place?"

"Not tonight, man. Tonight we locate her and find out where she's staying. Tomorrow we'll watch her and devise a plan. Things like this take time, Dennis, it's not something you can rush into, you dig?" Mark finished his beer and opened a second one.

"Right man, I get it. I'm just wondering what you have in mind. How do you see this thing playing out?"

"Tonight we locate her, tomorrow we follow her. Once she gets familiar with her surroundings she'll be more apt to let down her guard, meaning she'll walk off on her own and when she does, we'll get her. Or should I say *you* will get her and drag her off somewhere remote where I'll be at taking a pee. We'll pretend to scuffle and then you run off, easy as pie. You'll be wearing a ski mask and clothes you'll dispose of before heading back into the crowd."

"Then you'll comfort the maiden in distress." Dennis laughed. "Brilliant."

"Damn right! I'll take her to report the attack and I'll play the perfect knight in shining armor. Her crazy ideas will dissolve, she won't think of me as part of the evil establishment anymore, she'll see me as a great guy and then we'll live happily ever after."

"As part of the high social elite. You'll have a huge house on the top of a hill like old man Searfus and life will be beautiful," Dennis added with an evil grin before pulling a leather pouch out of his backpack.

"That's right man, just beautiful. If I can marry Al Searfus' only daughter can you imagine the possibilities?" Mark snickered.

"What's that, man?"

"It's weed, you want to try some?" Dennis pulled a glass pipe out of the pouch. He loaded it with a green substance that he pulled out of a baggie. From his pocket he retrieved a plastic lighter and held it in front of him.

"You're kidding right? All that talk about hippies, LSD, banana peels, and pot and here you are offering me some?"

"We're at a three day rock concert, don't you want to know what all the hype is about?"

"I don't know man, maybe," Mark confessed, and watched as Dennis taught him the basics.

His first few hits made him cough but once the effect took over he laughed. "This stuff is alright," he admitted, taking a drink of his beer. "Except that it makes me thirstier than hell."

"Yeah, you see? It's only pot. It's mellow, less than drinking a beer but just as enjoyable. It makes you feel calm, unless it makes you paranoid."

"Paranoid?"

"Sure, man, sometimes it can make you paranoid...but not usually."

"Shouldn't you have told me that before you gave it to me?"

"Why man, are you paranoid?" Dennis sat forward in his chair.

"I don't think so."

"Then don't worry about it, just go with the groove, man."

"How long does this shit last?"

"About an hour, maybe a little longer since it's your first time. You'll be fine by the time we go, I promise."

Mark settled himself into the second kitchen chair. "Do you want to know something crazy?" Mark asked, finishing another beer.

"Of course, I love crazy shit."

"I helped get rid of the Searfus boy," Mark said, laughing hysterically.

"You did what, man? I thought the son was in the military?"

"Oh yeah, he is. He's in the Marine Corps. He's been gone about two months now; he ended up getting deployed in the DMZ. Talk about being in the thick of the action, man, you can't get much more intense than that."

"So how are you responsible for his being there? I don't get it." Dennis stuffed some more weed into his pipe and lit up a second round.

"He came to me in February telling me how much he hated school. He said he wasn't good at studying and that sometimes he thought about going into the military. He wanted to get away from his father's domineering ways and thought it might give him a chance to grow up. Plus he wanted to give his father a reason to respect him, so I encouraged him to go. It was easy as pie, man, I have to tell you." Mark took another hit off of the pipe. "No wonder the US military loves getting young kids, they are so vulnerable. All I did was agree with all of his reasons for going. We had conversations about his grandfather and his uncle, who are both career military men. I told him that he could be just like them, make a name for himself that didn't include his father's title. He liked that idea.

"Over the course of a few months we became buddies; I called him, he called me. What a fucking stupid little dork, I could have talked him into anything. Yep, he became my buddy because I supported his every move. Just what every rich attention starved kid lacks. When it came time to enlist, I even went with him and, get this, he *thanked* me before leaving. Can you imagine that? I led the little mouse right into a trap, right where I wanted him, and he fucking *thanked* me."

Dennis took the pipe and lit what remained in the bowl, watching Mark closely. He knew the guy was an asshole, hell he himself was an asshole too, he couldn't deny that, but Mark's confession came as a complete surprise to Dennis. He had a kid brother in the Army. Sure, he would do just about anything for a buck— business was business, and he was an all-star when it came to making money— but he did have some moral code, remote as it may be.

When he thought of the young Searfus kid in the jungles of 'Nam he couldn't help but think of his own brother Jeremy, who had enlisted without anyone knowing it. Dennis missed his younger brother and he worried about him every day. Fortunately, Jeremy was in a relatively safe unit, but anything could happen over there.

The idea that Mark had helped young Richard Searfus get to 'Nam left a bitter taste in Dennis's mouth, but he was set to make a lot of money this weekend so he pushed the thought out of his mind and opened another beer.

Hell, he didn't have to like Mark Rhodes, but he had to work with the slimebag. He reminded himself that he was making a pool of money off the little shit at this event and that thought helped him hold his tongue and smile. In the back of his mind, however, he wondered what Rhodes was actually capable of. If he could manipulate a young kid into going into the Marines what was he going to expect Dennis to do for all that bread? For the first time he questioned his decision and wondered why he had come here.

"So you see, I helped Ricky Searfus right into the military, man. He was pure putty in my hands. Now he's out of the way, so papa bear has to think of alternatives. I mean, what are the chances that Ricky is going to walk in his father's footsteps?"

"You can't say that, he'll be back in a year. There's no telling what he'll do then, what is the kid, 18?"

"Yes, he's 18 and he enlisted, which means he's in for two years. If I'm lucky I'll be married to his sister by that time and the old man will see my potential over his. And there's always the chance that he won't come back at all. He's in a highly militarized zone, there's lots of crazy shit that happens in a place like that."

"Are you hoping that the kid gets *killed*? That's low, man, even for you."

"Hoping? No, I'm not hoping for it, but as I said before, he's in a major combat zone, anything is possible. You have to admit that if he didn't come back it would make my life a little easier, wouldn't it? And since I'm the one who pays you for all my undercover jobs that makes your life a little easier too."

Dennis smiled, but inside a red flag was waving. Mark Rhodes was a manipulator, sure, but wishing that a young man would never come back from Vietnam, that was an all-time low. Dennis had an opportunity to see deep into the man's soul and what he saw made him wish he wouldn't have come this weekend.

Chapter 32

The crowd pushed forward, and Ron's hand tightened around Katie's. Although the lines were moving quickly, Katie felt as if she were suffocating. Moonbeam was lost in the shuffle; she had tried to hold onto her but that bond had broken when a short hippie kid had bounced in front of her.

She and Ron made it to the front of the line and breathing heavily, Katie presented her ticket. On the other side of the ticket booths she found Moonbeam and Frog waiting, both separately and not looking at each other. Katie shrugged. She had to allow events to play out. There was nothing more she could do. Now it was up to the players themselves: Moonbeam, Frog, and Dylan, wherever he might be.

The fairground entrance was decorated with banners and flowers. Inside stood several frowning motorcycle police frowning. Anyone could tell they weren't happy to be there. Several hippie girls draped in flower headdresses approached them. They tried to hand the officers flowers but they were hesitant to accept.

As time passed and the young women continued to chat with the police, the men started to smile and laugh, obviously enjoying themselves. Soon they had accepted the flowers and they stuck them into their helmets. The hippie spectators applauded and the police officers smiled at the crowd. This rapport would continue to grow over the course of the three-day event. By the end of the third day they and their motorcycles were loaded with flowers and the officers were dancing with the concertgoers.

The sponsors of the Monterey Pop Festival wanted to have the best of everything available; the best bands, the best sound equipment, and because they knew there would be drug related problems, even a first aid clinic. The idea was that every problem would be taken care of swiftly without stopping the music.

The clinic was the first building Katie saw. It was hard to miss the large red cross. Location detected in case they needed it later, Katie turned her attention to more important things, the beauty of Monterey.

The weather was perfect. The temperature peaked at 67 degrees and there was a slight breeze blowing off of the ocean through the multitude of Monterey pines. The fairground, amongst all of this beauty, was decorated skillfully. Banners reading 'Monterey Pop' hung from lightpoles, which led the way to the concert field and the art and craft shows that surrounded it. There were flowers everywhere, and the main banner, identical to the one that was wrapped around the stage, read 'Music Love and Flowers. Monterey Pop Festival June 16-18th.'

Because record producer and concert promoter Lou Adler wanted to emphasize the theme, he had 150,000 cymbidium flowers flown in from Hawaii so that there were orchids everywhere, including on every chair— all 5,850 of them. The remainder of the flowers littered the stage and decorated the fairgrounds. This image of flowers and love would follow the psychedelic flower child generation.

When Moonbeam saw Katie walk through the gates she ran towards her, threw her arms around her friend and squealed. "This is the grooviest, isn't it, Katie? Can you believe that we're really here?"

"No, I can't," Katie answered. It was true; the idea that she would have a second chance to experience 1967 was still ludicrous and she often shook her head at the reality. Yet here she was, repeating her youth, and this time she had made it to the Monterey Pop Festival.

Katie looked at the crowd and marveled at how she was able to relive this part of her life. Silently she swore to the gods that she wouldn't waste her 'second chance.' This time around she would fix the mistakes that shouldn't have happened, or at least try.

"This place is far out. Can you feel the love?" Moonbeam asked, spinning in a circle so that her blue flowered hippie skirt swirled around her.

It was true; the vibes in the fairgrounds were peaceful and serene. Everywhere she looked people smiled, music played over the loudspeakers, and many of the crowd started to dance. As with most hippie events, love actually *could* be felt in the air.

"It's definitely cool; the vibes are truly out of sight," Katie replied, astonished once again at the creativity of her generation.

"Do you want to go shopping?" Moony asked the group out of the blue. "Shall we tour the specialty booths?"

Ron looked at his watch. "Sure, we can walk around; we have time. What do you say, Frog boy, you want to go shopping?"

"I think I'd rather check out my seat," he replied with a sour look. Katie glared at him. "Enough," she said, grabbing the front of his green tie-dyed shirt and shaking him.

"Hey!" he yelled as she pushed him to the side of a cement divider so that she could 'talk' to him.

"That's enough, Frog, quit with the attitude. What the fuck is wrong with you anyways?"

He didn't answer, just stared at her with a cocky grin on his face.

"Okay, Mr. Arrogant, let me explain something to you," she said in a whisper so she wouldn't disturb the vibes of the fairgrounds. "I get why you're leaving, I really do. Actually, it's the first smart thing that you've done, which makes me wonder who is really behind the plan."

"What's that supposed to mean?" Frog asked defensively.

"It means just how it sounds. You are a boy. You might think that you're a man, but really you just are an immature boy."

"Do you think this is helping?" he asked, his voice filled with sarcasm.

Katie wanted to shake him again, but refrained. "That girl loves you. I know it's stupid but is it's true, and you are acting like an idiot. Now, I understand why you're leaving by yourself and not taking her, and I thank you for that decision, but you had a long time to prepare for this and you didn't. You went ahead with whatever bad mistakes you made the first time around. I'm guessing that your world has come crashing in and you need to get out fast. That's cool, it really is, and at least you have the brains to do that. Now you need to ask yourself if you want to spend time here with us before you split. If all you want to do is make everyone else miserable then don't wait, leave now. If you can't be here and enjoy the time we all have together then I mean it, Frog, leave. Whatever you decide, don't ruin this for the rest of us, especially Moonbeam."

"Why would I want to ruin anything for Moony? Everything you're saying is bullshit."

"Is it, Frog? Is it really?"

"You make it sound like I'm a moron, that all I care about is money, and that's not true. You're right, despite the warnings I went ahead and got involved in something heavy. That was stupid. Now I want to fix this mess, and then I want to come back and get Moonbeam so I can spend the rest of my life with her. I may never get that chance but I do take full responsibility for letting the situation get out of control. So, with that said, haven't I paid enough? Moony won't look or talk to me. What am I supposed to do, fall at her knees? I can't make her talk to me, and maybe it's best that she's mad, that way it won't be such a shock when I leave."

"Frog, I don't have time for this. Any conversation we have isn't going to help anything. We both know the score. Just be smart and don't make Moonbeam unhappy."

She shoved him hard then turned and walked back to their friends without another look. Frog, sulking, stayed in the same spot 'thinking.'

"What was all that about?" Ron asked when she rejoined the group.

"It's past time that somebody put him in his place," she said, walking off with Moonbeam.

"What are you doing?" Ron called out.

"We're going shopping. You can come with us or you can stay and babysit Frog, it's your choice."

Ron glanced in both directions, at Frog, and then at Katie and Moonbeam, and finally shrugged. "I guess I need to babysit. Do you have your tickets?"

Katie nodded, waved goodbye, and then she and Moonbeam walked off toward the booths.

***

The girls approached the stadium, where several blocks of Western looking buildings filled with vendors and a score of concertgoers were also shopping. In one of the corners stood a giant golden Buddha with flowers and incense at his feet. Banners— some decorated with astrology signs, others with peace symbols— waved over the crowd's head. Everything that a hippie needed was on sale: paper dresses, handmade jewelry, posters, sandals, hippie clothing and even macrobiotic food.

On the main drag was a candle store called the Sticky Wicket. The deep aroma could be smelled along the street. Katie and Moonbeam walked by, breathing in deeply.

"It smells so far out we'll have to go in there before we leave. I'd really dig one of those groovy candles but I don't want to carry one around all day," Moonbeam said. "Oh look," she pointed at one of the shops, "candy apples, let's get one!" The candy apple booth had a multitude of sweets to offer. Fudge, divinity, peanut brittle, and caramel corn were interspersed among a large selection of candied apples.

The girls each selected an apple, paid for their treats, and then proceeded down a long row of booths.

The concertgoers were diverse. Katie looked at the people who passed by; many were hippies, but not all. There were conservatively dressed college students and businessmen with ties, which seemed odd to Katie. There were young people, old people, white people, brown people, black people, anyone who dug the music scene was at the festival. Many different groups of people all grooving on a beautiful California day. It was truly amazing.

The girls nibbled on their candied apples, making their way in and out of the shops where everything under the sun was sold. There was beautiful artwork, macramé plant hangers, and handmade jewelry. There was a pottery booth where a craftsman sat spinning a pot. In another booth a glass blower made beautiful pipes, hummingbirds, castles, and other glass paraphernalia.

One booth sold beautiful tapestries to hang on walls, along with Indian tie-dyed bedspreads. There were T-shirts and chokers, leather works with handcrafted belts, purses, headbands, and sandals. Another vendor sold exotic scented oils, which the girls just had to buy. There was a booth selling hippie clothing for men, women, and children. The clothes were expensive, designed to look like the stuff the real hippies bought in the secondhand stores on Haight. Everywhere you looked there were flowers. The hippies wore them, the straights wore them, and even the performers wore them.

When Katie and Moonbeam made their way into another store they came face to face with several members from the Hells Angels. Before they could exit, Joey, Sal, and Dave had already seen them so they had to be cordial. The men were looking at some handmade knives, which they set down when the girls approached.

"Well look who we have here, hippie fairy princesses. How you doing ladies? Long time no see, Moonbeam," Joey said, flashing a smile.

"Good to see you again ladies," Sal said. Dave nodded.

"Likewise." Katie smiled a phony grin.

Moonbeam nodded to Sal and Dave, who had turned their attention back to the knives, and then she frowned at Joey. "I was doing much better before I walked in here."

"Ouch. Be nice, little fairy princess, I don't bite." He reached a hand out to touch her arm but she stepped back to avoid him.

Joey smirked and turned his attention towards Katie, pretending to ignore his former love interest.

"Katie, how have you been?"

"I'm fine. Thanks for asking. Hey, where's Dylan, isn't he with you?"

"No, we got separated in traffic. I'm sure he's here by now, I just don't know where. I'll catch up with him later though. Do you want me to deliver a message?" He glanced at Moonbeam, who was still ignoring him.

"No message, just tell him that you saw me."

"Sure."

The girls walked away, anxious to get out of the store, especially Moonbeam, who had no intention of talking to the Angels. When they thought they were in the clear, Joey came running out of the store and Moonbeam cringed and swore under her breath.

"Hey, I just wanted to say I'm sorry about that party. Dylan and I had no idea that Ruby and Eva were going to be there. Dylan told me that they drugged you, Katie, and I'm really sorry about that too. At some point those two bitches will show up and rest assured, I intend to talk to them about that stunt."

"Thank you." Katie nodded and then she and Moonbeam walked away. When they were a good distance away Katie shook her head.

"What is it?" Moonbeam asked.

"I just don't get it. Why do you hate Joey so much? I know the party turned out to be a fiasco but it can't be just that. What is it about him that you don't like?"

"Everything. Joey has evilness about him. I don't know exactly how to explain it except to say that I can feel it. He tries to be sweet and he can come off as a great guy, jovial, fun, and good spirited, but underneath that façade there's another personality, his real one."

"And Dylan, do you hate him too?"

"Dylan? No why would I hate him? Dylan is the good boy trying real hard to be bad, that's why he attached himself to Joey the real bad boy. Inside Dylan there's a serious, caring guy. That person has been hurt so deeply that he's scared to emerge. In the right situation though, Dylan could be a real good guy, even if he doesn't believe it."

"You know all of this because you feel it?"

Moonbeam stopped walking and turned to face Katie. "If you open your heart, Katie, you'll be able to feel it too."

They resumed walking in silence. Katie thought about what Moonbeam had said and decided that her friend was right. She had closed her heart off many years ago and now, forty-five years in the past, she was still haunted by decisions she had made in her future. The irony was bittersweet. She smiled, vowing that she would change that part of herself so that she could learn to trust again.

"What time is it?" she asked.

"Quarter till four," Moonbeam said after glancing at her watch.

"We should head to the seats. Do you want to visit the bathrooms first?"

"The little fairy princess powder room?"

Katie laughed. "Yes, that's the place."

They made their way to the left side of a wooden building that read "Ladies". As expected, there was a line out the door and they settled themselves behind two girls dressed in miniskirts with perfectly teased bouffants and white lipstick. The two girls were discussing their recent graduation from high school and how they wanted to visit Haight-Ashbury during summer vacation and pretend to be hippies. Then in September, after they 'sowed their wild oats', they would return to San Jose and attend college.

The recent graduates were sharing a joint, and when Katie and Moonbeam joined the conversation they passed the smoke amongst all four of them. Katie explained that three months in Haight-Ashbury would only make them want to stay longer and suggested that they give themselves a year.

She wasn't sure who she was giving advice to when she told them to forgo school and concentrate on being young and free. She told them to look her up when they got to Frisco and proceeded to give them her address. When that conversation ended Moonbeam and Katie entered the elaborately painted bathroom where large flowers, an assortment of suns and moons, a few peace signs, and even the Hindu Ohm symbol were painted on whitewashed walls.

Comments in the women's room centered on how beautiful the artwork was, and Katie again wished for her cell phone so that she could take pictures of the great designs.

After using the facilities, Moonbeam and Katie headed towards the concert field. The piped in music that had been playing all afternoon had stopped, which meant the real concert was getting ready to start.

As they weaved through the crowd, someone from behind yelled their names and they turned to see Robin, Katie's former roommate, adorned in hippie clothing.

"I can't believe I found you here!" Robin yelled excitedly. She hugged them both.

"Man, I almost didn't recognize you. Where did you get the groovy clothes?" Moonbeam asked.

Robin looked at Katie and a sheepish grin crossed her face. "I hope you don't mind, Katie, but you left some clothes in the apartment. I was going to return them after the festival."

"I thought those threads looked vaguely familiar," Katie laughed. "They look totally groovy on you. Keep them."

The green Indian style skirt and the white flower patterned blouse did look good on Robin, and so did the long hair hanging freely and the peace symbol painted on her face. This was a very different Robin than the one she had known the first time around.

"Really? I can have them?"

Katie nodded and smiled at the girl who she now considered a close friend. Things certainly had changed.

"Why didn't you tell us you were coming?" Moonbeam asked.

"I didn't know that I was. I met this groovy guy who was playing guitar in one of the clubs in the Haight. He had a friend that cancelled on him at the last minute so he asked if I wanted to come. I don't know what came over me," Robin said. "I know this is so unlike anything I've ever done, but I jumped at the chance. We're here with a few of his friends and we have tents over at the football field. Where are you staying?"

"Outside the fairgrounds, we're camped near the parking lot," Katie answered.

"Out of sight, it's so groovy that we ran into each other. Hey, do you have a few minutes? I'd like you to meet my friend. Maybe you've seen him before, he lives in the neighborhood and he's always around playing tunes on his guitar. Man, this dude can really play too. If you've ever seen him then believe me, you would remember him."

"Sounds like a far out guy, we would love to meet him. Where is he?" Katie asked.

"Over here..." Robin started walking towards a grove of trees where a slim, bushy haired Hispanic man stood waiting.

"Hey, Carlos, I want you to meet my friends. We just hooked up at the bathroom, isn't that crazy?"

Carlos was dressed in jeans and a sleeveless tank top. When he saw the girls approaching he smiled broadly.

"These are my friends Katie and Moonbeam, and girls, this is my friend Carlos," Robin said cheerfully.

The young man reached out and shook both their hands while Katie stared at him. "What's your full name?" she asked after a long moment.

"Carlos Santana." He smiled. "Do I know you?"

"No, not officially, but you sure look familiar."

"You've probably seen me playing my guitar."

"Yeah, that's probably it. It's nice to formally meet you though. I'm told you play a mean guitar."

He grinned. "Yeah, they've told me that too."

Suddenly there was loud tapping over the sound system, and someone played a few guitar chords.

"Sounds like it's time to split and head back to the seats," Carlos said.

"Yes it does. It was great to meet you, Carlos, I hope I see you around the Haight sometime."

"Of course you will, I'm a permanent fixture." He laughed. "I even got to play guitar at the Fillmore last month when Bill Graham was desperate for musicians. Believe me, I'm around, but maybe we can meet up later? We'll be here all three days." He put his skinny arm around Robin's waist.

"That would be groovy, I'd love to hear you play," Katie said. And she really meant it. Who in their right mind would pass up the opportunity to hear Carlos Santana?

"Sure thing. Robin, did you tell them where our group is camped?" She nodded. "Cool, then come by tomorrow morning before the concert, or the morning after that, we'll be there."

Katie smiled warmly, and then she and Moonbeam said their goodbyes and headed for their seats. When they entered the arena it was already packed. Katie and Moonbeam presented their tickets to a middle-aged attendant and the man escorted them to the right-hand side of the stage and up a long aisle. When they got closer to the stage, Katie could see Frog and Ron, who had already taken their seats.

"Thanks," she uttered to their escort, and the girls started to pass through the row of already seated concertgoers. When they arrived in the middle of the row, Ron stood and took Katie's arm, helping her into her chair.

"There you are. I was worried that you might miss the beginning of the show." He kissed her.

"Nice seats, I'm impressed. How did you get these?"

"I have connections," he said with a wink.

His connection was the same man who made much of the acid that was being digested that weekend. Owsley Stanley was well known in the San Francisco music community. Anyone who worked for him had advantages, which also included great concert tickets.

Their seats were in the middle aisle, ten rows away from the stage. Far enough back so that they could see the whole stage without looking up awkwardly, yet close enough that they could see the performers perfectly.

The arena was circular with the large assembled stage at the front focal point. On either side of the circle were side boxes, which had been set up for the event. These seats had the benefit of a roof over the patron's head, shielding them from the weather. Next to these, also on the outside of the circle, were plain bleachers without a cover. The seats in the center were on the ground floor placed into three columns called 'orchestra sections.' Here, white chairs sat directly on the lawn facing the stage. Every seat in the stadium held one of the Hawaiian orchids. The only concertgoers who didn't get a flower were those holding 'standing passes'. These tickets allowed the patrons to stand or sit anywhere that wasn't taken by seat ticketholders.

The tickets were organized into four groups: the day show (matinee $5 for the best seats-$3.00 for standing tickets), the evening show ($6.50 for the same seats-$3.50 for standing tickets), a full day ($10), or a three-day pass ($30).

Those who didn't have a ticket could pay a dollar and get into the acreage surrounding the fairgrounds where they could camp and hear the bands for free.

At the end of the first day of the festival Monterey's motels, parks, and even a few private residences that rented out rooms were packed. The property that surrounded the fairgrounds was overflowing. Those who couldn't find a place slept in their cars or under trees.

Katie settled herself into her seat and scanned the arena, surprised at how many people were able to fit into the fairgrounds. The hordes of spectators seemed to go on forever and she found herself wondering how many bodies were out there.

Their row consisted of the four of them along with a string of straight-laced college students, probably young Republicans Katie decided. One of the girls, dressed in slim jeans that zipped on the side and sporting a bouffant hairdo with a dark green bow, had a bottle of bubbles she blew into the crowd. In front of Katie there was a hippie couple tripping on something, and beside them a couple who looked to be in their fifties.

In the row behind, a skinny hippie kid played a wooden flute and beside him an equally skinny hippie girl dressed in a flowing white gown danced to the music.

Everywhere that Katie looked people were happy. There was no stress here, no worries, this weekend truly *was* about music, flowers, and love.

The afternoon was getting cool. The ocean breeze blew over the crowd, and the audience put on jackets and sweaters as the sky grayed over.

Ron pulled his brown corduroy jacket over his shoulders and then pulled a joint out of the inside pocket. He lit it, took a toke, and passed it to Katie. As soon as the aroma hit the crowd others pulled their supply out, and soon a cloud of sweet smelling Mary Jane settled above them.

Katie reached over Ron and looked at Moonbeam's watch. 4:50 p.m. Right then, the field exploded with excitement when the background lights flashed and a band walked out on stage. Katie took a deep breath. This was it, the event that she had been waiting for, the one that she had missed forty-five years ago. Now, by some unknown powers, she was actually here and the excitement was overwhelming.

Brian Cole, bass guitarist for The Association, approached the mic. Lights flashed in the background and the crowd went wild with applause. The band strummed their instruments and their chosen spokesman addressed the crowd:

"With the influx of machines into our affluent society you see before you this evening a machine of our own construction. You see an Association machine composed of many intricate parts. The first being behind us, a semi replying percussinant invertebrater, or a drummer-er. In the center of the machine we see a digit flexing instuminater, or a guitar. Towards the other end of the machine we see a transistorized instruminater stamped made in Japan. To my immediate right you see another catapult of vibracated tambourine chingers. I am a consistent lowering flagellator. And last but not least, the largest single component in the machine, an alarm in floating vocalizer. This machine, when programed correctly, makes a variety of sounds and rhythmic patterns such as...one, two, one two three..."

After an elaborate guitar introduction, Russ Giguere reached for the microphone and started to sing.

"Every time I think that I'm the only one who's lonely
someone calls on me...and along comes Mary."

Katie bounced in her seat. This was beautiful, everything about it, the place, the people, and the times. Life was peaceful; their worst fear was the continuation of the Vietnam War. Life was easy and fun. A feeling of freshness was everywhere. It was a time when the young generation honestly believed that they would change the world.

Ron put his arm around Katie and she snuggled against him. She was grooving on the vibes when he pulled her close. Expecting a kiss, she was surprised when he whispered in her ear.

"What happens to me?"

"I don't know, Ron. We never hung out together. I never lived in your house and we never went to concerts together. I don't know what happened to you after I moved out of the city. The last I heard you were living in the house renting out rooms and doing whatever it is you do."

"So you have changed things; really changed them." His mind was obviously starting to tick with possibilities.

"I have," Katie answered. "Nothing major, at least not yet. But some stuff, yes, I've changed."

"So you don't think that you're destined to relive your past the same way?"

"No, I think my options are open just as they were before in 1967, meaning anything is possible."

"But what about the important things, stocks and bonds, sporting events... are they set in stone? Can you predict all of them?"

Katie glanced at the hippie chemist. His eyes seemed to darken and for a second she shivered, knowing what he was proposing. She had honestly never thought of the possibility of making money, but Ron had undoubtedly figured out a scheme.

"I think they are set. I have free will but the events that are happening around me are the same. For example, this Sunday the Chinese will drop their first hydrogen bomb and it will take the world by surprise."

"What does that mean?"

"It means watch and see, everything has happened just as I remember it. I seem to be the exception. I have free will, and so do the people around me. If they choose to, that is. I think there is a pull to do things the same way again unless something interrupts that process; like me knowing the outcome and changing it. As for the actual events, all of them have been the same as they were the first time around."

"What would you think about making money off of this little gift?" Ron asked, kissing her on the back of the head.

She hadn't thought about money, content with what her mother was sending, but those funds would soon be cut off, and then what would she do? She had asked herself that many times. Ron was right, there was money to be made, lots of it. All she had to do was remember past events.

Her winnings, whether they were made on the stock market or by betting on sporting events, could easily support her for the rest of her life. Since she was only 20 years old that gig could last a really long time.

At the conclusion of The Association's performance, she had allowed herself to dream about a future, a real one. In her dream world, her brother lived, her parents had no control over her life, and all of her dreams came true. Most importantly, in this fantasy world she never ended up with Mark Rhodes.

"What did you think of them?" Moonbeam asked, shaking her into the present.

"They were great. They harmonized beautifully and they put on an excellent show. The introduction on the machine comparison was a bit weird but still I thought they were great."

"I think they'll go far, don't you?" Moonbeam asked and Katie, not wanting to disappoint her friend, said nothing, but she knew their outcome.

The Monterey Pop Festival brought instant fame to many, but that was not the case for The Association. Their performance was left out of the original film version. So the weekend that made legends out of bands that had never been heard of outside of their region did nothing for them. As the first act of the festival, essentially they had been screwed.

Brian Cole would become one of the many casualties of the drug era, just missing the 27 Club by two years. He would die from an overdose of heroin on August 2, 1972 at the age of 29, but tonight his band was on fire and anything was possible.

***

Mark and Dennis left the Travelodge at quarter past three. They had a slight buzz going on after a handful of beers and were cheerful as they left for the festival.

The fairgrounds were a little over a mile from the motel and when they made it to the parking lot the place was overflowing. Mark couldn't park anywhere close to the stadium so they ended up in a lot down the street where the two had to hike in. Mark took a parking space in the very back of a far off lot. His red Porsche was an eye catcher, and with what he and Dennis were planning, they didn't need any recognition.

Dressed in jeans and dark shirts, the men tried to blend in with the other concertgoers; just two regular guys going to a pop concert, nothing special to look at or draw attention to.

By the time they made it to the gate the lines had died down so it didn't take long to get into the fairgrounds. Hungry from his first pot experience, Mark led his accomplice towards the food booths where he bought another beer, a hotdog, and a corn on the cob.

"Think we should check out our seats?" Dennis asked.

"Are you fucking crazy?" Mark asked. "There are lots of people here and we are just looking for one. Where do you suppose she is? Did you think she was just going to fall into our hands?"

"No, but I thought we might get to sit down and eat our meal, maybe see the beginning of the concert before we started playing detective."

"Look, man, that just doesn't make sense. Why would we do that?"

Dennis shrugged and took a bite of his hotdog. "Look around, man. Most people are still out walking around the shops. In a very short time they're going to be taking their seats and when they do that will be the best time to find Katie."

"Once everyone is seated in the stadium how are we supposed to find her? Did you think we could just walk up and down the aisles staring at people? You and I are going to watch separate gates into the arena. That way, chances are better that one of us will spot her, unless she's already seated. If you find her before I do then you watch her. You find out where she's sitting, who she's with, and how close our own seats are to hers. If I find her first, I'll do the same." Mark glanced at his watch. "It's 3:40 now, we'll meet here at 5:00. If neither of us has found her, then we'll work out another plan."

"Cool, that works. Which gate do you want?" Dennis asked, finishing his hotdog and washing it down with half of a beer.

"I'll take the west gate, you can take the east. Remember, right here at 5:00 o'clock," Mark repeated, heading away from Dennis.

As he'd predicted, an announcement of sorts was broadcast over the P.A. system and the crowd started to disperse quickly.

Mark stood at the side of the west opening of the stadium. He stared at the hordes of hippie girls dancing through the entrance. Every time he thought he saw Katie the woman in question turned out to be just another longhaired blonde hippie girl draped in flowers.

When he had stood watching for what seemed like hours and was close to giving up, he got lucky. Standing in line at the women's restroom he saw Katie and her hippie friend Moonbeam. They stood talking to two young girls, sharing a joint and laughing.

"Ahh, there you are you little fucking bitch," Mark said under his breath, smiling excitedly. He moved closer to the women's bathroom.

He stood hidden in a grove of trees watching Katie and Moonbeam disappear into the restroom for several minutes. When they emerged, he prepared himself to follow, but stopped when he heard a girl calling their names. Moments later, Katie's roommate, the one who had humiliated him during his recent trip to San Francisco, stepped into view and Mark's face contorted with hatred.

There were so many people he wanted to get even with, but this bitch, the one who had turned him down, the one who thought she was better than him, she had attacked his ego and he couldn't let her get away with that.

Never before had he been rejected in this way. Girls usually fell into his lap easily, all except these two. Both had rejected him, made him feel less of a man. Katie with her threatening Hells Angel boyfriend, and Robin, who made it clear that she thought he was a creepy sociopath. He was on his way to being a great man, something to make the Rhodes family name shine again, and these two had brought out the worst of his inferiorities. He hated both of them.

Now, both were standing in front of him, less than thirty feet away. He sat in the underbrush, watching his potential victims as he cracked his knuckles and fought for composure.

Katie Searfus was essential to his future. She was the key to his ambition, the key to loads of bread, and the key that would restore his family name by erasing the tarnished image his father and uncles had caused.

She was of the society he wanted to belong to. He had to have her as his wife, as the mother of blueblood pure society children. His progeny would be great and all of that rested on her shoulders. That was the reason he was here, the reason he had cleared out his entire savings account. He was dedicated to the scheme, willing to use every asset he had to make sure he got the girl. But deep inside he hated her and he wanted to watch her suffer.

He looked at her, examining her many faults. Sure, she was beautiful and she would produce beautiful children, but right now she was downtrodden, dirty, and living in San Francisco like an animal. She believed in free love and economic equality; her ludicrous ideas were no better than a commie's. The longer she stayed in the city the more damage she would do to her reputation as an eligible debutante. In so doing, she was ruining his future reputation too. Mark fumed. No future wife of his would continue to act like this.

Soon, the girls were on the move, following Robin towards a skinny Hispanic kid standing under some trees. A ten-minute conversation transpired, the minutes ticking by as sounds over the loudspeaker told the crowd that the concert was getting ready to start.

Finally the visit ended, the girls embraced, and then Mark followed close behind Katie and her friend, staying in the shadows of the crowd for cover.

He followed them into the arena and watched them present their tickets. Then showing his own ticket, he entered the event, staying behind the crowd for shelter as he watched Katie and Moonbeam move towards the stage.

They took their seats, Katie sitting next to the very same hippie dude who had assaulted him several months before on his trip to San Francisco.

"So, they are still together," Mark said to no one, his blood boiling when he watched Katie kiss his aggressor. She had brought the Hells Angel, substituting him for her hippie lover, knowing that she couldn't bring the derelict to her parents' party. Now the truth was clear, she was lying to everyone, her parents, their friends, but most importantly she had lied to *him,* and that made Mark furious.

Victim located, it was time for him to find his seat, and he hoped it was close so he could watch Katie.

His seat, which was in one of the covered side-boxes, overlooked the crowd, and Mark was ecstatic to find that he could indeed see Katie from where he was sitting. This was better than he could have hoped for. He was smiling from ear to ear when he left the arena, walking back to the destination he and Dennis had chosen as their meeting spot.

He moved along the paved pathway, his thoughts drifting to money. How much was Dennis willing to do for an extra five grand? A new scheme formed in Mark's head, one he wasn't willing to share with his accomplice just yet.

"There you are, man, I thought something happened to you. You're ten minutes late," Dennis said. "I didn't see any sign of her, what about you?"

"I saw her. I followed her too, and the best part is that our seats overlook hers. We'll be able to watch her as she comes and goes all three days, isn't that great?" Mark asked with a twinkle in his eye.

"Perfect," Dennis replied emotionlessly.

Chapter 33

Dylan pulled into the football field and looked at his watch: 3:00. He was late; there would be questions.

He parked next to the other bikes and searched for the campsite. It didn't take long before Chocolate George found him wandering.

"Hey, man, there you are. Where the fuck have you been, brother? Big Jim has been looking everywhere for you."

"Yeah? Well, here I am, what's up?"

George looked around, obviously expecting to see someone else, and a look of disappointment crossed his face when he realized that Dylan was alone. "Isn't Skinner with you?"

"Skinner? No man, I rode alone. Sorry I'm late; I decided to visit a friend. What's the deal with Skinner?" Dylan brushed his now greasy hair back from his face with his fingers.

"I don't know. We thought he was traveling with you. Now that you're here and you haven't seen him...I don't know, man. It sounds like he's missing."

A cold shiver ran through Dylan and his legs wobbled. He knew instinctively this was a bad sign.

"Anyway, Jim wants to see you man. He's expecting Skinner too, so he's going to be surprised to see you alone."

"Where can I find him?"

"You're in luck, man, he's at the campsite." George nodded towards the football field. "This way my friend."

George led Dylan to the right-hand side of the field where the Angels had set up a makeshift campsite. Multiple tents circled a barbeque pit where chairs and tables were placed. In the middle of the camp Big Jim stood smoking a cigar and drinking a Budweiser.

"There's your man," George said, and headed back to the parking lot.

Dylan swallowed hard, dreading the conversation he was about to have with Jim. The Angels' president was a good man. He was trying to do good things with the club and Dylan respected him. He didn't want to lie to this man. What he really wanted to do was to pull him aside and tell him everything, but that wasn't possible, not yet. He had to find a halfway point somewhere between the truth and the lie.

The first person he saw was Freddy. When Dylan walked into the camp the already intoxicated biker jumped up and hugged him.

"Hey, man, where's Skinner?" he asked, glancing around.

Dylan shook his head and Freddy gave him a puzzled look. Suddenly Big Jim was beside him and repeated the question.

"I don't know where he is, man, he left before I did. I rode solo and I stopped in Santa Cruz to visit a friend. We chugged a few beers before I left, and that's why I'm late."

Big Jim eyed him suspiciously, then he looked at the camp filled with prospects and hangarounds.

"Let's take a walk," he suggested, and Dylan reluctantly agreed.

When they were past earshot of the campsite, Jim stopped, crossed his arms in front of his muscular body, and shook his head. "What's going on?" he asked, staring deeply into Dylan's eyes.

"I-I honestly can't tell you because I d-don't really know," Dylan stammered.

"You know something; don't tell me that you don't. You're late to the clubhouse, then you're late to the campsite. Visiting a friend in Santa Cruz, really? I'm not accusing you of anything, but there's something not right, and you and I both know it. This isn't the first talk that we've had, Dylan. I asked you what was going on months ago when we were at the Be-In and you denied any involvement into anything outside the club. Now, here we are again, and I'm still asking questions, and you're still denying any knowledge about what we both know you're involved in."

"Man, you have to trust me," Dylan said. "I swear to you when the time is right you'll know everything. You're a good leader and I love this club and its members.

You have my full respect and I promise when I know what's really going on, then you will too, but right now..." Dylan glanced around nervously and lowered his voice, "the woods have ears."

Jim wasn't sure what to make of Dylan's confession so he said nothing. He looked out over the field, specifically towards their camp, and then he shook his head again. "I want to trust you, Dylan, I really do, but I'm not sure you've earned that trust. I *will* find out what's happening, and if I find out that you're on the wrong side, then we're going to be doing more than just talking." Big Jim finished his cigar, dropped the butt on the ground and used the toe of his boot to grind it into the lawn, and without another look he walked off.

"Fuck!" Dylan muttered to himself. Would this mess ever end? And if it did, what would be the outcome?

He walked back towards the campsite deep in thought. Now he had Big Jim doubting him and that was a bad thing. On top of that, Skinner was missing, and he couldn't forget it.

His mind replayed the last meeting he had with Sal and Dave. They had said Skinner's fate was turned over to the 'higher ups'. Did that mean what he thought it meant? Where was Skinner now? Was he alive or..." Dylan shivered.

"Hey, man, I need to talk to you." Surprised by the interruption, Dylan turned and saw Terry sitting on the lawn drinking a beer.

"Sure, man, what's up?" He took a seat beside Terry.

"This is what's up, man." Terry handed him a piece of crumpled paper which had a primitive map drawn on it.

"What's this, brother?"

"It's a map...to Eva and Ruby's tent."

Dylan's mouth dropped open and he stared at the piece of paper speechless.

"I saw them in town this morning when Chocolate George and I were getting breakfast. They're disguised as hippies, they're real convincing too, I almost didn't recognize them."

"Unreal, man, they're here? They're really fucking here?"

Terry nodded.

Dylan laughed. "Can you believe that? They surface to attend a concert, a fucking rock concert. They know we're looking for them, they know we're going to be here, but they come anyway. How dumb is that?"

Terry shrugged. "Maybe they're tired of hiding."

"Maybe. They should be. It's better to get this over with than to postpone the inevitable. I mean, how long would you be willing to stay on the run when it doesn't make sense to even try?"

"What's going to happen to them?"

"I don't know, man, I have to get together with Joey to figure that out. Why? Are you feeling bad for ratting on them?" Dylan asked.

"I know it's stupid, but yeah, I guess I kind of feel bad for them."

"You did the right thing, Terry." He slapped his fellow Angel on the back. "There isn't anything else you could have done. I know chicks can sometimes just fuck you up mentally, but right is always right."

Terry nodded.

"How on earth did you get a map out of them?"

"They offered me a bribe to keep my mouth shut."

"Really? And what did they offer you?"

"A threesome in their tent all weekend long."

Dylan whistled and then he laughed. "I can see how that would be tempting. I'm glad you did the right thing though, I wouldn't want to have to kick your ass again."

"Yeah, I wouldn't want to go through that again either."

"Thanks. man. Tell you what, when we decide what where going to do I'll let you in on the plan. How does that sound? That way you'll know exactly what they're facing before they do."

"Sure, man, I'd appreciate that. I know it sounds crazy, but I care what happens to them."

Dylan nodded. "It doesn't sound crazy at all. You're a good guy, Terry, don't let that get in your way."

***

When Dylan left the clubhouse that morning he had gone straight to the garage, knowing that he would have the place all to himself.

Besides stocking up on cash, which he had hidden in a steel lockbox at the garage, he took a gun and then searched Sal's and Dave's office hoping to find some evidence, anything that he might be able to use against them if he needed to.

Unfortunately, his search came up empty. Apart from a few phony invoices for accounting's sake, there was nothing that might lead him to the person responsible for his and Frog's impending demise.

Dylan left the garage disappointed but stocked with a good bundle of bread, enough to keep Frog and himself hidden for several months, but he was no closer to a solution, and that bothered him. *Who wanted him dead?* He repeated that question over and over. If he knew who was responsible, he could take control of the situation and fight back instead of watching his back around everyone. He had taken the long route to Monterey, telling himself that he needed the time to think.

Now that he had arrived he couldn't help but look at everyone as a potential suspect. Anyone could be responsible for his death, and that left an eerie, cold feeling that crept into his soul, something he just couldn't get away from. And on top of everything else, Skinner was missing. It was still early, and there was still a chance that he might show up. Perhaps he had done the same as Dylan, went back into the city to do his own investigation. But Dylan didn't think so. Somewhere deep inside he knew that Skinner was gone and that he and Frog were next in line.

Dylan took the piece of paper out of his pocket and looked at the childlike drawing. Several months ago he would have been thrilled to have this information but now, compared to everything else in his life, it felt trivial. The only advantage that he could think of was that it created a diversion from the rest of his problems.

He and Joey were estranged. It was hard to accept but it was true. The man he knew today was no longer the friend he had grown up with. They had both changed, and they had headed into very different directions.

Perhaps the information he held in his hand was a key to healing that bond. At least for a small amount of time he and Joey would be united on some common goal and that brief connection might restore something that they had lost.

Dylan headed towards the parking lot, trying to remember the devastation he had felt when his bike was ruined. He was hoping to regain the anger but found that his current situation made the incident seem minor in comparison.

The parking lot was loaded with people, many leaving to get to the fairgrounds and others who were just getting there to set up camps. There were people of every denomination and socioeconomic background, all coming together for one weekend. The hippies were right, it was beautiful. Dylan wished that all he had to do was to groove to the music, flowers and love, but for him the weekend wouldn't be as elegant as that.

***

Chocolate George was standing in the parking lot giving directions to newcomers when Dylan arrived.

"So what's the score, man?" Dylan asked.

George looked at his watch. "Concert should be starting soon. Everyone is heading there. Do you have your ticket?"

Dylan patted the pocket of his jacket. "Right next to my heart."

"Sweet, then that's it, man. Go trip on peace and love baby." George chuckled.

"Is everyone sitting together?"

"Not all of us. The tickets are in clusters of three to five seats, all in different areas of the arena. We're supposed to choose a meeting point there but we haven't done that yet. You'll find out when you get there. Tomorrow we're leaving the campsite as a group. Big Jim has something planned. I think we've been asked to help out, same as usual, they use us and abuse us. Anyway, the concert begins at noon. Jim wants us there at 11:00 for instructions. As far as tonight goes, high times, brother. Unless something changes, go groove, man. I'll be there soon. One of the prospects is taking my place in the parking lot."

"Cool, then I'll see you there. Hey, by the way, have you seen Joey?"

"Yeah man, he got here on time." George laughed, then he took some chocolate candies out of a white bag he was hiding in his vest pocket and popped one into his mouth.

"Ha, ha, ha, very funny. So where is he now, do you know?"

"He's at the concert. Sal, Dave and Joey all left about forty-five minutes ago. I'm not sure where they're sitting so don't ask me, but they're at the fairgrounds for sure."

"Far out. Then I guess I'm heading to the fairgrounds." Dylan jumped on his bike and kick started it then sped off on his Harley.

***

Dylan didn't have a problem finding Joey. When he walked into the fairgrounds Joey was talking to a group of Angels in the courtyard.

For the first time in his life Dylan dreaded approaching the one person he thought he would always be close to. The nervous feeling he had disturbed him but he brushed it away and, trying to act normal, walked over to the other Angels.

"Hey," he said when he walked up to the men.

"Dylan, you finally made it. What took you so long, brother?" Joey asked.

"I went through Santa Cruz, thought I'd drop in and see Dan Hodges as long as I was going through there."

Joey nodded. Dan had been a longtime friend for both of them.

"I told him you said hi," Dylan lied and Joey smiled.

"Listen, man, we got something to discuss." Dylan pulled the makeshift map out of his vest pocket. "This, my friend, is the location of our missing ladies."

"Ladies? Which ones?" Joey asked with a chuckle.

"The ones who fucked our bikes up, remember them?" Dylan let the information sink in.

"Eva and Ruby?" Joey asked, astonished.

"The very same. Right here under our noses, supposedly disguised as hippie chicks."

Joey laughed and studied the crude drawing on the piece of torn paper. "So, now what?"

"I was going to ask you the same thing."

"Wow, man, are you asking me for my gut feeling or what we should do?" Joey said with a smirk.

Dylan shrugged his shoulders. Again, the incident seemed trivial compared with everything else.

"You should do the right thing," Sal suggested, unexpectedly joining the conversation.

"He's right, do what the club wants you to do," Dave chipped in after moving away from the rest of the Hells Angels where they formed a private group to talk. "We already have enough suspicion surrounding us so let's not add to it."

"Okay, so what *is* the right thing?" Dylan asked.

"The right thing is to hit them up with their arrest warrant. Let the fuzz haul their asses off to jail. I'm not sure how much time they'll get but you can figure they'll be charged for the destruction of the bikes and then for avoiding arrest because they didn't turn themselves in, even though they knew there were warrants out. And, of course, everything depends on their current records. If they have past offenses then they could be facing five to seven years."

"And if they don't? What if their records are squeaky clean?" Dylan asked.

"Doubtful with those two, but if that were the case they are still looking at destruction of property and avoiding a warrant, maybe two or three years."

"Probation in a year and half?" Sal said.

"Or sooner," Joey piped in.

"They'll have to pay for the damage to the bikes as well," Dave said.

"Oh fuck yeah, they're going to pay for the damages!" Joey roared.

"Look, man, you don't have a choice. This has to be handled in the right way because this is a club issue. Meaning, whatever we decide, Big Jim and the First Skulls have to know about it," Dave said.

The bikers became quiet. Several seconds passed before Dylan spoke. "I think we should play their bluff. Let them think that Terry is on their side."

"What do you mean?" Joey asked.

"They gave this map to Terry with the promise of his silence. If he didn't tell us that they were here he was offered a kinky sex weekend."

Joey laughed. "Really? Trashy sluts."

"So we play a game with them, send Terry in tonight to make them think that everything is cool."

"Oh, Terry's going to love this," Joey laughed.

"Terry makes an appearance, maybe he takes some beers over and just hangs out for awhile, you dig? When he leaves, we have a prospect or two step in and watch them."

"Do the prospects get to watch when Terry's with the whores?" Sal chuckled.

"The visit is Terry's thing, what happens is up to him. However he wants to play his part, it's cool, and I don't want to know about it. The important thing is that he shows up. That will calm their nerves and make them think they've won. Once they've relaxed we can confront them."

"Tonight?" Joey asked.

"No man, not tonight. We want to confront them tomorrow at the fairgrounds with an officer of the law. It will be done nice and peaceful, no scene. That will score some points for the club and our problem will be solved. We'll look golden for the way we handled the situation and the bitches will go to jail," Dylan finished.

"Not quite as fun as I pictured our revenge would be. I thought we could get some hard ass biker chicks to kick their asses. But I guess this is the best way to handle it. Per the First Skull's directive, 'do nothing to taint the Hells Angels' name.'" Joey cracked his knuckles. "So we have a plan. Now what?"

"Now, go groove to music and check out the hippie chicks," Dave ordered.

"Hey man, speaking of hippie chicks, I saw Katie and Moonbeam," Joey said.

"Yeah? How did Moonbeam respond to you?" Dylan asked.

Joey shook his head. "Man, that chick hates me. I don't know why. Anyway, Katie said to tell you that I saw her, and now I have."

"Groovy." Dylan took a deep breath of fresh Monterey air.

"Let's go experience 'music, flowers and love'," Sal said, and the group split apart as each man left to look for their seat, which to Dylan's delight weren't anywhere near each other.

***

Dylan's seat turned out to be on the left-hand side of the arena, ground floor, about twenty-five rows away from the stage. The Association had already finished when he made it there, and a Canadian psychedelic rock band called The Paupers had taken the stage. The band was in the middle of an acid rock song, 'Magic People', and Dylan swayed to the music.

He located his seat easily and was surprised to find that he was sitting next to Terry and Chocolate George. This, he told himself, was a good omen.

"Hey, man, it's about time you showed up. Where the fuck have you been?" Terry asked.

"I was hanging out enjoying music, flowers and love," he said with a fake LSD induced voice.

Anxious to talk, Terry jumped over Chocolate George and landed on the seat next to Dylan's. "Is everything okay? Are the plans made?" he asked nervously.

"As a matter of fact, they are, my friend."

"Why does that sound bad?"

"Bad no, but it might sound like you're involved."

"Oh fuck, why man?"

"Don't freak, it's not a bummer." Dylan moved closer so that his fellow biker could hear him better. "Basically we're going to have the pigs pick the bitches up tomorrow at the fairgrounds, but we have to know where they are and to do that we'll need to have someone watching them."

"Man, I don't want to babysit those chicks. I turned them in, how am I supposed to spend time with them?"

"Relax, you don't have to babysit them, we're going to have one of the prospects do that. But you are going to have to make an appearance."

"An appearance?"

"You have to make them feel safe, let them know that everything is cool; that kind of an appearance. They're expecting you tonight so you'll call them on their bluff. After the concert you'll show up at their campground and pretend that you've taken the bait."

"Look, man, they're expecting me to ball them," Terry confessed.

"Yeah I know that, but that part of the trip, it's up to you, man. Whether you just visit or you spend some 'special time' with them, that's your bag, you dig what I'm saying? I don't want to know about that. All I want you to do is to make an appearance. Make them relax so they aren't looking over their shoulders all the time. Then you leave and they let their guard down. This is a winning situation, you give them comfort and at the same time you get even for the shit they left you to deal with. After a few beers, or whatever, you'll split and one of the prospects will watch over them tonight. Tomorrow the prospect will follow them into the park. That way we'll know where they are and when the time is right, we'll have them busted, can you dig it?"

"Yeah I dig, man, it sounds fair. Don't get me wrong, I'm not grooving on my part, but you're right, they do have it coming. As for having them busted by the pigs, I agree with that part too. It's the right thing to do. I'm glad the club decided not to handle it themselves."

"What do you mean, man? You know that the Hells Angels are a group of clean cut dependable Americans. Isn't that the part we're supposed to be playing, the one the First Skulls want us to adopt?" Dylan smiled cynically.

"Right man, isn't that the image we already have?" Terry laughed.

"Abso-fucking-lutely." Dylan reached over and stole a chocolate turtle out of George's white candy bag.

***

The day was magical, that was how Katie described it. Hours had passed quickly while the crowd peacefully grooved to the music.

After The Association, a Canadian psychedelic rock band took the stage. The Paupers played a forty-five minute gig and then, Lou Rawls, Beverly Martyn and Johnny Rivers did the same. Before she knew it, the hours had passed and The Animals' performance had begun.

Katie studied the bands, knowing beforehand how history would rate their performances. The Monterey Pop Festival, for a lack of better terms, was a changing of the guard between the British bands. Forerunners of the so called "British Invasion," The Beatles and The Rolling Stones couldn't attend. (The Beatles claimed their music was too complicated to perform on stage and two of the Stones, Mick Jagger and Keith Richards, had outstanding drug charges against them and were denied entry to the United States.) In their place the UK sent their best new bands: The Animals, The Who, and The Jimi Hendrix Experience.

As the sun went down over the Monterey Bay the night air chilled and Katie shivered. Despite several beers, a few joints, her warm knee length sweater, and the crowd beside her, she was still cold. Ron wrapped his arms around her and she leaned into his body happily, and then one of the songs she had been waiting for started, The Animals' rendition of 'Paint it Black'.

The screen behind the band flashed pictures of a girl with light brown hair. Close-ups of her eyes, teeth, lips and eventually odd flashes of different parts of her face graced the screen. These pictures moved faster until they eventually blended together into colorful oil mixed psychedelics.

As the colors swirled together on the screen behind them, John Weider took the forefront and began his long, beautiful fiddle introduction into 'Paint it Black.' The crowd went wild and with the night chill forgotten, Moonbeam and Katie were on their feet dancing to the music.

When Eric Burdon took the mic the stadium was already rocking, and when the song ended, the audience was on their feet grooving to one of the bands that would gain international fame from this concert. The result was spellbinding.

Although 'Paint it Black' was just a Rolling Stones' cover song, Katie had always believed that The Animals' version was better than the original, and tonight's performance had confirmed that. Between the music, the vibes of love and peace, and the beauty of their surroundings, Katie was caught in the moment. Like the thousands of people beside her, she found herself believing that this feeling of euphoria could actually last forever.

When The Animals finished their set the lights on the stage dimmed, and for a few minutes the crowd was silent.

With her ears still ringing, Katie turned to look at her friends. Moonbeam looked flushed and happy. Beside her however, Frog sat looking pathetic and despondent. He was clearly miserable. Katie suddenly felt guilty over her harsh treatment of him several hours prior. She nudged Ron in the shoulder and gestured towards their depressed friend.

"I think I should go sit with him for awhile," Ron said when he saw his demeanor.

"I think you should too," Katie agreed. She moved so that he could walk past her and Moonbeam, taking the hint, moved quickly to fill his vacant seat.

"The Animals were simply groovy," she gushed. "Just divine."

"Yes, they were," Katie agreed, and then nodded towards Frog. "What's happening with him?"

"Who the fuck cares? Lying piece of shit. Let him sit there and sulk."

"Wow, harsh."

"He was going to ditch me, think about that. I came up here believing that we had a future together, that we were going to Chet's commune where we would live this beautiful groovy life together. Now look."

"I agree that was a crappy way to find out. I would be angry too," Katie admitted.

"As I said, let him sit and sulk, he deserves it." Moonbeam started to bite at the corner of one of her fingernails.

"Maybe he does deserve it, but let's consider this. Frog is into something really bad. It's so bad that he might die for his mistake. Maybe you have your eyes closed, Annie. You want to believe that just crossing the Golden Gate Bridge will wipe out all of Frog's indiscretions. Maybe it's time that you open your eyes. You don't need, nor do you want to, take that kind of baggage on. That's one heavy load, baby. You have goals in life and you will achieve whatever you put your mind to, I've been there to see it." Katie brushed her friend's long auburn hair off of her shoulder. "Let him go, honey. I know you love him, but dying is a heavy price to pay for love, don't you agree?"

Moonbeam nodded.

"Let him go do whatever it is that he has to do. Contrary to popular belief, love does not conquer all. This time around he was forewarned, now it's up to him and Dylan to figure this out. If it were Frog alone, I'm not sure he would be able to do that, but if Dylan is involved, and I believe he is, then he'll figure something out."

"How do you know that? I mean that Dylan will find a way out of this, or is that just a guess?"

"Dylan is a survivor," Katie said. She remembered the night they had spent across the Golden Gate Bridge when she had declared him a daredevil. Maybe she had been wrong that night, or maybe Dylan was both, but one thing was for sure, he was most definitely a survivor.

"I hope you're right." Moonbeam wiped a tear away from her eye.

"I hope I am too." She realized that the conversation had shifted away from the main topic so she cleared her throat and tried again. "Moony, here's the main point. I'm afraid that you're letting your anger with Frog get in the way of reality. If you let him leave now, while you're angry and not talking, then what if something does happen? In the long run will you regret the time that you could have spent with him this weekend and didn't?"

Moonbeam didn't say a word but Katie knew that she had made her point. An immediate change came over her friend's demeanor. Her face softened and the lines on her forehead told Katie that Moonbeam was thinking about what she had just said, and that was a good thing.

Katie smiled and took a drink from her soda. She looked around the arena staring at the thousands of people who were packed together sharing this remarkable historical event. Abruptly everything changed. One second she was fine and in the next her heart was beating wildly. She stood and whirled about frantically, staring at the people around them.

"Did you see that?" she asked, suddenly terrified.

"See what? What's wrong?" Moonbeam stood and stared into the crowd. After seeing nothing out of the ordinary, nothing that might have caused Katie to react the way she did, she turned back, shaking her head in confusion. "What is it?"

"I don't know...." Katie sat down and reached shakily for the cup of soda. "I was fine, totally content and happy and then suddenly I felt like I was being watched. Not just watched, like I was being watched by someone who was threatening, someone who wanted to hurt me. This super creepy feeling came over me and I knew that I was being stared at. When I turned, I saw a flash of something that moved. Whoever it was, they knew that I saw them."

"I didn't see anybody and I was facing in the same direction that you turned. It was probably just your imagination. I told you that you need to relax and open your heart so that you can feel free again." Moonbeam glanced once again into the crowd.

"Maybe, but wow, what a trip. Look at my hands, they're still shaking. That was really strange, I have never felt that way before." Katie shook her head, disturbed by the incident.

"In all your sixty-six years?" Moonbeam asked with a laugh, trying to comfort her friend.

"Yeah, something like that."

"I sure wish you could tell me what will happen over the next few months," Moony said sadly.

"Yeah, I wish I could too, but my powers of 'foresight' only go so far."

Katie tried to act normal but she still felt uneasy. She was joking with Moonbeam but inside she knew that the threat was real. Someone was watching her. Whoever it was they were evil, because the hair on the back of her neck was still standing on end.

***

"I told you not to get that close," Dennis said when Mark returned to his seat.

"I told you so..." Mark mocked in a squeaky voice.

"Well I did, man, and you know it. Besides, no harm done, she didn't see you, not really."

"Close enough," Mark said, still panting from his sprint across the lawn. He retrieved his beer out of the cup holder in front of him and took a long drink out of the now warm beverage. "Much too close," he muttered. "From now on we stay strictly to the plan. That was my mistake and I know it was a big one. I just wanted to...see her."

"It's cool, man. As I said, no harm done. There's no way she could have seen you. You were much too fast. Look over there, she's laughing with her friend, she probably doesn't even remember."

"I don't know about that. I'm telling you she picked up on something, I know she did. I don't know if that's going to affect anything, but she sensed someone was watching her."

"It will work out, buddy, you'll see. Just sit back, be mellow, and enjoy the music."

The lights went out for a few seconds. When they returned there was a bright flash when Simon and Garfunkel walked onto the stage.

Mark counted to ten, willing himself to calm down. He tried to settle his rattled nerves by watching the harmonizing group but in the back of his mind he was worried. He knew that somehow Katie had sensed his presence and that disturbed him. He didn't want her to be on guard, looking over her shoulder and feeling uneasy, because then he and Dennis would have a hard time finding her alone. Now the idea that she might stay close to her friends for the entire concert upset him.

"Damn," he said aloud.

Dennis reached over and patted him on the back. "It's cool, dude, don't sweat it."

Mark was confused. He didn't know what had compelled him to get that close to her. Perhaps it was the beer or the funny stuff they were smoking earlier, but for some reason he had to see her up close. He had told himself that he loved her, but he wasn't sure if that was the case. He knew he wanted her, that he would do anything to have her, even if that something was crazy and unstable. That's why he had gone to look at her, just to know what his feelings for her really were.

Katie meant his career. With her family ties he could and would be a powerful man. Without her, he wasn't sure what he could achieve, and he didn't want to find out. Somewhere along the line he had become obsessed with her, he knew that. He told himself that it was love, but Mark wasn't even sure if he was capable of that.

That was why he ignored Dennis's warnings and ventured out on the field alone. All he wanted was to see her close enough so that he could tap into his feelings, if he actually had any. After all, he was risking a lot by throwing this weekend together. It was costing him a bundle, but if his plan was successful and it earned him her affections, then it would be worth it.

At first he was a good distance away from her, then he was drawn in closer and closer. When he was within several feet he stopped and stood admiring his obsession longer than he should have.

It was confusing. She was certainly beautiful, and he indeed felt something stir within him. Something that he had never felt for the other girls who had thrown themselves at him, but what that was, Mark wasn't sure. What he did know was that he had to have her, that he *would* have her, because his life depended on what she could give him. Mark had always gotten whatever he wanted his entire life...until her, and he was about to change all of that.

He watched for several minutes before she sensed him. As her head turned, Mark dove into the crowd. He picked a spot where tall hippies stood, and sat behind them on the lawn several feet away. He remained there for five to ten minutes, absolutely still.

When he was sure that Katie and her friend were no longer staring into the crowd he sprinted back towards the box seats where Dennis sat waiting.

What puzzled him the most was that after all of that his feelings still weren't clear, and he decided that perhaps he didn't really have feelings, not like other people did. It wasn't the first time he had thought about that. In fact, he had thought about that topic many times before.

What he did feel, if he was perfectly honest with himself, was desire. A desire so strong that he couldn't walk away. Whether that was love or not, Mark decided that it didn't matter.

No matter what his feelings for her really were, he knew that he would have her, and if he couldn't then maybe he could fix things so that nobody ever could.

***

Terry carried two six packs of Schlitz Malt Liquor across the fairgrounds parking lot. He wasn't sure how this would play out, he just wished that it was over.

He had drunk several swigs of tequila for courage before setting out from the football field, and now his nerves were so rattled he wished he had taken several more.

He followed Ruby's primitive map, looking for a cement divider next to a long grassed-in area under several large birch trees. According to the drawing, this marked the spot of the girls' tent.

Seven to ten feet behind him a young prospect named Spencer followed. When Terry walked away from this drama Spencer would stay and watch the girls until the plan unfolded tomorrow at the fairgrounds.

When he was about to give up and consider the map a fake, Terry saw the location and knew that he had found their campsite.

His heart pounded. He took several deep breaths and then made a beeline for a midsized green canvas tent. Eva and Ruby were sitting on lawn chairs talking to some of their hippie neighbors. He looked at his watch; it was 12:45 a.m.

"Hey there, honey. We weren't sure if you were going to show up," Ruby called out when she saw him. She tapped Eva on the shoulder and the tall redhead turned and smiled.

"Terry, baby! What a pleasant surprise, we were just talking about you. We were wondering if you were going to show up and then 'poof' here you are, just like magic."

"Just like Bewitched popped you in, man." Ruby laughed and twitched her nose like Samantha Stevens on the sit-com.

"I fucking love that show," Eva said. She imitated Ruby by attempting to wiggle her nose but failed miserably because of her level of intoxication.

The girls were already flying on something, Terry realized, and he breathed a sigh of relief. Deceiving them was going to be a hell of a lot easier than he had planned.

"Good evening, ladies. I thought I would bring you a nightcap and just check in to see how everything is going." He set the beers on the lawn and then plopped down beside them.

"It'sh sho groovy to shee you, Terry, thanksh for the beer," Eva slurred. She got off of the lawn chair and moved closer to Terry so that she could take a beer. She opened it quickly and took a long, thirsty drink. Then she sat on the lawn, settling herself so that she was almost sitting on Terry's lap, and leaned against his body.

"I can't stay long, ladies, I don't want anyone to get suspicious. I told them I was just going out for a walk and that I'd be back long before 2:00. But tomorrow I'll make up a valid excuse so I can stay with you all night long." He cracked a beer open and downed half a can in one gulp

Meanwhile, Ruby moved off of her chair. She sat on the lawn behind Terry so that she could massage his neck. Terry gave in to the pleasant sensation and closed his eyes. She lowered her red-stained lips close to his ear and whispered, "Do you want to move into the tent?" She ran her hands down the front of his chest and nibbled sensually on his ear.

"No. I mean, I would rather save this until tomorrow night. It's been a long day and I've done a lot of drugs. I wouldn't want to disappoint anybody, especially myself." He leaned forward so that he could reach another beer. Ruby dropped her arms and sat back on her heels, taking the hint.

The girls glanced at each other and then Eva said, "Sure, baby, whatever you want. It's your dime, so whatever turns you on." She finished her own beer and laid the empty can on the lawn beside her.

"I just wanted to stop by, have a few beers with my favorite ladies. I thought we could just groove for awhile and enjoy life, isn't that the hippie way?" he laughed through a mouth full of malt liquor.

"How should we know?" Eva said, opening another can.

"Isn't that what you are now?" he asked.

The girls ignored him.

"Hey, Terry, you want some drugs" Ruby asked. "We have Quaaludes, some LSD, and I think we have a few pink hearts left, although I'm not sure because we took most of them today."

"Hell no. Thanks for the offer, but I think I've had enough for today. I want to be coherent tomorrow so I can remember the concert, you dig?"

He pulled a joint out of his pocket and lit it, hoping that the herb would calm his nerves. Terry looked at his watch and decided he would stay another half hour before making his escape.

"Everything's alright isn't it, Terry?" Ruby asked suspiciously.

Terry passed her the joint. "Everything is groovy, baby." He kissed her. Once he got his point across he kissed Eva too. "Everything is beautiful." He finished the joint and lit another. Then he lay on the lawn looking up at the stars, his head spinning.

Seconds later, Eva laid her head on his shoulder. He hugged her and the guilt returned. He closed his eyes, just feeling the moment, and when he opened them again he realized that he had lain there for hours.

Terry rubbed his eyes and retrieved his arm, which by now was numb up to his shoulder, from beneath the sleeping Eva. He sat up and yawned, and then he looked at his watch, 3:15 a.m. It was definitely time to leave. He quietly drew a blanket over Eva, then looked into the tent to check on Ruby, who was officially passed out. Without making a sound, he walked out of the camp.

Thirty feet from the tent he saw Spencer and a hangaround named Billy. They were sitting beneath some trees smoking. When he walked up to them they stood and passed him a joint, which he accepted greedily.

"Sorry, man, we hope you're not frozen. When you fell asleep we didn't know what to do so we just left you there. We figured if we tried to get you up one of the girls would wake up too and then we would be fucked," Spencer said.

"It's cool, man, no harm done." Terry handed the joint back. "I'm just going to head back to the football field and get some real sleep." He started to walk off and tossed over his shoulder, "I'd like to remember some of the concert tomorrow."

The two-wannabe bikers looked at each other and nodded. They wanted to remember some of the concert too.

Chapter 34

Katie opened her eyes and blinked. Ron's van was hot and miserable inside. She pulled at her sweater, which had wrapped itself uncomfortably around her neck. On her way to the door she noticed that Moonbeam was gone and she wondered what time it was.

She slid the door open and the cool Monterey air invaded the stuffy compartment. Breathing in deeply, she jumped out of the VW and looked towards the grassed area searching for her friends. Moonbeam and Frog were nowhere in sight but she saw Ron sitting on a lawn chair drinking what looked like a cup of coffee.

Barefoot, she approached the campsite and pulled up another chair to sit beside him.

"Good morning," he said looking up from his steaming cup. "Would you like some java? It's only instant but it's better than nothing."

Katie pulled a ceramic cup out of a box and Ron filled it with boiling water. She selected a variety of packets out of a bowl on the table and poured the powdered contents into her cup. "Frog and Moony?" she asked, stirring the brew.

"Taking a walk, if you can believe that. They started talking this morning. Real freak out, I didn't see that one coming."

"Hmm, imagine that." Katie opened a package of multi-flavored pastries and slipped a bear claw out of the opening. "What time is it?" she asked, chewing on her sugary breakfast.

"Nearly ten. You had a good sleep."

"Wow, I guess so. What time did Moony get up?"

"About the same time as me, maybe seven o'clock. They've been gone for over an hour."

"That must be an interesting talk." Katie took another bite of her bear claw.

Ron pulled his own pastry out of the bag. "Yeah, it really surprised me. I thought they weren't going to talk for the rest of the trip, but what do I know?"

"What time do you think the gates will open?"

"The concert starts at 12:00, but they have all those booths so they're going to want to give people enough time to shop. I say they will start letting people in around 11:00, which means you should probably start getting ready."

"Yeah, I suppose I should. I wonder what the line to the women's bathroom will be like?" She ran her tongue over her teeth, which felt crusty from last night's snacks.

Ron shrugged and poured himself some hot water.

"I guess I'll get my stuff and find out."

She walked back to the van and retrieved her small toilet bag and then chose a clean shirt, undergarments, and a fresh hippie skirt before walking to a small bathroom.

Katie was surprised to find that there wasn't a line. She was able to freshen up, change her clothes, and even apply some makeup without being disturbed. When she finished, she headed back to the camp where Ron was busy packing up the odds and ends.

"You look refreshed and beautiful. Are you ready to go?"

"Shouldn't we wait for Moonbeam and Frog to return?" Katie asked.

"Nah, they have their tickets, let them have some alone time. We can't lose them, they're sitting next to us." Ron smiled as he put his arm around her.

"True, they know where to find us. Let's go."

Ron picked up a gray sweatshirt and tied it around his waist. He caught her hand, and the two set off for the concert.

When they got to the fairgrounds the staff had started to let people in, and although they had to stand in a line it was moving much faster than it had the day before.

Ron and Katie showed their tickets and entered the park for another day of music, flowers, and love.

It was June 17, 1967. Today, Canned Heat would start the show and the second band would be Big Brother and the Holding Company. Katie couldn't wait to see Janis's performance, knowing that it would be deemed one of her best.

"I've been thinking of this gift of yours, specifically on how you can make money," Ron said totally out of the blue.

"What?"

"Your gift."

"Oh yeah, right."

"When we get back I think we need to get a series of notebooks."

"Notebooks?"

"Yeah. You start making a list of everything you remember. The outcome of sporting events, stocks, companies to invest in, stuff like that."

"Notebooks? Really?"

"Sure, one notebook for each category. One for sporting events, the next for stocks and bonds, and another for random notes, you see what I mean? The more you go over this stuff, the more you'll remember. The more you remember the more money you make, you dig?"

"Yeah sure, I guess so."

"For the big sporting events we can go to Vegas. You know, stuff like the World Series, boxing events, and the Super Bowl. Do you know anything about hockey? If you do we can make bets on the Stanley Cup outcomes too."

"To be truthful, I don't know how much of that stuff I can remember. I mean, I can't just sit down and make a chronological list if that's what you're asking me to do."

Ron just looked at her.

"Maybe when teams are playing each other I might be able to remember who wins but I can't guarantee that. I was never really into sports. What I remember was games being played in the background while parties were going on. I might or I might not know the outcome, but I can tell you this for sure, I'm not going to be one hundred percent accurate."

"No, but I bet there are times when you're going to be seventy-five percent sure or higher. As I said before, the more you write this stuff down the more you'll remember. We just need to give you access to the material you're going to need."

"Access to what material?"

"Sports baby, you and I will become avid sports fans. The more you watch the more you'll remember."

Katie wasn't sure she wanted to put that much time and energy into something she didn't really enjoy, but she didn't say anything, hoping the topic would just blow over. There was a time and a place for a discussion like that and as far as she was concerned, this was neither.

"As for stocks and bonds, I bet you know more than you think. Once you start studying the *Wall Street Journal* and we get you up to date on the stock market, you'll be amazed at how much you remember. Your subconscious mind probably has a ton of information stored up. Think about it, how many years have you watched the news? That information has to be stored somewhere." He tapped Katie's temple. "All you have to do is start working your brain to remember. As soon as we get back I'll get a subscription to several journals and we can start studying them."

"Oh boy!" Katie said with false enthusiasm, making a face and hoping he would pick up on the vibes, but sadly he didn't.

"The big investments come later after we've built up capital. By then you'll be good at this, so we'll be able to invest in upcoming companies. I'm sure you know of several which can make us rich?"

Bored with the conversation, Katie's mind wandered and she found herself studying the other concertgoers.

"Maybe we can cash in on inventions. Are there any modern day devices that we don't have now?"

Katie laughed. "I don't think we'd be able to invent them."

"Why?"

"Future advancement is about computers. Everything is run by them, every business, every car, even generators have computer parts inside. Unless you know anything about computers, and I assure you that I don't, we're going to have a hard time inventing one."

Katie was only half listening to the conversation, continuing to search the faces in the crowd.

"Look over there, isn't that Mickey Dolenz?" She pointed to a young man with bushy hair who was dressed in Native American attire.

"Computers? What kind of computers?" Ron asked.

"There, isn't that Mickey Dolenz?" she repeated louder.

"What? Oh Mickey Dolenz, from The Monkees?" Ron stopped and stared at the young man who was several feet away. "Sure, I guess it could be," he replied. "Now back to these computers..."

Katie let go of his hand and walked over to the man in question. "I love your show and your music. I think you're going to go far in the music business. You might not believe that since you're viewed as a television show, but forty years from now people will still be listening to your tunes, even young people."

Mickey Dolenz looked at her and smiled. "Thank you, and what might your name be, pretty lady?" he asked with a bow that delighted Katie and she laughed.

"My name is Katie."

"Lady Katie, you have a beautiful day."

"I certainly will. You do the same." She started to walk away.

"Lady Katie," Mickey called, and she turned to look at him. He walked over and took a flower off of the lei he wore around his neck. "A beautiful rose for a beautiful lady." He handed her the white flower as he bowed.

Katie accepted the gift, curtsied, and then shoved it into her hair with an assortment of others she was collecting.

"That was odd," Ron said as Dolenz and his group walked away.

"I think it was glorious," Katie said happily.

"Hey, about these computers," Ron tried again, "are they large?"

"Large? No they aren't large, they're small. Well, they started large, but they get very small."

"Small?"

"Yeah real small, this big," she said, showing him the normal size of a cell phone.

"That's a computer?"

Katie saw a snow cone cart and ran towards it. "Can I have a large cherry?" she asked the youth manning the booth. She pulled out a quarter and handed it to him. Several seconds later, he passed Katie a large red cone and she sucked on the straw happily. "I love these things."

"Katie, computers, are they all that small?" Ron asked again.

"What? Oh computers, yeah some are that small. They're actually telephones. Handheld computers that the populace carries around with them."

"Carry around with them? Telephones that are really computers?"

"Yeah, sure. There are computers in different sizes. Telephones can be computers or you have the larger desk version, laptops that are about the size of a large book, and then there are tablets which are a bit smaller," she said in between bites of her ice treat.

"You mean regular people own them?"

"Of course, everyone has one, even school aged kids. I told you, in the time I came from it's the age of computers. The whole world is run by them, even countries that you would think of as Third World are run by computers. If all the computers suddenly stopped, ordinary life would be interrupted. In the long run people would starve, they wouldn't be able to do anything without them."

"Nothing?"

"Nothing. Computers run the finance world. You were talking about stocks— the stock market is computerized. Hell, a hotdog stand is computerized. All cars have a computer system that controls them. I think any electronic device has some form of computer installed. That's what runs the system. Without them the Twenty First Century would shut down. That snow cone made me thirsty, I sure could use a bottle of water."

"Any electronic device? Say, a lawn mower?"

"Sure a lawn mower, it probably has an automatic starter. That's a form of a computer. I suppose a bottle of water is out of the question. Let's see, not a Coke or a 7up unless they have diet, and that hasn't been invented yet so..."

"A toaster?"

"It probably has something computer related inside, something that tells it what to do. Maybe a lemonade."

"When does all of this happen?"

"All of what?" Katie walked towards the nearby lemonade stand with Ron trailing behind her.

"This computer takeover, when does it happen?"

"Oh wow, I don't know, let me think... It was gradual, you understand. It wasn't like one day we woke up and computers had taken over the world, it was a little bit at a time. I know Steve Jobs and Steve Wozniak built the first home computer in a garage. After that the whole market just exploded."

Katie stood in the lemonade line.

"Who are those dudes?"

"Steve Jobs and Steve Wozniak? They are the founders of Apple Computer. They built some of the first models in their garage."

"When was that?"

"Sometime in the seventies."

"Where are they now?"

"Now?" Katie laughed. "I believe they're still at Homestead High School. I don't think they'll graduate for another few years. Then I think you can find one or both of them at Cal State Berkeley."

"Cal Berkeley really? They're local boys?" Ron's brain was reeling.

"Yes they are." Katie got to the front of the line and ordered her lemonade. Stepping away from the stand, she sucked on her drink contently. "I think I need to pee now."

"What?"

"Pee, you know the bathroom?"

"Sure. You want me to walk you?"

"No. Not unless you have to go too. You can stay here and wait for me if you want."

"You're sure about them being at Homestead High School?"

Katie pretended not to hear him as she ran down the hill towards the bathroom.

"Apple Computers, Apple Computers," Ron muttered over and over...

***

Moonbeam woke and stared at Katie who was breathing heavily in her sleep. It had been a restless night and for the most part, she had been uncomfortable. She looked at her watch. It was only 7:00 a.m. She could try to sleep more, but knowing that it would be a waste of time she crawled out of the van instead.

The outside air was cold so she slipped her jacket around her shoulders before heading towards the bathroom.

When she passed the campsite she saw Frog sitting at the metal table. He seemed trancelike as he stared into a cup of what must have been coffee.

Hoping that he didn't see her, she slipped past him silently, making her way to the small wooden restrooms.

On the way back to the campsite she was freezing. Despite the cold water in the restrooms she had managed to wash herself, but now her hands were icy and she shivered.

"Do you want a cup of coffee?" Frog called out when he saw her returning.

She was going to ignore him but then she remembered what Katie had said. In fact, she had been thinking about that all night, which was one of the reasons she couldn't sleep. Her honest feelings, if Frog left now and never returned she would feel horribly guilty. That was the reason she decided to end the feud before the weekend was over.

"Sure." She approached the table and pulled a cup out of the box.

"It's just instant."

"That's alright, I don't like coffee anyway. I just want something warm to hold onto."

"Look..." he said, offering her the condiment bowl, "I don't know how to start this conversation..."

"I'm not surprised." Moonbeam settled herself into a chair.

"I know I'm dumb okay? You don't have to tell me."

He became quiet, thinking, and Moonbeam stared at him, waiting for an explanation.

"When I was a kid I grew up poor, me and my three sisters. Don't get me wrong, my parents did their best, we never really went without, but luxuries were very few. I was the youngest in the family, and everything I owned was used— bikes, skates, even clothing— which were given to me by older cousins. Hell, I never had anything new. I watched my parents struggle and I vowed that I would never live paycheck to paycheck, you dig? So I found ways to make extra bread on the side, selling stuff, delivering things, whatever I could.

"Most people came to the Haight to live the hippie life, you're one of them. Me, I came to live that life too, but I also knew there was cash to be made.

You know how I live, how I support myself. You know my lifestyle. When the Guthrie incident occurred, it freaked me out. I thought I was losing it, really losing it. The business opportunity came along and I accepted it without much thought.

"Then I started to see all this bread coming in, more money than I have ever seen in my lifetime. I have to say it went to my head and that made it hard to quit. I used Katie's knowledge to my advantage, I thought. Always in the back of my mind I knew I had time before pulling the plug since I wasn't supposed to disappear until August. That made it easy to keep going and I didn't think about the future. I mean yeah, the August deadline was there, but I figured I'd worry about that part later. I suppose you wonder how I thought I would get out of this."

Moonbeam nodded.

"I guess I just figured I'd split and it would all be cool, you know? Part of me thought I'd go back to Redding, another part said I'd find someplace new. It just didn't seem to matter that much to me, not compared to the dough I was bringing in. Nothing seemed important until you and I came together, and by that time it was already too late."

"But what about our plans?" Moonbeam asked, pulling on her floppy hippie hat.

"Moony, be realistic. Do you really think we can escape by going to Marin County?"

"I suppose not," she admitted.

"These people will follow me no matter where I go. That, baby, is the problem."

"But you could take me with you."

Frog had thought of that many times, but he knew that Dylan was right. Taking anyone with them endangered that person's life, and he wasn't going to allow anything to happen to her.

"No, baby, I can't, and you know why."

Moony looked down at her cup of coffee, willing herself not to cry.

"Hey, do I hear life out there?" Ron called from inside the tent before he walked out into the sunshine. "Ahh, a simply beautiful day." He headed towards them. "Good to see the two of you sitting together and talking."

Frog nodded but Moonbeam still stared silently into her cup.

"I'm off to the john so you two can carry on where you left off." Ron marched off to the bathroom with a bag and a change of clothes in his hands.

"Now what?" Moonbeam asked.

"I'm not sure. I want to tell you that I'll be back and that you have nothing to worry about, but that's not true. All I can say is that I love you, I really, really, do. I know that I don't deserve your forgiveness considering what's gone on and the lies that I've told you. This isn't the way a relationship is supposed to start, but then we never really had a beginning thanks to my stupidity." Frog sighed. "I can't tell you my plans Moony, but I can tell you that I will do everything possible to fix this mess so I can come back to you. If I can clear everything up then maybe we still have a chance together, a real one where I don't have to lie to protect you. Then we can go to Chet's commune or anyplace else in the world that you want to. But right now...you must see that it's impossible."

"Yes, I can see that. What I can't understand is why you let it get this far? You knew, Frog, you knew everything because Katie and old man Guthrie told you."

"Yes, they did, and I ignored them. I'm a fool, that's the explanation. I'm a fool and this is the only way out, I have to leave."

"I know," Moonbeam said sadly.

Frog wiped a tear off her cheek and then he leaned over the table and kissed her.

***

Katie walked towards the bathroom but as she got closer her pace slowed. Three Hells Angels stood outside staring at the door.

"What's going on?" she asked Terry, before noticing that he was standing beside Dylan.

"We have... an incident taking place."

"Can I use the facilities?"

Suddenly Dylan was beside her. He took her hand and led her away from the group. "Ruby and Eva are inside," he whispered.

"No shit? Ruby and Eva are here at the festival? The ones who wrecked your bike? The bitches that drugged me?" She stepped away so that she too could see the opening to the bathroom.

"Yeah, the very same."

"What are you going to do about it?" Katie asked.

"We are going to handle it as the peaceful American club that we are," Dylan smirked. "I'm surprised that you would ask."

Katie stared at him as if he wasn't all there.

"Sorry, inside Angels joke," he said with a chuckle. "George has gone to get the fuzz. This whole thing is going to be nice and peaceful. They have warrants so all we have to do is turn them in and the police will take it from there. Can you dig that?"

"I see. So why are so many of you guarding the women's bathroom?"

"Long story. Let's just say that this has been an all-night adventure." He nodded towards a prospect that yawned and rubbed his eyes.

"Hmm, so the two bitches who drugged me are in that bathroom right now?"

"Yep, that's about the extent of it. Now we're just waiting for the pigs to show up. Then this little incident will be over and everyone can go back to grooving to the weekend."

Katie stared at the bathroom then she stared at the backs of the Angels who were waiting outside. That's when she blew a fuse. All of a sudden all of her frustrations seemed to manifest into a ball of anger, and all she could see was red.

She took off the crown of flowers she was wearing, handed them to Dylan, and then stomped off towards the bathroom.

"What are you doing?" Dylan asked as she marched off.

"I'm going to kick their asses."

"Wait..." Dylan tried to grab her arm to stop her but she pulled away.

"Wait my ass. Those two have it coming. Oh boy, do they ever have it coming." She rubbed her hands together in anticipation.

"Those two have been in many fights and they are going to rip you apart if you start anything with them, Katie."

"Really? You want to make a bet?" Katie said before stomping off.

"Hey..." Dylan called out again, but she ignored him.

She passed the other Hells Angels. Joey winked at her and Big Jim tried to stop her.

"Hey there, little hippie princess. Remember me?" He jumped in front of her.

"Sure, you're the president. I met you at the party."

"That's right, you did."

"If you'll excuse me..." she said, stepping around him.

Jim gently took hold of her arm but she pushed him off and determinedly walked up the ramp that led to the bathroom. Inside there were several women washing their hands, someone flushed the toilet and unlocked the stall door. Katie glanced around the colorful interior and then she saw them. In the very back corner of the room, beneath a narrow window, stood the two biker girls dressed as hippies. They were sharing a cigarette, lost in conversation, so they didn't see Katie until she was standing directly in front of them.

Years of defense training separated her from the girl she had once been. Katie had taken classes in restraint training while she was going to college and those sessions had gradually taken her into martial arts.

She had taken classes for years, everything from Kick Boxing to Kung Fu. They had been her exercise classes, and although she wasn't learning the material to be tough, fifteen years of lessons had given her a knowledge that she was sure she could use if she ever needed to. Today she was going to find out.

"You." She pointed at Eva and before the biker chick could respond Katie punched her in the mouth and sent her spiraling backwards. Eva hit the basin with a thud and then went down on the floor clutching her bleeding mouth.

Ruby was shocked. For several seconds she stood paralyzed, her mouth open. When she finally responded she caught Katie's long hair and twisted it around her fist, but before she had a chance to punch her, Katie put her hand over Ruby's fist and shoved it into her own head, forcing Ruby to open her hand.

When Ruby realized that Katie was getting away she tried to take a swing, but Katie ducked. Since she didn't make contact, Ruby wobbled unsteadily on her feet and that's when Katie kicked her legs out from under her, and she too went down on the floor, hitting the back of her head hard on the ground.

Several hippie girls screamed and ran for the exit. In the meantime, Eva was able to get up but that didn't last long. With a roundhouse kick, Katie caught her in the shoulder and sent her flying forward across the floor.

"Fucking drug me, you skanks!" Katie yelled, and then wondered if they knew the term or if she was using it out of time context. "Two bit whores!" screeched in correction.

The front door opened and Moonbeam appeared.

"Are you alright, Katie?"

Moonbeam's sudden presence distracted Katie and Ruby was able to scramble to her feet so that she could take another swing. Katie felt it connect but she was able to stop her rival's fist and twist it behind her back. That's when Ruby started to yell and Katie lowered her body onto the floor where she held the girl's arm firmly in place.

"If you move, I break Ruby's arm, Eva. And if you think I can't do it you go right ahead and test me. Nobody drugs me, you got that?" Eva, who was on her feet leaning against the bathroom wall, nodded.

"Okay, man, we're sorry," Eva said with her arms raised above her head in surrender mode. "Now let her go before you fucking break her arm. We're going to jail, isn't that enough for you?"

"No, not really."

Dylan walked into the bathroom and saw Katie kneeling on the floor holding Ruby's arm up her back. He knelt beside her. "That's enough, a cop is on his way. Do you hear me? George is leading him over the hill right now, it's time to get the hell out of here."

Katie relaxed her grip and let Ruby go, watching as the tall redhead rolled on the floor, holding her arm.

The bathroom door opened again and Officer Mitch Powers, according to his nametag, walked in. He was one of the police at the entrance to the fairgrounds. Today he was adorned with flower leis, which made him look like he was on a Hawaiian vacation rather than a working cop on assignment.

"I hear we have some outstanding warrants." He looked around the bathroom and then at the two girls bleeding and sitting on the floor. He turned and looked at Dylan questioningly.

"Don't look at him," Katie said to the policeman. "I'm the one who hit them."

"You?" he asked in surprise.

"Sure, they were trying to get away. I thought it was my American duty to stop them." Katie tried to look sweet and innocent while she rubbed at her knuckles.

Dylan looked at the officer and shrugged. "What can I say, sir?"

"She's a fucking liar!" Eva screamed. "She walked in here and then she attacked us for no reason."

"Are you the two girls who have outstanding warrants?" the officer asked, staring at them.

"We were going to turn ourselves in after the concert," Eva said.

"Sure you were," Officer Powers said with a nod.

"What about her? Shouldn't she be arrested for assault? She can't just come in here and pound on us like that. I want to press charges," Ruby said. She pulled herself off the floor.

"You three," the officer, said pointing at Katie, Dylan, and Moonbeam, "out."

Without another word the three gladly left the bathroom.

"My hand hurts," Katie announced.

Dylan took her hand, kissed her knuckles, and then inspected them. "I guess they would hurt," he said. "They aren't broken though, just bruised and sprained. What you need is a bag of ice. Who would have ever known that you could fight like that, baby?"

The other Angels joined them then. They laughed and slapped her on the back in congratulations.

Ron saw the commotion from where he was standing and ran across the field in an attempt to get to Katie. When he arrived under a grove of trees she was out of the bathroom laughing with the Hells Angels and he stood on the sidelines watching, not sure what he should do.

Another officer wearing flowers around his neck arrived and without looking at anyone, he too entered the bathroom.

"I'll tell you what, baby, you were outstanding," Joey said. "I wanted some biker chicks to kick their asses but I got Mohammad Ali instead." He snorted laughter. "I only wish I could have seen it."

"No shit. When I went in there I wasn't sure what I would find, you should have seen her up on Ruby's back holding the bitch's arm behind her back and threatening to break it."

"Little fairy princess, way to take over the situation, baby. Tell you what, next time I need a chick for back up I'll give you a call," Big Jim joked.

A black and white pulled up and parked beside them. The bikers backed up, giving them space and once again became spectators.

Handcuffed and bleeding, Ruby and Eva were escorted out of the bathroom.

"Wait till we get out you little hippie bitch!" Ruby screamed.

"Any time, Ruby, any time," Katie said in a low voice.

"We'll work your ass over good, wait and see bitch!" Ruby yelled back.

Officer Powers turned and looked at Ruby. "Would that be a threat? We can charge you for that too."

"Fuck you!" Eva screamed at him.

"The two of you need to keep your mouths shut. Or maybe what you need me to do is to hand you over to this little lady so she can smack you around a few more times?"

"You can't do that, you fucking pig!" Ruby yelled belligerently.

Officer Powers shoved her into the police car and then pushed a silent Eva in beside her. Within minutes they were driven out of the fairgrounds, and because the police didn't want any added attention they used a side entrance, disappearing quickly. All except Officers Mitch Powers and Dale Edwards, who walked back to their turf at the park's entrance.

One problem solved, Katie thought. This had never happened the first time around and that gave her a feeling of promise. If she had free will and so did the people around her, maybe there was a happy ending waiting for all of them.

Ron remained on the sidelines watching Katie with the Angels, specifically the one she had walked out of the bathroom with. He seemed to Ron a bit too touchy with Katie, but of course she didn't do anything to stop his attentions either. Curious, he moved further into the trees so he wouldn't be seen.

***

"You can get some ice at the medic station. Do you want me to walk you there?" Dylan asked.

"Nah, I'll be fine. I'll hit up one of the drink booths, I'm sure they've got some ice they can give me."

"Concert should be starting soon," Big Jim called out, and he and several of the other men headed towards the arena.

"I guess we should go," Katie said, and Dylan nodded in agreement.

A screeching noise came over the PA system announcing that the concert was getting ready to start.

Katie turned to walk away but Dylan caught her arm and stepped in front of her, then he kissed her.

She was going to push him away but didn't, and the kiss ended up lasting much longer than either of them thought it would.

When Katie finally pulled away she stared at him, wondering again what it was about Dylan that made her heart beat just a little bit faster.

"I'll see you around," he said, and then he squeezed her hand once last time and walked away.

***

Ron wasn't sure what he'd just witnessed, but he knew that it hurt. He had heard talk about some Angel that Katie had been involved with, but he had never actually seen the guy. The biker never came around, and as far as Ron knew, Katie wasn't seeing him seriously, but that kiss was disturbing.

For starters, Katie had never reacted that way to his kisses. She wasn't the one who initiated the interaction, but she had certainly swooned at the biker's touch.

As the mystery biker walked away, the girls walked around the corner to the men's bathroom where they met up with Frog. Together, they headed towards the lemonade stand where Katie had left Ron waiting.

Ron watched their movements as he debated his next move. He could easily meet them at the lemonade stand but then what? Did he talk to Katie? Did he yell at her or demand answers? They weren't even officially dating, but he had thought that they had a future together.

Visibly shaken, he decided to walk by himself back to the arena and meet them at the seats. He told himself this would give him time to pull himself together so that he could think of a plan.

He wasn't sure what his feelings for Katie were. Up until several minutes ago he had believed that he was falling in love with her. But now he questioned himself.

A year ago Katie annoyed him. She was immature, giggly, and loud. Now she was a grown woman, and that maturity was what attracted him to her. She was beautiful, that was certainly a plus, but it was her mind that he was most interested in, or so he thought. He believed her story about time travel, it was the only explanation, and even though it seemed impossible there was too much evidence to the contrary. She was from the future and that reality opened a lot of doors. All she had to do was remember specific events in time, and that knowledge would make her filthy rich

What confused him now was his own involvement. He wanted Katie and he believed that he loved her, but he also had to admit that part of the attraction was the oddity of the situation. He had suspected that Katie was from the future for a long time, but when that was confirmed he had to admit that it drew him closer into her web. The novelty, the opportunities, they all intensified his feelings towards her. Now though, after what he had just witnessed, he wasn't sure what the truth was anymore.

When he arrived at the arena most of the seats were full. Someone was fiddling with the mic and that caused high squeals to go out over the PA system. They would be here soon and he needed to decide how he wanted to handle the biker kissing incident. He knew what he wanted to do, but that action wouldn't get him anywhere. He decided that he wouldn't say anything, he would just let the weekend go on as planned, and then he would go back to San Francisco and make decisions. One thing was for sure, that kiss between the biker and Katie would haunt him always.

***

Katie and her group were late to the show. When they arrived at their seats, Canned Heat's performance had already begun.

Canned Heat, taking their name from the slang term for Sterno, was a Los Angeles based band that played a combination of Blues Rock.

Alan "Blind Owl" Wilson and Henry Vestine were in the middle of a guitar solo when the threesome sat down. Bob Hite held the microphone and a blaring rendition of 'Rollin & Tumblin' burst forth.

Another member of the 27 Club, Katie realized, trying to count them all on her fingers. Brian Jones, Janis Joplin, Jimi Hendrix, Ron "Pigpen" McKernan (Grateful Dead drummer) and Wilson; all here today and all dying at the age of 27.

Alan Wilson would die from a drug overdose on September 3rd, 1970. His death would set off a chain reaction amongst the rock community. Fifteen days later Jimi Hendrix would die from asphyxiation (Sept. 18, 1970), and sixteen days after that (Oct. 4 1970), Janis Joplin would be found dead from a heroin overdose in a Los Angeles motel room. But today, June 17th 1967, they were all alive, at the peak of their talent, and they would all be making an appearance this weekend.

Katie sat next to Ron and noticed immediately that his body language had changed.

"What's wrong?" she asked.

"Nothing's wrong. What happened to you? You never came back from the bathroom."

"I had difficulties."

"Difficulties in the bathroom? Is that a woman thing?" he asked, trying to act normal even though she knew he was different.

"This one was." She showed him her hand.

"What the hell? What happened?"

"Remember the girls who drugged me back in January?"

He nodded.

"They just happened to be here in the woman's bathroom hiding because they had warrants out for their arrest."

"For drugging you?"

"No. These two girls ruined a couple of Hells Angels' bikes and then they avoided arrest. The Angels were waiting for the police to show up and I sort of lost it when I found out they were in there."

"Sort of lost it?"

"Yeah. I got this overwhelming compulsion to hit them so I did. I marched into the bathroom and took both of them down, can you believe it?"

"Biker chicks? How did you do that?"

"Fifteen years of martial arts training. It was the way I kept myself fit in my former life," she said proudly.

"Nice one. I bet they were surprised, and I bet the Angels were surprised too."

"Yeah, they were, but I was confident that I could whip their asses and I did."

Canned Heat's next song, "Dust My Broom" started , and Katie settled herself into her chair. She reached over to take Ron's hand and was puzzled at his resistance. She suddenly remembered Dylan's kiss and instinctively knew that Ron had seen her.

The knowledge made her heart beat faster. She hoped that she was wrong, but Ron's touch was cold. She realized that this would change things and before it drove her crazy she took a joint out of her canvas bag, pretending not to notice a difference in Ron's behavior. She lit the smoke and passed it to him.

Chapter 35

Moonbeam walked towards the soda stand debating her next move. They were stressed. Things were crazy and everyone needed a break, especially Katie. Her mind hadn't been free since the incident back in January. Of course, being a time traveler had changed Katie and that was okay, but Moonbeam hated to see her friend constantly on edge the way she was this weekend.

She stood in line behind a woman with a floppy yellow hat. After getting hit in the nose several times she backed away. At the window, Miss Floppy Hat ordered a Coke and a hotdog and then, none too soon for Moonbeam, moved out of the way.

"I'll have a large Coke," she said to the white haired woman behind the counter. Seconds later she walked away taking sips off the overflowing soda. She found an empty spot at one of the wooden tables and there she placed the cup ready to prepare her brew.

Moonbeam reached into her pocket and pulled out the last samples of Owsley Stanley's White Lighting and then without hesitation, dumped the contents into the cup and stirred the mixture with a paper straw.

She stopped when the straw was saturated and falling apart. *That should do it.* She headed back to the seats, still justifying her actions.

This would be good for all of them. It would give their minds a break, a mini groovy vacation. Katie would be able to search her soul, and that would help her come to terms with whatever actions she needed to take in the future. This was for Katie's benefit, and someday her friend would thank her.

Canned Heat had ended by the time Moonbeam got back to the seats. The microphone squealed. Big Brother and the Holding company were getting ready to start. With a tinge of guilt, she passed Katie the cup and watched as her friend gulped down much of the contents.

Seconds later the male members of Big Brother walked out on stage and Sam Andrews, James Gurley, Peter Albin and Dave Getz played a musical introduction. Janis Joplin stepped on the stage, held the microphone in both hands and sang a traditional blues song she had rearranged entitled, "Down On Me."

Janis was dressed in a gold lame pantsuit rather than the hippie garb she wore during her original Saturday performance. Katie looked around, and noticing that the performance was being filmed, smiled. Per her advice, Janis had agreed to be filmed by D.A. Pennebaker for his documentary. Did this mean that they wouldn't be giving a second performance on Sunday? (Originally Big Brother and the Holding Company played a second session on June 18th, after the band changed their minds and decided to be part of the film.)

Janis's strong voice rang out through the arena and the crowd stopped what they were doing, mesmerized by the performance.

Janis stomped her feet on the floor keeping time with the music. Holding the microphone with both hands, her rings shining in the daylight, she serenaded the crowd with her powerful voice. The raw emotion of her performance seemed to spill over into the audience as they grooved to the music.

Katie studied the crowd. Most of the spectators looked shocked, their mouths hanging open as they watched the hippie girl from Port Arthur, Texas slowly weave her way into instantaneous stardom.

Big Brother's second song, 'Combination of the Two' started, and Moonbeam tapped Ron on the shoulder and asked to change seats. Now at Katie's side, she leaned over and whispered. "So what is it about this chick that you dig so much?"

"Are you kidding? Just listen to her, she's unbelievable. She has a three-octave range, and if you listen very carefully, you'll notice that she can hit two notes at the same time."

"Oh I know she's great," Moony said, drinking the cola and then passing it back to Katie. "There are a lot of great singers from San Francisco, but what is it specifically about *her* that you dig?"

Katie didn't answer. She took a long drink off of the soda and watched Janis's performance, wondering what it was about the singer that just spelled star. Was it the raw emotion in her voice, or the way she seemed to pull the audience in and hold them captivated in the same way that she held the microphone? There was sadness in the girl, and that added to her mystique, making the draw unexplainable.

Janis Joplin was a victim of her own times. A young woman from a Jim Crow state transported into an environment based on love, free sex, and drugs, caught in a triangle with a talent so overwhelmingly powerful that in the end it devoured her. She wasn't alone in that fate, Katie realized. Jimi Hendrix also fell into that category, as did many of the other performers here at the festival.

"I don't know what it is," she finally answered. "I just dig her. Look around, everyone else digs her too." And that was an understatement. The effect Janis had on the audience was spellbinding.

Big Brother played their fifty-eight second song entitled 'Harry', a plea for Janis's missing dog to come home, and then the bluesy rock tune 'Roadblock.' This was followed by the highlight of their performance, the song that would truly launch her into star status, 'Ball and Chain,' a Big Mama Thornton tune made famous by Big Brother and the Holding Company.

According to history, the Saturday performance was a longer rendition of the song but it was missing the long psychedelic guitar introduction provided by Sam Andrews. Today, since they were being filmed during their first performance, the two shows seemed to be intertwined with an introduction by Sam that was stunning, but nowhere close to the Sunday version.

Janis stomped her feet in time, licked her pale lips, and held the mic in both hands. In a low voice that dramatically grew louder, she started to sing the blues ballad. The crowd, still wound up after 'Roadblock', a dance tune, slowed their movements and eventually returned to their seats.

Caught in the moment, the crowd stared at the stage and Katie in turn stared at the crowd.

A speechless Karen Black, future B-movie horror queen, sat holding an orange that she had been munching only moments earlier.

Even the bubble blower who had been actively keeping pace with the songs had stopped. She too stared at the stage, and the word that seemed to skip off of everyone's lips was, "Wow!"

Much too soon the song ended and the bubbly little singer skipped off the stage, disappearing into the curtains as the crowd, still mesmerized by the performance, sat quietly staring at the now empty stage.

Stagehands worked quickly moving musical equipment off and then back on as they prepared for the next band, probably the only band that could follow

Big Brother and the Holding Company after that performance, the hippies' favorite protest band, Country Joe and the Fish.

Moonbeam drank a good portion of the soda and passed it to Katie.

"Here, finish this." She bounced to her feet.

"Where are you going?" Katie asked, sipping on the paper cup.

"I'm going to the bathroom and then I might stroll a little bit, want to come?"

"Sure, I guess so." Katie looked at the stage. She had seen Country Joe and the Fish many times, and although she enjoyed their performances immensely, this might be a good time to slip away and try to make it backstage.

"Sure, I'll go with you." Finishing the last of the cola Katie rose to her feet and followed her friend down the aisle.

"Where are you off to?" Ron asked. Katie wasn't sure if it was her imagination but his words seemed to be filled with suspicion.

"To the bathroom, then we're going to walk around a bit, do you want to come with us?" She expected him to say yes, and was surprised when he declined. Ron was still in a huff, and she wasn't sure if she cared enough to start a conversation about his mood right now. So, still pretending that everything was fine, she followed Moonbeam out of the arena.

Katie carried the empty cup to the garbage container where she dumped it along with some candy wrappers.

"What was that about?" Moonbeam asked curiously.

Katie turned and just looked at her.

"It's obvious that something's wrong, Ron seems to be all uptight."

"I don't know exactly, but I have my suspicions."

"And?" Moonbeam quizzed.

"I think he saw Dylan kissing me at the bathrooms."

"That's a bummer. But it wasn't your fault, he kissed you, not the other way around."

"True… but it was some kiss."

"Nothing you can do about that now, baby, it's over. Don't trip, it's his bag not yours."

Katie nodded. Yes it was over, and after this weekend she would never see Dylan again.

"Are you going to talk to him about it?" Moony asked.

"No, I don't think I'll say anything unless he brings it up. What's the point? Ron and I aren't officially together, and I'm not officially with Dylan, that's for sure. I'm a single woman. I don't think I need to explain myself, do I?"

"When you put it that way…I guess not."

They walked the rest of the way to the bathroom in silence, each lost in their own thoughts.

When they were finished at the restrooms, Moonbeam nudged Katie.

"What do you want to do now, single lady?"

"Honestly?"

"Sure honestly."

"I want to try to get backstage so that I can see Janis."

"Janis Joplin, the singer?"

"Of course silly, who else would I be going backstage to see?"

"Can I come with you?" Moonbeam asked excitedly

"Yep, let's go."

The girls circled the stage until they came to a side gate where a set of stagehands sat patrolling. Young girls who were waiting unsuccessfully to get inside, surrounded them.

Katie and Moonbeam watched the girls' failed attempts for several minutes before a frustrated Katie finally excused herself to the front of the line.

"Excuse me," she repeated until one of the men finally acknowledged her presence.

"What do you want?"

"I'd like to get backstage to see Janis," she said, followed by his and the cluster of groupies' laughter.

"Right," he said with a smug grin. "You and everyone else who's standing here."

"She's going to want to see me, go ask her. My name is Katie and I'm her spiritualist."

He laughed harder this time, as did the groupies who were listening to the conversation.

"You might think that's funny, but she won't when she finds out that you turned away her friend without even checking with her first."

The stagehand studied her for a few seconds and then he stood from the stool where he was sitting. "Look, miss, if I walk back there and she doesn't know you I'm going to be real fucking upset."

"That's cool, because she does know me and she is going to want to see me. My name is Katie, I'm her spiritualist, and I'm here with my friend Annie."

With one last look he turned and walked towards the makeshift village behind the stage. Several minutes later he returned, staring at Katie as if he expected to recognize her as someone of importance.

"You," he said, pointing at her, "can go in, but only you. The place is crowded enough, no extra visitors allowed."

"Is that at Miss Joplin's request?" Katie asked.

"It's the way it is, take it or leave it," the stagehand snapped back. "You can go in but only you. Make a decision, yes or no." He turned his back on her.

"Never mind, Moony, I'll go back with you," Katie said, backing away from the gate.

"No, don't. You have a chance to go backstage, that's groovy, baby, you go do your thing. I'll just go back and hang out with the guys. I'll let them know that you're backstage visiting a celebrity."

Katie looked at the gate where the arrogant guard sat, his back still turned to the crowd.

"I don't know... I wouldn't feel right going without you."

"Oh, but you have to. This is your moment to shine. She's your friend and you're going backstage to visit her. Next time you see her maybe she'll let me come with you."

Katie looked towards the gated opening. "Are you sure?"

"Baby, go and do your thing," Moonbeam said, and then she hugged Katie and walked away.

Katie walked to the front of the line, where Mr. Personable was still ignoring those around him.

"I'm ready to go in now." She had to repeat herself several times before he finally turned and looked at her. Without a word he opened the six-foot high gate and let her walk inside.

"She's that way." He pointed. "She's standing in the street in front of the Hunt Club." He shoved Katie inside the yard and shut the wooden gate behind her.

"What an asshole," Katie muttered. She turned and studied the small community. Old looking buildings were arranged into several rows that resembled a small western town. About two-thirds of the way down the main street Katie saw the Hunt Club, and as promised, Janis and the rest of her band were standing outside talking to other performers.

Too shy to just walk into an ongoing conversation, Katie stayed on the sidelines waiting until Janis finally noticed her.

"Katie!" she called out smiling. "Hey everyone, this is Katie, she's my spiritualist."

She heard a chorus of greetings as she walked towards the outstretched arms of Janis Joplin, who hugged her vivaciously.

"You're golden, Katie, just golden baby."

"You were phenomenal," Katie said with a broad smile. "Absolutely breathtaking."

"Thanks, man. Listen, you have to have a drink with me." She took Katie's arm in her own and led her into the Hunt Club.

The small pub was set up as a western saloon with old wooden tables and chairs. Janis plopped herself down at one of them and gestured to Katie to join her. Seconds later a young waiter came to take their order.

"A half pint of Southern Comfort and two glasses," Janis said happily, taking Katie's hands into her own and staring into her eyes. "You're magical, baby. Everything that you told me came true. How on earth did you know?"

"It's a gift I guess, or maybe it's a curse."

The waiter returned and set two shot glasses and a bottle of southern whisky in front of the two women.

"Crazy man, you knew everything, even about the documentary. By the way, how do you like my garb?" she asked laughingly. "Hip threads, right?" She poured an equal amount of the amber liquid into the glasses.

"Super hip." Katie took a sip of her drink.

"Come on, baby, you can do a better drinking job than that. Haven't we been through this before?" Janis shot her own drink, and Katie followed her example.

"Yeah, I guess we have been through that before." Katie laughed, remembering their first talk the night she was taking posters from the Avalon.

"Now what?" Janis asked, pouring them each another drink.

"What do you mean? Now you're a star."

"I'm not sure what that even means," Janis laughed.

"It means that you will be constantly in the public eye. From here on out you will be photographed wherever you go and you'll be going a lot of places: New York frequently, Europe for concerts, and different states for television appearances. It means that your life as you know it has just changed dramatically."

Katie sipped her Southern Comfort. "It means that you're going to be under a lot of pressure and that might not be such a good thing."

Janis shook her head. "How can that not be a good thing? Fame man, it's all I ever wanted."

"Sure, but maybe you don't know what it is that you wanted, and now you're about to find out."

"Okay, man, explain. Maybe I've just had too much So Co, but I don't get what you're saying." Janis laughed, but this time it was more of a nervous chuckle. Katie realized that Janis believed in her. This, if played out correctly, could have a positive outcome.

"Are you asking me what's next? Do you want to know more of your saga?" Katie questioned, watching as the singer visibly shook.

"Wow, man, you're a fucking trip." Janis refilled both of the shot glasses.

"Well, do you?" Katie prompted the new rock star.

"Fuck man, the hair on the back of my neck is standing straight on end. This is creepy fucking shit, baby."

"It's only creepy because you know that what I'm about to tell you will come true."

"Okay, baby, shoot, but I sure hope that the shit you're about to tell me will be good."

Katie's head swirled with possibilities. What should she disclose? She had three years until that fateful day in October of 1970. She didn't want to get into Janis's final outcome yet, deciding instead to keep her predictions positive for now. Anything else could come later as long as Janis continued to trust her.

She took Janis's right hand in her own and studied the palm for several minutes, touching certain lines with her fingers and muttering to herself. Finally she dropped the singer's hand, sat back in her chair and with a chug off her Southern Comfort said,

"You're about to sign with one of the top managers in the music business, his name is Albert Grossman. You'll meet him here at the Monterey Pop Festival. I don't know if you have met him yet but you will. Bob Dylan, by the way, is one of his other clients. When you go back to San Francisco your band will release their first album, "Big Brother and the Holding Company," and you will have several minor hits off of the album.

"For the remainder of this year you'll have local wall-to-wall gigs, and the next one will be at the Diggers' Summer Solstice celebration in Golden Gate Park on the 21st. They'll be using equipment that they borrow from this weekend's event.

"At the beginning of 1968, I think maybe February, your group will begin its first East Coast tour starting in Philadelphia, and then going to New York City. But be careful, because by 1968, the tides will change and the band will be billed as 'Janis Joplin and Big Brother and the Holding Company.' Your fame will supersede the band's and the media coverage you'll be given will generate resentment among the other members."

"Me, man?" Janis grinned at the potential joke.

"Janis, *Time Magazine* will call you the most powerful singer to emerge from the white rock movement. You are a shooting star."

Janis stared, unable to speak. "That's heavy shit, baby," she remarked after a long moment.

"Very," Katie agreed. "And it's all true." Finished with her predictions for now, she took another drink out of the shot glass.

"But what about the band?" Janis asked.

"According to Grossman and others, you *are* the band. That popularity, *your* popularity, will become the problem."

"And?"

"You need to answer that, baby; my powers only go so far. That's it for now, that's all I can see." She sat back in her chair.

Always leave them wanting more.

"When will you be able to see more?" Janis asked.

"I don't know, a month or two, maybe, when some of the fluster surrounding you has died down."

"Fluster?"

"Yeah, fluster. Too many vibes to be able to see anything further for a while."

Katie scanned the bar, for the first time noticing the other patrons. Several tables away Peter Tork sat with two men she didn't know. Peter was joking around with a plastic wrapped candle that someone must have bought from the Sticky Wicket.

Other tables were packed with stagehands and a table or two where local 'Frisco bands sat chatting, and in the furthest corner closest to the bathrooms the unmistakable presence of Brian Jones, recognizable by his long, shaggy Beatles' haircut.

Katie's heart raced. She didn't want to make a scene, but sitting amongst rock stars from the '60s was definitely a high.

"Groovy place, right?" Janis commented, then she noticed Katie scanning the bar for familiar faces.

"It sure is."

In the back of the room a chair fell to the ground and the bar hushed. Brian Jones staggered a few steps and then picked up the chair he had knocked over. He smiled absently around at the others, pulled some change out of his front pocket, set it on the table and swaggered for the exit.

At this point in his brief life, Brian Jones was on a down spiraling train wreck. Difficulties within the Stones and losing his girlfriend of two years to Keith Richards only months before had affected him greatly. Always a drinker, Jones had become worse. This and his drug use would result in his firing from the Rolling Stones, and his decline would lead him to become a member of the 27 Club on July 3,1969.

He wove his way through the wooden tables, trying his best not to knock them over, and stopped suddenly beside Katie.

Katie rose from her seat, looking him directly in the eyes. "Don't go swimming. Stay away from pools."

He looked confused. "What is that supposed to mean?"

"She's my spiritualist," Janis tittered. "Tell you what, man, she's the best too. If she tells you not to swim I would fucking stay out of the water."

Brian stepped backwards, bumping into a table in his path, which slid a few inches across the floor. "Why can't I go swimming?"

"Because you're going to drown in a swimming pool."

Katie watched the color drain from his face. He turned away in fear and without another look staggered towards the doorway.

"So you just picked that up from the air, without even touching him?" Janis asked.

"Well, he did kind of bump into me but yeah, that's what I picked up." Katie sat back down beside Janis.

Suddenly Katie felt flushed, and she ran a hand over her sweating brow. Something was wrong, she didn't feel right.

"Are you really a spiritualist?" somebody asked, and Katie turned to find Peter Tork standing at their table.

She nodded.

"She sure fucking is!" Janis exclaimed.

"May I?" he asked. When Katie and Janis nodded their permission, he sat at their table.

"What can you tell me about my future?" he asked, showing Katie his hands.

She studied his right palm for a few minutes, running her fingers over the lines just to look official. "Mr. Tork, you are going to live a long life and during that time, even though you'll try to run away from it, you will always be a Monkee. Right now you're thinking that the T.V. show is just a stepping-stone to your career, but that's not the way it turns out. Even as an older man in your late sixties and early seventies you will still be touring and performing as a Monkee."

Peter laughed. "In my sixties I'm still going to be a Monkee?"

"Don't laugh. You'll make a lot of bread out of it and you'll have songs that will still be remembered decades from now."

"And I can go swimming?" he asked with a wide grin.

"Anytime you would like." Katie shook her head; the lights in the bar seemed to be trailing her.

Peter Tork kissed her hand in thanks and walked back to his friends.

"What is it?" Janis asked, offering her another shot of Southern Comfort.

"I don't know. Colors are starting to run together as if..."

"As if what, man? Like you're on an acid trip?"

And then Katie knew.

She banged the flat of her hand on the table. "Damn Moonbeam."

"Your friend?"

"Yep, we shared this large Coke. I'll bet she threw some LSD tabs into it."

"Well it's not your first trip is it?"

"No, I've been through this before." She almost added "forty-five years ago", but decided to leave that part out.

"Then I guess my advice would be to just go with it, groove to whatever happens, baby," Janis chuckled.

Just then, a man middle-aged man in a tweed sports jacket stepped into the bar, his eyes glancing over the crowd. When he saw Janis sitting at the table he smiled and approached.

"Miss Joplin?" he asked, extending his hand in introduction.

"Yes." She took his hand and stood from the table.

"My name is Albert Grossman. Perhaps you've heard of me? I work with Bob Dylan."

Janis turned abruptly. Her blue eyes met Katie's in astonishment.

"I was hoping that I might speak with you alone for a few minutes?" he asked.

"Of course," Janis said. "If you'll just give me a few minutes, I'd like to say goodbye to my friend."

Mr. Grossman nodded.

"Are you going to be okay, Katie?" Janis asked quietly. "I can get one of the stagehands to walk you back to your friends."

"No, I'll be fine. I've been through acid trips before. And I'm at a hippie event surrounded by love and peace, what could possibly happen?" She smiled at Janis. "You go ahead and do your thing, baby."

Janis hugged her. "I'll come by your place in a month or so if that's okay?"

"Anytime."

"Here, I want you to have this." Janis removed a strand of love beads from her neck and placed them around Katie's.

"Thank you, they're beautiful. I will cherish them, but you don't have to give me anything." Katie stared at the colorful strand of beads, which sparkled unnaturally in her drug haze.

"I know I don't have to, but I want to." Janis hugged her again and then she skipped off, anxious for her talk with Albert Grossman, a man who would become instrumental in advancing her career.

***

Dylan stood by the chain-linked fence smoking a joint. Big Jim's surprise mission had turned out to be a gig guarding the fences surrounding the arena so the teenyboppers couldn't hop over.

He'd been downtown early making phone calls and visiting Western Union. His plans were made and they were secure. Nobody would be able to search for them because he had used an assumed name, which he had documents to back up.

As far as Dylan was concerned he and Frog were set, just as good as gone. They would cut out sometime today, fleeing to a cabin in the mountains that he'd arranged. They would stay there until this heroin shit blew over.

Once safe, he would use his connections in the Bay Area to figure this whole mess out. Who wanted him and Frog dead? That was the question and

Dylan was determined to find the answer. Once he knew whom he was fighting, then he could involve the club and he would personally tell Big Jim everything.

"How long do we have to stand here?" Terry asked.

"We each put in an hour of duty and then you can go do your own thing, whatever that might be." Dylan passed him the joint.

"Who's on now, man?" Terry asked, nodding his head towards the arena where a band was playing.

"Some cat named Al Kooper, and then the Butterfield Blues Band performs," he said, taking a hit off the joint. "We'll be finished and back by the time Quicksilver Messenger Service comes on."

"Is that who you're anxious to see?" Terry asked.

"Not necessarily, although I do like our home grown bands the best."

"Me too."

"By the way, how do you feel about the Ruby and Eva thing now that it's over?" Dylan asked.

Terry dropped the last of the roach paper on the ground.

"I'm okay with it. I'm glad to have it done. What do you think they're going to do when they get out?"

Dylan snorted a laugh. "I think they're going to stay away from us."

"Do you really?"

"I don't know, man, does it really matter? I don't think they're going to come after us if that's what you're worried about."

"No, but I was wondering about their threats against Katie. Do you think they'll go looking for your little hippie when they're free?"

Dylan laughed again. "I think my little hippie can take care of herself."

"Yeah, I guess that's true enough."

A pair of young girls made it to the top of the fence and the bikers stopped them before they could jump over.

"Nope, you have to go back," Dylan said, raising his arms.

"Come on, man, be cool," a dark haired beauty of about fifteen said.

"Believe me, little lady, I am cool, but you still have to go back. We can't let you over the fence. We have our orders."

"What if I just jump?" a large Amazonian blonde girl asked Terry.

"Then whatever's left of you when you hit the ground will be escorted to the exit." Terry laughed at the two girls who suddenly looked defeated.

"Can you just tell us, are the Beatles inside?" the dark haired girl asked.

"Of course not. They aren't playing this weekend, why would they show up?" Dylan asked.

"Then I guess it's just a rumor?" the blonde said before dropping back over the fence."

The dark haired girl was about to jump too but Terry stopped her. "Where did you hear this rumor?" he asked, suddenly curious.

"We heard it from a friend who heard it off the radio. She said the disc jockey announced it this morning."

"What exactly was the announcement?"

"That the Beatles were going to make a surprise performance sometime this weekend. That's why we thought we would check it out."

"This was broadcast on the air?"

"That's what our friend told us." The dark haired teen dropped down from the fence.

"Fuck!" Terry said. "The Beatles? Can you imagine if that was actually broadcast over the airwaves? We would have hundreds of kids trying to climb over the fences!" Terry shook his head. "Man, that would be a motherfucker to patrol. Think about it."

"I don't want to," Dylan said just as five new heads looked over the top of the fence and asked about the Beatles.

Terry and Dylan looked at each other, swearing. Guarding the fences that surrounded the arena was going to be a lot harder than they had expected.

Dylan said a silent prayer, hoping that this Beatles rumor wouldn't postpone his and Frog's departure.

Chapter 36

Katie staggered. The sky was melting and it was beautiful. The wet colors fell to the ground and mixed together into exotic puddles that ran the full length of the fairgrounds.

"Red, blue, yellow, white..."

She pointed at the liquefied pools that only she could see. She was walking back to the arena, back to where her friends were waiting, but the trip was taking much too long. She tried to avoid the quagmire of colors so she wouldn't dye her feet, and there were laughing hyenas everywhere.

Not that the hyenas were bad, they weren't. She just had to avoid them because they wanted to pull her into teepees.

"Are you alright?" one of the hyenas asked as it snuck up behind her.

"I don't want to go to a tripping teepee," Katie repeated for the umpteenth time, stepping away from the laughing animal. This interruption caused her to place her foot in a combination of colors that dyed her skin several psychedelic shades.

"Hey, nobody said anything about a tripping teepee," the laughing creature answered. "All I asked was if you were alright?

"I was alright. I am still alright if your pack would just let me get back to my friends."

"My pack?" Dennis was confused. He realized then that Katie was flying on more than beer and weed.

"Go away! It's your fault that my feet are a strange color, you made me step in the puddles of melted sky."

"I did what?"

Katie didn't answer, she was too busy sidestepping invisible pools of psychedelic melted sky.

Dennis wasn't sure what to make out of the situation so he stood paralyzed, watching as she continued to walk, weaving oddly along a route that was going to take forever. At this rate she would never make it back to the arena before midnight.

This wasn't going to work; this chick was too fucked up. So much so that she wouldn't be able to remember anything that took place. Hell, she didn't even know that he was human.

While Katie continued to trip her way back to the arena, Dennis drifted into the underbrush where he had left Mark. He found the young executive sitting on a bench cleaning his fingernails with a pocketknife.

"Hey, man, what are you doing back? I thought we were meeting at the agreed spot." Mark closed the blade and put the knife back into his pocket.

"Mission aborted, man," Dennis said, taking a seat on the bench beside him.

"What are you talking about?"

"Dude, that chick of yours is fucked up, drugged out on something heavy. She thinks I belong to a pack."

"A pack of what?"

"Exactly!"

"What's that got to do with our plan?" Mark asked.

"Are you kidding? It has everything to do with it, man." Dennis shook his head. "She won't remember any of this tomorrow or even later tonight, so why bother?"

"She's that fucked up?"

There were several Native American teepees set up for drug-induced problems. These were intended as a safe place to 'trip' until one's journey was over.

"That and beyond, man. She's someplace else, someplace that you and I are not. You want to see?"

Dennis rose from the bench and led Mark a short distance and pointed through the trees.

"Look, right there you can see her from here, weaving in and out like a nutcase. She's stepping over different colors of dripping sky, she says."

To Dennis's surprise, Mark started to laugh. "Oh man, this is going to be great. We couldn't have it any better. Not only did we find her alone, but she's so tweaked out of her mind that we can convince her of anything." He clapped his hands in anticipation. "This is going to be great, just great."

He moved closer to the paved path and watched Katie continue her obscure dance across the pavement.

"Oh man, I love this. Okay, this is your time to shine, brother, go do your thing." Mark walked back to his seat on the wooden bench.

"Tell me you're kidding."

"Why would I be kidding?"

"You still want me to take her behind the fairgrounds?"

"Isn't that what we agreed on? Isn't that what I'm paying you for?"

"Sure, when you were going to save her from a bad guy and she was going to remember it. Now that she's in never never land, well I just figured it would change things."

"Why should it?"

Dennis stared at him and shook his head. He took a cigarette out of his shirt pocket and lit it.

"Look, man, nothing's changed. You take her to the back lot down by the creek and I'll be there waiting."

"Nothing's changed? How can you say that? This was supposed to be done at night and I was going to choose the time and the place. I was supposed to get her, pull her into the bushes, and put a knife to her throat just to scare her. Then you were supposed to appear out of nowhere and chase me off, end of story. Now, I'm not sure what our plan is."

"Okay, things have changed a little," Mark conceded, "but the end result is the same and let me remind you that you're making a lot of bread."

"Bread ain't shit if I end up in jail. Now I want to know what the plan is, because at this point I'm not sure. You're asking me to get a crazy person across the fairgrounds into a wooded area and then down an incline, that I understand. But from that point on what do you expect me to do?"

"I don't know exactly," Mark admitted. Now that he knew Katie was mentally incapacitated, he had many ideas dancing through his head.

"Well you better be sure dude, because I'm not walking into anything blind."

"Hey, man, shouldn't you be watching her so she doesn't disappear?"

Dennis walked back to the undergrowth and pointed through the trees. "That chick isn't going anywhere. She's circling the yard on some other fucking planet. Believe me, we have time to talk."

"I'm not sure, man. I still want to keep to the plan basically the same, but why move at night? In the condition that she's in it should be easy to coax her anywhere. Hell, tell her you're taking her to a pack meeting. Doesn't this make everything easier? You can convince her of a story and she'll go with you willingly, which is much safer than wearing a ski mask and abducting her."

"Sure it's easier. That's not what I'm asking. Now that she's flying high, what's going to happen once I bring her there? That's what I want to know."

"Are you suddenly developing a conscience, Dennis? You've done a lot of underhanded shit for me, my friend. I didn't expect this reaction from you."

"I'm the devil, I know that, but you've had me looking through records and gathering dirt on your opponents. This is different, this is physical. And yeah, I'm getting paid a lot of bread, but as I said before I'm not willing to go to jail for it."

"Fine, you want a plan, here's the plan." Mark stood from the bench still holding the knife and waved it around as he spoke. "Bring Katie to the creek. Once there you can put on the ski mask and come out of the bushes as a monster. Terrify the shit out of her and as planned I will take it from there."

Dennis shook his head.

"I'll raise the stakes."

"You're going to pay me more?"

"That's right, how does four thousand sound? Is that enough?"

"Let me get this straight. You want to pay me four grand to bring a whacked out chick to the creek. Then I put on a ski mask and I pretend to be a creature and I terrify her. You come out of the melting sky as the hero who chases the monster away?"

"Correct. See? Much easier than what we had planned before."

"Except that she isn't going to remember anything, so how is that going to win you the chick?"

"You let me worry about that, okay? All you've got to do is get her to the creek, play monster for a few minutes, and I'll take it from there."

"Man, I don't know. I'm getting a bad feeling about this."

"What are you, a hippie now? You come to one hippie event and you can 'feel the vibes'? Hey, you want the bread or not? If not, I can pay somebody else to do it. I'm sure I can find someone here who will take that amount of bread just to lead a chick to a creek."

"I don't like this," Dennis said to nobody as he made his way back to the paved walkway.

Mark pulled the blade out of his pocket and went back to cleaning his fingernails with the knife.

**

Dylan was exhausted after his two-hour gig of pulling teenaged kids off of the fence. By the time he was replaced, several of the Angels were discussing a plan to find the stupid bastard who had made the Beatles announcement and drag him behind their bikes.

Big Jim intervened by contacting the local radio station and the disc jockey retracted his earlier statement, but the damage was already done. Even though the DJ let the public know that the Beatles were not showing up at Monterey, the rumors continued, and the crowds of kids wanting to see the superstars grew larger.

As tired as he was, Dylan embraced the distraction. This was the perfect time to split. With the intent of finding Frog, he removed his colors and made his way back to the arena, avoiding any of the other Angels who were busy corralling teenagers.

Quicksilver Messenger Service was in the middle of their last song, 'Who Do You Love' when Dylan made his way into the concert. Rather than heading for his seat, he wandered closer to the stage where he knew Frog and the rest of Katie's group were sitting.

Miraculously, Frog was sitting alone amongst three empty chairs. Perhaps, Dylan thought, the Gods were actually on his side after all. He wandered up the aisle. When he came to Frog's seat he knelt beside him.

"Hey, man." He tapped Frog's arm and made him jump.

"Fuck!" Frog put his hand over his heart. "You scared the shit out of me, man. Don't ever do that."

"Sorry, man. Don't make a scene, but it's time to go. Try to act cool as you follow me out of the arena."

"Now?"

Dylan nodded and made his way back into the crowd.

Frog's heart sank and he dreaded what was to come, but he followed the biker. At Dylan's request, he had moved his bike in the morning. Now it sat further down the street in a lot closer to the freeway entrance.

Weaving in and out of concertgoers, Dylan led Frog towards a less populated back exit where they could make a fast getaway onto Highway 1.

Before either man dared speak, they were out of the fairgrounds and into a secluded spot close to their bikes.

"I almost didn't recognize you without your Hells Angel vest on," Frog said in a low voice.

"I can't escape and wear my colors at the same time can I? That would certainly draw unwanted attention."

"Yeah, I guess people would remember seeing a Hells Angel on the freeway."

"They sure as well would. We make a rumble where ever we roll," Dylan said with a chuckle.

"Do you want to tell me where we're going?" Frog asked.

"Nope."

"Come on, man, what if we get separated? You can't let me get on the road if I don't know where we're heading. Look, we're gone, who can I possibly tell our plans to?"

"Fine." Dylan stopped and looked around the deserted street just to make sure they were alone. "I've rented a cabin in North Lake Tahoe. That's where we're going. We'll hole up there until we can settle whatever this is. Do you know how to get there?"

"Vaguely."

"We get on Highway 1 heading north. We take the 156-East exit and follow that onto Highway 101. We'll be on 101 for an hour and then you'll see 680. Exit that to the north and in about seventy miles it will lead onto Interstate 80 East. You think you can remember all of that?"

"Got it. North side you say? Away from the casinos?"

"That's right, no casinos, just trees in every direction. It's nice, it's secluded, and best of all, it's away from the Bay Area where we can relax and think."

Dylan walked towards their bikes that were now visible in the distance. He was anxious to put as many miles as he could between himself and Monterey County.

"It's a long way," Frog said, trailing the biker.

"Yes, but we'll be safe there. We won't have to be looking over our shoulders constantly wondering when death will find us. You dig?"

Frog nodded.

"Look, if we can't make it all the way tonight then we'll just pull over someplace in the woods to crash. You brought a sleeping bag right?"

"Sure did. I brought everything on the list that you gave me and it's all packed on the back of my bike like you told me to do."

"Good."

They walked across the parking lot in silence and when they got to their rides, they stopped and stared at each.

"We'll, this is it, man, you ready?" Dylan tied a blue bandana around the bottom half of his face.

Frog pulled on a hooded sweatshirt and then a brown leather jacket on top of that and sat on his bike.

"Let's do this, man." Frog kick started the Honda into life and followed Dylan out of the parking lot.

***

"There isn't a fairy garden in the woods," Katie said, hands on hips, as she stared at the hyena that had come back a second time.

"Sure there is," Dennis said soothingly.

"You're just a nasty animal who needs to go back from where you came."

"Hey, come on, haven't I helped you get over the puddles of melting sky?"

"Well yeah, you have. And you've helped by keeping the other hyenas away."

"That's right, the ones who want to take you to the tripping teepees."

"True, but fairy gardens are only in storybooks," Katie insisted.

"Of course, but *you're* in a storybook."

She laughed and swirled in the melting colors that bounced around her. "No I'm not."

"You're not?" he asked, trying to sound puzzled.

"No, I'm at the Monterey Pop Festival," she told him, looking at the colored stains on her feet.

"Yep, and that's in a storybook." He snapped his fingers to get her attention away from the invisible things she was focusing on. "Look at me. What am I?"

"You're a laughing hyena."

"Right. Now look around the fairgrounds, how many hyenas are there?"

"Ohhh, too many."

"Think about it, if you're not in a story then why are you talking to a hyena?"

Katie tried to think of an answer but the question had confused her. She stopped and looked at his furry face. "I don't know," she admitted.

"Why is the sky melting and leaving puddles?"

"I don't know..."

"Because you're in a story, Katie. Can you tell me that you aren't?"

She shook her head trying to think. When she couldn't come up with an answer she stared at Dennis.

"You see? You're in a storybook, and if you'll let me, I can take you to a fairy garden."

A fairy garden. Katie thought of the possibilities "Are there lots of fairies?" she asked.

"So many you won't believe it." Dennis took her arm gently and started walking across the fairgrounds.

"You'll be able to wash your feet off there too, there's a creek."

"A fairy creek?"

"Yeah, with magical water. All those colors that you stepped in will wash off easily."

"Ohh! I'd like that. I don't want my skin to be psychedelic."

"I wouldn't want that either, but the fairy water will wash everything clean and you'll be sparkling again."

Katie looked at the stains on her feet. "I sure would like to be clean." She allowed the furry hyena to lead her towards the edge of the fairgrounds.

"Wait!" Katie stopped short. "What about the puddles?"

"It's fine, you can walk through them now because we're going to the magical creek to wash them off."

"Oh..." Katie said, rationalizing his statement.

"That's right, it doesn't matter now. You can get as much of the colored sky on you as you want since we're going to wash it off anyways," he said, and Katie giggled as she purposely stepped into the invisible colored pool. "See? There's no reason to walk funny anymore."

Now that Katie was no longer avoiding the colors on the ground the other hyenas seemed to lose interest in her. They stopped coming up to her and asking if she needed to go to a tripping teepee. Katie decided this was a good thing. She was lucky that she had found the one good hyena in the pack; the only one that she could trust.

"Do they bite?" she asked.

"Does who bite?"

"The fairies, silly, who else would I be taking about?"

"Oh yeah, the fairies. No, they don't bite, they're nice, you'll see."

"Can I hold one?"

"Sure, you can hold as many as you want."

"That's so groovy," Katie said. "Thanks for taking me."

"You're very welcome."

They arrived at the end of the fairgrounds where the woods started. Katie walked through the trees and nearly fell several times. She clung tightly onto Dennis's arm.

"I can't wait to see the fairies!"

"I know. We're getting close too. All we have to do is cross the road here, walk down a hill, and that's where the creek starts." She nearly slipped again and he caught her.

"Oh good!" She giggled, still holding his arm for balance when they crossed the road and wandered further into the trees.

Deep inside, Katie knew she was making a mistake, but believing that she was in dreamland she ignored her internal warnings and continued to follow the nice hyena into the woods.

Getting down the incline was difficult since the hill seemed to dissolve beneath her. After falling several times, she pushed her furry guide away and slid the rest of the way down the hill on her butt.

She landed at the bottom with a thud, then jumped to her feet and wiped her soiled back end.

"Friend?" she called out, turning to look for the hyena. "Oh friend, where did you go?" she asked, but her guide was gone.

Having come this far, Katie was determined to find the magical water, and so she held onto the trees for support and walked towards the sound of the creek.

"Oh hyena friend?" she called out one last time, and when she didn't receive an answer she continued to move towards the sound of the running water where, in her deluded state, she thought she could hear fairies talking.

***

When Katie landed at the bottom of the incline, Dennis headed into the woods to look for Mark. The girl was here, where the lunatic wanted her. Now all he had to do was don the ski mask and scare the shit out of her. Then, he could walk away from all of this and let Mr. Arrogant take over.

Come tomorrow, he would be four thousand dollars richer and this botched scheme would be over. He had learned a valuable lesson. He would never again involve himself in one of Mark Rhodes' plans, no matter how much money the scumbag was paying.

"Mark, where are you, man?" he called out when he reached the designated meeting spot. "Mark?"

"I'm here, be cool. You're fucking loud, man."

Mark was sitting on a downed log opening and closing his pocketknife.

"Okay, man, give me the mask so I can finish this thing. I want to get this shit over with."

Mark tossed him a red and black ski mask and Dennis quickly pulled it on. "How do you want me to play this?" he asked, watching as Mark threw the knife into a tree beside him.

"Anyway you want, as long as you give her a good scare. Once I hear her scream, I'll come to the rescue and take it from there."

Dennis walked back into the bushes. Several feet away he could see Katie at the creek's edge sitting on a boulder. He climbed down the embankment quietly and approached from the rear clutching the handle of a Swiss Army knife he normally carried in his pocket.

When he got close to the girl he could see that she was holding a maple leaf and talking to it. He shook his head. He was about to attack a chick that was so fucked up she thought she was talking to a fairy.

Dennis wasn't sure how he should go about this. This was the first time he had done anything violent towards a woman, and even though he knew nobody was going to be hurt for real, he was nervous. This just didn't feel right. But four grand was a lot of dough, and he had gambling debts that needed to be paid off. Easy money was always hard to come by, he reminded himself as he closed the knife and stuck it back into his pocket. He readied himself, silently counted to three, and then snuck up behind her.

"Aren't you a beautiful little thing?" Katie asked the leaf. "I'm so glad my feet are clean now. That magical water is wonderful."

This girl is a trip, Dennis thought to himself as he grabbed her from behind and pulled her off of the rock where she was sitting.

Katie landed in powdery soft dirt blinking rapidly and staring up at a dark blob that stood above her. The fairy she was holding only moments ago had flown off and was now safely hiding in a tree looking down at her.

"Do you know who I am?" the red and black creature questioned Katie. She shook her head.

"I'm the boogie man," he replied, and then he growled fiercely.

Katie scrambled to her feet. She was shocked but she stood silently waiting while he approached her. Fifteen years of martial arts had left an impact. Even now in her delirium she assumed a protective stance and prepared for combat as the thing came closer.

Before the monster had a chance to attack , Katie leaned inwards and bashed it hard in the nose.

The thing yelled and staggered several steps, clutching its now bleeding face.

Katie ran. At the edge of the embankment she fell to her knees and attempted to crawl up the melting cliff to safety. She tried to use the trees and shrubbery to balance her climb upwards, but was unexpectedly knocked off course when the thing captured her. Using the collar of her sweater, it pulled her backwards and she rolled down the hill.

Katie reached for at anything that she might be able to use as a weapon. When her tumbling body finally came to a stop she rose to her feet holding a broken tree branch and started swinging it wildly in front of her.

The masked creature jumped away, avoiding contact as she continued to swing the weapon.

Katie's drug crazed mind was in a frenzy trying to discern what was real and what was hallucination. What she knew for sure was that she was under attack and basically she knew how to protect herself. But in these *Alice in Wonderland* surroundings, where nothing was clear, that was difficult.

Her attacker appeared to change not only in size but also in shape. One second it was a giant, and in the next it was the size of the fairy who still watched from the tree. The sky no longer melted, now it wept, and its blood red tears ran down the trees and the hillside.

Katie tried to concentrate on her attacker, waiting for his next move, but someone or something knocked her to the ground. She rolled into the underbrush where she was pinned face down in the dirt so that she couldn't see her new abductor.

She shut her eyes and gathered all of her courage and then in one sudden move she bucked her nemesis off long enough to turn her head and look at him. In her drugged state her vision deceived her. What she saw was a dark shadow of a man with marble like shapes swirling kaleidoscope fashion over his features. This made recognition impossible but her attacker didn't know that.

Thinking that she'd seen his face, Mark acted fast. He tackled Katie to the ground where unable to move or even breathe, she shut her eyes and prayed.

"What the fuck, are you doing?" Dennis asked.

"Rescuing you, you fucking idiot, she was kicking your ass."

Dennis stood on the sidelines and watched the struggle. "Now what man?"

"Give me the ski mask and get the hell out of here."

"What?"

"You heard me, give me the fucking mask."

Dennis pulled the mask off of his face. "You don't want to wear this man, it's covered in blood. She got me good."

"I don't care, I don't want her to see any more of my face."

"Okay, man, it's your call, but I wouldn't want to be covered in somebody else's blood. Besides, you said it yourself, she already saw your face." He handed the stained mask over.

"Get the fuck out of here!" Mark yelled, and then holding Katie in place with his knees, he pulled the ski mask over his head.

When Katie felt his movements change she struggled, but Mark shoved her face into the dirt and temporarily stopped her from breathing.

"You heard me, get out of here," Mark repeated.

"What are you going to do, man?" Dennis wiped his bleeding nose. "This wasn't in our plan."

"The plans have changed, brother, your job is done. I'll take it from here."

In a last ditch effort to free herself, Katie bit into Mark's hand. He flinched, his eyes closed for a second, and then he slapped her hard.

"I told you, man, I don't like this. I need to know how this is going to end before I walk away. I'm already an accomplice, I'm not going to jail for your vendetta. This is over, man, you hear me? You said it yourself, nobody gets hurt. We've gone too far, let's go. Maybe she won't remember any of this and we can still get away.," Dennis pleaded.

"You want to know how this is going to end? It's going to end with you five grand richer. Walk away, man, and pretend this weekend never happened."

"Five grand," Dennis repeated the amount to himself. That kind of bread could pay off everything he owed and it would put money in his pocket too. With that thought, and against his own better judgment, Dennis walked out of the creek basin and left Mark alone with his tripping victim.

***

Frog and Dylan started their journey on Highway 1, the scenic roadway that runs along the Pacific Ocean, the full length of the state of California. The route was quiet but they experienced their first of many setbacks before they had driven a mile.

The change was subtle. At first the bike seemed to pull towards the right, but thinking that it was just the roadway, Dylan ignored it.

It wasn't until his bike started to wobble that he knew there was an actual problem, but by then it was too late. The tire bounced out of the frame and headed down the embankment. The bike slid across the roadway and Dylan was thrown in the opposite direction down the hill.

Gradually, he came to a stop in a pile of leaves and there he lay several seconds gasping for air and trying to understand what had happened. Then, cautiously, he sat to assess his injuries.

Meanwhile, Frog parked on the roadway and literally flew down the hill screaming his name.

"I'm here!" Dylan yelled back. He caught hold of a birch tree and pulled himself to his feet.

"Jesus Christ, man, are you alright?" Frog panted.

"I think so. Nothing seems to be broken." Dylan took a few steps away from the tree. "Yeah, I think I'm okay except for some scrapes and bruises. My bike, man, how bad is it?"

"Fuck! You think I took the time to look at your bike? I have no idea how your bike is. What the hell happened?"

"My tire, man. Everything was cool and then it popped out of the frame. I don't know how that happened. It was fine this morning when I rode it into town."

"You think somebody fucked with it?"

Dylan thought hard. The tires were new. He'd put them on himself when he rebuilt the bike. There was no way the bolts could have come loose by themselves, especially loose enough for the tire to actually come out of the frame. That was impossible.

"Yeah, man. I do," Dylan said, shocked at his own words. "I'll know more when I look at it but it sure doesn't sound good. Which way did the tire go, did you see it?"

"It's down there someplace. It couldn't have gone far, you pretty much followed it down in a straight line. Listen, I'm going topside to make sure your bike's out of the roadway. I'll be right back and then we'll search for it."

When Frog headed up the embankment Dylan started looking through the underbrush hoping to recover his lost tire but what he found instead caused him to scream and jump backwards.

"Fuck!" Dylan put his hand to his chest to steady his nerves. He closed his eyes for several seconds and breathing in deeply, trying to understand what he had seen.

He knelt in the dirt and moved several bushes out of the way before coming face to face with the dead body of Skinner.

"What is it man?" Frog called out. "Why did you shout?"

"Fuck man, fuck!" Dylan repeated, shaking his head.

Frog re-joined Dylan to see what the biker was staring at, and when he did he stopped short and his jaw fell open.

Skinner's body was blue and bloated. His dead eyes stared upwards at nothing, as if he were uttering a prayer.

"Wow, man, wow." Frog placed his hands on his head and paced back and forth. "Now what?"

Dylan briefly examined the body. Skinner had a broken jaw, multiple cuts on the face, and what looked like blunt force trauma to the back of the head.

"Someone beat him to death," Dylan concluded. "They bashed his head in with a crowbar or maybe a hammer. Either way, he met a grisly end." Dylan dropped the branches, allowing the underbrush to conceal the body. "My bike, man?"

"It's on the side of the road scratched to fuck, but I think you can still drive it, as long as we can find the wheel."

"Then let's get started. I want to get the fuck out of here."

"What about Skinner? Are we just going to leave him there?"

"Hell yeah. We can make an anonymous call when we're safely out of here, or better yet, I'll call Big Jim. But right now we aren't going to do anything except find my fucking tire so we can get the fuck out of here."

"I don't know, man. I don't like leaving him there. It just seems wrong."

"You want to end up like him?" Dylan asked. "Don't you get it? If I'm right, someone sabotaged my bike hoping to kill me. Skinner is gone, that means they're after *us* now!"

"Who?"

"That's the mystery, isn't it? If I knew the answer to that question then we wouldn't be splitting. Come on, man, help me find the tire. I want to get out of here as quickly as possible."

For several minutes they scrambled through the landscape searching for the missing tire. Finally, they split up to cover more territory. Frog trudged uphill to search higher ground, while Dylan moved down the mountainside.

Dylan was trying to act tough but inside he was trembling. Someone had tried to kill him. He hadn't examined the bike yet, but he knew he was going to find that it had been tampered with.

Skinner was dead, and he could have been dead too. This was no game, this was for real. Somebody wanted him and Frog gone, someone who knew where his bike had been parked. That meant that they were probably being followed right now, and that knowledge changed everything.

Frantically, he tossed bushes around and swearing until finally he heard Frog's voice screaming from the top of the bend.

"I've got it, man!"

"Thank God," Dylan mumbled. He turned and started to head up the hill but suddenly stopped and listened. Somewhere in the vicinity he could hear a girl let out a bloodcurdling scream and before he knew what was doing he found himself running down the hill towards the creek and the desperate screams beyond.

***

Mark waited a few minutes to allow Dennis time to walk away. He had begun to question his actions but for reasons unknown to himself he just couldn't stop. He tried to tell himself this wasn't what he wanted, that this was going to sabotage his future, but right now none of that mattered.

"You think you're better than everybody else don't you?" he whispered into Katie's tangled hair. "You're out playing hippie girl, one of the beautiful people, but you're really a hypocrite. A little rich bitch hypocrite who judges everybody without giving them a chance."

How *dare* she insult him? *He* was the one who had brought the Rhodes family name out of the gutter. He had worked hard to get where he was, and this little tramp wasn't going to get the better of him. Nobody would ever make a joke out of Mark Rhodes again.

Katie lay perfectly still, willing her mind sober. She knew this voice. It should be crystal clear who her attacker was, but the drugs in her system betrayed her and she found herself drifting in and out of reality.

"This could have gone so much differently," he said, twisting her long hair in his hands.

The change in leverage gave Katie an advantage. Ignoring the pain to her head she rolled her body into a position where she could free one of her legs, and then with all her might, she kicked her attacker in the chest and sent him reeling backwards. Then taking a rock beside her she hurled it, successfully clubbing her attacker in the head.

This was her one and only chance. Katie knew that if her attacker got her again he would kill her.

She tried to run up the hill but slipped and once again fell to her knees. Scrambling up the embankment, she deliberately kicked debris down in her path hoping to slow her pursuer. Her heart pounded so hard that she thought it might explode and the hallucinations persisted, despite the seriousness of her situation.

The being on the ground remained still for several minutes but then miraculously it sat up, reminding Katie of Michael Myers from *Halloween*. The monster rose to its feet.

"You fucking little bitch!" it screamed. "You're going to pay!"

Seconds later it headed up the hill, skillfully avoiding the rocks and dirt that Katie kicked downwards. Halfway up the hill it got her. She had only paused for a second to catch her breath and that was all it took. The thing made it over the avalanche of debris and caught her around the waist, knocking her to the ground. Now both of them slid down the incline.

Katie screamed and reached for rocks, sticks, anything in her path, but the thing pinned her arms uncomfortably to the ground.

"Oh yeah, now you're going to pay, Katie," it said and started to laugh evilly.

***

Dennis sat on the side of the hill far enough away so that he couldn't see the incident below, but he was close enough that he could hear the girl's screams. Many things floated through his mind as he struggled with the knowledge that Mark would probably rape and then kill this girl. Hell, not just any girl, this was Al Searfus' daughter. She was a socialite and her father had power and money. He could get anything he wanted, and what he was going to want was revenge.

He soon realized that people had seen them together. He had led Katie across the fairgrounds in plain sight. Plenty of people had seen them and any one of them could identify his face.

Al Searfus would never let this go. He would find the culprit and since no one had seen Mark except for Katie, it would be his word against that of a madman.

He heard Katie's frantic screams and decided that five thousand dollars wasn't worth what this was quickly becoming, a murder scene.

If he was arrested now, how many charges would he be facing? None as severe as rape and murder, that was for sure, and that was why he had to stop this before it went any further.

Maybe he could still turn this around. If he stopped what was happening, he could offer to testify against Mark and save himself. He might be able to avoid any jail time at all if he cooperated with law enforcement, but if he allowed Mark to kill her there were no options. He would go to jail for first degree murder since this was premeditated.

Katie screamed again. This time Dennis rose to his feet and ran towards the fairgrounds. He needed witnesses, and if he could find a cop along the way that would be even better.

***

That laugh! Katie knew that laugh. It belonged to her husband. He used to laugh that way when he ridiculed her and made her feel small. This monster above her was Mark. Hallucinations or not, there was only one creature that sounded like that.

"What do you want, Mark?" she screamed as loud as she could, and the recognition in her voice stopped him. "That's right, you fucking asshole, I know who you are! You're Mark Rhodes."

"Shut up!" the monster roared. "Shut the fuck up!"

Mark took a handful of dirt in his fist and shook it in her face. "You scream again and I'm going to shove this down your throat until you choke on it, you understand?"

"Go right ahead, you piece of shit! You think you're going to rape me, is that it? You're going to have to kill me first. I'll fight to the death. Don't think I'll give in and make it fucking easy for you."

Katie managed to get a hand loose and before he could stop her she gouged her fingernails into his lower arm causing him to scream.

"Fucking whore!" He caught her hand and pinned it to her side, but during the struggle she managed to scratch him again on his cheek.

"You see what I mean? I'll get some blows in too, you scumbag. How's that going to look on Monday morning when you have to show up at my father's office?" she asked. "Think about it, Mark, no job, not with marks like that on your body. Scratches can scar really bad too, mine will."

"Shut up!" he screamed. "You think this is a game?" he hissed as he shook her hard.

"Yeah, you fucking dick, I think this is a game."

Katie used all of her strength, and screaming at the top of her lungs, she fought back, moving her body erratically to loosen his grip. Finally she broke free. Mark tried to catch her but she dodged and then took a swing of her own, hitting him in the side of the head, knocking him off balance.

Still screaming, she rose to her feet and started to run but he took hold of her foot and pulled her back to the ground. Before she could move he wrapped his hand around her very long hair and shoved her face into the dirt, stopping her from breathing.

"Now, we're going to play this my way, do you understand?" He pulled his knife out of his pocket.

Katie struggled for air, the possibility of death passing through her mind.

Feeling a change come over her body, Mark eased up just enough so that she could lift her head an inch or two off the ground and take a breath.

"You still think this is a game, Katie?" He shoved her face back into the dirt.

For a few seconds he let her struggle and when he eased up again, he placed the blade of the knife next to her jugular. "You want to fight me now, Katie?

One move and I'll cut you. What do I have to lose? Think about it, killing you is my only way out."

He reached beneath her skirt and tore her panties away, and still holding the knife to her throat, he started to wrestle with his own clothing.

Katie swallowed hard, instinctively knowing what would happen next. Her options were limited, as Mark had just pointed out his only way was to kill her.

"This could have turned out so very differently. All you had to do was give me a chance," he said, leaning into her face as he straddled her body. "We could have had a good life together, you and I. I would have been a devoted family man. I would have taken real good care of you and you would have been happy. What's happening now is your fault. *You* did this, Katie, not me." Saliva dripped from his parted lips and fell on her cheek.

His breath smelled like alcohol and stale tobacco and she gagged. "That's not true," she managed to choke out.

"What did you say?"

She felt the blade slice into her skin, but intent on speaking her mind continued to talk. "I said you're a lousy cheating husband. A self-centered prick that only cares about himself. You were a lousy father and a lousy son-in-law who stole my family's business. There is nothing good about you, Mark Rhodes. It's better I die than spend my life with you aga—"

He shoved her head into the dirt to stop her from talking and fought to position himself above her and between her parted legs.

***

"Hey, you motherfucker!" Dylan bellowed as he charged towards his target.

The man, who was wearing a ski mask and whose pants were around his ankles, tried to run but Dylan was on top of him in an instant. He knocked the assailant to the ground and they rolled in the dirt fighting for dominance.

Dylan easily overpowered his opponent. He rolled on top of the man and continued to deliver a series of blows to his face and his body. The man tried to defend himself but he was no match for the larger biker. Eventually he gave up and just lay there moaning.

"That should keep you still, you fucking piece of shit. You make one move and I'm going to tear your head off."

In the distance Frog called Dylan's name and the girl who had yet to utter a sound repeated it.

"Dylan? Is that really you?"

Having recognized her voice, he turned his head and stared at her. *"Katie?"*

She was crying and trying to rise to her feet.

Dylan, dumbstruck, turned his attention back to the man on the ground. "Who the fuck, are you?" he demanded. He bent down and snagged the bloody mask off of the pained and bloody face of Mark Rhodes.

"You!" Dylan kicked him hard in the ribs.

Mark tried to crawl away in terror but Dylan kicked him again.

"Didn't I warn you? I told you man never to come near her again and I find you doing *what*?"

He gave him another kick to the ribs, and then Dylan held the front of Mark's shirt and pulled him into a sitting position against a tree. "Man, you better fucking say something."

"I'm sorry, man, I'm sorry," Mark blubbered.

"You're sorry? Are you for fucking real, man? You're fucking *sorry*?" Another kick to the ribs. The executive winced in pain.

"You make another move and I'll kill you. Do you dig?"

Mark nodded and coughed a clot of blood into his hand.

Katie was on her feet now, slowly walking towards them.

Dylan took another look at the crushed body of Mark Rhodes, and deciding that he wasn't going anywhere, rushed towards Katie. He met her halfway, wrapping his arms around her and lifting her slightly off of the ground, and kissed the top of her head.

"Katie, my God." He brushed the dirt, leaves and tears away from her face. "Are you alright?" he asked, pulling her trembling body closer to his.

She nodded.

"Katie, did he...? Because if he did, I'm going to kill the bastard." Dylan reached for the buck knife that was strapped to the ankle of his boot.

"No. You showed up before he could."

"I didn't, man," Mark gurgled. "You heard her, I didn't!"

"It doesn't matter, I should still kill you just on principal alone, you piece of fucking shit."

Dylan held the large knife in his hand and let go of Katie, walking towards his intended victim.

Just then Frog pushed through the trees. He stood mouth agape, studying the situation. "What the fuck?"

"This fucker tried to rape Katie," Dylan replied. "Now I'm going to cut his balls off."

"We have to go, man," Frog interrupted, snatching Dylan's arm to get his attention.

"What?" Dylan shook his head and stared at him.

"There's a whole crowd of people heading this way, pigs included. Katie's screams must have attracted them."

"Fuck! How far away?"

"A few minutes. They were just leaving the fairgrounds when I found you."

"Watch that asshole for a few minutes would you?" Dylan asked and Frog laughed.

"Him?" Frog nodded towards the damaged body of Mark Rhodes. "Sure, I'll watch him, but he doesn't look like he's going anywhere anytime soon."

Dylan took Katie by the hand and pulled her away from earshot. "Are you sure you're alright?" he asked.

"Apart from the hallucinations, and a few cuts and bruises, yes."

"Hallucinations?"

"Moonbeam shared a Coke with me earlier but she forgot to tell me that it was laced with LSD."

"Jesus, all this and you're strung out? What a bummer day." Dylan shook his head. "You think you're going to remember any of it?"

"With the fairy as my witnesses, no problem."

Dylan looked upwards, and seeing nothing out of the ordinary smiled. "Sure, something like that." He touched her face and then traced the long scratch across her neck, which Mark had made with his knife. "Motherfucker," he mumbled.

"I'm okay."

"Look, I have to go, baby. Help is going to be here soon. They're going to take care of you but I can't stay for the fireworks, you dig?"

"I remember why," Katie said dreamily.

He kissed her and pulled her into his body, holding her tightly. "I have to tell you something, Katie, and it's important, so try to remember." He tipped her head upwards and then stared into her heavily dilated eyes. "I love you. I have never said that to anyone else in my life but I have to tell you the truth in case I never come back. Remember the dream? The one in the hall? I told you about it when we took that ride across the Golden Gate Bridge?

Remember the girl in that hall, the one that I've dreamt about all of my life? You're that girl, Katie, I knew it the first time I met you. You're that girl that I've missed out on in every lifetime except this one."

Katie tried to follow his words but now that the threat had ended the fairy was flying above her and it was hard to ignore the beautiful colors that its wings spread across the sky.

"I'm going to fix this mess, I swear it. And when I do I'll be back, and I'll never let you get away from me again. Wait for me, Katie. I know you like Ron but you love me. Wait for me." He kissed her, and before the crowd of people descended over the hill he and Frog were gone.

She knew she should remember his words. She knew they were important and that they would make more sense tomorrow when the drugs wore off, but right now the sky was melting. And like the fairy that flew back into the trees to hide, his words drifted away into the approaching night.

Chapter 37

When Moonbeam returned without Katie, Ron was puzzled. Moonbeam explained that Katie had gone to see the singer from Big Brother and the Holding Company and that surprised him. Katie had mentioned the singer before but he had no idea that she knew her well enough to get backstage.

When minutes became hours, he grew suspicious. Ron remembered the kiss he had witnessed between Katie and the biker, and was sure she had disappeared with him.

Moonbeam started to trip then, giggling, which gradually turned into full-fledged hallucinations. During her delirium she admitted that she had shared acid laced Coke with Katie. Thinking the LSD might have lost some of its potency since the January Human Be-In, she had added an extra dose to the cup.

As Moonbeam's visions intensified, Ron became more and more concerned about Katie. By four o'clock, when she had been missing for nearly three hours, he decided it was time to go and look for her.

He wanted to go alone, but Moonbeam, feeling guilty, had insisted on joining him. Frog remained behind. His moodiness had intensified over the weekend and Ron had to admit it was a blessing to get away from him.

"Where did you see her last?" Ron asked.

"At the gate that leads backstage, where the butterflies live."

Ron took the drug-flying Moonbeam by the arm and they headed towards the gate that led backstage where several pompous young stagehands sat surrounded by giggling groupies. Ron pushed his way to the front of the line and addressed the young punk who was dead set on ignoring him.

"I'm looking for my friend, man. She went backstage several hours ago to see Janis Joplin."

The stagehand turned to evaluate Ron before actually acknowledging his presence.

"What do you want?" he asked disinterestedly.

"I want to know what time she left. I'm concerned. She's been gone for about three hours and she might be tripping. "

"What does she look like?" he asked with a bored yawn.

"About 5'6", long blonde hair, and barefoot. She was wearing a long green hippie skirt, a white poet's blouse, and a leather vest on top. She has a headband with green beads and a strand of flowers around her neck."

"Yeah, yeah I remember her. She was here about forty-five minutes. When she left she seemed pretty strung out. She was wandering out there for a long time," he said, pointing to the courtyard of the fairgrounds.

"Thanks, man." Ron collected Moonbeam, who was tracing lines on the wall with her fingers, and together they headed towards the courtyard where he hoped they would find Katie.

***

"This way, officers. Down there next to the creek, that's where I left them," Dennis said to Officer Powers and his partner Jones.

Dennis led the men into the trees. They were followed by a group of hippies they had collected on their walk over to the creek. Now the crowd was becoming a problem and Officer Jones shouted for them to stay back.

"Explain this to me again, young man?" Officer Powers asked Dennis.

"This guy I work with offered me a free ticket to the pop festival and two thousand dollars to help him out this weekend."

"Help him out?"

"That's right. There's this chick that he digs. She wouldn't give him the time of day and he was going to win her over this weekend."

"Win her over? Now, we're looking for a potential rapist?"

"He flipped, Officer, that's the only way I can explain it, he just completely flipped out and he's going to kill her if you don't stop him."

"And you're involved?"

"I was. I mean, in the beginning, it was just a game, something to get the girl to notice him. Stupid, I admit, but nobody was supposed to get hurt, you dig? As soon as I knew that the plan had changed and that the attack was for real, that's when I was out, man. That's when I came for your help."

"I see them, they're below us!" Officer Jones yelled, charging down the hill.

Officer Powers and Dennis ran too, and seconds later all three emerged into the lower landscape where Katie stood holding her clothing together. On the ground next to a cluster of trees lay a crumpled man coughing blood into his hands.

"What's going on here?" Officer Jones demanded. He pulled a two-way radio out of his belt holster. "I'm down by the creek across from the fairgrounds. We're going to need an ambulance and a couple of squad cars."

"Copy that," the dispatcher's voice said on the other end of the radio.

"Now, what is this?" he asked, looking at Katie.

"He attacked me." She pointed at the bleeding man who still lay on the ground. "He attacked me, tore my clothes, and tried to rape me."

Officer Powers removed his jacket and put it around Katie's shoulders. "What happened to him?"

"Someone beat him up." She looked at the cop with eyes that were heavily dilated.

Powers looked at Dennis. "Did you do this to him?"

"No, man, when I left to get help, he was the aggressor."

"Friend!" Katie exclaimed when she noticed Dennis. "Friend, you came back to save me!" She had a huge smile on her face which, despite the dire circumstances, made Dennis smile too.

"Yes," he said. "I came back to save you, Katie."

"So who worked you over?" Jones asked the very pale Mark Rhodes.

"Her biker boyfriend, that's who!" Mark mumbled in a low voice, which caused him to start coughing all over again.

"Miss, what happened to him?" Powers asked, shaking his head in disbelief. This was not what he expected.

"Someone beat him up."

"Who?"

"How should I know? It could have been a lot of people. He's hated by many, believe me. Maybe Tiffany tried to kill him. I can't blame her really, he's a miserable hyena."

"I told you, man. I told you the chick was fucked up on something," Dennis said.

A multitude of emergency vehicles pulled up to the roadway. Someone yelled at the crowd to stay back, and then several men walked into the clearing.

"What happened here?" the police lieutenant asked Jones while two paramedics knelt beside Mark Rhodes.

"The clown on the ground tried to rape the girl. Apparently he was interrupted."

"I'll say." Lt. Dixon whistled and shook his head. "How is he?"

The paramedics were carefully strapping Mark to a gurney. The young businessman's body was crushed but he was going to make a full recovery.

"Stable. Broken ribs, someone did a real number on him."

"Her boyfriend," Mark tried to say, but started to cough again.

"Miss, was your boyfriend here?" Lt. Dixon asked.

"There was a fairy, but he's gone now," Katie said, scanning the tops of the trees.

"She's intoxicated, sir," Jones explained.

Dixon shook his head. "Crazy hippie kids. Miss, can you look at me please?" When Katie did, he asked, "Can you tell me what happened?"

"He tried to rape me. The hyena friend brought me down to the creek to see the fairies and he attacked me. He...he ripped my clothes but someone came and stopped him."

"Did you know this someone?"

"Nope. Never seen him before in my life," Katie lied and then started to spin in the sunshine.

***

Ron and Moonbeam walked into the courtyard. For several minutes Ron searched for Katie. An attendant with a radio sat on one of the benches watching and then finally approached.

"Can I help you?" asked Herb, a balding man in his fifties.

"Yeah, maybe you can. Did you happen to see a girl with long blonde hair and a green skirt? She was probably acting a little strange since she had a 'special drink' before she wandered off by herself."

Herb scratched his head thinking and then nodded. "Sure I saw her. She's a pretty little thing. She was here for a long time dancing around the yard. I checked in with her a couple of times. There are several teepees set up for 'tripping,'" Herb said. "I wanted to take her there but she wouldn't have any part of it. I had several of the women attendants check in with her too, thinking that maybe she would go to one of the tents with them but she refused. Then along came her friend and she seemed happy to go off with him."

"Was he a biker with shaggy brown hair?" Ron asked, his jealousy rising.

"A biker? No, this guy wasn't a biker. This guy was clean cut, looked like he works on Wall Street. He had short, blondish hair, a crew cut I think, nice dress pants and a button down shirt."

"Where did he take her?" a desperate Ron asked.

"That way." Herb pointed to the other side of the fairgrounds. "She seemed happy to go with him, danced all the way."

"Thanks, man." Ron took Moonbeam by the hand dragged her along to the other side of the fairgrounds.

Short hair and business clothes? Ron didn't know anybody who fit that description unless it was the creep who had come to San Francisco looking for Katie months ago.

"Fuck! I bet it was him," he said aloud, remembering the confrontation at Katie's apartment. She had told him that the creep would never leave her alone. Had she gone off with him? No, she hated him, she had told Ron that, she wouldn't have gone with him willingly. Somehow, though, he knew that Mark Rhodes was involved and he shivered.

"Hey, man, a girl was raped down at the creek. I heard it on a cop's radio," a hippie announced to his friends just as Ron and Moonbeam were walking past. Ron dropped Moonbeam's hand and sprinted towards the creek where a crowd of people had formed.

***

"He's ready to go to the hospital," one of the medics announced.

Officer Jones officially arrested Mark and then the medics transported his gurney up the hillside.

"I'll have backup waiting at the hospital. They'll handcuff him to the bed and watch him until he can be moved to the jail. We have to make sure he doesn't try to make a run for it, you know what I mean?" Lt. Dixon said. "Now what about the girl?"

The paramedics had checked her over. Besides a few scrapes and bruises, Katie was fine, but she wasn't coherent enough to let her walk off by herself. That presented a problem.

Dennis was still giving a statement to the police. He too was on his way to jail, and the officers had no other choice but to take Katie with them. That meant taking her to either the hospital or the police station until she sobered up.

"Lieutenant Dixon, her boyfriend is here to claim her!" Powers yelled down the embankment.

"Her boyfriend?" Dixon assumed that this was the aggressor who had worked over the rapist. "Let him pass!" he yelled back.

Seconds later a tall hippie with shoulder length brown hair walked into the clearing.

"Katie!" He rushed to her side, took her thin body into his arms and hugged her.

"You're her boyfriend?" Dixon asked the newcomer.

"That's right, she's here with me," Ron said as he held a shaking Katie in his arms.

"Are you the one who beat up the would-be rapist?"

"Beat him up? Who Mark Rhodes?" a confused Ron asked.

"Let me see your hands, son."

Ron flipped his hands over several times so the police officer could examine them. "Nothing, not even a scratch," Dixon said to the other officers who looked on.

"What's happened?" Ron asked.

"Your girlfriend was allegedly attacked by an individual whose name you've already mentioned."

"Mark Rhodes," Ron said.

"That person is on his way to the hospital. Seems that before Mr. Rhodes had a chance to finish his attack, a vigilante stepped out of the woods and beat him up severely."

"A vigilante?"

"That's right. Broken ribs, maybe a punctured lung by the way he was bleeding. Rhodes said her boyfriend beat him up, any idea who he was talking about?"

"I'm her boyfriend, but I didn't do that."

"No you didn't, but someone did, and your girlfriend here is either not telling who that person is or she doesn't know. Whoever it was, that person saved her life. Too bad he didn't stick around so we could identify him."

"Who is that?" Ron asked, pointing to a handcuffed Dennis, who stood talking to the cops.

"That's the accomplice. Seems he came here with Mr. Rhodes. They had some cockamamie scheme to scare your girlfriend but it erupted into more, and that's when Mr. Drummond here turned his friend in."

"Mr. Drummond?"

"Have you ever seen him before?" Dixon asked. Ron shook his head.

"He works for my father," Katie singsonged. "He's a good hyena."

"Jesus Christ. So this whole scene was organized?" Ron asked in amazement. "You mean Mark Rhodes came here looking for her purposely to attack her? That sick motherfucker. I wish I *had* beaten the bastard up." He hugged Katie tighter. "Katie, baby, are you alright?" He pushed her body away from his so he could examine her wounds.

"She's fine, paramedics checked her. Just a few bumps and scratches. The worst is across her neck. Looks like Rhodes had her at knifepoint when he was interrupted. I'd like to get a statement from her but under her current condition that's impossible."

"What's going to happen next, Officer?"

"We were going to take her in since she isn't coherent enough to release on her own recognizance, but now that you're here that changes things."

"Can I take her?"

"That depends, son. We're going to need to speak to her about this. Obviously we can't talk to her now, but tomorrow we're going to need a statement."

"What time? I promise I'll have her there. Here, take down my information," Ron said as he reached for his wallet. "I can show you where we're camped too. That way you will know where she is at all times. Please, let me take her. I promise I'll watch over her and I'll have her at the police station whatever time you say."

"Lieutenant, we have a hippie girl here claiming to be Katie's friend, she's insisting on coming down," Officer Powers called down from the roadside.

Dixon looked at Ron and he nodded.

"Let her through!" the officer yelled up the roadside, and seconds later Moonbeam walked through the trees.

"Who are you?" Dixon asked.

"My name is Annie, I'm her friend." Moonbeam put her arms around Katie.

"She's staying with both of you?"

"That's right, Officer. Katie is here with both of us. We're staying here in the parking lot. I have a VW bus."

"Alright, I'll release her to the two of you, but you have to show my officers where you're staying. We'll come tomorrow morning for a statement. Don't go to the concert until we've met with you. Understood?"

"Got it, Officer. You have my word." Ron led both girls up the embankment.

At the top, Officer Jones handed Ron a plain gray blanket and pointed to the jacket Katie wore. "I'm sorry, I need that back."

Ron exchanged the blanket for the police jacket, and with an arm around each of the girls, walked away from the creek.

When the man in handcuffs realized they were leaving he shouted, "Stop! I need to talk to her! Katie, I have to tell you something!"

Officer Powers tried to shove Dennis into the squad car but he resisted. "It's important, you have to hear me! You want to know this, Katie, you really do."

"Friend?" Katie smiled at him and letting go of Ron, she drifted towards Dennis.

"It's about your brother, Katie. Mark talked your brother into signing up for the military. It was Mark's idea. He wanted to get rid of Richard so he could take over."

"Richard?"

"That's right, Katie, he went with him to the Marines recruiting office to sign up. He pretended to be Richard's friend. Mark convinced him of the advantages of going in the service. Richard believed him, he thought Mark was trying to help him and that's why he enlisted."

"Mark took him to sign up?" Katie asked, her brain trying to register what Dennis was telling her.

"He lied to your father, said he had a dentist appointment, but what he was really doing was taking Richard for his physical. He wanted to make sure that your brother didn't chicken out."

"Okay, big shot, you told her what you needed to, now get your ass into the squad car," Jones said as he pushed Dennis inside.

"Hey you," Dennis said, "her boyfriend, what's your name?"

"Ron."

"Listen, man, make sure she remembers what I told her okay? I know she's miles away right now on another planet most likely, but tomorrow she's going to want to know the truth about her brother. Please remind her."

Ron nodded and then Dennis let Jones shove him into the car.

Katie, Moonbeam, and Ron worked their way through the staring crowd, heading for Ron's van. When they reached the parking lot Katie stopped, took Ron around the waist, and hugged him.

"Thank you for helping me."

"You're welcome, baby. Come on, let's get back to the van so we can get you cleaned up and taken care of."

"Alright." She took his hand, but then stopped again, jumped into his arms and said. "I love you too, Dylan. Of course I'll wait for you."

Ron's body shook and his heart dropped into his stomach.

***

Katie opened one eye but her head hurt bad so she closed it again. She knew that something bad had happened and her mind fought to block the memories that were there, waiting to take over.

Go back to sleep she told herself, but Moonbeam knew she was awake, she could feel the hippie girl staring at her.

"Are you alright?" Moonbeam asked several times. "I know you're awake, I saw you open an eye."

"Then you know that I'm not okay. Go away." Katie pulled the blanket up over her head.

"We need to talk," Moonbeam insisted.

"Oh no, we have nothing to say to each other."

"I think we do."

"I think we don't." Katie turned over on her side, ignoring her friend.

"I was trying to be helpful," Moonbeam said in her own defense. "I thought I was giving you a break from stress. I thought an acid trip would be calming and that it would help you find peace."

"Really? Is that how you're going to try to explain this?" Katie asked harshly, abandoning the blanket and sitting up.

"It was a mistake. I'm sorry."

"It was a bad day to make a mistake."

"How did I know shit was going to hit the fan?" Moony wailed plaintively.

"That's not even the point, is it?"

"I thought—"

"It doesn't matter what you thought," Katie said with her voice raised, "you were wrong."

"I know that now, I just didn't know it yesterday."

"Not an excuse, Annie. Not even close to an excuse."

"I'm sorry," Moonbeam repeated. "I really hope you can forgive me."

Katie shook her head. "With all the years I've known you of course I'm going to forgive you but right now, I'm boiling mad."

Moonbeam smiled shyly. "They'll be here soon, you might want to clean up."

"Who will be here soon?"

"The police, to take your statement."

That's when her memory, what was left of it, came back. She dropped her head into her hands as her mind replayed the nightmare.

"Fuck, fuck, fuck!"

"I know it was a bad day..."

"I'm hot. I have to get out of this thing, move over." Katie reached for the door of the bus and then jumped into the lot breathing deeply. Moonbeam followed.

"How much do you remember?" Moonbeam asked.

"Not enough, too much... I don't know." Katie shook her head. "My head is fucking killing me."

"You want some aspirin? It will help."

"So would a lobotomy."

Katie walked towards the campsite where Ron was sitting alone drinking a cup of coffee. Frog was missing and she wondered briefly where he was, and then she remembered. Frog and Dylan were gone. She had seen them leave, hadn't she?

"And, how do you feel this bright, beautiful morning?" Ron asked sarcastically in between sips of coffee."

"Like fucking shit."

"I would think so. You put up a good fight though, I have to hand it to you; you're one tough little chick, Katie."

She didn't say anything. She pulled a clean cup out of a box and poured herself some instant coffee then sat in one of the camping chairs and shut her eyes. "So much for listening to Carlos Santana play the guitar this morning."

"Who?" Ron asked, but she ignored him.

For several minutes she sat, eyes closed, trying to remember everything that had happened, but the memories were difficult to reconstruct. The story seemed to be wrapped in fantasy, as if she were watching a movie rather than remembering what happened to her yesterday.

Moonbeam sat beside her. She held two white tablets, which she tried to hand to Katie. "Aspirin," she said, but Katie waved her away.

"Do you really expect me to take something that *you* give me? I mean, ever again, do you really think I would trust you enough to take aspirin from your hand?"

"But it *is* aspirin. I can show you the bottle. Look, here there's the letter B engraved in the top of the pills that stands for Bayer. Of course they're aspirin, what else could they be?"

"Belladonna?" Katie said sardonically.

"But that's poison, that doesn't even make sense."

A police car pulled into the lot and parked lengthwise behind Ron's bus. Two officers jumped out, one of them Lt. Dixon.

"Here they come," Moonbeam announced.

"Terrific." Katie sucked on her coffee and waited while the two cops approached and then sat at the metal table beside her, Ron and Moonbeam.

"How are you feeling this morning, Miss Searfus?" Lt. Dixon asked.

"Lousy."

"Have you taken any aspirin? It would probably help. I have some in the car."

Moonbeam opened her hand and showed the officers the two tablets she held.

"There you go," Dixon smiled. "Take those."

Katie glared at Moonbeam but accepted the aspirin and washed them down with a gulp of coffee.

"Ready to get started?" the police lieutenant asked.

"Sure, why not?" Katie straightened herself in the chair.

Lieutenant Dixon pulled a pen and a yellow writing tablet out of his bag. "How much do you remember?"

"Bits and pieces. It's a bit foggy, to tell you the truth."

Officer Dixon nodded. "Do you remember the attack?"

"Some of it, I don't know exactly. It's like a dream."

"Well, let's try, shall we? Do you remember who attacked you?"

"Yes, that I remember. His name is Mark Rhodes, he works for my father."

"How long have you known this individual?"

Tough question. She almost said forty-seven years, but stopped herself. How long had Mark been working for her father in 1967? She rubbed her hands together trying to think of an answer.

"Two or three years I guess. I don't *know* him, know him. He works for my father. I've seen him at events and a few family functions."

"Have you ever dated him?"

"No." She hadn't gone out with Mark until the end of 1967, after Richard died in 'Nam.

"What about the other man, Dennis Drummond, do you know him?"

"I don't know. I know he works for my father. I've heard the name before but until yesterday, I'm not sure if I've ever seen him."

"Why don't you tell me what you do remember?"

Katie sat forward, resting her elbows on the table. "I remember watching Big Brother and the Holding Company. Moonbeam brought a Coke back that we shared." She stopped a second and glared at her friend. "When the band ended, Moony and I left our seats to walk around. I know the singer of Big Brother, she's a friend of mine. Before leaving San Francisco she asked me to visit her backstage at the end of her band's set, so I did. Unfortunately, Moonbeam couldn't get in so she returned to the seats. Janis and I had some drinks together and then I left."

"Janis who?" Lt. Dixon.

Katie smiled, finding humor in his question. "Janis Joplin, she's the singer of Big Brother and the Holding Company."

"Right, your friend?"

Katie nodded. "By that time I was starting to fly."

Officer Dixon looked at her questioningly.

"Trip out. You know, on whatever it was that Moony added to the Coke."

"Oh, of course, trip out," Lt. Dixon repeated, adding that to his written notes.

"That's where my memory fogs." She stopped and sipped on her coffee, thinking. "I saw a lot of colors and my vision wasn't clear. People looked odd, fuzzy. You understand?"

"Not really, but continue..."

"Somewhere in that dream I met Mr. Drummond, and for drug induced reasons, I followed him to the creek. I'm not sure of the specifics, but we arrived and Mr. Drummond disappeared. That's when I was attacked by Mark Rhodes."

"So he was there, waiting for you?"

"Yeah, exactly."

"Go on."

"I tried to get away. I tried to climb the hill but he knocked me down. I remember he slapped me, and then he told me that the only way out was for him to kill me. He had a knife." Katie pointed to the scratch across her throat. "He cut my clothing and held the knife to my neck. Then someone stopped him."

"Someone, like the biker?"

Katie was surprised; had she mentioned Dylan?

"We know about your biker boyfriend. I had a little talk with Mark Rhodes last night after he was stabilized. Oh, and by the way, he has three broken ribs and a punctured lung, but they're expecting him to make a full recovery. Anyway, this conversation that Mark and I had, he said he couldn't remember the biker's full name but his first name is Dylan. Mark met him at a family party your parents held a few months ago?"

Katie's face flushed. She hadn't told Ron about that party, and now he knew she was keeping secrets. She looked up just as Ron excused himself from the table and walked away, heading towards the fairgrounds.

"Sorry, I should have spoken to you privately," Lt. Dixon said after the silent confrontation.

Katie sighed. "It's okay, you didn't do anything. I already blew that myself."

Lt. Dixon cleared his throat and then tried again. "Dylan is a Hells Angel, I understand. What can you tell me about him?"

Katie swallowed hard. She'd wanted to keep Dylan's name out of this but that was impossible now.

"His name is Dylan Taylor. Yes, Mark met him at my parents' home. They had a cocktail party in March, Dylan was my escort."

"And how does he fit in with this story?" Lt. Dixon looked up from his notepad.

"He showed up. I don't know how. All I know is that one minute I was face down in the dirt and in the next, Mark was trying to get away. Dylan caught him and that's why he's in the hospital."

"And what happened to Dylan Taylor? Where is he?"

"I don't know, he left. That's all I know. He worked Mark over and then he split."

"Why would he do that?"

"I have no idea."

"You have no idea, not even a guess?"

"No sir, I don't. He just left. That's when you showed up."

"I see." Lt. Dixon completed his notes and then he closed the pen and put it and the yellow pad back in his bag.

"Miss Searfus, we'll be in touch. We have all of your contact information I presume?" Katie nodded. Lt. Dixon handed her a business card. "If you remember anything, or there's something you want added to the report, don't hesitate to contact me."

"Of course." Katie looked at the card.

Lt. Dixon and his partner rose from the table. They started to walk away but Dixon stopped and turned towards Katie.

"Miss Searfus, you should call your parents today. They're worried."

Katie had forgotten all about her parents. She wondered how they would react to this news.

"You spoke to them?" she asked.

"Yes, this morning. They were...shocked. Your father said he's known the young man in question for several years, very upsetting news. Your parents said to tell you that they're sorry, whatever that means, and that they're waiting for your call."

Lt. Dixon and his partner walked away. Minutes later the police cruiser pulled out of the parking lot.

"You know you really should call them," Moonbeam urged. "I know you're upset with them, but they are your parents and I'm sure they're worried."

"I will. I'll call when we get into the fairgrounds," Katie said, wondering how that call was going to play out.

This was a new development, something she hadn't anticipated. How would this affect the bond she had with her parents? This could change everything, she realized, and for the first time she wondered if there was hope for a normal relationship with her family.

Chapter 38

When the police left, Katie and Moonbeam set off for the fairgrounds. They took their time, strolling through the parking lot, and sharing a doobie as they tried to settle their rattled nerves.

"Is it a bad time to ask about Frog?" Moonbeam said tentatively.

"What about Frog?"

"You're sure you saw him with Dylan?"

Katie nodded. "He was there alright, they both were. I was tripping really bad, but they were definitely there."

"So they got away."

"Yep, damn right they did." Katie pointed across the parking lot. "Hey look!" she exclaimed. "See that psychedelic bus over there?"

"Yeah, I've seen that bus before around the Haight."

"That's the Merry Pranksters' bus. Its name is Further, you know, of acid test fame."

"Oh yeah, the electric Kool-Aid acid tests right? That must have been fun driving across the country in that groovy bus and turning people on to LSD. What a beautiful thing."

"The main guy's name is Ken Kesey, he's an author. I think he has some property up in La Honda. Anyway, he's going to write this groovy book called, *One Flew over the Cuckoo's Nest*. They make a movie out of it. It's a great film too. I think it wins several Academy Awards."

"Oh yeah?"

They reached the main gate where Moonbeam finished the last of the joint and disposed of the roach paper on the ground.

***

Sunday morning, June 18, 1967, was calm. Ravi Shankar, an Indian sitar musician and composer, played a four-hour gig consisting of contemporary Indian tunes.

In the 1960s the hippies absorbed Eastern culture. They adopted much of the musical style and instruments, which they mixed with rock and roll. The outcome was called "the psychedelic experience."

During that Indian renaissance, Ravi Shankar rose to fame in the United States. Rated as one of the best contemporary Indian artists of all time, he began teaching Western musicians how to play the sitar. One of his students was George Harrison from the Beatles.

In June 1967, the Beatles released their LP *Sgt. Pepper's Lonely Hearts Club Band*, which quickly rose in the charts. Shankar's influence could clearly be heard on the album, which added to his fame. As a result, he was a highly sought after act, important enough to be one of the only musicians paid for his performance at the Monterey Pop Festival, receiving $3,000 for a four hour concert.

***

When they entered the fairgrounds Katie looked at Moonbeam's watch: 2:00. That gave them several hours to pull themselves together before the rock cluster of super bands started. Somewhere around five o'clock Buffalo Springfield would take the stage and from then until closing, roughly midnight, it would be one phenomenal act after another (The Who, the Grateful Dead, The Jimi Hendrix Experience, The Mamas and the Papas, and Scott McKenzie).

Katie was determined to see all of these acts come hell or high water, while sadly acknowledging that she had missed some of her favorites the night before (Moby Grape, The Byrds, Jefferson Airplane and Otis Redding). Just one more reason to hate Mark Rhodes.

"We're in. Now what?" Moonbeam asked.

"I guess that depends on what I *want* to do vs. what I *should* do."

"That's your bag, baby. I can't tell you what to do but you already know my opinion." Moonbeam shrugged her shoulders.

"I guess I should get this over with." Katie looked through her bag and seconds later came up with a handful of coins.

"I don't think it will cost that much," Moonbeam said.

"We are in Monterey," Katie reminded her.

"You can call them collect."

"Never. If I'm going to call, then I'm going to pay."

Katie walked to the phone booth next to the entrance. She dialed the number and dropped the correct amount of coins into the box. She stared at her bare feet, her heart beating wildly in her chest while she waited for the call to connect. Several clicks later, Pat Searfus answered the phone.

"Hello?"

"Mother."

"Katherine, thank God you called. We had a call from Lt. Dixon last night. We've been so worried. Honey, are you alright?" Her mother sounded frightened, something Katie had never heard before.

"I'm fine, a bit banged up but I'll be alright."

"How on earth did something like this happen?" Pat's frantic voice asked.

"What did Lt. Dixon tell you?"

"He said that you're at some concert in Monterey, that Mark Rhodes followed you there, and then he and a friend attacked you. Is that what really happened?"

"That's right, yesterday afternoon. He and Dennis Drummond, another of Dad's employees. They led me away from the concert and then...Mark attacked me."

Pat gasped. "Oh how awful. Thank God you're all right. I never saw something like this coming. Mark seemed like such a nice boy, a stable nice young man who was going places. How wrong I was." Katie could hear her mother pause and take a drag off of her cigarette. "I knew he had a thing for you but I never thought he was the psychotic type. Jesus, it just shows that you never really know anyone."

"I tried to tell you and father that there was something wrong with him."

"Yes, honey, you sure did. It's true you sensed something was wrong with him from the very beginning. I'm sorry your father and I missed that."

"Mark puts on a good act, that's all."

"Katherine, who was this other man? The one who stopped the attack?"

"What?"

"Lt. Dixon said that the attack was interrupted by another man, someone who saved you and then just disappeared."

"Yeah, that's true too."

"Was it the young man that you brought to the party?

"Yep, his name is Dylan Taylor."

"He just disappeared after the attack? Where did he go?"

"I don't know, he was there, and then he wasn't."

"The lieutenant said that he's a biker, someone affiliated with the Hells Angels?"

"That's right."

"Well, it's a good thing he was at the concert. What would have happened if he hadn't been?"

"Mark would have raped and killed me."

The line went silent. Pat was drinking; Katie could hear the ice cubes tinkling in the glass.

"Honey, your father's standing here. He wants to talk to you." Pat dropped the phone and before Katie could say a word her father's voice came over the line.

"Katie, are you alright?"

"Yeah, I'm fine. I'm sort of rattled but...I'm okay." Katie almost said that it was worth it just to get the legacy of Mark Rhodes off her back but remained silent.

"Honey, I'm so sorry that we tried to push that monster on you. Your mother and I believed that he was good husband material. How he was able to fool us, fool *me,* for three years, I don't know. Thank God you were able to see through his façade. I can't imagine what would have happened if you would have married him."

"I would have been miserable. He would have cheated on me with multiple women and then he would have weaseled himself into taking over the company. Once he did that then he would have walked away with a pregnant hussy named Tiffany. And worse of all, that child, her child would have ended up inheriting the firm. That's what would have happened."

Her father said nothing and Katie wondered if she had said too much.

"I guess it doesn't matter. He's in jail and he probably won't be working for you when he gets out?"

"*If* he gets out anytime soon. I have the best attorneys in San Francisco working on this. I'm hoping to keep that boy in the can for a very long time."

"Good, he needs to be locked up. I hope he rots in there," Katie said. "Dad, what do you know about the other guy in Mark's scheme? I know he works for you, or he did."

"Dennis Drummond? He's been with us a little over a year. He works beneath Mark, nothing special, just a gopher of sorts."

"Did Lt. Dixon tell you anything about him?"

"That he participated in your abduction and that Mark paid him for his part in the sick plan."

"Did he tell you about Richard?"

"What about Richard?"

"Before they hauled Dennis off, he told me something and I believe him."

"Go on..."

"He said that Mark was responsible for Richard's decision to join the Marine Corps."

"How can that be? They didn't even know each other."

"According to Dennis, Mark befriended Richard. He said they hung out a lot and that Mark used the opportunity to manipulate him. Dennis said Mark wanted Richard out of the way, and that's why he talked him into joining the service."

Al was silent, thinking. Katie heard more ice cubes rattling together. "Jesus Christ, what kind of a person *is* he?"

"A bad one."

"I'll destroy him, Katie. I'll destroy both of them; I swear it."

"Speaking of Dennis Drummond, he's not such a bad guy, not really. I'm not saying he's a great guy either, he obviously took money from the slimebag, but when he realized that I was going to be hurt for real he did the right thing. Even if the right thing meant that he was going to go to jail, he still made that choice."

"Are you saying we should go easy on him?" Al asked.

"I think you should use him to prosecute Mark. Dennis knows a lot about Mark's activities behind your back. Don't you want to know what those activities are?" Katie asked.

"Yes, actually I do. I bet you're right, Dennis knows a lot."

"Well, I'm at this concert with friends and they're waiting for me so I should..."

"Katie, wait. When are you coming home?"

"Home?"

"When are you coming to visit?"

"I don't know."

This was a turn of events that Katie hadn't expected. She had forty-five years of resentment built up towards her parents. Now, the reason for that anger had ended. Mark Rhodes was locked in a cell, and she was hopeful she would never see him again.

"There's good news," Al added, trying to keep Katie on the phone longer. "Richards coming home for a week in August. He's not sure of the date yet, but he'll find out soon."

Of course, Richard would be home in August, and Katie had been waiting anxiously for that visit, knowing that originally it was the last time she would see her brother alive.

"We'll see you then, won't we?"

"Yes, I'll be there." Katie was very confused now that her worldview had been completely altered.

"Well, we should really let you get back to your concert, I suppose. When you get back to the city give us a call. Don't be a stranger, Katie."

Katie didn't know how she should feel. She needed time to digest all the changes. At the moment, all she knew was that she felt numb.

"Are you feeling better?" Moonbeam asked her.

"I don't think 'better' is the right word. Confused or shocked would be closer to what I'm feeling."

"You'll figure it out. At least you're talking to them now, that's a good start."

Katie nodded. Moonbeam was right, that *was* a good start.

"What do you want to do now?" Moonbeam asked.

"Pee."

"What?"

"I need to pee really bad before I can decide anything. Do you need to go too?"

"No, I'm good. I'll wait here and watch the crowd. Everything's groovy."

"Okay, won't be a minute." Katie walked towards the wooden bathrooms, surprised that for once there wasn't a line.

She used the facilities and then washed her face in the sink. Nervously she examined her wounds in the mirror. She looked at herself and gasped. She knew she was banged up but she didn't expect so many scrapes and bruises. She truly looked as if she had been in a prizefight.

She thought about applying makeup but gave up, knowing that it would never cover the wounds effectively, especially the nasty one across her throat. She ran cold water over a paper towel and dabbed at the scratches. When she was finished she dried her face carefully and walked out of the bathroom.

Lost in her own thoughts she failed to see a group of black men standing under the trees.

"Katie!." one of them yelled. Startled, she turned towards the voice. "That's your name right? You were one of the chicks giving out free samples of LSD at the Human Be-In."

She recognized him immediately and smiled back. Huey P. Newton stood in full Black Panther attire with several men, one who looked like Bobby Seale, and a woman who looked remarkably like Angela Davis.

"Yeah, I sure was. I'm surprised you remember me though," she said as he walked towards her.

"I have a good memory. You gave my group a compliment; you said that we were doing great things for the people of Oakland."

"That's right, I did say that, and I still believe it's true."

"Ouch!" Huey said when he got close enough to notice the injuries on her face. "What happened to you?" He pulled a cigarette out of his pocket and lit it.

"I had a confrontation with a would-be suitor, but it's settled now."

"Wow, that's some confrontation. Anything I can do to help?"

"No, as I said it's all settled. Believe me, the guy who did this looks worse than I do. He's in jail so it's all cool."

"Damn, baby, you're all bruised up. Who is this clown?" Huey turned her face side-to-side looking at her wounds.

"A guy who wouldn't take no for an answer. A friend of mine interrupted him, or it would have been worse."

Several more members of the Black Panthers joined the group and wanting to leave, one of them yelled out, "Is everything cool, Huey?"

"All good, man, just give me a minute would you?" He turned back to Katie. "Listen, if he becomes a problem when he gets out just let me know, okay?"

"How would I find you?"

"In Oakland, baby. You come there and ask around. It's a piece of cake to find any one of us as long as you're a friend."

Katie smiled and he started to walk off. "Hey by the way," she called after him, "who did you come here to see?"

"Do you really need you ask? Jimi Hendrix of course."

"Of course." Katie waved goodbye to her new friend.

She found Moonbeam where she had left her, not far from the payphones.

"Not very warm today," she commented as she approached.

The day was cool, as Katie had predicted. It even looked as if it might rain. Katie knew, though, that the day would remain overcast, misty and cool, much like the emotions inside her, but it wouldn't rain..

"Who were you talking to?" Moonbeam asked.

"What?"

"The black man that you were talking to over by the bathrooms...isn't he a Black Panther?"

"Oh yeah, Huey Newton, he's a Panther alright."

"How on earth do you know him?" Moonbeam asked surprised and concerned.

"I met him at the Human Be-In when we were handing out LSD samples. I guess you could say we're friends." Katie never thought she would be referring to a member of the Black Panthers as a friend; how things had changed this time around.

"Isn't he scary?"

"Scary? No, not at all. He's actually a good guy. He offered to help me out with Mark if he comes back." Katie giggled, thinking of how Mark Rhodes would react to a visit by several members of the Black Panthers.

"They look scary, all of them."

"They aren't scary. They're just a bunch of guys trying to protect their own while trying to rise above the ridiculous racism in our country."

"But the news says—"

"The news is full of shit. Don't believe everything the media tells you."

The Black Panthers, a group unknown in January when they appeared at the Human Be-In, were now a well-known national phenomenon.

Their rise to fame came on May 2, 1967 when a group of thirty some-odd Black Panthers in traditional attire (black leather jackets, berets and dark sunglasses) crossed the lawn of the state capitol in Sacramento. Many were armed with shotguns, which they kept carefully aimed at the sky.

When they approached the capitol building, Governor Ronald Reagan was outside addressing a group of schoolchildren. When he caught sight of the Panthers he turned on his heels and ran inside.

The group approached, marching in tight formation, and when they reached the steps of the capitol they turned and faced the crowd.

Their leader, Bobby Seale, read a mandate addressed to "The American people in general and black people in particular." In it, he detailed the "terror, brutality, murder, and repression of black people" practiced by "the racist power structure of America," and concluded his speech by saying that "the time has come for black people to arm themselves against this terror before it is too late."

The Panthers then marched into the capitol building and onto the assembly floor where a debate over the Milford Act (an act aimed at prohibiting citizens from carrying loaded weapons on their persons or in their vehicles) was in session.

The result was chaos. State legislators dove under desks and screamed at the militant group not to shoot. Security guards quickly surrounded the Panthers, took their weapons away, and herded them into the hallway where, before being led into an elevator, a journalist yelled, "Wait, who are you?" A very young sixteen-year old, Bobby Hutton, yelled back, "We're the Black Panthers. We're black people with guns, what about it?"

Katie couldn't hide her amusement when she thought of the Black Panthers. She couldn't help but think of *Barbequing with Bobby Seal.* In 2014 he had become a cooking enthusiast known for his excellent DVDs and cookbooks on the subject.

Ultimately he would trade in his young militant ways for his declaration and bill of rights intended for all BBQ lovers.

"When in the course of human development it becomes necessary for us, the citizens of the Earth, to creatively improve the culinary art of barbe-que'n in our opposition to the overly commercialized bondage of "cue-be-rab" (barbecuing backwards); and to assume, within the realm of palatable biological reactions to which the laws of nature and nature's God entitle us, a decent respect for all the billions of human taste buds and savory barbeque desires; we the people declare a basic barbeque bill of rights, which impels us to help halt, eradicate, and ultimately stamp out "cue-be-rab!" (Bobby Seale 2009).

Time sure changed things. Katie wondered what the Panthers would say if she marched back right now and told them that the first African American president would be elected in 2008. Instead, she turned and watched them walk towards the arena.

***

Ron wasn't sure what he felt. Was it hurt, confusion, betrayal, or all three? What he did know is that he had to get away.

Today was the third and last day of the concert. For him it felt like they had arrived months ago, not just days. So much had happened, things he had never expected.

When they left 'Frisco, he thought that he and Katie were on their way to becoming a couple. Now he knew that would never happen. She was in love with a biker named Dylan. They might not be 'officially' together, but that didn't change things for Ron; he had no intentions of playing second best.

He had waited a long time for the right lady to come along. He thought that lady was Katie, but he was wrong. That put him back on the market, a place he was familiar with. The situation with Katie hurt, he couldn't lie about that, but he had to believe that somewhere out there he would find the right woman. All he needed now was to nurse his wounds. That was his intention when he arrived at the beer booth.

"I'll have two large ones," he told a robust woman behind the counter.

She filled the order, took the cash, and handed him two large beers. He finished the first of the beers in a single gulp. Then he wiped his mouth on the sleeve of his jacket and started on the next one.

A dark haired hippie girl watched his movements and several minutes later she approached him.

"Hey, don't I know you?" she asked.

Ron turned to look at her. She was pretty. She had long dark hair and chocolate colored eyes that seemed to twinkle in the daylight. He didn't know her name but she sure did look familiar. He shrugged.

"I know who you are," she said, snapping her fingers. "You're Katie's roommate, the guy that owns the house on Page Street."

"Ron," he said. "Guilty as charged."

"I'm Robin Crosby, Katie's former roommate." They shook hands.

"Oh yeah, Robin. I remember you. You were there the day I shoved her stalker freak to the ground."

"Yeah I sure was, that was groovy. I was hoping you would punch him in the face too, but I guess you're a lot nicer than I am."

"I should have."

"Where is Katie?" Robin asked, searching the area behind him.

"She's with Moony, I'm not sure where they are. I'm solo today."

"Oh, well I hope everything is okay?"

"To tell you the truth it's been a really long twenty-four hours. Katie is fine, she's here someplace as I said before, but yesterday afternoon she was attacked by the very same stalker dude, Mark Rhodes."

"What?"

"Yeah, the piece of shit followed her here. She wandered off alone and he coaxed her down to the creek where he tried to rape her."

"My God! Is she okay?"

"Yeah, apparently somebody named Dylan caught him in the act and beat the shit out of the asshole, sending him to the hospital."

"Damn, that's crazy. Was he arrested or just hospitalized?" Robin asked.

"Both. He was arrested and there's going to be a court case I would imagine."

"Wow, and she's here you say, walking around?"

"Katie's fine, don't worry. This guy Dylan, he got Mark Rhodes before he could really do anything to her. She has some minor scrapes and bruises, but nothing worse, thank God."

"My God, that's terrible. I just knew he would do something; maybe not this bad, but I knew he wasn't going to just walk away. That's why I thought it was a good idea for her to move into your place. I thought he might not bother her if she was living with male roommates, but I guess he was sicker than I thought."

"A lot sicker."

"You know he tried to ask me out, right?"

"Really?"

"Yeah, he called me from the Travelodge he was staying at, the same day as the confrontation. Get this, the freak wanted me to have dinner with him. Oh, he said he wanted to discuss Katie, but that was bullshit."

"What a prick."

"Yes, exactly. Listen, I know this might sound blunt, but why aren't you with her today? Shouldn't you be by her side?"

"What do you know about Dylan?"

"Dylan?" She blinked rapidly before she directed her gaze at the ground.

"So you do know something about him?"

"Not much. I've heard her talk about him, that's about it."

"Did you know that she loves him?"

"She's never said that to me, but I have gotten that impression."

"Yeah, well that's why I'm out here solo."

"Is she with Dylan?"

"No. From what I understand, Dylan and Frog are both gone."

"Gone?"

"Yeah, as I said before, it's been a rough twenty-four hours."

"I'm sorry."

"For what? It's not your fault. It's not anyone's fault I guess; it's just the way things turn out sometimes." He smiled weakly. "But usually this is how things turn out for me."

"I'm sorry that you're hurting," Robin said.

"Thanks."

"What are you going to do now, wander around all day and miss the rest of the concert?"

"I don't know. I haven't planned that far ahead. I don't think I want to go back to the seats yet, but then I'm not sure that I ever will."

"That's a bummer, man. The best part of the concert is coming up too. Buffalo Springfield's on next and then The Who, some group from the UK that is supposedly going places.

"Yeah, that's what I've heard. Oh well, maybe if I get drunk enough I'll go sit down for a while." Ron took a long drink of his beer.

"Why don't you come and sit with us?"

"What?"

"One of our friends had to split early, work I think. Anyway, his seat is open and I'm sure my friends won't mind if you join us.

"I don't know, man, I don't like to impose on anyone's gig, you know?"

Robin took a doobie out of her purse and lit it. "I'm new to this stuff." She took a few puffs. "It makes me cough."

"New to weed?" Ron accepted the joint from her outstretched hand and then puffed on it himself.

"I've been a sheltered child, but I'm coming out of my shell."

"Is that right?"

They both laughed.

"Seriously, it's true. I'm the intellectual type, college student. I don't get many chances to have fun, but from now on I think I'm going to make time."

"Right on, sister. So, where do you go to school?"

"San Francisco State, I'm pre-law.""

"A future lawyer."

"God willing." Robin sucked on the joint and coughed. "I love this stuff. Where has it been all my life?"

"It's been around, believe me."

"Have you been to college?" Robin asked.

"Yep, I did my stint. Chemistry major."

"Really, a chemist? That must be interesting."

"Oh yeah, especially these days," Ron chuckled. "It's been very helpful."

"So how about it? Do you want to join us?"

"First, who are 'we'?"

"Some chick named Simone, a guy named Bobby Eldridge, and Carlos, my date for the weekend."

"Carlos? Does he happen to play the guitar?"

"How did you know?"

"Katie happened to mention a guitarist named Carlos. I thought it might be the same person."

"You're right it is. Katie was supposed to come by our camp to hear him play. Now I know why she didn't make it."

"So this Carlos, he's a good guitarist?"

"That's an understatement. He's the best, that's why he's here; he wants to hear the other best, some cat named Jimi Hendrix."

"What's your friend's name again?" Ron asked, in better spirits now that the pot had brightened his mood.

"Carlos Santana. He's a regular in the Haight, maybe you've heard him play."

"No, I don't think so, but I'd like to. One of the best you say?"

"That's right."

"Groovy, does he have a manager?"

"A what?"

"A manager, do you know if he has one?" Ron's brain was reeling, making plans for the future. This guy would be famous, Katie had told him so.

"Wow, I don't know, I haven't asked him. You can ask him yourself when you meet him at the seats."

"Yeah, I guess I could do that."

"I've been gone a while, I should get back," Robin said. "I was only supposed to go for a pee, you dig? He's going to be wondering what happened to me if I don't get back soon."

"Right."

"So, are you coming with me or not?" she asked and Ron, who was slightly recovered from his broken heart, nodded and followed her.

I have to meet this young guitarist, he said to himself. This guy might be his goldmine.

***

Katie and Moonbeam settled into their seats, observing the crowd around them. There were people from all walks of life and that continued to amaze Katie. Strung out hippies sat with the well dressed and alongside families; various ages, ethnicities and subcultures all joining together in musical harmony.

Peter Tork stepped out on stage to address the audience.

"I'm here to fulfill a function this particular time around. One which I revel in and glory in, that of introducing the next group who are my favorites. Because of longstanding friendships with individuals as well as...I like the music." He chuckled. "I'd like to welcome now with a great big fat round of applause my favorite group, The Buffalo Springfield!"

The lights on the stage brightened and a psychedelic light show started . Colors swirled on the screen behind the stage and the band, consisting of Stephen Stills, Dewey Martin, Bruce Palmer, Richie Furay and David Crosby, stepped onto the stage.

After a short psychedelic musical introduction, the band broke into their famous song, "For What it's Worth." When they reached the chorus, everyone in the arena was on their feet dancing in the aisles.

"Stop children what's that sound? Everybody look what's going down," the crowd sang along with the band.

The second tune, a calmer one this time entitled "Clancy Can't Even Sing," settled the crowd, and many returned to their seats.

"I wonder where Ron is?" Moonbeam whispered.

"Hiding from me, I'm afraid," Katie whispered back.

"What happened between the two of you?"

"I told him I loved him."

"Really?"

"Yep, and then I called him Dylan."

"Wow, that's a real bummer."

Katie nodded. "Not much I can say to justify that comment, is there?"

The crowd around them swayed, flowers of every shade bounced on heads, necks, and decorated the arena. This was bliss, Katie felt, everyone together in peace, grooving as if nothing else in the world mattered.

When Buffalo Springfield ended, Katie's heart beat wildly. *The Who is next!* she thought to herself excitedly. She was about to watch their first US concert and unlike the rest of the audience, she knew how it would end.

This would be the first time that Peter Townshend, or anyone else for that matter, destroyed their instrument on stage. The crowd would go wild. She had seen the video, but now she was here in person watching the show live.

The Monterey Pop Festival was the changing of the guard for the British bands there. The keys to the Americas were handed over to The Animals, The Who, and the Jimi Hendrix Experience. These bands were unlike any that the crowd had ever witnessed before, and the excitement that they brought would explode, making them, as well as many other artists at the festival, overnight international sensations.

An announcer offered the following brief introduction and then history was made: "I'd like to introduce you to an act from England, who have been passed by slightly in America, but they won't be after this. And, this is a group who will destroy you completely in more ways than one. This is The Who, this one."

Band members Keith Moon, Peter Townshend, Roger Daltrey, and bass guitarist John Entwistle stepped onto an American stage for the first time, using borrowed amps since they left their high powered ones in England to save money.

Keith Moon, dressed in a long sleeved red silk shirt and love beads, set the tone with an elaborate drum solo that only he could deliver. As he basically went crazy on the drums, "Substitute" started. The sound drifted over the arena and the American counterculture got their first taste of the future of British rock and roll.

Behind the band the psychedelic oil show wrapped itself around a flashing green strobe light, which simply read, The Who.

Roger Daltrey took the mic in both hands and mesmerized the audience as he sang.

"You think we look pretty good together but I'm just a substitute for another guy
I was born with a plastic spoon in my mouth..."

sang the shaggy haired Daltrey, clad in a multicolored, fringed cape that encircled his body when he periodically spun around. On his left, a very young Peter Townshend wooed the crowd with his incredible talent on lead guitar. Dressed in a flowered shirt and ruffled cravat, Townshend swung his arms in his 180 degree trademark move as he played to his first American audience.

"These guys are great!" Moonbeam said.

"Just wait, you haven't seen anything yet," Katie said, preparing her.

"That drummer, he just goes insane doesn't he?" Moonbeam said, staring at Keith Moon.

"He's one of the best ever, but then again so is this band."

The set rolled by as the audience, enthralled by the band's unique moves, swayed and grooved to the music. And then the last song, the one that Katie had been waiting for. She knew the impact it would have on the audience so she smiled and rubbed her hands together in anticipation.

The Who and The Jimi Hendrix Experience, specifically Peter Townshend and Hendrix, were rivals. Both men, incredibly talented guitarists, had similar endings to their acts and both wanted to be the first to play that evening. Eventually, a coin toss by John Phillips of the Mamas and the Papas would decide the matter. Peter Townshend called the winning combination and The Who won. They were the first of the two bands to take the stage.

Pete Townshend innocently finished his song, "You Are Not Forgotten", and then the lights dimmed, Keith Moon changed the beat, and Roger Daltrey declared his loyalty to "My Generation."

Katie watched the band, but also the audience, waiting for their reaction to what she knew was the climax of their performance.

Towards the end of the song, Keith Moon delivered an outstanding drum solo and then Townsend joined in. At first he bounced his guitar against objects on the stage, catching it and still playing it in between hits. Then he progressed to throwing it on the ground, and finally deliberately demolishing the instrument by beating it repeatedly on the stage, swinging it like an axe.

The guitar broke into a million pieces, and a very shocked audience looked on. They gasped loudly when the preplanned smoke bombs went off behind the amps. Then, in mass confusion, stagehands jumped on the stage and tried to rescue expensive equipment, not knowing that the demolition and the explosions were part of the act. When it was over Pete's guitar lay in pieces on the stage as he, Roger Daltrey, and John Entwistle walked off stage.

Keith Moon, still in the heat of the moment, continued his solo, beating at his drums relentlessly. When finished, he kicked the drum set over and then casually walked off the stage ending The Who's first American performance.

***

Ron sat beside Robin. On her other side the guitarist known as Carlos leaned forward. Ron looked at the skinny kid. He had wild, curly hair and didn't really look like much, but even from where he was sitting, Ron could tell there was a presence about this young man. It was just a feeling but Ron thought the musician had star quality.

On stage, the Grateful Dead featuring Jerry Garcia, Bob Weir, Phil Lesh, Pigpen McKernan, and Bill Kreutzmann were on their last song, "Alligator/Caution Don't Stop on the Tracks." Ron had heard the Dead plenty of times but tonight they were different. Like many of the bands playing at the festival, tonight they were on fire.

Jerry Garcia's fingers flew over the strings and Pigpen McKernan's keyboard was smoking. Bob Weir told the audience "You know what folding chairs are for don't you? They're for folding up and dancing on." The crowd grooved and Ron swayed along with the rest of them, truly believing this was one of the Dead's best ever performances.

At the end of the number, the MC, a very nervous Peter Tork of the Monkees, entered the stage and talked briefly with bassist Phil Lesh, who prompted Tork to address the audience.

"There is a huge crowd outside that continues to try to climb over the fence. I guess it was rumored that the Beatles might be here." Tork laughed. "Since this is the last night and there's a lot of people outside the stadium, it makes sense to just open the gates and let them in." The crowd roared in approval, the gates were opened, and a huge mass of people from outside joined the stadium audience.

Ron didn't really know much about the next act except that they were from London and that the singer/guitarist was an American. He knew that Robin's friend was here specifically to see Hendrix and now that the Grateful Dead were finished with their set, Carlos was literally bouncing in anticipation.

"I love the Grateful Dead. No matter how many times I see them their act never gets old," Robin said excitedly. "They have so much energy when they perform."

"You don't even know about energy," Carlos said. "Wait until you hear this next guy. He is out of sight, man, just out of sight."

"How do you know him?" Ron asked. "I've never even heard of the dude before."

"Man, I'm a guitarist," Carlos said. "This guy you're about to see is the greatest guitarist of all time. The sounds he can get out of his instrument are out of this world."

Ron wasn't sure how one guitarist could be better than most of the others who had played here, but he decided to reserve his opinion until after the band's performance.

"Won't Moonbeam and Katie be worried about you?" Robin asked unexpectedly. "Do you think you should check in with them, just to let them know that you're alright?"

"I don't know. Katie's probably glad she doesn't have to face me. It would just be awkward. That is, if she even remembers. She was really fucked up."

"Maybe you should give her the benefit of the doubt, talk to her. You know? Maybe it was just the drug talking."

Ron shook his head. "You know that's not true. She has a real thing for this biker."

Robin looked down at her feet and said nothing.

"Look, I dig Katie," Ron said, "but I'm not going to be her consolation prize, you know what I mean? Now that I know she loves someone else, even if he's gone for good it doesn't matter, I can't go ahead with anything."

"I really am sorry," Robin said again.

"I'm not, it's better that I know the truth. This could have gone on for a lot longer and that just would have made it all worse." Robin smiled, and Ron thought she was pretty and kind. He liked her.

"You're going to have to face her on the ride home," Robin reminded him.

"Yep, I will."

"You're leaving in the morning?"

"When we get up, yeah, probably 10-ish. What about your group?" Ron asked.

"Same, whenever we get up and on the road."

The lights flashed, Carlos mumbled something in Spanish, and then the PA system announced Brian Jones' name. The lone Rolling Stone walked on stage ready to introduce the English band with an American singer.

His first words were inaudible since the crowd was applauding wildly, but they soon quieted so that Jones' voice could be heard.

"This next performer is the most exciting band I've ever heard, The Jimi Hendrix Experience."

The stage went dark, a guitar solo could be heard , and then with a flash the lights came on, illuminating the band. Seattle-born Jimi Hendrix was home to make his mark on the Americas.

Jimi was dressed in the height of London's hippie fashion: an orange frilled shirt, multicolored paisley jacket, tight red pants, and to top it off, a groovy headband and a purple feathered boa around his neck.

Ron had never seen anything like this. Right off the bat he understood why Carlos thought this guitarist was out of the ordinary. There was nobody like Jimi Hendrix. Ron was sure this band would take the country by storm.

The band finished their first song, "Killing Floor," and then Jimi spoke to the audience.

"Yeah, what's happening, brother?" he asked with an American Northwestern accent. "Here's another little thing we have called 'Foxy Lady.' My fingers will move as you see? You will hear the sound that you hear, but...dig this."

The Hendrix band erupted into a tune that had the whole audience stunned by his unbelievable talent.

"You've got to be all mine, Foxy Lady," he sang. The audience was electrified, just like the guitar he played.

"Is this guy groovy or what?" Carlos asked ,satisfied that his point had been made.

Ron nodded in disbelief. "This guy is unbelievable, Brian Jones is right."

By the second song, "Like a Rolling Stone," Jimi had lost the jacket and the boa, revealing his long sleeved frilly orange shirt and the black vest that covered it. Around his neck he wore a gold medallion that moved as he dipped and swayed to the music. And then he did something that Ron had never seen a performer do. On a break in the lyrics, Jimi Hendrix played the guitar with his teeth.

Ron looked at Carlos and nodded enthusiastically. "You're right man, this guy is the best."

The onlookers were lost in the performance. Ron glanced at the faces around him, noticing the look of pure amazement, which he was sure his own face revealed.

In the middle of "Hey Joe" Hendrix again played the guitar with his teeth, this time doing a whole solo without once looking up. The audience was awed. When his second solo included playing the guitar behind his head there were no words that could explain this man's talent.

"The Wind Cries Mary," slowed the set down, calming the audience, and then the next song, "Purple Haze", set the audience on fire again.

"Excuse me while I kiss the sky...whatever it is that girl put a spell on me...purple haze in my eyes."

A stoned chick behind Ron was rocking in her seat almost falling over, her eyes glassy and barely open.

Jimi continued to dip and sway, no break at all in his guitar playing. And then the final song, "Wild Thing."

At the beginning of the song Hendrix played the guitar upside down while it was behind his back. The start of the song was slow and Jimi appeared almost sensual in the way he played the instrument. He dipped to the floor and did a summersault across the stage and then with the guitar behind his back, played the chorus of the song.

The suggestive performance became even more sexual as Hendrix rubbed his guitar on the amp behind him and then slowly collapsed to the floor where he literally rode his guitar while still playing the strings.

Disappearing for a moment, Jimi stepped behind the stage, and when he reappeared he was holding a can. His guitar still lying on the ground, Jimi opened the can, recognizable now as lighter fluid. He squirted the contents on the guitar and then lowered himself to the floor where he kissed the head of his instrument. One match thrown onto the guitar was enough to burst it into flames to the screams and roars of the crowd.

Hendrix raised his guitar in true Pete Townshend style, and he too demolished his instrument, which in turn put out the fire. Before walking offstage Hendrix took the broken neck of the guitar and threw it into the audience.

"You see what I mean, man?" Carlos bubbled enthusiastically.

"Can you play like that?" Ron yelled over the roaring crowd.

"Almost, I just don't do any of the fancy shit." And for reasons unknown, Ron knew that Carlos was telling him the truth.

***

Katie was saddened that the weekend was coming to an end. They were in the middle of the Mamas and the Papas act, listening to "California Dreaming" when she realized that her world had drastically changed.

She had waited so long for this concert, knowing it would be a turning point, but that turning point had always seemed so far away and now that it was looming just around the corner, she felt numb.

She looked at Moonbeam happily singing along with the band, and wondered what the two of them would find when they returned to San Francisco. Frog and Dylan were gone, she didn't know if they would ever see them again, and that made her feel empty.

"*Monday, Monday*," Katie sang along with Denny Doherty knowing that, come tomorrow, she would be living the tune. This Monday would be a downer, she was sure of it.

Scott McKenzie walked on stage wearing a long silk robe like the rest of the band members. The Mamas and the Papas backed him up as he sang "San Francisco", the song John Phillips had written for the festival. The song that would become the mantra for the Summer of Love.

> *"If you're going to San Francisco*
> *be sure to wear some flowers in your hair.*
> *If you're going to San Francisco*
> *you're going to meet some gentle people there.*
> *All across the nation such a strange vibration*
> *people in motion there's a new generation with a new explanation."*

"Can you believe it's almost over, Moony?"

"I know, it went by so fast. Well, most of it anyways."

Mama Cass introduced the last song of the festival, the finale "Dancing in the Streets."

"Hey, you want to cut out before this huge crowd does?" Moony asked. Katie looked around the arena, which was overflowing with people now that the gates were wide open.

"Yeah I think I do. Otherwise it might take us an hour or more to get back to the parking lot."

"What about Ron?"

"What about him? I have to face him sometime, he's driving us home."

The girls walked to the exit with a horde of others who decided that leaving early was a good idea.

"Do you think they're safe?" Moony asked.

"Yes, I think they are," Katie said, knowing she was referring to Frog and Dylan.

"How can you be sure? I mean they could have been...killed when they left here."

"No, they're safe. Dylan is no dummy, and Frog will listen to him. I don't know where they'll go but I'm sure Dylan had this completely planned out beforehand."

"I sure hope you're right."

"I am."

The walk back to camp took longer than the two nights prior, and when they got there it was noisy. Many people were leaving the parking lot, trying to get on the highway before the concert actually ended. Katie was glad they weren't driving anywhere tonight. By the looks of the traffic it would take forever to get out of Monterey County; another reason Dylan had left the night before.

They arrived at the camp and as Katie had predicted, Ron was nowhere to be found. Fortunately the van was still there, which meant he was still planning on driving them home.

"Now what?" Moonbeam asked.

"Now we watch the traffic split and then we go to sleep in the van, the same as last night. When morning comes we'll go home to San Francisco where everything will be different for both of us."

"That's your best advice?"

"It's my only advice," Katie said. She poured herself a cup of cold black coffee, knowing that it was going to be a very long night.

Chapter 39

Robin Crosby called her next witness to the stand. Sixty-eight year old Dennis Drummond made his way across the room. With the use of a cane he limped into the witness chair and was sworn in by the bailiff.

Robin cleared her throat as she approached the witness. "Mr. Drummond, how many years have you been working for Mark Rhodes?"

"Forty-seven in April."

"And what is your job exactly?"

"I preform whatever's needed."

"Whatever's needed? What does that mean, Mr. Drummond?"

"It means that whatever Mr. Rhodes wanted me to do, I did."

"Can you give the court an example?"

"Objection, leading the witness," Brian Ebbes, Mark's lawyer called out.

Judge Allen didn't blink an eye. "Overruled. The witness will answer the question."

"An example.... well, I would go through company records, mostly private information. I learned to do background checks, basically playing private detective, investigating both clients and employees. My job essentially was to dig up any information that could be used against potential opponents."

"In case Mark needed it?"

"That's right. I dug up the dirt and Mr. Rhodes would use that information to his advantage. If someone were cheating on his wife or their income tax, I would know about it. Draft dodgers, homosexuals— not that any of that matters now— but there was a time it did, you understand. I would find out everything that I could, and then I would provide the information to Mr. Rhodes. He would use that knowledge in whatever way he deemed necessary."

"So you would do anything?" Robin asked.

"Within reason."

"Spying?"

"Sure, but no more than what the federal government uses against us ordinary citizens," Dennis answered, trying to justify his actions.

"So spying, extortion, blackmail, how about murder?" Robin raised her voice slightly on the last word to make sure the courtroom caught her question.

"Never!" Dennis's wrinkled face darkened.

"Okay, spying, extortion and blackmail but you drew the line at murder. Is that what you're telling me, Mr. Drummond?"

"No murders," Dennis repeated.

"How about false documentation, forged signatures? Have you seen much of that in your forty-seven years of service?"

Dennis smiled. "Much of my job dealt with forged or illegal documents."

"Can you be more specific?"

"I've changed documents, substituted documents for originals, transferred signatures from one to another. As I said before, whatever was needed, that's what I did."

"And did Mr. Rhodes use any of those tactics to inherit the company?"

"Objection!"

"Overruled," said the judge.

"Sure he did. When Mr. Searfus died, Mr. Rhodes hired multiple attorneys. Their primary job was to find loopholes in everything, any legal document attached to the firm as well as to the old man's will."

"What were they looking for?"

"Ways to negate old business deals. Mark assigned a full time staff to work on just that."

"During your time of employment, did the staff work on anything related to Katherine Rhodes?"

"Oh yeah. One of those old business deals had to do with Mrs. Rhodes. Mark was looking for a way to have his wife cut out of her father's will, more specifically, ownership rights to the company. He looked at every loophole imaginable and finally decided the easiest road to take was to have her deemed mentally incompetent."

"Mentally incompetent? How does one go about doing that?" Robin asked.

"First, we had to obtain her medical records. At the time Mrs. Rhodes was suffering from stress related illnesses, so it was easy. Mark had his attorney draw up some legal documentation. I think the way it was worded had to do with medical issues and mistakenly thinking it had to do with her health, Katherine signed the document. What it really did was to give proxy over to Mark, putting him in control of the corporation. Then he had the board vote her off due to her 'incompetence,' which she had unwittingly confirmed by signing the legal paperwork.

"Because of that signed document it was easy to vote her off the board and eventually eliminate her from the company altogether. The board members at the time actually believed that's what Katherine wanted, so essentially Mark duped them too."

"Objection, Your Honor, speculation."

"Overruled." Judge Allen glared at the defense attorney.

"When were you made aware of Mr. Rhodes' intentions of taking over the company?"

"When I was hired in 1965."

"What were you told about your job description?"

"Mark made it very clear that he wanted to take over the company and that he would be willing to do anything to obtain his goal. I was hired to work under the radar."

"And that was made clear to you from the very beginning of your employment?"

"Yes, ma'am."

"What can you tell the court about Mark's quest to eliminate the Searfus heirs?"

Dennis laughed wryly. "In 1967 Mark talked Richard Searfus into enlisting in the US Marine Corps. He wanted to make sure that the number one heir was out of the picture, at least temporarily, until he could take over. Once Richard was gone, Mark's first mission was to establish himself into a comfortable position in the firm so that when and if Richard came back he would be in charge of junior. Of course, he was hoping that Richard would make a career out of the Marines, ideally giving up his claims to the company so that Mark could move in and take over, but then conveniently for Mark, Richard died in 'Nam."

"And how did Mr. Rhodes react to the news of Richard Searfus' death?"

"Too damn happy. He joked about it. He took several of his special staff out for drinks to celebrate."

"Were you among them?"

"No, I had a kid brother in the service so Richard's death hit a little too close to home."

"But your colleagues attended?"

"They sure did."

"Why would Mark Rhodes do something like that?" Robin asked.

"Because with Richard gone he knew the company was his. Mark was a self-proclaimed ladies' man. The family was in mourning over Richard's death and that made stepping in easy, especially with Mr. Searfus' hippie daughter."

"Mr. Searfus' daughter?"

"That's right. Katherine was grieving, and in her sorrow, she fell right into Mark's plans. Within two months of Richard's death they were officially together, and within six months they were married. The rest was easy."

"Do you think that you played an important role in Mr. Rhodes' success?" Robin asked.

"Most definitely, and I was well paid for my part."

"Why do you think you were so valuable as an employee?"

"For my judgment skills. Mark was— is— impulsive. There were many times in our business relationship where I stopped him from making some pretty clear mistakes. Luckily for him he listened to me and that, I believe, is how he made it to the top of the firm."

"Can you share one of these bad judgment calls with the court?"

"In 1967 Mark Rhodes and I attended a three-day concert together. While there, he had some crazy idea and I stopped him from pursuing it."

"What was this crazy idea?"

"Mark wanted to play hero, he thought it might make Katherine like him. You see, up until that point, Miss Searfus wouldn't give him the time of day, so he came up with some lame brain idea. He was going to pay me to attack her, so he could run in and save her. The way Mark figured it, that would make him look like a hero." Dennis laughed, remembering.

"And you stopped this idea from occurring?"

"Damn right I did. I didn't want any part of it, no matter how much money he was willing to pay me."

"But you went to the concert?"

"Yeah, we went for all three days."

"And how was Mark Rhodes' behavior at the concert?"

"Agitated, obsessive. He spent most of his time following Katherine around."

"Following? Can you give the court an example?"

"Objection, Your Honor, speculation!" Ebbes, the defense attorney screeched again. "The witness can't make the presumption that Mr. Rhodes was obsessive or agitated! This is Mr. Drummonds' opinion and it has nothing to do with fact."

"Ms. Crosby, can you restate your question?" Judge Allen asked.

"Certainly, Your Honor. Mr. Drummond, during that weekend how did Mark Rhodes spend his time?"

"He followed Katherine Searfus around. He watched her from around corners or by hiding in trees and bushes. It was strange, but that was before I really knew Mr. Rhodes."

"Go on..." Robin prompted.

"Mark was prone to doing odd things, that's why our partnership was important. I kept him stable, on the straight and narrow, and he knew it."

"You kept him stable? How did you do that, Mr. Drummond?"

"Mark had a lot of harebrained ideas. Fortunately, he learned to trust me over the years. He would run his plans past me, and if I thought they were questionable, I would stop him in his tracks. That's how I kept him stable," Dennis said, shifting his body uncomfortably in the hard wooden chair.

"What if you hadn't been there?"

"I don't know. I always was there, so I'm not sure what he would have done without me."

"But you didn't fully trust his choices, is that right?"

"Yeah, that's right."

"Because he was impulsive and sometimes used bad judgment?"

"Yes, because of all of that."

"No further questions," Robin said. She walked away from the bench and sat beside Annie at the prosecution table. Across from them to their right sat Mark Rhodes and his attorney, Brian Ebbes.

Mark had aged in the past six months and he'd put on weight. His salon obtained tan was gone, all signs of Botox had worn off, and the color he normally rinsed in his hair was fading to gray. Now he looked like the little old man that he was, broken and weak.

Tiffany was no longer by his side. Robin had heard that she ran off with one of Mark's friends. The same man who looked remarkably like her son, Robbie.

Now Mark was alone with his attorney and occasionally his daughter Angela, who had returned from the Far East.

Angela was concerned about the future of the company. When her father's legal troubles started she returned from overseas fast to hire her own attorney, making sure that her interests were protected.

During the four months she had been back in the country, Annie could count the times Angela had visited her mother on one hand minus several fingers. Clearly, Angela was here for Angela and no other reason.

Brian Ebbes rose from the table, buttoned his jacket and approached the witness. At first he said nothing, pacing several times across the front of the courtroom for effect.

"Mr. Drummond," he said after a time, "you say that you have been employed by Mark Rhodes for the last forty-seven years?"

"Yes, that's right, I have."

"Yet," Mr. Ebbes referred to a document in his hand, "interestingly enough, you were living in Los Angeles for two of those years. Is that correct?"

"Yes but—"

"And you were working for an agency in Orange County."

"That's true too but—"

"But you were a consultant, is that what you want the court to believe?"

"That's right, I was a consultant. I did have an additional job but I continued my employment with Mr. Rhodes as well."

"So you would have the court believe that even though you were four hundred miles south and you had a full time job at the time, you were still actively involved in the Rhodes Corporation?"

"Yes that's correct."

"And how did you do that from such a long, long, distance?"

"I had guys who reported to me."

"And during that time Mr. Rhodes was able to function perfectly well without you around, isn't that right?"

"Yes, but my guys were on the case."

"But you made it seem as though Mr. Rhodes couldn't function without you, Mr. Drummond. As if he had all of his ideas and decisions run through you before making a move. That's what you told the court. You said that your rational decisions are how Mark Rhodes obtained and kept power."

"Yes but—"

"But for two years Mr. Rhodes did without your expertise and he ran the corporation just fine without your help. Isn't that right, Mr. Drummond?"

"Yes but—"

"No further questions, Your Honor."

Judge Allen formally released the witness from the stand.

Drummond's demeanor changed. Proud of his testimony but angry at this turn of events, his face grew solemn and hard as he left the stand. He avoided eye contact, especially with Mark Rhodes, who was glaring at him.

"Ms. Crosby, do you have another witness?" Judge Allen asked.

"Yes, Your Honor, I'd like to call Cheryl Alexander to the stand."

The thirty-something year old corporate attorney timidly took the stand where the bailiff swore her in.

"Ms. Alexander, can you tell the court how you know the defendant?"

"I work for Mr. Rhodes. At least I did before all of this took place."

"What job did you perform at the Rhodes Corporation?" Robin continued.

"I'm an attorney specializing in legal documentation," she mumbled.

"I'm sorry, I didn't hear you clearly. Can you please speak up?"

"I'm an attorney specializing in legal documentation," she repeated more clearly.

"Legal documentation? As I understand it, Mr. Rhodes had three attorneys that specialized in this field, you and two others?"

"Yes, that's right."

"Why did Mr. Rhodes need three attorneys who were all specialists in one field?"

Cheryl Alexander glanced at Mr. Rhodes, swallowed hard, and then turned her face away before answering.

"I'm sure I don't know."

"You don't know? There were three of you working on old, present and new documents, and you don't know why your coworkers were there?"

"I don't know."

"You sat beside these people every day. Are you trying to tell me that you didn't discuss cases or ask opinions? That none of you involved your coworkers in your cases? I find that hard to believe, Ms. Alexander. I'm an attorney too, and I can guarantee you that my colleagues have at least an inkling of what my cases are about."

"Maybe my coworkers aren't nosey like yours," Ms. Alexander snapped.

"Maybe, or maybe you're honoring your confidentiality agreement right now by not discussing your work with anyone. If that's the case I don't think your agreement is relevant when you're testifying, I think that would fall along the lines of perjury. You do realize that you've been sworn in, Ms. Alexander?"

"Of course I understand that, it's just that I don't fully understand the question."

"Were you required to sign a document when you were hired agreeing to keep your work confidential?"

"I don't know."

"You don't know, but you could have?"

"I could have, but frankly I don't remember."

"Let's see if we can refresh your memory, shall we? What company documents have you worked on?"

"Whichever ones I was asked to look at."

"What documents have you worked on, Ms. Alexander? It's a simple question really."

Cheryl tried to look at Mark but Robin blocked her view.

"Don't look at him, look at me."

Ms. Alexander did, but her face was flushed red with anger.

"What documents have you worked on?" Robin repeated.

"I've worked on old documents mostly, many from the 1960's and 70's."

"What possible relevance could documents that old have on the present day corporation?

"Many of them had to be revamped, modernized, you understand?"

"No, actually I don't understand. Give the court an example of a document that you specifically had to 'revamp' and why that was needed."

Cheryl was quiet. She swallowed several times nervously and then ran her hand through her shoulder length brown hair. "I worked on Mr. Searfus' will and the documents that turned the corporation over to his heirs," she said, almost in a whisper.

"His heirs? Who would that be?'

"It was an old will completed many years before his death. It mentioned both of Mr. Searfus' children, leaving equal parts to them."

"But there was only one surviving child," Robin stated.

"Yes, that's right, and the company was left, originally, to her."

"Her?"

"His daughter, Katherine Searfus Rhodes."

"I'm curious, why did Mr. Rhodes have you examining a will from 1973?"

"Mr. Rhodes was concerned over Katherine's mental capacity to run the company. Mr. Searfus had a clause in his will regarding 'sound mind' as a condition for administration of the firm. Mr. Rhodes felt that Katherine's medical issues fell within the boundaries of that clause. For the best interests of all, he took over the company. Today Rhodes Corporation is running smoothly and making a good profit. Obviously he did the right thing."

"In your opinion?"

"Yes, in my opinion."

"Ms. Alexander, did you ever meet Katherine Rhodes before the accident?"

"Once, at a cocktail party about a year ago."

"Did you converse with her?"

"I don't know. There were a lot of people at the party."

"So your opinion that Katherine wasn't able to run the company by herself was based on what evidence, since you can't remember whether you have ever talked to her or not?"

"It was based on medical records."

"Medical records that you've seen?"

Cheryl Alexander paused. She was sweating heavily, obviously uncomfortable with the questioning.

"Did you see the medical records, Ms. Alexander?" Robin repeated.

"Yes." She stared at her hands, which were curled protectively in her lap.

"So you looked at Ms. Rhodes' private medical records? Did she sign an authorization form for you to see them?"

"Mr. Rhodes had authorization."

"Are you sure? Did you see his authorization?"

"Well, not exactly."

"Are you a doctor, Ms. Alexander?"

"I'm an attorney."

"An attorney, not a doctor? Yet you went through medical records without the legal right to do so, and from those records, which I might add Mr. Rhodes didn't have authorization to use either, you made a medical diagnosis?"

"I didn't make a medical diagnosis. I simply drew up the prospective documents that needed to be signed by a trained physician."

"Papers drawn on documents that you had no right to have access to in the first place."

"I didn't have anything to do with the medical diagnosis, just the legal paperwork."

"Just the legal paperwork that you worked out after looking at Mr. Searfus' will and his daughter's private medical records, which Mr. Rhodes received fraudulently."

"Objection, Ms. Alexander isn't on trial here," Ebbes tried.

"No she isn't, but maybe she should be, as this is clearly illegal."

"Ms. Crosby, let's stay with the facts in this case," Judge Allen chided her.

"Of course, Your Honor, just the facts." Robin redirected her thoughts. "Ms. Alexander, you drew up documents using medical records provided by Mr. Rhodes. These records you took for face value assuming he had legal rights to them. You made the mistake of not checking to see if your client was telling you the truth. Therefore the documents that were signed by Katherine Rhodes were not legal to begin with."

"I don't know about that."

"Did you see legal documentation regarding the medical records before you went through them?"

"I told you I don't remember."

"And I told you that no legal authorization was given for anyone, including Mrs. Rhodes' husband, to go through those files. Files which were obtained under questionable circumstances."

"I don't know anything about that."

"Yet you went through Katherine's medical records trying to confirm a clause in her father's will. A clause that you knew would replace her as the rightful heir, and you did that without making sure that the documents you were using were obtained legally?"

"I told you, I don't remember."

"No further questions."

Mr. Ebbes took a sip of water then approached the bench. "Ms. Alexander ,did you willing participate in an investigation that you knew or suspected could be illegal?"

"Certainly not."

"When Mr. Rhodes asked you to go through old records did you think that his request was unusual?"

"No, not at all. Many corporations have clauses in their original documents. I've spent a lot of time going through old records for many employers.

"What do these documents have in common?"

"Most of them include a clause regarding the inheritor's ability to run the company. In this case, Mr. Rhodes was concerned, and of course he had a right to be."

"Because he was protecting his wife and her financial future?"

"Yes, in my opinion he was."

"No further questions."

Annie looked at Mark Rhodes and cringed when she saw a smile on the monster's face.

"The scum," she whispered to Robin.

"We've been through this before, Annie," Robin said quietly. "You have to let the case run its course. There's no telling how these things will turn out. Have some faith."

"I know, it's just that he and his daughter make me sick. Look at Angela, sitting there like a vulture hoping to cash in on her father's fall from grace."

"The apple doesn't fall far from the tree," Robin remarked.

"You're sure right about that."

Annie looked at her watch. It was four o'clock; another hour and court would be adjourned for the day, meaning that they would come back and do this all over again tomorrow. When would it ever end?

She shook her head and looked at the jury. She could tell they were obviously bored. All they wanted was to get this over with so that they could go home to their ordinary lives. She didn't blame them, she wanted the same thing, but it wasn't going to happen. During the past month this case had become high profile with massive media publicity. Annie was seen as the underdog who dared to take down the great empire of a distinguished member of the community. Whichever way this case turned out, her life would never be ordinary again.

The past six months had been hard. The court case was always looming in the back of her mind. She had been able to block Mark's requests for returned guardianship but that was only half of her battle. The rest had to do with taking over the firm, giving back what was Katherine's and then as guardian, managing the interests of her friend's estate.

With continued improvements in medicine, specifically stem cell research, there was always a chance that Katie would recover. Financially, Annie wanted to make sure that option was always possible. With her in charge of Katie's wellbeing, as well as her financial security, any new treatments that emerged could be promptly utilized.

If Mark was restored as guardian, or if Angela was able to take over the corporation, Annie knew what the outcome would be— her friend would spend the rest of her life in a nursing home with minimal medical care and no chance of a full recovery.

Annie was determined that wasn't going to happen, no matter how tiring the case became. She was in it for the long haul, and thankfully, so was Robin.

"Ms. Crosby, do you have any further witnesses?" Judge Allen asked.

"Not at this time, Your Honor. The prosecution rests."

Annie turned and stared at her.

"Mr. Ebbes, do you want to call your first witness?"

"Yes, Your Honor. The state calls Annie Sullivan to the stand."

Annie heard her name and held her breath. She knew this was coming, she just hadn't expected it today. Robin nodded in encouragement and mouthed the words that she would be all right.

She was nervous but managed to make it to the witness stand without tripping.

"Do you swear to tell the truth, the whole truth, and nothing but the truth so help you God?" the bailiff asked.

"I do."

Mr. Ebbes paced in front of the witness box without saying a word. Then he stopped directly in front of her and smiled. "How are you today, Ms. Sullivan?"

"I'm well, thank you."

"Ms. Sullivan, do you recall the telephone conversation that you had with Mr. Rhodes back in February 2014, where you discussed Mrs. Rhodes' legal guardianship?"

"Yes, I remember the conversation."

"Isn't it true that at that time Mark Rhodes was under a great deal of stress?"

"How would I know?"

"Did Mr. Rhodes confide in you during that conversation, telling you that he had a baby due in less than a month and that he was going through some legal issues of his own?"

"Yes, that's what he told me. Of course, I had called him after the hospital informed me that they were having problems getting him to consent to the medical procedures that Mrs. Rhodes needed to survive. During the conversation he told me he had too much on his plate. When I suggested that I take over guardianship Mr. Rhodes jumped at the opportunity, anxious to wipe his hands of his ex-wife's medical problems."

"Ms. Sullivan, that is speculation. When Mr. Rhodes signed over guardianship he did so with the understanding that after his son was born he would take back the care of his wife."

"That's not what he told me."

"Ms. Sullivan, isn't it true that you called with the intent of talking a distraught man into signing guardianship of his partner of forty-five years over to you?"

"No, that's not true. I took over guardianship of Katherine because Mark didn't want the responsibility. At the time he was in the middle of building a new family, which included filing for divorce from Katherine. A divorce which was stopped by the courts because of Mrs. Rhodes' medical condition."

"Was there a time limit set on guardianship?"

"No."

"But you couldn't locate Katherine's children at the time, isn't that true? In fact, her son still doesn't know about his mother's condition because he is working in an undisclosed location. Shouldn't her children have guardianship if their father is unable to perform the responsibility?"

"Her children were nowhere to be found."

"Then. But today her daughter is sitting right here in the courtroom."

"Her children weren't responding to phone calls. I've known Katherine Rhodes a long time, her children never respond to phone calls."

"Maybe to phone calls that they don't get?'

"Phone calls that they don't want." Annie turned to look at Angela. Of course she was here now since money and transference of the corporation were involved.

"Were there any time limits set on guardianship?" Mr. Ebbes repeated.

"No, I had my attorney draw up the paperwork. The word 'permanent' appears throughout the document. It would be real hard to miss it. Mark signed what he knew was a permanent document."

"According to you?"

"According to his signature and the multiple court appearances where guardianship has been repeatedly given to me."

"This was before Mrs. Rhodes' daughter Angela showed up."

"This was before Mrs. Rhodes' daughter Angela *bothered* to show up," Annie corrected,

"It's unusual for a non-relative to be granted such rights."

"Yes it is."

"A lot has happened since February," Ebbes said after several seconds of silence.

"That's true, a lot has happened."

"During that time Mr. Rhodes has reversed his decision for a divorce and the paperwork has been revoked. The family in question was inadvertently not formed, and Mr. Rhodes has remained with his legal wife. He has no intention of filing for divorce at this time. He has made his future plans clear that he is intent on caring for the woman he married forty-five years ago. This includes financial support by overseeing her inheritance. Isn't that what a marriage is supposed to be about, Ms. Sullivan?"

"A normal one, but not this one."

"Ms. Sullivan, that is your opinion, and the court is asking for facts. Should a spouse be responsible for their partner?"

"Yes," Annie replied, feeling pressured into her response.

"That's right, Ms. Sullivan. A spouse is supposed to be responsible for their other half and that is exactly what Mark Rhodes is trying to do. He turned guardianship over to you when he was unprepared emotionally to take on the task. That is no longer the case.

"Mr. Rhodes has made sure that the insurance company has taken care of his wife's needs and he has paid for any extras out of his own pocket. Katherine has been denied nothing in her care. Mr. Rhodes has handled his end perfectly, which means that we shouldn't even be here right now. The reason this case is still on the books is because it presents a financial gain for you, Ms. Sullivan, an opportunity that you're determined to profit from. Isn't that correct?"

"No, that's not correct. Katherine has received the best care possible because of my intervention. I'm the one who has been overseeing her care, not Mr. Rhodes."

"Can you prove that?"

"You can call the hospital or the insurance company and ask who they've been dealing with for the past six months. "

"I've done that, Ms. Sullivan," Mr. Ebbes said, holding a manila file over his head for the jury to see. "Here are the logs from the hospital where Ms. Rhodes is receiving long term care. As you can see, Mr. Rhodes has called there every day to check on his wife's progress and here..." he held up an additional file, "are the correspondence logs from the insurance company. As you can see, Mr. Rhodes has made an abundance of calls to them as well. Does that look like a neglectful husband who doesn't care about his wife?"

"No, but I'm sure you advised him to start making phone calls as soon as he hired you."

"Ms. Sullivan, isn't it true that by taking over Rhodes Corporation you stand to make a lot of money for yourself?"

"No. The profits from the company will be held in a medical trust for Ms. Rhodes. Nothing will come out of that account unless it's for her medical care."

"But you'll be taking over the company, meaning you'll be earning a salary to run things." Mr. Ebbes had a crooked smile on his face.

"Who said that I would be in charge of anything?" Annie asked.

"Then how do you plan on running the company? After all, you'll be cutting out the president, and I'm sure that will include other employees whom you feel might jeopardize your leadership. With those cuts how do you plan on continuing the positive growth the company has been experiencing?"

"Objection, Your Honor," Robin said. "This has nothing to do with Ms. Rhodes' care. Ms. Sullivan is not on trial here, and might I add that she already has legal guardianship."

"On the contrary, Your Honor," Ebbes countered, "this has everything to do with Ms. Rhodes' care. Ms. Sullivan is planning to take the company away from a productive president and a board of directors that he appointed. What's next? Is she going to place a comatose woman in charge? She said she's not planning on running the company, but someone has to. Who will that be? In the meantime, how is any of this going to benefit the corporation that is providing for Ms. Rhodes' continued treatment. With inexperienced employees how long will it take before things start to crumble, and when they do, what does that mean for Katherine Rhodes?"

"Mr. Ebbes, that is not a question it's a statement," Judge Allen cautioned. "Please rephrase what you're trying to ask the witness."

"Ms. Sullivan, how are you planning on running the company?"

"I have several business attorneys that specialize in cases like this, they will handle the transition. As for getting rid of trained employees, why would I do that? I have no intention of losing qualified workers. The company will be handled in the same way that it's always been run."

"Minus Mr. Rhodes?"

"I didn't say that. It's not my responsibility to say what happens to Mr. Rhodes, that's what the jury is for." Several people laughed, and Annie stopped herself from smiling.

"Are you saying you would allow Mr. Rhodes to continue to run things?"

"I'm saying that Mr. Rhodes is on trial and that the jury is responsible for deciding the outcome of this case. My responsibility is to Mrs. Rhodes. As her legal guardian I'm doing everything I can to protect her rights. Parts of those rights include the business she inherited from her father, the one that her husband had her unknowingly sign her name off of just before he filed for divorce.

"Those divorce papers, whether they were revoked or not, threatened to take the company away from her completely. Mark's fate rests on the jury's shoulders, and I trust that they will make the right decision. As for the corporation, the same people who are running it now will be running it as we go forward. The only changes will come from the decision of this court and from my business attorneys, who will be making small adjustments so that the company can continue to make positive strides in the transition."

"But the corporation is running perfectly now and Ms. Rhodes is getting the care that she needs, so what do you have to worry about? If it's not broken, why are you trying to fix it?"

"Things are running smoothly because I've had guardianship of Katherine over the past six months."

"Can you prove that? Do you have any way of showing the court that things would be different if you weren't involved?"

"I have logs showing the many times Mark and I have argued over Katherine's medical treatments. Treatments that wouldn't have taken place if I hadn't had authorization power."

"Allegedly. You can't say that they wouldn't have happened at all; that would be pure speculation. I repeat, do you have a way to prove to the court that your status as legal guardian has changed anything?"

"Only my word."

"No further questions."

Brian Ebbes returned to his seat next to Mark Rhodes. He was smiling, and it was easy to see that he was pleased with his performance.

Robin wasn't smiling. She appeared studious and stone faced as she approached the bench. Annie had never seen her this way and the change was puzzling.

"Ms. Sullivan, how many years have you known Katherine Rhodes?"

"I've known Katie for forty-six years."

"Can you tell the court how you first met?"

Annie smiled. The years seemed to disappear from her face. "Katie and I met in the summer of 1966. At the time I had been living in the Haight-Ashbury District for a little over six months, long enough to feel that I had a foothold on the way things worked. One day in early June a very naive Katie showed up in the Haight. She had just graduated from high school and she was there to make her mark on the world, much like all of us who were living in the neighborhood at the time.

"I was standing on a corner in front of a convenience store with a group of friends. We were having a debate about politics, something irrelevant I'm sure; just a couple of kids discussing how you think things should be when you're nineteen years old. Anyway, up comes this newbie, and she joined in the conversation. She was cool, we all liked her, and so in a sense I guess my group just adopted her. Katie and I immediately grew close, and I helped her learn the ropes. The rest is history."

"Can you tell the court who the members of that group were?"

"What?" Annie shook her head. The questions had taken an unexpected turn.

"Who were the members of the group that were standing in front of the convenience store, the ones who adopted Katie?"

"Let me see, there was myself obviously, my roommate Chet, his friend Barry Bog, Daphne Watson, and a guy we called Frog."

"This was a close group of friends?"

"We were more like family. Haight-Ashbury was a different time and to understand it you need to know what we, as a subculture, believed. We were going to change the world, make it a better place where money wasn't worshipped, a place where people could live in love and peace. We believed that everyone should be free to be themselves. Today it sounds crazy, but back then that's the way it was. The friends that we made in the Haight were close friends, the closest friends that I've ever known."

"Which explains why you feel compelled to protect Katherine Rhodes' life?"

Annie's heartbeat slowed. She had been wound up by the defense, ready to fight, now she became emotional and her eyes filled with tears.

"Katherine is the only true best friend that I've ever known. She is the sister that I should have had, and I would do anything to protect her. That's why I wanted guardianship, and that's why I'm fighting to keep it."

"Ms. Sullivan, how many years have you known Mark Rhodes?"

"I think about forty-four years."

"And during all of those years did Katherine ever talk to you about her relationship with her husband?"

"Yes, many times."

"What did she say about the relationship?"

"Objection, hearsay," Ebbes said.

"Your Honor, this is not hearsay, this is a factual conversation that is relevant to this case."

"The witness will answer the question."

"She told me of his many affairs, how embarrassing they were for her. She told me that he was emotionally cruel and that she wanted to leave him, but that her financial situation was such that it was easier to stay."

"Did she leave him, or was it the other way around?"

"He left her when his latest girlfriend got pregnant. He just walked out one day and moved in with the new girlfriend. Then he immediately filed for divorce from Katherine."

"In your opinion, why was Katherine out driving the night of her accident?"

"Katie had been served with divorce papers earlier in the day and knowing that her name was no longer on the corporation, she was sure that she was going to end up penniless. Katie was driving that night because Mark Rhodes had left her with no other options."

"Do you think she was trying to kill herself?"

"Undoubtedly."

"Objection!"

"No further questions, Ms. Sullivan."

Robin walked away from the stand with a huge smile on her face. It was the first time in the court case where she felt confident the verdict might just turn out in their favor after all.

Chapter 40

Somewhere around Truckee, California, Dylan flagged Frog over. It was midnight and the two bikers were freezing. Dylan saw a diner off of the highway and signaled for Frog to pull over.

Dylan parked his bike and dismounted, bending his frostbitten fingers.

"Man, I'm fucking freezing," Frog said, jumping off of his bike. "I'm so glad you decided to stop, I can't fucking feel my hands anymore and I need to take a piss something terrible."

"Yeah, I figured you were due for a break."

"Me? What about you, man?"

"Nah, I'm a seasoned biker remember? Listen, we're on the second part of my plan, I need to fill you in on some things. Let's get some coffee and talk."

The inside of the diner was quiet. Apart from a man sitting at a table by himself and a couple of young kids eating burgers in the back, the place was empty.

Dylan pulled his gloves off and sat down at the counter. He asked the waitress to bring two cups of coffee, and then he waited for Frog to come back from the bathroom.

It had been a long day but now he could breathe a sigh of relief. They were far from San Francisco, and Dylan hoped that meant that they were safe from the evils that followed.

"Man, my fucking fingers hurt. I had to run them under warm water so I could bend them." Frog sat beside Dylan and held the coffee mug for warmth he shut his eyes for several seconds, savoring the heat.

"Okay, man, listen up."

Frog opened his eyes and turned to look at Dylan.

"I have a buddy who he doesn't live far from here. We're going to his place and we're going to dump the bikes in his garage. He has an old beat up Ford he's loaning me. We're going to take the truck the rest of the way up to North Shore."

"Groovy, I'm glad that we're done with the bikes. Shit, does the truck have a heater?"

Dylan took a drink of his steaming coffee and cracked a wry smile. "Dude, you would never make it as a Hells Angel."

"Why, man, because of my Honda?"

"Yeah, *that* would be the reason," Dylan said sarcastically.

"What's next?" Frog asked, nursing his cup of coffee.

"Next we pick up the truck and then we head to Tahoe. I've already rented a cabin there, all we've got to do is pick up the key. We go shopping and fill the kitchen with food, then I make contact with some people back in the Bay. After that we just sit and wait."

"How long?"

"However long it takes, man."

The two finished their coffee and reluctantly returned to their bikes. Dylan led the way up a remote country road where, at the end of a long driveway, a dark house loomed menacingly.

He parked next to the wooden structure and then pulled on the garage door until the rotting wood released.

"Man, I've been here a hundred times, always for a fucking party," Dylan said fondly. "Best grooving place in the world to have one too, out here in the middle of nowhere. This is the first time I've been here slinking around and hiding in the darkness. I feel like a fucking prowler, man."

The garage was nearly bare, nothing inside except a workbench and tools. Dylan walked his bike inside and then peeled off his leather chaps and gloves.

"I won't be needing these for awhile."

Frog pulled his ride alongside Dylan's Harley and parked.

The old Ford sat in the front yard. Dylan shut the bikes inside the garage and approached the house, where he reached under the mat and retrieved a single key.

"Okay, man, let's go."

"Where's your friend? Shouldn't we check in with him first?" Frog asked.

"He's not here, he and his old lady are away. Weekend trip, I think. He left the truck key under the mat. We're supposed to leave the bikes and take the truck. Come on, man, let's go. We have another hour before we get to Tahoe."

Frog followed him to the old Ford, where Dylan unlocked the doors and they both jumped inside. The bench seat was split open and white fluff poked out of the tear, some of it falling on the ripped carpet below. Disregarding the interior, Frog closed the door and shivered.

"Man, this place is fucking cold."

"This is nothing, man, wait until we get a little further up. North Shore is a lot colder than this."

"Terrific."

Dylan pulled the truck onto the roadway heading east, where an entrance onto Interstate 80 let them back to the highway.

"The highway will split here in just a few minutes, we'll take 50, it will lead us to into Tahoe."

Dylan turned the radio on; the Beatles were singing about 'Lucy in the Sky with Diamonds'. When the engine was warm enough Dylan flipped the heater on.

"So, you want to tell me about that dude back in Monterey, the one you kicked the living shit out of?" Frog asked, curiosity finally getting the best of him.

"Not much to tell really. Back in March Katie asked me to take her to a cocktail party at her parents' house in Antioch. It was a real stuffy event, upscale shit with real snobs. You dig? The reason she wanted me to go was because of that loser. The one I just beat the living shit out of. Way back then the cat was already a problem, following her around and talking shit. I guess Ron had a confrontation with him in 'Frisco a few weeks earlier so the little asshole was fuming about that. Anyway, he was a pompous little fucker and he thought he was the cat's meow. You know the type? Makes you want to throw up on them," he laughed.

Frog nodded.

"He followed us around at the party. He kept trying to make me look stupid. After a few awkward episodes I took the little wimp outside and had a talk with him. I showed him my Hells Angel tattoo on my back and he just about pissed his pants." Dylan laughed uproariously at the memory. "I told him then that he needed to leave Katie alone but the arrogant little fucker obviously didn't listen. After the tire came off of my bike and we split to look for it, I heard a chick screaming. I didn't know it was Katie, but I could tell that the woman was frantic, yelling for her life. I couldn't ignore that, man. Next thing I knew I was running towards the screams. Imagine my surprise when I pulled into that cove and found the asshole from the party straddling

Katie. Man, I wanted to smash his fucking head in, slice him from ear to ear, you dig?"

"Yeah I think so." Frog imagined Moonbeam under the same circumstances and flinched. If it had been her he would have felt the same way. "So he didn't rape her did he?"

"She said that he didn't have the chance and I trust that she's telling me the truth. If I find out differently then we're going to have another play date in the future. Anyway, I lost it on the clown and I would have taken it further too except you stopped me."

"Yeah, we have enough troubles without you killing someone."

"Agreed man," Dylan said. "Anyway, I think I gave him a good lesson, at least I hope I did."

"How bad off do you think he was, man?"

"He has bumps, bruises, probably a few broken ribs. He'll live, but he deserved much worse."

"You're right, man, he did."

They drove the next ten miles in silence, both lost in their own thoughts. When they came to the turn off onto Highway 50, Dylan flicked the heat off.

"Fuck, man, talk about one extreme to another. Heater works all right, doesn't it?"

"No shit." Frog cracked his window a few inches, allowing a cool breeze to flow through the cab. "So what's the deal with you and Katie?"

"So what's the deal with you and Moonbeam?" Dylan shot back

"Touché. Do you love her?"

"Yep, something along those lines. What about Moony and you?"

"I love her, man, but I'm pretty sure that she hates me now."

"Nah, she doesn't hate you, man. I've seen the way the chick looks at you, Frog. She loves you."

"Not after this she won't. I've done everything you're not supposed to do in a relationship, man. I've lied to her, I've broken promises, all the things that aren't okay. You get my drift?"

"Yeah, clearly."

"Now she's got all the time in the world to think about me and us. Who knows how long we'll be gone? Contacting her is out of the question. After this, she'll dump me for sure. I bet by the time we come out of hiding she'll already have a new dude."

"Wow man, that's heavy. I'm sorry."

"Yeah, well I deserve it. Karma man. What about you and Katie?"

"Me and Katie?" Dylan laughed. "I don't know what we are man. I can tell you this, we seem to be drawn to each other. There's this pull...I've never felt anything like it with anyone else in my life."

"It's called love, man."

"Yep, something like that."

"How much has she told you about herself?"

"Told me about herself? What do you mean, man?"

"She obviously convinced you of something or we wouldn't be on our way to Lake Tahoe right now."

"Right, I see what you mean. You're talking about her premonitions?"

"Premonitions?" Frog laughed, he couldn't help himself. "Is that what she told you?"

"Yeah, why? Do you know something else, something that she's not telling me?"

"I must be tired, man, I'm talking stupid." Frog closed the window, which was now letting in too much air.

"Frog, tell me what you know. Don't you believe in Katie's premonitions?" Dylan was confused at the strange turn the conversation had taken.

"Oh I believe in them alright, why would I be here with you if I didn't? It's just I don't think I'd really call what Katie has premonitions."

"Is that so? And what would you call what Katie has?"

"Look, man it's not up to me to tell you anything. You should ask Katie yourself."

"You brought the conversation up, Frog, I didn't. Tell me what you know."

"I don't think Katie would want me to do that." Frog swallowed hard, regretting what he had started.

"Then maybe you shouldn't have brought the topic it up in the first place. Too late man, now you need to spill the beans. What do you know about Katie that I don't?"

Frog was disappointed in himself. Why on earth had he opened his mouth? Now he had no choice, he had to tell Dylan the truth.

"Katie... doesn't exactly have premonitions, man. It's more like she's been here and done this before."

"What?"

"Just like I said, man, she's been here in 1967 before. This is her second time around."

"She really believes that?"

"She knows it, man! She can tell you everything about the future. Even short term stuff that's going to happen in a day, a week or month. And here's the biggest trip of all, she's always right."

"Always?"

"Yeah, man. It's fucking heavy, I know."

"So you actually believe that she's from the future?

"Yeah, man, I believe it, and Moony believes it too. Just recently Ron found out, and now he's a believer."

"This makes no sense, man. What are you trying to say? That Katie's a time traveler?"

"Yep."

Dylan turned and looked at him, waiting for a punch line that didn't come.

"You remember the night of your Hells Angels party?" Frog asked. Dylan nodded. "That night Katie was drugged with something. We thought it was acid, and it was a heavy fucking dose too. When she woke up the next day she swore that she had returned from the future."

"The future?"

"Yeah, man, way in the future too, like forty something years. At first we doubted her but there comes a time when you have to believe because she's proven it over and over. It's true, man. She's from the future all right, she's the real deal."

"Then the premonition about you and I being killed?"

"She knows it's going to happen because it happened before, in her 1967."

"Holy fucking shit." Dylan wiped the sweat off of his brow.

"Yeah, man, that's how I felt at first too. It's creepy. I watched television with her and she would tell me the endings to every show. Movies too, first time showings, and she could tell me the whole flick. New songs on the radio, she'll know the words the first time the song's been played on the air. She knows other stuff about the future too."

"Like?"

"Like, she knew about the Monterey Pop Festival before it was ever planned. She knew Mohammad Ali was going to lose his title because of draft dodging, and she said that the Chinese would be setting off their first atom bomb this weekend. It hasn't happened yet, but just watch, man, she'll be right because she always is."

Dylan didn't know what to say. Maybe he was just overly tired, because he found himself believing the claims way too easily. Katie did know a lot about the future. If she told Frog, and practical as he was, he believed, then who was Dylan to question the validity?

"I know this is going to sound crazy, but this shit you're rapping about? I think I believe you. In some strange fucking way it actually makes sense. So, she's been this way since January?"

"That's right. At first Moony and I thought she might pop back at some point, wake up and not remember any of this, but that hasn't happened and we're going on six months. I guess at this point, she's here to stay."

"What has the last six months been like?"

"It's been crazy, man. Besides knowing that I'm supposed to die in August, Katie has been trying to change her own shit. Get this, man, that loser that you just worked over back in Monterey? The first time around, Katie fucking married him."

"She did *what*?"

"That's right, man, she married him. Can you fucking dig that?"

"Not at all." Dylan made a face of disgust.

"I guess she got sucked into the marriage. Her parents really dug the dude for some reason and they kept trying to push them together. Then when Katie's brother died in 'Nam she freaked and went home and married the guy."

"Wait a minute, Katie's brother's not dead, he's in the Marine Corps, but he's not—"

"Not yet, man, but it's coming; October I think."

"Richard is going to die in October?"

"According to Katie he is. He's in a really dangerous unit stationed close to the DMZ."

"Yeah, she told me he's in a unit that has a high casualty rate."

"Right, well, it does. Katie says they have a lot of inexperienced officers now that the war is expanding. She said that one of these newbies almost got her brother killed when he first got to 'Nam. This October, another newbie officer is supposed to get him killed. Since she hasn't been wrong once..."

"Damn, no wonder she was always off doing her own thing."

"Yeah, that's the reason. That and preventing herself from entering into a crappy marriage. Now that the marriage bit is off the table Katie is focused on saving her brother."

"So she knew back in January that her brother was going to end up in Vietnam?"

"I guess so."

"Why did she let him go?"

"What was she going to do, tie him up?" Frog asked with a chuckle.

Dylan turned and glanced at him. "I would have helped," the biker said in all seriousness.

"You would have helped her tie her brother up and keep him someplace hidden just to stop him from going into the Marines?"

"Sure man, why not? Ultimately I'd be doing the right thing."

"See, man, that's the difference between hippies and bikers, that's why we can never join forces and become one. Hippies want to solve the world's problems through love but your kind wants to solve violence with more violence."

"What are you talking about, hippie boy, we are joined."

"No, man, we're not."

"Sure we are, Frog. According to Katie we share the same grave for eternity, you can't get closer than that. Put it this way, if we can't trust each other then we're really fucked."

Frog couldn't argue with that.

***

The city of Tahoe loomed before them. It was 1:30 in the morning and they needed the key to the property that Dylan had rented. They pulled into a small strip mall off of the main road and there, next to a public telephone booth Dylan stopped the truck and yawned.

"We're here, man. All I've got to do now is to call my guy. He lives close to here and he's supposed to come and give me the key."

Dylan fished several loose papers out of his pocket and then, finding the one he was looking for, stuffed the rest into the empty ashtray.

"I'll be back in a minute."

Frog watched the biker as he made the call and then headed back towards the truck. He looked exhausted. Frog glanced into the rear view mirror and realized that he looked just as bad. A long stay in the mountains would do both of them good.

"He's on his way. I guess he lives across the street in those apartments because he said he was walking over."

"Cool, I can't wait to get somewhere, man."

"No kidding, me too. Look, there he is." Dylan jumped out of the truck and headed towards a short, balding man. They talked for a few minutes, shook hands, and then Dylan took the key and headed back to the truck.

"I got it, man, let's go shall we?"

"Fuck yeah!"

The cabin was up a long dirt road, on a secluded piece of land far away from any neighbors. The woods were quiet, and despite the porch light, which was left on in their honor, the night was completely black.

Frog jumped out of the truck and stood for a few seconds breathing the cool, fresh air. He stared at the star filled sky and for the first time in months actually felt safe.

"Nice place right?" Dylan asked as he walked past the hippie heading for the front door.

Dylan opened the door to the cabin and switched on the lights. He pulled two beers out of a small canvas bag and held one out to Frog.

"They're a bit warm but it's a beer, do you want one?" Dylan asked. Frog nodded, and he handed him a can.

"Thanks, man. Not just for the beer, I mean for everything. If left to my own devices, I'm not sure what I would have done. Money is a draw for me. I'm stupid for it, I know that. I had a deadline, Katie said August and I believed that, I guess I still do. Between you and me, if you hadn't pushed for us to leave I probably would have stuck it out a little longer. After all, it's late June, man, and that means I still have time."

Dylan shook his head. "Sure money is always a draw, but personally, I'd rather be alive. And you're welcome by the way. I'm glad to have you along. This is a drag but at least we have company."

"Yeah." Frog smiled and then drained half the can of warm beer in a gulp.

"You have to admit it's a great place to hole up, private and beautiful," Dylan said looking at the stars.

"Hell yeah, I love it up here. If we have to hide out, man, then this is the place to do it. How did you think to come here? It really is perfect."

"Tahoe and I have a long history. When I was a kid in foster care I used to attend camp up here in the summer. Joey and I both did. We loved it, waited all year for that trip, dreamed about it. It was the only good thing about being in the system. For that one week every year we would come here amongst all this beauty and just be kids, playing in the forest. It's the only place I've ever been in my life where I feel free. There's this sense of optimism that I get when I'm here. I don't know, maybe it has something to do with the clean air, but I start to think that anything is possible, and right now that's the kind of atmosphere we both need."

"Yeah man, I can dig that. The place sends out great vibes I can feel them."

"Tomorrow we'll go to the small market. It's about halfway down the main road just a few miles away from town. We'll buy supplies, enough to last us for about a month. There are some supplies in the truck already. If you haven't noticed, my buddy stocked the back well. There's food, blankets, a medical kit, cooking essentials, even a shotgun, plus the revolver that I brought from San Francisco."

"Guns, man, really?"

"You think this is a game, Frog? You bet your ass I brought guns. Anyway, as I was saying, I don't want us taking additional trips outside of the cabin. The more the locals see us, the more they'll talk. Which is the reason we need a good story too, something believable that we can tell the worker at the market. People in small towns talk too much. They're going to ask questions about us, wanting to know why two bachelors are staying at a cabin in the woods for so long. We want them to think that we're ordinary Joe Blows just here on a much-deserved summer fishing trip. So we'll be doing a lot of fishing. If the locals see us we want to look legit. That way we can avoid suspicion and plan our next move."

"Which will be?"

"Besides eating fish, making contact with my connections back in the Bay."

"Who are you going to contact? We don't know who the hell we can trust."

"We can trust Big Jim."

"How do you know that for sure?" Frog finished his beer and shivered.

"Big Jim is one of the First Skulls. The First Skulls are the good guys, they're the ones who are trying to restore the reputation of the club by cleaning things up. Big Jim isn't involved in any of this. As for anyone else, your guess is as good as mine."

"It's fucking freezing out here, man, why are we standing outside?" Frog wrapped his arms around himself and clenched his teeth.

"We're standing out here because it's beautiful. Look at the stars, Frog, they look so close you can almost touch them. We were as good as dead before we came here. Don't you want to stand here, look at the world and just feel alive?"

"Right man, I can dig it." Frog walked back to the truck and retrieved his jacket out of the front seat. On his way back he took two more beers out of the small canvas bag.

"About Katie, man..." Dylan said. He sat on the lawn still staring at the sky and within seconds, Frog sat beside him.

"Look, man, I thought we were done with that topic. I think you need to talk to Katie about her trip back in time, man. I already feel guilty about how much I've told you."

"Yet you did tell me, so now you're stuck. As I was saying about Katie, what has she told you about our situation? I thought it was a series of premonitions, and with the dreams that I've had since I was a kid, well, I believed her. But now that I know she's really talking about the past, that changes everything. Frankly, I'd like to hear what she's told you." Dylan pulled a doobie out of his jacket pocket, lit it, and took a long drag before passing it to Frog.

"You know Katie is going to skin me when she finds out that I've told you all of this." Frog took a long drag on the joint and then passed it back. He swallowed hard, looked at his hands, which he'd placed in his lap and picked at a hangnail.

"You already know that Katie changed after your party. At first she didn't tell us anything. All that we knew was that she was acting really strange. Then sometime around the Human Be-In, she finally told us the truth. She said that she was from the future, 2014, where she'd just had this real bad auto accident. Somewhere after that, when she got used to her new/old surroundings, she told me my fate. She said I would disappear at the end of summer, August to be exact, and that my body would never be found.

"I didn't want to believe her, I'm sure you know what I mean. After a while, though, it was undeniable. That's when I started to listen. Well I wanted to listen, but you know the rest, man."

"2014, for real?"

"That's what she said."

"What's the world like in forty-five years? Is it any better than it is now?" Dylan asked pulling a drag off of the joint.

Frog laughed. "Worse man, can you believe that?"

"Somehow that doesn't surprise me. Nothing ever seems to get better where politics are concerned. What about the war, it can't still be going on forty-five years in the future?"

"No it's not, according to Katie it ends in 1975."

"Wow, man, eight more years of this shit?"

"Yep, and we haven't hit the worst part of it yet. She said they start a lottery draft somewhere in 1968 so from what Katie said, we haven't seen anything yet."

"That's a drag, man. Who would think that shit would continue to go until the middle of the 70's? What a waste of lives."

"Yeah, but there are some positive things on their way. Katie said we walk on the moon in 1969 and that in 2008 we have a black president."

"For *real*, man?"

Frog nodded.

"That's cool, no more old white guys running the country into the ground."

"I don't know about that. Katie said by the time he inherits the country it's already screwed. According to her, Big Brother is everywhere. She said people carry pocket phones around with them so they can be reached anywhere, at any time."

"They carry phones in their pockets?"

"I know, that's what I said too. I guess they're computer controlled and battery operated. Not like the batteries we have now, these are rechargeable because you plug them into the wall, and she said something about touching the screen too, whatever that means."

"Wow, I hope I live to see all of that." Dylan finished off the smoke.

"Me too, man. At this point I just want to see September, but a long-term future, that would be groovy." Frog started to laugh. "Look at us man, two grown men sitting here talking about time travel and both of us actually believe it."

"I know, man, it's crazy, but what can you do? I have to believe it, I've had too many dreams that steer me to the same conclusions that Katie's confirmed."

"I've had dreams too." Frog said, shivering despite his warm jacket.

"You know this thing with Katie, it's a trip."

"No kidding!" Frog shook his head.

"Not just the time travel thing, it's more than that. It's the supernatural twist to all of this."

"I don't like thinking about that part. The hallway, old Guthrie, fuck man, that horrible wacked out maid with the rotting teeth. That whole scene just freaks me out. What a bummer trip!"

"I know, Frog, but it's a key in this thing that nobody has really considered."

"Because it's fucking creepy, that's why."

"Come on, you were just saying that we're two grown men. Now you're chicken to discuss dreams? I'm telling you, they're a big part of this."

"Okay, man, go ahead, let's talk about the eerie creepy shit. Let's do it tonight too, right before we go to bed so we can dream about it!"

"That hallway with all the doors, it has to mean something because we've all been there. I've dreamt of those doors my whole life, and that's not all. I'm sure I've felt Katie there. We never see each other, but I can always feel her when I'm there. Sometimes we come close to touching or almost seeing each other, but she's always just one step ahead of me.

"You know what I think? I think that we've done this before, Frog. I think that Katie's right. She's come back to fix things, and we're part of that game. We've all played this scene before and in between then and now, we've all been in that hallway."

"Then why don't we remember being here before?"

"Because we both died."

"And Katie?"

"I don't know, man. I'm not sure how it's all pieced together. It's a jigsaw puzzle that I haven't completed. But Katie and I, we have something between us that's different, and both of us can feel it, it's like a...like a tingling when we're together."

"That's fucking creepy, man."

"But it's true."

"Who do you think they are? The people who are after us, I mean. Who the fuck are they?" Frog asked.

"I don't know. Do you want to make a list of possible suspects and then take bets to see which one of us is right?" Dylan lit a new smoke and passed it off to an overly anxious Frog.

"Maybe. It wouldn't hurt would it? We can rate them and it could give us a rough figure of our most likely suspects."

"Like a star system?" Dylan laughed.

"Why not?"

"Look, man, that's not going to do us any good. If you want to talk then let's talk, but making calculations is a waste of fucking time."

"Do you have a better idea?"

"Yeah, process of elimination. Let's start with what we know for sure. Whoever wants us dead bumped off Skinner."

"Maybe."

"No maybe, man, it's the same person."

"I don't think we have enough information to say that for sure. His death could have nothing to do with ours."

"Come on, man, really?" Dylan shook his head.

"How long do you think Skinner was dead before you found him?"

"Considering the condition of his body, he'd been dead for a while. Rigor mortis sets in from between two to four hours, depending on the outside temperature, and it reaches its max at about twelve hours, then it lasts approximately seventy-two hours. The way he looked, I'd say Skinner died three days ago. He never made it to the concert man, put it that way." Dylan lit yet another joint, hit it, and passed it to Frog.

Frog took several puffs off the smoke and shook his head vigorously. "Man, I can't get the picture of Skinner's corpse out of my head, I don't know if I'll ever be able to. He looked so fucked up, like a monster out of a horror movie. I know he took a beating, Dylan, but fuck, man, he was all purple and bloated and shit. His skin was starting to peel off." Frog covered his face with his hands and cringed.

"That's what happens after a few days, bacteria and enzymes start breaking down the body. The pancreas fills with so much bacteria that it basically digests itself. When the rot works itself to the other organs, the body changes color. First it turns green, then purple, and eventually black. That's when you start to smell it. The bacteria create this gas, which of course smells awful. That gas causes the body to bloat, the eyes to bulge out of their sockets and the tongue to swell and stick out of the mouth."

"Great, man, thanks. That's what I really needed, a visual description of the picture that's haunting me. Now the image can permanently scar my psyche!"

"Sorry, man, I thought you wanted to know."

"No, man, I really don't want to think about Skinner changing colors." Frog took a deep toke off the smoke and glared at Dylan.

"Sorry, man. You hang with the Angels long enough you get a full education in forensic science. Anyway, as I was saying," Dylan said, clearing his throat, "let's start with what we do know. We know that the unpatched bikers could be involved, we know that Sal and Dave contacted them, and we know that whoever killed Skinner went to the concert."

"How do you know they went to the concert?"

"Great cover, man, think about it. You have the best alibi in the world when you're standing in a crowd of 50,000 people and many of them can identify you."

"True enough."

"Whoever this is, they wanted to stop Skinner's interference into the drug trade, and think about it, Frog, there are a lot of hands in this pot. It could be the bikers, it could be the guys from Oakland, shit, it could even be Dave or Sal for that matter. Skinner had a lot of people pissed off at him, but this is where the whole thing gets tricky. Why would Skinner's enemies go after us? What possible connection do we have with Skinner?"

"You're forgetting the thugs from Oakland, the ones who beat the fuck out of me. They could be after us, and it could be totally separate from the Skinner trip. They drove my ass out of Golden Gate Park, but they didn't stop the operation because you and Joey stepped in. They have good reason to be after both of us."

"No way, man. They are so far below our level of operation at this point. They wouldn't dare come after either one of us. To do so would be suicidal. They're small time thugs, they aren't looking to be martyrs. It's not them, Frog."

"Maybe the Mafia?"

"Why would the mob be after us? If they were involved then they would be after Dave and Sal, not us. We're little fish in their big pond. Nope, whoever this is, they're after us because our involvement scares the shit out of them."

"Scared of us? That's crazy. Why would anyone be scared of us?"

"Because you and I are changing, Frog. At first we were out for the profit, neither one of us having thought this thing out fully. We were in it for the bread, plain and simple. Now we're neck high in this shit, the operation is starting to make big bucks, about to hit the big time. I bet this is happening much faster than any of them thought it would. You and I, we started to rock their boat and Skinner..." Dylan laughed nervously, "Skinner was trying to sink it."

Dylan finished the rest of the joint, poured the last of his beer on the ground and then without another word, walked into the cabin.

***

Back in the Haight, the month of June raced by. As Katie had predicted, the Chinese exploded their first atomic weapon on June 18th. Muhammad Ali was convicted of draft dodging on June 20th, but was released on appeal. On that same day, the Fillmore Auditorium added to their venue. Instead of having shows just on the weekends they would now have them six nights a week, and their opening bill featured Jefferson Airplane and Jimi Hendrix.

The Diggers' Summer Solstice celebration took place on June 21st at Speedway Meadow in Golden Gate Park. Wooden stages were set up on the side and a flatbed truck served as a third stage. On one side the Diggers barbequed a lamb and fried hamburgers in shovels. Paper flowers decorated the park and a woman in a tent painted faces.

The Grateful Dead, Big Brother and the Holding Company, Quicksilver Messenger Service, and Mad River played, using Fender speakers and amps they borrowed from the Monterey Pop Festival.

Although it was a huge success, the old time hippies couldn't help but feel the difference. Their world was slowly coming to an end. The peaceful, beautiful neighborhood of love that they had created in Haight-Ashbury was changing. It was becoming too large to control and more newcomers were arriving daily. As the Diggers had feared, the publicity that The Human Be-In brought to the Haight District was starting to destroy it.

By the end of June, the US erupted when race riots swept the nation.

The first took place in Buffalo, New York on June 27th, when two hundred people were arrested. The next day, fourteen people were shot during the riots.

July 12th, race riots in New Jersey became violent. Twenty-six people were killed, fifteen hundred injured, and over one thousand arrested.

July 13th, race-related rioting broke out in Newark, New Jersey. When the violence ended four days later, twenty-seven people were dead.

On July 17th, riots shook Cairo, Illinois; on the 19th, Durham, North Carolina; on July 20th, Memphis, Tennessee; and on the 24th, Cambridge, Maryland.

The riots in Detroit led to the postponement of a Tigers-Orioles baseball game when the worst rioting of the summer took place between July 23-30. This disturbance left forty dead, two thousand injured, and five thousand homeless. The rioting and looting only stopped after President Johnson dispatched 4,700 paratroopers to the area.

Other uprisings took place in Toledo, Ohio; Rochester, New York; East Harlem and Pontiac, Michigan. This was the first time in a quarter century that the National Guard had been deployed.

By July 27th, in the wake of the riots, President Johnson appointed the Kerner Commission to assess the causes of racial violence. This act prompted H. Rap Brown, a known black militant, to announce that violence in the United States was "as American as Cherry Pie."

Despite the new commission, violence from race tensions continued, and on July 30th, four people were killed in Milwaukee.

Post Monterey Pop Haight-Ashbury was changed too.

The fully functioning free clinic offered medical care to the masses paid for by funds collected at the pop festival. The Diggers, who changed their name to the Free City Collective in July, continued tending to the needs of the neighborhood, but that job was becoming increasingly difficult as the population tripled.

Katie and Moonbeam's lives had also changed dramatically. With Frog and Dylan gone the girls' carefree party days drifted away. Moonbeam waited for word daily, thinking that the men might send a card or make a phone call, something to let them know that they were safe, but her hopes never materialized. The whereabouts of Frog and Dylan remained a mystery.

While Moonbeam learned to deal with her loneliness, Katie struggled with dramatic changes of her own. The first was minor but still upsetting. When they returned to the city she and Ron became indifferent towards each other. Although they had never talked about her blunder at the concert, they both knew that the episode was a deal breaker.

Now when they came face to face with each other there was an uncomfortable silence between them. Katie could still see the hurt in his eyes, and that knowledge made her feel terribly guilty.

Moonbeam told her that Ron was fine, that he was spending a lot of time at the lab; whose lab was anybody's guess. She also knew through the grapevine that he was spending a lot of time with Robin too, and that made her happy. Ron was looking for a mature woman who was going places in life. Now with Mark Rhodes out of the picture, Robin was certainly heading in the right direction.

On top of Katie's minor problems, her worldview had been shattered. For forty-five years she had dealt with a certain set of 'what ifs', and now that the main antagonist in her life had been removed forever, she was numb.

Katie knew that she should be ecstatic, and in a way she was, but her life had been so altered by her marriage that now she didn't know what to expect. Being faced with the unknown created a void that she had to fill before she could be whole again.

Mark Rhodes had pleaded guilty in a plea bargain to avoid an embarrassing trial. He was sentenced to five to seven years for kidnapping and attempted rape, and placed in Corcoran State Prison. Al Searfus vowed that he would keep the pressure on the authorities while he and his legal team searched for additional charges.

With Mark out of the picture, Katie didn't know how to relate to her parents. She hadn't called them since the festival but she had thought about them a lot. With her anger gone, she started to remember her childhood. There were good times before her parents' marriage deteriorated.

She remembered a family trip to Disneyland, several to the beach, and one special weekend where they had a picnic in the park. There had been some great Christmases too when the family had taken trips to the snow. At one time life had been pleasant in the Searfus family. Katie hadn't thought about the positive things in forty-five years, but now those good memories were popping up.

Richard would be home during the second week of August. Katie remembered that visit vividly. She and her father had a huge fight. The argument had started over politics and then expanded until Al told Katie exactly what he thought of "her kind", the no good longhaired hippie freaks that collectively were ruining the country.

It was an ugly fight and one Richard was drawn into. That interaction made Katie realize that the younger brother she had known all her life was gone, replaced by a person she didn't know.

Richard listened to the argument with quiet reserve. When the topic turned towards the Vietnam War he listened to their very different opinions without saying a word. When he'd heard enough, he rose from the couch and in a mannerism that Katie had never seen before, proceeded to let them know that they didn't have a clue as to what was going on. The conversation had ended when Richard marched out of the room, refusing to talk to either one of them. As Katie remembered, he walked out of the house, despite their mother's pleas, and went to a local bar where he had spent the rest of the evening drinking with a fellow Marine who was also home on leave.

Katie saw him only once more, and that visit was brief. Before he left from San Francisco Airport, they met for lunch. They discussed their views of the war, agreed to disagree, and then Richard boarded a TWA flight for Vietnam. That flight would take him away forever.

She had changed her path, and it was time to change Richard's. That mission was going to be an emotional rollercoaster.

Now that they were in the last week of July she was absorbed by the situation. All she could think of was her brother. She sat for hours each day trying to remember every specific detail, knowing that the more she could remember about Richard's death the more convincing her story would become.

Richard was shell-shocked when he came home. At the time she hadn't known what the problem was, but now that she was sixty-six years old she certainly did: PTSD (Post Traumatic Stress Disorder).

Katie had seen many vets come home with problems, some lasting lifetimes. What she really hoped was that her advanced knowledge of the Vietnam vets' plight would help her save her brother. Richard would be home in less than two weeks; she had to find a way to get through to him or it would be the last time she would ever see him.

When she wasn't thinking about the details of Richard's death she spent her time planning the conversation she was going to have with him. Sometime during their visit she would pull Richard away from their parents long enough to talk to him. She would take him into the backyard of their parents' house, and she would confront him and tell him the truth.

Katie was terrified. She knew she was only two weeks away from the most important event in her past. How this played out would decide the future for the Searfus family.

Chapter 41

Despite being physically and emotionally exhausted, Dylan had problems falling asleep. When sleep finally came it was restless. He tossed and turned, plagued by bad dreams, his mind in frenzy. Now that he was seemingly safe, bits of information surfaced, and he found himself evaluating every detail that had taken place over the last few months.

At 6:00 a.m., Dylan gave up trying to sleep. With their next move planned, it was time to get Frog up. The cabin was beautiful in daylight. It was nothing elaborate, just a traditional Tahoe hideaway, but the full oak interior was an excellent touch to the breathtaking woods outside the windows.

Frog had taken the room in the back of the house and as Dylan made his way down the long hallway he stopped several times to open draped windows. Finally he came to the partially opened door and knocked. An early riser, Frog sat straight up in bed.

"What is it, man?" he asked, wiping his sleep puffed eyes.

"I think we should get an early start. We have plenty to do before we can settle down. The quicker we get it all over with the better."

"Just give me a minute to pee and wash my face, and I'll be right with you."

Frog rose mechanically from the bed and marched towards the hall restroom. When he emerged, Dylan was sitting at the table sipping a cup of coffee.

"Want some?" Dylan asked.

When Frog nodded he pointed towards a percolator sitting on the kitchen counter. "Help yourself, man. There's some cream in the fridge if you need it, and I found some sugar cubes in the top cupboard too."

Frog fixed himself a cup of black coffee and then took a seat at the table. "Now what?" he asked in between sips.

"Now, we have to work on blending in."

"Blending in? Here?"

"Yeah, man, so we don't look different, you dig? We don't need any attention, Frog. What we need to do is to appear normal, just like everyone else who lives here."

"Okay."

"That means we both need a haircut."

"Fuck no! Do you know how long it took me to get my hair this long man? It's my pride and joy, you're not cutting it."

"Sorry, man."

"I can tuck it into a cap. It works, I've done it before."

"No, man, sorry, it's not good enough. And that's not all, we have to do something about your wardrobe too."

"My wardrobe?" Frog looked down at his Che Guevara T-shirt. "What's wrong with my threads, man? You're generally wrapped in black leather, you got nothing to say about my 'wardrobe', man."

"Am I in leather now? No, I have a long sleeved shirt, jeans, and a sweatshirt with no logo, nothing that's out of the ordinary. As soon as you chop my hair off I'm going to look just like anyone else in this small town. Nobody will take a second look and notice anything unusual about me. That's how you need to look too."

"What are you saying, man? No T-shirts?"

"I'm saying nothing that makes you look anti-establishment, or in your case, radical hippie. No political signs." Dylan pointed at the carved wooden peace sign Frog always wore around his neck. "Your T-shirt, come on, Frog that's a no brainer. No tie-dyed anything either. Nothing that says 'I'm different from you', and that starts with a haircut."

"Do you know how to cut hair?"

"Sure, I used to cut Joey's all the time when we were kids, and he used to cut mine. You think I had money to spend on shit like that? Sit down. We might as well get started."

"Now? You're just going to whack it off? I want to know before you do anything."

"Short man, clean cut, just a regular haircut that any square in America would wear."

"Wow, man, that's a fucking bummer. Are you for real?"

"Come on, Frog, it will grow back."

"Don't tell me that. It makes it even worse pointing out that I have to start growing it all over again."

"I know, and I'm sorry, but it's got to go, Frog."

Reluctantly Frog sat in the chair that Dylan pointed to.

"The easiest way to do this is to just whack it off while it's in a ponytail. Are you ready?"

"No."

Before Frog could protest it was too late. His ponytail, all fifteen inches of it, was lying on the cabin floor.

"Fuck man, look what you did. I said I wasn't ready!" Frog bellowed.

"A few seconds wasn't going to change anything, man. It had to come off."

"But you could have waited until I was ready, man. That was cold, brother, really fucking cold."

Frog stared sadly at his beloved hair, which was now lying, still neatly banded together, on the floor.

"Alright, Frog, you can sulk while I finish. You have a bowl cut man. You look just like a fucking blond Moe from the Three Stooges." Dylan laughed loudly.

"Very fucking funny! Go ahead man, you've already ruined my hippie-ness, you might as well kill it completely."

When Frog was 'clean cut' he rose from the chair and shook the excess hair off of his shoulders.

"Revenge time. Hand over the scissors."

Dylan did and without a word took his place at the table.

"What if I chop it all off?" Frog asked.

"Then I pin your ass to the floor and cut all yours off."

Frog finished with the best conservative haircut that he could pull off and then laid the scissors on the table.

"That's it, man. Now we both look like complete dorks. Are you happy?"

"Nope, not until you change your shirt. You still look like a walking target to the conservative people who live here. If you don't have anything plain I can loan you a shirt and we can buy some at the little market."

"Small market shirts? How tempting. No man, I'm cool. I have a few plain white ones, enough to get by."

"By the way, that leads me to another problem. What's your real name?"

"Curtis, why?"

"I can't walk around town calling you by the name of an animal can I? Don't you think that would sound pretty strange to the locals?"

"Right man, good point." Frog poured himself a second cup of coffee.

"Good. Let's get moving, Curtis, we have a lot to do."

"I'm almost scared to ask this, but what are we going to be doing?"

"First we unload the supplies from the truck, take inventory, and then we go shopping."

"That's easy. I can do that." Frog put his coffee mug on the counter and followed Dylan outside.

Dylan opened the back hutch of the camper shell and they both pulled boxes and supplies out of the back and transported them into the kitchen.

"When we get to town, we're going to split up. You're going to get the supplies, and I'm going to make a phone call," Dylan informed Frog as they brought the last of the load inside.

"A phone call? You said we were going to get settled here before you called anyone."

"Yeah I know but—"

"But you changed your mind already?"

"Last night I couldn't sleep so I tried to do a lot of planning. No matter what I tried to think about my thoughts kept returning to Skinner's rotting body lying in that ravine. I think it's time to call Big Jim, man. I know I said we would wait, but on second thought I think the faster the club steps in the better off we are."

"Right man, that makes sense. I can dig that."

Dylan returned to taking inventory while Frog changed into a plain white T-shirt. When he returned, the biker had already made a list.

"Let's go, I want to get this shit over with."

Dylan took his handgun off the table and stuck it into the waistband of his jeans. Then he covered it with his jacket.

"You're taking the gun?" Frog questioned.

Dylan said nothing. He'd discussed the two guns with Frog already and he wasn't going to go through it again. He walked past Frog on his way to the truck and started the ignition. Frog followed him outside and jumped in. They sat for several minutes while the engine on the old Ford heated up.

"Something else, man, we need a believable story to tell the locals. Once they find out that we're here long term they're going to start asking questions. We want to stop that shit before it even begins, you dig?"

"Sure man, I got it. Something like a death in the family?"

"Yeah, that could work."

They arrived at the market a little after 8:00 a.m.

Dylan yawned widely. He was exhausted, running on pure adrenaline. He knew that he wouldn't be able to relax fully until he'd taken that final step and called Big Jim.

"Now you've got this, right?" Dylan asked again.

"Come on, man. Please, don't make me go over the story again."

"I hope you have it, because what you tell this dude in the store reflects on this whole trip, you got me?"

"I know, I got you an hour ago. Listen , if you think I'm so inept why don't you just come with me?"

Dylan glared at him.

"Okay, timetables, I get it. You don't want to be in town too long, I got this. Go make your phone call, I'll get the supplies and give the salesperson our fishing story."

"Don't blow this, Frog."

"I told you, don't worry, I'm a businessman."

Dylan headed towards a phone booth in the back of an empty parking lot. He fished through his pockets and came away with a handful of change.

Stepping into the glass telephone booth, he closed the accordion styled door, dropped a dime in the box and dialed the number.

"Thirty-five cents for the next three minutes," the operator replied, and Dylan dropped the required coins into the box.

The call was answered on the second ring.

"Hells Angels, San Francisco Chapter."

"Terry, is that you?"

"Fuck, Dylan, where the hell are you? The Club's been going crazy trying to figure out what happened to you."

"I know, man, I'm sorry. I have some shit going down and I had to skip out for a while. Listen, I actually called to talk to Big Jim, is he around?"

"Yeah he's in the back, hang on a sec, I'll go get him." The line went silent, and several minutes later Big Jim's voice came over the line.

"Dylan, Jesus Christ, where the hell are you?"

"Man, I got a story to tell but it's got to be between just you and me. I'm in a situation where I don't know who I can trust."

The line went quiet for several seconds. "Call me at the garage, it's vacant. Sal and Dave don't use it anymore. Give me a few minutes to get out there."

"Got it, man." Dylan hung up and waited several minutes before calling the number. Big Jim answered immediately.

"Okay, Dylan, now we can talk in private. What the hell is going on?"

"I don't even know where I should start. I guess with Skinner. Have you found him yet?" Dylan asked.

"No, he's still missing." Jim's voice changed, and Dylan realized that he was hitting on a touchy subject.

"Well I found him, man, and I'm sorry to tell you this but...he's dead."

"*What?* Where?"

"His body is down a hill in Monterey. Frog and I found him when we were splitting."

"Dead how? Was it a motorcycle accident?"

"No. He was...he was beaten to death."

"Beaten to death? But who would want to do that to him?"

"That's a good question, because whoever killed Skinner is after me and Frog too."

"I'm going to take a wild guess and say that this has something to do with Sal and Dave?"

"That's right. I know you've suspected us for a long time. Well, I'm here now ready to tell you the whole story."

***

Frog walked into the small market. A string of beads announced his arrival and an older man stepped out from a back room to greet him.

"Well, hiya young fellow, what can I do for you this morning?"

"I have a list of things to pick up. My brother and I are up here for the summer on a fishing trip."

"The whole summer you say, you and your brother?"

"Yeah, that's right. We had a death in the family recently and...well my brother and I are up here fishing. You know, trying to relax and deal with our loss."

"Oh, I'm sorry to hear that. You came to the right place though; this is a beautiful, peaceful spot. It's a great place to recoup."

"Exactly, that's why we're here." Frog smiled at the older man and handed him the shopping list.

"Let's see, several types of fishing bait, canned beans, cereal, powdered milk, a pound of coffee, a bag of sugar, four six packs of Coca Cola, and two cases of Budweiser. I think I have everything on your list."

Hank, according to his nametag, busied himself collecting items throughout the store while Frog sucked down a complimentary cup of java. When everything on the list was priced and bagged he dropped a $20 bill down and told Hank to keep the change, all fifty-two cents worth. Frog gathered the lone grocery cart from outside the store and packed his paper bags inside. He pushed the cart to the truck, shooting a quick glance towards the phone booth where Dylan seemed to be deeply involved in a heated conversation.

**

"The business started back in November of last year, at least that's when I think the original deal went down. I wasn't there, you understand, but I've heard Dave talk about it several times.

"As far as I know, the upper members of the crew are bikers from multiple clubs. They came together and joined with an already established drug ring out of Oakland. Sal and Dave are part of the bikers who call themselves, 'The Unpatched'.

"Joey and I got involved in January, just before the Human Be-In. If you remember, that was the first time you asked me about my loyalty to the club."

Dylan could hear Big Jim sigh, clearly recalling the incident.

"I know that getting involved was a foolish decision, but I didn't expect it to get as big as it has. I thought that Joey and I were joining a small operation, just a little additional pocket cash to get us through the tough times." Dylan paused remembering how innocently the nightmare started . "Since Joey, Frog, and I joined the operation, the business has exploded and frictions within the group have started to take place. The latest problem and the most complicated was Skinner's continued investigation into it. Sal and Dave tried everything they could to get him off our tail. They even offered him a cut of the bread but he refused, and that's why he's lying in a ditch. Somewhere in the scheme of things, when I really understood what was going on, I wanted out and Frog, well he's not digging it anymore either."

"Why are you telling me this now? Why didn't you bring it to my attention ages ago when I first asked you? I could have stopped it then."

"Because I'm stupid, because it involves murder now, and I'm not keen on that shit, or maybe it's because Frog and I are next. There are a lot of reasons that I'm making this call, but one of the biggest, one you aren't going to believe even though it's true, is my loyalty to the Hells Angels."

"You're right, that's a hard pill to swallow. I have a hard time believing that at this point, but go on."

"I know I owe you an apology, Big Jim. I broke club rules and I wouldn't blame you if you de-patch me. God knows I deserve it. In the meantime, I need your help and maybe my information can still stop the operation before Skinner's body is discovered and the club's name gets dragged into this."

"Okay, point made." Jim went silent and Dylan could hear him open a can and suspecting that it was beer, he looked at his watch: 8:30 a.m.

"My call is that disturbing that it's causing you to drink?" Dylan asked. "Was that a Bud I heard you open?"

"Fuck yes I'm drinking. Do you want to know the truth? I'm mad as hell that you let this go on for as long as it has," Big Jim snapped. "I'd like nothing better than to toss your ass to the sharks. Lucky for you, unfortunate for us, that at present you're still a member of this club. The foolish mistakes you make still impact our name, and that reason, plus the fact that I lost a good friend out of this mess, is why the club will get involved. Don't you think that warrants an early morning beer?"

Dylan wished that he too had a Bud in his hand.

"Now, give me some information," Big Jim said. "First off, where can we find Skinner's body?"

"He's just outside of Monterey on Highway 1 heading north. Somewhere halfway between the entrance to the freeway and the first exit there's a steep hill that leads down to a creek. He's there about three-quarters of the way down under some bushes. The body is pretty decomposed by now, so you should be able to smell him."

"Where does Joey fit in with all of this? He's obviously involved and you haven't mentioned him. You and Frog are in hiding, and he's at the shop today working with Dave and Sal. Is that where his loyalty lies?"

"Yes, Joey's involved, but he's not one of the main players. He's just fucked up right now, caught up in this trip of having money. Once everything settles then I'll come back to the Bay and I'll deal with him.

"I know the two of you are close..."

"More than close. We grew up in foster care together. Joey is my brother. He's money hungry, but I guarantee he's not involved in anything higher up. That would be way out of character for him. Joey would prefer to do the little stuff, staying in the middle without choosing sides. He's just laying back doing as little as possible and collecting the cash. Anything more complicated than that would be too much work for him, Joey's lazy."

"I hope so, because when I send the boys out to investigate, they're going to be looking into everything and everybody."

"I understand."

"Now you're going to have to do something for me, Dylan. I want to know the names of every person who's involved, those who are Angels and those who are not. I want to know how far up the ladder this business goes, and I want to know the names of everyone, even if they're just pseudonyms. List their rank in the organization from the lowest to the highest person you can think of, and when that's finished call me with the report."

"I'll do that, but be aware, there are a lot of hands in this pot. This drug ring goes way up. I know some of the names and Frog knows others. Together we should be able to piece together a pretty good list of members, but it's going to take us a couple of days."

"That's fine, Dylan, take your time. In the meantime I'll have some guys out scouring the hillside in Monterey looking for Skinner's body."

"Right on, man."

"Dylan, are you and Frog safe?"

"Yeah, I'm not going to tell you where we are but we're safe enough."

"Good, stay there. Make a list of the names and call me back as soon as you can. We'll find Skinner and then the club will take it from there."

The line went silent.

"Dylan, are you there?" Big Jim asked after a long pause in the conversation.

"Yeah man, I'm here."

"Thanks for finally coming forward. You should have done it earlier, but the important thing is that you did contact me."

"Thanks, boss."

"That doesn't get you out of the shit can by the way. You got your dues to pay."

"Yeah, I know that too."

***

When Dylan got back to the truck, Frog was already sitting behind the wheel.

Dylan opened the passenger door and jumped in. "Did you get everything we need?"

"Yep, I got everything that was on the list."

"And the clerk?"

"He's cool man, a little old dude. I told him that we're brothers and that we're up here recouping from a death in the family. Nice guy, said he'd tell the locals that we're in mourning so they don't bother us."

"Good."

Frog started the truck and pulled the Ford onto the two-lane road heading back towards the cabin.

"How was the call?" Frog asked.

"It went all right. I told Jim where to find Skinner's body. He's sending some guys out to look for him now. Apart from that, you and I have some work to do."

"Work?"

"Yeah, Big Jim wants us to make a list of all the members we can think of. He wants us to rank them in order of importance so he knows who's in charge."

"That's heavy. If we turn over everyone's names then they're *all* going to be after us."

"They already are."

"No, not all of them, just some of them."

"Does it make a difference, Frog?"

"I don't know, man, maybe."

"When you come down to it, how many people can actually kill you?"

"All of them."

"One, man. That's all it takes, and we've already got that one out looking for us."

Dylan's thoughts drifted to the Bay where the Hells Angels held the difference between his and Frog's lives or deaths in the palm of their hands.

***

Katie turned the television on, adjusted the rabbit ears on top, and when the picture was clear enough— 'clear' being relative after watching a plasma— she plopped herself down on the couch ready to watch the morning news.

It was Tuesday, August 3, 1967. The newscasters were still talking about the most recent race riot in Washington, D.C., which had started on Sunday night. In the Middle East, Israel had taken over full control of Jerusalem. In the US, President Johnson announced plans to send another 45,000 troops to Vietnam.

Katie marveled at the old fashioned commercials. They never seemed to get old, especially the cigarette ads, which always showed a healthy cowboy riding through the sunset, or a beautiful actress dressed in diamonds to promote the product. This picture of the sultry sexy smoker always made Katie snicker, knowing the truth about the product.

In a little over a week, on August 14th, Richard would be home on leave. Even though she had rehearsed her arguments over and over and reviewed her facts regarding Richard's death so that she could recite them on cue, she was still nervous. Her mind raced constantly, and she found it difficult to do everyday normal activities, including eating and sleeping.

This morning she had given up on both, fixed herself a cup of strong coffee and watched the news. She was still astonished by how much media coverage the Vietnam conflict had. In later years the US would never broadcast a war over television. But this was 1967, before the Patriot Act when the government wasn't experienced on how media coverage affected the masses. They would never make that mistake again. The Vietnam War had taught the US a lot about deceiving the American people, especially when it came to wars where, in present day, journalists couldn't even take pictures of flag covered coffins.

KTVU, channel Two was locally owned and independently transmitting from Oakland in the 1960's. Katie watched their newscast and then flipped through the stations to watch *The Price is Right*, back to channel two for *Dialing For Dollars* with Pat McCormick, and then at 3:00, her eerie favorite, *Dark Shadows* on ABC channel 11.

Depression had kept her sitting in the same spot every day for weeks. Besides using the bathroom or occasionally making herself a sandwich, she lived in front of the T.V., simply waiting for the most important event in her life.

She knew that she was brought back for this purpose, saving Richard's life, and hopefully Dylan's and Frog's too. She felt like Sam Becket in *Quantum Leap,* except she didn't have invisible Al's help, and she certainly didn't have Ziggy the computer system. Instead, she had to rely on herself and hope that she could get it right this time. Until that event took place, Katie knew that she wouldn't really be whole. Plus there was a nagging part of her that couldn't help but wonder what would happen if she did get it right. Would she, like Sam Becket, leap out of this time period and perhaps pop back to the present, or somewhere else?

It was up to her now. Depending on how successfully she played this visit she could actually reverse the worst thing that had ever happened to her family. The key to her success depended on how Richard would respond to their conversation. With Mark out of the way, all Katie needed to do was to keep Richard alive. If she failed at that then she wasn't sure if she wanted to go back to either lifetime.

By mid-day Katie was tired of going over the same questions and possible scenarios in her tormented mind. She was considering a shower when someone knocked on the door. She almost ignored it but the person was persistent.

"I'm coming, I'm coming!" she hollered. "Hang on a second."

Katie unlatched the chain and lock and pulled the door open. To her surprise, Janis Joplin stood in the doorway smiling.

"Janis!"

"Hey, baby, good morning. Is it okay that I came by?"

"Of course, but it's not morning, it's past three o'clock." Katie threw the door wide open and a flamboyantly dressed Janis walked inside.

"As I said, baby, good morning, at least it's morning to me." She chuckled. "Hell it's a rare thing these days if I see noon. I know it's a lot to ask, me just popping over here and all, but do you think you can give me another reading? I can pay if you want."

"You don't have to pay me, come in. Sorry, the living room is filled with a lot of junk. I've been spending a lot of time in front of the tube."

Janis looked at the darkened room, the empty potato bags, the half-eaten package of red licorice, and at two empty bottles of Coca Cola.

"Wow, man, sugar party?" she remarked with a snicker.

"Kind of, but chips are salt." Katie smiled and pulled some magazines off the other half of the couch so that Janis could sit beside her.

"Chips are way better for you because they're salt and oil instead of sugar. What is it? A break up with some fucking dude?" Janis asked.

"Not exactly, but it does have to do with a man, you're right about that," Katie said in defense of the disheveled state she was caught in.

"Is there anything I can do to help?"

"No, unfortunately it's one of those things that I have to work out for myself, you dig?"

Janis nodded and then sat on the couch, sinking into the overstuffed cushions. "If this is a bad time, man, I can come back later."

"No, it's actually an okay time. It will help me get out of this funk, make me concentrate on something other than myself. That's a good thing, believe me."

"Okay, man, if you say so. Are you going to do my cards again?"

"No, I think this time I'll just read your palm and feel the vibes when I touch you."

"Like you did when Brian Jones bumped into you in the saloon at Monterey?"

"Yes, exactly, just like that."

Janis nodded, swallowed hard, and then offered both hands to Katie. For several seconds Katie closed her eyes and held Janis's fingers, pretending to feel the projected vibes and then she opened her eyes and studied Janis's right palm.

"You've been very busy."

"Yes, just like you said we've had a lot of local shows and they'll continue until the end of this year. We've already started our booking for '68 and again like you said, we'll be going back east and then all over the nation." Janis grinned. "It's been crazy, things haven't calmed down for a minute, and we have bodyguards at all the events now. In fact, Mr. Grossman wants me to take somebody with me even when I'm just walking around the streets in 'Frisco, but I'm not ready to play that bag yet. This is my home, man, people know me, I'm safe on these streets."

Katie nodded. Janis *was* perfectly safe on the streets of San Francisco, and she was safe in a swimming pool. What she needed was someone to save her from herself.

"Have you been drinking a lot?" Katie asked.

"No more than usual," Janis lied.

Katie stared at her and then reluctantly the hippie star fessed up. "Okay yeah, I've been partying heavy, but I've been celebrating, man. I need to get all of my partying out of the way now while I'm young because I won't be able to when I get old." Janis laughed at her own excuse, Katie didn't.

"Janis, you need to start taking better care of yourself, eat better, sleep natural hours when you can and the partying...I can see that it's going to become a problem."

Janis, used to predictions that sounded like she was walking in heaven, was quiet. Then she nodded, "You're right, I don't take very good care of myself."

"I know." Katie continued to study Janis' palm. "Is someone trying to convince you to split from the band and go out on your own?" Katie asked, knowing full well that her new manager, Al Grossman, was becoming a source of friction in the band.

"You can tell that from my *palm*?" Janis asked. Katie nodded. Janis swallowed and stared at her feet. "Mr. Grossman says that I can do better without Big Brother. He thinks they're holding me back."

"Are you starting to believe that too?"

"Hell no. I've been talking to Mr. Grossman about signing the whole band, not just me."

That would happen, but it wouldn't stop Janis' manager from pushing her towards a solo career.

"He tells you that the band isn't as good as you are?" Janis nodded. "That they're holding you back from becoming a singing sensation?" Janis nodded again.

"Mr. Grossman says that they aren't good enough on their instruments. That if I had better musicians...maybe some horns..."

"He's wrong, Janis. It's a mistake to leave Big Brother. You'll regret it always, and you'll never feel right about it afterwards."

"I was afraid of that," Janis muttered.

"He's going to make it seem like you have to do it or you're not going to get anywhere. It's not the truth. If you leave Big Brother the guilt you feel...well that's really going to affect you moving forward. The band is your family away from your real family. You don't want to leave that connection, believe me."

"Mr. Grossman can be very persuasive. What if he makes me choose?"

"You're the star, Janis, do you really think he wants to cut that tie? And if he does, let him."

"Really? But what about my career?"

"You're going places, with or without the likes of Mr. Albert Grossman." That was what Janis wanted to hear.

"Now about your health. Your drinking is starting to affect you physically."

"I'm young, I can handle it."

"Can you?"

"Okay, maybe I've been doing too much partying but hell, I'm having a good time and this is a great place to be in my life. After all, man, I'm only twenty-four. I mean really, how much damage can I do to myself? Shit, cells and stuff regenerate themselves, right?"

"Not in the liver."

Janis laughed a nervous chuckle and pulled her hand back as if she'd just been burned. "Wow, man. Maybe this reading thing isn't such a good idea." She started to gather her belongings.

"Maybe it's the best reading you'll ever have."

"Well, it sure isn't starting out like that."

"Depends on what you take away from it, you dig?"

"I don't know, man, your readings are always creepy, but this one..."

"What if this one has the power to save your life someday?" Katie asked. "What I can see in your hand is that the cells in your liver are changing because of the alcohol you're consuming."

"How can you see that?"

"You see this line here?" Katie fabricated. "That's the line that shows your liver function. Do you see the breaks in the line here, and here? That shows the beginning of liver damage."

"Really, man?" Janis pulled her hand away and stared at the line in question, seeing the breaks that Katie had pointed out. She rubbed that part of her palm. "This is a bummer. I thought you were going to give me some more groovy news, I didn't expect a downer trip."

"I can give you great news. You'll be playing at the Hollywood Bowl next month and in the beginning of '68, just as you told me, you'll be on an East Coast tour. Everything you touch from here on out will turn to gold. By next March the band will be billed as 'Janis Joplin and Big Brother and the Holding company'. That's when your problems will start. Al Grossman will push for a split between you and the band and eventually you'll relent and break away. But that change is months away. By June of '68, Big Brother's second album will nearly be complete. Before it's released it will already hit gold status. By the middle of '68 you'll be on television shows galore, especially the *Dick Cavett Show,* and by the end of the year you'll be world famous, on a European tour."

"That's all good, man!"

"Everything about your career is good, better than good really, it's fabulous. You are going places, that's undeniable."

"So my health is the problem?"

"Oh yeah, it's going to become a big problem."

"Like how, man? I'm healthy."

"I told you that this might be the most important reading I ever give, depending on what you take away from it."

The color drained from Janis's face.

"I'm serious about that. The question is, do you want to know the truth, even if it's unpleasant?"

"I don't know, baby, now you're scaring me."

"This reading could have the potential of saving your life someday."

"Seriously?" Janis pulled a bottle of Southern Comfort out of her bag and took a swig. Seeing the look on Katie's face, she recapped the bottle and put it away.

"Well, do you want to know?" Katie asked, stone-faced.

Janis leaned her head on the back of the couch and covered her face with her hands.

"Never mind, I don't have to tell you anything right now. You've got a lot of time before anything bad happens but I'd watch my health if I were you, and I mean that seriously. If you keep going in the direction that you're moving now then your habits will get worse and then—"

"Stop, man. You asked me a question and you're giving me the answer before I decide whether I want to hear it or not."

"You're right, I'm sorry. It is your decision. I'm just saying that if you want to know...well you know where to find me."

Katie walked across the room and changed the television back to channel two just in time to watch hand puppets Charlie and Humphrey, created by KTVU's own Pat McCormick. Charley was a horse that wore a sea captain's hat, and Humphrey Hambone was his bulldog sidekick. (Eventually Humphrey wore a trademark Oakland Raiders sweater sent to him by Sonny Barger of the Oakland Hells Angels.)

"I love this show." Janis said. "I like *Dialing For Dollars* too."

"I know." Katie smiled. "You'll write a song about it."

"I will?" Janis swallowed hard. She twisted her hands together and then announced with a pained look on her face "Okay, man, tell me."

"You have time, Janis, you don't have to hear it now."

"But I will eventually."

"No, you can decide that you never want to know and never contact me again."

Janis nodded, she had thought of that possibility.

"No, man, I have to know, it will drive me crazy. Please tell me."

"Are you sure?"

"Yeah, man, I'm sure."

Katie turned the television off. "Let me see your hands again." She returned to studying Janis' palms, running her finger along several different lines as she tried desperately to weave a convincing story together in seconds.

"As I said before, the cells in your liver are changing. I know you're young but your drinking is already starting to affect your body. You're experiencing early signs that could lead to cirrhosis of the liver."

"That's pretty fucking scary."

"Isn't it though?"

Janis stared into Katie's unblinking eyes.

"That's not all, Janis. Your drug use... that's what's really going to get the best of you."

"What drug use, man? I barely use at all anymore."

"Maybe not, but you've shot speed in the past and you almost killed yourself then."

"Where are you getting all of this, man? This shit can't be written all over my palms."

"Do you remember how Brian Jones bumped into me? How I was able to feel what his future was going to be unless he changes things?"

Janis nodded.

"That's how I know."

"By touching me?"

"That's right, from touching you," Katie lied. "You might not be using now, or if you are maybe you're not using needles, but you will, and it will be heroin this time around."

"I tried it once but I haven't done it again. Well maybe a few times, but not recently," Janis confessed.

"It will be like that, you'll try it, and then move on and then you'll go back to it and try it again. It's like the pull of a magnet. As your career grows so will your drug use and alcohol use. You'll try to get off of the drugs and you'll be successful but then you'll start to think that you're cured, and there is no cure. The only treatment is to abstain completely, and you won't be able to do that, not for very long. You'll believe that you can use heroin recreationally without getting hooked again, but you're wrong.

"One day the odds will be against you. You'll have too much to drink, a few too many pills, and on top of that you'll shoot up. It won't be regular heroin either, it will be some super potent batch and the combination will—"

"You're kidding right? You're making this up." Janis face was blanched white and her hands shaking. She believed, Katie could tell, and she almost smiled.

"I wish I was kidding, but I'm not. You've seen my predictions come true. Inside you know that what I'm telling you is the truth."

"No, this is silly. It's just a game, like cards right? I'm a survivor, I know that."

"Brian Jones will be found dead in his swimming pool on July 3, 1969. The coroner will say that his death was from drowning and that his body had high levels of alcohol and intoxicating drugs. Jimi Hendrix will choke to death on his own vomit, he'll die September 18th 1970, and sixteen days later, you'll be found in a motel room in Los Angeles."

"Wait, you've never touched Jimi Hendrix. How can you know that?"

"The name of the place they'll find you in is called the Landmark Motel. You'll go out for a late night dinner after leaving the recording studio to a place called The Beanery. You'll have a few shots of tequila and then you'll go back to the motel. You'll shoot up in the room and then you'll go to the lobby for a pack of cigarettes. You'll seem fine; you'll chat with the motel worker for a few minutes and then you'll head back to your room. That's when the lethal combination will hit you. You won't even have a chance to smoke a cigarette.

"You'll have two friends who are supposed to show up that night, neither will. The voice recording that you're supposed to make the next day, so that you can finish off another album, won't happen. Instead, the album will include one instrumental track and the record will be released after you're gone."

"When is this supposed to happen?"

"Sometime during the night of October 3, 1970. You won't live to see the sun rise on the 4th."

"Fuck!"

"That's three years from now, Janis. You can change this."

"Fuck!"

Janis stood. She was pasty white and blended with the wall behind her.

"The pusher, the guy who sells you the smack, I think his name is Dave. His tester is gone that weekend so he markets his batch without having anyone sample it. It's strong, very strong, between 50%-80% pure. Eight people will die that weekend from the same batch, and you will be one of them."

"Fuck!" She gathered her belongings . "I don't think I can hear any more of this right now. I need some fresh air." Janis turned on shaking legs and walked out of the yellow Victorian house.

Chapter 42

For the past two months, Big Jim had been in investigative mode. As Dylan had predicted, the drug ring had a long ladder. Most of the players used false identities, so tracking them was difficult. What Jim did know, was that taking the whole drug ring down was virtually impossible.

After several meetings with the First Skulls, the Angels' course of action was clear. They needed to keep their names out of the media and to do that, they needed to be ready to negotiate. The real challenge was finding who they needed to negotiate with. The club was instructed to leave Sal, Dave and Joey alone while they concentrated on the bigger fish in the bowl. As for Sal and Dave, Big Jim had special plans in mind for them.

Dylan and Frog's list had been informative but almost worthless. These people were pros; they didn't use their own names. Many times one person had multiple identities. Piecing out who each of them was more problematic than it was worth. The Angels had resorted to what they did best. They watched their suspects and learned everything they could about the people they knew were involved.

Skinner's body was found where Dylan said it would be. Despite the badly decomposed form, it was still possible to tell that his death wasn't an accident. Of course, for an accident to occur there needed a bike present, and Skinner's wasn't found.

Jim had Skinner's remains removed from the gully without media attention. Through other club 'connections', Randal Skinner's cause of death on his certificate was listed as accidental. It was well understood that the Hells Angels would be handing the actual killers. This was how the First Skulls wanted the situation handled.

Now in the second week of August, Big Jim sat in his office at the Dogpatch clubhouse reviewing his notes. Despite his investigative work and the long hours of labor his men had put in, his notes were vague. These people knew what they were doing. Even with his Angel contacts he couldn't compete with the mastermind of this drug organization. The cover up was just too complex for the club to unravel alone.

In the main room, a telephone rang. Several minutes later Terry knocked on Big Jim's partially opened door. "Hey boss, the guy on the phone wants to talk to you."

"Who is it?"

"He wouldn't say."

"What did he say?"

"He said that you were going to want to talk to him."

Big Jim followed Terry to the next room where the telephone sat on a paper-cluttered desk. He sat at the desk and pushed some of the unorganized piles out of the way before taking the receiver.

"This is Jim."

"Mr. Jim, how nice to talk to you. My name is Calvin, I think you've been looking for me."

It took Big Jim a few seconds to realize who he was talking to. His mind flashed between the players on his list and then he remembered Frog's description of the businessman in Oakland. The one who had saved him from being turned over to the Black Panthers as a car thief; the one who had tried to get him safely out of the city of Oakland.

"Yes, actually I have been looking for you."

"I heard from several sources that your men have been following my men. Did you think that we wouldn't notice Hells Angels watching us?"

"We are a little hard to miss aren't we? Sure, I knew you would notice, but I needed to draw you out some way, Calvin, so that we could have a little chat."

"And here I am personally calling you. I have to admit the suspense is killing me. I've been wondering for days why the San Francisco Hells Angels might be looking for me. Please tell me what this all about?"

"If you don't mind, I think I'd rather do this in person."

"I expected as much. Shall I send a car over to get you? It's much easier that way, I assure you."

"You want to pick me up? And you're expecting me to come alone?"

"Sadly, Jim, trust is what this world is lacking. My driver, Peter, will be there in less than an hour, no weapons."

The line went dead. Jim rubbed his forehead. He had expected a meeting with one of the main organizers but he hadn't expected to be picked up in a car, which most assuredly would turn out to be a limo. The idea of going alone was not appealing but what choice did he have? Sometimes being the president of the San Francisco Chapter of the Hells Angels came with a price, and this was one of those times.

***

Katie's brother arrived on Tuesday, August 15, 1967. Her father and mother had picked him up from the airport and according to her parents, Richard had slept for the first two days of his visit.

On Saturday, August 19th, Katie was invited to dinner at her parents' house. This time she was alone, vulnerable, and incredibly nervous.

Her father sent a taxi to pick her up at 5:30 and Katie, who had packed an overnight bag just in case she decided to stay, reluctantly stepped into the yellow cab. An hour later the driver pulled up in front of the house in Antioch.

Katie's father saw the cab and stepped out on the porch to greet her. He paid the driver and then hugged her. "Katie, it's good to see you. Your mother and I were so worried when Lt. Dixon called. I'm so sorry about what happened."

"It's not your fault that Mark Rhodes is a mental case."

"No, but it is my fault that your mother and I pushed him on you."

Katie couldn't argue.

"Listen, before we go inside, I want to talk to you about your brother."

"My brother?"

"That's right, he's different. Quiet and kind of moody. He doesn't like a lot of questions. Actually, he doesn't like to talk at all."

"Shell shocked," Katie said.

"Yes, I suppose it's something like that."

"Okay, anything else?"

"Your mother. She's been drinking a lot more over the last few days, stress. It's hard for her to see your brother this way."

Katie nodded. It was going to be difficult for her to see Richard like this too.

They both walked into the house, which was darker than normal.

"Lights?" Katie asked.

"Candles, your mother's idea. She thinks it makes things…serene."

In the background Johnny Cash sang, 'I Walk the Line.' The house felt gloomy and a shiver ran through Katie's body.

Her mother was sitting on a chair in the dining room and Richard was on the couch, both staring blankly at the TV, where Yul Brynner and Deborah Kerr danced in elaborate costumes. Katie walked into the room and her mother rose to greet her.

"Katherine, darling, it's good to see you."

She hugged Katie. Katie closed her eyes. Her mother smelled familiar, like cigarettes and gin. Katie's childhood flashed before her.

When Katie walked towards Richard on the couch, he rose. He didn't say anything, just embraced her and then almost robotically sat back down.

Katie tried to think of something to say but she was tongue-tied. What was she supposed to do? Ask him something stupid, like, how are you?

She dove into a conversation immediately by mentioning Mark Rhodes.

"I suppose you heard what happened to me at the Pop Festival?" she asked, and Richard nodded.

"I did hear about that. Is the loser still locked up?" he asked in a low monotone voice.

"Yes, he is." Katie swallowed hard, and then asked her next question. "I didn't know that you and Mark were friends."

"Katherine, why don't you tell us about San Francisco?" her mother asked, trying to change the conversation from a topic she found offensive.

"Turns out that he wasn't a friend after all. It's a good thing he's in jail or I would blow his brains out," Richard said, sounding chillingly honest.

"Too bad he's not out on bail, I would have enjoyed that." Katie grinned and Richard smiled too.

"Oh look, Al, my baby boy is smiling." The ice cubes in Pat's glass jingled and she nearly fell off her chair. Richard glared at her, looked at Katie and then rolled his eyes.

"So you heard what Dennis Drummond said about Mark Rhodes? How he deliberately convinced you to leave college and go into the Marines?"

Al nodded. "I told him."

"Imagine that guy working as dad's protégé all these years while secretly stabbing all of us in the back." Richard shook his head in disgust.

"I hope he gets butt raped in prison," Katie commented.

"Katherine! I can't believe you would talk like that," Pat slurred, taking another sip of her gin and tonic.

"Well it's the truth. I hope it happens more than once too. I hope some big, hairy, tattooed inmate takes a special liking to him and decides to use Mark as his special boy toy."

Richard laughed.

"Katherine!"

Katie smiled. It was good to hear her brother laugh.

"I need a drink," she said, and scurried to the drink tray in the hallway where she made herself a martini, hoping that the rush of alcohol would steady her nerves. "Does anyone want anything?" When nobody answered she made her way back into the living room.

Katie sat next to her brother and sipped her drink. Richard and their mother had gone back to staring at the television.

"How about we turn on a few lights? I like candles and all, but this feels like we're sitting in a morgue."

"This is relaxing," Pat answered without looking away from the T.V.

"No, this is depressing."

This time her father nodded in agreement and went for a light switch in the hall. The sudden illumination took the eerie feeling out of the room, especially when Al blew out some of the candles.

"Way to go Dad, that's much better." Katie nodded. "Next question, why are we watching television and listening to the stereo at the same time?"

"Because it's relaxing," Pat replied.

"No, not really, it's kind of annoying." Katie took a few more sips of her martini. So far the drink hadn't done anything to improve her mood, perhaps she needed to drink it a little faster.

Richard watched her. "You might want to take it easy on that," he suggested.

"I need a smoke. Do you want to come outside with me?"

"Do you smoke now?" Pat asked. "It's okay, dear, you can smoke in here with me." Pat pulled her pack of cigarettes out of her leopard print cigarette purse, shoved one into her mouth, lit it hurriedly, and then sucked in deeply.

The smoke rose into the air and wrapped itself around the ceiling, hanging there like a dark cloud.

"Actually, I think I need to get some fresh air," Katie said, rising from the sofa. She could feel the martini now, her body felt warm and flushed and as she'd hoped, she felt more relaxed.

"I'll go with you." Richard followed her towards the sliding glass door.

***

Within an hour of the call, a limo pulled up in front of the Hells Angels' clubhouse. The driver, who verified that his name was indeed Peter, exited the car and helped Big Jim into the back.

He sat in the back surrounded by expensive alcohols and fine crystal glasses. He remembered mafia movies that he had seen and wondered if Peter was taking him someplace to be bumped off. Despite the fear that had settled in his stomach, Jim allowed Peter to shut the door of the limo and then drive away from the Dogpatch.

They crossed the Bay Bridge and headed into Oakland. Peter suggested a drink several times but Jim declined. As tempting as the offer was, he was determined to have a clear head when he met the mysterious Calvin.

Peter headed towards Jack London Square, where he parked the limo in front of a fancy steak house.

"We're here, sir." Peter slid the car into a VIP parking space.

"Enjoy your lunch, sir. I'll be here when you're ready to leave."

Relieved that his ride had ended in a nice place rather than at the bottom of the bay, Big Jim jumped out of the car and headed into the restaurant.

The place was dark. It took several minutes before his eyes adjusted to the lighting, and when they did, he stood in the entry hall studying his surroundings.

Tito's Steak house had steps down to the main floor where booths with real tablecloths adorned with peach colored candles lined two sides of the room. In the middle, antique style tables were sporadically spaced so waiters in tuxedos could easily lift heavy trays safely between the patrons.

The host, who called himself Doug, greeted Big Jim at the door and escorted him down the steps and through the semi-populated tables. In the very back of the restaurant he opened a side door and led Jim into a private dining room where an Armani suited black businessman stood when he entered the room.

"Big Jim, how good to meet you." Calvin held his manicured hand out as a peace offering.

Big Jim grasped his hand and the two formally introduced themselves.

"I hope you like a good steak, Jim," Calvin said. "I had my people save us some very fine filet mignon for our lunch this afternoon."

"A good steak sounds fine to me," Big Jim said.

"Now what kind of wine do you prefer, Jim, red or white?"

Jim was shocked. This was not at all what he expected. No one in his life had ever asked him about wine before.

"Wine?"

"Of course, a gentleman never discusses business before a nice meal. Please, red or white?"

"I'll trust your judgment. Which do you prefer?"

"Ahhh, myself I like Cabernet, but occasionally I like a good pinot noir if I can find one."

"Cabernet is fine."

"Very well. Anthony, can you get us my usual?" he asked the tuxedoed Asian man who stood in the dimly lit corner of the room.

"Of course, sir."

Anthony disappeared for several minutes. When he returned he was carrying a wine bottle in one hand and two glasses in the other. He set the glasses down and opened the bottle, pouring a small amount into Calvin's glass and allowing him to taste the contents.

"Very nice." Calvin smacked his lips and Anthony filled Calvin's glass half full and then he did the same for Jim.

"Wonderful taste of oak blending with just a hint of wild cherry."

Jim tasted the wine and agreed the blend tasted okay. As far as oak and cherries were concerned, all he could taste was wine, but since he generally drank Budweiser he wasn't sure his approval meant anything.

Anthony took their steak orders and then rushed to the kitchen, leaving the two men alone with the bottle of wine.

"I'm sure you'll like the food here Jim, it's such a delightful place. Exquisite really.

Jim surveyed his surroundings. The insides of the restaurant and this private room were fancy that was for sure, but he cared little for such things and wished he were back in the Dogpatch Saloon where he could really feel at home.

Their meals arrived. Anthony placed the dishes in front of them, refilled their wine glasses and left so they could eat in private.

"So, Jim, are you a native San Franciscan?"

"Yes, born and raised. How about you, are you a local boy?"

"Indeed, Oakland born and raised."

"The Bay Area is a great place to grow up."

"That depends, are you talking about the weather, entertainment, or advancements and opportunities for everyone?"

Calvin chewed his perfectly cooked steak, savoring the dish. Big Jim munched his down, wishing he had ketchup and considered asking for a bottle, but Calvin started talking about the different ingredients and how their 'special touch' made the dish what it was. In his opinion this steak was perfect and Jim took that as a hint that maybe this time he should eat his meal without smothering it in ketchup.

"Well the weather is nice. The entertainment in the city is fine too, but as for advancements and opportunities, things are pretty much fucked for everyone unless they have a relative in the system."

Calvin smiled. As crude as this biker was he liked him. Jim was honest, and Calvin respected that.

When the meal was over and the dishes cleared, Calvin ordered another bottle of wine as he and Jim sat back to discuss business.

"I must say, Jim, I'm at a loss. I know that some of your men are involved in a business deal with my organization, but I'm not really clear what that has to do with the Angels or why several of my key figures have been followed during the past few weeks."

"Calvin, I have a problem. I'm hoping that with your help we might be able to solve an issue that could otherwise bring unwanted attention to both of us."

"Unwanted attention? From whom?"

"The media, police, people that you and I don't want to deal with."

"I'm listening."

Calvin poured the remainder of the second bottle of wine into both of their empty glasses.

"I'm sure you're aware of the Hells Angels' reputation," Big Jim said.

"Naturally."

"The higher ups in our club are trying to clean that image up. It's gotten to the point where we can't ride our bikes in peace without someone getting all over our backs. The pigs and the media are all there waiting to pounce on anything we do wrong."

"Yes, I'm aware," Calvin nodded.

"In order to make those changes we've been doing a lot of community service. We're trying to get the people of San Francisco to know us so that they aren't scared every time we ride down the street."

"I see, and what does that have to do with me?"

"Your organization contains several of our members. Members who were warned about bringing negative attention to the club, defying our rules, or running non-approved business operations beyond club orders. What I want is to take my people out of this."

"And why should I care about your so called club rules, especially when I don't understand what any of this has to do with me?"

"For one, the murder of Randal Skinner."

"Murder?" Calvin shook his head. He was obviously shocked.

"That's right, we found his body in Monterey. We figure he died on the way to the festival. He'd been beaten to death."

"And you think I had something to do with that?"

"I'm not sure what I think, so I'm going to ask you outright, did you?"

"Certainly not. I have heard of Skinner, though, and I know that his actions were starting to cause problems in my operation. Several of your guys actually turned the problem over to my higher ups quite recently. However, I want you to know, Jim, that I am not involved in this man's death. If you're thinking that we organized a hit, then you're wrong. Perhaps the men from your own club are responsible, but we most assuredly are not."

"That's good to know. It gives me a starting point as to where I need to look next. As for my men, the ones who are working with you, I want them out, and I want it done quietly."

"Jim you do understand that pulling your men out won't solve anything? Heavy drugs are coming to San Francisco and there isn't a soul who can stop that. The Black Panthers have tried to keep them out of Oakland, but of course they haven't been successful and neither will you. Someone is going to bring merchandise in when there's a market for it. That, my friend, is the way of the world."

"I realize that, I'm not trying to stop anything. All I'm asking is for my men to be out, especially if they're the ones who are responsible for Skinner's murder."

"A murder you think was caused because of their involvement in my business operation?"

"That's right."

"You are correct I don't want any publicity regarding that. Where, may I ask, is Mr. Skinner's body now?"

"He's buried. The club took care of the evidence and his death has been ruled an accident. We know otherwise, and as a club we are ready to clear up this mess in the easiest and most effective way."

"I could have my men clear the mess up for you," Calvin offered, finishing his glass of wine.

"Unnecessary, we prefer to handle our own problems."

"Very well, and who are these men that you want out of my operation?"

"Dave, Sal, Joey, Dylan Taylor, and a hippie called Frog."

"Oh yes, Frog." Calvin laughed. "I remember Frog, I met him in Oakland. I had to save him from a crowd of angry men who thought he'd stolen an old van. Frog isn't a biker, why are you including him on your list?"

"Frog is a friend of the club, he comes with the rest of my boys."

"A friend to the club? I guess I'm not clear, I thought you were taking your men out to 'deal with' them quietly. Now you're telling me that you want Frog out because he's a friend of the club."

"When Skinner was killed, Dylan and Frog became targets. They're presently in hiding. Before this meeting I suspected that you had put a hit out on them too."

Calvin laughed. "That's preposterous."

"Which means if you didn't order a hit, then I have a lot more detective work left to do. But at least now I have a pretty good idea of who I'm going to be investigating."

"Take your people, Jim. I have no use of them. Their positions can be filled immediately. I have many possibilities waiting in line. Your men are starting to bring attention my way and as you said, that's a problem. All five of your boys are free to go. I hope that will solve both of our problems."

"I hope you're right." Big Jim rose from the table ready to take Peter's limo back to San Francisco.

***

Katie and Richard walked into the backyard. The sun was just starting to set when they sat on a bench that overlooked the horizon.

"Mom and Dad driving you crazy?" she asked.

"That's an understatement."

Katie pulled a joint out of her bag and smelled it. "Purple Haze, California grown. I bet it's better than the shit you get over there."

"Not necessarily, we get some really good ganja. Strange shit, looks almost black, but I'll tell you what, some of it is out of this world."

Katie handed Richard the pre-rolled smoke and watched as her brother lit up.

"Tastes good," he said after a deep drag.

"Yes it's good, I have a friend who grows it, and contrary to what you might think, 60's weed is as good as it gets. The debates on THC content that are to come are just ridiculous."

Richard laughed. "You're an odd one, Katie. What does that even mean?"

"Nothing yet, but someday it will." Katie took a sip off of the martini she carried and set it on the brick patio so she could take the joint from her brother.

"See, I told you to go easy on that shit." Richard picked the glass up and drained it. He set the glass down and then sucked in deeply on the joint, all the while staring at the sun just coming down over the horizon. "It's beautiful." He passed the joint to his sister.

"Very." Katie finished the smoke and disposed of the discolored paper on the ground.

"It feels strange to be home... different," Richard stated. "No, on second thought I'm the one who's different; home is still the same place."

"I can't say that I understand, but I want to."

"Mom and Dad, Jesus! You can't believe the fucking questions they ask. Finally I just stopped talking. What's the point? I didn't come here for them to cheer me up."

"What about your friends?"

"What about my friends? You mean people like Davis and Arnold? What do I have in common with them? I tried. I went out with them and...I just didn't belong. I'm not like them anymore. I'm not like anyone here anymore." Richard sighed. "I want to go back, can you believe that? I couldn't wait for this week to come, and now that I'm here all I can think about is going back. I don't fit in here. I don't know who I am anymore, that's disturbing. If I feel this way on a visit, what's it going to be like when I finally come back? I haven't been gone that long, but look how much I've already changed."

Katie thought of a song not yet written. In 1982, the Charlie Daniels Band would epitomize the way most Vietnam vets felt about returning. The title, 'I'm Still in Saigon,' said it all. In the song the singer explains that the only place where he ever really knew who he was, was in Vietnam.

That, she imagined, was how Richard was feeling now.

"It's called post-traumatic stress disorder, Richard."

"What?"

"All veterans come home feeling that way, you're not alone."

"How would you know that?" Richard asked.

Katie shrugged. "You've come home expecting things to feel the same but as you said, you've changed. That isn't a bad thing, it's just the way it is. When you come home for good you'll have to find a new niche in this world. It will take time but eventually..."

"That's just it, I don't think I'm going to be coming home."

"What are you talking about?" Katie asked. This visit was turning out to be much different than the first time around when they had spent their time arguing about the war. This time Richard was confiding in her.

"Let's be real, Katie, do you know where I'm stationed? Right outside of the DMZ, one of the most dangerous spots in the war. I'm no fool, the odds are against me."

"You shouldn't say that."

"I shouldn't say it, just think it you mean?"

"I guess it would be foolish for me to say neither."

Richard smiled. "Thanks for being honest. That's the worst part about this visit, everyone is pretending that everything is the same as it was when I left. I watch everyone stumbling over their words because they don't know what to say to me. I see the fear in their eyes when they realize that I've changed, but you...well at least you're not pretending."

"It's tempting." She laughed, so did Richard.

"Hey, I know a spot where you'll feel at home. Let's go to Ike's, that little bar down on the main street, it's where the vets hang out. I'll buy you a drink."

"You're going to take me to a place where I can visit with the rest of the damaged?

"No, a place where you can mingle with kindred souls. Or would you rather stay home and hang out with Mom and Dad?"

Richard was fast to get off of the bench. "Hell no, anything's better than that. Let's go."

Instead of going back into the house Richard and Katie sneaked out of the side gate and headed towards the neighborhood dive bar, which was within walking distance.

"I told you to come and stay with me in 'Frisco when you came for your visit, you should have listened."

"With all the hippies? You know what they say about the soldiers? They say that we're rapists and baby killers. I really don't think I would like it there."

"People are stupid, who cares what any of them think?"

For the next few minutes they walked in silence as Katie framed her warning conversation, wondering when and where to bring the topic up. She had a speech memorized, but now that she was here with Richard she wasn't sure it was the way to handle things. Perhaps taking the evening one step at a time would be a better plan.

When they got to Ike's, Richard held the door open. Katie walked into the dimly lit bar and smiled. As she had predicted, this was a place where Richard would feel at home. Richard studied the rectangular shaped bar, noticing the other soldiers, who just like him, were home from the war.

They took a seat at the bar and both ordered a beer and a shot of tequila. Since they had skipped out before dinner, they decided to share a burger and fries.

"Do you think they've noticed that we're gone yet?" Katie asked.

"Not a chance. Mom is too blitzed and Dad, well he's not far behind."

The bartender arrived with their drinks, two ice-cold bottles of Coors and two shot glasses of tequila.

"Here's looking at you, kid," Richard said, imitating Bogart and then they both chugged the tequila and bit into a salt covered lemon.

In the middle of the room several vets crowded around a pool table. Others stood at the bar and still more sat drinking at tables. The atmosphere was friendly and pleasant.

"You're right, I do fit in here," Richard admitted, sipping on his beer. "How did you know about this place?"

"You would be surprised at the things I know."

"You're different, Katie, you've changed too. I don't know how to explain it but you seem...older...wiser."

Their burger arrived. Katie asked for a second plate and she split the meal into two portions.

They sat eating and drinking their beers as they watched the activity around them. Beside the pool table several men played dice. The jukebox played music Richard had listened to in 'Nam, and he found himself drifting into a space where he felt content.

"Who's the guy who saved you? The one who beat Mark to a pulp?" Richard asked out of the blue.

"That would be Dylan."

"It was a good thing Dylan went to the concert."

"Yeah, a very good thing. I'd probably be dead now if he didn't find me when he did."

"Mom says he's a Hells Angel? Really, Katie, you're involved with a biker? That doesn't seem like your style. Aren't hippies and bikers complete opposites?"

"One would think." Katie laughed. "First off, we aren't involved, not really. We've never done anything but kiss. Secondly, he isn't around anymore, so the relationship is finished before it got a chance to start."

"Where is he?"

"Now that's a story in itself. Actually, I have a lot of stories I could tell you. As far as Dylan goes, he has his own agenda. He left right after the concert, right after he helped me." Katie paused and swallowed, remembering the attack. "He was on his way out of town when he found me actually. As soon as he knew I was safe he was gone."

"Is he gone for good?"

"I don't know. I'd like to say no but I can't answer that."

"You haven't heard from him in two months?"

"No, and I don't expect to hear from him anytime soon either. He and Frog, well I just hope they're safe."

"Frog. I know I've heard that name before. He's your hippie friend right?"

"That's right, he's Moonbeam's, I mean Annie's, boyfriend."

"And he's gone too?"

"Yep, he's with Dylan, hopefully safe, and as I said before I don't expect to hear from either of them anytime soon."

"What about Annie, has she heard from Frog?"

"Nope, she checks the mailbox every day hoping that today's the day she'll get a letter or a card but she's wasting her time. It will be a long time before we hear from them, if we hear from them."

"None of that makes sense."

"I know, it's not supposed to. Anyway, Dylan's not my main concern at the moment." She finished off her beer. Richard gulped down the last of his own and then ordered two more and two more tequilas.

"What if he wasn't gone?" Richard asked.

"You're persistent. If he wasn't gone and things were different...I don't know, maybe then he would be my future but that's not the case. Dylan and I are... we're like two souls who meet in every lifetime but never manage to get together."

"That's an odd thing to say."

"I am odd, haven't you noticed?"

The bartender brought their new drinks and collected the discarded remains of dinner.

"Do you really think you won't be coming home?"

Richard took a few sips off of his beer and then nodded. "I won't come home, Katie. I know that for a fact, I can feel it. I dream about it too, it's only a matter of time before my number is up."

"But what if you had information that could change that?"

Richard didn't answer. He stared at her, really stared at her. For several minutes he remained quiet then another round of shots arrived. He toasted his sister and they chugged the tequilas. They sipped at their beers in silence and then unexpectedly Richard turned and looked at her. "Who are you, Katie, and why are you so different?"

"I'm an old soul."

"Yes you are, but you never were before. I feel like I'm talking to a person I don't know. I mean, it's you, of course, you remember everything about our past, you look like you, but you're not the Katie that I know."

"Now that's a real odd thing to say."

"Is it?"

What was she supposed to say? This was an unforeseen obstacle she couldn't explain so she decided not to try.

"Yeah, it's a real odd thing to say," she repeated.

Richard stared at her, waiting for an answer that didn't come. Instead, she said something that was so unexpected that he forgot the question he had just asked.

"You get a lot of inexperienced commanders, don't you?"

The question took Richard by surprise. Even though the tequila had already dulled his senses he blinked rapidly as he tried to understand where the conversation was going.

"What do you mean?"

"I mean one nearly got you killed, you know the one who managed to get himself blown up by a land mine. Despite that fiasco you're still getting untrained officers, right? Ones who can potentially endanger their troops?"

Katie had studied the battle her brother had died in for forty-five years. She had read everything ever written on the topic. It was easy to rattle the facts off the top of her head, and in her drunken state she decided to do just that.

"Who the fuck are you, Katie? How can you know any of that?" Richard ordered more tequila and chugged his fast without going through the salt and lemon ritual.

"You'll get more bad commanders, some will be worse than others. Eventually you'll get some cat named Becker, a real loser. He'll be transferred from operations to the front because of a mistake he makes there. They'll send him to Camp Carroll to get rid of him."

"Trace Becker?" Richard asked. He was confused, his head swimming with the effects of the tequila.

"That's right, you're going to have him. The higher ups think that putting Becker in a combat zone where all he has to do is follow orders is a good idea, but it's not."

"I know Becker, he just transferred in the day before I left." Richard was startled. A chill crept up his spine and he shivered. "How do you know any of this?"

"Becker is going to get the whole platoon killed, thirty-six men plus himself. It will happen in October."

"What are you talking about, Katie? This is getting really fucking creepy."

"It will be called Operation Kingfisher and it will take place in September. On the 21st the 2/4 Marines start a search and destroy mission where they encounter a NVA regiment. Since they're lacking in tank support, because heavy rains knocked out roads and bridges, that becomes a problem. The dense vegetation and the close proximity to the enemy restricts them from receiving either reinforcements or air support.

"After a daylong battle the Marines suffer with sixteen dead and one hundred eighteen wounded while trying to break free from the enemy's kill zone. At dusk the battalion withdraws, and because of the NVA's presence they can't return to pick up their dead for three weeks. That's the beginning of a siege, which will last from September until October 31st.

"In the second week of October the 2/4 will relieve another unit's mission to defend a recently built bridge. The construction of the bridge reopens a vital road to Con Thien that has been washed out by the Monsoons. The bridge has to be defended because if it's destroyed it will cut off the only supply line that leads to Con Thien.

"But I'm not in the 2/4, Katie."

"I know that, Richard, you're in the 2/9. Your platoon will go in as reinforcements somewhere around the 26th or 27th of October."

"My platoon?"

"That's right, under the command of Captain Becker."

"Wait a minute, Katie, this isn't making any sense."

"Becker panics. He doesn't do well in emergencies. He already knows that but for the sake of his men he tries to fake it. Under the pressure of being bombarded with artillery, he makes a decision that doesn't coincide with the mission. The men of the 2/9 must have known that he was wrong. They had been there long enough to know when a commander was running on fear, but what could they do? They had to follow orders; to do otherwise would be mutiny. And so they followed him to their deaths. None returned, all thirty-six men killed in action."

"How can you say these things? How do you know about Con Thein Base, or about the divisions that are stationed near me? You can' t know any of these things, it isn't possible."

"When Operation Kingfisher starts you're going to think about this conversation. You'll play it over and over in your mind so you need to remember as much as you can about what I'm telling you. Right now I know it sounds like science fiction. Like something you'd watch on Star Trek, but when it starts to play out, just exactly the way I tell you that it will, you're going to think back on this conversation a lot."

"What is this, Katie?"

"This is about my premonitions, Richard, one of my many dreams that come true. The same way that I know that you led your unit back safely after your lieutenant died and stranded you in the jungle."

"You don't have premonitions, you never had them before, not ever!"

"You said it yourself. I'm different. You asked me why. This is why, Richard. I can see the future, and I know that you won't live past the 27th of October."

"Stop this, Katie, fucking stop it."

Richard stood from his stool abruptly. Everyone in the small bar suddenly turned and stared.

"You're talking crazy because you're drunk!"

"I'm talking crazy because it's the truth and you need to hear it. Becker will lead you down a hill thinking that he's taking you to the objective but he's wrong. Down that hill is a whole regiment of NVA. He'll tell you to hold your position, but if you do they'll surround you. Enemy reinforcements will arrive, but yours won't. Your platoon fights valiantly, but you can only hold out for so long before your ammo is gone. Somewhere on the night of the 27th that fight comes to an end, and you n Richard's head swam. He started to hyperventilate and held onto the bar for support thinking that any moment he might go down.

"When you find yourself in that position you'll know I was telling you the truth and here's the most important part. Remember this, Richard, this will save your life and the lives of the men you convince to go with you."

Richard swayed and Katie jumped off of the stool and held his arm, turning him towards her. She shook him to get his attention. When he turned to look at her his eyes were watering.

"Go up the hill, Richard. I know it's a rugged climb, Becker will tell you that the only way out is down, but he's wrong. You're surrounded and there is no way out. Don't head towards the flatlands because troops of NVA are marching towards your location. The only way out is *up*. Climb, and then head towards Gia Bihn and the Red River Delta."

"The Delta is flatland." Richard shook his head.

"I didn't say to go there I said to head *towards* the Delta, towards Gia Bihn and away from An Kha."

"How do you know the names of these places? How do you know about the terrain and the Delta?"

"I know because everything I'm telling you is the truth. If you don't take steps to stop it then the events that I'm describing will happen and your dreams will come true, you'll never return from Vietnam."

**

When Big Jim returned from his lunch with Calvin he gathered his men together and they decided to pay Dave and Sal a little visit.

When the posse of twelve bikes pulled up in front of the shop, Dave tapped Sal on the shoulder and pointed out of the window. Before the group of bikers could descend upon them they stepped out on the sidewalk to greet them.

"Hey, brothers, what a surprise," Dave said. "I'm not sure if we're really ready for company though."

"We need to talk." Jim strode past both men and entered the garage.

"Hey, what is this?" Sal asked. He backed himself against the wall so the twelve men could enter the building without knocking him down.

"This, my friends, is a little conversation that we're going to have," Sal said sternly, "one that's well past due, and I bet you have a pretty good idea of what it's going to be about."

"Not true, man, I don't know what this is or why you're here," Dave said with a fake smile.

"That's not true. You know exactly why we're here. I bet you've known that this meeting was coming for a long time."

Dave laughed, trying to act innocent. "I'm sure I don't know what you're talking about, man."

"I'm talking about a heroin ring, one that you and your boys are involved in."

"Look around, man, all we're doing is running a gara—" Sal started.

Jim shoved him into the wall and shook him hard. "Don't fucking play games with me, you little shit. I've already been to see Calvin and we had a very interesting conversation about your involvement. *Former* involvement, I should say, because you're out."

"What are you talking about, man?" Dave asked.

"I'm saying that I've been to see your boss, Calvin, the fancy businessman in Oakland. He and I made a deal. The two of you, as well as everyone else in our club, are out. Do you understand? You're done."

Sal's face turned beet red and he trembled in anger. "You can't decide what we can and can't do." Terry and Chocolate George stepped closer, ready to curb any movement he made with force.

"Oh yes I can, as long as you're in this club, which by the way is a short lived status. Now, I've got some questions, and how the two of you answer them will determine your future." Big Jim turned and pointed at Freddy. "Get some chairs, we're going to be here a while."

Freddy and several other Angels pulled chairs in from the offices and from the entry room. Before heading back into the garage, Freddy put the closed sign in the window and pulled down the front blinds.

When he returned to the garage, Big Jim had Dave and Sal sitting in chairs. They were facing the Angels' president listening attentively.

"First question." Big Jim cleared his throat. "Who's responsible for Skinner's death?"

"Skinner's death?" Dave asked shaking his head in confusion. "Skinner is dead?"

Big Jim smacked him hard in the head. "Come on, man, don't fucking play games with me!"

"Fuck man." Dave held the spot were Jim struck him; it was already bruising. "There's no need for that, shit. I'm serious, man, this is the first I've heard about Skinner's death."

"He's right, man," Sal said. "We turned the situation over to Calvin's people. We didn't know they had him taken out so quickly."

"They didn't take him out," Jim said. "Calvin insinuated that you did."

"Hell no, man, that's not true! We turned the situation over to Calvin a week ago. If he says that they aren't the ones who had him whacked, it sure as fuck wasn't us."

"They're lying, let's just shoot them," Freddy said, and the other bikers laughed. Sal and Dave didn't, they looked terrified.

"We didn't have anything to do with Skinner's death, that's the God's honest truth!" Sal yelled.

Chocolate George stepped close to Jim and whispered, "I think they're telling the truth."

Jim stared at the men seated before them. For some reason he believed them too, which left a bigger problem. If Dave and Sal had nothing to do with Skinner's death, then who killed him?

Jim shook his head. None of this made sense. "You are officially removed from the Hells Angels. Regardless of what happened to Skinner, the facts remain. You went behind the club's back and you got involved in a business you were told not to. One which you knew could threaten your membership in the club. For your actions you are hereby de-patched."

"Freddy, Mikey, and Danny are going to escort you to the state line between California and Nevada. You're going to step over that line and you are never going to enter California again. You are officially out of the Angels and you're banned from ever joining any other state chapters. If you ever come back to California then the club with deal with you further, if you know what I mean?"

Sal and Dave stared at the floor. They looked relieved. It was clear they had expected worse, but then so had the rest of the Angels.

"That's it?" Terry asked, remembering his own beating at the hands of Dylan and Joey.

"God knows if it were solely up to me the punishment would be much worse, but the First Skulls are serious about cleaning up the club's reputation. A harsh punishment with media attention isn't worth the positive ground we've made with our charity work."

Jim made an inconspicuous thumb up sign directed towards Freddy, and the biker smiled. Jim couldn't say more but the gesture's meaning couldn't have been clearer to Jim's longtime friend. Sal and Dave might think they were off the hook, but they still had a punishment waiting when they got to the state line.

Jim turned his attention back to the ex-Angels. "Before you relocate, every club tattoo that you have needs be covered up with solid black ink or removed completely, your choice. Are you ready to get started?"

Dave and Sal nodded, and then both men removed their shirts, revealing the famous Hells Angels' death head tattoo on their backs. Freddy and Terry pulled out tattoo guns and plenty of black ink and sat beside Sal and Dave, ready to perform the cover-ups.

***

Katie and Richard sat in the airport staring out the window. Today was the day that Richard was returning to his post in Vietnam.

They hadn't seen each other since their party night at Ike's Bar, and they hadn't spoken about the odd events of the night either. When Katie picked him up in a taxicab her father had ordered, Richard acted normal. There was no talk of premonitions or odd behavior. In fact, Katie wondered if he had blanked out the whole conversation.

When they arrived at the airport she followed him to the gate he was leaving from and there they sat, side by side with other soldiers and their families. Katie marveled at how relaxed air security was in 1967. She found it hard to believe that she and others were able to just walk to the gates where aircrafts left from and sit with travelers until their departure time.

They sat in silence. Katie wanted to bring up their evening together and resume the conversation that they had left 'for another time'. Now that they were both sober, she was reluctant. What if Richard didn't remember her warnings? She sat nervously, hoping that he might bring up the topic. When he didn't, and the minutes continued to tick by, she finally got up the nerve.

"I was serious the other night when I gave you my warnings."

"I know." Richard took her right hand in his own and squeezed her fingers. "I've got this, Katie Cat. You don't have anything to worry about." ever come home."

Chapter 43

Chocolate George had been following this person of interest in a Dodge Dart that he'd rented several days before. It was strange driving a car; he missed his bike. However, his gut told him that he was on to something big. This wasn't the person he'd been assigned to watch, but he was sure that this guy was guilty of something. Innocent men didn't run, and by the looks of things his suspect was getting ready to do just that. George just didn't know when.

George followed him to a donut shop and then to a storage unit in South City where he collected what looked to be all of his belongings. These items he took with him and then headed back into the city, and then east on Highway 80.

When they hit Fairfield, about an hour outside of San Francisco, George realized that this was the day his suspect was splitting for good, and he had every intention of following.

George realized that he couldn't do this alone. It had gone too far and he needed to call Big Jim for assistance. He couldn't do that until the man he followed stopped to rest. For now, he followed, wondering where they were heading, and hoping that a half tank of gas was enough to get him there.

***

Two months in the mountains was a long time. Frog and Dylan were bored. They had run out of conversations weeks before, and fishing had become a chore that neither had any interest in. They spent their days reading the limited material they could find in the cabin, which consisted mostly of fishing and hunting magazines along with some lame romance novels that had been left behind by a previous renter.

Dylan insisted that their provisions run out completely before they could make another trip to the small market, which by now seemed like a haven to Frog. He couldn't wait to get out of the cabin and go anywhere as long as it didn't involve a fishing pole.

When the stale bread was gone and they were on the last of the canned goods, Dylan finally agreed that a trip to the market was necessary. Frog was ecstatic. He had even agreed to a haircut without complaint.

They intended to leave early in the morning but things didn't turn out that way. When they woke they discovered that they had a plumbing leak, which fortunately Dylan was able to fix without bringing in outside repairmen

By the time he was finished it was already half past two. If they'd had any food left, they would have put off the market for the next day, but with everything gone except a bottle of apple juice and a box of raisins, both agreed that the market trip had to take place today.

Frog donned his usual white T-shirt, placed his Giants baseball cap on his head, and the two set out for the market. Hank recognized Frog the minute he walked in and he smiled broadly.

"Hey there, young'un. I wondered if I'd see you again. Is this your brother?" he asked, looking at the clean-cut version of Dylan.

"Yes sir, this is my brother Dylan."

"Nice to meet you, Dylan, sorry to hear about your family's loss."

"Thank you. It was rough for a while, but I got to tell you, it's really helped being up here amongst all this beauty," Dylan replied.

"Yep, it's a healing spot. Lake Tahoe is God's country." Hank looked at Frog. "I'm sorry young man, I don't think I caught your name the last time you were in."

"My name is Curtis." Frog offered his hand and shook Hank's.

"Well, it's nice to meet both you boys. What can I do for you today?" Hank asked.

"We need a few supplies," Dylan said.

Hank took the shopping list from Curtis and looked it over. "Yep, I think I have all of this. Let me get that for you." Hank started to gather the supplies.

Frog happened to glance in a side mirror and the sight made him chuckle. The image was too good to keep to himself so he tapped Dylan on the shoulder and pointed towards their reflection. In the mirror, two shorthaired straights stood staring back at them; each could have passed as the boy next door, someone like Rickie Nelson or Dobie Gillis.

Dylan studied their reflection and stifled a laugh. He wished he had a camera to capture this moment for eternity and vowed silently that when they got out of this he would never look like the man in mirror again.

Hank set the last of their supplies on the counter. "Yep, I got everything."

"Great." Dylan reached for his wallet. "How much do I owe you, Hank?"

"Let's see... that's $17.50."

Dylan handed him a $20.00 bill.

"How long are you thinking of staying?" Hank asked.

"To be honest, I'm not sure," Dylan said, pocketing his change. "I guess we're staying until it feels right to go home."

"I understand. Hey, you boys know that there's an electrical storm coming in tonight, don't you?"

The cabin where Dylan and Frog were staying was void of luxuries, including a television, a radio, or even a telephone. This was the first they had heard of a storm coming their way.

"An electrical storm?" Frog echoed.

"That's right. It's unusual up here, but sometimes we get them in the summer months. Nothing to really worry about, just stay out of the lightning, that's my advice. In other words, it would be a bad time to go out fishing."

"Right, good advice. What time is this storm supposed to hit?" Frog asked.

"Weatherman said it would be here sometime after 6:00. It's early yet, you got plenty of time to get home."

"Thanks for the information, Hank." Frog smiled.

Dylan and Frog gathered their supplies in the lone shopping cart and walked to the truck where they loaded the boxes into the camper shell. When they were finished, Frog took the cart back, waved a final good bye to Hank, and he and Dylan drove off.

"You know what would be great, man?" Frog asked.

"What?"

"A pizza and a beer. Think about it, man. An ice-cold fucking glass of brew and a combination pizza? Just beautiful, man."

"No, Frog."

"Come on, man, this is fucking torture. It's isolation and it's against the Geneva Convention... something like cruel and unusual punishment."

"You're so fucking dramatic, Frog."

"Think about it, man. Steaming mouthwatering pizza and a great ass beer to go with it. Doesn't that sound groovy? How can you pass that up?"

"It sounds stupid."

"Why? Look at us, we're complete fucking dorks just like all the other fucking dorks in this town. How can it possibly hurt anything to have a pizza and a couple of cold ones?"

Dylan knew he should say no but he had to admit, they did look inconspicuous. He remembered their reflection in the mirror and laughed.

"You're right, we look like boys next door, but here's the thing— we have that electrical storm coming in. We really should go back to the cabin."

"It's only 3:00, dude. Besides that, we already know that we don't die in an electrical storm."

"See, that's kind of thinking that almost got you killed, thinking that Katie's predictions are set in stone. You can't trust that shit, man."

"Come on, man, one pizza. Even if we just pick it up and take it home. Please, man, be reasonable. I'm starving for real food."

Dylan hated to admit it but Frog was right. What could one visit to the town hurt? The locals already knew that they were here for an extended period of time. It was perfectly safe to get a pizza and maybe even a few beers.

"Okay," Dylan agreed reluctantly. "But you have to act cool, okay? No hippie shit, you got that?"

"Hippie shit? What's that supposed to mean?"

"It means you don't talk political hippie shit to anyone, including me, and you try to act...you know, normal."

"Right. And this coming from a Hells Angel."

"Do I fucking look like a Hells Angel, Frog?"

"Do I fucking look like a hippie, Dylan?"

"Okay man, point made."

***

Carl's Pizza Parlor looked like an old time log cabin. It was on the corner of the street next to a laundromat surrounded by trees. Dylan entered the parking lot and pulled into a space. He turned and stared at Frog.

"Come on, man, I got it okay?" Frog said, anticipating what Dylan would say. "Don't talk like a hippie. I got it. I'll pass as a fucking straight, you'll see." Frog opened the door of the truck and jumped out, then he walked towards the redwood cabin with Dylan following close behind.

The inside of the pizza parlor was busy. Kids were playing on pinball machines, which clicked and clunked out random rhythms. Frog and Dylan entered a short line and, looking at the menu above, debated pizzas. As with everything else in their two months together, pizza was another thing they couldn't agree on.

They ended up with a large half pepperoni and half combination. With two large mugs of specialty brewed beer, the men sat down at a table in the back, as far away from the game noises as they could.

For the first few minutes they didn't talk. Both studied the other patrons in the restaurant, who were too busy with their own lives to notice them. Dylan wondered how different it would be if the hippie Frog and the wing skull vested Hells Angel had walked inside instead. Now that would have attracted attention.

"Here's to another fifty years," Dylan toasted. He and Frog touched glasses and gulped down the ice-cold microbrew.

"I got to tell you, Curtis, this was a good idea. I think both of us need to just relax and be normal for a while, just like ordinary people again."

"See man, I told you everything would be cool." They sipped at their beers and when their pizza order was called Dylan brought the steaming dish back to their table along with paper plates and napkins.

They settled in quietly, munching their dinner and enjoying the atmosphere. The jukebox played a multitude of Beach Boy tunes, which Frog and Dylan weren't especially fond of, but nevertheless, this outing seemed like a luxury.

"Hey, man, do you know what the date is?" Frog asked in between mouthfuls of pizza.

Dylan had to think for several seconds and even then he wasn't sure. The past two months had blurred together so he wasn't even sure what day of the week it was most of the time.

"No, I don't think I do, not for sure. I guess it's somewhere around August 14th or 15th."

"Yeah, it's the 15th, and that means we only have sixteen days left in August."

"Very good math skills, congratulations, man."

"No man, don't you get it? That means that we've almost made it to September."

"So?" Dylan bit into the last slice of pepperoni pizza.

"So, we're supposed to die in August. We've almost made it to where we don't have to worry anymore."

Dylan shook his head. "No man, you can't think that way. It's not safe until this shit is solved. It doesn't matter if it's September or October, the timetable can be off. How many times have we gone over this?"

"But you don't know that for sure, it's just a guess."

Dylan had learned not to argue with Frog. The self-proclaimed businessman had a million explanations so that he always came back to whatever idea he believed to be right. In this case it was the month of August, and Dylan knew that no matter what he said, Frog was going to believe what he wanted to until he was proven wrong.

"Okay, man, whatever you say."

"What are you going to do when this is over?" Frog asked.

"You know, I'm not sure. I haven't thought about that. Can you believe it? I've been so concerned about getting through this alive that I haven't thought about what I would do when, or if it ever ended. What about you, man? What are your plans?"

"I'm going back to 'Frisco and I'm going to find Moonbeam. Hopefully she's still single and she'll at least talk to me. If she will, then I'm going to go to that commune, the one she's always talking about where Chet settled. I'm going to live off the land and do whatever it is she wants to do. Just be content, you dig?"

"Yeah I do."

"What about Katie?"

"Oh, I'm going back for Katie, that I'm sure of. I told her I would. From there...well, I don't know. I guess we'll just play it by ear, if she'll have me that is."

"Well here's to the next two weeks going by quickly so that this shit can finally come to an end," Dylan toasted. He refrained from explaining to Frog yet again that the beginning of September meant nothing.

One beer led to another and before they knew it, it was late afternoon and the electrical storm Hank had warned them about had begun. The first crack of lighting took them off guard but then, remembering the weather report, they both knew that they had stayed much too long in town.

"Fuck man, what time is it?" Frog asked.

Dylan looked at his watch. It was already 6:30. They had been here for nearly four hours.

"Damn, man, we have to get back before this storm gets worse." They finished their beers and rose from the booth, heading out into the dark clouded sky.

When they had entered the restaurant it had been overcast but nothing like this. Now the clouds were black. The wind had picked up, and an occasional flash of lightning lit up the sky.

They climbed into the truck and started the twenty-minute drive back to the cabin. The wind was picking up. Trees swayed wildly, and now on top of the lightning there was the accompanying boom of thunder. Hank had told them that it wasn't going to rain, but Dylan had his doubts. To him it looked as if it would start to pour at any minute. The tug of the high winds forced Dylan to drive at a snail's pace. He concentrated on keeping the truck on the road but it was difficult.

"Fuck, Hank wasn't kidding about the weather," he said.

There was a loud bang. It happened so fast that Dylan thought someone had tried to shoot them. The front tire on the truck blew out and it hydroplaned through the water across the pavement, coming to a stop just before hitting a redwood fence. Dylan and Frog breathed a sigh of relief.

"What the fuck was that?" Frog gasped.

"It's just a blowout. Fucking scared the shit out of me though." He laughed nervously. "Now this is going to be fun. Frog, the jack and the spare tire are in the camper shell buried under the supplies. Help me move the shit around."

When they got out of the truck the wind hit them full force nearly knocking them down. With some maneuvering they managed to move the items from Hank's store so that they could find the tire, jack, and toolbox.

It had begun to rain, and from the looks of things it wasn't going to clear up anytime soon. Thunder and lightning continued and now that the rain was coming down too, Dylan was sure that the storm was just going to get worse.

"Let's get this over with as quickly as possible so we can get back to the cabin." Dylan set the jack up and turned the crank. When the truck was several feet off the ground, he started to work on the bolts, which were hard to turn because of rust and the damage it had caused.

Changing the tire took much longer than they had expected. By the time the truck was ready to move they were soaked and Dylan's hands were cut and bleeding. He wrapped some paper napkins around them so he would be able to drive.

Dylan pulled the truck back on the road and turned the heater to high. They sat in front of the vents shivering. This was a miserable night to be out for a drive. They had made a huge mistake by staying at the pizza parlor so long.

When they arrived at the cabin it was dark, ten past 9:00. The nights were ending sooner now that summer was coming to an end. Several weeks earlier it would have still been light.

The porch light was out. At first, Dylan thought that it had burned out but then he noticed that the house was completely dark too. He had left the kitchen light on, he was sure of it.

"Fucking power's out. The storm must have knocked out a power line."

The thunder blared, lightning lit their surrounds and as Dylan had predicted, the rain was coming down harder.

"We need a flashlight and some candles. Do we have any?" Frog asked.

"I think we have better than that. I saw a camping lantern in the garage. You stay here and keep the lights on so I can see what I'm doing."

Dylan found the camping lantern in the garage. He searched his pockets for his lighter but remembered that he had left it on the seat of the truck. He found the lantern and was ready to head back to the truck but came to an abrupt stop when the truck lights suddenly went out.

"What the fuck? Frog, I told you to keep the lights on!" he yelled, knowing full well that the sound of his voice would never travel in this weather.

Fully expecting Frog to turn the lights back on, he waited patiently. When he remained in the dark after several minutes he assumed that the battery in the truck had gone dead, why else would the lights shut off?

He headed in what he believed to be the way back to the truck thinking all he needed was his lighter and then he and Frog could get inside the cabin away from all this rain.

Dylan pulled the hood of his jacket over his head. Keeping his head low so that the pounding rain couldn't hit him in the face he moved towards the parked Ford.

He was about ten feet away when he realized that the passenger side door was standing wide open. Curious now, he ran the rest of the way to the truck and when he got there he found an empty cab. Frog was gone.

Dylan reached into the truck and found that Frog wasn't the only thing missing, so were the keys. That apparently was the reason the lights had gone out.

He found his lighter easily. Knowing that he couldn't light the lantern outside in this weather he climbed into the truck and shut the door. He prayed that the old lantern would work, and lit the mantle. To his relief the old clunker lit the first time around and the inside of the truck illuminated.

Dylan blinked several times trying to adjust to the brightness. Immediately he noticed blood smeared on the passenger side window and the seat where Frog had been sitting only minutes before.

Instinctively he put out the light, hoping that he hadn't been seen by whoever had taken Frog.

He crawled out of the truck and headed into the forest. Knowing that heading towards the house would make him a target, Dylan decided to take his chances in the trees where at least he could take cover if the suspect had a firearm.

Meanwhile the storm raged. The lightning lit up the sky, adding an eerie glow to the trees. The rain was still coming down hard and the thunder was deafening. Dylan's mind raced. He searched for a safe hiding place while his eyes scanned every corner of the forest. With his .45 in hand, he zigzagged through the redwoods.

He settled into a cluster of trees which would not only keep the rain off of him but would act as a shield. He sat shivering in the cold, trying to understand what the hell was going on.

Who took Frog? he asked himself and wondered if the hippie was already in the dirt grave that he had dreamed about his whole life.

It was August 15th and he was in the woods running for his life pursued by someone who wanted him dead. Katie was right about her prediction. More than likely he and Frog would both die here tonight.

Dylan sat with his back against a tree trunk. He waited for his attacker, knowing that one of them would never leave the woods of Lake Tahoe alive. He just didn't know which one.

***

Chocolate George kept a good distance from the man he was following. His rented Dodge was a godsend; not once had the man taken a second notice of the inconspicuous vehicle. Unlike his motorcycle, which would have been a spectacle, this family car was easy to overlook.

After an hour and a half on the road his suspect had finally stopped for a break. While he enjoyed a meal at Sambos, George used the time to call Big Jim. Jim was mad at first because George had made decisions on his own, but he quickly came around and agreed that George was on to something important.

They had reached Davis, just outside the capitol city of Sacramento. George was fairly certain the man was heading towards Nevada. He just didn't know if he was taking Highway 80 towards Reno or Highway 50 towards Lake Tahoe.

Jim sent club members for backup. Some headed up Highway 80 East while he, Terry, and a few prospects headed up Highway 50. Both groups would make periodic calls to the clubhouse hoping that George would phone with new information. George was instructed to continue following his suspect until the club caught up with him.

***

Frog woke in a freshly dug hole chillingly similar to the description Katie had given him of his final resting place. His head was killing him and his eyes were blurring. It was easy to tell that he had been clubbed on the head and disposed of. Frog tried to move but found out quickly that his arms and legs had been bound with rope. This, he realized, was it. If he couldn't do anything to get out of this, he would die just as Katie had predicted.

Frog checked the strength of his bindings and smiled. They seemed tight enough and most people would be stymied for a way to get out, but not Frog. Frog had learned early about knots; he had been fascinated with them. His sisters had been relentless tying him up with their jump ropes, and as a result, he was skilled in untying knots and could get out of almost any bindings.

An amateur had tied this knot. This person didn't know what they were doing and that was their mistake. The primitive knots were easy to get out of and within minutes Frog had his bindings off and was scurrying up the side of the hole. When he reached the top he moved into the heavy forest hoping to find cover so that when the madman who had left him to die found out that he had freed himself he would be a great distance away.

Then he remembered the shotgun in the truck. If he could get that gun then at least he would have a fighting chance. Katie had been right about everything. Although it was probably a lost cause, Frog was going to go down fighting. At least with a gun he could hope to take the asshole with him when he died.

His head throbbed, but he had been through worse. As a kid he had grown up on dirt bikes, and he had taken more falls than he could remember. Although he probably had a concussion, this was nothing compared to some of the wounds he had received as a child. He had lived then, and he was determined to live now.

The storm was worse. Visibility between lightning strikes was next to nothing. When the electrical storm did light up the sky the effect was gloomy, casting unusual shadows against the already dark landscape.

Frog carefully moved north towards the cabin, searching everywhere for the lunatic who attacked him. When he reached the cabin's lot he darted across the yard and hid in the shadows, watching and waiting for the madman.

***

Dylan sat with his back against the trees watching his surroundings. Something whizzed by his head and he realized that the object was a bullet. He remembered the blowout on the truck and his first impression that it had been shot out. Now he wondered if even then they had been under attack.

Instinctively, Dylan shot back in the direction the bullet came from and then realized that he had made a mistake. If the gunman was shooting off a random bullet just to scare him, Dylan had given his attacker his exact location.

He scrambled, trying to get away from the cluster of trees as quickly as possible, but it was too late. This time the bullet grazed his shoulder. The shooter knew exactly where he was, and if he didn't move quickly the next shot would kill him.

On his stomach now, Dylan scurried under some bushes and then belly crawled towards a thickened area in the woods. He could hear someone approaching. He fought for control, his heart beating wildly in his chest. He lay flat under a thicket of bushes, aiming forward at what he knew was coming through the darkness.

The shadow appeared and Dylan fired. Someone screeched, bushes shook, and his aggressor withdrew.

Dylan sat patiently listening to the storm around him, hoping beyond reason that he had just chased his attacker away.

***

When Frog found the truck he looked around carefully for his assailant. He needed the rifle. The inside of the cab was warm and there was a part of him that wanted to hide inside and hope for the best, but he realized that was out of the question. His attacker would eventually check the truck and when he did...Frog wasn't going to allow himself to be cornered, even if he did have a shotgun for protection.

He picked up the gun and filled his pocket with shells before scurrying back to the safety of the forest where he found a hiding place to plan his next move. He thought he heard gunshots somewhere, but the rain and the continual thunder that resonated over the landscape muffled the sounds. Since Frog couldn't detect where the shots were coming from, he continued to head west, looking for a spot where he could sit and wait for his assailant.

***

Chocolate George turned right onto the exit that led towards Lake Tahoe, again glad that he had rented the car because a storm was heading their way, and according to the radio it was going to be a real doozy. At their current speed, they should reach Lake Tahoe in less than an hour. He hoped that the suspect he was following might rest long enough for him to make a call to the clubhouse.

What George couldn't understand was why anyone would escape by going to Lake Tahoe. He would have done things much differently, but then again he wasn't on the run.

Whatever this lunatic had in mind, George was sure he was involved in Skinner's death. That too was a mystery to George; he couldn't understand why this person would have any grudges against Skinner.

It wasn't his job to figure any of this out, though. All he was supposed to do was to keep the suspect in sight so that the Angels could take care of the situation when they arrived. Until then, George would do what he needed to do. All he wished was that he had a pint of chocolate milk to keep him company and decided he would buy some when he was finally able to catch a rest.

***

Dylan hid, waiting for his assailant to return. Undoubtedly he would come back, because this person plainly wanted him dead. Despite the scuffles he had with the stranger, he hadn't been able to get a glimpse of his face. This guy was clever. He had planned this in advance, and the weather was helping him.

The water dripped from the bush he was hiding beneath. He was drenched and shaking but he sat diligently, waiting for his opponent to arrive.

His mind in overdrive, he reviewed potential suspects. Was it Calvin's people, the hoods from Oakland that they had taken customers away from? Could it be Sal and Dave? And if it was, how on earth had they found them? Nobody knew that he and Frog were hiding in Tahoe. He hadn't even told Big Jim where they were. Was it possible that whoever was out there had followed them here two months ago? If that were the case, why hadn't that person attacked them sooner? None of this made sense. The only thing that was clear was that a man with a gun, probably a .38 by the sound of the weapon, was hunting him down, and that person had more than likely already killed Frog.

The lightning was close. Dylan actually thought that it might hit the forest where he hid. The thunder continued to boom. The rain slowed after he took refuge in the woods, but now it pounded the hillside and the wind intensified.

Every cell in Dylan's body told him to run but he knew that running would turn him into a moving target. He hid in the underbrush waiting for the mysterious shooter to arrive, hoping that when he did the lightning would allow him enough visibility to get off the first shot.

***

Chocolate George was glad when his suspect pulled over at a coffee shop. He hoped the man would take a long break but he must have been aware of the approaching storm. The stop was quick, just long enough to get a cup of coffee and use the john. This guy was anxious to get somewhere, that was clear.

Despite the short stop, George had been able to call the clubhouse and update them on his location. He told the prospect on the phone where they were and hoped that Big Jim and Terry weren't far behind.

When they hit the city of North Lake Tahoe, his suspect stopped at a payphone and made a quick call. And then within moments made an upward climb into the mountains. George gave him a few minutes to get ahead and then he carefully drove up the weaving road behind him.

This guy was heading somewhere and it was more than just escaping the club; he had an agenda. Everything about this adventure felt wrong. George shivered. This was going to be bad, he just knew it.

At the end of the winding road was a log cabin far from any neighbors. The first thing his suspect did was to cut the power line, which didn't make sense considering the size of the storm that was blowing in. The power undoubtedly would have gone out on its own; this guy was desperate.

George parked the car a good distance from the site and trailing behind on foot, he followed, watching from the safety of the trees. The man checked the cabin and used a key from beneath the welcome mat to enter. He was inside for several minutes and then he came back outside and shut the door behind him. He sat on the front porch where he seemed to be waiting for someone.

George stayed hidden, watching the black clouds roll in. When the electrical storm started he expected the man to leave, but he ignored the weather, which was clearly going to get much worse. He remained seated on the porch watching the road before him. Chocolate George settled into the underbrush where he took a pint of chocolate milk out of his jacket pocket and finally enjoyed his treat.

***

Big Jim pulled into the rest stop at the top of the summit. He called the clubhouse and was happy to find that George had called in. The prospect told him that George had arrived in Lake Tahoe nearly two hours ago and that the man he was following seemed to be heading to a property in the hills.

The storm was blinding on motorcycles and even though it was miserable they had pushed forward, eventually making it to the outskirts of North Lake Tahoe. They were close enough now, and Jim wasn't about to give up.

Following a hunch, Big Jim, Terry, and a prospect named Toe stopped at a small café and then a small market along the way. They discovered that George and a dark haired man had been there several hours before. According to the clerk at the market, someone resembling Chocolate George had bought several containers of chocolate milk before heading up Miller's Road where several cabins were located.

The clerk said the cabins were all rentals, so he had assumed that both men were staying in the area. He advised them not to try to climb the hill in the storm, especially on motorcycles, but they ignored him.

With the thunder banging and the lightning illuminating the nights sky, the three men made their way up the hill in the blinding rain. They kept their bikes' lights on high beam as they climbed the tedious hill, pushing against the wind.

***

Dylan hid in the underbrush listening for the arrival of his opponent, but couldn't hear anything over the thunder and heavy downpour. When the man arrived in the clearing Dylan hesitated, at first thinking that his mind was playing tricks on him. When the man moved and the brush around him shook he knew this was for real

When the next bolt of lightning sparked the sky he made his move. He fired, but the bullet went high and missed the target. Swearing, he rolled out of the way knowing that his attacker would be sending a hail of bullets his way.

Luckily for Dylan there was a slight hill behind him, which he conveniently slid down. As he crawled into another patch of bushes, his attacker opened fire.

He counted the shots— 1,2,3,4— and then the night went quiet again. He heard rustling in the trees above and knew that his assailant was searching the landing for a body.

Lightning illuminated the sky again, and for the first time he caught an image of the man above.

He could see for only a second, not long enough to get a good look but what he could tell was that the man was stocky and about medium height. Thunder drowned out the sounds around him and he didn't dare move, knowing that the man above knew undoubtedly that he had missed his mark.

Now he was searching for Dylan, and if he heard anything he would shoot first and ask questions later.

Dylan held his breath, waiting for the next strike of lightning and hoping that he could see something, anything, that would let him know that his assailant hadn't followed him down the hill.

His hopes were dashed when the sky lit and he saw the boots of the man who searched for him. His opponent was standing directly in front of him.

Dylan aimed the gun upwards but he didn't get the chance to shoot. Before he could do anything he was yanked out of his hiding place and thrown on the ground. He tried to roll but the air had been knocked out of him and for several seconds he lay there gasping.

The figure above him kicked the gun out of his hand and then began to laugh.

***

Frog wandered through the woods, periodically hearing gunfire, but the storm was so loud he couldn't pinpoint the location. He could feel warm blood trickling down the side of his face from his head wound. He was sure that he needed stiches but there was nothing he could do now. His head was throbbing painfully and the concussion threw him off balance, but he trudged forward looking for the source of the gunshots.

The ground was slick. It had been a long time since these woods had seen rain and the dirt was slow to absorb the abundance of water. Several times he nearly slipped in the mud but managed to catch himself before he went down.

The shotgun he held was heavy but he was used to carrying a weapon. As a child growing up in Redding he had many opportunities to shoot a gun and as luck had it, his grandfather was a skilled hunter who'd taught him everything he knew. Frog could operate the weapon and he knew how to track a target. He might object to the use of firearms but when shit hit the fan as it had tonight, even a hippie had to defend himself.

His courage was restored on his creep through the woods, and for the first time tonight he realized that the tables had turned. Now he had become the hunter and he was seeking his assailant, knowing that when he found him he would gladly blow the motherfucker away.

***

Chocolate George saw the truck coming up the hill. The man on the porch saw the headlights too and disappeared into the woods, but George could still see him standing in the shadows watching the truck pull into the driveway.

It was hard to see the front of the house through the downpour, so George crept closer to get a better look at the scene about to unfold.

One man got out of the truck and walked into the detached garage. Using only the lights from the old Ford, he seemed to be searching for something. That's when the suspect made his move. He dashed out of the darkness towards the truck and, using the handle of what looked to be a gun, knocked the passenger in the head several times before snatching the keys out of the ignition. This immediately shut off the headlights, and he dragged his victim into the woods.

George was torn. What he should do next? Ultimately he headed into the forest following his suspect, where he watched the attacker tie up his unconscious victim and kick him into a hole.

When he was finished, the suspect headed back to the cabin. George knew that he was going back for the second victim and he wished he had a weapon. He also wondered how far away Big Jim was and prayed that he would get here before George had to intervene.

***

Dylan braced himself for the kick he knew was coming. When it did, he caught the leg of his aggressor. Pulling backwards, he successfully knocked his opponent off of his feet, and before the man could adjust, Dylan pounded him in the back of the head.

The man reached for his weapon but Dylan was too fast; he hit him again and knocked his arms away. Thunder boomed and lightning lit up the sky. His assailant lay face down in the dirt and struggled to get up.

Dylan hit him hard and his attacker held the back of his head in defense. Then unexpectedly, the man rolled over and knocked Dylan off balance. Suddenly he was the one on top and he was holding a gun to Dylan's head. It was only then that Dylan realized who his attacker was.

Totally stunned, he stopped struggling and became motionless, giving the man on top an advantage. He grabbed Dylan's neck and started to strangle him but Dylan fought back. The pair rolled in the mud, each trying to gain the upper hand. Lightning struck again and the thunder was deafening. Dylan managed to grab a rock as they rolled, and he used it to knock his attacker off. When the man landed next to him, Dylan tried to rise but stopped and looked at him. Joey lay on the ground beside him pointing a loaded .38 Special at his head.

"I bet you're surprised to see me, brother." Joey laughed, Dylan didn't.

"Lake Tahoe? How predictable you are, Dylan. Really? The same place we came as kids, and you couldn't think of a better hiding place than this?"

"It's you, all this time, the one person I never suspected... What about Skinner man, did you kill him too?"

"Fuck yeah, I killed the stupid motherfucker. He's the one who caused this gig to go downhill in the first place, him and his fucking investigation. He's the cause of everything and I should have killed his ass earlier, way back at the Be-In when he first started asking questions. But I didn't. I let Sal and Dave handle the fucker and look what's happened now. 'Let the unpatched bikers handle the situation,' that's what everyone told me. When? When would that have happened, Dylan? Skinner was ready to go to the club for fuck's sake, and they hadn't done anything to stop him, so I had to. Hell yes I killed him, and you want to know what? I enjoyed every second of it."

"And his bike?"

"It's it Mexico man, I sold it. Motherfucker is costing me a future of millions, he sure as hell owes me his fucking ride."

"I don't believe this is really happening."

"Oh believe it, it's happening."

"Why man? Why would you want to kill me? We're brothers."

"You aren't my brother. We were just a couple of kids who used each other to get where we are today, and I would have continued to use you too except you stopped helping my cause. Now, you're a liability, man, you dig? If you're not an asset then why am I keeping you around?"

"What are you talking about?"

"You ruined my gig, man, you and that fucking little hippie bastard. We had a groovy thing going. Millions, man, we could have made *millions*. A conscience? Dylan, when did you develop that? When you met that fucking little hippie whore?"

"Hey man, I—"

"What? You want to rush me and defend your lady's honor?" Joey laughed. "Go right ahead. I'm waiting for you."

Dylan hesitated.

"What? Is it because I'm holding a thirty-eight or because you're chicken shit?" Joey tossed the weapon aside. "There, now we're on equal terms. Let's see if you can do it, lover boy. Come on, kick my ass. I've been waiting for this fight for a long fucking time."

***

The first cabin that Jim and the Angels passed had lights on, and so did the second. When they came to the third and final cabin, it and the surrounding land was pitch black.

"Here!" Big Jim said, dismounting his bike. "This is where we're going to find them, I can feel it."

"I sure hope so. Where do we even begin?" Terry asked. He glanced at the vast amount of land they had to cover and shook his head. Next to him the two prospects parked their bikes and all four headed towards the completely black cabin.

"We start here at the house!" Jim yelled though the raging storm so his men could hear him. "If we don't find anything at the house then we spread out into the forest."

The weather drowned out most of the sounds but in the distance Jim thought he could hear gunfire. Now he was convinced that he had found the right location, something was definitely going down. All he needed to do was find the source of the gun battle.

***

Dylan threw the first punch with his left fist. It clipped Joey in the jaw and knocked him off balance. Before he could get in a punch, Dylan hit him again, and this time he slammed into a tree.

Joey was tough, he could take a good punch. He came back with a vengeance. He hit Dylan in the ribs, and Dylan buckled and went down on his knees. He knew that Joey was going to kick him; he had seen him in enough fights to know his strategy. Dylan counterattacked and knocked Joey into the mud next to him. They fought for control, rolling over and over in the blood, mud, and the pouring rain.

***

Chocolate George watched the fight between Joey and who he now recognized as Dylan. This was a shock. He had known that Joey was involved in Skinner's murder and he knew that the biker had a purpose coming up here in this weather, but he had never imagined this. Joey and Dylan were tight; they were brothers after all, having grown up in foster care together. George was confused.

He wished again for a weapon, watching helplessly. Now they were fist fighting and George hoped that Dylan would be able to bring his assailant down. If he couldn't, Chocolate George would be forced to step in, something he'd been told not to do unless it was absolutely necessary.

George looked down the road hoping that Big Jim and Terry would get here before this nightmare got worse.

***

Big Jim and the others waited for more gunfire and when it didn't come they walked into the forest hoping to hear something that might show them the way. Just then, several rounds went off, this time louder and more intense. They were close, all they needed to do was change direction and head east. There in the foreground was a cluster of trees that surrounded an area of the forest they couldn't see into. That was the location of the gunfight.

When they arrived at the clearing two men were rolling in the mud. Across from them Chocolate George stood watching.

Jim and his group moved closer to the battle, slipping through the mud as they made their way towards who they now recognized as Joey and Dylan.

Joey was on top of Dylan, and this time he wasn't going to give in. He was tired of playing fair. The game was fun at first, but now it was tiring and it needed to end. Joey pulled a switchblade out of his boot and, holding Dylan down with his knees, steadied his hand ready to slice his brother's throat.

Chocolate George lunged, but Joey saw him coming and sidestepped the attack. Dylan coughed and was finally able to rise to his feet. Jim, Terry, and the prospects emerged from the forest and watched in disbelief as Joey picked up the thirty-eight and pointed it at Dylan's head.

***

Frog hated rain. He'd never realized that until today, and he swore that if he ever got out of this mess he would never walk in it again.

Since the water couldn't sink into the ground fast enough, it had started to flood, and lake sized puddles were forming all around him.

Again he heard gunfire, and knew he was close. It was coming from a cluster of trees to the left. He ran but slid in the mud and went down hard, hitting his already throbbing head. He lay there several seconds, tempted to give up and stay in the safety of the mud, but another shot rang out and he climbed to his feet and ran towards the battle.

This time he made it to the clearing without slipping. What he saw was confusing. He wasn't sure what he expected, but this wasn't it.

Ten feet away Joey picked a gun up off the ground. He raised the weapon and pointed it at Dylan's head, ready to shoot. Frog was fast. He pointed the shotgun at Joey's chest and pulled the trigger. Joey dropped the gun and fell face first into the mud next to Dylan's feet.

***

The First Skulls and their connections handled the unfortunate incident. As with Skinner's demise, it was discreet, and no questions were asked.

The death certificate stated that Joey had been killed in a bike accident and since his only known relative was Dylan, no one would cause difficulties for the club.

They could have gone through legal channels, but that would have brought unwanted negative publicity to the San Francisco Chapter. A quiet end to this fiasco was just what everybody needed. Now that it was over and Joey's ashes had been scattered in the wilderness, it was time to put this behind them and move forward.

That was easier for some than others. Dylan was traumatized. His best friend was dead, and Frog had taken a man's life. Even though Dylan knew he had to pull the trigger, he also knew that Frog needed time to understand and accept his actions

This morning, Saturday, August 19th, 1967, the traumatic incident was over. Jim and the boys were riding back to 'Frisco and the cabin Dylan had rented was turned back over to the owner.

Dylan sat outside the vacated cabin and waited for the Angels to leave.

"You sure you won't come with us?" Jim asked.

"How can I, man? My head is so fucking messed up. I don't know what to think anymore. I won't be any good to anyone until I sort this shit out."

"We might be able to help you with that."

"What? I thought I was being considered for de-patching?"

"Yeah, well, maybe you've redeemed yourself," Big Jim said.

"I appreciate that, I really do. Right now, though, I just need to find myself."

"Understood. We'll be there waiting for when you're ready to come back." Dylan and Jim embraced. "Be careful, young man. Trouble seems to follow you."

"No shit, you've noticed that too?"

"What about Frog?" Jim asked.

"I don't know. At one point he wanted to go back to 'Frisco... but that was before all this."

Frog overheard his name and walked towards them. "What's that? You guys talking about me?"

"Hey, man, what are you going to do now?" Dylan asked.

"What do you mean? I thought we were driving the truck back and then we were going to pick up our bikes?"

"We are, but what are you going to do after that?"

Frog took a seat beside Dylan and scratched his short blond hair.

"I don't know, man. What are you going to do?"

"I'm going on the road. I'm just going to ride until I've had enough, and then I'll decide what to do next," Dylan answered.

"On the road?"

"Yep. Just be free, man. Travel where I want, no responsibilities. I've got to get my head together, you dig?"

"Yeah, man, I dig. You think you might want company? I'm pretty hot on my Honda these days."

"Really? I thought you wanted to get back to Moony? You know, join the commune and live off the land and all that."

"Yeah that was before. Now...I don't know who I am, Dylan. I know I had to do what I did, it's just hard to accept, you know?"

"Yeah, I think I do. Sure man, you can come with me. After all, we were supposed to share a grave for eternity, remember?"

"We still might."

"Fuck, I hope not." Dylan laughed, and for the first time in days, Frog laughed too.

"If you guys are going to hug, fucking get it over with already. I've got to leave, I've had too much fresh air and city life is calling me," Jim groused. He turned to Frog. "You know you're welcome to come with us, right, Frog?"

"What, me and my Honda?"

"Well we'd have to do something about that." Jim laughed. "If you ever want to join us, Frog, I think you've earned that. You'll have to start out as a prospect, but we'll go easy on you."

"Thanks, man, I'll consider it. For now, though, I think I'm going with Dylan somewhere on the road so I can get my head straight."

Jim said his last goodbyes and then headed to his Harley.

Terry hugged Dylan and followed Jim to the bikes.

"Be careful, Dylan, I won't be around to protect you," Chocolate George said with a grin.

Dylan hugged him tightly. "Thanks, man, for everything. If you wouldn't have gotten involved... Well, I owe you, big time."

"Yeah you do, Dylan. When you to get back to 'Frisco I'm going to make you pay up." George laughed and waved good-bye to Dylan and Frog. Their engines fired up and then he and the rest of the Angels were gone.

Chapter 44

In August of 1967 the last of the summer race riots came to an end. On the 3rd, Lyndon Johnson announced that he was sending 45,000 more troops to Vietnam.

In the Haight, things were changing too. Hordes of underage runaways, some as young as thirteen or fourteen, had descended upon the city. With no place to live, many were camping in doorways or in Golden Gate and Buena Vista Parks. Junkies were a common sight and drug lords fought over territories. What had been a love and peace neighborhood was fast becoming a dangerous place.

The Diggers tried to keep up with the influx of newbies, but trying to find homes for everybody was impossible. The Free Frame of Reference was struggling too. There were just too many bodies to feed. It was a small neighborhood, and accommodating everyone was just no longer possible.

Crime was rampant; rapes, robberies, and heavy drug offenses became common, everyday occurrences.

Between Aug.6th- and 8th, two known drug dealers were murdered in the neighborhood. John Kent "Shob" Carter and William "Superspade" Thomas were both rumored to have been eliminated by the mob, which by now was one of the many groups who fought for territory rights in the Haight.

On August 7th Beatle George Harrison and his wife, Patti Boyd visited the Haight. With a slew of followers, George and Patti walked up Haight Street, into Golden Gate Park, and settled in an area known as Hippie Hill. He was handed a guitar but declined to play.

Later George said that he had expected Haight-Ashbury to be a special place, a creative and artistic spot filled with beautiful people. What he found instead was a bunch of dirty, spotty faced underage kids, all strung out of their minds. Even mothers and their babies looked stoned. That was how much the neighborhood had changed. Just a short time earlier George would have found a very different Haight-Ashbury.

The Diggers had been against publicizing the Summer of Love. They had warned that bringing media attention to the good thing they had would destroy it. As it turned out, they were right. The Summer of Love was destroying itself.

Katie's and Moonbeam's lives had changed too. They still lived in the house on Page Street, but it felt different. Ron was seeing Robin now, and Katie was happy for them, but still things were awkward between her and Ron. He avoided her when he could, and when they did happen to meet face to face they were cordial but cold, saying little to each other. The change made Katie sad, and she hoped for the day when they could be friends, putting any bad feelings behind them.

Moonbeam was now working at the Psychedelic Shop part time. Ron and Jay hired her for late afternoon until closing. In the morning hours she frequented Golden Gate Park, sometimes at the children's playground or in front of the museum where she read palms and the Tarot for the tourists. She also tried to keep Frog's business alive by selling out the rest of his merchandise and restocking. She wasn't as good as Frog, but she did her best and at least was able to keep the small business afloat.

Moony had taken Frog's disappearance hard. Every day she checked the mailbox for a letter, and when the phone rang she rushed to answer it. Katie tried to tell her that they wouldn't hear anything from the men for months, but still she continued to hope.

After Richard had gone back to Vietnam, Katie felt like she was caught in a void, a stagnant place where she couldn't do anything but wait. She still received her mother's checks, now with an added bonus, but she took odd jobs as well; anything to keep her mind busy.

Sometimes she still handed out Owsley's LSD samples at events, and other times she helped Moonbeam at the shop. When she had nothing else planned, she even helped the Diggers in the Panhandle who were still trying to feed the masses. She did all of this to keep herself from thinking, which would surely drive her crazy at this crucial point in her own history.

There were still free concerts in the park; the Grateful Dead, Big Brother and the Holding Company, Country Joe and the Fish, and a slew of others played, but the neighborhood and the events weren't the same. The old feeling of perfect harmony just wasn't there anymore.

Life in the Haight had started to get ugly. The runaways got younger and younger, pimps and drug dealers were everywhere. It was impossible to find places for everyone to live, even though the Diggers still tried. Many ended up staying in the street or at the two parks (Golden Gate and Buena Vista, one at either end of Haight street.) The district was filled with homeless addicts and alcoholics. It wasn't safe to walk the streets late at night anymore, and sometimes it wasn't even safe in the daylight. Most of the longtime hippies talked about leaving, even the Grateful Dead.

One day towards the end of August, Moonbeam and Katie were at home watching television, something they rarely did anymore. Someone banged on the front door and when Katie answered, she was shocked. On the porch stood three Hells Angels: Big Jim, Terry, and Chocolate George.

Fearing the worst at the sight of the bikers, she put her hand over her mouth and waited for the bad news they were surely here to deliver.

"It's okay," Big Jim said quickly when he saw her reaction. "Dylan and Frog are safe; they're just fine. I'm sorry if we frightened you. We just...we wanted to talk to you and Moonbeam, if she's around? We have an update and some messages to give you two."

"Yes, of course, come in." Katie opened the door wide, her body trembling with the rush of adrenaline. She willed herself to calm down.

When Moonbeam saw them walk into the parlor she rose from the couch and stared at the bikers, frightened by their visit.

"It's alright," Katie told her, "they're here to let us know that Dylan and Frog are safe."

Moonbeam's eyes filled with tears. "Oh thank God." She put her hand over her mouth and let out a gasp of relief.

"May we?" Big Jim asked, gesturing towards the couches.

"Of course, I'm sorry. Please come in and have a seat. I didn't mean to be rude, it's just, you scared the shit out of me." Moony giggled.

"Can we get you anything?" Katie asked. "I think we have beer in the fridge."

"Sure, a beer would be groovy," Terry responded, licking his lips.

Katie disappeared into the kitchen and came out with a six-pack of Pabst Blue Ribbon and happily handed out cans.

"We just got back from Tahoe," Jim said. He stopped to open his can of beer and then took a large gulp of the amber brew. The two women stared at him waiting silently. "When Dylan and Frog left the pop festival they rented a cabin in North Shore. That's where they've been these past few months. Dylan called and told us of their unfortunate situation, and we've been playing detective ever since. I don't want to get into the specifics of their business dealings, that's for them to tell you, but I am happy to let you know that the mystery has been solved and that your old men are safe and sound."

"How was it solved? They were hiding from someone who wanted them dead. Did you find out who that someone was?" Katie asked.

"Yes we found him and he's gone," Jim said. "He... died in a motorcycle crash."

"Who was it?" Katie persisted.

"Joey, Dylan's foster brother," Jim confessed after a brief silence.

"Joey?" Moonbeam said in shock.

"That's right. It blew our minds too."

"Damn, who would have thought it would be Joey? I never...I dated him briefly, remember?"

Big Jim nodded. "You were at the party at the Dogpatch."

"I'm sorry with the way it turned out," Big Jim said. "As you can imagine the news has...affected Dylan greatly."

"I bet." Katie remembered the conversations she had with Dylan regarding his foster brother. She couldn't imagine what it would be like to find out something horrible about your best friend.

"Are they coming back soon?" Moonbeam asked.

"That's why we're here," Terry replied.

"Dylan and Frog have a lot on their minds. There's a lot more to the story but you probably guessed that. It's just not our place to tell you anything else. Point is, it's going to take them sometime to get over this...incident, to put their heads together, you dig?" Big Jim said.

Moonbeam's eyes brimmed with tears again. "You mean they aren't coming back at all?"

"Oh they're coming back all right, just not now," Chocolate George spoke up. "They said to tell both of you that they'll be back but that they need some time first. Dylan said they're going on the road for a while. We don't know where, but he said that you'd understand."

Katie nodded. She did understand, but Moonbeam stared back at him blankly.

"As for you, Miss Moonbeam, Frog wanted me to give you this." George leaned across the couch and handed her a small sealed envelope.

"Thank you." She stared at the note but did not open it.

"Well that's it, ladies. That's all we have to tell you. I wish the news was better, but your men are safe." Jim drained his beer and rose to his feet. "If there's anything we can do for either one of you, call the clubhouse. I mean that."

"Thank you, we appreciate that. If we need anything we'll call, I promise," Katie promised.

The three Angels followed the girls to the door, hugged them goodbye, and then left.

When they were gone Katie turned to Moonbeam. "Well, are you going to stare at the envelope all night, or are you going to open it?"

Moonbeam held the white envelope in her hands, turning it over several times. "I don't know if I want to."

"What do you mean? You've checked the mailbox every day for months now. Here you are finally with a note, and you don't want to open it? That doesn't make any sense. They're safe, Moony. No matter where they're going they're safe, this thing is over."

"But what if it's not?"

"Is that why you're scared to open the letter, because you think he's going to tell you that's it's still ongoing?"

"Maybe."

"No, Moony, it's over. Open the envelope and find out."

Moonbeam resisted. She even pushed on the envelope to see if she could read any of the print inside, but gave up when she couldn't.

"Go ahead, Moony."

Moonbeam tore the envelope open and pulled out the single sheet of paper. She looked at it, smiled, then shoved it in the pocket of her faded 501's.

"He said that he loves me, that it's all over, and that he'll go anywhere in the world that I want to, but he needs to get his head together first. That's why he and Dylan are going on the road."

"It's over," Katie said. They hugged each other in relief and happiness.

***

August 24, 1967 started just like any other day in the Haight. It was sunny and the weatherman said the temperature would be in the high 60's, beautiful by San Francisco's standards. Moonbeam and Katie had gotten out early. They had a lot to do before the afternoon when Moonbeam had to be at work and Katie to the Panhandle where she was helping the Diggers hand out the four o'clock meal.

Today was Thursday. In the Haight that meant it was the unofficial start to the weekend. College students from all over the Bay Area, who rarely had classes on Friday, started to arrive. These 'weekend hippies' would drive into the district and party until Sunday, when they would drag themselves back to places like San Jose, Redwood City, and Mountain View to attend classes on Monday morning.

Today was no exception. Along with the multitude of street kids and the regular drunks and junkies, there were the familiar faces of people they saw every weekend. Some of these Katie and Moonbeam knew and they greeted them as they made their way down Haight Street.

In the week since the Angels' visit, the girls had finally started to discuss a future beyond the stagnant condition they were living in. They decided it was time to get out of the Haight before the whole house of cards came tumbling down. Katie obviously knew that would happen much sooner than anyone was ready for.

They had gotten used to the idea that Frog's and Dylan's ordeal was over, thinking that the worst had already happened. When the two men were ready to come back, Moonbeam and Katie wanted to be someplace better. Anywhere except the Haight, watching the dream the original hippies had created come to a corrupt and ugly end.

Katie continued to worry about Richard. She had yet to hear anything from him but she knew that up until October her brother would be safe. She had called her parents once. She was glad to find that Mark Rhodes had been sentenced to a seven-year stay in San Quentin. Her father was still working on ruining his life when he got out, but Katie was fairly sure that had already happened.

She also learned that Dennis Drummond had been sentenced to three years, minus time for testifying against Mark Rhodes and time already served. He was looking at eighteen months in Folsom Prison, far away from Mark Rhodes.

Katie felt that she owed something to Dennis. He came back for her, and he had brought help. Dylan had taken care of the immediate threat, but Dennis had stayed loyal to his word. It was his testimony that had sent Mark away, and she was grateful to him.

She asked her father to give Dennis a job when he got out, and her father had promised to think about it. She wasn't sure why she thought Dennis was good inside, but she did. She remembered his kind face and how he had been her 'good hyena,' her savior among all the bad things she had seen that day.

The call to her parents had been several weeks ago. She knew she should call again soon, but it was difficult getting over forty-five years of resentment overnight. But she was trying and that, according to Moonbeam, was the best that she could expect from herself right now.

They were halfway down Haight Street when they waved at two Hells Angels standing on the sidewalk talking with a group of hippies. Chocolate George and Hairy Henry Kot waved back.

The Angels' presence brought back the conversation they had last week, and suddenly Katie and Moonbeam felt the absence of Dylan and Frog.

"They must have had one hell of a time up in Tahoe. I wish I knew what really went down," Moonbeam said, the exact thing Katie was thinking.

"I do too."

"What do you think the real story is?"

"If I were guessing?"

"Yep."

"I don't know, I have to think about it."

They walked past the Psychedelic Shop. Jay saw them and called out the door, "Moonbeam, don't forget that you're working today!"

"Yeah, I know. It's only 1:00. I don't start until 3:00. Don't worry, I haven't forgotten."

"Okay, I just wanted to make sure."

"Big date tonight?" Moony asked, and Jay blushed the color of his red T-shirt.

"Not a big date, just a... date, date."

"Don't worry, Jay, I'll be back way before then."

Their mission today was to meet a man named Cory. He was a distributor that Frog used for cheap materials: T-shirts, beads, leather scraps, and miscellaneous items. Before he left, Frog had a regular meeting with Cory every Thursday at 1:30. They would meet in a parking lot at the end of Haight Street. Now Moonbeam consistently kept the appointment and continued to trade with him. Sometimes she paid Cory in cash and other times in Owsley's samples, but today she was paying him in pot.

Chet had visited recently and his commune was growing several successful crops. He had left a pound of premium weed for Moonbeam who, like Frog before her, used it as bargaining currency. In the Haight, weed was money.

"You want to know what I think? I think that Frog and Dylan tried to get out of the drug business," Katie said. "They took off from the pop festival and holed up in a cabin in Lake Tahoe. Somewhere along the line things fell apart and Joey ended up on the wrong side. Because of his connection to Dylan he knew exactly where to find them."

"And?" Moonbeam prodded.

"And Joey died."

"Joey died how?"

"In a bike crash."

Moonbeam rolled her eyes. "Right, sure he did. You don't believe that and neither do I. What do you think really happened to Joey?"

"I think that I don't want to know. And I think that you don't want to know either. Some secrets are better left buried."

Katie and Moonbeam turned into the parking lot and just like clockwork, Cory was there waiting. After a brief exchange of merchandise Cory left and so did the girls, heading back up Haight Street the way that they had come. They carried a large paper bag each, filled to the top with odds and ends that Moonbeam would turn into jewelry and other unique hippie constructions.

"How long do you think they'll be gone?" Moonbeam asked.

"Now that's the question, isn't it? This supposedly went down on the fifteenth of August. If I were going on the road I would head east, and I would make stops along the way. How far I would go would depend on how much I was trying to forget. From the sounds of this, something very heavy went down in those woods. Just knowing that Joey and Dylan came to blows...that those blows resulted in Joey's death, well Dylan's got to be a mess."

"And Frog?"

"Maybe he's just trying to be a good friend, or maybe he was heavily involved in this shit too. I'm sure we'll eventually find out...or maybe we won't. I guess in the long run it doesn't matter. The important thing is that Dylan and Frog are free from the drug ring and that the person who was going to send them to an early grave is...dead. As for how long they'll be gone, this is August, maybe they'll be back before Christmas."

"That long?"

"That depends on how traumatic the event was for both of them. My guess...well, they won't be back for a long time."

Moonbeam accepted the information as fact. Despite her hopes for an earlier reunion, Katie was right. Something heavy had taken place in the mountains, and it was going to take the men time to recover.

Further down the street people screamed. Everyone on Haight stopped and stared towards the sound. The screams intensified and within seconds it seemed as though anyone close to the Straight Theater was in a panic.

Moonbeam and Katie looked at each other; something bad had happened. They held their bags tightly, knowing that they had to get their merchandise home, and moved quickly, weaving in and out of the spectators who stood frozen in place.

When they got to the Psychedelic Shop, Kerry Bug and Nathan approached them. It was easy to tell that the teens were in shock, both looked several shades lighter than normal, and they were shaking. The sound of an ambulance blared from lower Haight Street.

"What is it? What's happened?" Katie asked them.

"It's Chocolate George," Nathan said.

"What about Chocolate George?" Moonbeam asked.

'He's been in an accident, right there." Nathan pointed towards the Straight Theater. "He was making a right-hand turn and his mud flap hooked onto the bumper of the car in front of him, some old '55 Chevy. When the car moved George's bike flipped him off and he landed...on his head."

Katie remembered now, how could she have forgotten? She and Moonbeam had just seen George and his friend Hairy Henry maybe forty-five minutes earlier. If she had remembered the date, perhaps she could have stopped this. Katie blamed herself. She should have known.

"He's still alive," Kerry Bug said. "When we left he had a pulse. Maybe they can do something at the hospital, I don't know. He banged his head pretty fucking hard when he came down on it, so..."

Katie knew he was still alive, he would be. They would take him to the hospital and they would work on George, trying to keep him alive, but he would be pronounced dead from massive head injuries.

People in the street were crying. George was a beloved character among the hippies and the street people. He was always happy and joking around but more importantly, he always had a good word to say about everybody.

Katie remembered George's death and the wake that followed four days later. How on earth had the event slipped her mind?

They moved further down the street, still weaving between the people that stood in place. When they reached the site of the accident, the police had sealed the area off. An ambulance's lights flashed and Hells Angels continued to arrive in droves. Hairy Henry was crying. He stood with Freddy and several Angels Katie didn't know. Big Jim arrived with Terry and they drove their Harleys over the curb to get around the stalled cars. Katie and Moonbeam passed by them unnoticed.

"Will he live?" Moonbeam asked. Katie shook her head, and her eyes filled with tears. She had made a mistake. If she hadn't been so tied up in her own affairs, she could have stopped this from happening. How many more mistakes would she make? Her thoughts drifted to her brother, hoping that he would take her advice so that another tragedy, like this one, could be avoided.

***

On August 28th, Chocolate George Hendricks' body, which was cremated with two quarts of chocolate milk so that he would never get thirsty, was delivered to Cypress Lawn Cemetery in Colma. Two hundred Hells Angels from chapters all across the state of California escorted the white hearse through the streets of San Francisco. The Angels then headed to Golden Gate Park where three hundred hippies from the Haight joined them as they held a party in honor of Chocolate George.

At one point Emmett Grogan, one of the Diggers, showed up with a thousand beers on ice in the back of a pickup. The crowd drank the beer and then had a snowball fight in August. George would have loved the way his party turned out.

Katie and Moonbeam were among the crowd who gathered in the park. A stage was erected and the Grateful Dead, George's favorite band, and Big Brother and the Holding Company performed.

Since Big Brother and the Holding Company were the Angels' cover band, Janis knew the bikers well, and she had taken a special liking to George, who had become a good friend. She had taken George's death hard like many others in the Haight, and now as she performed, Katie noticed that the singer looked tired and her eyes were red rimmed like many others on this sad occasion.

Katie and Moonbeam sat on the lawn watching Big Brothers' performance and the hippies and Angels partying around them.

As with most gatherings there were drugs and singing and dancing in the streets. The usual hippies and bikers were there, but there were others who had come just for the funeral. Katie saw who she thought was Sonny Barger talking with Big Jim.

"George sure was loved," Katie commented.

Moonbeam nodded. "He would have dug this party."

Terry and Freddy walked by on their way to join the conversation with Big Jim and Barger. The girls watched them silently pass by.

Katie sighed. "This is too sad."

"Now what?" Moonbeam asked.

Katie studied her; her eyes were red rimmed too. "What do you mean?"

"I mean what happens next? What happens to the Haight and everyone who started all this grooviness?"

"What do you mean what happens? You're watching it take place. Haight-Ashbury can't accommodate this many people. You see what's happening, all the teenyboppers are getting younger and younger, the Diggers can't find places for everyone anymore, and they can't feed everyone either. What happens is the bad element moves in, and the hippies move out. Some go home, back to school, some move north, and lots settle in Oregon. Others move to Marin County where they live in communes and the rest just drift away like people do. The neighborhood deteriorates because of overcrowding, homelessness, hunger, and severe drug problems. Crime goes crazy, and the peace loving hippies can't live here anymore. There won't even be attempts to clean it up until the mid-1970's, and that's a long time off. Basically the dream dies."

"That's sad."

"That's life. It's filled with disappointments."

"How long until it..."

"Implodes?"

"Yeah."

"It's nearly the end of August now. By 1968 it will be falling apart, and by the end of the year nobody will really be left; not anyone who can get out that is. Drug addicts, dealers, runaways, prostitutes and their pimps... they'll be all that's left."

"And where will we be?"

"Well originally, you went to Marin County and I went home and got married, after...after Richard's death in October. This time around who knows where we'll be?"

"Are you coming to Marin with me? If I go that is?"

"Yeah, I believe I am. Where else am I going to go? Home? Not a chance of that happening, and I'm sure as shit not going to get married anytime soon so...yeah I'm coming with you."

"Regardless of...Richard's outcome?"

"Richard's outcome..." Katie took a deep breath and shook her head.

"I'm sorry, maybe I shouldn't have said that."

"It's okay, I have to think about it, don't I? After all, that day is getting close."

"But your meeting with him, it went well, right? You said he listened to you."

"He did, and he believed me. Now it's up to him. I'd like to think that he'll do the right thing, but when the time comes who knows what will happen?"

"You said that all he had to do is go up a hill and he'll be okay."

"It's a lot more complicated than that. He has to get more than thirty other soldiers to agree to follow him, or he has to sneak off on his own. What he's going to be doing is against orders, and that's a court martial at best."

"It's a hell of a lot better than dying."

"For you, for me, yeah, but we aren't there in the middle of that jungle surrounded by the North Vietnamese Army. There's going to be a lot of pressure on him. Richard's a good soldier, he's going to feel obligated to obey orders."

"Not if the orders are going to get him killed he won't."

"I hope you're right. We'll find out soon. As I said before, the day is getting closer, October 27th to be exact. The last time, my parents got the telegram on November 5th. My mother called me in the afternoon. I remember it was exactly three because I looked at the clock."

"And then you went home?"

"And then Mark Rhodes helped me pack up my stuff and together we moved me home. That was on the 12ᵗʰ of November. Mark and I were married on the 15ᵗʰ of December. We had a Christmas wedding, thinking that it would cheer everyone up."

"Did it?"

"Did it what?"

"Cheer everyone up?"

Katie smiled sadly. "No, I don't think so."

"So what about this time?"

"This time, wow, I don't know. I'm not going home no matter how the Richard situation turns out. I guess we go to Marin County and we try the communal life you're always talking about."

"We'll be happy, you'll see."

"You were last time. You liked it there. I remember your letters were filled with adventures, I was jealous."

"Well this time you'll be with me, and we'll have adventures together."

They hugged each other and smiled.

"When do we move?" Moonbeam asked. "Shouldn't we start planning?"

"We are planning, but we're going to do it slowly. We're going to know exactly where we're going, make sure it's a place that both of us like, and then we'll pick a date. But I can't go anywhere until..."

"Until after October," Moonbeam finished.

"That's right. I know it's silly to stay in the city but for some reason...I just can't move on until I know."

"I guess that makes sense. It gives us time too. I mean, maybe the guys will be back by then, who knows?"

"Yeah, maybe they will be."

The party around them continued. Bikers and hippies grooving in love and peace just like any other Be-In, but this one was different. This one was signaling the end of an era. With Chocolate George dead, everything was different.

***

People partied throughout the afternoon, and toasts were made in George's honor. When the sun dipped low, people started to split, everyone except the locals who watched the crowds disperse.

A dark haired hippie girl walked up to Katie and said, "Hey, your friend wants to talk to you."

"My friend?"

"Yeah, man, the singer chick from Big Brother. She saw you in the crowd and asked me to get your attention."

"Janis?"

"Yeah, man, Janis, she sent me. She's over there next to the stage."

Katie glanced behind her and saw Janis gesturing towards her.

"Thanks," Katie said to the young hippie who nodded and walked off.

"Come with me, Moony."

"No, you're her fortuneteller, you go see what she wants. I'm tired anyway, so I'm going to head back to the house."

Moonbeam called to a hippie they both knew, and the man turned around and waited for her to catch up. Katie watched them walk away talking and smoking a doobie that he produced from a jacket pocket, then she walked over to the stage.

"Hey, baby, I saw you out there grooving to the music. Bummer occasion though, isn't it?"

Katie nodded.

"You're looking better than the last time I saw you. How's the guy situation coming along?" Janis asked.

"Oh that... it's ongoing, but it's better than the last time I saw you. You guys were great by the way, but then you always are."

"Thanks man, I appreciate that. Hey, about the last time I saw you, you know at your pad? Sorry about the way I just up and split like that. It wasn't cool of me."

"I completely understand. I would have probably done the same, considering the reading I gave you."

"Yeah, about that reading, man, it was trippy. I got to say it's messed with my mind. It's made me think a lot."

"That's good I hope."

"Yeah, man, it's good. Freaky as hell." Janis laughed and shook her head.

"So you're probably not ready for another reading anytime soon?"

"I don't know, man, would it be better than the last one?"

"I sure hope so." Katie smiled, but she couldn't cover up the sadness in her eyes.

"I guess I never marry?" Janis asked, showing Katie her hand.

Katie took it and pretended to study the lines in her palm.

"You'll be engaged but..."

"But I'll die before I get married?"

Katie nodded.

"Is he a good guy? I mean, do you think it would have worked out?"

Katie laughed. "His name is Seth, same as your father's, and no, he's not a good guy at all. He's a lot younger than you, and I don't think it would have lasted. I think you just wanted to be married and he was there. He's a scammer. Be careful of him, and my advice, I don't think you want to marry him. He ends up in a series of robberies, ugly stuff really."

"That figures. My choice in men." Janis shook her head. "Well, according to you I guess I don't get the chance to marry anyone."

"That's really up to you, isn't it?"

Janis looked at the bottle of Southern Comfort in her bag and thought about the recent needle marks on her arm. "Yeah, I guess it is."

"You can change things, Janis!"

"Can I?" Janis asked.

Katie nodded. "I know what I am now," Katie suddenly said.

Janis looked perplexed. "What you are?"

"That first day when I met you at the Avalon, remember?"

Janis laughed. "When you were five fingering the posters?"

"Yeah, that day. We went out in the back lot and you asked me who I was."

"Oh yeah, man, I remember that. You didn't have an answer."

"Not then I didn't, but I do now."

"And?"

"I'm a fixer, Janis. I'm meant to stop things from happening that should never take place. That's who I am, that's my purpose in this world."

"Fixing things like my overdose?"

"That's right, like your overdosing, or stopping my brother from dying in Vietnam."

"And Brian Jones from drowning in a swimming pool?"

"Maybe, if he takes my advice. Just like you, because you can change things too."

"Hey man," a male voice called from the sidelines. Both women turned and found Jerry Garcia smiling back at them.

"Are you Janis' spiritualist, the one she's always talking about?"

"This is her, man. This is Katie, my personal fortuneteller."

"Groovy! Can you read my fortune, Katie?"

Katie smiled. "I sure can."

"Be careful, man, she's blatantly honest, you might not want to hear what she's going to tell you," Janis warned.

"I want to hear." Jerry, adorned in one of his trademark long sleeve striped shirts, walked towards them holding out both of his hands.

Katie took the right one in hers and then pretended to study the lines. The circuits in her head worked overtime as she remembered the history of the Grateful Dead. Finally, satisfied that she had her story straight, she looked up from his palm.

"The Grateful Dead will be world famous. The Monterey Pop Festival has made that happen for you. You'll perform together as a group for the next thirty years. In between albums and touring with the Dead, you'll have your own musical career, but you'll always remain one of the Grateful Dead."

Jerry grinned.

"You're married now, and you have a four year old daughter named Heather, isn't that right?"

Jerry nodded, the skepticism which had been so clearly written on his face instantly disappearing. Now he was shocked and his demeanor changed.

"You'll marry three times. Your next wife is currently a member of the Merry Pranksters."

"The Merry Pranksters?" Jerry asked. "Who is she?"

"I think they call her Mountain Girl. You'll have two daughters together." Katie stopped and looked at him; Jerry's mouth was agape as he stared at her intently. "Your third wife will be your widow."

"See, man? I told you to be careful," Janis said. "Her predictions can be fucking scary as shit."

"Go on..." Jerry replied.

"You just don't take care of yourself. You'll gain a lot of weight, you'll take it off unhealthily, and then you'll gain it back plus more. You'll end up with diabetes."

"I have diabetes in my family," he admitted.

"Even your illness won't be incentive enough for you to get healthy. Your drug use, mostly heroin and cocaine, will get the best of you and your heart will fail. You'll be fifty three years old."

"Fuck!" Jerry snatched his hand away as if it had been burned and rubbed it across his blue and red-striped shirt.

"What did I tell you, fucking creepy right?" Janis said.

Jerry backed up a few steps. "Thanks for the reading, I think."

"Man you can change that shit easy, Jerry. Don't gain a ton of weight," Janis told him. "Me, man? The drugs get me. I only have three years left. At least you get married a dozen times and have a baseball team of girls. Shit, I have nothing."

"Wow, that really is a bummer, Janis, three years?" Jerry asked.

Katie nodded. "But you can both change things, can't you see that? Now that you know the truth you can fix what shouldn't happen."

Chapter 45

The return trip to Vietnam was worse because Richard knew what he was going back to.

During the trip he was haunted by his conversation with Katie. He wanted to believe that it was the alcohol talking but he knew differently. She knew way too much about everything; the landscape, the names of bases, cities she couldn't possibly know about, and which troops would be involved in battles yet to come. Information that in-depth had to be more than just intoxication.

When Richard made it back to Camp Carroll, he was exhausted, not only physically, but also mentally. Katie's premonition was all he could think about.

The jeep pulled into camp and stopped next to the Flagpole.

"We're here, Private Searfus," the driver announced.

Richard picked up his bag, jumped out of the jeep.

"Hey, Searfus."

Richard looked across the courtyard where Clemmings and Clark stood outside the enlisted men's club. He walked over to the pub, dropped his bag at the door, and entered the stuffy wooden structure. The smell of heavy sweat and stale beer hit him, immediately reminding him that he was really back in Vietnam.

"I bet it's great to be back," Clemmings told him with a snort.

"Oh yeah, fucking terrific." Richard popped open a warm can of Beer 33.

"I bet you missed that shit too, didn't you?"

"Fuck yeah, as I was opening cans of ice cold Bud I was dreaming of a warm Beer 33."

"That's okay, man, we were enjoying them for you," Clark said jovially.

"Where is everyone?" Richard asked.

"Out on patrol, same old bullshit. You know the routine."

Richard nodded. "Why aren't you with them?"

"They have to leave someone behind to mind the big guns don't they? We're it."

Corporal Hodges walked in and plopped himself down on a stool next to Richard. "Hey, Clipper John, you came back."

"Yeah, I did."

"That was stupid, wasn't it?" Hodges asked, opening his own Beer 33.

Richard laughed. "Yeah I guess it was. Any action while I was gone?"

"No, surprisingly it's been quiet." Clemmings knocked on the wooden table in front of him. "A few odd scuffles here and there but for the most part... So tell us, how was stateside?"

"Fucking odd, man, really fucking odd."

"I've heard that from a lot from guys when they get back. That's why I went to Australia on my R and R. I wanted to see something new instead of trying to relive something that I couldn't." Clark opened another can of beer.

"You were smart. I don't know what I was thinking." Richard shook his head.

Hodges pulled a pack of cigarettes out of his pocket, slid one into his mouth, and lit it. "It gave you a glimpse of what it's going to be like when you get back. Now you know what to expect. Maybe that's a good thing."

The recurring feeling that he wouldn't make it home came back, and then just as quickly he remembered Katie telling him how to survive. His head started to spin, but he contributed the sensation to the high humidity. Inside he knew otherwise.

"So they're out with Captain Becker?" Richard asked.

"That's right," Clemmings answered.

"How is the guy?"

"Like any fresh meat in a combat zone." Hodges laughed. "Did you expect more?"

"I was hoping for more."

"He can follow orders, that's about it. Rumor has it that he fucked up someplace else and was transferred here," Clark said.

Richard nodded, Katie had said as much.

"At least he hasn't made any dire mistakes yet," Hodges remarked.

"Is he that bad?" Richard asked, already knowing the answer.

Clemmings shrugged. "Who knows? It's still too early to tell. He doesn't get a high rating mind you, but whether he's stupid enough to get himself blown up like Lt. Franco, well that verdict's still out."

"We've been through worse, we'll survive him," Hodges added and laughed.

"Will we?" Richard asked, and for a brief second thought about revealing his sister's premonition to the group but then just as quickly, he changed his mind.

***

Vietnam had a single rainy season, monsoon season. Rainfall during the remainder of the year was infrequent. For coastal areas and parts of the central highlands facing northeast, the monsoon season ran from September to January. These regions received torrential rain from typhoons, which moved in from the South China Sea.

The monsoon season of September 1967 was especially brutal. As a result, major bridges, imperative to ongoing American missions, were washed out.

August had been uneventful in the DMZ, but September dawned with new violence. Between September 4th and the 21st, the US Marines engaged in multiple battles with NVA forces east and south of Con Thein.

In early October, heavy monsoons washed out the bridge leading to Con Thein Base and it had to be rebuilt immediately; this was one of Katie's predictions. From there Richard watched as every single one of her prophesies unfolded one right after another.

On September 21st, the 2/4 Marines started their search and destroy mission and as Katie had described, they encountered an NVA regiment. Their lack of tank support since the heavy rains had knocked out roads and bridges quickly became a problem. The dense vegetation and the close proximity to the enemy restricted them from receiving reinforcements or air support.

After a day long battle, the Marines suffered sixteen dead and one hundred eighteen wounded. At dusk the battalion withdrew and because of the NVA's presence, just as Katie had said, they weren't able to retrieve their dead for another three weeks. That was the beginning of a siege, which would last until the end of October.

In the second week of October, the 2/4 were placed on a mission to defend the recently built bridge to Con Thien. The construction of the bridge reopened a vital road that, if destroyed, would cut off the only supply line leading to the 'Hill of Angels" (Con Thein), a US Marine combat base located in the DMZ less than two miles away from the border of North Vietnam. During the war, it was a prime location for fierce fighting.

On October 25, the 2/4 Marines performed a sweep, looking for mines and troops north of Route 561. Although they didn't come in contact with the enemy, the progress was slow because of heavy undergrowth. Finally exhausted, they set up a night position but were quickly located and then bombarded by the North Vietnamese Army. Several officers were killed and they and the wounded were evacuated by helicopter. Lieutenant Colonel John Studt was flown in to take over command.

On the 26th, the 2/4 marines moved north and secured their objective at 1300. There they came under heavy NVA mortar and gunfire attack. Two helicopters were shot down attempting to pick up casualties. Lt. Col. Studt called for reinforcements and F Company, who were left behind to guard the unit's ammunition, the 3/3 marines, and part of the 2/9, under Captain Trace Becker's command, were called in from the north. Both units arrived at dusk and then heavy fighting ensued.

Richard kept up on troop news through a series of sources. One of these was Walter the jeep transport driver. Walter was a gossip who brought news from a fifty-mile radius everywhere and anywhere he delivered soldiers.

As word of Operation Kingfisher made its way around Camp Carroll, members of the 2/9 were certain that for a change they were going to be left out of the battle, but Richard knew otherwise. October ticked by, and he waited for the day when his company would be pulled into the ongoing nightmare.

Thoughts of desertion, or a self-inflicted injury entered his mind, but he knew that he couldn't go through with a cowardly act. How could he leave his entire troop to perish while he planned for his own escape? Richard was a better man than that, and so he waited with the rest of the company until the dreaded day finally arrived.

On the 26th of October, he and the other men from H Company were pulled into a briefing. They were told that they were being deployed. Their mission was to locate and reinforce part of the 2/4, who were under heavy enemy attack.

Richard realized then that this was it; the end that he had been waiting for. Every man in his company would be dead within hours. He knew that it would happen the night of the 27th and 28th. Katie's prediction, that he would never see the sunrise on the 28th, was about to come true.

Feeling numb, Richard walked with the rest of the men and boarded the Chinook chopper, which would fly them into the jungles near An Kha.

**

During the Vietnam War, the US used a personnel rotation policy that defied military logic. Officers spent a year in the country, but only six months under troop command. This policy was particularly destabilizing to combat troops. The motive for the military protocol was to ensure that all of their military leaders were properly exposed to combat with the assumption that the Vietnam War would be a short one. Instead, it became the nation's longest, but once a bureaucracy as large as the US military set a rule in place, it was beyond the power of mortal man to change it.

Rotation of officers assured that the troops would forever be in the hands of inexperience commanders. Just as an officer was getting the hang of things they were on their way out, and a fresh, poorly trained one was coming in.

Along with officers who were inexperienced, there were others who were harsh, completely inept, or overzealous for personal fame.

With the Vietnam War becoming more and more vilified at home, US soldiers were increasingly unwilling to go into harm's way. They expected their leaders to have a similar sense of self-preservation, even if these motives were obstructive to the war. Commanders who frequently took dangerous or suicidal missions were unpopular with the men. If the officer was seen as low quality or endangering the lives of his men, lower ranking soldiers used the threat of fragging. Sometimes a warning would be given to the target by placing a grenade pin on his bed, indicating that if his actions continued a fragging would take place.

Richard's unit arrived at dusk, as Katie had told him they would. Captain Becker assembled his men according to units and as Richard knew he would, ordered them to hold their current position.

Aware of the Marines' arrival, the NVA immediately called in reinforcements, who continued to deploy during the night. The American's, however, were cut off from outside help and had no possible way of getting a helicopter in, even if they needed one.

When Richard's troop jumped out of the chopper, they pulled their shovels out of their packs and started to dig a series of foxholes. When they had enough coverage, they crawled into the trenches and waited for their orders, studying the terrain.

Richard was especially nervous, knowing that within the next twenty-four hours the whole platoon would fall victim to the NVA. He looked at the young faces around him and knew that every one of them would die unless he could somehow change things.

Torres was sitting beside Richard. He jumped and covered his head when an explosion overhead sent a rush of dirt into their hole.

"Fuck, man, here we go again." Torres uttered a prayer and then crossed himself. Beside him, Lewis did the same.

"What are we supposed to do now?" Lewis asked.

"Wait until the idiot gives us the order to shoot or to move camp," Owens answered in between puffs on a Pall Mall cigarette.

Further down the trench a young private from F Company 2/4 pulled a cloth wrapped bundle out of his pack and proceeded to shoot up.

"Go easy on that shit, Davis," the man next to him said.

"Why, man? If I'm going to die I want to be stoned as fuck."

A third soldier, who'd watched Davis, pulled out his own 'stash' and followed suit.

Owens shook his head. "I've never understood that."

"What?" Richard asked.

"That," he said, nodding toward the two soldiers. "When I'm going into battle I want my head to be clear so I know what I'm doing, you dig?"

"I understand that," Richard said, "but I also understand their side. Hell, haven't you ever thought about it? It would numb everything. Sure, you'd still be here, but you wouldn't feel a thing."

"Never, man. I'm a booze only type of guy."

Torres looked at him questioningly.

"Okay, booze and a little weed," he admitted. "Anything harder, though, it's just not for me."

"It's not about that," Richard said.

"No, I know what it's about, man, it's about escaping all of this. Me? I just want to live through it."

Richard knew that wouldn't happen, not this time. No matter where their heads were, every single man in their platoon would die before morning. At the moment he had to agree with Davis; if you had to be here you might as well be stoned as fuck.

Artillery fire went off somewhere to the right and the men dropped lower into the hole. Gunfire continued, but nothing came close. Eventually they sat up, carefully leaning their backs against the safety of the foxhole.

Trace Becker appeared above them. He called his lieutenants together, talked to them briefly, and then sent them out, undoubtedly to give orders to the enlisted men. Lt. Dey jumped into the hole beside Richard just long enough to tell the men to hold their fire. According to Dey, the officers were working on coordinates, trying to locate the missing 2/4 unit that was cut off on the Vietnamese side.

Within seconds, Lt. Dey jumped out of the hole and walked away, leaving the men filled with curiosity.

"What's that supposed to fucking mean?" Lewis asked.

"It means that they're getting ready to move us," Owens answered. "If they weren't they would already have us firing at the enemy."

Richard looked at his watch: 1800. He wondered when Becker would decide to move them down the hill and hoped that it wouldn't be anytime soon. He swallowed nervously and looked up. As Katie had said, it was a steep climb straight up rugged terrain. It would be easy to tumble down, especially for the guys who had just shot up. The climb itself looked as if it would kill them. This was going to be even harder than he had anticipated.

Seconds later, Corporal Hodges jumped into their hole. "Do you know what they're fucking planning?"

The men shook their heads.

"Clemmings and I just overheard Dey and Becker. Stupid motherfucker's got us on some suicide mission."

"Come again?" Torres said.

"Becker's been on the radio with the higher ups. Everyone's uptight about this missing 2/4 unit."

"Missing? I thought we were sent to reinforce them?" Lewis said. "Now they're missing?"

"Out of radio frequency, or their radio is fucked up," Hodges explained.

"Anyway, get this, they were asking for volunteers to head into undisclosed areas, that happen to cross over into North Vietnam. That dumb fuck Becker volunteered us. He said that he saw a path and he suspects that it leads to the missing 2/4 unit that we're all looking for."

"*What?*" Owens shouted.

"Exactly as it sounds, man. This Becker dude is taking us on some path that he knows leads into North Vietnam. According to his calculations that's where the missing 2/4 unit is held up."

"And if his calculations are wrong?" Torres asked.

"Then we could be walking into a slaughter." Hodges pulled a cigarette out of his pocket, stuck it in his mouth, and lit it. "A full-fledged slaughter."

"Why would he want to accept a mission like that?" Owens said. "Does he have a death wish?"

"Supposedly he's from some bigwig military family. He has a grandfather who's a four star general and his daddy is heavily decorated too. Becker's a fuck up who got kicked out of his last job for incompetence. Imagine the feather this mission will put in his cap if his hunch is dead on. According to his talk with high command, he's convinced that he's right."

"What are we going to do?" Lewis asked.

"What do you mean what are we going to do?" Hodges asked. "You're in the US Marine Corps, soldier, you do what they tell you to do."

"Fuck," Owens said in defeat.

Hodges jumped out of their foxhole and headed back towards his own.

"Fuck," Owens repeated.

Richard had sat silently listening to the conversation. He felt as if he were outside his body looking down, waiting for the confrontation, which he knew would end all of their lives.

"Do you believe in premonitions?" he whispered to Torres.

Torres scooted closer. "What man?"

"You know, occult, premonitions, stuff like that?"

"Yeah, man, I do. Do you know what Santeria is?"

Richard shook his head.

"It's a mixture of Roman Catholicism and a Caribbean religion. My grandfather was a Santero a priest in the Santeria religion. He was a very powerful man in the faith."

"Is it something like voodoo?"

"Not voodoo, not at all. But it has qualities that are voodoo like. My grandfather had dreams that came true and my mother said he used to put powerful spells on his enemies. She used to panic when her father-in-law came to visit. She would tell us kids to hide our hairbrushes and to never to leave fingernail clippings or blood on anything. I remember once flushing tons of tissues down the toilet after I had a nose bleed." Torres shook his head at the memories. "He was one freaky dude, that's all I got to say."

"Then you believe in all of that...spooky stuff?"

"Absolutely. I've seen too many witchy things to believe otherwise."

"Then I've got something to tell you, man, and it's really freaky."

"Go ahead."

"When I was home on leave I went out with my sister. We had a few drinks and then she started talking real crazy."

"Crazy?"

"Yeah, man. She said she had a premonition, but I think it was something much stronger than that. I swear, man, she has second sight. The things she knew... well, there's just no way, it's impossible."

"My grandfather had the gift, I know what you mean, man. He was always predicting the future." Torres nodded.

"That night, she told me everything that's currently happening to us right this minute, being here, man, this whole battle scene. She told me back in August that the NVA would start attacking in September. She knew that the bridge to Con Thein would be washed out. She told me that the 2/4 would be sent in to protect the newly built bridge and how on a routine sweep they would be ambushed."

"She knew all of *that*?"

"That's not all, man, there's more." Richard wallowed hard. "She knew that Captain Becker would lead a platoon into the battle as reinforcements. She also knew that he would make a mistake, and he would lead thirty-two men on a trail downhill, and that trail would be the wrong one. Instead of finding the objective, his path would take them to a regiment of North Vietnamese soldiers. According to her, all thirty-two men, including Becker and his senior officers, die. That platoon is ours, Torres, and all of us are going to die if we follow his orders."

Torres was quiet. He absorbed the news calmly and then shook his head. "Is that all she said?"

"No, she told me the only way out of this battle, the one and only way that we can survive."

"Which is?"

Richard lowered his voice, "Mutiny. Going against direct orders."

"Maybe not, perhaps we can talk to him, reason with him or something," Torres suggested.

"And tell him what, man? Katie's premonition? No way will he listen to that. You heard what Hodges said; this is the guy's one chance to redeem himself in his family's eyes. If he's right, which he believes he is, then he'll be a hero. Do you think Katie's premonition can sway him away from that glory?"

"Then what do we do, follow orders and die?"

"I don't know, man, I've been thinking about that for months, and now that the time is here...well, I just don't know."

"You said she told you the way out?"

"She sure did. She said we needed to climb."

They both looked up. Torres whistled. "That's going to be one steep motherfucking climb."

"I know."

***

Trace Becker was thirty-three years old, and he'd been trying to find his niche in the world for the past ten years. He had a lot of pressure on his shoulders since he'd come from a long line of successful military leaders. The Becker family had officers in every American war all the way back to the Revolution, and they were proud of that accomplishment.

Not only were they officers in the military, Becker's family decedents had all been decorated war heroes. His grandfather, a four star general, had earned a Congressional Medal of Honor during World War I when he saved his whole unit.

His father, another successful general, helped defeat Hitler's regime in 1945 when his unit marched into Berlin. And his older brother had only been in the military a year longer than Trace and he was already decorated, having earned several medals for leading his troop into battles.

Now it was his turn. So far, his military career had been less than exemplary. Trace had a knack for getting himself into schemes that at first sounded great and then later turned out to be disasters. That's what had happened to him at his last assignment in operations. Not this time. This time he was sure he was on his way to greatness.

Once he led his platoon of men down the path he knew was hidden in the shrubbery below, they would find the missing 2/4 unit, reinforce their numbers, and together they would come out victors. How could they not? After all, Trace's men would be pursuing their own into North Vietnam. They would defeat the NVA on their own turf and then he would save the missing unit and deliver them and his own platoon back to safety. As for the men who wouldn't make it back from this mission, well, war was war. At least the majority of them were young and single without families. In Trace's mind, that made their lives expendable.

***

By 1900 the ceasefire was still in effect. Becker didn't want to give away the platoon's current location, and Richard knew why. Becker was waiting for the okay and then he would move H Company of the 2/9 along with F Company of the 2/4 into a failed mission which would take all of their lives.

After much discussion, Richard and Torres decided that there was only one thing they could do. They had to talk to the rest of the men in the company and try to convince them that the suicide mission they were on had to be stopped.

Hodges, Clemmings, and Clark had spread the word, and by now all thirty-two men knew they were going to be moving into enemy territory as soon as the okay came from upper command.

It was easy to convince Lewis and Owens despite— or maybe because of— the fact they had overheard the conversation about Katie's premonition and the stories about Torres's grandfather. Regardless of the reason, none of the men trusted their commanders enough to follow them down an unmapped trail into enemy territory. Now it was time to take their concerns to the rest of the men, starting with the rest of H Company. Richard snuck out of his foxhole and jumped into theirs.

"Hey, Searfus," Clemmings greeted him. "Do you have a smoke on you?"

"No, I don't smoke cigarettes."

"I know. I wasn't talking about a cigarette." Clemmings grinned and Richard, understanding immediately, pulled a pre-rolled joint out of his pocket.

"Ahh man, you never disappoint me." Clemmings reached for the joint and lit it.

"So what do you think about this idiot Becker?" Clark asked. He was sitting in the foxhole, back against the dirt wall, drinking an extra warm can of Beer 33 he had brought with him.

"Actually, that's what I'm here to talk to you about. This dude, he's going to get all of us killed."

"That could very well happen." Clemmings passed the joint back to Richard, who took a long drag. "But there's not much we can do about it."

"Isn't there?" Richard asked.

"What are you talking about?"

"Listen, man, I know it sounds crazy, but if we take that path down to the river and we cross it, we're going to die, every single one of us." Richard passed the rest of the joint to Clark, who finished off the smoke.

"You don't know that," Hodges stated.

"Actually, I do know that. I can just... feel it. If we go down that hill, we're done. Becker is wrong. That path doesn't take us to the missing 2/4 unit. He's going to deliver us right into the hands of the enemy. There's a whole regiment of NVA down that hill waiting for us."

"Hey, man, be careful what you say," Hodges scolded.

"I'm serious, Hodges."

Clemmings pulled Richard closer. "Shut your mouth, man. Are you fucking stupid?"

"No, man, I'm right."

Clemmings, Clark, and Hodges stared at each other.

"Searfus, what the fuck are you suggesting?" Clemmings finally asked.

"I'm saying that Becker is incompetent. He's on a glory mission to impress his father, a four star general, and that's all that matters. I'm saying he's wrong and that he's going to get all of us killed."

"From what we heard, you're probably right." Hodges nodded in agreement. He had overheard Becker make the deal with upper command. "But it's the Marines man, we don't have a say so in any of this."

"Do you really believe that? Even if the man is leading every single one of us to our deaths?" Richard asked, raising his voice slightly so that several men further down the hole turned and looked at them.

Clemmings shook him. "Fucking lower your voice, Searfus. What you're discussing can get us court martialed."

"It's better than dying."

"I don't want to hear any of this," Clemmings said, stepping away.

"I do," Hodges said. "What do you know, how do you know it, and what are you proposing to do about it?"

"I know that Becker is wrong. I know that down below there's a whole regiment of NVA waiting for us. I know that it doesn't matter whether we cross the river or head in either direction. Even if we take the flatlands, we're going to end up meeting the enemy, hundreds of them against the thirty-two of us. I know that if we go along with Becker's scheme all of us, including him and his senior officers, will be dead before first light tomorrow."

"And you know this how?"

"That's the hard part. I can't explain it. I just know that it's true."

"And you want us to take your word for it? That's fucking crazy, Searfus, you must know that."

"I know it sounds crazy, but I also know it's the truth. We die, every single one of us, before morning if we follow him."

"You just *know* this?"

"That's right, I just know it."

"Not good enough, not for me, Searfus." Hodges returned to rubbing his M16 down with a rag.

Richard looked at Clark, who had remained quiet throughout his story.

"Don't look at me, buddy. If you want me to listen then you've got to come clean. How do you know what you're telling us is the truth? And don't tell me any bullshit like 'I can't explain it' either. You and I know that's a crock of shit."

"Okay. I'll tell you how I know, but keep in mind it's weird as fuck."

"Try us," Clark said.

Richard settled himself in the hole and lowered his voice. "When I was home on leave I had this conversation with my sister. We were drinking at the time, so at first I thought it was the alcohol talking, but then she started to tell me things... things she couldn't possibly know..."

Clemmings moved in closer. Although he pretended that he wasn't interested in the conversation, Richard knew he was listening.

When Richard finished his explanation, the men stood mouths agape, staring at him. Even the other men in the foxhole who couldn't help but overhear the conversation were silent.

"She knew all that?" Hodges asked. "The names of towns and everything?"

"That's right, man, and she knew it back in August. Everything she told me that night has come true. Every specific detail."

"How come you didn't tell us this sooner?" Clark asked skeptically.

"Really, man, do you need to ask me that?"

"You're right, I would have thought you were crazy," Hodges admitted.

"What now?" Clark asked.

Torres hopped into the now crowded foxhole. "I'll tell you what now. All we need is for some stupid asshole to shoot off several random bullets just like this." He turned his M16 in the direction of the enemy and fired several shots. "You see, now the gooks know exactly where we are so Becker's sneak attack is ruined." Torres smiled broadly. "Now, maybe we have a fighting chance, no pun intended."

From outside the foxhole commanders screamed as they searched for the man who had let off the random shots. However, before they could find Torres and haul him off, the explosions, which until now had been aimed over their heads, were coming directly towards them.

***

After the random shots, the enemy started to shell their location. Captain Trace Becker had no choice but to give the order for his men to open fire. With that directive, rocket launchers, grenade launchers, and an M-60 machine gun were mounted in place. When they were given the directive to shoot, the jungle erupted in battle.

Within minutes artillery fire and mortar explosions lit up the night's sky. Richard and Owens lowered themselves further into the foxhole, and when there was a break in incoming fire they got off an occasional shot. But they were outnumbered and everybody knew it. Their only consolation was that they didn't seem to be the NVA's main target.

The diversion in firepower gave Becker additional reasons to believe that the trail he intended to follow was the right path. Still believing that the missing 2/4 were being pelted with the brunt of the NVA's weaponry, he wove a plan together, hoping that he could still come out of this battle as a hero.

Meanwhile, bullets from a DP 7.62mm light machine gun sprayed an array of ammunition their way. Six hundred rounds later the gun stopped, and from one of the foxholes an American grenade launcher set off a series of Mark-2 hand grenades propelled by a rifle-mounted launcher.

"Thanks, Torres, this is way fucking better than taking a mountain trail," Owens rattled off in between explosions.

"Fuck you, Owens, you ungrateful turd."

A nearby explosion knocked rocks and debris into their hole. A stone about the size of a golf ball hit Lewis in the head and he yelped. Thinking that he'd been shot he sat back in the hole and covered his head, waiting to pass out. When darkness didn't come and a knot formed on his forehead instead, Lewis was relieved and started to laugh hysterically.

They launched more grenades and then there was the sound of the M-60 flooding the nights sky with a hail of bullets. From a hole beside theirs men screamed and dirt sprayed around them when one of the NVA's bombs finally hit its mark.

"Who was in that hole?" Torres asked, eyes wide, frightened. Richard and Owens shrugged.

There was screaming beside them. The medic, Alexander, was working on somebody, and then it suddenly became dark and silent until a new round of artillery hit their way.

Lewis moaned; the bump on his head ached. Although it was much better than a bullet, he still felt off balance and dizzy. *Concussion*, he told himself uneasily as he crawled to the spot where his buddies were shooting and aimed his own rifle towards the NVA.

Someone from above yelled, "Mahoney and Gilbert are both dead!"

The dead men were from F Company 2/4. Men that Richard and his troop didn't know, somehow that made the casualties easier.

Not our men. Richard went back to spraying bullets towards the North Vietnamese side.

In the confusion someone dropped into their hole. Richard and Owens turned simultaneously to see Clemmings crawling towards them in the darkness.

"How do we get out of this fucking shit, Searfus?"

Richard pointed at the cliff, which looked especially volatile in the darkness. "We climb," he said. "It's the only way out. The flatlands and the path down to the river are flooded with NVA troops, and more are coming all the time."

"Then we need to start planning something because Becker is pulling men off the battle. He's still planning on taking that path down the river. Nothing has changed, Searfus. He still thinks the 2/4 is down there and he's determined to drag us down with him."

"You're fucking kidding?" Torres said.

"Man, I really fucking wish I were. Hodges and I heard him talking to his officers, arguing actually. They're all telling him this is a bad idea but he won't listen. Lt. Dey will be here soon to move us out."

"Fuck, man, what do we do?" Lewis asked.

"Jesus, Lewis, you have one hell of a knot on your head, brother," Clemmings said, just noticing the injury and leaned closer so that he could see Lewis clearly.

"I know, I got hit in the head with something."

"Good fucking thing it wasn't a bullet," Owens told him.

"I know." Lewis smiled and rubbed at the knot on his head affectionately.

"Now what?" Owens repeated.

"I heard some of the guys are going to try to talk to the lieutenants. Tell them that we're all uncomfortable with this mission. Whether the officers can do something about it or not, I don't know."

"And if not?" Torres asked. "If the stupid motherfucker won't listen to reason and he's determined to take us down that path, then what?"

"I don't know, man." Clemmings shook his head.

Artillery fire knocked them down further in the hole, and for a few minutes the noise around them was deafening, and then as quickly as it started, the shelling stopped.

There was the sound of thunder overhead and rain fell from the sky in what seemed like buckets.

"Great, man, that's all we need," Owens groused.

Clemmings jumped out of their hole and headed for his own.

The rain continued to pelt down around them, filling the hole so that their ankles were quickly disappearing under the muck. It was no surprise when Lt. Dey suddenly jumped in beside them.

"Start packing up, men," he ordered. "We're moving position."

Lightning lit up the sky, and seconds later came a thunderous roar so loud that the earth beneath their feet seemed to vibrate.

"Captain Becker wants to use the weather as a diversion to move us to lower ground, closer to the objective," Lt. Dey explained.

Richard tried to remain silent but couldn't. Before he knew what he was doing he was already talking. "Lieutenant, this mission is a bad idea, it's going to get all of us killed."

"I don't think you're in a position to question command are you, Searfus?"

"I don't have to question it because you already know it's a mistake sir, I can see it on your face."

Lt. Dey indeed looked pale, and Richard could tell he was frightened. Unlike Captain Becker, he wasn't seeking fame and glory. With a wife and two children back in Arizona, all he wanted was to do his duty and then go home to his family.

"We're Marines, Searfus, we do our job," he said, but all the men in the foxhole saw the doubt on his face.

"We're all going to die." Searfus repeated. "An NVA regiment is down that path and more are arriving as reinforcements. If we head into the lowlands we'll be completely surrounded. It will be too late to get out, sir. We'll all die there, every single one of us."

"What are you talking about, soldier? Get your gear together, Private, that's an order."

"It's true, sir," Torres cut in. "When he told me I thought he was crazy too, but it's all happened exactly as his sister said it would."

"Are the two of you high?" Lieutenant Dey asked. "I'm going to pretend that this conversation never happened, soldiers. Now get your gear together immediately."

"Yes, sir."

Gunfire erupted somewhere but it wasn't directed towards them. Richard hoped the NVA had moved positions.

"I'm not going, man," Torres said as soon as Lt. Dey was gone. "My birthday's in two weeks. I want to turn 20, man. I'm not going."

"I'm not going either. I've already got a fucking concussion," Lewis said, rubbing the knot on his forehead. "I'd rather be court martialed. I'll gladly go to jail rather than die out here."

"Calm down, man," Owens replied. "None of us are going, but we need a plan and we need to let the rest of H Company know. Hell, we owe it to them. Maybe some of them will want to come with us."

Lightning flashed and thunder exploded. In the blink of an eye Clemmings and Hodges were there in the hole beside them.

"We tried to talk to Lieutenant Dey, but he wouldn't listen," Hodges said.

"We tried to talk to him too." Torres shook his head.

"We did talk to a few of the 2/4. They're going to have a discussion amongst themselves. So far there are fifteen of us that agree with a revolt," Clemmings informed them.

"A revolt?" Richard asked.

"That's right, what were you thinking?" Hodges asked.

"I was thinking of heading up the hill."

"All fifteen of us just head up the hill together?"

"I didn't think of that part," Richard said.

"Well we have. Listen, there was another radio transmission that came in for Becker. We're supposed to move out at 2300, that's two hours from now. Between now and then we're going to have this organized. We'll know how, when, and how many of us are going by then. Searfus and Owens, we want to take you back to our hole."

The men followed Clemmings and Hodges, and after a slight trot across the muddy clay surface they were jumping into another hole.

Clark and two other men nodded at them in greeting and then they all sat down.

"What happened to the shelling?" Richard asked.

"Radio communication said that the NVA are focusing on their other target. The torrential rain that's blowing towards them is making it difficult to bomb us," Clark replied.

"Shame about that," Richard said with a chuckle.

"Okay, the way I see it, we can do this one of two ways," Hodges said as he scooted closer to the other men. "When Becker gives the call to move out we lag behind, maybe have someone up ahead cause a distraction which helps us so we can disperse."

"You want us to wait for two hours?" Owens asked.

"Which takes us to choice number two," Hodges said. "We can start evacuating men now, two at a time."

"You think the officers won't notice men disappearing?" Richard asked.

"Eventually, but how many men will we have out before that happens?" Hodges asked.

"We can just refuse to go," Clark suggested.

"Right, and have Becker shoot us?" Hodges said.

"He wouldn't do that," Clark argued. "This is the Marine Corps for fuck's sake, they aren't going to just shoot us."

"That fucking crazy bastard? Are you kidding? We're out here in the middle of fuck all, do you really think the regular rules apply?"

"Hell yeah, he'll shoot us as deserters, why shouldn't he?" Clemmings interjected.

"Then we go back to the second plan. Anyone who wants to leave does, but they do it in an organized fashion. We leave in pairs and from different locations on the hill. Clemmings and I will organize this into shifts," Hodges said.

"Searfus, once we're up, which direction do we head towards so that we can get the fuck out of here?"

"Head towards Gia Bihn and the Red River Delta, away from An Kha. That way," he said, pointing for emphasis.

"How many men in your hole?" Clark asked.

"Six, and all six of us want to go."

"Good, then the men in your hole go first. When you're up we start to rotate foxholes until the officers catch up with us."

Owens nodded. "If this downpour continues we have a decent chance to stay unnoticed."

"Maybe, but in case we don't, put out the word that it's every man for himself."

**

"Lewis, do you think you can make it up the hill or am I going to have to drag you?" Torres asked in all seriousness.

"I don't know, man. I'm going to try but I have to be honest, my vision is fuzzy and I just don't feel right."

For those reasons, Lewis and Torres were chosen as the first to leave the foxhole. The next group to leave would the three men from F Company 2/4, two of whom were still under the influence of the heroin they had shot into their veins several hours earlier.

"I'll leave the hole first, and then I'll help you, if you need it that is," Torres said to Lewis. "When we head up the hill you'll go before me, that way if you start to fall I can help you."

Lewis nodded. The bump on his head was large and badly bruised; his pupils were dilated too. From the look of the injury Lewis had a moderate concussion but despite that, he was anxious to leave. Richard could tell that he was pushing himself beyond his limit, and he hoped that Lewis could keep up the stamina until he and Torres had reached the top of the hill.

"Now remember, that way." Owens pointed to the right. "Don't climb anywhere near here, try to make it to a spot that's out of eyeshot. Even though we have heavy rain coverage, I don't want anyone taking unnecessary chances. You got that?"

Torres and Lewis nodded.

"Now, you do know which way to head when you get to the top of the hill?"

Before either man could answer Richard was pointing out directions. "Gia Bihn is that way, and beyond it the Red River Delta. There's An Kha, make sure you're always heading away from it. We'll meet at the banyan tree near the rock pile. Remember where we went on our first outing away from Camp Carroll?"

Everyone nodded except for the members of F Company who stared at him blankly. Richard turned towards them and pointed again. "You see that location? That's An Kha. As long as your back is always facing away from that hill you'll find us."

The three men nodded.

"We got it, man. I'm ready. Let's do this, Lewis." Torres jumped out of the hole and then he helped an off balance Lewis to his feet.

They set out across the rain-saturated landscape and soon disappeared into the blinding downpour. Richard watched them until they were out of sight and then he said a prayer, thanking the powers that be for the gift of rainfall on this specific day. If he got out of this, he vowed that he would never again complain about the rain in Vietnam.

***

Torres and Lewis walked away from the rest of the platoon heading east. When they were several minutes away from camp, Torres stopped and pointed upwards. "There, you see that cluster of trees on the side of the hill? You can hold on to those for support."

Overhead, thunder boomed and lightning shot across the sky. Finding his footing, Lewis looked up and shook his head. Then he started to climb. As he had expected, the going was rough. His equilibrium was off and he felt top heavy. Several times Torres had to put a hand on his back to steady him, and this was before they came to the steepest part of the hill. Once there, Lewis decided that there was only one way he could continue to climb. He got down on all fours and slid himself through the mud and debris, holding on to rocks and trees along his way.

Back in the hole, Owens pointed at Davis and the two men who were assisting him, one of whom looked more fucked up than Davis did.

"You're up," he said. "You head to the left of the hill and find a place to climb away from here. Once up, reverse direction and head that way, you got it?" Owens asked. Seconds later the three men were out of the hole, and the perpetual rain drowned out their images almost immediately.

"We're next, Searfus. Just a few more minutes and we'll be out of this death trap."

Richard knew that this was only the beginning. It was barely 2100; the battle below would continue until 0200. What would happen between now and then was anybody's guess.

Torres pulled himself to the top of the cliff then reached below and dragged a mud caked Lewis the rest of the way up. They both lay there in the rain for several minutes, panting as buckets of water washed over them.

"Now what?" Lewis asked.

"Now we get our asses out of here," Torres replied.

"What about the others? Shouldn't we wait for them to make sure there aren't any problems?"

"I would say yes, but you don't look so good, partner. I'm not sure how much more your body is going to be able to take."

"I'm tough man."

"Yeah, you're tough, but I swear I've never see a knot on anyone's head like that motherfucker. That rock got you good."

"True, but I can keep up, you'll see."

"Then let's go, tough boy." Torres pulled him to his feet and had to steady him immediately. "You see what I mean, man? At some point you're just not going to be able to go on. When that happens I want to be as far away from here as we can get."

The two men pushed forward, heading towards the Red River Delta.

***

"It's our turn, man. We'll head that way." Owens pointed towards the cliff.

Seconds later they were out of the hole, and like the men before them, they were heading along the cliff bed, searching for the best spot to make the steep climb to safety.

Meanwhile the battle, which had been silent for the better part of an hour, started up again. Suddenly their position was being bombarded with gunfire, which caused Richard and Owens to run further along the cliff. Once clear from the blasts they started to climb the hill, listening to the sounds of the battle behind them.

The combination of mud and gravel made the climb tedious. Several times their feet were washed out from under them as water ran continuously down the landscape. Using the underbrush to steady their climb, they continued upwards.

Below, a rocket launched by the Vietnamese hit close to the Marines' foxholes. Several seconds later, they heard gunfire. Then there was the sound of the M-60 launching five hundred bullets towards the enemy. The crack of thunder sounded and then a tree close to the encampment exploded in flames. That's when the men who wanted to leave made a run for it. Soon there were ten bodies scrambling up the hill beside Richard and Owens.

Richard could still hear the sound of battle raging and he could hear screams below. He held onto a tree, steadied his body, and then lurched forward onto his knees. From there he pulled himself up the hill by grasping the boulders around him. It was slow going but the rocks were firmly in place, making the climb much easier than it would be on foot.

Beside him he could hear other men climbing the slippery ledge. When he and Owens finally made it to the top, they lay there several seconds before flipping over and climbing to their feet to assist other men who had nearly made it to the top of the ridge. One of these men was Hodges. He clasped both Richard's and Owens' hands and then together they pulled him the rest of the way up the hill.

Behind him Clemmings made his way to the top unassisted, and then he too lay on the cold ground catching his breath.

"Clark?" Richard asked. Clemmings shook his head.

Lightning flashed. This time a tree on the other side of the battlefield was burning. The diversion temporarily stopped the NVA from shelling.

There was the sound of feet beside them as several men ran past. From below came the sound of gunfire. Captain Becker was now shooting at the dissenters. He was yelling, his voice miraculously rising above the storm as the wind carried the sound upwards.

"I'm going to court martial all of you, do you understand?" he bellowed. "As God is my witness, I'll make every single one of you pay!"

Then the Vietnamese launched an artillery attack.

"Let's go." Owens shook Richard to get his attention. "It's time, man, let's go. We have to get the fuck out of here now."

"What about the others, the men who are left behind? What if they decide they want to leave? Shouldn't we wait for them?"

"It's too late, man. If they try to leave now the officers will shot them. There's nothing more that we can do. We have to go, Searfus. Every man for himself, remember?"

Richard nodded, and a pang of guilt stabbed at him. He knew that Owens was right, but he also knew that they were leaving men behind to die. Even if there was nothing more that he could do for them, he still felt responsible. He had known that this day was coming. He should have planned for its arrival, but he didn't. Now he stood at the side of the cliff looking down. There were fifteen men, three officers, and Captain Becker below, and all of them would meet their death before dawn. For Richard, nothing would ever feel right again.

*****

They walked in silence, heading towards the Red River Delta. The sound of battle seemed to follow them, and at one point they actually thought they were under attack, but quickly realized that the battle they heard was coming from behind them.

Hodges and Clemmings took the lead, with Owens and Richard following close behind. The pounding rain, booming thunder, and lightning flashes continued. They marched, scanning the terrain, hoping to see more of their men but also watched diligently for the enemy.

Clemmings estimated that they had at least a six mile walk ahead of them. With the rain pounding down, he figured it would take them close to three hours. About forty-five minutes into the trip they stopped under a large umbrella tree to rest. Sharing a canteen of water, they tried to calm their rattled nerves.

"Is everyone alright?" Hodges asked.

They all nodded, but the mood was solemn. They had lost a lot of men today. Knowing that they should have been among the dead didn't change things.

"Did you hear something?" Owens asked, jumping to his feet. "I think someone's in the bushes."

The other men jumped to their feet too, M16s poised and ready.

"Hey, man, don't shoot, it's me." Torres emerged from the shadows, his hands held high. When he was sure the other men recognized him he lowered them. "I'm so glad to find you guys," he called loudly, trying to be heard over the rain. "It's Lewis, he's in the bushes. We had to stop, there's no way he can walk any further."

"The concussion?" Richard asked and Torres nodded.

"He did good though, I gotta hand it to him. Dude's a real trooper, that's for damn sure."

"We'll have to make a stretcher." Owens pulled a blanket out of his pack. Richard and Torres cut some branches off of the tree to fashion a stretcher, and several minutes later they were ready to carry Lewis out of the lowlands.

Partway into their walk they heard a loud whistle behind them and stopped.

Richard pulled his gun close, ready to use it if necessary, but quickly put it down when he realized that the newcomer was Lt. Dey. The officer who stood before them was drenched. He looked pale and broken.

"They're all dead," he said, shaking his head. "Every single one of them. Becker gave the order to head down the trail just like you said he would, Searfus. The men were reluctant to go, but there was little they could do except follow his orders. Becker made it clear that any dissenters would be shot on sight so the men were scared. We were halfway down the landing when I changed my mind. I couldn't go, I just couldn't."

Lt. Dey swallowed and wiped the water off of his face with his already wet sleeve. "I have twins, a boy and a girl, they were born in June. I've never seen them except in pictures and I just couldn't...I couldn't leave, not now." He sighed heavily. "Before I left for 'Nam, Maryanne was hormonal. Pregnant women can be very emotional, maybe someday you boys will find out. She told me one day that she had a dream that I died in battle before I got to see my babies."

Richard could hear the lieutenant's voice crack, and the officer let out a nervous laugh.

"I told her it would never happen, that she was only worried because of her pregnancy, but she didn't believe me. Until the day I left she swore that dream was true. When I was walking down that path with Captain Becker, I knew her dream was about to come true. I knew that I was walking right to my death and then I couldn't go any further. I lagged behind, pretending that I needed to monitor the men at the back of the line, but when I got the chance I hid in the jungle. Once they got far enough ahead I planned to go back to the cliff were I left you."

Lt. Dey stopped speaking, his face pained, and for a moment he fought for emotional control. "It happened so fast," he continued. "I could barely see them from where I was hidden, but I knew they arrived at the river. They were trying to cross and then from out of nowhere shots rang out. I walked closer so I could see what was happening. The men in the river were running, trying to get to the safety of the trees. When I left they were surrounded. I couldn't do anything to help them so I left. I could hear the men being slaughtered and I did nothing." Lt. Dey hung his head in sorrow.

"There was nothing you could have done without getting yourself killed too," Richard said.

"I know, but it doesn't make this any easier. When I left they were dying. I could hear them. I thought only of my wife and babies while I headed back to that cliff."

"You did the right thing," Richard told him. "We all did the right thing, we couldn't save everyone. Lt. Dey I'm glad that you're going home to your wife and babies, they need you more than this war does. I know you feel guilty, we all do, but we're alive. There are people at home who are going to be awfully happy about that."

The lieutenant nodded, and then the group silently moved forward, each man locked in his own thoughts, heading for the banyan tree were they knew the rest of their men were waiting.

***

At 0200 they finally arrived at the meeting spot. By then the rain had broken, and surprisingly, the sky had cleared. The humidity returned, and soon so did the mosquitoes.

There were ten men waiting. When they realized that Lt. Dey was in attendance, the men stood and saluted. Lt. Dey started to laugh.

"Really?" he said. "Don't you know that we are all in this together?"

The men relaxed.

"Now what?" a man from F Company asked.

"Now we head towards the main road. It shouldn't be long before someone sees us and picks us up," the lieutenant said.

"Then we can turn ourselves in for mutiny," Owen added.

"Mutiny?" Lt. Dey asked.

Owens looked at him. "Should we call it desertion instead?"

"Wait a minute..." Lt. Dey gestured for his men to come closer. "Nobody said anything about mutiny. What were we supposed to do? Captain Becker broke our platoon in half. He took half of the men with him and he left the other half with me. When I realized that they were surrounded and that there was nothing that we could do with seventeen men, I gave the order to retreat. Does anyone's story differ from my own?" When no one answered the lieutenant led his men towards the main road that led back to Camp Carroll.

Chapter 46

Even though the Summer of Love has been represented as a utopia of hippie art, music and culture, it was the beginning of the end for the Haight District.

While the hippie culture was at its height in popularity, the Haight neighborhood was beginning its long descent into degeneracy.

The district's main problem was that it physically could not handle the amount of kids that were moving in. The newcomers ended up living in small quarters, sometimes as many as ten kids or more sharing a room. Others who couldn't find shelter were living on the street in cold weather they hadn't expected. Summers in San Francisco aren't known for warm temperatures. These conditions caused illnesses that were easily passed through the overpopulated community. On top of that, unsanitary conditions, drug use, and sexually transmitted diseases from the 'free love' movement were taking their toll.

The young people who came to Haight in 1965 and 1966 had gone to college. Most were from upper middle class families, with fathers who held high positions in corporations, but the kids who came in the spring and summer of 1967 came from completely different backgrounds. Some were runaways as young as 14 from abusive homes, others were high school dropouts. There were religious fanatics, hardcore drug dealers, thugs, and of course plenty of pimps looking for potential prostitutes.

Rape and other types of assault against young women became commonplace. In fact, Emmett Grogan from the Diggers said in September of 1967, *"Rape is as common as bullshit on Haight Street."*

The murder rate, incidents of physical assault, and burglaries increased tenfold. Even the Diggers' free store, Trip Without a Ticket, was robbed.

As a result, many of the kids who had come to Haight in the spring looking for love, hope, beauty, and a new way of life were returning home. Instead of the utopia they had expected, they were sick, out of money, and found themselves living in dangerous surroundings.

Likewise, many of the original hippies, including members of the Grateful Dead and some of the original Diggers, fled. Hundreds headed for rural areas outside of San Francisco were they founded or moved into already established communes in the countryside.

As life changed in the Haight, ordinary life in America continued to go on, and of course, so did the Vietnam War.

On September 9, 1967, Rowan and Martin's *Laugh In* aired as a one-time special. It quickly became a regular series where Goldie Hawn, with slogans written on her bikinied body, danced as the 'sock it to me' girl. On September 17th, *Mission Impossible* premiered on CBS.

On September 23rd, the Soviets signed a pact with North Vietnam to send more aid to Hanoi, and on the 26th Hanoi rejected yet another United States peace proposal.

For Katie and Moonbeam, as well as many original hippies still living in the Haight, life had deteriorated. It wasn't safe to walk down the streets at night even when two women were walking together. For months they had talked about moving to Marin County and joining a commune, but Katie hesitated.

She didn't want to leave San Francisco, not until she had heard one way or another about Richard's fate.

The girls still lived in the house on Page, but life was very different. Although they still had friends in the neighborhood, many others were leaving. Even Robin had moved, and she was now living closer to the university.

To show their discontent for the media takeover of their way of life, local residents planned a protest for early October. This march, known as "The Death of Hippie", signified the end of the neighborhood the originals had built, a society that in their eyes that no longer existed.

In late September 1967, the shops on Haight started displaying flyers proclaiming "Funeral Notice for Hippie". Friends were invited to attend services starting at sunrise, October 6, 1967 (the first anniversary of LSD being made illegal). The event thrown by the Diggers and the Haight-Ashbury Switchboard, a place where hippies left messages for others and where families could keep in touch with people living in the district, would be held at the top of Buena Vista Park, San Francisco's oldest.

Moonbeam squinted at the clock. 5:00 a.m. She couldn't believe it. She hadn't woken up at this hour since...well, never, she realized. Katie was adamant too. They were going to the Death of Hippie event, a celebration that started at Buena Vista Park at sunrise, paraded down Haight Street, and then ended at the Panhandle. Last night she and Katie had pulled together a few 'hippie artifacts,' which they were taking with them. These would be added to the cardboard coffin the Diggers planned to cremate.

"Hurry up, you don't want to be late do you?" Katie urged.

"Certainly not," Moonbeam answered sarcastically. Truth was, she didn't want to go. Last night they had gone to a street party. Katie called it a pre-funeral wake, but what it really was, was a party.

Katie had repeatedly reminded her that they were waking before dawn, but she had still drunk too much cheap beer. Now her temples were throbbing.

"Okay, okay," she said, finally rising from the bed. She put on a pair of faded Levis and a long sleeve T-shirt, then ran her fingers through her long auburn hair. Ten minutes later, they were leaving the house and wrapping jackets around their shoulders.

Katie carried a paper bag with their 'hippie' belongings and they proceeded down Haight, walking with other early morning risers who were heading in the same direction.

When they got to the top of hill, about eighty people had assembled. As promised, a large cardboard coffin, lid open, lay on the cement. Participants placed their hippie trinkets inside— beads, bells, bits of clothing, feathers, and the local underground papers, the *San Francisco Oracle* and the *Berkeley Barb*.

Katie took their items out of the paper bag and laid them inside the coffin along with all of the others. Then she and Moonbeam took one of the white tear candles and a stapled agenda. The agenda had the words to the very long ceremony they would recite on their way down Haight Street.

On the cement next to the makeshift coffin Peter Coyote, Peter Berg, Emmett Grogan, and others ceremonially burned hippie trinkets, including pot and copies of newspapers. At dawn the fires stopped, musicians played a rendition of *Taps* at the first ray of sunshine, and then around 6:30, the actual ceremony started.

"October sixth, nineteen hundred and sixty seven. Media created the hippie with your hungry consent. Be somebody. Careers are to be had for the enterprising hippie," Emmett Grogan read as a chorus of voices joined him.

The coffin, decorated with a dead hippie holding flowers in his hand, and the words *"Hippie, Son of Media"* clearly printed on the side was ready to go. At the front of the procession one of the Diggers was dressed as a mortician, behind him the pall bearers, also Diggers, wore large papier mache animal heads. Together they led the funeral progression down the hill and out of the park heading towards the main street. The participants read their prewritten scripts as they slowly made their way down Haight Street.

"Your face on TV, your style immortalized without soul in the captions of the Chronicle. NBC says you exist. Death of hippie end/finished hippie gone, goodbye, goodbye Hippie death."

They marched down Haight, occasionally stopping to read from the script that foretold the end of an era. And it was true, Katie knew that more than anyone else. Soon, all of the originals would be gone.

As they slowly made their way towards Golden Gate Park they passed under a banner that was stretched across Haight: "Death of Hippie Freebie, *i.e.* Birth of the Free Man."

Their destination was the Psychedelic Shop, which had filled its windows with signs: "Nebraska Needs You More"; "Be Free"; "Don't Mourn For Me "; "Organize".

The procession stopped in front of the Jay and Rob's shop there they lowered the coffin. Many in the parade got down on their knees while the main players performed an exorcism while the crowd recited:

"You are free. We are free. Do not be recreated. Believe only your own incarnate spirit. Create, Be.... Do not be created. This is your land, your city. No one can portion it out to you. The Haight-Ashbury was portioned to us by Media-Police and the tourists who came to the Zoo to see the captive animals and we growled fiercely behind the bars we accepted and now we are no longer hippies and never were."

The Psychedelic Shop played loud music, trying to cover up the noise of a girl screaming. Somewhere inside the shop, the girl was on a bad acid trip and she continued to wail throughout the eerie ceremony. Even the full blast record player couldn't drown out her screams, which somehow added irony to the event.

Incense smoke encircled the crowd and the progression moved forward again; the parade participants rose to their feet and followed.

They arrived at the Panhandle at close to 8:30 a.m. The streets were becoming crowded as people headed off to work, school, and many of the locals were just getting up.

The cardboard coffin effigy was readied for cremation as the ceremony came to an end. The crowd turned to the last page of the agenda. Here, with the coffin lowered to the ground, they read the rest of the funeral script:

"Do not be bought with a picture, a phrase...Do not be captured in words. The city is ours. You are you. Take what is yours. The boundaries are down. San Francisco is free, now the truth is out."

The preamble to the Constitution of the United States was recited, and then the hippie coffin was cremated. A group of spectators, many of whom didn't understand the significance of the event, watched on.

When it was over, the participants cleaned up the ashes and leftover debris. Then they quietly dispersed.

Katie and Moonbeam headed down Haight Street. They stopped in front of the Psychedelic Shop with many others who had gathered.

The day before the Death of Hippie, Ron Diebel and Jay Thelin gave away everything in the store to customers who came in. Right after the funeral, the Psychedelic Shop was closing for good. Katie and Moonbeam watched as the men locked the store for the last time.

As it turned out, they would be the first of many to close up shop. Numerous other merchants in the Haight were also in debt, and they too were getting ready to lose their stores. The merchants, along with everyone else, had partied hard during the Summer of Love, and now it was costing them their livelihood.

When the funeral ended, Big Brother and the Holding Company, along with several other local Haight bands, gave a free concert in the Panhandle. Hippies brought plenty of drugs to commemorate the event, but the mood was solemn. Everyone who was an original in the Haight knew that it was the last party, the end to something that had been glorious.

***

On October 9, 1967, Latin American freedom fighter, guerrilla leader, and revolutionist Che Guevara was executed while attempting to incite a revolt in Bolivia.

On October 17, *Hair*, subtitled *The American Tribal Love/Rock Musical*, premiered off Broadway.

On October 21, tens of thousands of Vietnam War protesters marched in Washington, D.C. On the same day, the "March on the Pentagon", protesting American involvement in Vietnam, drew 50,000 protesters.

In the Haight, the Grateful Dead's house was raided yet again on October 2nd. This time Pigpen, the group's drummer, was arrested on drug charges.

Daily sweeps of Haight-Ashbury by the police were now a daily occurrence. On the premise of looking for underage runaways, they sometimes made several sweeps a day. Any man who couldn't produce his draft card was either a draft dodger or an underage teen, and would be taken into custody. The 'Man' was everywhere.

Katie and Moonbeam counted down the days until the end of October. Originally, her parents had received the telegram of Richard's death on November 5th. She remembered the day well. In the morning something had just felt *wrong*. Her mother had called her close to noon in tears, and Katie had known immediately that her brother was gone.

On the night of October 27th, she and Moonbeam had gone out. Hoping to keep Richard off her mind, they had visited with friends and had a few drinks in Pall Mall, the neighborhood bar, but the Haight just wasn't the same. The Psychedelic Shop had been a meeting point, and with the store gone it was a reminder that their era of harmony and peace had come to an end.

Moonbeam and Katie had been to Chet's commune in Marin several times. They liked it there, and had decided to make a permanent move to the hog farm at the end of November.

When they first arrived they would be living in the main house, but eventually wanted to get their own trailers and settle themselves on the five acre land with the idea that their men would be joining them at some point.

Friends moved out of the neighborhood on a daily basis. It seemed many were going back to school or back to whatever they had been doing before the Summer of Love had taken place. The Haight was a sad place now, just a remnant of what it had once been, but Katie couldn't leave, not yet.

On the morning of November 5th, Katie woke early. The night before she had tossed and turned, knowing that by noon she would know something when the phone either rang, or it didn't.

If her mother didn't call it would be a positive sign, but if the phone rang...she wasn't sure how she would handle the news a second time around. Either way, she was moving to the country at the end of the month; that was a promise she meant to keep.

Katie watched the minutes tick by on the 'Felix the Cat' clock. At 9:00 a.m. she made a second pot of coffee and sat down at the table still in her nightgown. From the end of the hall she heard a noise and turned just in time to see Moonbeam walk into the kitchen.

"Hey you. Is everything alright?" Moonbeam asked with a yawn.

"So far so good." Katie stirred her coffee nervously.

"I'm never going to get used to you drinking that stuff." Moonbeam put the kettle on the burner to make herself a cup of herbal tea.

"Would you believe it if I tell you that you'll be drinking the stuff too by the time you turn 30?"

"I will not, and stop it. You know how I feel about hearing all the creepy future stuff. Thanks, but I'll just find out when I get there."

"Last time the call came about noon," Katie said.

"So what are you going to do till then, drink coffee?"

"Maybe."

"How about some breakfast?"

"I don't think I can eat. I just don't have an appetite right now."

Moonbeam nodded. "You don't mind if I make something for myself do you?"

"Of course not, go right ahead." Katie tapped on her cup nervously.

"Why don't you just call your parents?" Moonbeam suggested.

"They won't know anything yet. A soldier came to the door with...it. The telegram, I mean." Katie swallowed hard. "My mother called me the minute he left, I think, or maybe she called my father first."

"Okay, just this once to keep your mind off this I'll let you tell me something about the future." Moonbeam smiled.

Katie chuckled. "Really? Okay, what do you want to know?"

"Who did I marry?" She took a gulp of her dandelion tea.

"Which time? You marry twice and both times you divorce. *You* leave, you dig? Not the other way around."

"The first one?"

"I told you, he's a podiatrist named Jerry."

"Jerry? Where and when do I meet him?"

"Not for a long while. You go through your commune stage, and then you go back to school to be a journalist. You meet Jerry in the university."

"The podiatrist?"

"That's right. Don't laugh, he has a lot of money."

"That can't be why I marry him."

"No, it isn't. I guess you marry him because Frog is gone and he's a substitute. This time, who knows what will happen?"

Moonbeam finished cooking herself an egg and cheese omelet. She split it in half on two plates and set one in front of Katie.

"I'm not hungry," Katie protested.

"You should try to eat something and then we'll smoke some weed and wait for a phone call we hope we don't get."

***

The phone rang at ll:45. Katie gasped.

"My God, Moony. I can't answer it." Her eyes filled with tears. "Can you get it for me?"

Moonbeam reached for the phone, her hands shaking.

"Hello? Yes, Mrs. Searfus, this is Annie, Katie's friend. Let me get her for you."

She pulled the phone away from her ear and handed it to Katie.

Tears streamed down her face as Katie clutched the receiver. She held it to her ear and closed her eyes. "Hello, Mother."

"Katie, darling, is something wrong?" Her mother asked. "You sound as if you've been crying."

"No, I'm fine, I... I just got up."

"Oh I see. I hope you're not coming down with a cold. It's going around, you know. Lucy Bridges and her husband had it last weekend."

"What?" Katie shook her head in confusion. This was not the conversation she'd been expecting.

"A cold, dear. You really are incoherent this morning aren't you? I hope you're not hyped up on some type of drug, Katherine."

"No, I'm fine. I told you I just got up. What is it, Mother, what's happened?" she asked, anxious to understand the reason for Pat's call.

"Oh yes. I had a call from your brother this morning."

"Richard? A call? When?"

"Yes, a call. I just got off the phone with him a few minutes ago. It was a strange conversation, actually. He insisted that I phone you immediately to give you an odd message. He said he would have called you himself but you've changed your number so frequently that he wasn't sure where to try, so he called me instead." There was a pause and Katie could hear her mother light a cigarette.

"What did he say?"

"I'm getting there, dear, hang on a sec." Pat took a long puff on her Virginia Slim. "He said to tell you that he and seventeen men went up the hill."

Katie dropped the phone and started to sob. Thinking the worst, Moonbeam grabbed for the receiver.

"Mrs. Searfus, this is Annie again. Is something wrong?"

"No, dear everything is fine here. What's wrong with Katie? Is she on some kind of funny drug?"

"Is Richard alright?"

"He's fine. I just called to tell Katie some crazy message. He said that he and seventeen men made it up a hill. Does that mean anything to you?"

Katie was laughing now in between her sobs.

"I did it, Annie." She rubbed her eyes. "I saved him and I saved seventeen other men too. Men who can now go home to their families."

Moonbeam broke into a huge smile and found her own eyes watering. "Strangely, Mrs. Searfus, what you just told me means a whole lot."

***

November 1967 was cold and wet. Katie and Moonbeam walked down Haight huddling under a red and white umbrella. They walked by the free clinic, which was packed these days as several nasty illnesses made their way through the neighborhood. Everyone seemed to be sick.

Katie pulled her sweater closer to her body as she fought the bitter wind blowing off the San Francisco Bay.

"I never thought I would say this, but I'm going to be awfully glad to get away from here," Moonbeam confessed.

"Me too, the sooner the better. Think about it, by this time next week we'll be in the country surrounded by beauty." Katie smiled at the thought.

"I just wish..."

"Don't say it, I know what you wish, and it's better to let it lie. I don't want you getting sad again."

"Yeah, you're right. Better I don't think about them."

A gust of wind hit them full force, bringing with it a splash of cold water. For a few seconds the girls closed their eyes.

"Damn, I hope it's warmer on the other side of the Golden Gate Bridge," Moonbeam commented.

"It will be warmer. I mean, it's going to be winter wherever we move, but we won't have that biting cold coming off of the bay."

"Groovy, I can't wait. I'm tired of being cold all the time."

Behind them a motorcycle pulled up next to the curb and stopped. They both turned around.

Big Jim smiled broadly, jumped off his bike, and headed towards them.

To get out of the rain the three moved under a store canopy to talk and Katie closed the umbrella.

"So you two are really leaving?" Big Jim asked.

"Yeah, not far though, on the other side of the bridge to Marin County."

"A commune?" Jim asked. The two smiling girls nodded.

"Damn, nobody is going to be left."

"Sadly, I'm afraid that's true," Katie said.

"Hey, don't get all sad on me." Big Jim smiled. "I've been looking for you girls."

"Do you have a message for us?" Moonbeam asked excitedly.

"No, I'm sorry I don't. I'm here for another reason. We're having a party tomorrow night at the clubhouse and we wanted to make sure that you're coming."

"Us?" Moonbeam asked. "I don't know, Jim, the last time we attended a party at your place...well, I'm not sure I want to relive that experience. No offense.

"None taken, but I really can't accept no as an answer. Not this time. See, the guys know that the two of you are splitting from 'Frisco and they wanted do something special for you. That's why you've got to come to the party tomorrow night."

"Well..." Katie looked at him skeptically.

"It's not going to be like the last time, I promise. Eva and Ruby are still in the can, so they won't be there. I will personally guarantee your safety and the purity of all of your drinks."

Katie laughed.

"Terry and I will pick you up at 7:00 and we'll make sure you get home safely too."

The girls looked at each other then simultaneously nodded.

"Great. Then Terry and I will see you around 7:00. Dress warm, we'll probably end up in the backyard at some point. You know how the clubhouse is set up, you can't help but party outside."

Big Jim jumped back on his Harley and swiftly drove off into traffic. Katie opened the umbrella and they huddled beneath it as they continued on with their journey.

"Another Hells Angels' party, God help us," Katie said as they walked down Haight Street.

***

Seven o'clock arrived much too quickly. The rain had stopped several hours before, but it was still cold and windy, and neither girl was looking forward to an icy motorcycle ride to the other side of the city.

True to their word, the two bikers showed up at 7:00 and pulled into the empty driveway.

"Well, here we go again," Moonbeam said as she buttoned her rabbit fur coat. "Don't you fucking drink anything funny you hear me?

Katie laughed. "You got it."

Minutes later they found themselves on the back of a bike heading for the Dogpatch on the other side of the city.

The front of the clubhouse was packed with bikes and bikers were already partying on the front lawn.

Big Jim hurried them inside. "Let's get you some clean beers, right out of the bottles," he said with a chuckle.

The inside of the house was warm. Big Jim handed them each a bottle of beer, which he purposely opened in front of them. They were standing in the kitchen talking when Freddy walked in with a cake box and set it on the table.

"My favorite, beer and cake!" one of the bikers yelled out.

"Shut up, man, this is a special cake!" Freddy yelled back. He pulled the lid off of the box to reveal the skull winged Hells Angels insignia.

"Look at that, man, ain't it fucking beautiful?" Freddy asked. The bikers gawked at the work of art making sounds of admiration and wonder until Freddy took a handful of cake and shoved it into his mouth.

"Knock it off, Freddy. Man, that's fucking disgusting!" Big Jim yelled from the doorway. "Cut it up right!"

One of the bikers pulled out a stack of paper plates and another pulled a proper knife out of a drawer and started cutting up pieces.

Big Jim supervised the process and then took two slices, one for himself, and the other for Katie.

"See? We aren't so bad." Big Jim smiled. "We've lost so many of our friends this year, it's too bad that you and Moony are moving too. I understand why, don't get me wrong, the Haight is a dumping ground now. Still, life as we know it is changing."

"Life is always changing," Katie said sagely, "that's the one thing you can be sure of."

"Hey ,can I show you something outside for a minute?" Big Jim asked her. Katie looked for Moony, and seeing that she was in a deep conversation with Terry nodded.

"Umm, sure."

They stepped outside onto the porch and Big Jim pointed towards a corner of the yard. "Can you take a walk over to that corner and tell me what you think about that rosebush back there?"

"What?"

"The rosebush, can you take a look at it and tell me if it's wild or if someone planted it?"

Katie looked at Jim as if he were crazy. "Are you serious?"

"Can you tell the difference?" he asked in all seriousness.

"The difference between a wild rose bush and a domesticated one?"

"That's right, can you?"

"I suppose I can." She followed him down the rickety back steps.

"Go on now. You go look and then you tell me which it is." He pointed towards the back corner of the yard.

"You're not going to come with me?"

"Go on, humor an old biker and go back there by yourself," he said with a smile.

Jim pointed towards the corner of the yard again and Katie's curiosity got the best of her. She walked into the darkest shadows of the yard, and there standing next to the garage was the figure of a man. The lone figure approached. Katie placed her hand over her mouth and took a step backwards.

Dylan walked into the light and smiled. He held out a bouquet of red long stemmed roses. "These are for you."

Katie rushed towards him and threw her arms around his neck.

"My God, Dylan! You're back and you're safe!" she cried into his jacket. "Frog?" she asked anxiously.

"He's out front meeting Moony." Dylan kissed her and ran his fingers through her long hair.

"Baby, I missed you," he said, pulling her close. "I *really* missed you."

Dylan swung her through the air and she giggled. When he set her down she hung her head.

"I'm so sorry about Joey."

Dylan sighed deeply. "Me too, baby, me too. Joey was...an opportunist I'm afraid. It's going to take me a long time to get over all of this. Tell you what though, while I'm getting over my past I'm anxious to move ahead with my future, especially if that future is with you."

Katie pulled away.

"What is it?" Dylan asked. "What's wrong?"

"There are things you should know about me before we plan a future together..." Katie said nervously. "Once you know the truth, well, you might change your mind."

"The truth? What, that you're from the future?"

Katie looked at him confused. "How do you know that?"

"Frog told me. At first I thought he was crazy, but then I realized that it makes sense. Actually, it's the only thing about this nightmare that *does* make sense." He stepped closer and put his arms around her. "2014?"

"That's right. I was driving my Porsche through the rain and I went over the cliff and hit a tree. I thought I'd wake up in the hospital, but I didn't, I woke up on Ron's couch. I don't know how, it just happened."

"Shhh, Katie. It happened because it was supposed to. It happened so that things could turn out right. If not for you, Frog and I would be in a ditch."

"And my brother would be dead too."

"Richard? He's *alive*? Is it over?"

"Yes, it's over. He called my mother a week and half ago to let her know that he was all right. He has five months left in 'Nam. I just hope—"

"He'll be fine," Dylan said, cutting her off before she could voice her thought. "You were sent back to make sure of that. Katie, you and I are meant to be together. You must feel it too."

She nodded. For reasons she couldn't understand, she *could* feel that. She could feel it very strongly.

"You came back to make things right. Part of making things right involves us. I don't care if you think you're twenty, sixty or eighty, I still love you and I want to be with you always."

"Sixty-six."

"Well you don't look a day over thirty," Dylan said and she swatted his hand playfully. Dylan caught her wrist and pulled her close. "Oh, Katie, I can' t tell you how good it feels to hold you." He shut his eyes and sniffed her hair, which smelled distinctly of summer flowers.

"Now what?"

"Now we go to Marin County," Dylan stated. "Isn't that the plan?"

"We? Does that mean that you're coming with me?"

"To a commune to live off the land?" He laughed. "Sure, why not? It's something I haven't tried before."

"What about the club?"

"The club is there, it always will be. I had a talk with Big Jim when I first got back." Dylan hung his head. "Right now I just can't belong to the Angels, there's just too many memories. I'm not saying that I'll never go back, I'm just saying that for now the club's not important to me. I love the club, don't get me wrong, but right now, this minute, the only thing that's important to me is you."

Dylan pulled her into the shadows of the garage and kissed her.

***

Terry nudged Moonbeam's arm and she turned towards him questioningly.

"There's someone in the front yard who wants to talk to you," he told her.

Moonbeam shook her head

"I'm serious," he said. Terry took her by the hand and led her through the house.

"Who is it?" Moonbeam asked.

"Oh believe me, you're going to want to see this guy."

They walked out on the porch and Moonbeam looked around. "I don't see anybody..."

"Hey!" somebody called from the side of the garage and Terry pointed.

Moonbeam descended the stairs, her heart beating wildly in her chest. Deep inside she knew who she was going to see on the other side of the wall, but until she saw him for herself she couldn't believe it.

Frog was standing in the shadows. When Moonbeam walked up he stepped in front of her and smiled.

"Hi, I brought you these," he said, holding out a bouquet of roses.

Moonbeam said nothing. After months of imagining this day, she couldn't believe it was really happening. She blinked her eyes twice and shook her head. When Frog was still there, she smiled and accepted the flowers.

"I know you're probably mad at me, and I have no right to assume anything, but if you'll have me I'd like to go to Marin County with you."

Moonbeam's eyes brimmed with tears and she flew into his outstretched arms.

"You're back!" she sobbed. "You're really back!"

Frog cradled her and kissed the top of her head. "I'm sorry, Moony. I'm sorry about everything. I should have listened to Katie...I shouldn't have lied to you."

"No, you shouldn't have," she murmured, breaking the embrace. "That was wrong."

Frog wiped the tears from her face. "Yes, it was wrong." He kissed her again. For several minutes they stood in the cold breeze clinging to each other.

"Your hair..." Moonbeam reached up and touched Frog's sandy blond hair, which barely covered the top of his ears.

"I know. I look like one of the Beach Boys don't I?"

"You look wonderful." She smiled. "I can't believe that you're really here."

"Me either, I feel like I'm still on a bike."

"How is the old Honda?" she asked, looking around for the red 350.

"Traded it in." He pointed to a black Panhead. "That's my ride now. It's a '58 I picked up in Colorado when the old Honda conked out for good."

"Geez, so you're a biker now?"

Frog laughed and stroked her long auburn hair. "Hardly, although I'm not sure that I'm the peace loving hippie you loved either."

Moonbeam leaned her body against his and Frog's arms encircled her.

"I'm not the same person that I used to be, Annie. I... I killed a man," he admitted. "I had to, it was either him or us, so I shot him."

"Joey?" she asked and he nodded.

"The truth is, I don't know who I am anymore. All I do know is that I love you, Annie, and that I had to come back to you. I don't have the right to just storm in and assume that you'll have me back, but I'm asking you now if you'll consider it?"

Moonbeam kissed him. "I love you too, Curtis, but if you want me then you're going to have to prove it. I'm going to Chet's commune next week. If you really love me you'll follow me there."

"Baby, I would follow you anywhere." He kissed her again, and they kept at it for quite some time.

Chapter 47

The court case continued for another week. During that time, Brian Ebbes called several character witnesses who provided positive testimonies regarding Mark Rhodes' humanitarianism, work ethics, and professionalism.

At one point, Angela took the stand, which turned out to be a bad decision for the defense. On cross-examination, Katie's daughter had erupted into a fit of anger that included yelling at Judge Allen. She had been evicted from the courtroom for the duration of the trial, although her attorney was there daily to represent her interests.

This morning, Annie and Robin hoped that this would be the last day of the trial. Before adjourning the previous afternoon, Robin was sure the jury was close to deliberating. The two women met at the front entrance of the courthouse. Annie was carrying two cups of coffee from Starbucks, and she handed one of the paper cups to her friend.

"Well this should be it," Robin said, smiling brightly.

"God, I sure hope so." Annie opened the lid and blew on the steaming coffee.

"Have some faith, Annie."

"What do you think?" Annie asked, the same question she had asked every morning for the past two months.

Robin shook her head. "It could go either way. You know how I feel about guessing the outcome of cases, it's never a good idea, it just jinxes things."

"That's silly."

"No, Annie, it's not." Robin led the way into the courthouse and then down the long hall that led to room C-25. Once inside they sat at the prosecution table quietly sipping their lattes.

From the table beside theirs, Brian Ebbes nodded and Mark Rhodes looked away, refusing to lock eyes with the enemy.

Several minutes later Judge Allen entered the room, and everyone stood. From the side door the jury was escorted into their seats by the bailiff and court began. The Judge nodded to Mr. Ebbes, and the attorney stood, ready to address the jury.

"Ladies and Gentlemen of the jury, I am here this morning to wrap up the defense's case. You see before you a businessman. He's not a schemer, he's not a planner who consciously destroys other people's lives, steals medical records, or uses every means possible to disinherit his own wife. He is merely a hardworking man trying to provide the best for his family while running a corporation to the best of his ability.

"Is he perfect? By no means, but is any man?" Brian chuckled for effect, then paused and made sure to make eye contact with every member of the jury. "Did he stray from his marriage? Regrettably he did, but he also protected his wife's business interests for years. He provided well for his family, and despite the death of Mr. Searfus' son Richard, he compensated for that loss and kept the family company running when it could have very easily shut down. Here he is today." Mr. Ebbes swept his arm toward his client. "He sits at that desk calmly, even though he's under attack for those same actions. Actions that kept the company thriving and his family fed. For that loyalty he's facing a jail sentence.

"If given the chance, Mr. Rhodes would keep that company running, and he would provide for Mrs. Rhodes' every need. Temporarily, he put that job into Ms. Sullivan's hands, believing that was the best option at the time. That is no longer the case. Mr. Rhodes is prepared to set up a trust fund for his wife's needs as he continues to push the company ahead in this new age of technology.

"Can the company run without him? Perhaps, but profits would certainly take a loss, and that wouldn't be in the best interests of anyone, especially Mrs. Rhodes, who needs around the clock care.

"That's why I'm asking you, the members of this jury, to do the right thing. Let the Rhodes family take care of their own. Who could possibly be better at caring for Katherine's wellbeing than her daughter and her husband of forty-four years? Allow them to continue to run the company in the same way it's been run, which, I might add, has been successfully done. Turning the business over to a comatose woman is not the answer, neither is allowing Katherine Rhodes to be under the care of a legal guardianship that she didn't consent to. Make the right decision, ladies and gentlemen. Restore legal guardianship to the Rhodes family where it belongs. Allow that man, who has taken care of this family for over forty years, continue to do so. It's the only thing that makes sense, and it's the only thing that's right. Thank you, ladies and gentlemen of the jury. The defense rests."

Judge Allen turned his chair around and looked at the seven women and five men of the jury. "Ladies and gentlemen, if you'll follow Mr. Erickson, our bailiff, he'll lead you to a private room where you can deliberate freely. Take as much time as you need, and if you want clarification on any of the charges or on any of the testimony, please ask."

The jury members quietly shuffled out of their seats and followed the court bailiff out the side door, disappearing into the hallway.

"Well that's it for now," Robin said, rising from the table.

"Now what?" Annie asked hesitantly, rising from her chair.

"Now we go to lunch, shopping, have our nails done. You name it. Until I get a call that the jury is ready, there's no reason to hang around here."

The door opened and a man dressed in blue jeans and a black leather jacket entered the courtroom.

"Ahhh, our lunch date is here," Robin said with a grin.

Annie turned and saw a much older Terry approaching. She walked halfway to meet him. "Terry, my god, this is a surprise." She hugged him tightly.

"Moony, you never look any older."

"You're such a liar, but I love you anyway."

"Well, let's get going you two, I'm starving." Robin threw her bag over her shoulder. "I'll drive. We're going to DiMaggio's, my treat."

Robin pulled her BMW into the restaurant's parking lot, which thankfully wasn't far from the courthouse. Terry jumped out of the back seat and opened Annie's door.

"Are you still riding?" Annie asked as they walked into DiMaggio's lobby.

"I sure am, every chance I get. Well, weather and health permitting." He chuckled. "I have arthritis these days, mostly in my hands and my knees. It can make riding the old Harley painful sometimes."

Annie and Robin nodded. They knew the pain arthritis caused in the joints because they suffered from the condition themselves.

Robin gave her name to the hostess and they were escorted to a table overlooking the bay. Seconds later the waiter arrived to take their drink orders, and a basket of sourdough bread with whipped butter was set in the center of the table.

"Are you still in the San Francisco Chapter of Hells Angels?" Annie asked.

"I am. I don't flaunt the colors unless I'm on a run with the club though. I've been doing this a long time, you know."

The drinks arrived and Terry took a sip from his Pepsi.

"Who's still around from the old days?" Annie asked.

"Hmmm...." Terry scratched his balding head thinking. "You remember Freddy?"

Annie nodded.

"Him for one. We lost Big Jim two years ago, cancer. That was a terrible thing." He shook his head and took another drink off his cola.

The waiter took their lunch orders and once again disappeared.

"What about Dylan?" Annie asked.

"He's still down in Long Beach, he still rides too. I don't know if he's in a club though, I haven't talked to him in awhile."

Robin seemed distracted; her eyes kept darting towards the doorway as if she were expecting someone else.

"What is it?" Annie finally asked.

"Oh nothing." She took a gulp from her own soft drink.

Annie stared at her questioningly.

"How's Katie?" Terry asked.

Annie took a deep breath before answering. "She's the same really. She's getting the best medical care, I've made sure of that. That's why this case is so important to me, I want that to continue."

Their meals arrived and for the next ten minutes the group ate quietly. Then Robin's telephone rang and she looked down at the number. "I have to take this call." She excused herself from the table.

"The jury?" Terry asked.

Annie shook her head. "This quickly, I doubt it."

"I guess it's been rough, I mean the court case and everything?"

"It has been. Mark's been fighting tooth and nail. I won't lie, the stress has been something terrible."

"And you're sure of this? Permanent guardianship is a big deal."

"If I don't keep guardianship those bastards will let her die. Horrid people, all of them. As for the company, that was fraudulently stolen from Katie by that swindler of a husband. Then there's Angela, who would gladly kill her mother today if she could get her hands on the inheritance and the company. My God, you should have seen how they had to remove that girl from the courtroom. Honestly, yelling and screaming at the judge."

"It was a good move for your case." Terry smiled, deepening the lines on his face.

"How'd you end up here today?" Annie asked.

"Robin called me. Well, actually, I talk to her and Ron frequently. I love it when Ron tells me about the new varieties of weed he comes up with. Can you imagine if we would have had that stuff back in the day?"

They both laughed.

"I wanted to be here for the outcome of the trial. Robin's fairly sure it will come sometime today and...well ,I just felt the need to be there in the courtroom when the verdict is read. Do you know what I mean?"

"Yes, I do." Annie nodded.

"After that, I thought the three of us might take a drive over to the nursing home and give her the news in person. If it's good news that is." Terry smiled, showing a set of perfectly white dentures.

The front door opened, Robin was back, but she wasn't alone. At first Annie couldn't see the man behind her but when he came into focus, Annie rose from the table.

"My God!" She held her hand over her mouth as Robin and the newcomer approached. "Did you know about this?" she asked, and Terry nodded.

Robin and Annie's ex-husband arrived at the table. Annie felt her eyes start to water and she fought back the tears.

"Hi, Annie." He reached for her hand. "I know this is a surprise, it was Robin's idea," Curtis mumbled.

"Yes it was," Robin said, "and I stand by my decision. We'll aren't you going to hug her?" Robin nudged Curtis, and he did. He put his arms around Annie's small body and pulled her gently towards him.

Curtis shut his eyes, remembering how she used to smell like summer flowers, and detecting the familiar fragrance for just a second, he smiled. The years seemed to disappear and he was Frog again, holding his beloved Moonbeam.

Much too quickly the embrace ended, and they were just two older people with the stories of their lives etched across their wrinkled faces.

"Come sit down." Robin pushed him towards an empty chair at the table.

"How many years has it been since you've seen each other?" Terry asked.

"Thirty-four?" Curtis said.

"About that," Annie said. "We saw each other at Big Jim's daughter's wedding."

Curtis nodded. "But we didn't talk to each other."

"Because we were both married to other people," Annie reminded him.

Annie smiled at Curtis, but then she turned and glared at Robin. "I can't believe you called him."

Robin smiled back sweetly. "I can't believe I waited so long."

"How long were the two of you married?" Terry asked, finishing his Shrimp Louie salad.

"Three years," Annie answered.

"Not long, why did you split up?"

"Because we were stupid," Curtis said flatly.

Robin's phone beeped and she looked at the text. "I can't believe it, this soon?"

"What?" Annie asked.

"It's the jury, they're finished deliberating. We need to get back to the courthouse." She flagged down the waiter so she could pay the check.

"Are you coming with us?" Annie asked her ex-husband.

"That's the plan." He smiled. "Robin thought it would be nice if we were all there when the verdict was read. I guess something like a reunion for old hippies."

Annie chuckled.

"I've missed you, Annie." He patted her hand affectionately.

"I've missed you too, Curtis."

They smiled at each other, both noticing that the spark they'd once felt was still there buried deep inside.

"Let's go," Robin prompted.

Curtis wrapped his hand around Annie's and they headed for the door.

***

The courtroom was cool. Annie pulled her sweater around her shoulders.

Judge Allen entered and they all rose. Annie looked behind her. Curtis, who was sitting in the spectator seats with Terry, smiled and gave her an encouraging thumb up.

Mark Rhodes and his attorney walked into the courtroom. Mark kept his eyes lowered, making sure he didn't make eye contact with anyone.

Annie tried to glare at him, but the attempt was futile. Angela's attorney, Michael Tran, walked in and took a seat at the defense table. Then the courtroom doors were shut and locked, and the jury entered through the special doorway.

"All rise," said the court bailiff.

When everyone was on their feet, Judge Allen asked, "Has the jury reached a verdict?"

The foreman of the twelve member jury stepped forward to a microphone. "We have, Your Honor."

"Proceed," said Judge Allen

The foreman read the sheet of paper she held in her hands:

"We the jury in the case of Rhodes vs. The State of California find the following: on count one, using fraudulent means to acquire medical records, guilty. On count two, falsifying company records, guilty. On count three, embezzlement of company funds, guilty. On count four, perjury, guilty and on count five, insurance fraud, guilty."

Annie gasped, and Robin hugged her.

Mark Rhodes looked shocked. This was not the verdict he had been expecting. His lawyer talked to him encouragingly, but his face was frozen into a permanent scowl.

In the spectator section shouts of happiness and excited talking arose as several photographers from local news stations shot pictures of the disgraced businessman.

Judge Allen banged his gavel on the desk. "I'll have silence in the courtroom." The excitement in the room stopped immediately, and everyone except for Mark Rhodes and his attorney took a seat.

"Mr. Rhodes," Judge Allen said, "you have been found guilty on all five charges."

"We're going to appeal," Brian Ebbes called out.

"I'm sure you are, but in the meantime, I'm here to pass sentence, and I'm going to do that." Judge Allen looked directly at the defendant. "Mr. Rhodes, we have heard testimony from several people over the course of this trial. Most have claimed that you used company funds for your own advantage and that you underhandedly took a corporation away from the rightful heir. Personally, I'm shocked that we didn't arrive at this point much sooner, but we're here now.

"In February you knowingly signed over custody rights of your deathly ill wife to Ms. Sullivan. It was done under legal means, and from the testimony here I'd say that it was documentation that you wanted drawn up so that you could escape the responsibility of your wife's care. I also believe you would have left that document in place without another thought, except that the other charges in this case finally caught up with you. After closely examining Al Searfus' will, dated September 7, 1966 , I am confident that Mr. Searfus intended to leave his company to his children, Richard and Katherine. With Richard deceased, that company was the sole property of his daughter, Katherine Allison Searfus Rhodes. Although there seems to be a clause regarding 'sound mind', that document has been altered so many times it's basically worthless.

"It is hereby ordered that the Rhodes Corporation, formally known as the Searfus Corporation, is to be returned to Katherine Rhodes immediately. As for her custodial care, I believe it is best to leave it in the hands of Annie Sullivan."

"But her daughter?" Angela's attorney, Michael Tran piped up.

"Mrs. Rhodes' daughter is unreliable, out of the country more than she's here, and as documentation from the hospital and nursing home show, hasn't responded to phone calls regarding her mother's condition. Her behavior in this court of law causes me concern. Unless something drastically changes, and I doubt that it will, the care of Mrs. Rhodes is best left in the hands of her current guardian, Annie Sullivan."

Judge Allen paused. He took a long drink of water.

"Mr. Rhodes," he said, "as a family man myself, your actions puzzle me, but I'm not here to pass judgment on your morality, only on your crimes."

"Yes, Your Honor," Mark managed to mumble.

"On count one, using fraudulent means to acquire medical records, I give you the maximum penalty of eighteen months. On count two, falsifying company records, I give you the maximum penalty of twenty-five years. On count three, embezzlement of company funds, I give you the maximum penalty of twenty-five years. On count four, perjury, I give you the maximum penalty of one year. And on count five, insurance fraud, I give you the maximum penalty of fifteen years."

Mark's mouth dropped open. His attorney kept repeating that he 'shouldn't worry because they would win on appeal', but Mark looked terrified. Annie watched him being led away in handcuffs and she smiled.

We won. She still could not believe the outcome.

"We did it, Annie, we actually did it." Robin hugged her tightly and laughed joyously.

"I can't believe it," Annie said.

Behind them, Terry and Curtis were yelling and the press was trying to get a few last minute shots as the CEO of Rhodes Corporation was led away in shackles. A few more pictures of Annie, the new custodial owner of the Rhodes Corporation, and the press was gone.

"Now for a celebration," Robin said. "Let's go tell Katie the good news."

***

When the group arrived at St. Mary's Nursing Facility, Ron Diebel was already there. Ron still had long hair fastened in a ponytail that ran halfway down his back, but now it was gray, and his skin was wrinkled. Despite that, Annie would have recognized him anywhere. Some people just looked like themselves no matter how much they aged. Ron was one of those people.

Ron kissed Robin and congratulated her on her victory. Then he hugged Annie and greeted Curtis and Terry excitedly.

"Look at you Frog." Ron laughed. "Short gray hair, a dress shirt and slacks, who would have known?"

"I know." Curtis laughed. "We've all changed so much. Me with my short hair, you with your gray ponytail, and Terry balding."

"What about us?" Robin asked.

"Well..." He turned to study the ladies.

"Robin, you look like a successful mature business woman, still as beautiful as always. And, Moony, you still look like that beautiful little hippie girl who used to run around Haight-Ashbury barefoot even in the winter. The only difference is that your hair is shorter and the auburn has turned lighter. But your eyes still sparkle the same way that made me love you."

Annie blushed.

"Shall we?" Robin suggested, pointing towards door to Katie's room. The group of old friends nodded and quietly entered the room where a comatose Katie lay hooked up to wires and tubes and an I.V.

"Hey, honey," Annie said quietly. "Look who I've brought with me." She walked over to the bed and took Katie's hand in her own. She brushed the gray hair out of her eyes, while pointing at the three men who walked through the doorway. "You remember Terry, Frog, and Ron? They're here, baby. We're all here, Robin and me included. We came to celebrate with you. Do you hear me, Katie? We got him, honey it's all over. Robin put the bastard in jail for twenty-five years. Mark is sixty-seven, that will make him over ninety before he's eligible for parole. He's going to spend the rest of his life behind bars. As for the little hussy he left you for, she's gone, and the kid...." Annie snickered, "well let's just say the DNA test proved that Mark isn't the father. What he did, he did for nothing, Katie, because that's all he got in the end. The company is yours, and I'll make sure it's run correctly. I won't take a penny from it, I promise. All the profits will go into a trust fund that will be spent on you. Anything, and I mean *anything* that might bring you back to us, money isn't going to be a problem. When the time comes I'll make sure the corporation is split between your children, but until then I'll manage it on your behalf." Annie kissed her on the forehead and stepped away from the bed.

Robin knelt beside her and held her hand. "We're all here, Katie, everyone who loves you, and we're always going to be. Come back to us, we all miss you." Robin kissed her cheek and smiled.

"Hey, baby, remember me?" Terry asked. "When you get better I'm going to take you on a ride. Your choice, honey, on my bike or in my '57 Chevy. I bet you're surprised that I still have that."

"We all love you, Katie," Frog called out.

"We really do," Ron agreed. "We all miss you too, but you'd be happy today, my friend. Robin really gave it to that son of a bitch that you married." Ron pulled a perfectly rolled joint, one of his 'special batch', out of his shirt pocket. "And this is for you, honey. I call it Katie Kush."

Ron lit the king sized smoke and took a big toke before passing it around the room. The old friends celebrated for more than an hour, telling stories and reminiscing about the old days. Ron produced his iPod and a set of mini speakers and they listened to the music of their youth, Jefferson Airplane, Jimi Hendrix and the Grateful Dead. One of the nurses in the home supplied them with a few bottles of cola. With paper cups they toasted to their old friend's health. Around midnight, the friends left the hospital and went their separate ways once again.

***

Curtis followed Annie to her car on the premise of keeping her safe, but they both knew that he had another motive in mind.

"I really enjoyed spending the day with you." He took her hand into his own. "I'd really like to see you again, if it's all right with you, I'd like to call you sometime."

"I'd like that too."

"We were stupid kids..."

"I know we were."

"I thought we'd be young forever, you know? I just always thought there would be more time. That if you and I were supposed to be together, it would happen. Then the years kept drifting by, more and more of them, and I was afraid to call you."

"I know that too." She touched his face.

"Don't be mad at Robin for calling me."

"It was a nasty trick. She should have asked me first."

"Would you have gone along with it?" Curtis asked.

Annie laughed. "No."

"That's why she didn't tell you."

Annie pulled her car keys out of her coat pocket and fumbled with them.

"I guess I should let you get on the road, it's late." Cutis helped her with the car door.

"Yes it is," Annie said, yawning. "I haven't been up this late in many years."

"Me either."

"Thanks for being there today. I'm sure someplace inside it meant a lot to Katie."

"It meant a lot to me too."

They stared at each other for a few seconds and then Curtis reached out and stroked her cheek with his hand. "You know, I never stopped loving you."

"I never stopped loving you either, Curtis."

Curtis kissed her, and for just a second they were Frog and Moonbeam all over again.

***

Dylan and Frog walked into the barn, both wearing bib overalls. When the girls saw them they started to laugh.

"Look at the two of you," Katie said. "What a couple of farmers you've become. Who would have known that several months ago you were a longhaired hippie entrepreneur and you a hard ass Hells Angel?"

"Yeah, yeah, yeah, very funny." Dylan pulled her close and kissed the tip of her nose.

They had been living in Marin County since the middle of November, and now it was December 31st. When they first arrived, the couples had moved into the main house along with Chet and his old lady Jillian, but it was too crowded. They quickly bought their own trailers and along with others who occupied the property, they set up house on the five-acre farm they called "The Pig Sty". There were twenty-seven people on the commune now, and they were completely self-sufficient. Along with the pigs that they raised, they also had an assortment of vegetables that they grew and canned themselves.

Katie had to admit that life on the pig farm was good. Life with Dylan was all she needed. Daily she thanked God for her second chance. When Richard's ordeal was over she thought she might flash back to the present, Sam Becker style, but when she didn't she was thankful.

Katie wasn't sure how all of this was possible. Sometimes she still tried to figure it out. She only hoped though, that whatever had brought her here would never return her. In the meantime, she planned to live a full life in her past with the man that she loved and her best friend.

Tonight was New Year's Eve 1967. She couldn't believe it. She was starting another year in her own past. Miraculous as that sounded, it was true.

She had talked to her parents several times, and they were well. In fact, they were both trying to stop drinking. Katie was proud of them. She and Dylan had spent Thanksgiving with her family, and when her brother had called for the occasion she had talked to him extensively about his ordeal.

Richard was being transferred out of Vietnam in a month, and he would be stationed in Germany for eighteen months. Needless to say, he was excited about leaving South East Asia.

Katie had asked when he was getting out of the military and was surprised to find that he was considering a career in the Marines. Richard sounded happy, and that in itself was a miracle.

Moonbeam and Frog were happy too. He had quickly become a learned farmer and was good at marketing any crops they had left over, which always put money in the commune's pocket. Sometimes when they needed cash,

Katie would bet on sporting events. She even put some money in the stock market, which of course was doing well. It was nice to know the outcome before the events took place. She could always count on her memory to get them by in times of need, if they ever had any.

Moonbeam and Frog had thought of getting married on the farm, and when Katie had told her that in present day she had no children, Annie decided to do something about that. Now she was several months pregnant and deciding whether she should do the right thing before or after the birth of the baby. Katie was sure that whichever way she decided, life for her, Frog, and the baby would be happy.

"Aren't the two of you supposed to be cooking or something?" Frog asked them as he hugged Moonbeam and kissed her on the neck.

"It's already done, silly, we've been cooking all day."

"All thirteen of you ladies?" he asked, and she nodded. "That must make for a very crowded kitchen."

"We all have our different tasks, so we don't get into each other's way."

"I'll bet." Frog and Dylan laughed.

"Dinner's at 7:00 sharp, and you can't come dressed like that," Katie told them both.

"I don't know why, we're living on a pig farm," Dylan replied.

Katie kissed him. "I'm not even going to respond to that."

"We're going inside to get ready, are you coming up soon?" Moonbeam asked while she and Katie headed towards their separate trailers.

"Yep, we're just going to feed the last pen of pigs, put the tools away, and then we'll be there."

***

Seventeen people sat around the enormous homemade wooden table. In the middle of it, a carved turkey sat waiting. On another large platter was half a roasted pig, and in bowls encircling the feast, mashed potatoes, gravy, cauliflower and yams, all home grown on the Pig Sty. Several bottles of wine were opened and poured into ceramic cups that had been made on the commune.

At the head of the table was the founder of the commune, Chet, and by his side his ladylove, Jillian.

Chet tapped on the side of his wine cup with a spoon to get the attention of everyone at the table. When all eyes were focused on him he stood and addressed his friends.

"We have come such a long way in the year that we have been here; from a dream to a reality, where we can all live in peace and harmony. To you, my friends, I make this toast. May all of your dreams come true in 1968." He lifted his cup into the air.

"Mine already have," Katie whispered into Dylan's ear.

Dylan turned and smiled at her. "So have mine."

They held their glasses high, toasted to the New Year, and then Dylan kissed her.

***

When the group left, Maria, Katie's nurse, cleaned up the mess. She was happy that Katie's friends had thrown her a party and was certain that somewhere inside Katie knew they were there. Sometimes she felt as if Katie was present. There were other times when she was someplace else entirely, but today when her friends were there, Katie was with them. Maria had noticed a distinct smile on her patient's face, a smile that she had seen several times before, one that always made Maria happy.

Maria had taken a special liking to this woman. Even though she was in a coma and non-communicative, Maria had felt something for her. Maybe it was how closely her own life mirrored the woman in the bed.

Like Katie, her husband had left her for a younger woman. Dr. Reynolds said that Katie had tried to take her own life in an auto accident when she thought she was being left penniless. Maria knew how that felt because the same thing had happened to her. When it did she had thought about driving over a cliff too. Instead, she was here working at St. Mary's Nursing Facility. Katie reminded her daily of how close she had come to driving her car off of the road, and how she could have easily ended up in a coma as well. Or even dead.

Perhaps it was her good mood or maybe it was for sentimental reasons, she wasn't sure. Normally she would never let a visitor in this late, but this visitor was different, who wouldn't let her in?

When the woman showed up and asked to see Katie, Maria had escorted the seventy something year old woman through the hospital corridor and then into Katie's private room. Maria found a chair in the lobby and sat it next to Katie's bed. She wondered how this visitor could possibly know her patient and thought of asking, but quickly changed her mind.

"I'll leave you alone with Katie. If you need anything I'll be right out here in the lobby."

The older woman nodded and smiled at Maria. When Maria was gone the woman sat a large bouquet of exotic flowers in a vase next to another on the dresser. Curious, she stopped to read the card. It was addressed to Katie from the US Marines Corps and Torres, Clemmings, Owens, Hodges, and Lewis had signed it. They wrote that they loved her and that they hoped she'd get better soon.

"I guess you have friends in the military huh?" She sat at Katie's bedside and took her chilled hand in her own. "Hey, baby, look at you! Haven't we changed?" She looked at Katie closely. "I heard about your accident yesterday on the news. You know, the court case and all. I'm sorry. If I had known I would have come sooner. I'm glad to hear that your attorney won your case and that your slimy old man is going to prison." She laughed a nervous chuckle and then her eyes started to water.

"I know deep inside you can hear me, Katie. They say people in comas can hear music, stories..." she swallowed hard, "and they can especially tell when people are talking to them. That's how I know you're here with me now."

The visitor brushed her long unruly hair out of her blue eyes and fastened it back in a crude ponytail. Then she leaned forward again and took Katie's hand in both of her own.

"Thank you, Katie for everything you did. You were right; I did get into some really heavy shit. I know I should have listened to you but I didn't." She hung her head and stifled a sob. "I was young, famous, and into myself. I didn't want to think about my own mortality, I just wanted to party.

"It almost happened, Katie. Almost. But your premonition and your repeated warnings finally rang true. Better late than never, right girlfriend?"

She laughed a raspy laugh. "I was there in Los Angeles just like you said I would be. A month earlier I had started shooting up again. I knew it was stupid, but I did it anyway. I thought I was a pro at injecting smack. What a fool I was.

"I met that guy, the one you said I would. You were right about him too, he had my father's first name, but he was nothing like my dad." She swallowed and rubbed at her eyes, which were now puffy and red.

"October 3, 1970 happened just as you said it would. I was in L.A., and I was staying at the Landmark Motor Hotel. I was in room 105, just like you said I would be, and I had contacted a pusher named Dave. My friends were supposed to come that night, Peggy and my so-called fiancée Seth, but neither showed up. I'd recorded that day, and I was tired. We went to Barney's Beanery and I had those tequila toasts you were talking about. Hell, I even dropped a few Vicodin. Earlier that day I'd bought the H and it was waiting for me back in my hotel room. And then I had this flashback... that's what stopped me. No kidding, man, it really was. I was standing there in the hotel and then like magic your premonition flashed through my mind. It was crazy, Katie, it was like you were there screaming at me. I saw your face and then I thought of my family, my parents, my brother Michael and my sister, Laura. I thought of what my OD would do to them, and I stopped myself.

"I'd gone out to the lobby as you said I would but I didn't shoot up first. I bought the cigarettes and I talked to the man at the front desk. All the while my body was aching for that fix, but I didn't take it, Katie."

She wept, and then reached for a tissue from the box on the dresser. "I would have done it, I would have. I was so close. Every cell in my body called out for that fix, and I didn't take it. I stayed in that lobby for ten or fifteen minutes fighting that craving. Finally, I asked the desk clerk to walk me back to my room, and he did. I gave him my balloon pack and I asked him to flush it down the toilet. I handed him a $50 tip, too. Then I waited in my room for my friends who never showed up. I sat up all night staring out the window just to make sure that I saw the sunrise on October the 4th. When I did, I broke down and cried because I knew I should have been dead."

Janis wiped at her nose with the tissue.

"I called my family in the morning and I talked to my parents, and my brother and sister. Then I recorded that last song on the *Pearl* LP, 'Buried in the Blues', with Big Brother and the Holding Company. You see, I took your advice on that too." She wiped her eyes on the same tissue. "Al Grossman wanted me to branch out on my own, just like you said he would, but I didn't go through with it. I stayed with Big Brother and the Holding Company, and I'm glad I did. The guys in the band, they've helped me through a lot

"I went to rehab, Katie, a good one, and I stayed there for months. I knew how close I had come to my own death. To this day I believe I would be gone if not for you. I read later that seven people died that weekend from Dave's smack. I should have been the eighth.

"Now here we are, two old broads, and you're in here." Janis looked around the depressing room and sighed. "The worst part is that there isn't anything that I can do to help you. I feel so helpless about that because I owe you so much. I wish I could change things for you, my friend," she said with a sigh. "I would do anything to help you if I could." Janis squeezed Katie's hand. "I'm married. Did you know that?"

"I dumped Seth. Boy, you were right about him too, not a good guy. I married Kris. It took him years to get around to asking me, but he finally did."

Katie's finger twitched, and Janis jumped. Thinking that she might be coming out of her coma the singer stopped and stared at her. When nothing else happened, Janis took it as a sign that Katie was listening.

"I'm sure you've heard of my husband, his last name is Kristofferson, he's a singer too. In fact he wrote 'Bobby McGee' for me to record, but you probably know that." She smiled thinking of her husband. "We have a daughter. Her name is Amanda, she's thirty-four years old now. She has a daughter and a son. I look at them sometimes, and I know that they're a complete miracle."

Maria stuck her head in the door. "Is everything alright?"

"Oh sure. I'll be leaving in just a few minutes if that's alright?" Janis asked.

"Of course, Ms. Joplin, take your time. By the way, I love your music, both yours and your husband's."

Janis smiled warmly, and Maria shut the door.

"I wouldn't have any of it without you, Katie. No family, no husband, and I wouldn't have the great relationship that I share with my family either. From the bottom of my heart I thank you."

Janis rose from the chair. It took her a few seconds to stretch her old legs. "Getting old is a drag, Mick Jagger was right about that." She pushed the chair out of her way. "Which reminds me... Jerry Garcia and Brian Jones send their regards. So does Jimi Hendrix. I know you never talked to him yourself, but I told him what you said and...well, he changed things too." Janis flashed her trademark grin. "Well, I guess I should let that nurse get home to her family. Thanks again, my friend." She squeezed Katie's hand one last time then leaned over and kissed her on the cheek. "Wherever you are right now, I hope that it's groovy."

She turned to leave but stopped herself. "I almost forgot," she said, turning around completely. Some old lady with really bad teeth met me outside the nursing facility and she asked me to give you this. What significance it has I have no idea." Janis chuckled then pulled an old rusty key out of her bag. "She said that this would mean something to you. I don't know if it does or doesn't, but I promised her that I would place it in your hands."

Janis sat the key on Katie's chest and gently wrapped her hands around it.

"Goodbye, my friend," she said, and then Janis Joplin was gone.

Katie was left in her private room alone, holding a key that she would have recognized immediately as the one that opened the endless doorways.

Epilogue

When the bells went off, Barry Bog was frightened. He had never heard them before, and he'd been here for a very long time. He wasn't the only one who was scared. He heard random screams in the hallway from others who didn't know what was going on.

"What is it?" Guthrie asked.

"Man, I don't fucking know."

A soldier from one of the world wars ran past. Barry tried to stop him but failed.

"Where's the fire?" someone asked and turning abruptly, Barry came face to face with Jim Morrison.

"Man, I don't think there is a fire."

"Then what's with the alarm?" Jim asked confused. He looked up and down the hallway.

Barry and Guthrie both shrugged. "We don't know. We're trying to figure that out too," Barry said.

Other guests continued to run past them, terrified by the bells that wouldn't stop ringing.

"Never mind all of this," Morrison said, shaking his head. "We're missing some of the band, have you seen them?"

The sound of the bells changed, becoming periodic bursts from a trumpet, and a multi-colored mist dispensed from the vents.

"Groovy colors man," Guthrie said.

Morrison grabbed the front of Barry's shirt and repeated his question. "Have you seen any of the missing band members?"

"What?" Barry asked, removing the singer's hands from the front of his shirt. "Mind the threads." He straightened his clothing.

"Sorry, man." Morrison swallowed and pushed his bushy hair out of his eyes. "Some of our group is missing. Have you seen anybody leave the 27 Club room?"

A lightshow commenced, colors rolling around them. Music replaced the blasts of noise. Guthrie tugged on Barry's sleeve. "Let's go, man," he whispered, licking his lips and thinking that there must be some good old Thunderbird around here someplace.

Barry focused, ignoring the noise and colors around him. "No, Jim, I don't think I saw anyone leave your room. Who's missing?"

"Wait man, I can't remember, let me think..." Morrison's memory hadn't recovered fully from the drugs he'd taken in life. Sometimes he had memory lapses, and the inhabitants of the endless hallways had come to expect that. Barry stepped back and let Morrison have some space, which always seemed to help.

"Oh yeah, now I remember," Jim said and snapped his fingers. "We haven't been able to find Janis, Hendrix, or Brian."

Barry shook his head. "No man, I haven't seen any of them."

"Then I better get a move on, I've got to find them! We're supposed to perform tonight. Hey, if you see them..."

"We'll make sure to let them know that you're looking for them," Guthrie assured him.

"Thanks, man." Morrison waved and headed down the hallway looking for his friends.

The concert hall doors opened automatically; something was going on inside.

"Come on, man," Barry said, nudging Guthrie in the shoulder. "Let's find out what the hell's going on."

"Sure, man, I'm mighty thirsty." Guthrie licked his lips as he followed Barry and a group of others towards the main hall.

The auditorium was dark except for the stage, where psychedelic colors flashed across the screen.

"What's happening?" everyone was asking when they strolled through the room, trying to find seats in the darkness.

The music stopped and the multi-colored mist was gone. Now there was just a room full of people waiting for someone to address them.

"I wish I had some Thunderbird. What kind of party is this?" Guthrie whispered. "Where's the refreshment table?"

Barry patted him on the arm sympathetically.

The psychedelic colors stopped. For several seconds the room went dark and then overhead lights flashed on.

"Ladies and gentlemen, we've had a success," a small balding man with horn-rimmed glasses announced. He stood at a wooden podium, which hadn't been there minutes before.

"A success?" There were gasps in the room and the sound of voices talking excitedly. Then the announcer, who Barry had never seen before, was back at the podium asking for quiet.

"A success means that we've chosen a new candidate."

Confetti fell from the ceiling and the lights flashed off. When they came back on, several young girls dressed in Victorian clothing wove through the crowd passing out paper horns.

"This calls for a party my friends. The last time we saw a success this big...well, I think it was in 1922." The small man cheered and so did everyone else in the room. Horns were blown, the audience called for musicians, and in the back of the room a champagne fountain magically appeared out of nowhere.

"Ah, now that's more like it!" Guthrie yelled. "I wonder if they have any Thunderbird?" He rushed towards the self-service bar.

"I wonder who the lucky soul is? The one who's going to get a second chance?" a ballerina in a pink tutu asked Barry.

"I don't know," Barry said.

Several US presidents were huddled together debating the topic. They took bets, hoping that one of them would be the next lucky traveler.

William Randolph Hearst pulled his wallet out of his pocket and looked for someone to 'pay off.' Barry wondered how Hearst had managed to bring his wallet along when his own pot had been confiscated.

A band walked on stage. Barry recognized Duke Ellington and sighed. He hated it when they played the oldies.

Guthrie was back, holding two glasses of champagne. Barry reached for one, but Guthrie pulled it away.

"Come on, man, there's a whole fucking fountain of the stuff," Barry told him. Guthrie looked at the fountain and reluctantly handed a glass of bubbly to his friend.

"So what's this all about?" Guthrie asked. "Not that I don't enjoy a party. Hell, I'll celebrate anything," he said proudly, draining his first glass of champagne.

"You don't say?" Barry asked sarcastically.

"I'm serious, Barry, I'll celebrate anything," Guthrie repeated. "By the way, what exactly is going on?"

"I've never seen this before, but it seems as if Katie and Frog have been successful."

"Well damn! I didn't think the boy had it in him. I'll drink to that!" Guthrie pulled Barry's glass away from him and finished off the contents.

"Hey, man, really? Do I mess with your food or drinks?" Barry said.

"Sorry, man, it was an accident."

"Are you listening?"

"Yeah, man, I'm listening. You said that Katie and Frog were successful. What does that mean?"

"It means they were able to change the past. They made things right," Barry explained.

"That's far out, man," Guthrie said. "What happens now?"

"Now, some lucky bastard gets another chance."

"How soon before that happens?" Guthrie asked licking his lips. He looked at the fountain, craving more of the bubbly brew.

"I don't know, man. When someone fails they come back right away. Well, after that miserable hag takes a go at them." Barry shuddered thinking of the horrid woman with the rotting green teeth. "We don't get a party when that happens."

"That's a bummer, man. I'm sure glad I'm here for the first successful party. Hey, do you think they have larger cups?"

"Why, man? Like I said, there's a whole fucking fountain of the stuff. They aren't going to run out anytime soon." Barry shook his shaggy head.

"I know, man, but I have to keep walking over there," Guthrie said, his voice fading as he headed towards the drink table again.

Barry watched his friend go and shook his head. *Some people are just never going to change.*

"Mr. Bog?"

Barry turned and found the short, balding announcer from the podium staring at him.

"That's me, man."

"Would you come with me please?"

"Why, man, what's this about?"

"Well, you can't find out if you don't come with me, now can you?" The round man chuckled.

"But I don't know you, man," Barry said.

"Suspicious, Mr. Bog? Might I point out that you're trapped in a hallway?"

"That's true, man, but—"

The plump man smiled. "You're safe, Mr. Bog, I promise you."

"Okay, man, you have a point. I'll trust you, but first I need to tell my friend where I'm going," Barry said.

Am I being sent somewhere else, maybe to another hallway?

"What's going on here?" Guthrie asked when he returned holding a steel coffee mug filled with sparkling wine.

"This dude's taking me someplace, man," Barry complained.

"Taking you someplace? Why, man?" Guthrie asked the newcomer.

"Because, gentlemen..." The balding man stepped closer and lowered his voice. "Mr. Bog is getting a second chance."

"Me?" Barry said, pointing to himself in shock.

"Keep your voice down, Mr. Bog. For God's sake, don't let the presidents or Gandhi overhear you." The announcer looked around nervously.

"Me?" Barry said again, a huge smile appearing on his face.

"That's far out, brother." Guthrie congratulated him with pat on the shoulder.

"Now would you come with me?"

"Yeah, man, just give me a second."

The announcer took several steps back and waited. He crossed his arms in front of his body and tapped his foot impatiently.

"Guthrie, this is it, man. I get a chance to change things, can you believe it?" he asked excitedly.

"That's excellent, man, but what am I going to do without you?" the old man asked.

"You'll make friends. There are a lot of groovy people here; you just need to give them a chance."

"I don't know, man. I don't know any of them." Guthrie shook his head sadly, looking around the hall.

"For instance, over there that's Edger Allen Poe. You like his stories. Go make friends. He's sitting all by himself, and he likes to drink."

"He does?"

The announcer huffed and looked as his wrist as if there was such a thing as time in the hallway.

"Look, man, I'll do everything I can for you down there. I'll try to get you off the streets," Barry promised his friend.

"That won't happen brother, don't waste your time."

"Don't say that, man. Everyone can be helped, it's never too late. I can help you!"

"When you get back to the Haight it will be what, 1965? By then... well, don't bother, Barry, I mean that. Just buy me a hot meal once in awhile and a bottle of Thunderbird. That will do me just fine." Guthrie tapped his friend on the shoulder. "You better get going before they choose someone else. This guy over here looks like he's about ready to blow a fuse." Guthrie laughed and pointed at the red-faced announcer.

"You're right, man. I'll be seeing you." Barry hugged the old man and said goodbye.

"Okay, I'm ready," Barry said to the chubby, balding announcer.

"Well, it's about time," he said crankily. "Come with me."

Barry followed him into the hallway, making sure to shut the assembly room door behind him.

"This way, Mr. Bog." He led Barry down the hallway and then around a corner, where he randomly disappeared.

"What the fuck? Hey, man, where did you go?" Barry yelled into the deserted corridor.

"Did I lose my chance?" he called out. "Look, man, I'm sorry I took so long." For several minutes Barry walked up and down the hall looking for the chubby old man, but the announcer was nowhere to be found.

"Okay, man, I guess I lost my chance. That's cool. Can I go back to the party now?"

The lights in the hallway dimmed, and when they came back on Barry wasn't alone. The old hag maid was with him and she was holding an old rusty key.

Barry was several feet away, but he could smell her.

"You!"

"That's right, Barry, it's me." She laughed, holding the old key out in front of her. "You didn't think you'd get to leave without seeing me one last time, did you?"

"I was hoping..." Barry admitted, stepping back, this time into the wall.

The maid stepped closer. Still wagging the antique key in front of her face she pulled something else out of her apron pocket. Barry gasped when he saw it was a syringe.

"What the fuck?"

"That's right, Barry, it's your drug of choice. Do remember all the good times you had together?" She waved the yellow filled hypodermic needle. "I'm going to give you a taste of what you've been missing before I send you on your way. Just think of it as a bon voyage present." She laughed, showing green stained teeth and gums.

"No, man, get that shit away from me. That's what killed me the first time around." He tried to move away from the hag but was still backed into the wall. The old maid encircled him and stopped him from moving in any direction. Then painfully she jabbed him in the arm with the blunt needle and twisted the syringe mercilessly.

"There you are, Barry. Good and high for your trip back to the past."

The hag pulled the needle out of Barry's arm, laughing as she unlocked the door Barry was leaning against.

"Mind the fall, Barry, that first step is a bitch."

She tossed him through the doorway.

Barry fell into the void and spun through the darkness. He tried to scream but he couldn't utter a sound, and fell silently into an abyss of blackness with his mouth wide open. From above he could still hear the old hag cackling in the hallway.

About the Author

Diane Sager was raised and resides in the San Francisco Bay Area with her husband, three dogs, a cat and an African Grey Parrot named Storm. She holds a fascination for all things macabre and has developed a deep knowledge of horror, serial killers, vampires, zombies, the Tarot, world religions, witchcraft and the occult.

This former high school teacher of emotionally disturbed and high-risk youth is now dedicated to full time writing. Diane also writes under the name of D.S Sager.

www.ingramcontent.com/pod-product-compliance
Lightning Source LLC
Chambersburg PA
CBHW080816020726
47501CB00009B/2316